I0831366

Then Again

Then Again

Rick Boling

THEN AGAIN

Manufactured in the United States of America

First WordMerchant edition published 2015

10 9 8 7 6 5 4 3 2 1

WordMerchant Publishing
Post Office Box 1764
New Port Richey, FL 34656
www.wmpublishing.com

ISBN 978-0-692-55480-7

Cover and Interior Design by R. LeBeaux
Madisons Photo by Jimmy Powell
Author Photo by Steven Kelley

For

Burt Kempner

And

Jonni Gill

HERE ABOUT THE BEACH I WANDERED
NOURISHING A YOUTH SUBLIME
WITH THE FAIRY TALES OF SCIENCE
AND THE LONG RESULT OF TIME.

- Lord Alfred Tennyson

IT IS OFTEN STATED THAT OF ALL THE THEORIES PROPOSED IN THIS CENTURY, THE SILLIEST IS QUANTUM THEORY. SOME SAY THE ONLY THING QUANTUM THEORY HAS GOING FOR IT, IN FACT, IS THAT IT IS UNQUESTIONABLY CORRECT.

- Michio Kaku

PERHAPS IT IS MUSIC THAT WILL SAVE THE WORLD.

- Shinichi Suzuki

CONTENTS

Part One

Now

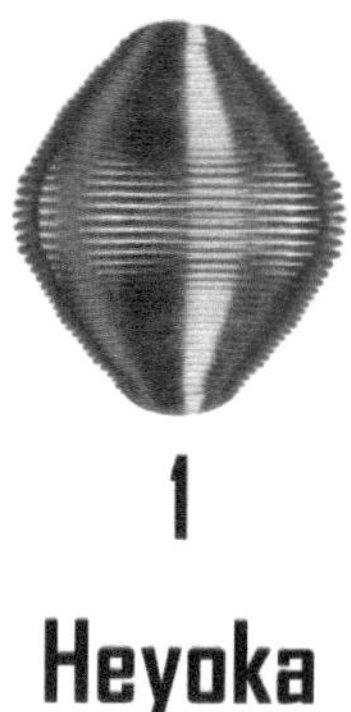

1

Heyoka

I first met Heyoka Husereau D'Ailleboust in Lyon, France, at a small concert bar called LeMusique. I was backstage in the room labeled Cabine D'essayage—which I assumed translated into "cramped closet you may use as a dressing room"—slamming down a couple of last-minute Jacks to make sure my liver remembered who was boss, when Mariah Carey came in and delivered a note written on a crinkled drink napkin. On second glance, I decided it wasn't really Mariah Carey, only a pudgy barmaid with big boobs who might have passed for a distant cousin of hers to someone high on half a quart of Tennessee whiskey.

Despite the crinkles, after I flattened out the napkin, the handwriting was clear and a little effeminate. At first I thought the note might have been an offer by one of my two remaining female fans to introduce me to some elaborate variation of coital acrobatics, but no such luck; the note turned out to be a simple, though peculiar, request. Unaccompanied by currency of any denomination, or even the offer of a drink, it read:

> *I was wondering if you might consider playing "Florida in my Bones." It's a song I remember from my college days, and hearing it has an uncanny way of transporting me back in time ... reliving fond memories, if you know what I mean.*

Thanks,
Heyoka (A lifelong fan)

There might have been ten people in the world who remembered ***Florida in my Bones***, an obscure little tune that had been included as a last-minute filler on the B side of my first album. And the odds against one of those ten people finding me at this dead-end gig nearly 5,000 miles from the Sunshine State were astronomical.

Like most of my more recent venues, LeMusique was what we over-the-hill touring musicians like to call an "intimate room," as if we preferred performing for a few dozen drunks instead of a stadium full of 50,000 screaming fans. Of course, I'd never starred in one of those stadium gigs myself. The closest I'd ever come was on a shared tour in 1975, shortly after ***Robin's Song***, my first national release, peaked at number nineteen on the Billboard charts. I served as the opening act for another non-superstar one-hit-wonder by the name of Danny O'Donnell, who's single, ***I've Got a Rose for You***, briefly hit number five, then disappeared for all time into that vast dustbin of forgotten bubblegum ditties. Danny and I performed at a few fairly large venues on that tour, though we never drew more than ten thousand, and there wasn't a lot of screaming.

Still, somewhere among the few cells that remained operative in my oxygen-deprived brain, this particular request lit a spark of long-suppressed ego, and I decided to search the music files on my laptop for the lyrics. Luckily—or maybe not—I found them, and by the time the MC knocked to let me know I was on in three minutes, I had put together a reasonable facsimile of the original chord arrangement. Hitting the high notes with my aging James-Earl-Jones of a voice, however, was going to be a different story.

It was seventeen paces from the lovely Cabine D'essayage to my stool on the tiny, darkened stage, and I made it without tripping. Unfortunately, my night vision had long ago gone the way of the cassette tape, and when the curtain lifted I was caught trying frantically to return the stool to an upright position. This might have been embarrassing had I not managed to turn it into a humorous imitation of a Jim-Carrey pratfall.

As the nervous laughter died down, I took my seat and squinted at the invisible audience in a futile attempt to see beyond the glare of the spotlight and identify someone who looked like a Heyoka. The name was, to me at least, non-gender-specific, but even if I could have seen anything other than a swarm of Technicolor fireflies, I would have had little chance of singling out my one faithful fan. I could still sense an undercurrent of empathetic anxiety in the room, so I decided to start with one of my sure-fire, ice-breaking opening lines.

"Sorry to disappoint you, but I only know two songs," I said. "And I always do one of them first." I curled my arthritic claw of a left hand around the neck of my Martin D-28, then looked up and added, "This is the other one." And over a ripple of chuckles I launched into the goof song I'd written decades before about always returning to the Sunshine State.

I've left this old state when I'm hurtin'
I've left it when I'm feelin' fine
But when I'm done funnin' and flirtin'
I keep wanderin' back to the palm trees and sunshine

As my eyes adjusted to the dim atmosphere, I started to make out a couple of faces in the crowd.

I've drunk moonshine in Pikeville
Felt Montana's wind chill
But no matter how far I roam
I always end up headin' home
That Florida sun's shinin' deep in my bones

God, I thought, *did I really write this crap?* And just then, while I played a little unplanned guitar interlude in order to give me time to catch a breath, I saw a row of brilliant white teeth floating behind a table close to the stage.

I've woken up mornin's
To wildflowers swarmin'
'Long the old Santa Fe Railroad line
I've stood looking over
Fields covered with clover
In the foothills of ol' Caroline

The teeth had to belong to this Heyoka character. No one else could be enjoying this stupid song enough to smile that broadly in public.

I've tried the Big Easy
I've let Vegas squeeze me
But no matter how far I roam
I always end up headin' home
That Florida sun's shinin' deep in my bones

And, much to my chagrin, it did not look like a female.

I've seen sunsets on mountains
Bellagio's fountains
Sat under a tall redwood tree
But when snow's a fallin'
I still hear the callin'
Of the surf and the sand and the sea

In fact, judging from the shadow that hovered behind those teeth, the owner was a rather large male person.

I've seen fall in Ontario
The Yucatan in Mexico
But no matter how far I roam
I always end up headin' home
That Florida sun's shinin' deep in my bones

I had to look down in order to finish with the complicated Flamenco -style riff I surprised myself by remembering, and when I glanced back out at the crowd, those teeth were flashing like a lighthouse on meth behind two large, clapping hands.

As is often the case, one enthusiastic fan's applause was contagious, and that contagion repeated itself after each song in my 50-minute set, eliciting half-hearted ovations from an audience that otherwise couldn't have cared less. Applause, however, was applause, and regardless of its insincerity, I was transported back to those few years early in my career when I had a small but dedicated contingent of admirers. Which was why, once I was back in the Cabine D'essayage and heard the inevitable knock, I resisted the urge to yell GO AWAY and opened the door.

MY FIRST CLEAR VIEW of Heyoka Husereau D'Ailleboust nearly knocked me sober. For one thing, he was huge, and—probably due to an autonomic fright response—my senses sharpened and my bleary vision cleared. The smile was still there, but it now protruded from the lower half of a deeply weathered face the color and texture of ruddy sandstone carved by centuries of water erosion. His mountainous nose swept out and down like an undulating inverted ski slope and, in contrast to the smile, there was a notable downcast to his triangular eyes, the pupils of which resembled pools of liquid onyx. Taken as a whole, his countenance projected a combination of intelligence and humor, infused with a touch of melancholy.

I tried to shake off my initial shock and formulate some kind of greeting when, without preamble, he said, "Buy you a drink?"

It was clear that the tiny dressing closet offered no possibility of accommodating two people, so I followed him into the bar. We made our way through the sparse crowd and headed for the attached dining room, where he motioned toward an empty booth overseen by a large oil painting of the late Jacques Morel. I'd met Morel—a celebrated singer-songwriter often referred to as the French James Taylor—back in the eighties, when he was single handedly putting LeMusique on the map as one of France's premier musical destinations. In the years since then, the club had become known more for its cuisine than its musical offerings, and today the restaurant's three-star Michelin rating made it a favorite among English-speaking tourists. Which is why I happened to be among the few fading American stars hired to play for the concert bar's dwindling audiences.

"Jack," Heyoka said the moment we sat down. I thought he was referring to the painting until he glanced up at a waitress who seemed to have appeared out of thin air. "Single Barrel. Two glasses. Ice. Bring the bottle and leave it." As abrupt as his words were, he said them with that warm smile, and it was obvious the petite young server understood his truncated descriptions, because she turned on her heel and left. I was about to ask how he knew my preferred form of liver assault, when he said, "Firewater. The bane of many a red man like me. And, of course, of one Rix Vaughn as well. Wonder if it's that small percentage of Powhatan in your blood. You think?"

I considered mentioning that my folks had told me we were distantly related to Pocahontas, but I had no idea what tribe she belonged to. Besides, I had been essentially struck dumb by this strange encounter, and couldn't get my voice working.

He must have noticed my puzzled expression, because he chuckled. "Sorry. I guess you're a little confused. What say we start over?" He reached out a massive paw. "I'm Heyoka. Heyoka Husereau D'Ailleboust to be more precise. I'm pretty well known among a certain international cadre of physicists, though I'm sure you've never heard of me. In that sense we're a lot alike, except that I *have* heard of you. In fact, I'm probably one of your biggest fans."

"I, uh ..." I stammered, shaking his hand. "That's ... interesting." Thankfully, the waitress returned at that moment, placing a bottle of Jack between us, along with two large tumblers and an ice bucket. She proceeded to crack the bottle and drop ice cubes into our glasses with a set of tongs, but she stopped short of pouring. Instead, she stepped back and stood with her hands clasped in front of her, as if waiting for further instructions. By then I was in serious need of a drink, and had to resist the urge to grab the bottle.

"Is this okay?" Heyoka asked. "Or would you prefer a nipple?" His tone was one of intentional humor, not condescension, and I decided to reply in kind.

"What I'd really prefer is a funnel," I said. "But this will do." He gave a quick nod to the waitress—whose nametag, I noticed, read "Aurélie"—and she evaporated into the darkness while he poured us both a drink.

"To my favorite old folkie," he said, holding out his glass. I clinked it with mine and we both drank; him a sip, me a one-gulp drain.

"So," I said, reaching for the bottle, "how is it that you know so much about me? And what brings you to this aging bistro at the edge of European nowhere?"

"Long story." He took another small sip, then put the glass down and tapped on the rim with a gnarled finger. "I'd like to tell you all about it, but that will take some time. Speaking of time, since this is your last night, and you don't have any other engagements until the one at Le Barclay in Bordeaux three weeks from now, why don't you come stay at my place? I've got an extra room, and that would give us time to get to know each other."

I should have been shocked at his detailed knowledge of my schedule; however, by then I was past being surprised. Not only that, but I had a feeling I knew what this was all about. "Are you propositioning me?" I asked. "I'm not anti-gay, mind you, but I think you should know that I'm straight."

This time he laughed out loud, and when I didn't respond, he sucked in a breath and said, "Oh, man. I just realized how that must have sounded." He shook his head to clear away the last few giggles. "To be perfectly honest, I am propositioning you, but not in that way. I have no interest in sex, at least not with other men. I'm simply offering you a place to stay at no expense for the next few weeks. Room, board, conversation, and maybe a little music, if that's agreeable. I really am a fan, you know. Plus, I'd love to pick your brain about string theory."

I thought for a moment. Touring solo in Europe on a shoestring budget, with an agent who was close to cutting me loose, was a little hairy to say the least. So the prospect of three weeks without expenses was something I could hardly dismiss out of hand. Even if it meant spending that time in some hovel with a total stranger who was nutty enough to admit being a fan of someone as obscure as I'd become over the last couple of decades.

"String theory?" I said. "I've heard of it, but I'm no physicist, and I have no idea what it means.'"

"It means," he said, "are you still using GHS Phosphor Bronzes on your D28? What about the Hannabach Titanyls for your Ramirez? What's the trick to playing that weird counterpoint Travis-pick you use on ***City Strings***? Plus a few other questions I have. I play too, by the way. Though compared to you ... well, there is no comparison. As for physics, I want to talk a little about that as well, but I'm mostly interested in your music and your career."

Before I could think of a response, Aurélie materialized beside the table again. "Look," he said, "why don't you let me buy you dinner? That way you'll have time to consider my offer."

Thankful for the distraction, I nodded my agreement, whereupon he said to Aurélie, "Bring Mr. Vaughn a bloody filet, half a dozen seared scallops—from the sea, not the bay—a baked potato with butter, no sour cream, and some fresh asparagus. I'll have the usual. Oh, and bring us a bottomless basket of garlic bread." Aurélie glanced at me for approval, and when I tilted my head in acquiescence, she faded into the murky surroundings.

While we waited for the food, I again asked how he knew so much about me.

A trick of the light made his ebony eyes gleam as he looked across the table and said, "You will soon come to understand that I have an unusual talent for gleaning information directly from the ether." His voice lowered a notch, adding a sense of drama. "You see, I have this device called a computer, and it's connected to a sub-etheric information source called the Internet, wherein can be found a website called rvaughn.com, plus a Facebook fan page that contains a rather detailed profile of a singer-songwriter by the name of Rix Vaughn."

"Right," I said. I had forgotten about my website and Facebook page, neither of which interested me in the least. But I knew my agent employed a publicity service that kept them updated with my irregular schedule, which would explain how this oddball had known where to find me and where my next gig would be. However, the profile—also written by the publicist—was mostly bullshit hype and did not contain personal details such as my preference for Jack Daniels, bloody steak, and seared sea scallops. I was about to confront Heyoka with this fact when he continued.

"As for the rest of it, there's a little matter of your multiple run-ins with the law over the years, and the resulting news stories, which are also available on the Web for anyone who wishes to spend a little time searching. Plus, though you may not be aware of it, a few of your former, shall we say, groupies, have given interviews to various media outlets, detailing things like your favorite foods, your early heroin addiction, and your penchant for large quantities of a certain brand of Tennessee whiskey. You should Google yourself sometime. You'd be surprised how much is out there."

We bantered for a while, mostly about trivialities not available through the ubiquitous Google search engine, and by the time the food arrived I was convinced that this strange man really was a die-hard fan of mine.

I had not been able to afford the food at LeMusique, contenting myself with less expensive fare at a few local cafes in Lyon's market district. There was nothing to complain about in that pedestrian cuisine, however, it couldn't hold a candle to what we were served by Aurélie. At the peak of my career, I'd been much more popular in Europe than in the US, and I'd eaten at some of the most revered culinary destinations on that continent. Those now-distant memories came back to me as I carved into fork-tender, cannibal-rare steak, boat-fresh scallops seared golden brown, a potato dripping with sweet clarified butter, and straw-thin asparagus steamed to perfection. "The usual" for Heyoka, was a bowl of shelled mussels in white wine sauce over a bed of fluffy saffron rice, the aroma of which almost made me wish I'd opted for his choice.

Between bites, I asked him to tell me something about himself, and when he hesitated I reminded him that I, too, had a computer that connected to the Internet. "Well," he said, "If you want the whole story, you'll have to take me up on my offer. But ... okay, a short version...

"I was born on the Yankton Sioux Reservation in South Dakota and grew up in abject poverty. Early on, however, I had ... let's call it a revelation. Anyway, I realized I had a talent for mathematics, and by the time I reached middle school I had bypassed all my peers and was applying for admission to several prestigious universities. At age 16, I was offered a full scholarship to Ecole Polytechnique Fédérale de Lausanne, with all travel and living expenses paid. That's not too far from here, by the way. Just north of Lake Geneva in Switzerland. After earning a doctorate in quantum mechanics, I returned to the states to accept a position at MIT as an adjunct professor of theoretical mathematics, where I began developing several unorthodox theories in particle physics—theories that baffled my peers and eventually earned me the nickname "Hey Joker." Unbeknownst to my detractors, this was a fairly accurate description of the Lakota Sioux meaning of Heyoka."

"Okay," I said when he didn't continue. "I give up. What does it mean?"

"Heyoka?" he said. "Heyoka is a spirit in Lakota Sioux mythology reputed to be a trickster. Historians unfamiliar with Native American spiritual beliefs often describe him as being evil or nefarious, but he's really only a harmless clown who makes those he inhabits do things backward or unconventionally. The name was handed down to me from my ancestors seven generations removed, and it actually fits me quite well."

"So, you're a tricky, unconventional, physicist clown?"

"Many of my fellow physicists would say so," he said, scraping up the last of his rice with a slice of garlic bread. "However, if you want to know the specific reasons why, you're going to have to spend some time with me at my home."

Practicality and common sense were now joined by curiosity, and I made a decision to accept his hospitality. I might have been stupid to take up with a complete stranger on a moment's notice, but given my current situation I didn't have a hell of a lot to lose.

Our meal was capped off by an excellent Crème Brûlée, served in individual ramekins and caramelized at the table with a miniature propane torch expertly wielded by Aurélie. After Heyoka signed for what had to be a substantial bill, my worries about having to sleep in a hovel were somewhat allayed. However, when we reached the parking lot and a valet drove up in a scruffy looking, elderly Citroen, I began to wonder what I'd let myself in for. I had taken a step toward the curb when a young oriental fellow brushed past us and took possession of the odd little car. The next vehicle in line was of a make I didn't recognize, though I was reminded of a black Maserati I'd seen at an auto show years before.

"I took the liberty of having your equipment sent on ahead," Heyoka said as the car slowed to a stop in front of us. "If anything is missing, we can pick it up tomorrow."

I thought about commenting on his presumptuousness, but I couldn't come up with a plausible reason to object, so I merely stood and watched while the doors of the low-slung sedan slid out and back to reveal an elegant interior of beige leather. After we were inside, the doors slipped back into place without a sound, and I sank into a seat that came alive, shaping itself to my body. Seat restraints of a semi-rigid, yet comfortably resilient, material emerged from behind and above, settling against me until I felt as if I had merged organically with the car.

We negotiated the narrow, lamp-lit streets of Old-Town Lyon, careful to avoid the few late-night pedestrians that straggled over damp cobblestones. A few minutes later we approached the Peripherique at the edge of town, and it was only then, when the car accelerated up the entrance ramp, that I realized there was no sound of an engine.

"What is this thing," I asked, as we merged with the light traffic on the perimeter highway.

"Thing?" he said. "Oh, you mean the car. It's a little something I came up with myself. Runs on a small, closed-cycle nuclear fuel cell. Daimler made the body for me, based on a modified Maserati design, and the drive train—all except for the power supply—was assembled by a friend of mine who used to work for BMW." He passed his hand over something in the sunken dashboard, and I heard the strains of my own song, ***This Poor Boy's Still a Fool,*** emanating from a surround-sound system with reproduction of such pristine clarity it was like listening to myself play live. I was so absorbed by the realistic quality of the music, it didn't occur to me right away that the song had never been released and wasn't on any of my early albums or later CDs. I started to say something about this, but he preempted me.

"It's a shame this one was never released," he said. "It's a nice little song, and I love the line, 'frozen paper words won't make tomorrow yesterday.'"

"Thank you," I said. "But I'd like to know where you got that recording? The song never appeared on any of my albums, and I'm almost positive I have the only copy of the master tape. Plus, this is obviously digital, and even though I did eventually digitize it, it's not available as an MP3 and wasn't included on any of my later CDs."

"Right," he said. "And what would you say if I told you I had a copy of ***Sunday Morning Sentinel*** as well?

"I'd say you were full of shit if I didn't already know there was something weird going on here." ***Poor Boy*** had been written to serve as the B side of ***Sunday Morning Sentinel,*** a song of tremendous promise that was never released due to one of the stupidest decisions I'd ever made in my life. I was about to ask how much more he knew when I noticed we were approaching the exit for my hotel. Before I could tell him to get in the right lane, he whipped around a long line of traffic and pulled onto the off ramp.

"The Hotel Orientale, right?" he said, as we turned a corner and entered the parking lot of my humble living quarters. To a foreigner, 'Hotel Orientale' might have sounded a little exotic, but in English the name was simply "Eastern Hotel," Lyon's version of a Best Western. Not terrible digs, but nothing to write home about, even if I'd had a home to write to.

Heyoka waited in the car while I went up to the room and gathered my few belongings. Over the years, my once-extensive collection of travel accessories had, of necessity, dwindled to the bare essentials, so all I had to retrieve was my suitcase, toiletries, a hanging clothes bag, and couple of bottles of Jack. I took a moment to refill my hip flask, then returned to the car and jammed my meager possessions into its small trunk. I was walking toward the office to settle up and check out, when Heyoka rolled down the window and said, "Don't worry about that. It's taken care of." He offered no further explanation as I climbed back into the car, and I decided not to ask any questions until we were back on the highway.

We soon turned onto A42 and headed northeast toward a full moon that bathed the rolling countryside in a milky satin mist. I waited until the traffic thinned and we were moving along at a steady clip, before raising my voice in order to be heard over the music. "So," I yelled, "are you going to explain all this, or what?"

The sound system, apparently reacting to my attempt at conversation, lowered in volume until it was no louder than elevator Muzak. "Of course," he said in the relative quiet. "The explanation, however, is complicated and will require some demonstrations I can only provide after we get to my place."

"And where, exactly, is your place?"

"In the foothills outside Saint-Genis-Pouilly, not far from Geneva. We should be there shortly."

The way I calculated it, Geneva was over ninety miles from Lyon, and we'd barely left the outskirts of town. Which meant that 'shortly' would be over an hour unless we were traveling unusually fast. I hadn't paid much attention to our immediate surroundings, and when I glanced out the side window into the shimmering yellow haze, I noticed things were moving by in a blur.

"How fast are we going, anyway?" I asked.

"Let's see," he said, looking straight ahead at a greenish iridescence that hovered in the air near the windshield. "Looks like about 180 kilometers an hour. So, maybe twenty-five minutes?"

I couldn't think of anything more to say, so I took a swig from my flask and relaxed into the embrace of the form-fitting seat as the sound of my own music rose again, filling the car like a live concert.

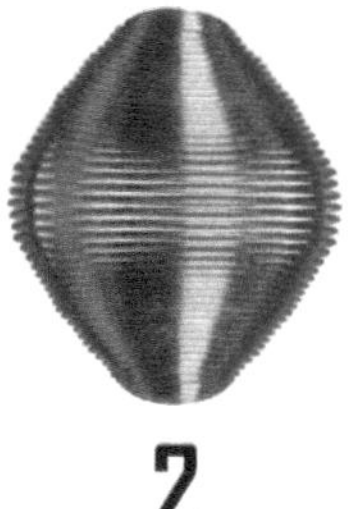

2

The Villa D'Ailleboust

Given the fancy car and expensive meal, I wasn't surprised to find that Heyoka's "place" turned out to be far from a hovel. However, by the time we wound our way up through several narrow passes in the heavily wooded hills, I had begun to wonder if we weren't headed for a primitive retreat with teepees for sleeping quarters. The few glimpses I caught of the moon through the canopy of tall conifers made it appear to grow larger with each mile traveled. And when we broke through the tree cover into a small ravine, the once silver-dollar-sized satellite had transformed into a pearlescent beach ball, illuminating everything from the glistening waters of a serpentine river to the jagged cliffs that rose on either side of the canyon.

The now-unpaved road was smooth for one that cut through such wild terrain; and, like a faithful old workhorse, the car seemed to follow it instinctively, with only an occasional nudge on the steering wheel from its unconcerned driver. By the time I had drained the last few drops from my flask, I could still see no signs of a house, or even a teepee. I was thinking about asking the typical kid's question, "Are we there yet," when we turned toward what appeared to be a collision course with the trunk of a fir tree. I held my breath as we swerved around it and headed up a steep, twisted driveway surrounded by more dense forest.

The Villa D'Ailleboust was announced by a carved wooden sign, under which stretched a gated entrance reminiscent of one that might have guarded a cattle ranch in the western US. The gate swung open to reveal an almost vertical climb that led to a sprawling, multi-level log structure perched atop a promontory studded with boulders and stunted scrub pine. Awash in the moon's soft yellow glow, the complex looked like something Disney might have designed to house a nostalgic reenactment of Buffalo Bill's Wild West Show.

We cruised to a stop at the glass-fronted entrance, and two strapping young men appeared to unload the trunk. Heyoka greeted each of these valets like friends, rather than servants, introducing them to me with brief descriptions and names I would not remember. A third—an oriental gentleman I recognized as the Citroen driver from back at the club—escorted us up a split-log stairway, into an enormous room with thirty-foot-high vaulted ceilings of knotty pine supported by thick beams of cedar. A majestic elk-horn chandelier hung from the apex, shedding subdued light on an assortment of rustic wooden furniture upholstered in woven fabric of typical Native American design. Across the back of the room, windows stretched from floor to ceiling, framing a moonlit silhouette of the distant Jura Mountains.

Despite the villa's backwoods appearance, it was clear that Heyoka had spared no expense in recreating an atmosphere both comfortable and decoratively familiar. And, had I not known where we were, I could easily have mistaken those mountains for the Colorado Rockies.

Being early September, the weather wasn't cold yet, but here in the higher elevations it was chilly at night, which explained the roaring fire that filled a random-stone fireplace. I was staring out at the magnificent mountain vista when Heyoka came up beside me and laid a hand on my back. "Whaddya think?" he said. "Sorta reminds me of home. Not you, though, I guess. What with that sand in your shoes and sunshine in your bones."

Home for me had always been the two-dimensional landscape of Florida, although I had long ago tired of sandy beaches and boring, flat terrain. I'd fallen in love with mountains while touring the western US and vacationing in the Carolinas; and why I always ended up back in the Sunshine State remained a mystery. At one point my pigeon-like proclivity had to do with friends and family, however, my folks were long dead and I'd lost touch with most of my childhood friends. For more than twenty years, I'd made the road my home, hopping from hotel to hotel, with an occasional longer stay in a rented apartment when the gigs dried up. Royalties from my early albums and later CD compilations provided a meager, but fairly steady income, and on a few rare occasions a new artist would cover one of my songs on an MP3, adding a little extra bread to my dwindling cash flow. I'd even had one of my tunes included in a couple of hip-hop remixes.

I let Heyoka steer me away from the windows to a couch in front of the fireplace, where I was presented with a tall glass of whiskey by my new oriental friend, whom Heyoka addressed as Fred. This was one name I decided I should commit to memory, if only for the fact that he was the provider of my favorite beverage. I took a long drink and sank back into the cushions, breathing in the aroma of cedar and other earthy smells that permeated the atmosphere. I still had many questions, but before I could sort out my thoughts, Heyoka spoke up.

"I really do appreciate your agreeing to spend some time with me," he said, walking to the fireplace to stab at the logs with a poker. "And despite what I suspect you have interpreted as a mysterious reluctance on my part to explain my reasons for the invitation, I can assure you there's nothing sinister about them. I do have somewhat of an ulterior motive, though it's nothing that need concern you. It's just that it's a little too complicated for a decent explanation tonight. In fact, like I said, it's going to take a few demonstrations and a good bit of convincing for you to even begin to understand."

The agitated fire flared up, releasing a wave of warmth that rolled over my skin like invisible fog. When Heyoka was satisfied with the adjustment of the logs, he stepped away from the fireplace and reached to retrieve something from a nearby shelf. "Since it's already pretty late," he said, "about all I can manage tonight is a brief preview." He sat down on an identical couch opposite me and slid the thing across the coffee table between us. I was about to set my glass down, when Fred approached and whisked it from my hand, I hoped in order to refill it. "Go ahead," Heyoka said when I looked at the rectangular object. "It's something I think you will find fascinating."

The flat, black object looked like an oversized iPad, though there were no visible controls. Its surface felt cold like steel when I picked it up, but it weighed almost nothing. I looked at Heyoka for a clue as to what I should do next, but all he did was smile. And when I glanced down at the device again, I was staring at a 3D image that covered the surface from edge to edge. It wasn't a hologram because it didn't protrude above the surface, however, the image had such depth and color saturation, it seemed as if I were looking through a window at something happening in real time.

The scene was familiar, though I couldn't quite place the location: a pavilion or bandstand, with a crowd of thousands sitting on green benches in front of it. And then, while I was wracking my brain to remember, the camera, or whatever was providing the view, started to zoom in. The sensation was one of traveling forward into the scene, coming closer and closer to the bandstand until I could make out an orchestra surrounded by dozens of American flags. In front, center stage, stood a small boy, dressed in a red-white-and-blue Uncle-Sam costume, his mouth open, obviously frozen in mid-note of a song.

"Fourth of July, 1951," said Heyoka. "Little Richard Voniossi makes his first major personal appearance in front of seven thousand cheering patriots at Williams Park in St. Petersburg, Florida."

I was dumbstruck. Not only was this an event I had long forgotten, but as it came back to me, I remembered that the only photos I'd ever seen of it were black-and-white shots taken by local newspapers. Tears welled up in my eyes as I recalled that day and the incredible lady who convinced me I could wow the huge crowd with my powerful soprano voice: Mrs. Henderson—Carol—the music teacher who had given me my first taste of applause. Before then, I had only performed as a soloist with the youth choir. And back in those days, applause in church was strictly forbidden. From the day of that performance forward, my desire for applause became an addiction.

I looked at Heyoka, whose beaming smile seemed to light up the room. And when I looked back down, the picture had disappeared, replaced by another; this one of me and Carol sitting together at the piano, her pointing at the sheet music, and me staring at the ceiling while I played. The view then shifted, panning around the 3D image until I could see the exasperated look on Carol's face.

"She never could get you to look at the music," Heyoka said. "You were too clever for that. Savant-like, almost."

"I know," I whispered, still shell-shocked by the intimate realism of the image. I'd always had an incredible ear. Before alcohol and drugs began to interfere with my musical abilities, I could memorize any song almost instantly. Once I'd tediously worked out a tune from the sheet music, I refused to look at it again, and that drove Mrs. Henderson crazy because she knew it would keep me from learning to sight read.

Unfortunately, that talent applied only to remembering tunes and lyrics; when it came to the rote memorization required to make even average grades in school, I was a disaster.

Absorbed by bittersweet memories, I had momentarily forgotten the impossibility of the images that sparked them, and when I came back to the present, the magic contraption fell from my hands and landed on the floor between my feet.

"Don't worry," said Heyoka. "You couldn't break it if you ran over it with a tank."

Just then, Fred arrived with my glass, once again filled to the brim. I took it in a shaking hand and drained it. "Wha..." I gasped as the warmth of the whiskey burned its way down my throat. "What the hell is going on here? Where did you get these ... these, whatever they are?"

"All in good time, my friend. All in good time. I hate to keep saying it, but the explanation is complicated and will require other demonstrations that can only happen in certain special places under certain special conditions. For now, let's just say there's more where that came from. Much more."

"More what?" I shouted, my anger overcoming my sense of awe.

"More memories, Rix. A lifetime of them if you choose. And you must understand that it is your choice. If you don't wish to see them, to relive those moments in your past, then all you have to do is say so." He walked over to retrieve the now-blank screen from the floor. "Tell you what, you're probably whipped. So why don't we get some sleep and start again in the morning when we're both a little more lucid?"

The suggestion of sleep brought on an involuntary yawn, and I realized he was right about my being whipped. In fact, I was nearly dead drunk. However, I wasn't about to give up yet. "Look," I said, "you can't leave me hanging like this. I may be exhausted, but I won't be able to sleep unless I know what's going on. So I'd appreciate an explanation. Even if it has to be an abbreviated one, I at least need some inkling of what I've let myself in for here."

"An inkling ..." he said, turning to face me with his neon smile. "I suppose I could offer something like that tonight."

When he didn't continue I said, "I'm listening."

"You understand that I'm not going to go into any details until tomorrow?"

I nodded.

"Okay, let me think." He paused, glancing up at the rafters. "How about if I pose a question? It's a question you'll need to answer sooner or later anyway, so maybe it's best if you hear it now. That way you can sleep on it. If you consider carefully, the question will reveal the essence of what I have in mind, but I can't elaborate until tomorrow. Will that work for you?"

With what was left of my abused neurons once again drowning in a bath of ethyl alcohol, there was little chance I could comprehend any kind of complicated explanation, so I figured it was best to accept his compromise. Besides, it didn't look like I had much choice in the matter. I tried to get my brain to communicate with my mouth, but the connection was so weak, all I could manage was a grunt and a shrug.

Heyoka walked back to the couch and sat down, placing the viewer in front of him on the table. "Have you ever wished you could live your life over again?" he asked. "Or, to put it more succinctly: if you were offered the chance to go back to some point in your past and become your younger self, while still retaining all your accumulated wisdom and memories, would you choose to do so? And if you did, what point would you go back to, and what, if anything, would you change?"

I opened my mouth, but he held up a hand to stop me. "Fred," he said to the oriental, who had remained in the shadows near a doorway. "Show Mr. Vaughn to his room. Oh, and along the way, show him where the kitchen is, in case he finds himself in need of a snack before morning." Then, turning to me, he added, "There's a small bar in your room, should you want a nightcap, or perhaps an Alka-Seltzer. I'll see you whenever you choose to rise tomorrow."

I hadn't intended to ask any questions. In fact, I had no idea why I'd opened my mouth, except maybe to laugh at this ridiculous old coot and his nutty questions. Still, as I followed Fred to the restaurant-sized kitchen, then on down a long hall to my equally-impressive room, I couldn't stop my brain from spinning. And it wasn't only because of the booze.

After pacing for a while, I sat down on the massive feather bed, above which hung a stuffed bobcat preparing to pounce from a tree limb. The rough-hewn bedframe squeaked as I lay back and looked up at the sleek animal, feeling intimidated by the imaginary threat. Outside the tall windows, the mountain scene had faded into a fuzzy charcoal rendering in the waning moonlight. And with the dark closing in around me, I realized for the first time that I was trapped in this isolated complex. I reached into my pocket and pulled out my iPhone, not at all surprised to find there were no bars. So, not only was I several miles from nowhere with no transportation save what my host could provide, I also had no way to communicate with the outside world. Should I wish to leave, it would be Heyoka's choice to provide me with the means to do so.

Or not.

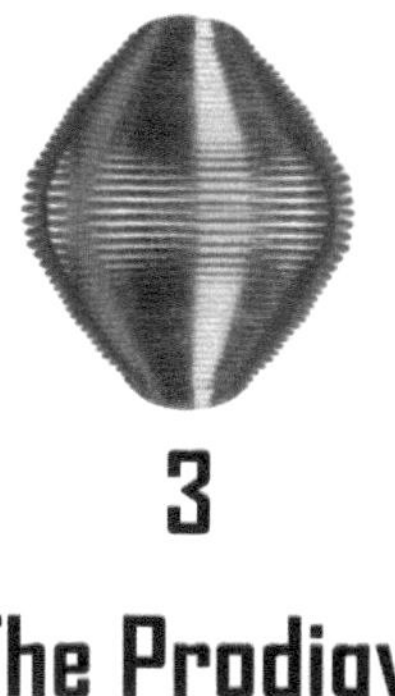

3
The Prodigy

There was a time when I could zoom down the aisles of a gigantic neural superstore, select from millions of memory fragments, and instantly reassemble almost any episode in my past. Unfortunately, I'd done most of my shopping over the years in the pharmacy and liquor departments of that superstore, and by the time I woke up in Heyoka's guestroom I was lucky if I could remember how I got there, let alone the details of my early life. Nowadays, gaining even minimal access to those memories required a sensory stimulus: an odor, a sound, or, as in the case of his little demonstration the night before, a picture.

I hadn't thought about Mrs. Henderson in decades, and was amazed at how quickly my memories of her came back when I saw the incredibly lifelike images on that magical viewer. The experience was like looking through a window into the past; as if I were a disembodied spirit with total, but secret access to those intimate moments. And, apparently, the pictures had initiated an ongoing recall process, because when I began to emerge from the alcoholic catatonia of the night before into that nebulous dreamland between sleep and wakefulness, I once again found myself traveling back—this time to the day I met the woman who would become my musical mentor.

THE MOTIVATION FOR MY first encounter with Carol Henderson was food. Mush to be exact. I had just turned four, and was playing in our side yard when the aroma of something frying caught my attention. This drew me to the outside staircase that led to the second-floor apartment Carol rented from us, and before Mom could stop me, I climbed the stairs and peered through her screen door. When Carol saw me, she opened the door and, waving at Mom to indicate it was okay, invited me in. I followed her to the kitchen and stood waiting while she went to the stove.

"You like mush?" she asked, flipping something in a big iron skillet.

I didn't care for the sound of that word, figuring it must be something like the icky cream of wheat Mom used to force me to eat. But when Carol held the frying pan down for me to see, there was nothing mushy about what was in it. Instead, sizzling alongside several strips of bacon, were three thick yellow patties, fried light brown. When she asked if I wanted to try one, I decided to take a chance. She served it with butter, warm maple syrup, and crisp bacon, and the moment I tasted that sweet, cornmeal pancake, my friendship with Carol Henderson was sealed. After I finished, she wiped my face with a damp towel and led me into her living room where I found myself in a wonderland of musical instruments. Other than an occasional song on the radio and the distant sound of the choir I could hear from the nursery at church, I'd never had much exposure to music. So, at first, I had no idea what the items in that musical menagerie were.

Carol must have seen the curiosity in my eyes, because she took me by the hand and led me around the room, introducing me to each instrument. The assortment included an upright piano, a small organ, a cello, a saxophone, and a bright golden trumpet that lay alongside two violins on a table. And when she reached down to tap out a simple tune on the piano, my life was changed forever. By the time Mom came up to see what was going on, I had learned to play Happy Birthday, Jingle Bells, and a few other one-finger tunes, while Carol accompanied me on the lower keys.

It wasn't long before she had me singing along with the music, and after we serenaded Mom with a couple of vocal duets, the two of them retired to the breakfast room for coffee, leaving me to fiddle around on the piano. They talked for a long time, and when we left to go back downstairs, Mom asked if I would like to visit with Carol again. Of course I said yes, and for the next several days, I spent at least three hours every afternoon in the upstairs apartment. I had soon memorized dozens of songs, plus the names of all the notes. And, despite my small fingers, I even learned to use my left hand a little.

At the end of a week, Carol sat me down at the breakfast table and got real serious. "Richard," she said, "this is important, so I want you to listen to me carefully." I took a bite of the banana she'd peeled for me, and waited. "You have a special gift," she continued. "I know you won't understand this just yet, but it's called perfect pitch. What that means is you can do something only a very few others can, maybe one in ten thousand. That's a big number, so … let me see … Has your dad ever taken you to a baseball game at Al Lang Field?"

"Uh-huh," I mumbled through a mouthful of banana.

"Okay, imagine the stands there are full, not one empty seat."

I closed my eyes and tried to picture it. "That would be a lot of people," I said.

"Right. And you know what? Al Lang only holds about seven thousand. So let's say we added some onto that, about another half as many as the full stands would hold. You know what a half is?" I nodded. "Great. So with the full stands and another half of the full stands, that would be about ten thousand people. And if you were there, you would be the only one in the crowd who had perfect pitch."

"What's perfect pitch?" I asked.

"I'll show you," she said, getting up. I started to follow her into the living room, but she shook her head. "No, I want you to stay here and listen."

Confused, I sat back down, and a few seconds later I heard her play a note on the piano. "Can you tell me what that note is," she said loud enough for me to hear from the other room.

"B-flat," I said.

"Right. How about this one?"

"D."

"Good. Good. Now let's try a chord. Can you tell me all the notes in this chord?"

"C, E, and G."

"Wonderful," she cried. "Wonderful, Richard." She came back and sat down at the table. "That's what perfect pitch is. Being able to tell what the notes are without looking."

"But, can't everybody do that?" I asked. "It seems so easy. Can't you do it?"

"Nope. I'd give my eyeteeth if I could, but I wasn't born with that ability. Like I said, only about one in ten thousand people have perfect pitch, and half of them probably don't even know it because they may never have learned anything about music. What makes your talent even better is that you have an amazing musical memory. That is, you only need to hear a song once in order to remember it. It's what they call an ear for music, and when you add that to your perfect pitch, you'd probably be one in a million."

"How much is a million?"

She thought for a moment, then said, "How high can you count?"

"To a hundred. Mom says I could count to a thousand just by adding one hundred to each number and then two hundred and three hundred, until I got to nine-hundred-and-ninety-nine, then the next number would be one thousand. But that would take too long."

"Okay, think about how long it takes just to count to one hundred. I once read that if you wanted to count to a million, it would take twenty -three days, counting all day and all night without stopping."

"Wow! That's a lot."

"It sure is," she said. "So you see, being one in a million is really special. But that's not all. As an extra bonus, God gave you one more thing."

"Oh, yeah? What?

"He gave you a beautiful singing voice. And when you add all those things together, perfect pitch, musical memory, and a beautiful voice ... well, it would be hard to say how many people have that kind of talent, but certainly not many. All I know is that it means God gave you a wonderful gift, something you should develop and share with others. Would you like to do that?"

"I guess. You mean I should teach people how to do what I do?"

"No," she said. "Unfortunately, you can't. It's not something you can teach, you have to be born with it. What I mean is you need to learn as much as you can about music, and then play and sing for other people."

"Like the people on the radio or in the choir at church?"

"Exactly. Do you think you'd like to do that?"

"I dunno. Sounds kind of scary, being in front of lots of people."

"Well, it can be at first, but you'll get used to it. And once you do, you're going to find that the people you perform for will be really happy because you did. And they're going to show you that happiness in ways that will make you very happy as well. Do you know what applause is?"

"You mean when people clap their hands? I've heard that on the radio when one of the bands finishes a song."

"How about at the baseball game, when someone hits a home run? You know how the people cheer and clap to show how happy they are?"

"Sure. I do it too. It's fun."

"What do you think it would feel like if you were that guy who hit the home run? If you were the one who made all those people happy?"

"Good, I guess." I was letting my mind wander, seeing myself running around the bases while all the people cheered and clapped for me. I liked the feeling, but I was really more interested in learning about music than hearing the applause. I felt that way right up until the day, three years later, when I stood in front of seven thousand cheering fans at William's Park on Independence Day.

THE THUNDEROUS APPLAUSE FADED into a constant thrum of pain, as the memories dimmed and I succumbed to the waking consequences of a dehydrated brain. This was a familiar condition for me, ever since I'd sworn off drugs and replaced them with a daily quart or so of whiskey. Thank God Heyoka had fed me, or I probably would not have been ambulatory. I stumbled to the small bar and drank four tall glasses of water, adding the thoughtfully provided Alka Seltzer to the last. Another half hour on the bed, and I was ready for something more substantial. Not food yet, but maybe a Bloody Mary? I found the makings at the bar and was working on my second, when a knock on the door startled me. But it was only Fred, proffering a breakfast tray. He placed the tray on a folding table, then stood back, waiting. I lifted each of the three domed covers one-by-one, replacing them over a steaming western omelet, three strips of crisp bacon, and a bowl of cheese grits—my preferred hangover repast.

When I nodded my approval, he said, "Heyoka would like to see you in the music room, whenever you feel up to it. There is no need to hurry, but because this complex can be a bit confusing, here is a map." He handed me a two-page diagram. I glanced at it, flipped to the second page, then looked up at him. "Those are the two levels, although there are actually three. The third—the lab—would be off to the right of the second page. It is below, mostly underground, but you needn't worry about that. Heyoka will take you there when the time comes. The music room, as you can see, is on the second level, directly above the Great Room you were in last night. The elevator is down the hall to your left. Or, if you prefer, there are stairs at the end of the hall. Again, please understand that there is no rush, so do take your time. You'll find towels and other things in the bathroom, and if you need anything else, we'll do our best to provide it for you."

After Fred left, I managed to eat most of the breakfast without throwing up. Then, after a short nap, I took a shower, shaved, and brushed my teeth. When I emerged from the bathroom, except for a little residual sandpaper at the back of my tongue, I felt almost human again. I dressed in jeans and an ancient Grateful Dead t-shirt, and headed out the door in search of the elevator.

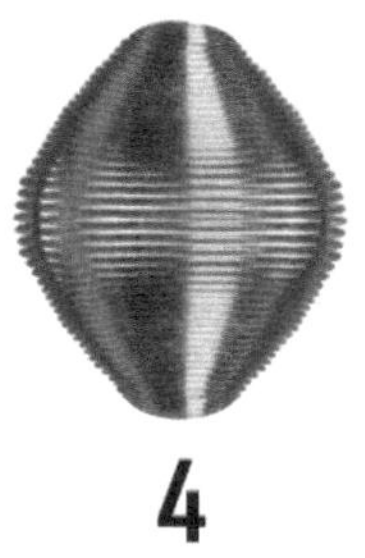

4
The Fiasco

The music room, like the Great Room downstairs, was framed on two sides by large windows that looked out on a crisp, green canopy of towering conifers. Paneled in redwood with beams of pecky cypress crisscrossing the high ceiling, it had the feel of a huge tree house suspended among the swaying limbs. When combined with my still-fragile condition, the sensation of movement led to a mild attack of vertigo. I reached to steady myself on what turned out to be a grand piano, then tore my eyes away from the windows to survey the room's contents.

What I saw reminded me of Carol's living room, though a much larger and more elaborate version. Scattered around the black-lacquered Steinway were several guitars, a banjo, a couple of mandolins, and even a sitar. A glass-fronted cabinet containing what appeared to be an antique baroque guitar hung on one non-windowed wall. A dozen or so other stringed instruments were displayed on either side of the cabinet, among which I recognized a balalaika, a bouzouki, and a Japanese shamisen. There were violins as well, and below all of them stood a beautifully inlaid harpsichord, its open lid painted with a scene of a naked woman playing a viola da gamba.

Still dizzy, I turned toward the other wall, which was covered with an array of speaker cabinets surrounding a flat-screen monitor that looked to be at least eight feet wide. Underneath, on one side, stood a

Korg Kronos 88-key synthesizer, and on the other, a huge mixdown board covered with hundreds of faders, pots, compressors and equalizers. A computer terminal sat between these on a curved Plexiglas stand, with a high-backed, sculpted-leather swivel chair in front.

I'd been so focused on the room's contents, I hadn't thought to look for Heyoka, who surprised me when he spun around in the chair and flashed his magnetic smile. "Whaddya think?" he said, repeating his words from the night before. "I tried my best to blend the old with the new here."

"It's ... It's, incredible," I said, gaining my bearings and leaving the safety of the piano to wander over and stand in front of the harpsichord. I pointed at the slender, hourglass-shaped guitar in the glass cabinet. "That can't be a Torres."

"Oh yes it can," said Heyoka, his eyes glowing with pride. "First epoch, as I'm sure you can tell by the shape and the tuning scrolls. Bone nut and saddle, gut strings, no signature. I had it authenticated by curators at the Museo de la Música in Barcelona."

Antonio Torres was the Stradivari of classical guitar builders, and his earlier instruments were essentially priceless. "I thought guitars from his first epoch could only be found in museums," I said, slipping behind the harpsichord to get a closer look.

"For the most part that's true, although a very few do reside in private collections. Many of his early guitars were lost to time, discarded because they weren't labeled, or destroyed during the Spanish-Moroccan War. Or, in the case of this one, hidden, along with other treasures, behind a cellar wall, only to be later abandoned by a family fleeing for their lives."

"Abandoned," I murmured. "So, how did you happen to come by it?"

"Ah, that, my friend, is another one of those questions that will require a complex answer. We'll talk about it later. As for your obvious desire to have a closer look, sorry, but that case is vacuum-sealed and cannot be opened without endangering the instrument's preservation. Besides, you've studied diagrams of many Torres guitars, so no secrets remain to be found. And, unfortunately, playing it would be a disappointment. Unlike the early Cremona violins by Stradivari and Guarneri, which represent the pinnacle of violin construction and have improved with age, the acoustic guitar has continued to evolve from the days when Torres introduced the sound-board concept and fan bracing still used today. Shapes have changed, materials have improved, bracing designs have been refined. In fact, your Ramirez is probably a much better sounding instrument than those produced in the nineteenth century."

"Right," I said, still fascinated by being within arm's reach of an authentic first-epoch Torres. In the early days of my career, I'd become obsessed with all aspects of the guitar: its history, evolution, and design. I'd even worked for a while as an apprentice to the renowned luthier, Harley Day, at his shop in St. Petersburg, where I learned to construct and repair classical and Flamenco guitars. The only Torres I'd ever seen, other than in photos and diagrams, was at the Museo de la Música, while on tour in Spain, but I hadn't been allowed this close to that one.

Suddenly, I was jerked from my reverie by the sound of my own voice. And when I looked over at the giant monitor, I saw it had come to life with a video of me playing guitar in a studio. As with the pictures of the night before, I recognized the setting but couldn't place it right away. Until, that is, I realized the song was ***Sunday Morning Sentinel***. I must have made my way over to the sound wall, because the next thing I knew, Heyoka had relinquished the chair, and I was leaning back in it, immersed in the memory of that recording session and the events leading up to it.

IT WAS THE FALL of 1972. I'd just returned from honeymoon number two, during which I'd barely escaped death-by-sex with my second former-groupie-child-bride. I was sleeping soundly in the aftermath of another morning attack of Kama-Sutra-style intercourse, when my brain—apparently unconcerned about the body's need for rest—went into overdrive, spewing out the lyrics to a new song.

Up to that point, most of the songs I'd written had been met with yawns from record producers because they didn't adhere to the golden rule of pop hits, which said all songs must include a "hook line." This one, however, did have a hook line. Not only that, but the line ended with the word "Peace," a prospect on the mind of almost every young American at the time. The song told an emotional story about the anticipated withdrawal of American troops from Vietnam, and after I had the melody and chord arrangement worked out, I felt sure I was sitting on a blockbuster that could make me a superstar.

After putting together a demo tape with the help of a friend who owned a local recording studio, the two of us took off for Muscle Shoals, Alabama to try and peddle the song. Back then, Muscle Shoals was a recording mecca of pop music, and after a couple of strikeouts, we were granted an audience with a producer who handled some of the biggest acts in the business. Thus began the saga of one of the stupidest, most egocentric, and costly mistakes of my life.

Timing was important, since the song's impact would be lost once the troops were withdrawn—and the expanding anti-war protests were moving the country rapidly in that direction.

The producer liked the song, but there was a catch. It seemed he had a stable of vocalists to whom he owed his loyalty, and he wanted one of them to sing it. I, on the other hand, was convinced the song was strong enough to make a star out of an unknown artist like me. Reactions from two other producers were similarly positive, however, the same condition applied: they would agree to produce the record and distribute it without delay, but only if they could have their own artists sing it.

Still intent on finding a producer who would accept me as the singer, we ended up in Nashville, where a major country music publisher by the name of John Denny agreed to produce the song with me as the artist. The only caveat was that he would have to get commitments for airplay from at least seventy deejays across the country before releasing the record nationally. With dreams of superstardom blocking out all common sense, I accepted his offer on the spot, and spent the next couple of weeks collaborating with some of the best studio musicians in Nashville to produce the record.

Looking back, it was my ego that drove me to accept Denny's sketchy terms without considering the pitfalls. Had I taken time to think things through, I would have realized that a country music producer's network of deejays might not be too enthusiastic about airing a mainstream pop single by an unknown artist.

Though I would never know for sure what might have happened if I'd swallowed my pride and let someone else sing the song, at the very least I could have avoided several months of intense anxiety waiting for a phone call that never came.

AS THE VIDEO OF me working in the studio with Denny and the boys began to fade, I was startled to find myself in Heyoka's music room. The dreamlike trip back in time had seemed so real, so vivid, it was as if my memories had been digitized and turned into a virtual reality game, with me as the central character.

Heyoka waited a few moments while I gathered my senses, then said, "Sorry about that, Rix. I know those memories must be painful for you."

"No shit," I said, thinking about the months that had followed that studio session.

Of course, Denny had only garnered commitments from 30 or so DJs when, in March of 1973, the last American troops were withdrawn from Vietnam, and the war, at least so far as the US was concerned, came to an abrupt end. As a consequence, ***Sunday Morning Sentinel,*** my star-making commercial masterpiece, lost any chance of becoming even a minor hit and was never released.

In the aftermath of that colossal act of ego-maniacal stupidity, I took the master tape—which Denny graciously offered to send me—, packed it away in a box labeled "Dumb Shit," and went on a drug binge that would probably have killed the average non-user. I awoke from that psychedelic fantasyland several months later, lying in a pool of vomit on the floor of a leaky cabin in the north-Georgia woods.

"So," Heyoka said, once again jerking me from my memories. "How about some lunch?"

Still staring at the blank screen, I shook the cobwebs from my brain and muttered the words that had become my mantra over the past decade: "How about a drink?"

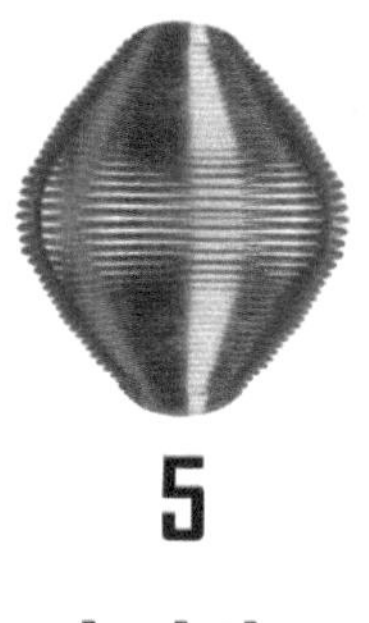

5
Probabilities

Standing in a corner of the music room was an odd-looking bass fiddle, larger than life, stringless, with highly polished maple sides and front. I hadn't noticed the oversized instrument until Heyoka pointed at it with a slender remote, and the ebony fingerboard separated down the center to reveal a well-stocked bar. "Help yourself," he said. "But I think you probably ought to eat something as well. How about a couple of Coney Island chili dogs?"

"Right," I said, wandering over to the fiddle-bar and pouring myself a drink. One of my favorite foods in the world was chili dogs from Coney Island in St. Pete. I'd been eating there since I was old enough to spin around on one of their chrome-rimmed soda-shop stools, and I'd tried for years without success to duplicate their recipe for chili sauce. "I suppose you're going to tell me you have the original chili-sauce recipe from Coney Island in St. Pete."

"I'll let you be the judge of that," he said, signaling toward a table and chairs that stood in the corner where the two windowed walls came together. As we took our seats, Fred came in wheeling a wooden cart, upon which rested a larger version of the silver domes that had kept my breakfast warm. When he lifted the dome, there, on familiar, heavy, stoneware plates, sat four steaming chili dogs.

"As you know," Heyoka said, "the perfect Coney Island chili dog not only requires a generous wooden spoonful of secret chili sauce, it must be constructed in the traditional manner: institutional hot dogs grilled crisp, soft steamed buns for the excess juice to seep into, onions haphazardly chopped, and good old cheap yellow mustard. Go ahead, see what you think."

I lifted one of the dogs, careful to support the soggy bun, sniffed it, took a bite, and was transported back to that ancient downtown greasy spoon, with its fly-encrusted screen doors, dusty old ceiling fans, and that little window into the parking lot through which "coloreds" were served back in the '50s. I finished off my two dogs before Heyoka was through with his first, and when he offered me the remaining one, I didn't hesitate to accept. After the traditional belch, I wiped my mouth with an authentic, flimsy paper napkin, and leaned back in the chair.

"Okay," I said, "That was great. But I think I've had enough of your magic tricks. It's time for the promised explanation."

"Yes," he said, "it is. However, you're still going to have to be patient with me. I need to set the stage with some things that are going to be difficult to believe. Tell me, what do you know about probabilities?"

"About what most folks know, I guess. I know that if I throw snake eyes ten times in a row, there's a good probability the next toss won't be snake eyes. I know that I'll probably drink about a quart of your Jack Daniels before I hit the sack tonight, and that I'll probably have a headache in the morning. I know there is a very slim probability that banjo over there is in tune, because I've never heard a banjo that *was* in tune. What else is there to know about probabilities?"

"Much, my friend. Did you know that this table's existence depends on probabilities, or as we physicists often say, potentiality? That even though it may feel solid to you, it is ninety-nine-point-ninety-nine -percent empty space, and the only reason you perceive it as a solid object is because of probabilities?"

"Yeah, I've seen all that gobbledygook on the science channels with Stephen Hawking and those dudes. Muons and bosons and quarks and flavors. Makes about as much sense to me as fairy dust and leprechauns. You physicist fellows seem to come up with a theory then go looking for something that will prove it. It's like you create it yourselves, tell it where and what to be, and when you look for it, there it is, right where you put it in your mathematical formulas. I know my understanding of this crap is about as intellectually perceptive as an armadillo's might be of a bus that's about to turn it into roadkill, but I can't help wondering if any of these things ever existed before you thought them up and went looking for them."

"You have no idea how close that is to the truth," he said. "How close it is to the true nature of matter or energy as seen through the prism of quantum mechanics. The fact is that subatomic particles, the basic building blocks of matter, *don't* exist, at least not with certainty in specific places. Until, that is, we go 'looking for them,' as you put it. In the meantime they only have a tendency or a probability to exist. What's really weird is that once we look for them and try to measure them, they show up in a definite place, but only for that infinitesimally small moment. Between measurements, we really don't know where they are or what path they took to get to the point in space-time where we observed them. To make things even more fairy-dust like, we don't know where they go afterward. They simply seem to disappear until the next measurement."

"I'm assuming you know how nutty that sounds." I said.

"Oh, sure. Even physicists can't explain it, at least in terms that would apply to what we think of as the real world, the macro world where we see and touch so-called solid objects. Enrico Fermi, a world renowned physicist and one of the fathers of the atomic bomb, was once reported to have said that anyone who claims to understand quantum mechanics doesn't know what he's talking about."

"So, you're telling me that this table is almost totally empty space, and you're basing that fact on something you can't pin down, don't understand, and couldn't explain if you did? By that reasoning I could tell you that I have God in my pocket, and expect you to believe it, even though I can't show Him to you, can't tell you how He got there, can't say where He came from or where He's going."

"That's a good analogy, but you're wrong about one thing. Even though I may not be able to totally understand it, I *can* explain the concepts mathematically. Unfortunately, such an explanation would make about as much sense to you as an opera sung in Swahili. The point is that these things *don't* make sense. Just as religious miracles, or paranormal claims, or Native American rain dances make no sense from a scientific standpoint. Still, some people—even some scientists—believe in such supernatural things, and many insist they have proof."

"Yeah," I said, "I used to be one of them. Then I grew up and joined the real world."

"Well, that might pose a problem. But for the moment—for the purposes of this explanation—I'd like to ask that you try to forget all your preconceived notions of reality. That shouldn't be too hard considering the fact that you've already experienced some things you think were magic tricks. What I'm going to try to get across is not only difficult to explain, it will no doubt strike you as the ramblings of a lunatic. But before you jump to any conclusions, I urge you to savor the taste of chili dogs in the back of your throat, or remember the participatory reality created by those pictures and the video I showed you. Can you do that for me—give me the benefit of the doubt for the next few minutes?"

I started to chuckle, but when I looked in his eyes I saw a kind of pleading. Nothing in his demeanor suggested an intention to deceive; on the contrary, what I sensed was a fervent desire for me to listen and try my best to understand. And he was right about the chili dogs and the uncanny realism of those moments he'd plucked from my past.

"Look," I said, "I'm a skeptic, okay? It's a skill I've honed over decades of being conned and fucked over like you wouldn't believe. But even though I tend to question everything, I still like to think of myself as an open-minded guy, so I won't dismiss what you have to say without giving it some careful thought. I may have to think of it as purely hypothetical, but you give me your best explanation, and I promise to listen with as few preconceived notions as I can manage."

"That's' all I could hope for," he said. Then he closed his eyes and remained silent for a long time. Finally, he blinked a couple of times, sighed deeply, and told me this story:

> I said earlier that I'd had a revelation when I was quite young, and by that I was referring to what we Lakota Sioux call a Hembleciya or vision quest. This is a big deal in our culture that normally happens in the early teen years as a rite of passage into adulthood. Mine, however, took place at age seven, much to the ridicule of my friends and elders. Fortunately, I had a medicine man who perceived in me a spiritual maturity others couldn't yet see. Anyway, like your first introduction to music, that experience changed my life dramatically, so I want to start off by telling you a little about what happened.

The quest began with some ritual purification and spiritual preparation ceremonies I won't go into. But the main part involved a solitary trip up into the hills, where I fasted for several days in order to seek communion with my ancestors. Of course, most modern scientists would attribute such a communion to hallucinations brought on by physical deprivation and mental fatigue. On the other hand, these same scientists believe in the more-or-less fantastical concepts of quantum mechanics we've been discussing. Where you draw the line between fantasy and reality—if there is a line—is up to you. All I can say is that what I learned during that quest helped build the foundation for my future as a physicist and answered many questions I would only later know enough to ask. Those questions had to do with the transitive nature of chronological time, the insubstantiality of matter and energy, and the holographic reality of the universe. And although I was a long way from developing the mathematical skills I would one day acquire, I did believe what I experienced was real.

During my vision I seemed to travel to another dimension, a mysterious vantage point from which I could see the complex interplay of subatomic particles depicted as a dance, not unlike the dances we Native Americans often perform to bring us closer to nature. The particles themselves appeared as vibrating or oscillating strings, creating the music for this dance. Parallel to this, I saw these strings represented in numbers, like a mathematical translation. And even though I had no idea what the equations meant, I realized that all this so-called spiritual stuff was actually rooted in a digital realm of complex mathematics. The overwhelming impression I came away with was of an infinite universe made up of random vibratory patterns that could be resolved into a kind of harmonic stasis through the simple act of observation. Just as the random vibrations of guitar strings can be manipulated through touch to create the harmonic beauty of a chord or melody.

Many years later, while I was studying some of the ancient philosophers' theories, I began to equate this orchestral perception with what Pythagoras called the music or harmony of the spheres. It was Pythagoras, by the way, who first discovered that the pitch of a musical note is directly related to the length of the string that produces it, and that the intervals between harmonious sound frequencies could be expressed as numerical ratios. This, to me, explained the numbers I was visualizing during my quest. It also led me to take up music and learn to play the guitar, but that's another story.

The great takeaway from that experience only became evident after many years of theoretical experimentation and spiritual meditation, during which I began to develop some extraordinary skills. I soon found that I could observe this realm of subatomic vibration in two different, yet equally serviceable ways: one spiritual, the other scientific. And it was then that the significance of my youthful vision quest began to come into focus. Unfortunately, by that time I was so steeped in the egocentric pursuit of fame as a theoretical mathematician, I was having a hard time seeing the forest for the trees, so to speak. And when I realized this narrow viewpoint was holding me back, I decided to return to the source of my enlightenment, even though I knew it would lead to ostracism from the academic world of my peers.

When I tried to explain to some of my more liberal colleagues that I wanted to work from both ends of the spectrum, to combine my spiritual insights with traditional mathematical formulae, I was written off as a nut case. But despite the criticism, I felt sure I was on to something—so sure that I resigned from my various positions and traveled back to South Dakota to solicit the advice of Billy Skywalker, my medicine man. There, I was embraced by my tribe like a prodigal son, and Billy, who was then in his nineties, recommended another vision quest. He organized a sweat and some other preparatory rituals, and soon I was on my way up into the hills, with only my pouch containing a few herbs and sacred relics, and a small skin of water.

As before, I fasted for days, hoping to receive guidance from my ancestors. I can't say how long I was up there, only that I was nearly dead from starvation and completely delirious before I had my second vision. Again, I was transported to that other dimension, only this time what I saw seemed different. Looking back, I don't think anything had changed, only my way of perceiving things, and I assumed this was because my intellect and spiritual awareness had matured. Whatever the reason, I saw the entirety of space-time as a dynamic landscape of oscillating strings and numbers, much like an orchestra performing a probability symphony, with the vibrating strings playing the melody and the numbers representing the time signature. The experience was staggering, both intellectually and spiritually, and I was so enthralled that I began to imagine myself as the maestro, directing and manipulating the rhythm of this cosmic orchestra. I tried my best to influence the music, but I was unsuccessful, and I realized I was going to need some assistance in the form of consultation with some of my colleagues in order to move to the next stage. After talking it over with Billy, I decided to return to the academic world and expand my knowledge in hopes of learning how to become a conductor rather than just a member of the audience.

The only problem with my plan was that, in order to accomplish this goal, I needed access to specific researchers at the cutting edge of quantum physics and theoretical chemistry. And since I was unemployed, with dwindling financial resources, I had to find a way to accumulate a certain amount of wealth in order to reposition myself geographically, socially, and academically. Up until that time I'd never given much thought to making money, but once I realized I was going to need a substantial amount of it, I put my acquired knowledge to work developing ideas that might have some practical application. It wasn't long before I was applying for patents and signing contracts with pharmaceutical companies and manufacturers in the aerospace industry.

The first of these patents was for a little thing I called an HHDR Photon Engine, a super-miniature, wave-based generator that today serves as the power source for some of the more advanced medical 3D imaging devices. This led to the development of a few other products and processes, and I eventually parlayed these into what most folks would probably think of as a small fortune.

If you're wondering why I chose to settle so far from my homeland, the reason is that I wanted to be in close proximity to the most advanced quantum physics facility in the world. You've probably never heard of it, but it's called CERN and it houses the LHC, or Large Hadron Collider, the largest supercollider ever built. This location, coupled with my willingness to provide several generous grants and endowments, gave me the opportunity to once again consult with the top researchers in quantum physics and biochemistry, and even to have occasional access to the LHC.

That was about ten years ago, and since then I've come up with a set of algorithms that combine experimental quantum mechanics with a synthesis of the chemicals that effect the brain during spiritual or transcendental experiences. By duplicating the brain chemistry that results from the complex interplay of physical and spiritual forces involved in these experiences, and combining it with a unique magnetic accelerative environment, I've been able to do some rather amazing things. You've seen a few simple, though somewhat limited examples, and if you found those demonstrations to be magical, let me assure you that, in the words of Randy Bachman, "You ain't seen nothin' yet!"

Anyway, I'm sure you're about to write all this off as so much supernatural horse manure, but before you do, consider that the greatest minds of today believe in things that cannot be seen, touched, understood, or validated in any way except through mathematical computation and a few rudimentary experiments in supercolliders. How much of a leap would it take, then, to accept that there is a way to observe and interact with these strange phenomena from a new vantage point? A vantage point that results from combining the illogical precepts of quantum mechanics with the seemingly preternatural power of spirituality as expressed through chemistry. Certainly this concept is no more fantastic than those the scientific community has already accepted as fact.

Think about it…

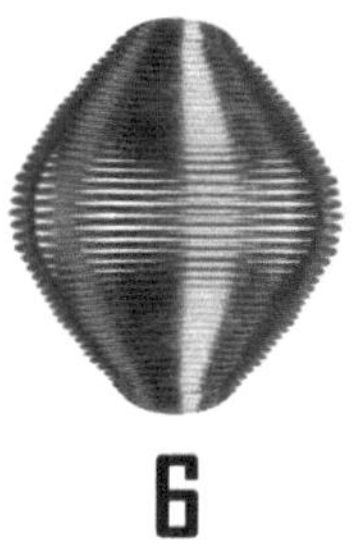

6
The Showdown

Heyoka's speech sobered me like the flashing blue lights of a cop car appearing in my rearview mirror. Wheels spun in my head as I tried to comprehend the convoluted explanation he'd offered. But clear comprehension was beyond my intellectual capacity, and I soon realized that accepting his story as the unvarnished truth would require a serious leap of faith. Problem was, I had abandoned my faith in the supernatural as a teenager, when my devoutly religious parents, going against all church doctrine, decided to get a divorce. Upon hearing this news, I had locked myself in my room for three days, praying to God with all my might, asking Him to keep them together. In a way, my self-imposed exile was like Heyoka's vision quest, except that it did not provide the desired results.

The story Heyoka told was compelling, mainly because I had personally experienced some rather astonishing evidence of his claimed abilities. I could easily attribute this to the random musings of a drunken mind. But as heavy a drinker as I'd become, I'd never hallucinated on alcohol the way I had on LSD, nor had I ever blacked out or lost track of time. My memory had become fuzzy and I tended to forget things I should remember, but that fact only made those trips back in time seem more amazing. Finally, I decided to admit my confusion.

"You're going to have to slow down," I said, retreating to the fiddle bar, pouring myself a drink, downing it, then pouring another and returning to the table. "I really do want to give you the benefit of the doubt and believe what you say, but a lot of it is beyond me. So why don't you skip the scientific jargon and explain what you mean in plain English? And while you're at it, I'd like to know why you're telling me these things, why you're giving me these demonstrations."

"Okay," he said, "I'll give it my best shot. The explanation has to do with my ability to observe the past from a position outside space-time. All the complicated stuff about string theory and music of the spheres is irrelevant, other than to explain that I'm able to view the universe from a unique perspective. More important is the fact that I can move about in that outside realm at will, poking my head in where and when I want, to observe and, if I choose, record, any event I wish."

I started to say something, but he held up a hand. "Please let me finish," he said. "The second stage of this ability, which I have yet to fully demonstrate to you, lies in the fact that I can now share it. I've given you a glimpse with those photos and the video, but I didn't want to blow your mind all at once by introducing you to the full experience, at least not until we talked and you were prepared both mentally and emotionally to handle it.

"The third stage—which is still speculative at this point—would be actual manipulation of the probabilities associated with your past life. That is, to send you—or someone else if need be—back in time to reenter your own existence at an earlier date, abandoning your current life for the chance to begin again from a certain moment in your past."

"So," I said, "what you're saying is you've invented a time machine? I thought time travel was impossible."

"Not exactly a time machine like the ones you see in the movies. You can't, for instance, enter the past physically, only as an observer. Or, in the case of stage two, as a sort of vicarious participant in your own former life. The old science-fiction version of time travel isn't possible because it leads to paradox. If you were to travel bodily into the past, there would be—or would have been—two of you, and the second you could do something that would change the first you's future, leading to paradoxical impossibilities. These kinds of illogical situations are most often described using what's called the 'grandfather paradox,' which was first portrayed by René Barjavel in his 1943 book ***Le Voyageur Imprudent***. In Barjavel's example, a man goes back in time and kills his grandfather before he is old enough to impregnate a woman. Consequently, the man's father is never born, nor is he, so he wouldn't have been around to travel back in time to begin with. I've studied the possibility of overcoming the paradox problems associated with physical time travel, and my calculations tell me that the universe simply does not allow scenarios that could result in paradox."

"What about travelling into the future?"

"Again, impossible. And that one is simple. Basically, the future hasn't happened yet, so there's no future to travel to. Einstein's postulation that the past, present, and future all exist simultaneously was, I'm sorry to say, incorrect. Time moves in a straight line, ending in the here and now. Nothing exists beyond the present."

"So let me get this straight," I said, scratching an imaginary itch on my head. "You're saying you can step outside this straight timeline, then poke around in the past and reenter it at any point you want. But only as an observer?"

"Right. At least in stages one and two. That's how I managed to get the original recipe for Coney Island chili sauce and record those images and the video. I wanted to keep the shock factor to a minimum, so I eased into it by first mentioning a few facts about your life that aren't generally known. Then I followed that up with the 3D photos and the virtual-reality video. Finally, I thought it would be good to have something you could interact with physically, so I looked around for things you liked to eat when you were growing up. I could have gone with the steak sandwich from Triplets, or spaghetti from Pandal's, but there was something about Coney Island's secret chili sauce that I thought might be more convincing."

I was trying to absorb all this without my brain freezing up. Dealing with the conflict between things I had experienced and what was left of my common sense felt like having my skull filled with hardening concrete. I opened my mouth a couple of times, but nothing came out, so I stared into my empty glass while Heyoka continued.

"Listen," he said, flashing his trademark smile, "I can see you're confused, and I'm sorry for that. The problem I have is that delving any further into an explanation of the physics involved is almost impossible. That part of the process is, as far as I know, unique and inexplicable, except mathematically, and even math can't explain everything. Which makes it impossible to comprehend by anyone other than myself. Of course, there could be others who have stumbled on something similar, and that might explain many extraordinary phenomena recorded in various historical and religious texts. I've spent a lot of time investigating this possibility, and the closest I've come was observing some monks at a Shaolin Monastery in 794 AD who appeared to enter other dimensions from time to time. But during those observations I couldn't be sure what the monks were actually doing or how. The point is that the best I can do is demonstrate the results of my time travels, so I've been trying to show you things from your past in such a way that their reality would be undeniable."

I was beginning to recover a little, and the cement seemed to be slowly draining from my brain, probably due to the infusion of alcohol. I considered getting another drink, but stopped myself, figuring if I got too drunk I would have no chance of being able to think clearly.

"Okay," I said, swirling the remaining ice cubes in my glass. "Speaking hypothetically, let's say I accept what you're claiming. But if I can't change the past because of this paradox thing, what good would it be to go back and start over from a certain point in my younger life? I'd just have to live everything all over again exactly as it was, only with my adult brain, which would make it even more miserable and frustrating."

"That's not how it will work, Rix. The process involves something we call the multiverse or, to put it another way, alternate realities. And you will definitely have free will to conduct your new life in any way you see fit. But exactly how this happens will take a while to explain, and right now I've got some calls to make and papers to sign. Besides, you could probably do with a break in order to clear your mind. I should be finished in about an hour, so why don't you play around with my digital recording studio while you're waiting?"

AFTER HEYOKA LEFT, I sat in front of the computer console and brought the huge wall monitor to life. The array of programming he had was impressive, and under any other circumstances I would have been intrigued. But all I could think about were those vivid depictions of the past. I'd often bemoaned the fact that I didn't have this kind of setup when I was growing up, thinking what an incredible body of music I could have produced if I hadn't had to work six or seven nights a week playing other people's music in cover bands. I was in my thirties before I finally managed to get a record contract and start spending my off time writing and working in a studio. But by then I was deep into the drug scene, and I'd expended most of my creative juices playing ***Proud Mary*** six times a night and covering hundreds of other rock tunes.

Even though I was still not totally convinced, I began to wonder what might happen if I took Heyoka up on his offer. Could I go back and change all that? Of course, even if I did, the digital recording technology of today wouldn't be available for decades, so I'd have to work with the same primitive equipment I'd been privy to back then. And with my knowledge of what was to come, I wondered if I could deal with the frustration. But at least I might be able to alter the way I used my musical gifts. Maybe I could keep myself from putting so much emphasis on the ego gratification of becoming a local rock star. After a couple of years playing sock hops and local parties in my early teens, I'd gotten a fake ID and graduated to nightclub work, wasting my talents on drunks and feeding my ego on occasional scatterings of applause and the sexual favors of admiring women.

If I did go back, about the only thing I could change would be the way I attacked life. I didn't even know if I could alter my addictive behavior, since that seemed to be genetically or environmentally ingrained in my personality. Hell, I didn't know if I even wanted to. What if my creativity was inextricably tied to the effects of the drugs? After all, I hadn't written a damned thing since I kicked the drug habit and substituted an ocean of alcohol. Of course, the other side of the story was that decades of drug abuse and alcoholism had left me with serious health problems. According to my last round of blood work and some other tests, my liver was failing, my kidneys were in bad shape, my cholesterol was through the roof, and my diverticulitis had advanced to a dangerous level. Plus, I knew my brain was atrophying as well. Clear memories were a thing of the past, which made those vivid flashbacks Heyoka had shown me all the more convincing.

Early in my career I had possessed a musical memory that was the envy of my peers. In fact, at one point in time I had over five-hundred songs stored in my head, and I could fake a couple of hundred more simply because I'd happened to hear them on the radio or a juke box or on the B side of some obscure album. But those days were long gone. Now I had to carry around a ream of cheat sheets and sit behind a music stand.

The frightening thing was, I had no intention of giving up alcohol, which seemed to indicate I had a death wish. And all indications were that I would soon be fulfilling that wish. What, then, did I have to lose by taking Heyoka up on his offer? Even if it turned out to be a load of crap, there wasn't much more damage I could inflict on myself than I already had.

Still, something nagged at the back of my mind. For one thing, I didn't like feeling trapped here, fattened up on booze and food like an animal being prepared for slaughter, or a guinea pig in a cage awaiting a bizarre scientific experiment. As futile and hopeless as my life had become, I wasn't quite ready to trade it in for some unknown, mystical alternative.

I was doodling on the synthesizer keyboard, deep in thought, when Heyoka returned. "So, what do you think?" he said, pulling the leather chair over and sitting down. "About the equipment, I mean."

"State of the art," I said. "Impressive library of samples. Given a little time I could probably assemble an entire philharmonic orchestra, not to mention a fair imitation of the Mormon Tabernacle Choir."

"I'm sure you could, and I'd love to hear you try. But for now let's get back to our earlier discussion."

"We can do that," I said. "But first I'd like you to answer one simple question. Why me? Out of all the billions of people in the world, why would you seek out an aging, alcoholic, has-been to play your little games with?"

"Legitimate question," he said. "And I promise to answer it. However, before we go any further you need to understand that this is no game. Everything I've told you so far is absolutely true, from the story of my first vision quest to my latest experiments and calculations. I admit that the stage-three process has yet to be tested, but there is no reason to believe it won't be successful. Even in the unlikely event that something goes wrong, the risk to you is miniscule."

Finally, we were getting to the crux of the matter, and I didn't like it. Before answering, I adjusted the keyboard input to imitate a pipe organ and started improvising an old horror-movie soundtrack from the '50s. "Sorry," I said over the music, "but I'm having a vision of my own, and it's not a good one. In fact, it brings to mind the writings of Mary Shelley. Victor Frankenstein was, after all, born and raised not far from here. And it's now obvious that I've been conned by a mad scientist who lives in a castle—wooden though it may be—ominously perched on a promontory in the mountains. A castle that contains an underground laboratory, no less. Not only that, but this mad scientist now wants me to participate in some mysterious experiment."

"I see your point," he said. "But there's one thing you haven't taken into consideration, and that is that you are free to leave at any time. Just say the word, and I'll have you back at the Hotel Orientale in less than an hour. I'll even take care of the bill for the duration of your stay. Believe me, Rix, you are not a prisoner here. In fact, I'll prove it to you."

The moment those words left his lips, Fred appeared. "Fred," he said, "Pull the Citroen around front and leave the keys in it." Then, motioning for me to follow, he strolled across the room and out the door.

I caught up with him at the elevator, and we rode down together without speaking. By the time we reached the front entrance, the Citroen was idling in the driveway. "I want you to get in the car and drive out of here," he said. "There's a GPS that will guide you. Go as far as you feel is necessary in order to convince yourself that I'm not going to stop you. If you're not back within the hour, I promise I'll have your things, along with a case of Jack Daniels, sent to the hotel and taken to your room, which will already be paid for."

I'd played my share of poker over the years, but for the life of me I couldn't read this guy's tells. Either that or there were no tells to read. If this was a bluff, it would be easy enough to find out: just get in the car and try to drive back to Lyon. And, after considering things for a moment, I decided to do precisely that.

I climbed into the cramped driver's seat and was putting the car in gear, when Heyoka stepped to the open passenger-side window and leaned in. "You know," he said, "in case you decide to return, the next thing I want to do is take you back to 1965 and give you a glimpse of your late father."

As I pulled away, his final words echoed in my head, bringing back memories of a song I'd written for my dad many years after he died. It was another of those songs that had come to me in a dream, this one so vivid and detailed it seemed supernatural, as if the lyrics were delivered to me by my dead father. Of course, I was doing a lot of drugs back then, so I eventually chalked the whole thing up to my chemically altered state of mind. Now, however, after hearing Heyoka's story, I wasn't so sure. And remembering all his talk about probabilities, I wondered how probable it was that the lyrics I'd written decades before would reflect some of the theories he'd expounded on, theories I'd heard for the first time today.

The song had appeared on the last album I recorded, and one of the lines that popped into my head was: *As yesterday weaves itself into tomorrow, long-finished stories are yet to be told.* But what really screwed with my mind were the words that seemed to foreshadow the experiment he wanted to conduct, the two words that made up the title: ***Beginning Again***.

I passed through the open gate and was about half a mile down the winding road, when I jammed on the brakes, pulled off on the narrow shoulder, and turned around. Then I headed back up the hill to Heyoka's wooden castle.

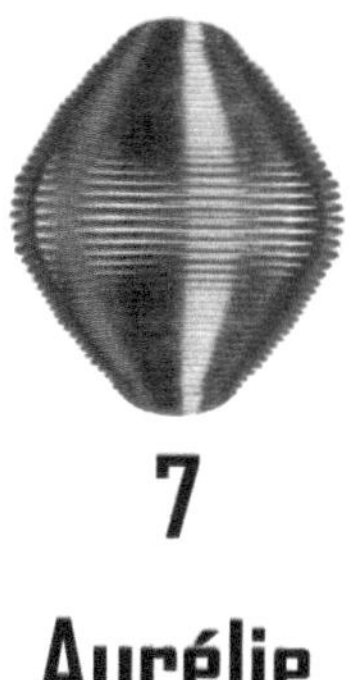

7

Aurélie

Twilight was settling in as I pulled up to the entrance, where Fred sat waiting on the front steps. After I rolled to a stop we switched places, and he drove the car down the driveway and out of view. I entered the cathedral-like main room and was about to turn into the hall when the scene outside the windows stopped me. The sun had dipped behind the mountain tops, scattering brilliant red and gold ribbons on a lacy bank of clouds. I stood mesmerized by the spectacle until a female voice broke through the silence.

"Heyoka asked me to bring you this," said Aurélie, who, like the night before at the restaurant, seemed to have materialized out of thin air. She handed me a tall glass of whiskey, which I accepted with a shaky hand and drank half of before the oddness of her presence at the villa registered. I thought about asking what she was doing here, but I was even more curious about her Midwestern accent. She hadn't spoken while serving as our waitress, and despite her name and facial features, it was clear she had not been raised in France.

"You don't sound French," I said.

"Nope," she answered. "Born in Canada, grew up mostly in South Dakota. My given name was … well, let's just say it was problematical. So as soon as I reached the age of consent, I changed it."

"But you look—"

"My father was Inuit, my mother French Canadian. I got my brains from him and my looks from her."

"She must have been a pretty lady," I said. "So what was this problematical name you were given?"

"That's a rather personal question, but since I know you changed Richard Voniossi to Rix Vaughn, and that you hated your middle name, Llewellyn, I guess I can tell you mine. The Inuit did not have surnames, that is until the government started requiring them for various legal reasons. My family chose Kunayak, and my full name at birth was A'akuluujjusi Kunayak, so I'm sure you can understand why I wanted to change it. I took the name from Aurélie Claudel, a French model and descendant of the famous sculptress Camille Claudel. Today, I go by the single name Aurélie."

"Fascinating," I said. "Lovely name. Anything else I should know about you?"

"Me? Not really. Except maybe that I'm not as young as I look," she said with a wink and a smile.

I'd paid little attention to her the night before, but here, with the firelight flickering like a halo of lightning bugs behind her hair, I was struck by the familiarity of her simple, almost peasant-like beauty. She was petite and slender, with auburn hair cropped in a short afro that framed a heart-shaped face. Her azure eyes, shadowed by long lashes, looked down on a delicate nose and a wide, generous mouth. Gone was the velvet beret that had held her hair in check; and the black-and-white waitress uniform had been replaced by stone-washed jeans and a loose-fitting t-shirt featuring a photograph of Jeff Bridges as Dude Lebowski.

I must have been staring because she did a little pirouette, then struck a hip-cocked pose and bowed her head in a mock finale. "Sorry," I said. "Didn't mean to stare. I was a little surprised to see you here is all. Don't you have to work tonight?"

"I work for Heyoka," she said, relaxing the pose. When she saw my confusion, she added, "Let me guess, you didn't know he owns LeMusique."

"Seems like there's a lot I don't know about Heyoka," I said, obeying her come-hither signal to follow her into the hallway. Though the jeans weren't tight, I could tell she had a well-proportioned body by the way her hips and thighs brushed against the soft denim. And when she glanced back over her shoulder, the familiarity I'd sensed before hit home. In the subdued light of the hallway, with her profile illuminated by the subtle glow of a wall lamp, she could have passed for my third wife's twin sister.

"You shouldn't blame him for that," she said, pointing to the open elevator door. "He's a brainy guy, but a little absent minded at times. He's also one of the most honest men I've ever known, and I can assure you he's not trying to hide anything. It just doesn't occur to him that it might be necessary sometimes to ... Rix? Are you okay?"

I was stunned by her resemblance to the only woman I had ever truly loved, and when I tried to answer, nothing came out.

"Rix?" she said again. My legs had turned to rubber, and it was all I could do to keep my balance as another vivid memory swept me back in time ...

Robin and I had splurged that warm summer night, with a trip to Atlanta, dinner at our favorite Italian restaurant, and a special showing of ***Gone With The Wind*** *at the historic Fox Theater. Upon returning to our tiny cabin in the north-Georgia woods, we were greeted by a sight one might be privy to once in a lifetime, and then only if they are very, very lucky.*

Most easterners are familiar with fireflies, or lightning bugs as we southerners call them, but few, if any, have ever seen the kind of living fireworks we found ourselves in the midst of when we parked in the dirt driveway next to our ramshackle home. To say they lit up the sky would be an understatement. It was impossible to count them, but there were thousands, if not tens of thousands, flashing their iridescent beacons among the dense forest that surrounded us. The spectacle was so bright I could make out the color of Robin's blue chiffon dress in the midnight darkness, and the vision of her standing there, framed in that ethereal light, had stayed with me ever since.

"Hey!" Aurélie said, startling me back to the present. Seeing her bathed in the soft glow of the wall lamp, I realized my earlier vision of her, backlit by the sparkling effect of the fire, had triggered the flashback.

"I ... uh ... Sorry," I said. "Little déjà vu there." I raised my glass and drained it, hoping the whiskey would dissolve the growing lump in my throat. "I was thinking how much you remind me of ..." But I stopped in mid-sentence. If I'd finished, it would have sounded like I was trying to hit on her, which was the furthest thing from my mind at that moment. It wasn't that I had a problem with bedding women half my age, or that she hadn't awakened my sleeping libido. It was just that for decades my sexual fantasies had been dominated by memories of Robin, and seeing her come to life before my eyes had knocked me for a loop.

"I remind you of what?" she said.

I didn't want to answer, but since I'd already started, I thought it would seem rude if I refused. "Just someone I used to know," I said, my voice hoarse with emotion. "But that was a long, long time ago." I managed to straighten up and lean on the wall next to the open elevator door. "Anyway, if you're taking me to see Heyoka, maybe we should get going."

"Oh," she said. "Sure. He's waiting for us in the lab." She took hold of my arm and steered me into the elevator. We waited for the door to close, then she pressed her palm against a small blank screen next to the controls. I heard a faint beep, and when she took her hand away the screen was flashing with a red arrow pointing down.

The elevator ride took quite a while, though there were no lights to show how far we traveled. I did, however, have the sensation of floating, which indicated we were descending rapidly. The awkwardness between us increased until the silence became nerve wracking, so I was happy to feel my weight return as we slowed to a stop. I took a step toward the door, and when it didn't open, I looked at Aurélie.

"It'll be a few more minutes," she said. Again, there was a sensation of rapid movement, but no loss of gravity. Instead, I felt myself being pushed toward the wall until I was forced to lean on it for support. Aurélie, on the other hand, leaned into the movement, obviously familiar with how to compensate for the nuances of this strange, underground journey.

When the elevator stopped again, the door opened on a small chamber reminiscent of the airlocks I'd seen in a few science-fiction movies. As we stepped out, the door closed, and three ceramic-looking triangular panels drew together in front of it, meeting with a muted click in the center. A faint whirring sound indicated some sort of seal being engaged, and a moment later a purple mist began to fill the chamber.

"It's okay," Aurélie said, sensing my anxiety. "The lab complex includes several sterile clean rooms, so we try to keep the overall environment as uncontaminated as possible. Heyoka has developed this bacteria-neutralizing nanofog to cleanse our skin and clothes before we enter."

Within seconds the mist dissipated, and the wall before us split in triangular sections identical to the ones that had closed in front of the elevator door. I expected some sort of Star-Trek scene, or maybe a room full of tables laden with bubbling beakers and glowing glass tubes, so I was surprised to see an antiquated office, featuring a scarred wooden desk piled with books and papers. Behind the desk sat a bespectacled Heyoka, seemingly unaware of our presence until Aurélie cleared her throat.

"And this," she said, "is the Master's study. As you can see, it's modeled on Albert Einstein's office, which you may know rivaled Mark Twain's in sheer messiness. I've tried to get him to let me clean and organize it, but he refuses."

"Don't mind my pretty protégé," Heyoka said, coming around the desk to shake my hand. "She's a pain in the ass sometimes, but I love her just the same. Who wouldn't? She's not only got the looks of a virgin teenager, but the brains of a massive parallel supercomputer. She could do with a little breast augmentation, but, like me, she refuses."

This light-hearted banter seemed to come naturally to them, the sarcasm tinged with faux exasperation.

"For your information," Aurélie said, taking my empty glass, "I am neither a teenage virgin nor a human computer. I happen to be thirty-six years old, and my educational credentials include a high-school diploma and a couple of wasted years in college before they booted me out. The only reason he thinks I'm smart is that I once managed to pull a Will-Hunting by arranging a group of symbols and numbers into the solution to some arcane mathematical conundrum called the 'Yang–Mills existence and mass gap problem.' Though I had no idea where it came from or what it meant, apparently that momentary flash of insight was stupendous enough for this aging cretin to kidnap me and make me his slave."

She went to a small sideboard between two bookcases, and poured me another drink. "As for the virgin part," she continued, handing me the refilled glass, "he wouldn't know the first thing about that, since he's a eunuch. Of course, I have no proof of that. But the fact that I don't means I'm either right or he's an asexual old fuddy-duddy."

"Enough of this mutual-admiration crap," Heyoka said, returning to his desk chair. "I'm glad you decided to come back, Rix. And, again, let me assure you that you are free to leave at any time. But since you're here, I have to assume you're at least curious to see what we've been up to, so I've asked Aurélie to give you a little tour while I finish a few things. She knows everything there is to know about our endeavors and the science behind them, so feel free to ask any questions you want. In fact, you might want to ask her about the multiverse and alternate realities I mentioned earlier. She may be a smartass, but she's a lot better than I am at coming up with simple explanations for complex scientific concepts."

"What he means is, I talk in English, rather than quantum Klingon," Aurélie said. "Come on, let's leave this cranky old Injun to his musings."

"Have fun," he said, as she led me along a narrow path between teetering stacks of books and journals. "But be careful. She's been awfully horny lately."

"Humff," she said. "As if you would know."

We rounded a corner into a corridor that wasn't visible from the office. Soft light radiated from smooth translucent walls, cool to the touch. Except for our muffled footfalls on the resilient flooring, the silence was so penetrating I felt it in my ears, like the increased pressure when a plane descends toward a landing.

About a hundred yards along, we came to another airlock that opened when we approached. "This is going to be just like the one beside the elevator," she said as the panels closed behind us. The same misting operation took place, and after the second set of panels separated, she led me onto a platform next to what looked like a miniature bullet train. The train car stood in an open space cut in the side of a tunnel about 12-feet in diameter. A metal bench protruded from the opposite wall, apparently to provide seating for people awaiting the car's arrival.

We had barely made it onto the platform when a window in the curved surface of the car slid up and out of sight to reveal two rows of seats separated by an access space. Each row contained four contoured chairs, and an aisle down the middle split them into sets of two. "Pick a seat," she said. "The trip will take about ten minutes."

I chose a seat next to the aisle and waited while the same kind of form fitting-restraints I remembered from Heyoka's car closed around me. Aurélie sat across from me and pointed to my glass. "You should drink some of that," she said. "We'll be accelerating and decelerating rapidly, so there's going to be some jostling. You'll be pushed back into the seat a bit, then forward into the restraints as we come to a stop."

A brief whining sound prodded me into action, and I managed to drink half the whiskey before the window slid closed and I felt myself being pressed into the seat. The G-force increased for about a minute, then let up until it felt like we were floating.

"I supposed this is all part of that CERN thing Heyoka told me about," I said a little too loudly. Being accustomed to airliners and commuter trains, I'd tried to speak over noise that wasn't there. In fact, as in the corridor, the silence was almost total, and the acoustics were deader than a sound booth in a recording studio. "It's some kind of international scientific complex, right?" I said, lowering my voice. "With a big supercollider?"

"Not exactly," she said. "I mean, you're right about CERN and the LHC, but not about this being part of it. The lab, as we affectionately call this collection of tunnels, shafts and underground chambers, is a privately funded research facility, designed by Heyoka, and constructed by a team of Native American technicians."

"You've got to be kidding," I said. "These shafts and tunnels had to have been cut through solid bedrock. And judging from the distances we've traveled so far, the entire thing has to be huge."

"It is huge, Rix. This tunnel alone is over six kilometers long, and there are several others for delivery of materials and maintenance supplies. The offices and storage areas, back where we left Heyoka, are about the size of an average Holiday Inn, and the central lab structure is perhaps two-thirds the diameter of the Superdome and twice as tall. Surrounding that are several anterooms and research labs and the ecosphere stabilization system, which includes the water and power plants. Finally, there is the computer processing and data center, though that doesn't take up much room in this dimension."

"Now you're losing me," I said. "If you're going to start talking about other dimensions, you'll have to bring things down to my level and go real slow. But tell me something: if this isn't part of some government-sponsored operation, who financed it? The excavation and construction must have run in the tens of millions. Not to mention the cost of acquiring the rights to build it here."

"Total cost was over two billion if you include the political payoffs it took to secure the cooperation of both France and Switzerland. As for who paid for it, that would be Heyoka."

"Give me a break. I mean he said he'd amassed what some people might think of as a small fortune, but two billion dollars? I don't think that qualifies as small. Where would he get that kind of money?"

Before she could answer the car began to shudder like a plane hitting an air pocket. Seeing my alarm, Aurélie reached across the aisle and laid a hand on my arm. "Don't worry," she said. "We're passing under the outer ring of the LHC. The vibration is caused by the interaction of the collider's magnetic field with our Maglev drive. It'll be over in a second."

After the vibrations faded I took a moment to gather myself, then said, "Okay. That was ... interesting. Now, about the money?"

"Well," she said, "there's no real mystery there, although few people know the extent of Heyoka's fortune or its origins. He's become a very private person over the past decade, mainly because of the ridicule he's been held up to by attempting to go public with some of his theories. Plus, he doesn't want the publicity and invasion of privacy that would result from being known as a multi-billionaire."

"Multi-billionaire," I murmured. "So, you're saying you can't tell me any more than that?"

"Oh, no. Not at all. He's told me to be completely open and honest with you, which is quite a compliment, actually. But before we get into that, there's something you need to understand about Heyoka. As successful as he's been financially, he doesn't think of his wealth as anything more than a means to an end. Don't get the idea he's obsessed with making money, because he's not. The only things he's obsessed with are science, mathematics, and music. And, of course, his privacy. Especially when it comes to this particular project.

"As for where the money came from, Heyoka owns an interest in some of the most profitable corporations in the world, mostly as a result of shared patents for his inventions. Back in the sixties and seventies he did independent research for a little firm you might have heard of called Intel, coming up with an idea that led to the development of the first commercial microprocessor. Before that he helped Texas Instruments perfect the first integrated circuit. Although he's never gotten—nor has he asked for—any public credit for these contributions, he *did* reap the financial benefits, and he used them to make some very shrewd investments in the healthcare and aerospace sectors. Today, he holds patents on several medical devices and a raft of other inventions and processes he developed for various aerospace companies and NASA."

"Good God," I said. "How does one man find time to do all that? And what about this ostracism crap? With all those accomplishments, why would he be considered an outcast among his own colleagues?"

"In case you haven't already figured it out, Heyoka is a genius of the first order, but he's also a rebel. Not only does he refuse to work as anyone's employee, his more recent theories have led to negative reactions from many of his scientific brethren. Which is why he decided to retreat into semi-seclusion. He still consults with a few of his more open-minded colleagues, but they wouldn't dare reveal their association with him and be branded as supporters of his bizarre ideas and unconventional research endeavors."

"Endeavors?" I said. "You mean there are other screwball experiments going on down here besides messing around with alternate realities and multiverses?"

"Many. We have other divisions working on things like antigravity, cold fusion, quantum teleportation, nucleosynthesis, fuel-cell technology, genetic engineering, and computer consciousness."

"Right," I said, still trying to wrap my mind around all this. "So what you're saying is that he's, I don't know, on some other planet intellectually?"

"Metaphorically speaking, he is, but you shouldn't let that make you think he isn't a regular guy. Even though he's accomplished goals few other physicists or mathematicians on the planet have ever dreamt of, some of his greatest loves are simple things like fishing and nature and music. Especially, I might add, the music of one Rix Vaughn."

"Yeah, so he's told me. I still don't get it, though. With his brains and money he could have access to any superstar in the world. So why in the hell would he take an interest in a broken-down old guitar picker like me?"

"That's a question you'll have to ask him, and I wouldn't be so quick to sell yourself short. Heyoka sees something special in you, and the chances of him being mistaken are in the billion-to-one range. Besides, I like your music, too, and I've got a collection of recordings that includes the entire discology of every singer-songwriter who ever lived."

"I guess I should thank you for the compliment," I said. "But as I'm sure you know I'm way out of my league when it comes to understanding all this tech-speak about quantum physics. He said you were good at explaining things, so ..."

"Don't worry, I plan to do a lot of explaining once we get to the lab where I can use some sensory aids to help you grasp things. As for being out of your league, I think it's time you came clean about that and stopped playing dumb. Heyoka told me you've been a lay student of science and a reader of SF all your life. Things will go a lot faster if you don't make me teach you how to add two-and-two, or explain the difference between a leopard and a lepton."

"There's a difference?" I said, allowing a smile to crack my lips. "Listen, maybe you're right about what I know and what I don't, but you must also be aware that I'm a right brainer, that I think in analog rather than digital terms. When it comes to interpreting mathematical equations I'm about as competent as a retarded groundhog. I could never even learn to sight-read music for Christ's sake, and I failed every algebra class I took before dropping out of high school."

"Yes," she said, "but you're not stupid. Far from it, actually. Your IQ ..."

"I know. I know. My folks made a big deal out of it back when I was a kid. But somehow having a genius IQ never translated into being good at learning stuff, especially when I was a cog in that mind-numbing production line they call school. The thing is, I think and memorize in the abstract. I need symbolic examples, everyday analogies I can relate to tangible things I'm familiar with. I do understand a little about multiple universes and the proposed vibratory aspects of string theory, but only because I can equate them to the indeterminate nature of musical improvisation and the overtones of plucked strings. I have no understanding of the science behind those theories because I've never been able to visualize the world of quantum mechanics."

"I can appreciate those limitations, Rix, and hopefully I'll be able to explain things visually or metaphorically, using analogies and everyday language. We'll see about that. But right now you'd better brace yourself for deceleration, or you're liable to end up with a non-metaphoric puddle of Jack Daniels in your lap.

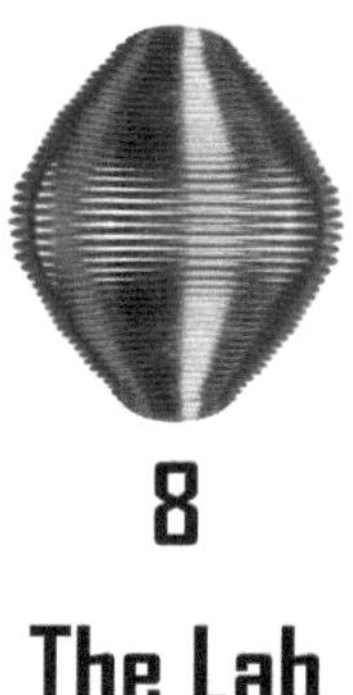

8

The Lab

After exiting another airlock and negotiating a series of labyrinthian corridors, we ended up in a long, curved passageway dotted on either side with an occasional smooth recess. We passed several of these indentations before Aurélie stopped and turned to face one. A small panel at the side glowed with the letters NIFS.

"This is our NIFS Complex," she said, as the skin of the recess separated along a previously invisible center line. I followed her into a tear-shaped atrium, from which five evenly spaced hallways split off like arms of a starfish. "The acronym stands for Nonlinear Interdimensional Feedback Studies, but don't waste your time trying to figure out what that means. I'll do my best to explain what we're doing here later."

We entered the first hallway on the left and walked to the end, where another portal opened into a room that reminded me of an IMAX theater I'd once visited at the Kennedy Space Center. Except for the floor, the room was spherical, and the walls glowed with a milky translucency. Two high-backed desk chairs sat in the center, surrounded by a circular desk with a panoramic computer screen that stretched halfway around. A portion of the desk split away to allow us inside the circle, closing behind us after we entered.

Aurélie motioned for me to sit. "So," she said, settling into the other chair and spinning around to face me, "what would you like to talk about first?"

I was still carrying my empty glass, and when I held it up, she reached down and pulled out a file drawer. "Sorry," she said, retrieving a bottle of Jack, "I don't have any ice in here, but at least you won't go thirsty." She poured some of the brown liquid into my glass while I tried to sort through the hundred-or-so questions banging around in my head, one of which occurred to me as I took a tentative sip.

"Before we get into all the technical mumbo-jumbo, I'm curious about this." I held up the half-filled glass. "To be more specific, why is it that you and Heyoka seem so intent on keeping me supplied with whiskey? Judging from what you know about me, you must be aware that I'm killing myself with this crap, so I'm wondering if you're trying to hasten my death."

"No … not at all." Her hesitation made it clear the question had taken her by surprise, and I watched as her once-confident demeanor faded into nervous confusion. She opened her mouth again, but all she could manage was an exasperated sigh.

"What?" I said. "Doesn't Heyoka's order to be open and honest cover the beverages you serve me?"

"It does," she said, resting the bottle on a knee. "I was going to explain about that, but I wanted to wait until we discussed a few other things first."

"It's spiked," I said, realizing for the first time that the vivid memories, the uncanny sense of traveling back in time, had probably been helped along by a chemical stimulant, most likely an hallucinogen. "You've been drugging me."

"Look, Rix," she said. "In the first place, we mean you no harm. The concoction we've been passing off as Jack Daniels is far less harmful than the real thing, while producing a nearly identical kick, complete with simulated hangover symptoms."

"Concoction," I said, taking another sip. "Sure does taste like Jack." I wasn't worried about being drugged. Besides, it wouldn't make much sense for them to go to all this trouble just to poison me. "Do you want to explain, or should I keep on drinking until I'm comatose and don't give a shit anymore?"

"You could drink a couple of gallons without becoming comatose," she said. "In fact, you'd probably drown before there were any adverse health effects. The host beverage is a nontoxic simulacrum of aged Tennessee whiskey, with a simple alkaloid base, some artificial flavors and coloring, and a tiny infusion of psychoactive compounds designed to mimic the high of alcohol. The neuroimaging enhancement—the chemical matrix that stimulates and clarifies memory—is something that evolved out of Heyoka's efforts to duplicate changes in the brain that occur during so-called spiritual experiences. And you should know that the miniscule quantities you've been ingesting have only provided a preliminary introduction to some pretty amazing things. The next stage, which we refer to as Stage Two, will, if you chose to continue, involve participatory experiences you won't be able to tell from the real thing."

"Been there, done that," I said with a smile. "Sounds a lot like LSD or Ecstasy."

"There's no comparison," she said. "Those synthetics cause hallucinations, dream states that warp reality. This, on the other hand,"—she held up the bottle—"stimulates real memories, things that have actually happened, with no alteration whatsoever. You may have forgotten details of your past on a conscious level, but all the information—the raw data—remains stored in your subconscious. And under the right circumstances that data can be reconstituted into clear and precise memories. Several cultures have learned how to access these subconscious reserves through physical deprivation, meditation, or the ingestion of certain plant materials, sometimes even going back in history to retrieve what might be called communal or collective memories. But until now no one has come up with a way to duplicate such processes in the lab."

"Far out," I said, sniffing the glass. "What's in it, exactly?"

"That's hard to explain unless you happen to be familiar with a branch of science called supramolecular chemistry. The original formulation has been reintegrated at the molecular level into something that would be unrecognizable to your average chemist. If I were to go back to its chemical origins, I could point to ingredients like acetylcholine, scopolamine, salvinorin A, sodium thiopental, mescaline, nicotine, and a few other odds and ends. But that has little to do with the formula in its present state. The algorithms evolved from a breakdown of reactions in the brain that result from some of those chemical compounds working in concert with activities like fasting, self

-induced pain, yoga, thermal extremes, and a myriad of other physical and environmental influences."

"Doesn't sound like much fun," I said. "Pain, starvation, body contortions? Not exactly my cup of tea."

"You're missing the point, Rix. What Heyoka's been able to do is duplicate these effects without the discomfort, specifically so he could work with other subjects in a laboratory setting. At first this only allowed for observation, but recently he's managed to expand the process, combining it with some non-chemical influences that enhance the effects to allow for benign participation. That is, re-experiencing episodes without being able to alter them."

"So, that's what's been happening to me?"

"To some extent, yes," she said, turning back to the computer desk. "Although you have yet to experience the full participatory iteration of the process. That will come in Stage Two, if you're willing to move on." She moved her fingers over the desk as if typing on an invisible keyboard, and the milky surface of the sphere that surrounded us came alive, resolving into an animated image of me and my dad strolling down a hospital hall. There was no sound, but the wrap-around visuals were astonishingly realistic.

"These projections will give you a two-dimensional preview of what you will see in much more vivid detail during the first phase of Stage Two."

Dad and I were standing in the coffee shop after he'd finished his morning rounds, then the scene dissolved into another; this one of me at age sixteen, sitting in my '55 Thunderbird with Susan Wilson. I remembered the moment well, since it was the night I finally talked her into having sex. I watched while we got out of the car and spread a blanket on the ground, then as we were about to lie down, the image faded and the sphere went blank.

"I think we'd better stop that one there," Aurélie said with a chuckle as the walls began to glow with that milky light.

I shook the memory from my mind and leaned forward in the chair. "What you're saying is that I can pick and choose the moments in time I want, then relive them as if I'm there again?"

"Yep," she said, turning her chair around to face me. "But you can't change anything. You have to relive them exactly the way they happened."

"Then what's all this talk about going back and starting over with my adult mind and doing things differently if I choose."

"That," she said, "is Stage Three, which will involve actual mental transference, the insertion of your current consciousness into yourself as a younger person. It's something Heyoka has been working toward for a long time, and it involves far more than chemical inducement." She spun back around to the desk. After a few more hand movements, the light dimmed again and something began to materialize above us. As the holographic image descended, it resolved into an odd-looking elliptical structure wrapped with a silver tube that formed a continuous angled spiral.

"This," she said, "is our version of a particle accelerator. In miniature, of course. The real one is on the other side of that wall." She pointed to the wall opposite the entrance. "It's similar to the LHC, however, it is not a collider. It is a continuous accelerator, able to move subatomic particles at velocities that come so close to the speed of light the difference cannot be measured."

"Right," I said. "If it's not a collider, then where do you get the subatomic particles?"

"See," she said, "you do know more than you let on. Unfortunately, the answer to that question is almost impossible to illustrate visually, so let me try an analogy you should be able to conceptualize."

"I wouldn't count on it, but don't let that stop you."

"Okay. First a little mumbo-jumbo, then I've got an idea about relating it to something you're familiar with. Briefly, when matter is accelerated to the speed of light, it gets stretched out, forming something like a plasma. In this state, matter becomes divisible into its smallest component parts, which are all basically different manifestations of one thing: an oscillating or vibrating string. The importance of this phenomenon, at least for us, is that the acceleration of these strings can, under the right conditions, lead to a state of intense sympathetic vibration, causing a rift or gateway in the fabric of space-time. It's not unlike the frequency overload that leads to audio feedback, which, as I'm sure you know, if left unchecked can rip the cones of speakers, not to mention a few eardrums. You might say we're plucking the strings of the universe until they vibrate so wildly they crack the cone of the space-time continuum."

"Interesting," I said. "Kind of like how sympathetic vibrations of a high note can shatter a wineglass."

"Exactly," she said. "Why didn't I think of that?"

"Probably because you weren't suggesting the total destruction of space-time, only a crack. In any case, believe it or not, I get it. Well, I don't really *get* it, but at least it doesn't sound like complete nonsense. One thing I'd like to know, though, is how you manage to achieve that kind of acceleration in a device that is obviously much smaller in overall size than the LHC, and that looks to be far too compact to accommodate the huge magnets necessary to create such acceleration."

"To understand that you'll have to accept some of the precepts of quantum physics." She waved a hand over the desk, and the accelerator was replaced by a transparent globe about the size of a soccer ball. "I'm sure you're familiar with the fact that what we think of as solid matter is mostly empty space."

"Heyoka and I already had that conversation" I said. "At the time I was playing dumb, as you call it. But even though I've read a lot about the subatomic world, I more-or-less have to take those concepts on faith because they're too bizarre for me to grasp in a realistic sense."

"Don't feel bad, nobody can rationalize the data in terms of everyday realism. However, I might be able to help you visualize what we're talking about if you can think of this globe as an atom. As you can see, it appears to be empty. That's because at this scale the components of an atom would be too small to be seen. We would have to blow the globe up to more than a mile in diameter before the nucleus would be visible, and then it would only be the size of a tiny pebble. And the electrons would be smaller still, say like grains of sand. So there's a lot of empty space inside."

"If you say so," I said.

"I say so. Anyway, Heyoka has developed a method of compressing matter. That is, squeezing out most of the empty space until it becomes super dense." As she said this, the globe shrank until it was no larger than a BB, then expanded again, morphing into the original image of the accelerator. "Our acceleration tube is made of this super-dense material, and, unlike the single circular tube of the LHC, it wraps around in a continuous serpentine spiral, a little like a closed double helix. If unwound, it would be as long as the collider tube, but only about one-fifth the diameter."

"Sounds like a good idea," I said. "But it still doesn't explain the lack of magnetic fields. And, if I'm not mistaken, that kind of acceleration would also require temperatures near absolute zero."

"You are not mistaken, however, in order to understand how these things are accomplished you would have to be able to comprehend some complicated scientific theories. To put it in the simplest terms possible, this super-densification process not only produces an incredibly strong and highly magnetized material, that material is able to absorb and concentrate the thermodynamic properties of its immediate environment with extreme efficiency. The reason you don't see any magnets is because the *entire tube* is the magnet, and its proximity to the super-cooled LHC enhances the effect of our own advanced, cryogenic cooling system, allowing for temperatures even lower than those that surround the CERN collider. In case you haven't already figured it out, we are directly below the center of the LHC."

As mind-boggling as her explanations were, I couldn't believe she was making them up; what would be the point? There was no denying that the facility was vast and scientifically sophisticated, and unless I chose to dismiss what she said out of hand, I had little choice but to accept it as the truth. "Let me ask you something," I said. "You say this Stage Two is more realistic than the Stage-One memories I've been experiencing?"

"Yes. Far more."

"And the Stage-Three thing is what you want me to be the guinea pig for?"

"Guinea pig is a harsh way of putting it, but I suppose you could say that."

"Okay, what I'm wondering is, has anyone even tested Stage Two?"

"Absolutely. Heyoka, of course, and Fred and myself. If you're worried about it, I can assure you there is absolutely no danger involved. But listen, you don't have to make a decision right now. You can wait as long as you like. Talk it over with Fred if you want to. And to reiterate what Heyoka said, you are under no obligation to do anything at all. You can stay here indefinitely, or go back to Lyon tomorrow."

"Maybe so, but if that's true, why the subtle con?"

"Come on, Rix," she said. "You can't really believe you would have gone along with all this if we'd told you everything up front. If you hadn't been introduced to these ideas a little at a time, you'd have been running for the exits, accusing us of being lunatics. It may seem like a con to you, but if it was, why would Heyoka invite you to leave, or pay for your hotel bill, or offer to pay your expenses for the duration of your stay in Lyon? Face it, this is a legitimate proposal, one you are free to either accept or reject."

"But I was drugged," I said. "Without my consent."

"Granted, but not until you arrived here at the villa. You voluntarily agreed to take Heyoka up on his offer of hospitality back at the restaurant, and at that time you were under the sole influence of unadulterated Jack Daniels, both your own and some that came straight from the bar. The drugs were only used to give you a taste of what's possible. They have no power over your decision-making processes. Think about it, do you feel like you are being chemically coerced? That we've robbed you of your free will? If so, you can go back to the villa and refuse any more drinks or food from us. I know you have a private stash of whiskey. If you want, you can return to your tour, take a year to make sure there's nothing of ours left in your system. The offer will still stand. The fact is that none of this will work without your complete, voluntary cooperation, so we wouldn't force you into anything you don't want to do even if we could."

I leaned back in the chair and watched the accelerator spin like top in slow motion. Even though I was trying to think of some way to dismiss what she said, I knew it didn't matter. My life was a wreck, and there was no chance of dodging the inevitable. If my luck held out, I had maybe two more years of deteriorating health and increasing misery before I landed in a nursing home. Or worse, in the morgue. So what if the whole thing turned out to be an elaborate hoax? At least I might be able to go out with some great memories, one of which had already been sparked by the woman sitting across from me.

"You're staring again," Aurélie said, touching my arm. "You know, Rix, my resemblance to Robin was not part of the plan. Some kind of karmic anomaly, maybe, but certainly not deliberate. I've been working with Heyoka for over twenty years, since long before we knew any details about your past."

I was no longer capable of being shocked by what they knew about my life, so it didn't strike me as odd that she would be aware of the memories her resemblance to Robin had conjured up. Still, I wasn't convinced this hadn't been part of their plan. "Why should I believe you?" I said. "For all I know you're her reincarnation. Maybe Heyoka inserted her mind into your body. Or maybe you're not even real, just a chemically induced hallucination."

"Could be," she said. "But considering your experience with hallucinogens, you should be able to tell the difference by now. As for my being a reincarnation of Robin, that's out of the question. We have to take into consideration the ethical ramifications of what we do, and replacing one person's persona with another's would be like committing murder. Seriously, Rix, this isn't Voodoo or some kind of evil brain swapping experiment from an old horror movie. Just because we choose not to be restricted by the arbitrary boundaries of 'legitimate' science doesn't mean we aren't compassionate human beings."

"It may not be Voodoo, but it sure sounds—"

"Hold on," she glanced over her shoulder at the computer screen where a light had begun to pulse. After a couple of seconds the light faded and she turned back. "Unfortunately," she said, "Heyoka's going to be tied up for a while, so we won't be able to include him in our conversation until the morning. Why don't we grab something to eat, and I'll try to answer any other questions you have. We can do that here in the cafeteria, or we can go back to the villa. Whichever you prefer."

"This place has a cafeteria?" I said, rising to follow her toward the entrance.

"It has a lot more than that," she told me as we emerged from the IMAX room. "In addition to several specialized labs and workshops, there are dorms for the staff, temporary sleeping quarters for visitors, a lounge, and even a game room. At times there are over fifty of us working here: technicians, maintenance personnel, researchers, data-entry folks, and the like. So, what do you think? Should we head back to the villa or tough it out here?"

"Tough it out? Is the food that bad?"

"Actually, no. It's just sandwiches and salads and two or three hot entrees, but they're all freshly prepared twenty-four-seven, and they're a lot more appetizing than what you'd get from your average institutional food service. Plus, since we're probably going to be coming right back in the morning, we could bed down here and avoid the long commute."

"Bed down? You and me?" I said with a smile.

"Sure ... Oh, sorry, I didn't mean ..."

"Kidding," I said. "Not that I wouldn't like to." I waited for some reaction: anger or maybe revulsion. But her expression remained passive.

"I'm flattered, Rix," she finally said, without the sarcasm I might have expected. "Don't get the wrong idea, but I have to admit the thought has crossed my mind. The thing is, we've got more important things to worry about right now, and I wouldn't want you to think I was trying to entice you with sex. You're having a hard enough time trusting us as it is."

"You've thought about it? I find that hard to believe. I mean, I'm old enough to be your—"

"Look," she said, interrupting me, "your age doesn't enter into the equation. Whether or not you like to admit it, you're a fascinating character with extraordinary talents. I've been a fan ever since Heyoka introduced me to your music, and I'm no different from any other woman when it comes to being sexually attracted to musicians. But you and I both know other issues are involved here, not the least of which is that you wouldn't be making love to me, you'd be making love to that memory of yours. And I'm not sure I could handle being a surrogate." She paused a beat. "Now, are we going or staying?"

"Staying, I guess. If you're sure you can trust me."

She gave a quick, non-committal nod and headed along the corridor in front of me.

AURÉLIE WAS RIGHT, OF course, at least about my thinking of her as a substitute. Decades had passed since I'd seen Robin, and she still haunted my dreams. Like most of the positive things in my life, I'd managed to fuck that one up royally, and I'd never forgiven myself. Could I go back and change things? And if I did, how would it affect the rest of my new life?

I'd read enough to know that time-travel could be a complicated matter, even without the problem of paradox, which Heyoka said wouldn't happen because I would be entering an alternate reality. But one thing that couldn't be avoided was what science-fiction writers called the butterfly effect, which referred to the idea that every change a time traveler makes in the past, no matter how small or subtle, will spread into the future like ripples from a pebble dropped in a pond, affecting everything in its path. How strong those effects would be and how far into the future the ripples would extend were questions left up to the writers. And their opinions—which were all over the map—could hardly be relied upon. After all, they were *fiction* writers, not scientists citing objective studies.

As we approached another recess in the wall, I noticed a sign above it. It was the only entrance I'd seen so far that was identified with anything other than an acronym. "Second Chance Café" it said, and I wondered if the name had been chosen for my benefit.

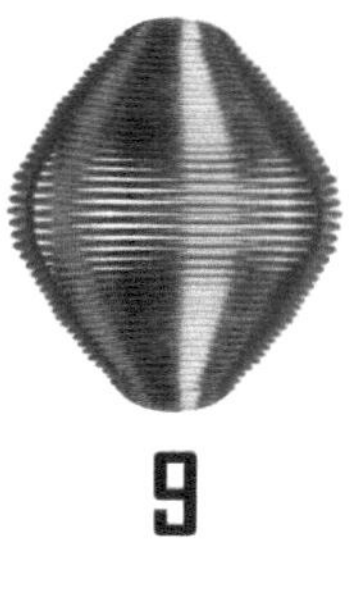

9
Playing By Ear

Aurélie's description of the food at the Second Chance Café turned out to be an understatement. The bacon-cheeseburger I ordered was excellent, as was a basket of the thinnest, crispiest, beer-battered onion rings I'd ever tasted. I had to be satisfied with lemonade, since they did not serve liquor, but she promised we would retire to the lounge after we finished, where there was a small wet bar. I asked her if the whiskey there was spiked, and she assured me that, other than a couple of bottles of fake Jack, the rest of the liquor was authentic.

"I think there's some George Dickel," she said, "and maybe a Canadian blend or two. I don't mean to push it, but you might consider sticking with our simulation. As I'm sure you know by now, it's as good as the real thing, and it not only sharpens memories, but it will help you think more clearly in general."

After sharing a slice of peanut-butter pie, we left the cafeteria and headed down the hall. We'd gone about 50 yards when she stopped in front of an entranceway labeled, simply, "Lounge." The door opened into a large, circular room with several semi-private arrangements of overstuffed chairs around the perimeter. A panorama of animated nature scenes lined the walls, separated by curtains to simulate windows. In the center of the room stood a self-serve bar, surrounded by a scattering of tables and chairs. A dozen or so people sat at the tables, some working on iPads and notebooks, others staring up at flat-screen TV monitors suspended from the domed ceiling.

We made our way to a small alcove next to a faux window that looked out on a rolling surf. Whitecaps glistened under a full moon. Aurélie flicked her fingers over a glowing panel built into the arm of her chair, and the seascape dissolved into a valley of brilliant wildflowers. The scene brought back memories of something I'd once seen on a hike into the High Sierras. I remembered being stunned by the multicolored spectacle, nearly brought to tears by its surreal beauty.

"This one reminds me of ***Parable***," she said. "'A thousand wild imaginings were singing in the trees, and as I strolled in silence through the flowers …'"

"I wrote that song in a valley very much like that."

"It's always been one of my favorites," she said. "The lyrics are so powerful I can close my eyes and imagine being there."

"My producer didn't think much of it. No hook line, he said. Too long. Too mushy. Album material at best. Not unlike a lot of my music. Writing for commercial consumption was never my bag."

"Would you change that if you had the chance?" she asked.

"I don't know. Maybe. Maybe not. If I'd applied my talents in a more commercial way, I probably could have come up with a bunch of hits. But they would have been artificial contrivances, like pages out of a marketing plan instead of music that came from the heart."

"That might be true," she said, "but if you had a string of major hits, you could still write the good stuff, and you'd have a much larger audience to hear it."

"Right. Like the politician who sacrifices his values to get elected because his campaign manager convinces him that if he sells a piece of his soul early in his career he'll be in a more powerful position to do good later. The problem with that is, power itself corrupts, as some famous dude once said."

"That dude would be Lord Acton. And the actual quote is, 'Power tends to corrupt, and absolute power corrupts absolutely. Great men are almost always bad men.'"

"How do you remember things like that?" I said. "There must be thousands of famous quotes from thousands of famous people, and I couldn't remember one of them if my life depended on it. Let alone who said it."

"I remember quotes the same way you remember the words and arrangements to songs. Your brain is wired to respond to music and lyrics, whereas mine is wired to respond to science and philosophy. In those categories I have an almost photographic memory, but when it comes to music, I couldn't find middle C on a piano, let alone identify musical notes simply by hearing them."

"Yeah, well, different strokes for different folks, I guess. My point is that money and fame also corrupt. If I'd gotten rich off writing commercial junk, who knows how that would have changed my perception of what was important? I could very well have fallen in love with the *idea* of being rich. In which case I probably would have continued writing junk, and you would never have become a fan. I managed to write a few fairly commercial songs, but I never once set out to write with the idea in mind of sacrificing my musical integrity to sell a million records. Which, of course, is why I never sold a million records."

She closed her eyes for a moment, then opened them and looked down at her drink. "You know, Rix," she said, "that's one thing we're not going to be able to help you with. There's no way we can predict the long-term consequences of changes you choose to make. We could say this or that should result in something specific, but the consequences will depend upon how you deal with the reverberations of those changes. Heyoka can help you understand the process, but he can't predict the long-term outcome."

"You mean he can't step out of time and see what the results will be?"

"Unfortunately, that's not how it works. I'm sure he told you he can't see into the future, for the simple reason that the future doesn't exist until ... well, until it happens."

"He mentioned that," I said. "I thought it was weird given all the other things he says he can do, but it does make a kind of logical sense. I mean, how could anyone see something that hasn't even happened yet?"

"I know almost everything we're talking about seems impossible," she said. "But that's one thing that actually is. Tell you what, let's go over and get a drink. I need a few minutes to clear my mind, and when we get back I'll try to explain."

I followed her to the bar, where she grabbed a bottle of Jack and held it up for my approval. I thought about it, then decided she might be right about their concoction helping me to think better. Surprisingly, she poured us both a drink from the same bottle.

We returned to our alcove and clinked glasses before sitting down. "In case you're wondering," she said, taking a sip of her drink, "I happen to be a fan of Jack Daniels myself, especially this particular variety. Like I said, it helps sharpen the general thinking process, and we're both going to need every bit of help we can get in that department."

"No argument here," I said, tilting my glass and draining it.

She spent the next few minutes trying to explain the theory of alternate realities and multiple universes, but she might as well have been speaking Greek. When I finally told her to forget the explanation and just tell me what it meant, she shrugged. "What it means is, your new reality will split from the life you have already lived, and you will begin an alternate existence starting at that point in time. From then on you'll be creating a new future, and we can't observe the future. Any future."

"That's a scary prospect, you know. Real scary, in fact. I've never been much of a gambler, and I'm not sure I want to start by rolling the dice into a future I can't foresee."

"But you've been doing that all your life," she said. "We all have. Every choice we make involves a gamble. Granted, some are educated choices, but there are never any guarantees. Life would be an unmitigated bore if we knew the outcome of every move we made before we made it."

"Yeah, well, I don't have a very good track record when it comes to making choices. And I doubt I'd be much better at it in a new existence." I stood and walked to the bar, returning with the bottle of fake Jack. I filled our glasses, then sat down and studied the window scene, which now showed a crystalline mountain lake. As I watched, raindrops began to fall, creating multiple overlapping circles on the otherwise-still water. I was trying to see a pattern in those complex interactions, when Aurélie broke the silence.

"With all the experience you have under your belt, don't you think you'd be able to make better choices? How many times have you said things like, 'If I only had …' or 'Damn, I wish I'd …?' The alternatives could turn out to be just as bad, but I doubt it. You already know the consequences of one course of action, so at least those dice you're rolling will be loaded in your favor."

"Maybe so," I said. "However, there's one thing you're not taking into consideration, and that is how badly I've treated my brain over the years. I don't have a tenth of the mental capacity I had when I was twenty, and my memory is about on a par with that of an Alzheimer's patient. So taking this brain back to an earlier time would probably result in more of a disaster than the first time around."

"That's where you're wrong," she said. "For one thing, though you may not realize it, your brain is already under repair." She held up her half-filled glass and smiled. "And although we won't be transferring the actual organ, in Stage Two you'll be reliving many periods in your early life, which will make those faded memories seem like they happened yesterday. After the actual transfer, your mind—which is separate from your brain—will not only retain those memories, but will also retain the wisdom you've accumulated over the years."

"My mind is separate from my brain?"

"Yes," she said. "Strange as it may sound, the mind or consciousness is an independent entity. That two-pounds or so of gray matter in your skull is only a rather sophisticated repository. If you think of the brain as a computer hard drive and your consciousness as the software and data base, the transfer process would be similar to moving all the software and data from one computer to another. Except in this case we can't use a direct connection. Instead, we have to extract your consciousness, creating a sort of disembodied persona, then move that persona into an alternate universe where we can implant it in the brain of a younger you."

"A disembodied persona …" I said. "Sounds like a ghost or a soul."

"You could use that analogy," she said. "However, belief in the afterlife is a matter of faith, not science, and to say such a thing as a soul exists would mean jumping into a quagmire of differing theologies we would rather avoid. Consciousness, on the other hand, is something we know exists because it is evident in the transition between life and death. Defining it beyond that is virtually impossible. Knowing consciousness exists and can be manipulated does not mean we know what it is."

"You guys are a trip," I said. "You con me, drug me, then have the audacity to ask me to let you experiment on a nebulous thing in my head you can't even define? Why should I trust you? You haven't even proven your claims about the drug cocktail you've been feeding me. Except for a few interesting flashbacks—which are nothing new for me—I have yet to notice any overall improvement in my memory. In fact, a few minutes ago I tried to remember how to find my way back to the villa and realized there was not a chance in hell."

"That's short-term memory, Rix. It will be the last to come back because it's the most difficult to restore. Your long-term memory should already be filling in at a pretty rapid pace."

"According to you."

"You don't have to take my word for it," she said with a condescending smirk. "Test it out for yourself. I know you have to use cheat sheets nowadays to remember most of your repertoire, so pick out an obscure song from the '60s, one you may have only played once in your life, and see if anything comes to mind. Better yet, how about something from your childhood as a boy soprano, like ***La Donna È Mobile***."

"Oh, sure, like I'm supposed to remember an Italian aria from half a century ..." But before I could finish the sentence, I heard that song playing in my mind, with all the words and music clear as a bell. Sung by Mario Lanza, no less. From there, I went on to some of the earliest rock and folk music I could think of, the lyrics and arrangements flowing through my head like medley. I must have gotten lost in the memories, because they didn't stop until I heard Aurélie calling my name. When I looked at her, she was smiling like a Cheshire cat.

"The woman is fickle," she said. "In case you didn't know, that's what ***La Donna È Mobile*** means in English. You probably haven't thought of that song since you were forced—against your will, I might add—to sing it at a recital when you were eleven years old."

She was right, not only about my age, but about the fact that I hated having to learn the song. Back then, before I rebelled against classical music and opera, I'd been forced to sing more songs in Italian and Latin than in English. And I had to memorize them phonetically because I never could learn to speak any foreign language. In Spanish class, I was always called on to read out loud because my accent and inflections were perfect, but I failed the subject just the same.

"What does fickle mean, anyway?" I said.

"Fickle? I don't know, shifty? Ephemeral? Flirtatious?"

"Sounds kind of like this French-Canadian-Inuit girl I know."

"Come on," she said, pulling me to my feet. "I think we'd better call it a night before we get into a verbal battle you are sure to lose."

"Oh, yeah?" I said, following her unsteadily into the hallway. "I wouldn't count on that. I may be no match for you in the brains department, but I'm pretty damned good at arguing. Hell, I drove off two loving and faithful wives using nothing more than sarcasm and nasty rhetoric. And, yes, I am intimately aware of what the word rhetoric means, he says with artificial eloquence."

I AWOKE WITH MY arms wrapped around Robin's soft body, hoping for a nice session of morning sex. Unfortunately, when I opened my eyes, I realized the reason she seemed so soft was because she was a pillow. As the events of the night before tried to push through the cloud of a simulated hangover, I began to recall a few details from my conversation with Aurélie, none of which were encouraging. It wasn't only the fact that I had to go into this mind trip blind, with no way to know the consequences of any changes I might try to make, she'd told me it was going to be a one-way street; no do-overs or coming back. After that, my recollection of the conversation degenerated into a drunken haze.

"You mad at me?" said a voice, barely audible over what sounded like the hum of an air conditioner. I rolled over to see Aurélie leaning on one elbow in a bed about three feet from mine.

"Mad?" I said, looking past her at an open door, through which I could see the blurry outline of a sink. *Hotel room*. I thought. "Where are we?"

"You don't remember?" she said, sitting up and wrapping the bedspread around her.

"Remember what? Hey, I thought that stuff was supposed to turn me into a memory savant."

"It will, Rix, but you sort of overdid things last night, so it'll take a while for the hangover effects to wear off. In case you've forgotten, you brought the bottle back here and, by the time we got through wrestling, you'd emptied it."

"Wrestling?"

"Give it a while," she said. "How about some breakfast?"

BREAKFAST AT THE SECOND Chance Café brought back memories of the Waffle House, my favorite after-hours eatery in the States. After scarfing down a waffle, a side of sausage, and a glass of ice-cold milk, I felt almost human again. Between bites I managed to drag a few details of our alleged wrestling match out of Aurélie. She didn't call it attempted rape, and she wasn't upset with me, but I did find out why my nuts were aching; apparently it had something to do with her knee.

Back at the lounge, we were joined by Heyoka, who apologized for bailing out on us the night before. "It's the damned money," he said as we sat under a scene of a forest glen with grazing deer and foraging squirrels. "If I didn't have to screw with that, I'd have all the time in the world. So, did you pump my little friend here?"

I looked at Aurélie and she shrugged. "He knows not of what he speaks. I'm sure he meant pump me for information."

"I meant it both ways, my dear. But I won't press you on your bedroom antics. Rix, I assume you got her to answer some questions?"

"Some," I said.

"And the answers only added to your discomfiture?"

"Good guess."

"Don't let that discourage you. It's always darkest before the dawn. Or maybe I'm thinking of the calm before the storm. I'm not very good with quotes and sayings like our human data bank here." He winked at Aurélie. "In any case, there are important things we need to discuss that I doubt she got into last night. Things you'll need to think about before you make a decision."

"There's more?" I said. "Having to draw to a metaphorical inside straight isn't enough?"

"Oh, I can assure you the odds of success are far more favorable than that. In fact, I would give the process at least a ninety-nine-point-three-percent chance of working perfectly. We've done all manner of preliminary experiments and calculations and—"

"I'm not doubting what you can do," I said. "I'm doubting my ability to make the right choices the second time around. Aurélie told me I'll only have one shot, that I can't come back and try again. She also made it clear that you can't help me because you can't see into my new future any more than you can see into my current one."

"That's true, Rix. However, I *can* give you some insight into things you'll have to deal with."

"And those would be?"

He looked at Aurélie. "What do you think Ms. Kunayak? You want to take this one?"

She frowned. "I don't know, Mr. Diddlybust. What are we talking about? The frustration factor?"

I rolled my eyes. "Oh, great. On top of everything else, there's a frustration factor?"

"To be perfectly honest, yes," Heyoka said. "And the severity of that frustration will depend on how far back you choose to go. If you were to go back to yesterday, or even last year, there would be little if any. If, on the other hand, you choose to go back to your childhood ... But here, let me illustrate." He nodded at Aurélie, who flicked her fingers over the panel in her chair. "Tell me," he continued, "are you familiar with the film ***Bicentennial Man***?"

"Based on Asimov's novelette ***The Positronic Man***. Seen it many times."

"Good. Then let me use Andrew the robot as a metaphoric example." He directed my attention to the video window, where the forest glen had been replaced by an early scene from the movie showing Andrew being uncrated. "This is Andrew as we first see him, primitive but certainly humanoid. Note the artificial appearance, the jerky mechanical movements. Now let's compare the primitive version to the technically evolved model." Half the scene was replaced by a clip from later in the film, showing Andrew as he looked toward the end. "Here he is at his most advanced. As you can see, his physical appearance and movements are exactly like those of a real human being. Likewise, his positronic brain has evolved considerably."

"Okay, so what does this have to do with me?" I asked.

"I'll get to that in a minute. For now, let's say we do this." The head of the later Andrew opened and his brain floated out, inserting itself into the head of the earlier model. "Transplanting Andrew's advanced computer processing capabilities into his more primitive body would create a robot with all the computational power and memory of the later version. However, that robot would be limited by the earlier model's less sophisticated physical abilities and appearance, which could lead to problems. For example, even though its new brain might *think* it can, this hybrid Andrew probably wouldn't be able to handle delicate objects without breaking them. And he certainly couldn't pass as a human being, either physically or intellectually."

As he said this, the robots were replaced by an image of me as a young boy holding my first guitar. "What we'll be doing," he continued, "is essentially the same thing. When we transplant your older human consciousness into a younger version of yourself, you'll find you are limited by your less-mature body."

"Limited?" I said, trying to imagine such a scenario. "How exactly?"

"One example would be the disappearance of the years of musical training and practice that have conditioned your voice and fingers to do certain things almost autonomically. Think about it. What if you went back to the day you picked up your first guitar? Imagine the frustration of knowing how to play, but not being able to get your fingers to do what you wanted them to. Not only would your hands be smaller, they would lack the strength and dexterity to execute the complex chord changes and fingerstyle patterns you perform today without conscious thought. Even though your brain is sending the correct commands, those neurological signals would be going to appendages that could not obey them."

I watched my younger self struggle to play a simple bar chord, remembering the months of practice it took before my aching fingers became calloused and the muscles in my hands grew strong enough to press all six strings against the frets at once.

"In addition," he said, "gone would be the years of private voice lessons that conditioned your vocal chords and taught you how to eliminate the break between your falsetto and your normal tenor voice, giving you a nearly four-octave range. You would remember how to do all these things, but it would take years of maturing and practice to raise them to their current levels of perfection."

"That shouldn't be a problem," I said. "I've always practiced a lot, and I enjoy the process of perfecting my technique."

"Maybe so," he said, "but you'll probably find it frustrating not being able to do with perfection what your mind says you should be able to."

"If I decide to go back that far, I'll deal with those things," I said. "What else?"

"Quite a lot, actually. For example, if you went back to your early teen years, you would run into even more serious conflicts between your biological age and your advanced mental capacity. These would be most pronounced in the inevitable tug-of-war between your juvenile endocrine system and your adult desires."

"Endocrine system." I repeated. "That's glands and hormones, right?"

"It is, and that system is especially volatile during puberty. It's hard to say how this interaction will play out, but one problem may arise when you become uncontrollably horny—which you will from time to time—and your adult mind wants you to proposition someone Aurélie's age. Also, since you would know a lot more about sex than other kids your age, that knowledge could become a major frustration when you find yourself trying to perform in ways your body is not yet mature enough to allow."

"Wonderful," I said, unable to conceal my growing despair, "Anything else I should be considering?"

"There are many things, Rix," he said. "So many in fact that there's no way we can know what they all are or how they will interact with each other. Obviously, there are no medical or psychological studies of the phenomena, since it's never been observed before. Consequently, you'll be on your own when it comes to figuring out how to cope."

"So, what you're saying is that I'm going to have to play it by ear."

"You are," he said. "And although it may seem like a difficult thing to face, there's probably no one on earth who could handle it any better than you. After all, you've been playing by ear all your life. You don't need a road map any more than you need sheet music. All you need are your instincts and your memories. In fact, that's one reason why I chose you."

"What, my ability to improvise? That's not unique among musicians."

"Yes, but there are few who can do it as nimbly and seamlessly as you," he said. "Being able to think on your feet will be a great asset when it comes to confronting situations that arise unexpectedly. And believe me, you're going to face many of those. One of the things you do better than just about anyone is what you musicians call faking it. Your years of working in cover bands honed that skill to perfection, and it will serve you well."

He glanced at the video screen, where the image had changed to one of me fronting The Madisons, the last band I worked with before striking out on my own. We were basically a blues-rock group, although we played all kinds of venues, from teen concerts, to frat parties, to social gatherings for retirees where we had to take requests for ancient standards we'd never played.

"But the real reason I sought you out goes much deeper than that," Heyoka continued as the image shimmered and dissolved into another scene, this one of a darkened stage with a spotlight on me performing solo. "You know, I wasn't lying when I said I was one of your biggest fans. I've been following your career for many decades, not for scientific reasons, but because I love your music. You wouldn't be aware of it, but I've attended dozens of your concerts and club performances over the years, and I've always felt you deserved more notoriety than you were afforded."

While he spoke, the screen began to show a montage of my solo career, starting in the early days after a couple of my songs had charted, and running through the decades that followed. Seeing the venues change from concert halls to small auditoriums to "intimate" nightclub settings was depressing, but even worse was watching my hair lose its color while my smooth, tanned skin faded to chalky parchment like a decomposing corpse.

"During those years," he went on, "I was developing the techniques I've been using to simulate the kind of observational time travel I experienced on my vision quests. And once I had that process perfected, I began to think about carrying it one step further, from observation and benign participation, to actual transference of consciousness. It may come as a surprise to you, but one of the things that sparked my interest in this came from wondering how you might have fared if you'd made different choices in your life. So, in a way, you were the one who inspired me in the first place."

That cement-mixer feeling started to invade my brain again, and I had a strong urge to get out of there. Though I'd never been claustrophobic, the walls seemed to be closing in, and I had trouble breathing. "I need to get out of here," I said, starting to rise. But before I could get to my feet it felt as if a hand grenade exploded in my chest and everything went black.

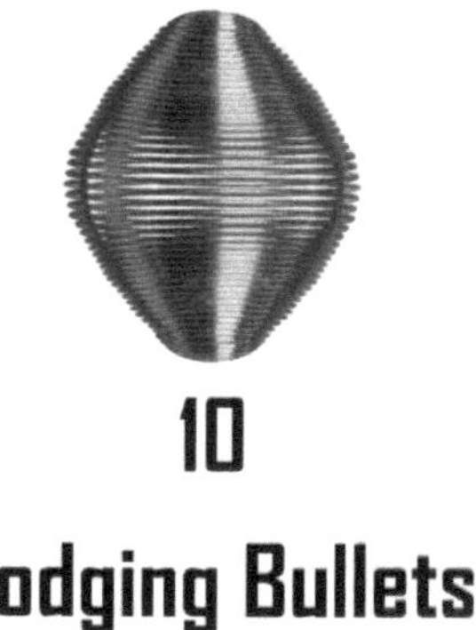

10
Dodging Bullets

Rix? Hey, Rixter!" The voice thrummed against my skull like a roll of thunder. "Come on, Rix, it's time to wake up." My eyelids felt like they had been plastered shut, but after a few tries I managed to crack through the goo and open a slit. "That's good," said the voice, which I now recognized as Aurélie's. "Can you squeeze my hand?" I felt her fingers wiggle against my palm and I managed a weak squeeze, whereupon she let out a whoop. "He's baaack," she said, returning my grip. That's when I felt the log someone had stuck in my throat, and the beeps and buzzes increased in volume around me until I could no longer think.

MY SECOND AWAKENING WAS a bit less unpleasant. For one thing, the log seemed to be gone from my throat, and the calliope of hospital sounds was muted. "Water," I managed to croak over the melting asphalt on the back of my tongue.

"It's only a little ice," Aurélie said, as a cool moisture spread across my lips. "We can't give you water until you're able to sit up."

"Whaa … haa …?"

"Okay," she said, "Now don't freak out on me, but you had a little heart attack. During the cardiac catheterization they found a blocked artery, so they did a balloon angioplasty and inserted a stent. There was minimal damage to your heart muscle, but the angioplasty released a cloud of plaque into your bloodstream, some of which ended up in your brain causing a couple of minor ischemic strokes. Anyway, barring any setbacks, they say you should be up and around in a couple of weeks. The surgeon did mention that your kidneys and liver are in bad shape, and he had a few choice words about cleaning up your act, so we should talk about that when we get back to the villa. For now, you need to rest and give yourself time to heal."

"Mmmmm," I said. And the room went dark again.

THE NEXT FEW DAYS were a jumble of tests and dreams and removal of life-support equipment, through all of which Aurélie remained by my side. She was always there when I woke up, sometimes accompanied by Heyoka, who seemed much more concerned about my condition than I might have expected. Aurélie, on the other hand, was upbeat: joking around, reading to me, and cajoling me into playing Scrabble—in order to exercise my recovering synapses, she said. I'd developed what I thought was a sizable vocabulary from years of songwriting, but I was no match for the human data bank. As soon as I was ambulatory, physical therapists took over, and it wasn't long before I was almost back to normal, with only a slight limp and a little numbness on the right side of my face.

Since it was clear I was not going to make it to my gig in Bordeaux, Aurélie had taken it upon herself to contact my agent and explain the situation, a gesture I found reassuring because it seemed like they were acknowledging the fact that, if I chose to, I could refuse their offer and resume my tour, such as it was. The heart attack, however, had served as a wakeup call. I knew I'd dodged a bullet from a gun that was still cocked and loaded, and that I'd be hard pressed to survive the next round as anything more than a human turnip.

Back at the villa, Aurélie and I settled into a routine of daily, therapeutic walks punctuated by humorous innuendo and futile debate over the sex that was not to be. Once I agreed to go through with the experiment, her argument turned from the surrogate excuse to one based on the fact that I wasn't going to be around to spend the rest of my short life with her. And my rebuttal that we should take the opportunity while we had it fell flat. Besides, she said, if we fell in love and I decided not to go back, Heyoka would never forgive her, and that was apparently more important than a few rolls in the hay with me.

During one of our walks, I asked if she would ever consider going back herself, and she said there was no reason, that she was satisfied with her life as it had evolved so far. "I can't say how I'd feel if I were in your shoes," she said. "I'm hoping I have a long way to go, but even if I don't, I tend to think that one time around will be enough for me. If I did go back, I wouldn't know what to change."

"That's what I'm thinking," I said. "I mean, I've had some ideas, but how do I know what the consequences will be? If you believe the science-fiction writers, I could step on a twig or swat a fly, and the butterfly effect might end up causing a nuclear war."

"I don't think that's true," she said, as we negotiated a narrow trail behind the villa. "I'm not sure any particular change you make will have much of an impact beyond your own immediate future. It's like the ripples in a pond that radiate from a dropped stone. Unless you continue to drop more stones, the ripples dissipate and the water becomes calm again, just as the opposing forces of yin and yang tend to balance things over time."

"You a Buddhist?"

"I'm a mathematician using Buddhist terminology to describe a proven theorem called LLN, or the law of large numbers, something you probably think of as the law of averages. Christians might refer to it as reaping what you sow. Casino operators call it the odds. It doesn't matter how you describe it—yin-yang, divine justice, karma—it all comes down to a mathematical certainty: things always average out over time."

"Karma," I said. "I've always thought that made a certain kind of logical sense. Unfortunately, I've seen little evidence of it in real life. Some of the biggest assholes in the world seem to be doing just fine, prospering, having loads of fun, all at the expense of others about whom they couldn't give less of a damn. If there is this averaging out factor, then I'm thinking it would require more than one lifetime to play out, which would mean reincarnation. And isn't that what Heyoka's trying to do: develop a scientifically acceptable version of reincarnation? I mean, you're giving a soul, or a consciousness as you call it, a second chance by transplanting it into a new body."

"I guess you could look at it that way," she said.

"And that brings to mind something I've been thinking about. Heyoka has never said there would be any limitations on what I choose to do in my new life, other than those I put on myself. But what you seem to be suggesting is that there are balancing forces out there that would limit the effects of the choices I make. And if that's true, I'm wondering what would happen if I used my knowledge of past events to make a bunch of money, or publish hit songs before the original writers come up with them."

"I don't know," she said, stopping at a spot that looked out over the valley below. We sat together on a fallen tree, and she twiddled with the leaves on a tiny branch that clung to the life ebbing from its host. "If I were to speculate, I'd have to say there would be a price to pay. I have no idea what that price would be, but it seems to me you'd have to settle the account sooner or later. Would you do that, Rix? Take advantage of your knowledge just to get rich or hurt others by stealing their material?"

"Nah," I said. "Money never meant much to me, and fame wouldn't mean a thing if it didn't come from my own creativity. I have my own style and that's not going to change. I might make different decisions about how to apply my talents, who to befriend, what options to choose when it comes to venues and producers and agents and such. But I would never steal someone else's material. Of course, I couldn't avoid being influenced by the music I've heard, but I'd try my best not to let that influence result in outright copies. After twenty years of working in cover bands, there's nothing I hate more than playing other people's music."

"I'm glad," she said, touching my hand. "In spite of all your shortcomings and errors in judgment, I like this version of Rix Vaughn. At least the essence of him. Strip away some of the bad decisions, and I think what you'd have left is a pretty good guy."

"You should speak to my ex-wives and a few dozen groupies before passing judgment on the purity of my soul. I talk a good game, and I even believe a lot of what I say, but there's some awful stinky stuff in my background that proves I don't always listen to that little angel perched on my right shoulder. In fact, for most of my life I've been more prone to the yang than the yin."

"But don't you see," she said, "that kind of honesty is a perfect example of what I'm talking about. The fact that you're willing to admit those things about yourself demonstrates one of your most admirable traits: you say what you believe to be true, even if it means being candid about your own shortcomings. I knew this long before I met you, because it comes through in your music, which, at times, is almost painfully honest."

"What makes you think that?" I said. "How do you know it isn't all fabricated bullshit?"

"Anyone who really listens to your songs knows it isn't, Rix. Honesty isn't something you can fake. Oh, there are a lot of young superstars nowadays that sing about their broken hearts and love affairs gone wrong, then claim the songs came from personal experiences. But anyone with a discerning ear can recognize that the lyrics are contrived to pluck the heartstrings of teens and tweens. Sad tales of love gone wrong. Angry tirades against former lovers. Gangsta rap that plays on the sexism and bigotry many hold secretly in their hearts. It's all *supposed* to be honest, but most of it reeks of deliberate commercial manipulation. And you said it yourself: you never set out to write with commercial possibilities in mind."

"Lot of good it's done me, this so-called honesty."

"That all depends on how you define 'good,' as Bill Clinton might say. You know as well as I do that the reason most music sells has little to do with quality, it has to do with connections and money spent on promotion. There are thousands of struggling singers and musicians out there right now who are just as talented as the few dozen who've made it big. Their only problem is that they don't have the right industry connections, or the money to promote themselves independently. The Internet was supposed to level the playing field, but that turned into a vast wasteland of untalented wannabes. Even if it hadn't, the minimal exposure provided to independents by the Web could never compete with the money and vast promotional capabilities of the major record labels."

"Yeah, well, I guess the cream has a harder time rising to the top nowadays, but the fact is it never was that easy. And I'm not talking about myself here. If you want to know where all the new Dylans or Taylors or Jackson Brownes are—the songwriters whose words actually mean something— most of them are stuck in bars, working for union scale and a few dollars shoved in a mason jar by drunks requesting songs the artists despise."

"Maybe you could figure a way to change all that," she said. "Maybe, with your knowledge of the industry, you could go back and

... I don't know, become a producer or something. Sell that piece of your soul to get rich and be the benefactor of the unknown singer-songwriter. It's not written in stone that you would automatically turn into a scumbag as Lord Acton suggested."

"Fat chance," I said, but the idea lit a spark in my brain. I didn't know what that spark was exactly, or how I could fan it into a flame. Still, it was something to think about.

We sat silently after that, snuggling together in the early evening chill while another spectacular sunset spread iridescent colors across the darkening sky. Like nervous teenagers exploring the boundaries of intimacy, we intertwined fingers, refusing to move until the gathering darkness threatened our safe return. Finally, with little more than the pale glow of a crescent moon to light our way, we rose and walked hand-in-hand toward the fading silhouette of the villa.

Part Two

Then

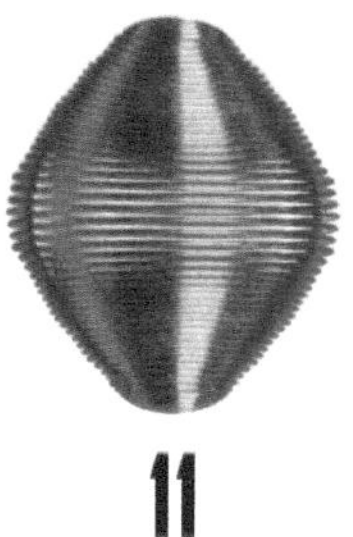

11
Coming Attractions

We spent the following weeks conditioning my brain for Stage Two. Little by little the active ingredients in Heyoka's chemical stew were strengthened to the point that the results became evident. Not only was I able to remember details of my life long obscured by a fog of alcohol and drugs, I'd almost beaten Aurélie at Scrabble a couple of times. The only problem was the headaches, which sometimes lasted for hours, and were often so severe I could sense her entering my darkened room simply by the movement of air.

Heyoka didn't want me taking pain killers, especially opiates, because he said they would interfere with the rejuvenation process. So he had Fred come in and try to adjust my Qi, whatever that was. Fred, it turns out, had spent many years studying Chinese medicine in Tibet and was adept in the ancient arts of acupuncture and something called Qigong. While he stuck me with needles and taught me how to breathe, move, and visualize, Heyoka continued to adjust the chemicals until the headaches subsided. We waited another week to make sure they were gone for good, and a few days later I was deemed ready to enter the next phase.

Aurélie and I made the long trip back to the lab and returned to the NIFS Complex, where we took a different hallway that ended at another airlock. "What you're going to experience here will be much more realistic than the previews I showed you before," she said, as we emerged from the airlock into a small circular chamber. A translucent dome took up most of the floor space, and when she passed her hand over a panel on the wall, the dome rose to reveal a comfortable-looking recliner. "This procedure combines sophisticated spatial manipulation with advanced holographic imagery, giving you the ability to adjust the point of view to your liking. Essentially, you're going to be a fly on the wall, observing a linear montage of your entire life. Go ahead, take a seat."

I started to sit, then hesitated. "I'm not sure I like the idea of sharing all the gory details of my past with you," I said with a smile.

"That bad, huh?" She pushed on my chest until I fell into the recliner. "Well, you don't have to worry about airing your dirty laundry. Much as I'd love to, I won't be enjoying the show with you. I'll be monitoring your progress, but this will be a private exhibition, for your eyes only."

As the chair adjusted to form-fit my body, she positioned my hands over some controls on the armrests. "Use the trackpad under your right hand to change the visual perspective," she said. "Under your left is a slider, similar to a fader on a mixdown board. Push forward to speed up the action, pull back to slow things down. The buttons on either side of the trackpad allow you to skip ahead or back in three-month segments."

I felt for the slider and trackpad, then located the skip buttons. "I assume the right button is for skipping forward?" I said.

"You assume correctly, and I suggest you use it often. A digital readout in the lower-left corner of your visual field will keep you abreast of how much real time has elapsed, so keep an eye on that and try to move along at a pretty fast clip. If you get involved in the details of too many events, the process could take days or even weeks. Remember, this is only a preview to help you choose which periods to relive during Stage Two. Now try to relax, and let me know when you're ready."

I made sure my fingers were touching the controls, then gave a quick nod.

"Okay," she said. "We're going to start in the delivery room."

I experienced a moment of claustrophobic panic as the dome descended around me, cutting off all sound. Seconds later, a brilliant flash of light left me blinking away stars. When my vision cleared, I was looking down at my mother writhing in pain on a hospital bed. Even though I couldn't hear her screams, seeing her in agony was gut wrenching, and I stabbed at the forward skip button until I saw myself as a toddler stumbling through thick white sand toward a rolling surf. With the progress back at normal speed, I experimented with the trackpad, using it like a joystick to circle around and view the scene from various angles.

Spellbound by the sensation of disembodied weightlessness, I watched Mom sweep me up in her arms while I struggled to release myself from her grip. She held me tight as she waded into the water, where I laughed and splashed and grabbed at her swimming cap. After wrestling with my slippery body for about five minutes, she decided she'd had enough and headed for shore.

Back on the beach, we used paper cups and a plastic bucket to build a crude sandcastle near the edge of the water, then waited for the incoming tide to wash it away. We were rinsing sand off under the public showers when I remembered what Aurélie had said and looked at the real-time digital readout. Over an hour had passed, so I pushed forward on the slider, and soon the playback took on an eerie resemblance to the fabled near-death, life-flashing-before-your-eyes experience.

Even at fast-forward, it was fascinating to watch myself grow and change, but I knew I would not want to start over that far back, so I used the skip button to jump past the more mundane phases of my childhood. I slowed things down again when I saw myself studying music with Carol Henderson, reveling in the replay of those innocent days before I rebelled against choir solos and stuffy opera recitals. 'The Devil's music,' Carol called it, blaming my exodus on the increasing popularity of Rock & Roll and R&B. She begged me to stick with the classical stuff, but the dream of stardom—a fantasy bolstered by Elvis and Chuck Berry and dozens of other emerging rock stars—was far too enticing.

My mother, bless her heart, refused to take Carol's side in the matter. Even though she had hoped for another Great Caruso or Mario Lanza, she believed in allowing me unfettered creative freedom. She even opened a charge account at the local music store, giving me permission to sign for all the 45s I wanted. And when my twelfth birthday rolled around, she talked my dad into buying me an electric guitar—a Gibson Les Paul Jr. with a sunburst finish. Seeing that guitar brought to mind one of my greatest regrets: that over the years I'd managed to destroy, sell, or hock dozens of instruments, each one associated with an important stage in my progression as a musician. These included the Les Paul, which today would be worth somewhere north of six grand, not to mention its sentimental value as a milestone in my development as a guitarist.

I lingered on the scene of my dad presenting me with the Les Paul on the morning of my birthday, then skipped ahead until I approached the end of my twelfth year. And it was only then that I started thinking about points in time I might want to revisit.

Shortly after my thirteenth birthday, I became infatuated with a girl who would change the future course of my life. Pat was older than me, and she not only ended my virginity, but within two short years she transformed me from a nerdy child prodigy into a street-wise rocker. She also introduced me to alcohol and drugs, laying the groundwork for the addictions that would plague me for the rest of my days. I'd forgotten how badly our affair had ended until I noticed the growing animosity between us. And, not wanting to relive our painful breakup, I skipped ahead, slowing down again in my later teens. For a while I became mesmerized, watching myself with all that youthful energy, practicing for hours a day and working with musicians I hadn't seen in years.

I was so absorbed in this era that I failed to keep a close eye on the digital readout, and three hours of real time passed before I reached my mid-twenties and the tumultuous period that would both define me as an artist and set the stage for my downhill slide. It was a decade that began with my decision to go solo and ran through the worst of my drug abuse; a time of free love, passionate obsession, and devastating loss that served as the prologue for my slow, steady descent into has-been obscurity.

Morbid curiosity kept me from speeding through those years, and three more hours of real time elapsed before I noticed the subtle changes in my appearance I'd seen when Heyoka flashed through the venues of my declining solo career. I had no desire to observe my aging deterioration in detail, so I skipped ahead until I saw myself on stage at LeMusique, then pressed the button one last time, putting an end to the review.

REEXAMINING THE HIGHS AND lows of an entire lifetime in less than eight hours was emotionally exhausting, and I emerged from the experience weakened both mentally and physically. The headaches returned, and my listlessness and lack of energy worried Aurélie, so she had Heyoka call in the surgeon and neurologist to take a look at me. Their verdict was that my recovery had been slowed, though not derailed, and that I needed at least a week of bed rest. Aurélie insisted on two weeks, and, to make sure I complied, she moved into my room, sleeping on a rollaway bed and checking my vital signs at regular intervals. One side benefit of this arrangement was that she spent almost all her spare time with me, applying cold compresses, massaging my neck, and talking about her past to help take my mind off the pain.

Aurélie's early childhood had been confusing. A precocious child with savant-like intelligence, she was speaking in complete sentences before she was one year old, and had mastered simple mathematics by age two. Her parents—both alcoholics—constantly argued over religion and politics, often fighting in front of her and ignoring her questions. When they occasionally gave in to her foot-stomping demands to be heard, their answers were incomprehensible.

Her mother, a staunch Roman Catholic, could not accept her father's belief that all living and non-living things—people, animals, inanimate objects, even forces of nature—had a spirit. About the only thing they agreed on was that the human spirit or soul lived on after death. For her mother, this meant entering heaven or hell or purgatory; for her father, it meant crossing over into the 'spirit world.' Priests verses shamans; prayer and hymns verses charms and dances; masks and body paint verses Sunday finery—all very confusing to a little girl whose emotional development hadn't yet caught up with her extraordinary intellect.

Her parents divorced when she was three, and because of their alcoholism and history of abusive behavior, she was placed in a foster home while Child Welfare agents searched for a qualified family member to assume custody. She remained in foster care until a maiden aunt on her mother's side agreed—after a little arm twisting—to take her in. Shortly thereafter, the aunt moved to South Dakota where Aurélie spent the rest of her youth and young adulthood.

Though not much more pleasant than her previous home environment (unbeknownst to the Welfare agents, the aunt also had a drinking problem) she made the best of things, entering school at the age of four, and immersing herself in her studies. She breezed through grade school and junior high, skipping several grades and advancing to high school before she turned twelve.

A high-school physics teacher was first to recognize her unique mathematical intuition. He introduced her to Heyoka, who befriended the aunt and took the spunky young girl under his intellectual wing. At Heyoka's urging, she began to explore the complexities of higher mathematics and quantum physics, though her rebellious nature caused her no end of problems in dealing with the conservative orthodoxy of traditional science. Heyoka paid for her to attend a private college, where she often challenged her professors, coming up with unconventional proofs of hypotheses that had confounded mathematicians for decades. This friction eventually led to her expulsion—not because she was wrong, but because jealousy and bruised egos would not allow her superiors to admit that a student could surpass them in their chosen fields.

Her parents, who had reconciled and split several times, eventually moved to South Dakota, sniffing an opportunity to share in Heyoka's largess. That plan would fail; however, their proximity presented Aurélie with the opportunity to visit them more often. Unfortunately, her unshakable opinions on what she referred to as "the mythology of religion," clashed with their spiritual practices, leading to sometimes vehement arguments over her refusal to accept any belief in the supernatural. She did, however, find Heyoka's pursuit of scientific explanations for so-called spiritual phenomena fascinating, adding her considerable skills to his in developing the procedures they were now testing on me.

When I suggested to her that the invisible entity she called consciousness could very well be what others referred to as the spirit or soul, she agreed, with reservations.

"I don't mind the labels people use to describe consciousness," she said. "But to say something is non-material or spiritual because it can't be seen is incorrect. We can't *see* subatomic particles, but we know they exist as material elements because of the evidence they leave behind as they travel. The same is true of consciousness. Even before Heyoka proved its existence as something independent of the body, many in the scientific community were warming to the idea, mainly because we've never been able to understand precisely what happens at the moment of death. We know the physical causes of death, but the question has always been: what is the essence of life that abandons the body? Where does it go and why? At the present time science doesn't have the answers to those questions. That time will come, however. Just as our description of the atom went from theoretical postulation to mathematical proof to visual evidence, one day we will be able to isolate, examine, and describe consciousness in scientific terms."

"Speaking of labels," I said, "what about the most famous one? I know you think belief in a supernatural god is silly, but one thing I've always had a problem with is that science can't explain what started everything. Saying it was the Big Bang only begs the question: what came before? Then what came before that and so on into infinity. Even if it's a never-ending cycle of expansion and collapse, logic seems to dictate that there had to be a beginning, something that created the original universe or at least drafted the blueprint. And since science can't explain where it all came from except by citing unproven theoretical postulations, what's wrong with some people calling it God?"

"Ascribing a name to something we don't yet understand is okay with me," she said, "so long as we never stop trying to explain it. But when it comes to clarifying theories about the origins of the universe, you can throw logic out the window. As with quantum mechanics, standard human logic fails when we attempt to explain even basic aspects of the macro world, such as its incomprehensible distances and the anomalies of the space-time continuum."

Though sometimes perplexing and mildly contentious, I enjoyed our talks, and after a while it became clear that the chemical brain scrubbing was doing wonders for my overall mental acuity. Another thing I noticed was that Aurélie no longer treated me with condescending sarcasm as she had earlier. As a consequence, our conversations became more relaxed and personal. She would often hold my hands while I talked about the things I regretted in my past, and these were gestures that seemed to suggest affection rather than scientific curiosity.

This new level of intimacy made it difficult for me to ignore the desire I'd managed to suppress ever since she'd convinced me sex was out of the question. I tried broaching the subject by urging her to talk about her love life, but she wouldn't take the bait, saying only that after a few years of teenage sexual rebellion and a couple of failed love affairs in her early twenties, she'd given up on finding a mate and become absorbed in her work with Heyoka. Though her abbreviated, matter-of-fact explanation left little room for discussion, I sensed a melancholy in her voice, and it saddened me to think of her as an old maid in the making, trapped in a loveless world of intellectual isolation.

During those two weeks, Aurélie kept me from dwelling on the playback of my life by distracting me with instructions on how things would work in Stage Two. She told me I would be in a dreamlike narcohypnosis, and that time would be compressed as it seems to be during REM sleep. Consequently, each period I chose to relive could last months or even years, while only a day or two would pass in real time. She also cautioned me against becoming too emotionally involved.

"Your body will be in a state similar to suspended animation, but it can still be affected by the emotions you experience. You need to remember that these events have already happened and try not to let the bad stuff upset you too much. Because the stress of the procedure will tax your already fragile metabolism, we've decided to limit you to three trips back, each to last no longer than three years. We'll be monitoring your physiology, watching for any negative changes, and if things start getting too stressful, we'll have to pull you out. Otherwise, you'll be in control of each trip's duration. By concentrating on a key word, you can stop and return any time you wish, so we have to think of a word that wouldn't normally enter your mind."

I suggested we use "Aurélie" or "Heyoka," but she said those names were too fresh in my memory. We finally decided on "Husereau," assuming Heyoka's middle name was not likely to cross my mind unless I deliberately tried to think of it.

After we had gone over all the instructions, and I no longer showed any signs of mental fatigue, Aurélie suggested I start considering which periods I should relive. And that, she said, was a decision I would have to make on my own.

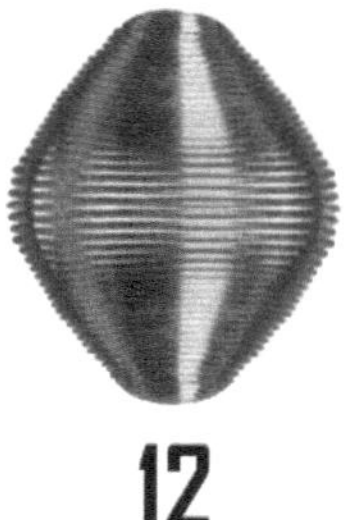

12
Sword of Damocles

My ability to think clearly continued to improve with the daily consumption of Heyoka's ever-changing mixture of chemicals; however, my decision-making skills didn't seem to be enhanced at all. Aurélie said the reason I was having difficulty making these decisions was because they were more emotional than intellectual. And she was right. There were so many things I wished I could have done differently, and so many ways those actions might intertwine with other aspects of my life, that choosing which periods to relive became an enormous challenge.

I found myself considering even relatively minor incidents, times when my selfish actions had hurt others. It was as if Aurélie's reference to karma had stimulated a desire to make amends now that I had a second chance. I wondered if this wasn't a last-ditch attempt to cleanse my soul; like the atheist who becomes a Christian convert on his death bed, or a corporate raider who donates his fortune to charity. Did motivation matter so long as the outcome proved beneficial to everyone involved?

Those thoughts led me down a convoluted path of speculation, and I soon realized Heyoka was right when he said it would be impossible to predict the long-term consequences of my choices. Any change I made would interact with other factors in ways so complex that attempting to forecast the end result turned into an exercise in futility.

Like ripples in a pond, there would be overlaps causing new perturbations that could lead to results as bad or worse than the original outcomes.

Heyoka seemed confident in my ability to play things by ear, that all I needed were my instincts and memories to make the right choices or deal effectively with the wrong ones. That sounded good, but I still wasn't convinced that messing around with fate would be quite so simple. Every time I considered the possible ramifications of correcting a particular transgression, I ended up slogging through a murky swamp of unpredictable possibilities.

Some of my regrets had to do with girls I had bedded; innocent—or maybe not—adolescents whose fascination with even a minor recording star like me had combined with their naïveté to make them vulnerable. The playback had reminded me of my coldhearted attitude toward many of these young women, an attitude mostly attributable to the fact that I was stoned or drunk at the time. Several had been one-night stands, sometimes with tearful aftermaths that resulted in stalking-like pursuit from town to town. Others were girls who seemed intent on attaining bragging rights, like old-west gunslingers adding notches to their six-shooters.

In later years, I'd crossed paths with a few of them, some happily married with kids; some who had become 'professional' groupies, or roadies traveling with the entourages of stars more famous than I would ever be. Still others were druggies or alcoholics, lost souls in continual pursuit of unattainable relationships with entertainers of almost any stripe. How much my uncaring indifference had contributed to their futile search for emotional fulfillment I would never know. Nor would I know what happened to the ones I'd never seen or heard from again. Had they fallen into intractable depression, maybe become self-destructive? Was I giving myself too much credit, accepting too much blame? If they'd never met me, would they have been better off, or had our encounters served as valuable life lessons?

Then there were the career decisions: the struggle for creative independence that led me away from working with other musicians I admired; the refusal to compromise my musical integrity for commercial gain; agents and promoters I'd screwed by not showing up for gigs; recording sessions I'd missed because I was too stoned or hung -over to give a shit. Among these was perhaps the worst judgment call

I'd ever made: my stubborn refusal to let someone else sing ***Sunday Morning Sentinel*** and assure its national release before the war ended.

At first, a simple reversal of that ego-driven act of stupidity seemed like a no-brainer. But when I thought a little deeper I realized there were several possible scenarios to consider, each with its own unforeseeable permutations. For example, if I went back to my teens and tried to clean up my act, would I end up with the necessary industry connections a decade later? Even if I did manage to plot the same general course, would the changes in my early life spread out over time, leading to an altered future in which I wouldn't have a chance to make the demo tape? Or what if we got in a car wreck on the way to Muscle Shoals?

On the other hand, if I started over when I was, say, ten or twelve, perhaps that would open up entirely new vistas, opportunities I hadn't been presented with before. Maybe I could avoid drugs and alcohol, and with a clearer mind I would make better choices from then on. The problem there was that some of my most productive bursts of creativity had been influenced by mind-altering chemicals of one kind or another, and I didn't know if I was willing to chance trading that for the benefits of a cleaner lifestyle. Besides, my actions would be governed by my adult mind, and even though my body would not yet be addicted, I might not be able to control the psychological cravings.

What, then, would be the point of going back at all? If I couldn't change my proclivity for substance abuse, I would end up in the same shape I was in now: physically deteriorating and facing the prospect of a miserable, premature death. Did I really want to go through that all over again?

Finally, there was Robin. If I went back to my early youth, would I be able to follow a path that would bring us together again? Given the potential of the butterfly effect, would she even be interested in me if we did meet? I knew it was partly my addictions that had attracted her in the first place. Sexual chemistry played a role, but it was her mothering instinct that turned what might have been a brief tryst into a loving quest to save me from the ravages of alcohol and drugs. She'd failed, of course, and I had no idea if there was anything I could do to change that.

After a while, the frustration of attempting to determine the ultimate outcome of alterations in my previous behavior led me into a kind of emotional paralysis. Had it not been for Aurélie's calm understanding, my abrupt, often-angry responses to her reasonable questions and suggestions would have driven a wedge between us. Instead, my descent into hopeless confusion seemed to bring us closer.

I had painted myself into a paradoxical corner from which neither logic nor guesswork could show the way out. And I was about to tell them to forget the whole thing, when Aurélie had a sudden change of heart.

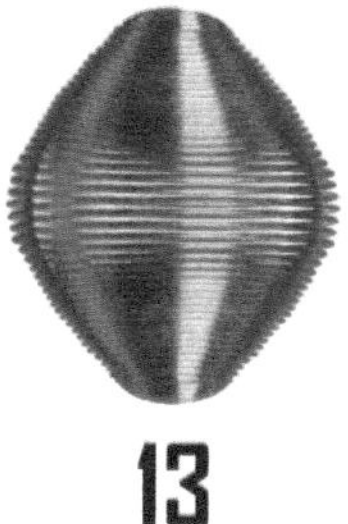

13
Till Death Do Us Part

I first thought Aurélie's capitulation was a mercenary attempt to make sure I stuck with the program. And when I later confronted her, she admitted that was partly true. Whether her initial motivation was dictated by a dedication to seeing the project come to fruition, or there was a more personal reason, didn't matter to me. What mattered was that her acquiescence drew me back from the brink of despair into a fantasy I'd been dreaming of since I'd first seen her bathed in the sparkling light of Heyoka's fireplace.

As we lay in the naked afterglow of the most mind-blowing sex I could remember since I'd been with Robin, I asked her what she meant by 'partly.'

"I meant saving the program wasn't the only reason I changed my mind," she said. When she didn't continue, I turned to her and cocked an eyebrow. "Okay," she sighed, "but you have to promise you won't get angry."

"As long as you don't try to bullshit me," I said. "Why don't we start with that ambush in the shower?"

"Oh, that. I was thinking about ***Robin's Song***. You know the line: *Loving in a veil of soapsuds*? I assumed making love in the shower was something you and Robin enjoyed, so I did my best."

"Pretty analytical," I said. "Was that the plan, to imitate Robin? I thought your major objection to our having sex was that I would be making love to her memory."

"It was, Rix. And it still is. But I could tell you were about to lose your mind dealing with the confusion and fear of what could happen if you went back, and I wanted to give you a taste of the positive things you could experience again. Not only that, but I ... well, I'm human, goddammit, and I hadn't had sex in so long I'd forgotten what it was like. I know I can't compare to Robin because you two had something special. But I guess I was being a little selfish, trying to kill two birds with one fuck, so to speak."

"One!" I said. "What about the other two? You were amazing, by the way. And I didn't even need my Viagra. Problem is, now I don't want to go back. Even if I only have a year or two left in this life, if I can spend that time with you—"

"Oh, no you don't. You're not going to use me as an excuse. Look, Rix, I'm not Robin. Not even a decent stand-in for her. You were horny and needy as hell, so you let your imagination take over. It was make believe. You have to understand that. The point is, you can have the real thing again if you want. I'm sure of it. All you have to do is ... now wait. Don't start ... We can't ..."

I didn't let her finish.

OUR FOURTH ATTEMPT TO achieve terminal orgasm was nearly successful, for me at least. And once Aurélie realized the danger such frenetic sexual activity might pose for someone in my condition, she refused to allow physical intimacy of any kind. I argued and begged, but when she threatened to check out and turn me over to Fred, I gave up and promised to stop bugging her about it. The fact was, simply being with her—holding hands, listening to her talk, indulging in an occasional chaste hug—was worth the frustration. And even though we both knew the chemistry was still there—that under any other circumstances we'd be jumping each other's bones every time the door closed behind her—we also knew there was no hope for a prolonged relationship between us. Not to mention that the sex might kill me prematurely.

A couple of weeks later I was readmitted to the hospital for a full health-status evaluation, after which the doctors informed me that I might have another eighteen months to live, the last six of which would not be pleasant. Although the angioplasty and stent had temporarily cleared my artery, my heart function was hovering around 45-percent, and the remnants of that cloud of plaque had left me vulnerable to additional blockages and strokes. Plus, I had stage-2 cirrhosis, deteriorating kidneys, advanced pulmonary edema, and a funky gall bladder. Because of my degenerating condition, I wasn't a transplant candidate; a moot point, since my body wouldn't be able to tolerate the trauma of major surgery anyway.

The irony of it all was that I'd fallen in love with someone more than thirty years my junior; and our age difference would not change in my alternate existence. I tried to think of ways Aurélie could go back with me, maybe inhabit the body of someone closer to my age, but she reminded me that doing so would be tantamount to murder. Besides, she would never abandon Heyoka, especially when they were about to complete the most important phase of the project. I was wracking my brain, trying to come up with a workable alternative, when it occurred to me that their research might go beyond Stage Three.

"We haven't thought that far ahead," she told me when I asked. "Right now, all our eggs are in one basket, so to speak. If everything goes as planned—which I'm sure it will, by the way—we'll evaluate the results and see if we can go anywhere from there. But we can't even speculate until we have some data to study."

"So there's a chance the project could continue?"

"A chance, yes. After we go over everything, other possibilities may present themselves. What those possibilities might be we won't know until all the data is in. Even then, we may choose to shut things down and seal the results. Unlike our other research, mind transference involves complex ethical considerations, and disseminating our methods could lead to abuse by unscrupulous entrepreneurs whose only interest is making a buck."

"But you can't see into my new future, so how will you know what the ultimate results are."

"We won't," she said. "The best we can do is monitor your progress for a while and make an evaluation based on what we see. It'll be a judgment call, and a difficult one at that. If the results appear to be positive or even neutral, then maybe we'll consider moving ahead. But we can't be sure what the pitfalls might be until we study at least a few years of results."

"If you're going to monitor me, can we communicate?"

"That remains to be seen. There's no way to know if contacting someone in an alternate universe is possible because we've never been through Stage Three before."

Although she refused to speculate on future possibilities, the fact that they had not yet decided to end the project with Stage Three gave me reason to hope. Hope for what, I didn't know, but I was so fearful of going back, I needed a lifeline to hang onto, even if that lifeline was woven from a few tenuous maybes.

Whatever the future held, I now had little choice but to fulfill my end of the bargain. Not only because I had made a commitment, but because the alternative was a slow, torturous decline, during which I would suffer the added frustration of being denied sexual intimacy with Aurélie. Even if I died quickly from another stroke or heart attack, I would still be dead. Or worse, I could end up as a vegetable. I was scared, but I wasn't about to let fear keep me from accepting a second chance at life.

HAVING DECIDED TO GO ahead with the project, the first order of business was to choose the three periods I wanted to relive in preparation for a final decision. Although Heyoka tried not to let on, I could tell he was growing impatient, most likely worried that I might have another stroke and destroy his careful repair work on my brain. I'd been stalling, but it was now clear that time was running out. So I told Aurélie to go ahead and schedule the Stage-Two previews, promising to make my decision within twenty four hours.

I went to bed that night hoping against hope that the answers, like many of my best songs, would come to me in a dream. Unfortunately, my dreams were no help. In the only one I could remember, I was on *Let's Make a Deal,* wearing a Grim-Reaper costume and trying to draw Monty Hall's attention by jumping up and down like an idiot. I was eventually selected, and by the time I got to the stage Heyoka had taken Monty's place as host. I ended up as the final contestant, and while Aurélie presented the three doors, Heyoka told me the rules had been changed: instead of choosing one of the three doors, I would have to guess what was behind each of them in order to win the Grand Prize of reincarnation.

I awoke at three a.m. in a cold sweat, with Aurélie hovering over me calling my name. After trying unsuccessfully to go back to sleep, I said the hell with it and convinced her I needed coffee. I was a little unsteady on my feet, so she held my arm as we walked down the hall to the kitchen, where we were surprised to find Heyoka and Fred sitting at the breakfast table playing Liar's Poker.

"Guess the insomnia's catching tonight," Heyoka said, glancing up from his folded one-dollar bill. "Coffee's on. Grab a cup and join us."

We poured ourselves some coffee, then sat down at the table. "Who's winning?" Aurélie asked, warming her hands on her mug.

"Fred, of course," said Heyoka. "He always was a better liar than me."

"It has nothing to do with dishonesty," Fred said. "It's all about probabilities."

"Wrong!" said Aurélie. "It's all about numbers and guess work, with a little bit of bluff thrown in for good measure. Bluff being a euphemism for lying."

"So says the numbers expert," Heyoka grumbled. "By the way, Rix, if she ever tries to hook you into a game, don't take her up on it. She'll win before you finish reading the serial number on your bill. So, have you come to a decision yet?"

I looked at the ceiling, then shook my head.

"Well, maybe you should stop trying. When I'm stumped, I've found what works best is to forget all the pertinent facts and play something like Rock-Scissors-Paper, or consult the Tarot cards. Anything that's completely random and makes no logical sense. How about it, Aurélie? Got any ideas? Maybe something numerical?"

"You know I don't believe in using random numbers to solve complex problems. And, for Rix, this one's pretty damned complex. Still," she said, looking at me, "if you're really at the end of your rope…"

"I am," I said. "And my rope ends in a hangman's noose. I'm ready for anything. Even a random drawing, if that's what it takes."

"Speaking as Dirk Gently," said Fred, "I believe in the fundamental interconnectedness of all things. Which means there is no such thing as randomness. Everything is connected to everything else. And that goes for numbers, too. You can choose any set of numbers and make it relate to whatever your problem is."

"Dirk Gently?" Heyoka said.

"Character in the last two novels Douglas Adams published," said Aurélie. "You know, the guy who wrote ***The Hitchhiker's Guide to the Galaxy*** series. The one who gave us the 'ultimate answer to life, the universe, and everything?'"

Heyoka looked bewildered.

"It's always nice when we find something we know and he doesn't, "Fred said.

"Okay, Fred," I said. "So give me a set of numbers."

"Let's see," he said, scratching his cheek with a finger. "I guess we'd have to come up with a set, or a piece of a set, that would relate to specific times in your past. Different chronological ages. Right?"

"You got it," I said. "Any ideas?"

He thought for a moment, then said, "Fibonacci."

When he didn't elaborate, I said, "Of course, why didn't I think of that? What the hell is a Fibonacci?"

"It's a number sequence," said Aurélie. "It starts with zero, then one, then one again, and after that each number is the sum of the previous two. So, from there it would be two, three, five, eight, thirteen, twenty one, thirty four, fifty five, eighty nine, and so on. You said you didn't want to go back to your preteen days, and you haven't yet reached eighty nine, which leaves thirteen, twenty one, thirty four, and fifty five. If you're serious about trying anything, why not choose three of those? At least that makes it only a three-out-of-four choice."

"Absolutely!" I said. "Problem solved. Fifty five is too old, so thirteen, twenty one, and thirty four it is. Let's just hope Dirk was right. If not, I may have to go with forty two, and leave it at that."

"Where does forty two come from?" Heyoka asked.

The three of us looked at each other and smiled. Finally, Fred said, "It's the answer."

"The answer to what?"

"THE ULTIMATE QUESTION OF LIFE, THE UNIVERSE, AND EVERYTHING!" we all said in unison.

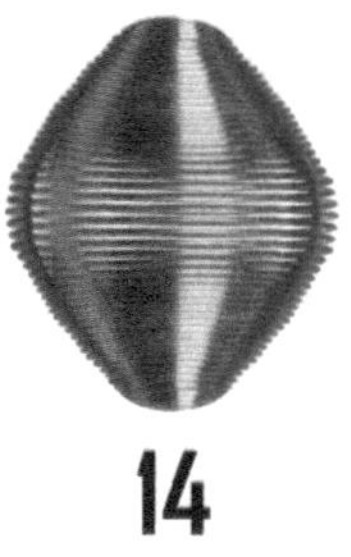

14
Catch 42

Over the years, Doug Adams offered several explanations for how he came up with the number 42, none of them having to do with science or mathematics. In one of these, he told an interviewer the number didn't mean anything at all. "It was a joke," he said. "It had to be an ordinary, smallish number, so I sat at my desk, stared into the garden and thought '42 will do.'" This made about as much sense as my arbitrary choosing of three numbers from the Fibonacci sequence, which, Aurélie later told me, was devised by an ancient Italian mathematician trying to solve a problem involving rabbit reproduction.

On the positive side, the decision put an end to my frustration, so I thanked Fred for his help, went back to my room, and slept like a log until Aurélie woke me around noon the following day with a breakfast tray. While I ate, she explained what I should expect during Stage Two.

"It's not going to be anything like the other presentations," she said. "In fact, at first it's going to seem more like a medical procedure than a visual reenactment." I stopped with a forkful of eggs halfway to my mouth. "Don't let that worry you," she continued. "There's absolutely no danger involved. I just don't want you to freak out when you see all the equipment."

When I didn't move, she said, "You can eat that now."

I looked at the fork, opened my mouth, scraped the eggs off with my teeth, and began to chew. After swallowing with an audible gulp, I asked, "What do you mean by 'all the equipment?' I've already seen some pretty weird stuff. Is there something even weirder about this?"

"Oh, no. Not weird, exactly. It'll be kind of like you're back in the hospital, rather than in one of our projection chambers. You know, hooked up to a bunch of high-tech gadgetry, lots of beeping and other sounds, maybe a little discomfort."

"Discomfort?"

"Not much, Rix. I promise. Some needles and probes and contacts and things. A helmet of sorts. But once we get started, everything will disappear, and you'll be perfectly comfortable. As I told you earlier, the experience will be indistinguishable from reality. You will not be observing, you will actually *be* yourself at a younger age, going through your life as it was back then. The only difference is you won't be able to control anything or communicate with your younger self, so you may feel a little frustrated. You'll get used to that pretty quick, though. I know, because I've done it. Now stop acting like a baby and finish your breakfast. We need to get moving."

BACK AT THE NIFS complex, we took a different hallway to another airlock and entered a room that looked like something out of a Star Trek movie. Several technicians sat at consoles around the curved walls, staring up at a bank of computer screens aglow with all manner of graphs and waveforms and digital readouts. In the center of the room, on a raised platform, stood a contraption reminiscent of a dentist's chair, above which an array of tubes and odd-looking instruments hung from an oval cowling.

"You know," I said, as Aurélie led me toward the chair, "I have a particular aversion to dentists." I stopped five feet short of the platform. "A shrink might call it a phobia."

"Really," Aurélie said, pulling on my arm.

I stood firm, refusing to move any closer. "Yes, really. It started when I was a kid and never went away. They're all liars, you know. And their biggest lie is always some variation of 'This is only going to hurt a little.' Strikingly similar to what you told me about this procedure, I'd say. Not only that, but now you want me to sit in a dentist's chair."

"It's not a dentist's chair, Rix. And I wasn't lying, unless you consider getting a blood test unusually painful. We'll be tapping a couple of blood vessels with needles so small you probably won't even feel them, and the rest is just a bunch of non-invasive sensors. We have to do these things so we can monitor your vital signs and brain activity, and deliver certain drugs to slow your metabolism. I promise you won't even have to open your mouth."

Still nervous, I stopped resisting and let her guide me into the chair. Technicians gathered around, placing contacts at various spots on my body and positioning my head under a helmet festooned with blinking lights. With all the confusion and activity, I hardly felt them insert the needles in my arm and upper leg, and the other procedures weren't that uncomfortable. Aurélie held my hand through the entire procedure, squeezing now and then and assuring me they would be finished soon.

"Another dentist lie," I said. "I can't remember how many times I've heard 'I'm almost through,' or 'Just another couple of minutes,' then had to wait an eon before they stopped drilling or pulling or scraping." As if responding to my accusation, the team of technicians began to drift away, leaving me feeling like a newly decorated Christmas tree.

"Okay," said Aurélie. "Now we're going to give you something to help you relax. I'll be right here the whole time, though you won't be aware of my presence. In a moment, you will wake up on the morning of your thirteenth birthday."

Within seconds, my vision began to blur and a feeling of calm blotted out my anxiety. As the room around me dissolved into a gray mist, I heard Aurélie's voice echo in the distance. "Be sure to remember your key word," she said. Then the gray turned to black.

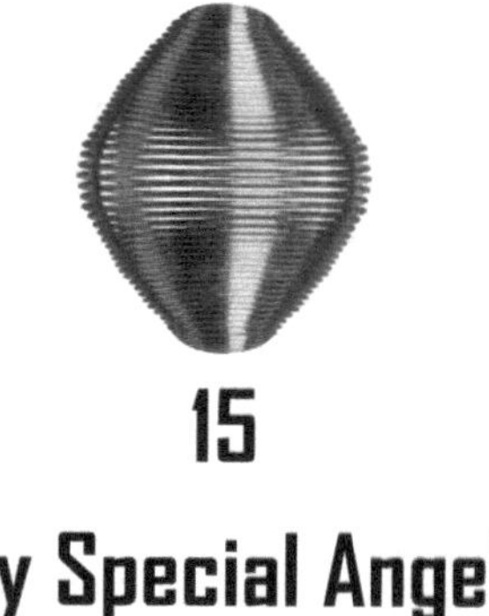

15
My Special Angel

I rolled over and tried to unwind from a tangle of sheets, while my aching nuts attested to the fact that I'd almost made it to the end of another wet dream. The sexual frustrations of adolescence had recently begun to plague me on a daily basis, and I was beginning to think I had some type of abnormality because I didn't seem to be able to control my own body. And it wasn't only in my dreams; I was often embarrassed in school by spontaneous erections that seemed to come out of nowhere. I had started to deal with this one, when Mom breezed into my room and stopped me cold.

"Happy birthday, Ricky," she said, leaning to kiss me on the forehead. "Too bad it's a school day. Only two more till your party, though. C'mon now, time to get up."

MY MORNING RITUAL IN those days consisted of the standard bathroom stuff, followed by twenty minutes of weight lifting in an effort to put some muscle on what was still a fairly skinny physique. I had no way of knowing I would soon experience a growth spurt that would turn me into a six-foot-two, 180-pound, Paul Newman look-alike. Of course, the older me knew, and I also knew what awaited me downstairs was the guitar of my dreams, a brand-new Fender Stratocaster. Aurélie had warned me about the frustration of not being able to convey information to my younger self. But she also said I would get used to the limitation pretty quick, so I did my best to stop trying and enjoy hitching a ride on the younger me's brain.

At the time of my thirteenth birthday I was nursing an enormous crush on one Pat Williams, a tall, willowy ninth grader, with a face like Audrey Hepburn and a loose, suggestive attitude that reeked of sexuality. Pat sat two rows down from me in Chorus class, and so far all I'd managed to do was make a fool of myself passing love notes to her that elicited only sad, condescending head shakes. The fact that I had by far the best voice of anyone in the class did nothing to improve my chances with her; until, that is, the school held its annual talent show.

By then I had made the transition from classical music to rock, and had organized a group of school buddies into four-piece combo. We were still playing in my garage, learning tunes by Elvis Presley, Chuck Berry, Paul Anka and the like. But at the talent show, my rendition of the Bobby Helms hit, ***You Are My Special Angel*** blew the crowd away and began the process of worming me into Pat's heart. I caught her eye early on, and while I sang the slow, pretty ballad, I used every ounce of showmanship I could muster to convey my love for her through that unique musical connection. I didn't hear the applause, nor did I give much thought to the fact that we won the contest, because my entire world was swallowed up in Pat's eyes. And later that night, when the phone rang and Mom yelled for me to pick up the receiver in the hall, I nearly fainted when I heard her voice.

"Ricky," she said. "It's Pat. From Chorus?" I was still trying to get my mouth working when she continued. "I wanted to tell you how great you were tonight. And, well, to apologize for the way I've treated you this year. I was wondering if we could get together some time. Maybe get a Coke at The Corner Shoppe or something."

"Uh ... sure," I stammered. "Sure. Anytime." Then, feeling somewhat emboldened, I said, "How about coming over for a swim? I've got a pool."

"That sounds great," she said.

Thus began my first legitimate love affair, and my realization that rock music could offer more than I'd ever dreamed.

Pat came over the next Saturday, unfortunately with her sixteen-year-old boyfriend in his brand new '57 Chevy. I was devastated, but I kept up a good front, joking around and graciously accepting my third-wheel status while we swam and listened to records. My faked nonchalance apparently paid off, because later, when her boyfriend was in the bathroom, Pat told me she'd like to come back sometime without him—and for the rest of the afternoon, I couldn't get out of the pool for fear she would notice the bulge in my bathing trunks. Finally, when she said they had to leave, I waited until they went to change, then ran up to my bedroom and put on a loose-fitting terrycloth bathrobe.

I made it back to the patio in time to walk them to the car, and right before they drove away, Pat leaned out the window and reached for my hand. "You know," she said, "I've got a birthday coming up in two weeks. Maybe you'd like to come to my party?" Again, I was rendered speechless, but I managed to squeeze her fingers and nod.

As I watched them disappear around the corner, it occurred to me that school was about to let out for the summer, and that Mom had suggested I might want to throw an end-of-the-year pool party for some of my friends. So I decided to ask if I could turn it into a birthday party for Pat. Mom said it was okay with her, and when I asked Pat, she went through the standard routine of, 'Oh, I wouldn't want to put you to any trouble,' then, 'Are you sure it's okay with your parents,' and finally, 'That's so sweet of you, Ricky.'

There was no way to know how she actually felt about me; whether she was attracted only by my singing or something more serious was going on. After all, she was almost two years older than me, and in junior high school two years was an eternity. Whatever had caused her change of heart, I planned to make the best of the opportunity, and the first thing I decided to do was try to act more mature.

For the last two weeks of school, I refrained from note-passing and other nerdy behavior. I even managed to fake a sort of suave indifference, offering perfunctory smiles when I passed Pat in the hall, and paying little attention to her in Chorus. Meanwhile, I worked frantically to prepare for the party, putting up the badminton net, cleaning the cabanas and scrubbing the tiles around the pool, and convincing Mom to let the band set up outside for a mini concert. I also spent my entire savings on Pat's birthday gift, soliciting the help of a Jeweler friend of Dad's to design a gold charm in the shape of an electric guitar and inlay it with a tiny diamond. This was a little scary, because at our age giving a girl a piece of jewelry could be interpreted as asking her to go steady. But since it would be only one among many charms on the bracelet she always wore, I figured I could get away with it.

Although I would have preferred the party to be a more intimate affair, I told Pat to invite whoever she wanted, and, between her friends and mine, more than fifty kids showed up. I talked our drummer Paul—who had just gotten his license—into driving me over to pick her up, and was thrilled when she agreed, because it meant she wouldn't be arriving with a date. On the way back from her house, we were jammed together in the front seat of his dad's Thunderbird, and the feel of her body against mine caused the inevitable hard on. Fortunately, the new pair of tight jeans I wore kept things from showing too much.

Mom made her famous barbecued hamburgers, and the party came off great, with lots of raucous pool fun and only two minor accidents that Dad treated with a little first aid. We topped it off with a set of live music, which had everybody dancing and cheering after each song. The old bitch across the street called the cops to complain about the noise, but by the time they arrived we had packed up our instruments. Besides, Dad knew every cop on the force, many of whom were his patients, so the two they sent out ended up eating hamburgers and telling stories about the bitch, who was notorious for filing complaints over everything from cats in heat to loud mufflers.

There was so much going on that I didn't have a chance to spend any private time with Pat until she was through opening her presents and everyone had finished eating cake and ice cream. I saved my present until the crowd started to thin out, and when I took her by the hand and led her to the unoccupied back porch, she didn't protest or resist. We sat beside each other on the Rattan couch, and I handed her the tiny box, whereupon she tilted her head and gave me a narrow-eyed look, as if I had overstepped my bounds.

"Hey," I said. "Don't worry, it's not an engagement ring or anything."

"I know, Ricky," she said. "But you shouldn't have done this. The party was the best gift of all. I … I don't know what to say."

"You don't have to say anything. Just open it."

She hesitated a moment before removing the top of the box to reveal a black-velvet snap case. She flipped it open and stared at the charm for a long time without speaking. Finally, she looked up, and when I saw tears in her eyes, it felt like I'd been hit in the chest with a bowling ball.

I opened my mouth to speak, but before I could get a word out her lips were on mine and her tongue was halfway down my throat.

I'd heard of French kissing, but up until that moment the only girl I'd ever kissed was an eleven-year-old cousin visiting from Ohio the previous summer. That was more-or-less an experiment, with clinking teeth, lots of giggling, and not a hint of passion. So I was a rank amateur when it came to kissing technique. Thankfully, however, something instinctive took over, and our tongues danced to the same rhythm until Pat pulled away and leaned her head on my shoulder. "Do you think we could find someplace a little more private?" she whispered.

A few of the older kids had paired off and disappeared into various hideaways, one of which was the dark hallway on the second floor. And when I stood and held out my hand, she let me lead her through the kitchen and up the stairs.

There was only one couple making out in the hall, so we moved as far away from them as we could and leaned against the wall in a dark corner. Pat wrapped her arms around my neck and nibbled at my lips as she pulled me with her to the floor. We were just getting comfortable in each other's arms, when the hall light came on and Mom's voice drifted up from below.

"Okay, you guys," she said with a humorous 'gotcha' in her voice. "Time to break it up."

Pat and I waited while the other couple straightened their clothes and disappeared into the stairwell. Then, as we got to our feet, I felt her hand drift down between my legs. "To be continued," she said, giving me a gentle squeeze. "If that's okay with you."

THAT SUMMER WOULD MARK my coming-of-age. I not only lost my virginity, I had my first taste of alcohol and smoked my first joint; all at the behest of my new girlfriend, who, it turned out, was far more experienced in the ways of the world than I might have guessed. A slut, many of my friends called her, though I never thought of her that way. Pat grew up on the proverbial wrong side of the tracks, with an abusive father and a food-addicted mother who weighed in at 350 pounds and spent most of her time criticizing everything her daughter did. Who wouldn't turn to alcohol and sex for solace and personal affirmation?

Besides, Pat loved me, or so she claimed. And I never saw any evidence to the contrary.

Music served as the catalyst for our age difference, as the band started to get paying gigs, playing parties and teen dances around town. And, although she was obviously enamored with my singing, in our quiet moments together, she made it a point to tell me her affection went much deeper than mere admiration for my vocal talents. She was also frank with me about my budding career, at one point advising me to "Scrape off that bunch of losers, and hook up with some real musicians, or you're going to end up going nowhere."

But that was two years down the road. And for most of those two years we were inseparable. Not only as lovers, but as collaborators. It turned out Pat was a lot smarter than anyone gave her credit for, especially when it came to understanding the local rock scene and coming up with ideas on how to promote the group. She was first to suggest we wear matching suits, negotiating with a menswear store to provide them at a discount in exchange for our mentioning the store at all our gigs. Next, she went to work on my dad, convincing him to set us up with our own sound system. She even acted as our agent, using her looks and charm to book us weekend gigs that ranged from birthday parties to school dances to sock hops at the local YMCA.

On the negative side, there was the booze and, later on, the drugs, both of which seemed to be career enhancing at the time. And there *were* tangible benefits, not the least of which was how alcohol reduced my inhibitions and nervousness about performing, turning me into a kind of wild man on stage and allowing me to emulate stars like Chuck Berry and Jerry Lee Lewis. Unfortunately, this new bravado also gave me a false sense of invincibility, creating an ego-inflated arrogance that spilled over into my off-stage persona. What I didn't realize at the time was that, even though I was maturing as a performer, I was still going through all the hormonal changes and emotional upheaval of adolescence. And it was the combination of all these factors that would leave me ill prepared for the shock of my parents' divorce.

Once again, Pat provided my support structure, comforting me and distracting me with sex and booze. She had her driver's license by then and access to her mother's station wagon, since the 350-pound behemoth could no longer fit in the car. Although I was an emotional basket case for a while, after I'd gone through all the stages of grief brought on by the divorce, I found myself entering a new life of almost complete autonomy. With Dad no longer around to serve as an authority figure, Mom had no power to discipline me, so I could do pretty much anything I wanted. And what I wanted, other than playing music, was to spend time with Pat, drinking and trying to break the world record for teenage orgasms.

The divorce also laid the groundwork for a new, more profitable relationship with my dad, at least from a monetary standpoint. It seemed he was dealing with a lot of guilt after leaving Mom for his young receptionist, and this translated into financial benefits for me—every time I stopped by his office for a visit, he would hand me a ten dollar bill. Plus, he was much more vulnerable to Pat's solicitations for help in promoting the band, a fact that would play a major role in establishing my reputation as a local rock star.

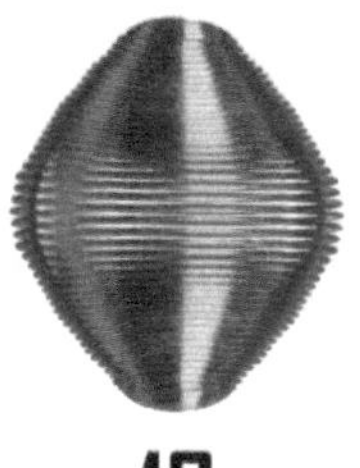

16

The Skip School Flu

Decades before ***Ferris Bueller's Day Off*** hit the Big Screen, my friends and I were perfecting the art of undetected truancy. And by the time I turned fifteen and entered high school, we were experts at it. Pat served as our forger, copying our parents' handwriting in authentic-looking excuse notes that often cited common illnesses. We jokingly referred to these maladies as the 'vacationitis,' or the 'skip school flu,' and one day Pat suggested I put those terms to music.

Most of our truant days were spent on a vacant stretch of beach property owned by Paul's dad, where we had built a roomy hut out of scrap wood and palm fronds. Inside the hut we dug two holes, one for a cooler, the other for empty beer cans, covering them with removable boards hidden under the blanket that served as the hut's carpet. As might be expected, we were all pretty high the day Pat came up with the idea for ***Skip School Flu***. Consequently, I wrote my first original song under the influence of a mind-altering substance, initiating a trend that would continue for decades.

Loose and uninhibited, I started spewing out nonsensical lyrics, while Tom and I grabbed our acoustic guitars and fooled around with some chords. Before long Paul joined in on the bongos and Sam began experimenting on his bass fiddle. Pat ran to the car to get a notebook, and by the time she returned we had put together a simple chord arrangement. It took me a while to rough out the lyrics to the first verse, but after that the words started to flow more easily.

Pat scribbled as I built a story song out of the various school-skipping schemes we'd tried at one time or another. These included fake phone calls Pat had made to the assistant principal, those forged excuse notes, and the granddaddy of them all: the day we called all the phones at the school from payphones, then left the receivers off the hook and hung 'Out of Order' signs on the phone booths. It was an elaborate plan, designed to tie up all the school's phone lines so they couldn't call and check on the sixty or so students who had agreed to skip en-masse that day.

I continued to work on the song for the next few days, refining the lyrics and melody. And when the band debuted it at the Saturday night YMCA sock hop, the crowd went wild. Ever the promoter, Pat's next move was to get Dad to pay for printing a promotional brochure. The three-fold pamphlet, printed on glossy paper, featured an action photo of the band, above the legend, "The Nite Cats, Singing Their Smash Hit, ***Skip School Flu***." Of course, there was no record to qualify the song as a hit, but Pat had a plan.

We needed to raise five-hundred dollars in order to pay the local recording studio for a package deal that included studio time and a pressing of a thousand 45s. Pat got Dad to kick in three-hundred, but that left us two-hundred short. So at our next few gigs she passed through the audience with a fishbowl, while we played the song and made a plea for donations to the "***Skip School Flu*** Record Fund." We also solicited donations from the kids at school, and within three weeks we had raised the rest of the money.

After convincing Mom to cosign for a checking account, we took our bag of cash and coins to the bank and deposited a total of five-hundred-ten dollars and seventy cents. Then it was off to the recording studio, where we booked a session for the following week. The package deal included only four hours of recording time, so we practiced like crazy for the next few days, and when we got to the studio it took us less than an hour to finalize the recording. We were about to pack up our instruments, when the engineer said over the intercom, "Okay, guys, let's hear the flip side."

In our excitement we'd completely forgotten the record would need a flip side, and we were going into panic mode when Pat came up with another one of her brilliant ideas.

"What about that jungle crap you guys are always screwing around with at the beach?" she asked. "It never made any sense to me, but everybody seems to love it." By "jungle crap," she meant this weird African chant thing we did, usually late in the evening after consuming a substantial amount of beer.

It had all started one night when Paul was playing an African beat on his conga drum and I chimed in with a drunken imitation of natives in the old Tarzan movies. Before long Tom picked up the bongos and Sam turned his bass fiddle over, slapping the back in a syncopated rhythm. There were no real lyrics, only guttural sounds like what I thought a tribe of African head hunters might make. After a while everybody was adding their own variations, which often included humorous sexual references and profanity. It was goofy and unstructured, but the beach-party crowd always requested it, and next to ***Skip School Flu*** it was the most popular "song" we had.

With nothing else original in our repertoire, everyone quickly agreed, and Pat went to the sound booth to ask the engineer if we could take a break in order to bring in some extra instruments. He said to make it quick, so we all scattered, arriving back a half-hour later with the conga, two sets of bongos, a pair of maracas, and Sam's bass fiddle. We also called several beach-party regulars, and by the time we were ready to record, fifteen rowdy high schoolers were jammed into the cramped studio space around us. Pat explained to the engineer that the unruly entourage was necessary for the performance, and after we got everyone settled down, he gave us the signal and started to roll tape.

What followed was one of the most hilarious recording sessions I would ever experience. The first take was so saturated with profanity and off-color humor, there was no way it would have made it onto a record. The engineer quickly caught on to what we were trying to do, and during the playback he pointed out the areas we needed to clean up. The second take was a little less offensive, but still way too nasty, so we tried to disguise the words better on the third one. By then the studio manager had joined the engineer, and the two of them became our coconspirators, tweaking the tracks and suggesting ways we could keep some of the bad stuff in without stepping over the line.

During the next five takes, the manager and engineer laughed so hard they could barely talk at times. Meanwhile Paul and I kept refining the offensive words and phrases, garbling them to the point that they could only be understood by someone with a dirty mind paying close attention. Eventually we put together a version that loosely adhered to their guidelines, and after adding some reverb and a little overdubbing, they gave the track their stamp of approval.

For lack of a better name, we called the song ***Jungle***, and we left the studio relieved, with both an A and B side of our new record ready for pressing. Of course, we knew no radio station would ever play the B side, not only because ***Jungle*** didn't qualify as a rock or pop song, but because it was far too gross. It would, however, have its day in the sun—or out of the sun, actually, since it was destined to become somewhat of an underground cult phenomenon.

I discovered this several years later at a college fraternity, where my group, The Madisons, was playing a weekend gig. I was walking down the hall on my way to the bathroom when I heard the strains of ***Jungle*** drifting from one of the rooms. I opened the door to find a bunch of frat boys, drinking beer, pounding on bongos, and singing along with the words we'd tried to disguise. It seemed that our impromptu flip side had been taped and copied dozens, or perhaps hundreds of times, and had become a favorite among college students all over the country. In fact, the kid who owned that particular copy said he was from California, and that he'd gotten it from a friend at Berkeley.

IT TOOK THREE WEEKS for the records to arrive, and once we had them in hand, Pat and I went around to all the local radio stations, begging them to play it. Most of the DJs agreed, some airing it on the spot. And the ones who didn't were so deluged with requests (orchestrated, of course, by Pat) they were forced to call and ask us to come back and bring them a copy.

As soon as the song hit the airwaves, we made the rounds of the local music stores, who were already turning away customers because they had no idea where to get a supply of the records. Most bought a couple of dozen, even though we wouldn't give them the discount they were accustomed to. Since we had paid around fifty cents apiece for the records, we decided to sell them wholesale for seventy-five, so we could realize a profit on our investment. And, at all our gigs, we sold them for the standard retail price of ninety eight cents.

Those were heady days. Despite not having a record contract with a major label, we did have a hit record, at least on the west coast of Florida. Pat doubled down on her promotional efforts, using the record's popularity as an excuse to increase our performance fees. She even set up a couple of private dances, renting local halls and advertising with fliers we would stick under the windshield wipers of cars at all the high schools.

Eventually, however, we saturated the market, and sales began to lag, then stopped altogether. And, without a follow-up record, let alone an album, the group fell back into the mediocrity it deserved, since we really were only a bunch of amateurs with nothing to recommend us except our one hit and me as a still-developing rock singer.

Then one day out of the blue, we got a call from the manager at the studio where we'd cut the record. It seemed an executive at a new Nashville label called Diddy Bop Records had somehow gotten hold of a copy of ***Skip School Flu*** and wanted to talk to us about a possible recording contract. They'd found the studio through the information on the label, and asked the manager to have us contact them. Pat made the call, and when they invited us to come to their offices for a meeting, we dropped everything, took the money we'd made from our record sales, and headed for Music City USA.

THERE WERE MANY FACTORS that led Pat and me to split up, not the least of which were the pills I swiped from my mom for that trip to Nashville. Back then, the amphetamines that would one day become known as 'speed' or 'bennies' were considered relatively harmless diet pills, and Dad was getting tons of free samples from pharmaceutical salesmen. And, since Mom was always struggling with her weight, there were sample bottles of Dexedrine and Dexamyl all over the house. Pat and I had experimented with the pills, and we knew one of their effects was to keep you awake for prolonged periods of time, particularly if you were suffering from the sleepiness brought on by drinking alcohol.

Before we left, I went through the house and filled a large bottle with dozens of 20-miligram pills, justifying the theft by telling myself that since we planned to drive straight through we would need them to keep from falling asleep on the road. Of course, we both knew we would be using them to get high as well, and once we were on the road, we did just that. Add in a cooler full of malt liquor, and we had the perfect formula for a fifteen-hour, non-stop argument.

The war of words started off with trivialities, joking complaints concerning insignificant things that irritated us about each other. But as the miles rolled on and more pills were consumed, the light-hearted bickering turned to anger and screaming, mainly over our long-festering disagreement about how I was wasting my time with "that bunch of losers."

Reliving the episode, I could now see that, even though she was high as a kite, Pat was sincere in her criticism; that her objections came from a desire to help me get past the career stagnation caused by carrying the rest of the band on my shoulders. At the time, however, being drunk and stoned myself, I wasn't about to give in and admit she was right.

Mental exhaustion often led to long periods of angry silence, which would then be punctuated by flurries of insulting epithets that exploded between us like shards of broken glass. And by the time we reached Nashville, I think we both knew our relationship was over. When we showed up at the address we'd been given, only to find an abandoned suite of offices, we couldn't even manage to direct our mutual anger at the assholes who had conned us into making the long trip for nothing.

We spent a restless night at a motel on the outskirts of town, sleeping in separate beds and not speaking except to mumble necessary things about the use of the bathroom the next morning. And after a quick breakfast at a nearby Toddle House, we headed off on a silent fifteen-hour trek home.

The emotional wounds we inflicted on each other during that trip added up to what would one day be referred to in legal terms as 'irreconcilable differences,' and it wasn't long before our relationship had deteriorated to the point that it was no longer salvageable. Everything came to a head two days before my sixteenth birthday, when our final argument escalated into a physical confrontation. The next morning, she left a tearful note and disappeared. And I never saw or heard from her again.

AT THE STROKE OF midnight, I found myself back in the dentist chair, bathed in sweat and trying to shake off the memories of those last few weeks before I turned sixteen. After they administered some drugs to calm me down, Aurélie took me to the sleeping quarters we'd occupied before at the lab, where she held my hands and tried to talk me down from the trauma caused by my trip back in time.

During the earlier previews I'd breezed through my two years with Pat without slowing or stopping, because I had no desire to watch our relationship fall apart. But after living through that period again, I was surprised to find that the painful experience had been somewhat enlightening. Observing things from a more objective viewpoint, I could now see that my affair with Pat had been both a blessing and a curse. A blessing in the sense that it provided the exposure I needed to solidify my reputation as one of the most talented musicians in the area; a curse because it set me on a long, destructive road of substance abuse.

The downside manifested itself subtly, starting with alcohol and pot, and eventually leading to those early experiments with amphetamines. After Pat left, the combination of pills and alcohol often sent me into fits of rage over the inability of my band members to keep up with me musically. Fortunately, this all worked itself out in a more-or-less natural way, when Tom and Paul left for college, and Sam, who was actually quite talented on the electric bass, accepted an offer to join another popular local group called The Midnighters.

The dissolution of the Nite Cats began a stretch of time during which I did nothing but hone my skills on the guitar. When I emerged six months later from my self-imposed musical exile, I was ten times the guitarist I'd been when I started. And it was only then that the advice Pat had tried to drum into my head hit home and my real career began.

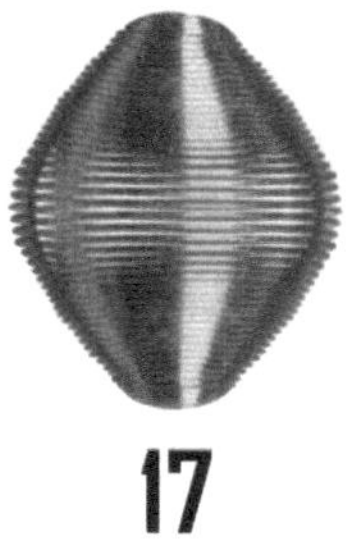

17

Rest In Peace

"What happens to *this* me after the transfer?" I asked Heyoka. Aurélie had ordered me to take some time off after that first session, and Heyoka had jumped at the chance to pick my brain about guitar technique.

"Damn!" he said, as he struggled to imitate one of my Travis picks.

"It's those big hands of yours," I said. "Why don't you try it on a classical? The wider string separation will help."

"Good idea. I've got an old Pimentel around here someplace." He returned the D28 to its stand and glanced around the music room. "Now, if I can only remember where it is."

"About my question?"

"Question? Oh, right. Well, your being, your actual self, will no longer be here. It will be in the time you have chosen, residing in your younger body. As for the body you presently occupy, it will die."

"That's a rather unpleasant thought."

"It shouldn't be, Rix," he said, rising and walking across the room. "We both know your current body is pretty well shot. And, as I said, *you* will be elsewhere. What's left here will be nothing but a human-shaped slab of dead meat with no consciousness or spirit."

The mental image of my dead body gave me chills. "So," I said, "What do you plan to do with this slab of meat after I'm out of it?"

"That's entirely up to you," he yelled over his shoulder as he rummaged around in a closet. "Ah, here she is." He came back to the stool carrying a molded fiberglass case. "You're familiar with Pimentel, I assume," he said, lifting out a timeworn classical guitar.

"Lorenzo?" I said. "Spent an afternoon at his shop once when I was out in Albuquerque. Heard he passed away a while back."

"Yes, after a long battle with prostate cancer. This is an early one built by the old man himself before he moved to the states. I have a later model, done with the Native American rosettes and purflings the family became famous for. But when it comes to classicals, I prefer the traditional over the modern. There's something about the tone and projection that seems to get lost in all the fancy decoration and supposed innovative design." He plucked a rapid series of arpeggios and the bright sound filled the room."

"Not bad," I said, surprised at his proficiency, which hadn't been evident on the steel-string. "Speaking of dying, I think I'd like to be buried back home."

"Where, St. Pete?"

"If it's not too much of a problem. How do you plan to explain my death, anyway?"

"Natural causes. We can cremate the body here and send the ashes back. Unless you'd rather it be embalmed and sent back whole. Either way, you'll have to let us know who to send it to."

"Man, this is creepy." I had several old friends living in the Suncoast area, but most were aging musicians; not exactly the type of folks who would be interested in seeing to the disposition of my corpse. "Why don't you talk to my agent? I'm sure he'd like to play it up in the press and take advantage of the inevitable spike in sales death always seems to generate."

"I'll have Fred arrange everything. We'll pay for a fancy funeral and make sure the obit gets lots of international coverage. Maybe you'd like to write it?"

"Not a chance," I said. "And you can forget about a funeral or a formal memorial service, because no one would show up. A musician's wake, on the other hand, might draw a couple of dozen, especially if there's lots of free booze and food."

"Musician's wake?"

"It's a tradition. At least among the musicians in my circle. It's basically an excuse to get drunk and have a jam session. We usually record the whole thing and anyone who wants will say something nice about the deceased. Then we give the recording to the family so they'll have something to remember him or her by."

"Ah, I see. A musician's wake it shall be then."

18
Lost And Found

After we finished Heyoka's guitar lesson, I retired to my room. I had planned to take a nap, but every time I dozed off I was awakened by dreams of Pat and those final few days before she disappeared. I'd heard a rumor that she'd enrolled at Florida State University, but in those days—before personal computers and the Internet—the only way to confirm the rumor would have been to call her parents, and I wasn't about to suck up my pride and make that call. Ever since my trip back in time, however, I'd been wondering how her life had evolved post-Rix, and it occurred to me that I could probably find at least some of the details on the Web.

Abandoning the nap, I went to the desk and cranked up my laptop. A Google search for "Pat Williams" resulted in over nine million hits, so I started adding terms to hone things down. I tried "St. Petersburg" to no avail, then "St. Pete High," which led me to an alumni site, but she wasn't listed as a member. I was about to give up, when my newly rejuvenated brain clicked into gear and I remembered her mother's name was Glenda. A search of obituaries in St. Pete brought up a "Glenda Williams," who had passed away in 1983 and was survived by "daughter Patricia" and "husband Alfonse." Next, I tried "Alfonse Williams," and hit pay dirt.

Her father's obit mentioned "daughter Patricia Scarletti," which I assumed was her married name. My agent had set me up with a

Linkedin account, and a search of that site brought up only eight results for "Patricia Scarletti." Five of the profiles included photos, and hers was the third one I clicked on. She had posted a picture that complimented her; it was obviously taken years earlier. And with her face still vivid in my mind from the session, I recognized her instantly. She was apparently single again, and her resume listed her as the owner of "PWS Consulting - Management Consultation and Applied Psychology." After that, I was stuck.

On one hand, I wanted to satisfy my curiosity; on the other, I was reluctant to contact her for fear she would still be carrying a grudge. And then there was her intimidating Curriculum Vitae, which included doctorates in psychology and communications, and a master's in anthropology—needless to say, a far cry from my high-school dropout status. Curiosity won out, but I decided to check Facebook first, rather than e-mail or call directly. I found Pat's page, which was loaded with photos of her kids and grandkids, plus lots of posts about Jesus, fundamentalist religion, and conservative politicians and causes. I was about to send her a personal message, but I stopped to reconsider.

I'd had this experience before. After my agent first set up my Facebook page, I spent a good deal of time looking up old friends with whom I had lost contact, and was often startled by how people had changed over the years. Back in our high-school days, my friends and I would occasionally get into mild religious and political debates, but these amounted to little more than momentary distractions from our preferred discussions of sex, sports, and rock 'n' roll. Having grown up in a liberal family, I was always shocked to discover that many of my friends had turned out to be right-wing religious fanatics, and I found myself getting into heated online arguments. I soon tired of this and quit messing with Facebook altogether.

Now I was faced with another possible reunion, one that would be superficial at best, confrontational at worst. And what was the point? I had already satisfied my curiosity: Pat was alive, apparently successful and happy, with a bunch of kids and grandkids. What more did I need to know? Our affair had ended on a bad note, and unless I could manage to bite my tongue, our reunion would end the same way. I mulled this over for all of thirty seconds before deciding not to pursue things any further, although thinking about it did remind me of my frustrating attempt years earlier to find Robin.

One of my first Internet searches was for Robin Barbary. I spent days searching for her, but after our short marriage had been annulled she seemed to have dropped off the face of the earth. I even paid one of those online locating services, which turned out to be a waste of money. In a way, I was almost happy to have failed in this endeavor, because it would have killed me to learn she'd gone on to marry some conservative asshole, or joined the Church of Scientology, or become a member of the Tea Party.

Fact was, I didn't know much about Robin's political leanings or religious beliefs, since we seldom discussed those things during our brief time together. I did recall her praying occasionally, though she never suggested we attend church. All I really remembered was her kindness and patience and loving affection. And, of course, the sex; the astonishingly sensual passion that had never been equaled until Aurélie not only equaled it, but surpassed it by a country mile.

Oddly, other than a striking physical resemblance, Aurélie and Robin had little in common. Robin was quiet and reserved, as if she were trying to hide her real self from me. She seldom talked about her life or background, concentrating instead on mine and demonstrating an uncanny ability to draw me out in ways no other woman ever had before. It seemed her only goal was to see to my wellbeing, which mostly had to do with keeping me away from heroin and the other drugs that were dragging me into the gutter.

Aurélie, on the other hand, was outgoing and sometimes demanding; sympathetic, but practical, and certainly not overly emotional as Robin had often been. Sex with Aurélie was different as well, though not entirely. There was nothing desperate or feverish about Robin's lovemaking, whereas Aurélie had been uninhibited and passionate. Both experiences, however, held a magical quality that went far beyond the physical. This was especially true with Aurélie, whose willingness to share her most personal thoughts and desires made our relationship more meaningful and fulfilling.

Unfortunately, that small taste of fulfillment was short-lived. Instead of finding salvation in Aurélie's arms, the heartache I'd carried for Robin had been replaced by a new one, a pain that went far deeper. Not only was Aurélie now untouchable sexually, in all other respects we remained close, and I had to endure my frustration while seeing her on daily basis. I tried not to let that frustration show when we were together, but as the days passed it became harder and harder to restrain myself, pretending benign acceptance while trying to convey the love I felt for her.

As I approached my next trip back in time, I was again having second thoughts. And were it not for my increasing physical weakness reminding me of how little time I had left, I would have resumed my pleadings for intimacy with Aurélie and refused to continue. As it was, however, I held my tongue, following her into the chamber and submitting once again to the technicians' elaborate operation of preparing me for a second walk down memory lane.

"I know it's hard," Aurélie said, after they had returned to their consoles and left us alone. "But try not to get too caught up in this. As real as it seems, you have to remember that it's only another preview. Like before, you won't be able to change anything or communicate with your younger self. And unless we have to bring you out sooner, or you signal us that you want to come back, you will remain in the past for three years."

"Got it," I said.

"Hang in there," she whispered, kissing me on the cheek. "And happy twenty-first birthday."

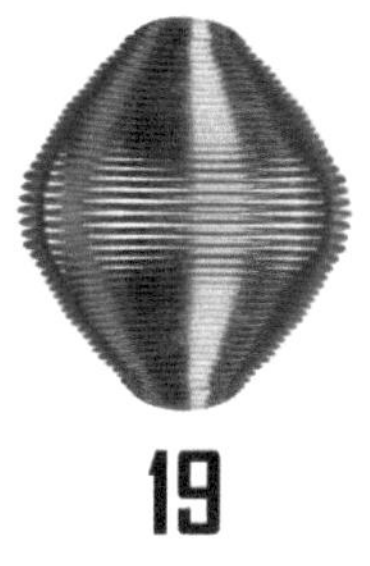

19

Legal At Last

Turning twenty one was somewhat of an anticlimax for me, since I'd been using a fake ID for five years and working in nightclubs for much of that time. But the anticlimax threatened to turn into a real one when I awoke cuddled against the naked body of a woman. Careful not to shake the bed, I slipped out of her limp embrace and watched as her sleep-crusted eyes blinked open and a shy, embarrassed smile spread over her face.

"Happy birthday," she said. She hesitated for a moment, then leaned forward to give me a soft, trembling kiss. Her cheeks were faintly creased from the wrinkled pillowcase, but the creases faded quickly, revealing an attractive young lady, perhaps in her early twenties.

"Uh, thanks," I said, the gravel in my throat making the words sound like they came from a ninety-year-old derelict. "Sorry, but I'm a little hazy here. Maybe you could fill me in on last night?"

"Not surprising." she said, swinging her legs off the bed. "You were awfully drunk. We should probably wait until the haze clears before getting into the nitty-gritty details." She reached for a pack of cigarettes, lit one with a slim gold lighter, and blew a cloud of smoke toward the ceiling. "I'm Carla, by the way. And, no, I'm not a hooker, if that's what you're thinking. In fact, most of the time I'm a rather respectable college student." Before turning to look at me, she grabbed a shirt—my shirt, actually—from the floor, sliding her arms into the sleeves and leaving the unbuttoned front draped loosely over her breasts. "I happened to be with some friends on our monthly Girls Night Out when I fell in love with the handsome singer. I overheard the bartender wishing you happy birthday, so I caught you between sets and said I wanted to be your birthday present."

"Girls Night Out?" I said. "Does that mean there's a boyfriend or a husband?" This was not an unusual situation for me. I was often propositioned by attached women, and more than once those encounters had led to trouble.

"Nope," she said. "I'm between boyfriends at the moment, just hanging out at the beach for a well-deserved couple of days respite from scholastic drudgery. So, unless you'd rather I didn't, I can stay until tomorrow."

"No, no. Not at all. I mean, you should definitely stay."

"Great! How about some breakfast? I'm buying."

SO, TELL ME ABOUT The Madisons," Carla said as we picked at the remnants of the breakfast she'd ordered from Room Service.

"Long story," I said. "Probably bore you to death."

"Try me. I've seen you before, you know. About three years ago in Atlanta at an after-hours place called The Steak and Trumpet. I was with my folks at the time, so I couldn't talk to you or anything, but I never forgot that voice of yours. You had a different band then. Something like The Ornamentals or The Instrumentals—"

"The Continentals," I said. "Eight-piece group with a horn section."

"Right. The Continentals. So what happened to them?"

I drained the last of my orange juice, then looked at her skeptically. "You seriously want to know?"

"I do," she said. "In fact, I'd love to hear your life story, but I'll settle for whatever happened to magically bring us together again."

"I'd say that had more to do with your showing up at the club last night than anything. We play here pretty often."

"Really? Well then, Surfside just became my favorite nightclub in the universe."

Surfside Inn was one of our regular venues. In fact, whenever The Madisons had a long enough break between private gigs, we were almost always booked at the Clearwater-Beach resort, a sprawling complex encompassing a hotel, several pools, two restaurants, and a two-hundred-seat lounge that consistently placed first in local surveys of popular nightspots. I was about to mention this when a knock on the door stopped me.

Our visitor was the maid looking to clean up and change the linens. I asked her to skip my room for today, then told her to wait while I went back to retrieve the breakfast cart. After she left with the cart, I closed the door and turned around to see Carla pointing at my crotch. I pulled the front of my robe out and looked down, then shook my head in mock dismay.

"Not that, dummy," she said. "The Do Not Disturb sign."

I slapped my forehead, grabbed the hanging sign, slipped it over the outside handle, and closed the door. I turned around and started to take a bow, but Carla had disappeared.

"Out here," she yelled from the balcony. I walked over, parted the drapes, and stepped out into the warm humid air. A vague, salty smell of decaying sea life mingled with the unmistakable odor of marijuana as she handed me a lit joint. "I found this on the night stand," she said in bits and spurts, trying to hold the smoke in her lungs as long as possible. "It's pretty powerful stuff. What is it?"

"It's called 'Gainesville Green,'" I said taking a hit. "Some students in the agricultural school at UF have been trying to develop a cannabis hybrid with a higher THC content. This is from one of their early batches."

"Interesting. How do you happen to come by it?

"We play a lot of frat parties at UF and FSU," I said, holding the joint out for her.

"No thanks," she said. "I mean it's amazing and all, but I don't think I need any more right now. Why don't you sit down and tell me all about The Madisons? You guys are incredible, by the way. When we first walked in last night, I remember thinking there had to be an entire orchestra playing. You were in the middle of some Ray Charles thing, ***You Are My Sunshine*** I think it was, and when I looked at the stage I couldn't believe there were only four of you. How do you do that?"

"Magic," I said. The grass was already making my head swim, so I dropped into the chair opposite her and knocked the flame from the end of the joint into an ashtray on the table between us. "Okay, The Madisons. Stop me if this gets too longwinded. I tend to get carried away talking about musical stuff, especially when I'm stoned."

When I didn't go on she said, "If this is what you call getting carried away, you must think I'm a mind reader."

"Sorry," I said. "The story's a little complicated. Anyway, the original idea for the group came about when I met this weird scientist who was developing ways to clone the human brain. I talked those three guys you saw on the stage last night into volunteering as test subjects, and after a couple of failed experiments this scientist managed to copy my brain and insert it into each of their heads. The result was a group where all the members had identical talents, musical tastes, and temperaments, something unheard of in the annals of rock history."

For a moment there I had her going. But then she broke through the high and came back to reality. "Right," she said. "And I'm Mary Poppins. Are you gonna tell me the real story, or do I have to unfurl my umbrella and float away on the breeze?"

"Just wanted to make sure you were paying attention," I said. "But, you know, sometimes it seems like that story's more truth than fiction. You'd be amazed how much alike the four of us are. Every once in a while, we'll all switch instruments for a set, and if we do it late enough in the evening, the audience doesn't even notice."

"Now *that* I might be able to believe," she said. "Although I can't imagine you as a drummer. I mean, what a waste."

"It would be a waste," I said. "I can hold my own on the drums, but I'm not in Jimmy's league by a long shot. Nor can I play sax anywhere near as good as Billy. But I can handle either for one set. My main instrument is the guitar, though I spend half my time playing organ. In fact, that organ is one of the main reasons we can create the sound we do with only four pieces."

"If you want to know what I think, your 'main instrument' is your voice. But that's neither here nor there. Come on, let's hear the real story."

"Well, it isn't quite as interesting as the brain cloning, so don't say I didn't warn you. I guess it all started while I was on the road with *The Continentals*. I don't know if you remember, but Jimmy was the drummer in that group as well. He and I have been friends since high school, and not long after we started traveling with *The Continentals*, we began to realize how much of a problem dealing with eight opinionated musicians could be. By the time we hit Atlanta, we were both sick of having to play referee all the time to keep things from falling apart, so we started talking about forming a smaller band.

"What we wanted to do was put together a tight-knit group of maybe four or five guys, and we had a good idea who two of those guys should be. One was Kenny, a Julliard-trained musician who gave up the cello for the guitar, and since then had become one of the most sought-after rock guitarists in the southeast. And the other was Billy, who, in addition to playing sax solos that would make John Coltrane weep, was an accomplished keyboardist. The problem was they were working in other bands at the time. So when things finally blew up in Atlanta, Jimmy and I headed back here, hoping to think of some way to entice them into joining us."

"Gee," she said, "all their names end in Y." It was obvious the grass was screwing with her head. "Hey, I just realized I don't even know your name."

Figuring I would get her off on a tangent and change the subject, I said, "Actually, at the time, I went by Ricky, so I guess all four of us had names ending in Y."

"At the time? You mean you changed it?"

"I did. I'd always hated my birth name, so about a year ago I had it legally changed to Rix. Rix Vaughn."

"Rix Vaughn," she murmured. "Sexy. It fits you well." The shirt had fallen open, and the sight of her naked breast sent my stoned libido into overdrive. I was about to suggest we retire to the bed, when she said, "So what happened when you got back?"

The mercurial nature of THC, I thought, pausing for a moment to refocus on the story. "I guess you could say it was sort of serendipitous the way things turned out. Jimmy and I hadn't had any luck finding Billy and Kenny, so we booked a gig at the Skyway Lounge in St. Pete as a duo, just organ and drums, with both of us singing. The Skyway has always had this Sunday afternoon jam session that usually draws a lot of musicians from around the region, and one Sunday the two of them showed up together. They were still with other bands at the time, but when we got to talking it became clear they weren't happy. The conversation soon turned into a mutual-admiration love fest, with all of us complimenting each other and kicking around ideas for what we wanted musically. And when we asked them to sit in with us, something magic happened."

"See," she said, "I told you what brought us together again was magical. So what made this chance meeting so special?"

"Well, in addition to the way we clicked on stage, they'd been just as frustrated as we were trying to find like-minded, similarly-talented artists. I don't mean to brag or anything, but Jimmy and I had been through this several times. What happens is a few mediocre wannabes will hook up with one or two serious musicians who then end up carrying the band on their shoulders."

"Yeah," she said. "I know what you mean."

"You do? Are you a musician?"

"Oh, no, I didn't mean it like that. I was thinking of study groups. You know, kids who get together and agree to research a particular course, then offer their summaries to the group. In most cases, maybe one or two actually do the work, while the rest hang around making excuses and benefiting from what the others bring to the table. Anyway, that's beside the point. Go on, please."

"You sure this isn't boring you? I mean, for someone who's not a musician—"

"Will you please stop saying that?" she said. "I told you I wanted to hear the story, and I meant it. I know you probably think I'm some kind of ignorant slut, and I couldn't blame you after finding me in your bed this morning. I'm no Miss Goody Two Shoes, mind you, but neither am I a shallow-minded, starry-eyed teenybopper. I swear on my father's grave I've never done anything like this before. I like you, Rix, and not only because of your amazing voice. You seem like a nice person, and I'd like to get to know you better. So I really am interested in hearing about how you got where you are, and nothing you say is going to bore me."

"Hey," I said, "I *do not* think you're an ignorant slut. I wasn't suggesting anything of the kind, I was only worried that—"

"I know. I know," she said, looking down and pulling the shirt together. "I'm sorry. I guess I'm being a little oversensitive. So please just forget it and go on with the story."

Fascinating, I thought. *Not your typical one-night stand.* I was staring at her face, thinking what a nice tan she had, when I realized from her indignant expression that I was supposed to be talking. "Uh, right. Okay. So we're at the Skyway and we start jamming, and it's like we've been playing together for years. I mean, you cannot imagine the chemistry, the silent communication, the perfect synchronization of thought and rhythm and vocal harmonies. We even took requests from some older folks for songs no other rock group could hope to know, and between Billy and me, we were able to pull them off.

"At one point, because it was approaching the holidays, someone asked us to play ***The Christmas Song***. You know, 'Chestnuts roasting on an open fire?' That's not a simple arrangement by a long shot, nor is it an easy song to sing. But when I looked at Billy and shrugged to let him know I had no idea what the chord arrangement was, he said, 'If you can sing it, I can play it.' So we switched places and he took over on the organ, while I stood up and sang. And man, did we nail it. Even the younger folks in the crowd applauded, and applause from an audience of drunks and other musicians is pretty hard to come by.

"Anyway, we agreed to get together at Jimmy's and talk about forming a group. That meeting turned into a four-hour jam session, and by the time we split up, Kenny and Billy had decided to give up the security of their current gigs and take a chance with us. We considered adding a bass player, but Billy said we wouldn't need one if I could get a Kruger Bass Unit for the organ pedals and add a second Leslie. So—"

"Whoa," she said, interrupting me. "You lost me there. "What's a Kruger Bass Unit, and who are these two Leslies? I didn't see any girls on the stage last night."

"The Leslies aren't girls," I said. "They're those big wooden speaker cabinets on either side of the stage. They're one of the things that give the Hammond organ its unique sound and strong bass projection. The Kruger is an electronic gadget that enhances the punch of the bass pedals, making them sound almost exactly like a bass guitar. Billy taught me how to run bass lines on the pedals, and he also showed me all kinds of new ways to use the stops on the organ to emulate horns and other instruments."

She started to interrupt me again, but I held up a hand. "Stops are adjustable slides on the organ that change the tone and pitch of the keys. And if you know how to use them, you can reproduce just about any sound, including those of other instruments and even the human voice. Remember I said earlier the Hammond was one of the main reasons we can create the sound we do with only four pieces?" She nodded. "Well, that's what I meant. With the Kruger and the extra Leslie, and with Billy's knowledge of how to use them, we eliminated the need for a bass player and added everything from simulated horn and string sections to virtual choirs for backup vocals, and even solos mimicking everything from flutes and trumpets to violas and oboes."

By then she had gone glassy eyed, and I figured I'd finally managed to bore her with all the details. But when I stopped talking, she perked up. "You know," she said, "that's a great story, and I do love your music, but I'm wondering why you would want to make career out of playing other people's songs. Seems to me with your talent you should be writing your own. I mean, being able to mimic hit records is cool, but it won't make you a star. And in my estimation, you deserve to be one."

Maybe she *was* a mind reader after all. Without my even hinting at it, she'd climbed into my head and discovered the one thing I'd been craving ever since the Nashville fiasco with ***Skip School Flu***. It wasn't that I didn't love being a part of The Madisons; I did. After all, we were making great money and were one of the most popular bands in Florida. But I didn't want to do this for the rest of my life. I'd seen too many musicians who had, and most of them ended up wasting away in some hotel piano bar, taking requests and hoping people would fill their jars with tips so they could pay the rent and keep themselves in booze.

"Hello?" she said. "Are you still in there, or have you left on the Cannabis Express?"

"Uh, sorry. Lost my train of thought there for a minute."

"So, about what I said? Don't you have any interest in writing your own material?"

"Yeah, sure," I said. "But I've had a couple of bad experiences with that already, and I'm not real good at handling rejection. Besides, the market is starting to be dominated by all this cheesy bubblegum stuff, what with The Beatles and the so-called British Invasion. And I have no desire to write that kind of crap."

"That so-called crap is making a lot of people rich and famous, you know. And most of them couldn't hold a candle to you when it comes to singing." She retrieved the half-smoked joint, lighting it and taking a hit. She handed it to me and I put it out again.

"No shit?" I said. "I'm not saying I couldn't write that stuff. In fact, if you were to set me down in a state-of-the-art studio like Lennon and those guys, give me a ton of drugs and leave me alone for a while, I could probably write a hundred silly, hook-line songs. The problem is, that's not what I want."

"What do you want, Rix?" she said, touching my hand. "Do you even know?"

I started to answer, but after I thought about it I realized I *didn't* know. My career so far had been a whirlwind of ego and fun and booze and drugs, and I'd never stopped to think much about the future. Now that I'd been confronted head-on with the question, I couldn't come up with an answer. I liked working with The Madisons, but not really in clubs where we had to play six or seven nights a week, repeating the popular songs of the day over and over. And lately the frat parties and other private gigs had started to dry up, probably because of our refusal to play stuff by the Beatles and other Top-40 bands we found musically laughable. Our mainstay was traditional rock and blues which we embellished with our own complex arrangements, plus a little light jazz and a few standards thrown in for the older crowds. We'd decided early on that Beatlemania was a passing fad, but we'd obviously been wrong. More and more it was looking like we were destined to become mainly a club group, and that was something I definitely did not want.

"Boy, you are some thinker," Carla said when I didn't answer her. "I wasn't trying to screw with your head, but maybe that's not such an easy question for you to answer. How about if we drop the subject for now?"

When I looked up, she leaned to kiss me, and the anxiety over my indecision evaporated. The kiss was tender, not overly suggestive, and the feeling of sincerity and caring it conveyed took me by surprise. I let her pull me to my feet, and she put her arms around me. Like the kiss, her embrace seemed intended to comfort rather than to suggest something sexual. Still, the longer we remained in each other's arms, the harder it was to keep from responding. And when she felt my erection, she pushed me away.

"You know," she said. "I didn't mean to propose anything by that. I could sense your confusion and was worried I'd ventured into forbidden territory. So the hug was more of an apology than an effort to seduce you. On the other hand ..." And this time the kiss left no question about what she wanted.

I HAD NO MEMORY of what had happened the night before with Carla, so my initial criteria for judging what she was all about came solely from her 'birthday gift.' And waking up to find someone I had no recollection of talking to naked in my bed hadn't, as she'd suggested, left me with a terribly high opinion of her as a person. Since then, however, I'd been forced to reevaluate my first impression. Not only was she intelligent and empathetic, but when we made love that afternoon, her demeanor was far from aggressive or slutty. She was quietly sensual in her responses, though once we got comfortable with each other she became almost recklessly passionate. We fit together as if she were a mold into which I'd been poured, and our numerous orgasms were synchronized so perfectly we never had to say a word.

After we'd worn each other out, we lay side-by-side for a long time without speaking, until she finally turned and snuggled into my neck. "I was going to ask if you enjoyed that as much as I did," she said, "but I think it would be a somewhat rhetorical question, don't you?"

"God, yes," I said. "I'm not sure what happened there, but it was amazing. By the way, I *would* like to know about last night. Because if it was anything like this, I might have to give up alcohol so I never miss—"

"Nothing happened," she said. "You were too drunk."

"You mean I couldn't—"

"I mean you passed out. Then this morning, when I woke up, you were staring at me, so I kissed you, hoping, I have to admit, that you might be willing at some point to make love to me. Thanks, by the way. I'm not terribly experienced, but I did my best. And it seemed to work out pretty good."

"You have a gift for understatement." I said. "As for your supposed lack of experience, I find that hard to believe. In fact, if you were so inclined, you could probably teach a course in—" She clapped a hand over my mouth.

"Look," she said. "I told you this was a first for me. I'm not a whore, Rix, and I don't make a habit of screwing guys I've never met before. Maybe trying to seduce you last night wasn't the most sensible thing I've ever done, but I was pretty drunk myself. And I'm *not* lying about my sexual naïveté, so don't go making insinuations about my supposed expertise. I—"

"Hold on a minute," I said, tearing her hand away from my mouth. "I was kidding, dammit! I believe you, okay? And I'm definitely glad you chose me to lose your good sense over. So don't get all pissed off at me for making a little joke."

"Okay, then," she said, nibbling on my ear. "Just so we're clear. Hey, don't you have to work tonight?"

"Shit!" I said. "What time is it?"

UNSHAVEN AND A LITTLE disheveled, I made it to the lounge at thirteen minutes after nine and took over for Kenny who was struggling with the high harmony to the Righteous Brothers' ***You've Lost That Lovin' Feelin'***. This was a duet Billy and I usually sang together, and we slid into our version without the crowd knowing anything was amiss. Carla stood at the side of the dance floor near the stage, beaming up at me, and when we finished the song, I turned and smiled sheepishly at Jimmy. "Sorry, man," I said. "I was—"

"And here's a little tune by The Temptations," Jimmy announced over the mike, ignoring me. "It features our own David Ruffin impersonator, Rix Vaughn, just back from a tour of our newly remodeled men's room here at Surfside." Kenny was already playing the intro to ***My Girl,*** and as a collective chuckle rippled through the crowd, Jimmy stood and pointed a drumstick at Carla. "Rix would like to dedicate this to his new fiancé. So let's all give the two of them a nice hand."

When I turned back to the audience, red in the face from embarrassment and anger, I noticed that, instead of shying away, Carla was bowing to the applauding audience. *Great,* I thought. *Just what I needed.* I got through the song without a hitch, and by the time it was over I had lost the anger and resigned myself to the fact that I deserved the humiliation for being late. The rest of the set went smoothly, and when I joined Carla during the break, I apologized for Jimmy's little prank.

"No problem," she said. "Though I was wondering if you wanted a civil ceremony, or if we should go for a big church wedding."

"Very funny," I said, finishing off my double bourbon and signaling the waitress for another.

"You'd better slow down," she whispered in my ear. "Didn't you say something about not wanting to miss anything again?"

I was trying to think of a clever retort, when the sound of firecrackers rang out from behind us. I turned around, but couldn't see anything for the scramble of bodies running toward the exits. "Rix?" Carla said as I started to rise. I looked down to see her grasping her neck in an attempt to stop the blood squirting through her fingers. "I think I've been shot."

20

R & R

The next several weeks were a nightmare. The surgeon said I probably saved Carla's life by wrapping my shirt around her neck and applying constant pressure until the ambulance arrived. Fragments of the bullet—a .32-caliber hollow-point fired by some lunatic seeking revenge on his former girlfriend—had nicked Carla's carotid artery, and the blood loss was substantial.

For a while it looked like she might not survive, and when she came out of the medically-induced coma, there was a question about how much mental impairment there would be due to the loss of blood and reduced oxygen to her brain. Though everyone tried to convince me I was not in any way responsible for what happened, I still felt guilty. Not only that, but during the brief time we'd spent with each other something seemed to click between us. It was a lot like the feeling I had when The Madisons first played together at the Skyway lounge.

I think the most compelling thing, the thing that grabbed me by the heart, was the look in her eyes when she first opened them. My initial impression of her eyes had been that they were large for her face, pale blue, and somewhat mysterious looking. But when she finally awoke from the coma, I saw they were almost colorless, the only blue being a watery hint of aquamarine. Staring into them, it seemed as if I could see into her soul, a lost and frightened soul, silently screaming for help. She would later tell me what I'd seen was real; that at that moment she had been overwhelmed with fear because she couldn't make her mouth respond to the signals she was trying to send from her oxygen-deprived brain.

After that initial breakthrough, her recovery was slow and arduous, beginning with fundamental things like learning to talk again, which she would later describe as "reestablishing the connection between my brain and my mouth." Ironically, she'd been majoring in Communications, which probably helped her with the speech therapy and in regaining her ability to form coherent sentences. One thing I came to understand and admire was her innate intelligence, which she used along with her communication skills to develop alternate methods of expressing herself.

People often see the inability to speak clearly as a sign of stupidity or even ignorance, and up until that point I had been guilty of the same kind of unreasoned prejudice. But even before Carly spoke her first words—a garbled version of "I want out of here"—I knew she was struggling to articulate her needs and desires. I soon learned to interpret her eye movements and facial expressions, so that long before she could speak clearly we were communicating in a way only the two of us could understand. These signals were eventually joined by hand gestures and body language as the physical therapy began to take hold, and I was often called upon by the doctors and therapists to help them understand her responses to their questions.

Having no obligations during the daytime, other than an occasional band rehearsal, I spent hours at her bedside, ignoring the nurses who tried in vain to enforce the hospital's arcane visitation rules. These breaches of hospital policy were ameliorated by the fact that I often brought my guitar and would serenade the staff with requests. Occasionally I was joined by other members of the band, and Jimmy would periodically report on her progress to the crowd at Surfside. Even some of the bartenders and waitresses started visiting, and her room was always filled with flowers courtesy of the club's owner.

As I predicted, our private gigs continued to dry up, which resulted in The Madisons becoming Surfside's de facto house band. Before long practically everyone in Clearwater knew who we were, including the nurses and other staff at the hospital; and our semi-celebrity status afforded us extra leeway when it came to bending the rules.

At first, Carla's mother—who turned out to be as attractive and feisty as her daughter—drove over from Sarasota every day. But after she saw the constant attention and bedside vigilance being provided by me and the other band members, she realized her daily trips were not necessary. So she resumed her obligations as owner of a fancy clothing boutique on St. Armand's Key, restricting her visits to the store's slower days at the beginning of the week.

As the weeks passed and Carla became more lucid and ambulatory, she returned to her earlier inquiries about my career. But I managed to sidestep them, while demanding that she tell me more about herself. At first she refused, citing her inability to speak clearly, but as her verbal skills began to return and I kept bugging her, she finally relented.

"So," she said one day, speaking slowly but with near-perfect clarity, "what would you like to know? And don't say you want to know how I learned to fuck so expertly. God I hate that word."

"Really?" I said. "Why?"

"I don't know. It's just one of those words that sound crass to me. Like pu ... pussy or cunt or cock."

"Doesn't sound like you have a problem saying them," I said, tickling her ribs.

"Stop it," she said. "I don't have a problem referring to those words as parts of speech, but I never use them in con ... conversation because they make a person sound ignorant."

"Sounds like a typical English major. What *are* you majoring in anyway?'

"Marketing and Communications," she said, "with a minor in English Lit."

"I see. So what do you want to be when you grow up?"

She jabbed me in the side. "I am gr ... grown up, thank you very much. And before this happened, I'd hoped to get into the movie business. Not as an actress or anything, but maybe as a publicity agent or with a big advertising firm that handles pro ... promotion for some of the major studios."

"Far out," I said. "Sounds like fun."

"It would be, but I'm a realist, and I know I'll probably never be a hundred percent again. I'll most likely end up teaching elementary school kids how to spell and punctuate and write little poems their mommies can hang on the refrigerator."

"That's odd," I said, "unlike me, you know what you want, but you're giving up before you even get started. Who says you can't get back to a hundred percent? Not the doctors, that's for sure."

"Who says you have to waste your talents playing for a bu ... bunch of drunks who only half listen to your music, instead of shooting for the stars?"

"Touché," I said, laying my head on her chest.

"What is it, Rix?" she asked, her voice softening. "What are you so sc ... scared of?"

"I'm not scared!" I said, though I wasn't sure that was the truth. "Maybe I just don't want to give up the security of working with a successful group of musicians I like and admire. Or maybe I'm like you, figuring the chances are slim that I could ever break into the Big Time. I've been talking to a producer lately, playing him some of my original songs, and he keeps telling me I have to write more commercial stuff. You know, with hook lines and repetition and something called pathos. Hell, I don't even know what that word means."

"Pathos?" she said. "It means stir ... stirring emotions. Something personal that evokes passion or sorrow or tenderness. That's what all those writers of what you call bubblegum are doing. What makes it sound so silly to you is that they're writing for teenagers, kids who are going through all the emotional confusion of puberty and adolescence. The kids don't hear the silliness. All they hear is words that res ... resonate with their own emotions, their crushes and breakups and parental grievances. And, of course, their sexual frustrations, though the writers have to disguise those references with innuendo and double -meaning phrases."

"Sounds like you should be a songwriter," I grumbled. "I sure as shit don't want to write that kind of crap. I write from my own experiences so I can feel the emotions myself, not fake them for a bunch of teenyboppers. The first song I ever wrote was pretty juvenile and silly, but at least it came from things I had experienced."

"What was that?" she asked, running her fingers through my hair.

"Just some stupid little thing about skipping school. And, no, I'm not going to play it for you. I've written a few songs since then, but from what the producer says, they aren't very commercial."

"Well, if you're not going to play me your stupid little song, then what about some of the others? Hey, here's an idea: why don't you write a song about this whole experience? It's almost stranger than fiction, and it is, after all, real."

"Yeah, right," I said, but the idea lingered in the back of my mind. I'd always had a hard time refusing a challenge, and for days thereafter all I could think about was how to put some of the emotions we were both feeling down on paper. I actually ended up writing three songs, but only one of them struck me as being something she might like. Two weeks later, when we were left alone in her hospital room, I pulled out my guitar and, without any introduction, started to sing ...

And sometimes she will tell me
That she thinks she's kind of slow
And wonders if the world sees her that way
And I laugh at her a little, and I cry inside to know
That I can't find the reassuring words I want to say

And then she smiles
And I can see somehow that she has all the answers
Though she doesn't seem to understand or know
And then she laughs
And I feel sorry for the ones who cannot know her
And hear her gentle words and watch her grow

For she is love and all around her shines a rainbow
And she is hope and holds the promise of the sparrow
She is peace and in her eyes
This old world loses its disguise
And I thank God, for this I know
She is tomorrow

"Damn," she said, tears threatening to choke her words. "That's incredible, Rix. And believe it or not, it has all those elements you were talking about. Not only that, but it yanks at the heartstrings, mine at least. There has to be more though. You can't leave it there."

"There is," I said, "but it gets a little flaky after that. The rest of it still needs a lot of work."

"So do I," she said, "but I'm not ashamed of being a work in progress. Come on, let's hear what you've got so far. Please? Maybe I can help."

I hated playing anything I wasn't yet satisfied with, but her offer to help was intriguing. "Okay," I said. "But don't say I didn't warn you." I started out with a little instrumental break I'd been working on, hoping the complex fingerstyle solo would distract her from the unrefined lyrics. But once I'd exhausted the stall, I knew I had to get on with it, so I took a deep breath and continued ...

There are days that I'm so caught up
In the frenzy and the fray
I forget to feel her presence in my world
Then suddenly I realize another precious day
Has come and gone without my little girl

But then she'll softly tell me
That I really am all right
Though I feel I must have surely gone insane
And I feel for all the others who must make it through the night
Without her there to laugh away the rain.

For when she smiles
I somehow realize that she has all the answers
Though she doesn't seem to understand or know
And when she laughs
I find myself in tears of joy that I was chosen
To hold her fragile love and watch it grow

For she is love and all around her shines a rainbow
And she is hope and holds the promise of the sparrow
She is peace and in her eyes
This old world loses its disguise
And I thank God, for this I know
She is tomorrow

And this time, the tears came in earnest.

IT WAS ALL WRONG, of course—our relationship—based on guilt and pity and the emotional upheaval of the shooting. We were married in the hospital, mainly because she wanted to get out of there, and the doctors wouldn't discharge her unless someone could be with her twenty-four-seven for the first few weeks. Since I worked at night and her mom worked during the day, I rented an apartment near the Skyway Bridge, halfway between Clearwater and Sarasota, and we split the caretaking duties. Things went well for a while, but as Carla struggled to regain her physical and mental abilities, she often took her frustration out on me, and I soon lost patience with her emotional tirades.

She did keep her promise to help with my writing, though, and even though our collaborations often led to vehement arguments, her input had a positive effect. In fact, ***She is Tomorrow*** and two other songs we worked on together made it onto my first album years later, and I made sure she was credited and received royalties for her half of the writing.

The marriage lasted two years, and our divorce was as amicable as could be expected. There were no kids to support, and she demanded no alimony. We stayed in touch for a while, but when she moved to California to take a job teaching communication skills to students recovering from brain injuries, our letters and phone calls became fewer and farther between, eventually stopping altogether except for an occasional birthday or Christmas card.

Her legacy, however, would live on in my life. She turned me on to poetry and folk music, which led me to discover the genius of Bob Dylan, who I had ignored up until then because I couldn't stand his voice. She also taught me a lot about syntax and composition and other aspects of writing I'd ignored in my less-than-illustrious career as an indifferent high-school student. And, of course, the sex was great, even when we weren't getting along.

Probably her single most important contribution to my career was the way she constantly harped on my musical cowardice, admonishing me to forget about The Madisons and break out on my own. As it had been with Pat, this was also one of the reasons for our frequent fights, and she never let up even after we split. In fact, the first letter I got from her ended with a PS that said, "Someday you're going to have to stop basking in the comfort and security of The Madisons, and take a chance."

Those words would eventually lead me to leave the band and strike out on my own. It was the toughest decision of my life at the time, not only because it led to many years of instability and frustration, but because it meant leaving a group of close friends and musical collaborators, the likes of which I would never find again. The Madisons broke up shortly after I left, with Billy going on to get a degree in chemistry and abandoning music except for an occasional gig as a sideman with his uncle's Guy-Lombardo type orchestra. Kenny died a few years later in a horrific car accident, and Jimmy ended up doing the piano-bar thing until he died of an overdose at the age of fifty.

A couple of months after the breakup, we were surprised to find ourselves at the same local bar one Sunday night, though what we thought was a coincidence turned out to be part of a plan. We were laughing and talking about old times, when the lights came up and couple of dozen local musicians walked out of the back room holding a cake aglow with five candles; one for each of the five years The Madisons had been together. They also presented us with four gold-plated Zippo lighters inscribed with our names and the name of the group, along with a plaque that read: "In commemoration of The Madisons, the finest band ever to hit the West Coast of Florida." There followed the best jam session I ever participated in, with every one of our musician friends joining us at one time or another, and the unfettered freedom of not having to play to a crowd of unappreciative assholes whose only interest was in getting laid or losing themselves in a bottle of booze.

I spent the rest of that year struggling to write and work as a single, while delving into stronger drugs in a futile effort to enhance my creativity. The gigs were sparse, mostly playing for tips at the last few remaining coffee houses, or doing dinner hours at intimate restaurants along the beach. To keep from going broke I also did a lot of studio work, writing and singing silly radio jingles for local businesses. It was during this time that I met the luthier Harley Day and became fascinated with the idea of building classical guitars. I was so strung out and frustrated by then, I decided to take him up on his offer to hire me as an apprentice, trading the ego satisfaction of performing on stage for the challenge of carving the perfect bridge or neck with a razor-sharp chisel.

As my twenty-fourth year came to a close, I was more lost and confused than I'd ever been in my life. The night before my birthday, angry and resentful over how my career had stalled, I sat on the seawall behind my apartment with a bottle of rum and that chisel, contemplating the most efficient way to carve death out of the veins in my wrist.

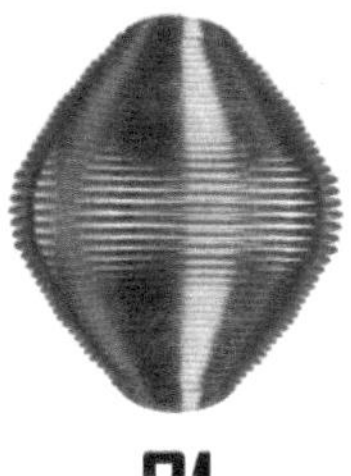

21

Georgia On My Mind

Do you want to talk about it?" Aurélie said. We were sitting in the lounge under a panorama of the Grand Canyon projected on the simulated window next to our table.

"Talk about what?" I said, taking a drink of the fake Jack I'd come to enjoy more than the real stuff.

"Whatever it is that's been bothering you ever since you returned from 1968. Judging by your physiological reactions there at the end, I'd have to assume it was a pretty painful episode."

"It's all painful, Aurie," I said. "Why do you think I'm agreeing to take a chance on a do-over?"

"I understand, and I'm sorry. But tell me something: why do you keep rubbing your wrist? I'm worried you're having circulation problems, and if that's the case we need to—"

I stopped her by holding my arm up and turning it so she could see the spidery white lines, almost invisible now after more than forty years. She leaned forward and stared for a moment, then gasped, touching my skin and running her fingers over the web of ancient scars.

"Oh, shit," she said. "I'm sorry. I didn't mean to dredge up old wounds."

"The hell you didn't!" I said. "That's all you've been doing from the start."

"But, but Rix, it's the only way we can help you make a decision."

"I know, goddammit. And I'm not blaming you. It's just that it's like having my guts ripped out every time I relive some of that stuff. As for this"—I pulled my hand back and rubbed my wrist again—"it's no big deal. It only bothered me because I hadn't thought about it in a long time and I wasn't prepared. I skipped over a lot during the earlier preview, and having to live through those episodes now can be a little shocking. Anyway, it didn't work, so let's forget it, okay?"

"Okay. Sure. So what about the next trip? You know, you don't have to bother with it if you've already made up your mind."

"I haven't," I said. "I keep thinking the farther back I go the more chances I'll have to make positive changes, but I don't know if that's true. So many of my later accomplishments depended on luck and being in the right place at the right time. By 1978, I'd had two top-forty hits, and even though that didn't make me a superstar, at least it was more than ninety-nine percent of the other struggling singer-songwriters had managed. So I have to decide if I'm willing to take a chance on screwing all that up by going back before then and trying things when I have no way of knowing what the repercussions might be."

She didn't answer. Hell, there weren't any answers. With all their extraordinary scientific breakthroughs, neither she nor Heyoka had given much thought to the human factor: the emotional consequences and unpredictable results of their experiment. But that's what guinea pigs were for, weren't they? I'd never been a big fan of PITA, but now that I'd become a research animal I could sympathize with their efforts.

As the Grand Canyon dissolved into a misty forest scene of deer and chipmunks and fluttering birds, I thought back to those days in Georgia when Robin and I had lived in that leaky little two-room cabin on a hundred acres of virgin hardwoods. It was there that I'd discovered something new, something so alien to my city-boy lifestyle it seemed as if I'd been transported to another planet. But those memories were bittersweet, and I had no desire to revisit them.

"I need to take a nap," I said.

Aurélie nodded. "Why don't we head back to the villa? You'll be more comfortable sleeping in your own bed."

My own bed, I thought. It had been decades since I'd slept in a bed I could call my own. Even here, although I did feel at home and comfortable, it wasn't really *my* bed or *my* home. And with all the memories and remorse beginning to hammer at my sanity, that thought alone was enough to drive me deeper into depression. I closed my eyes and did my best to clear my mind. "Good idea," I said. "Sorry I'm being such a stick-in-the-mud. I'm a little freaked out right now is all."

"It's perfectly understandable, Rix," she said, rising and reaching for my hand. "I can give you something to help you sleep if you'd like."

"Thanks but no thanks. I'm having a hard time keeping my eyes open as it is."

We didn't speak on the way back to the villa, and when we reached the door to my bedroom, she hugged me. "Call if you need anything," she said. As she turned and started down the hall, I thought about changing my mind and asking her to come in, but I knew that would only lead to more frustration. Besides, I really was dead on my feet.

Closing the door behind me, I stumbled to the bed and fell on my face, kicking my shoes off and pulling a pillow over my head. The fragrance of some night-blooming flower drifted in from an open window, again reminding me of those days in the north-Georgia woods. I tried to sweep the memory from my mind by repeating my mantra, but the mere act of meditating—ironically, a practice I'd learned from Robin—brought it into even clearer focus.

One drawback to the effects of Heyoka's magical elixir was that the memory enhancement was universal: everything became crystal clear, even those bits I preferred not to remember. There were many positive things about that era, awakenings and flashes of creativity that could only have occurred in that specific place and time. But there were also details I was happy had been blurred by drugs and the tricks an aging mind plays to protect one from emotional whacks to the heart. Now, however, those filters had been removed, and the memories were nearly as vivid as the ones evoked by Aurélie's elaborate gadgetry.

Unable to stop my mind from replaying the past, I decided to try and recall the events of 1973 that led to my self-imposed exile from civilization. I remembered the whole scenario had been set in motion by a phone call from my old boss, Harley Day, shortly after the ***Sunday Morning Sentinel*** debacle.

WHEN THE PHONE RANG that morning, I figured it was a bill collector, or maybe my uncle looking for another payment on the loan he'd given me to pay for the trip to Muscle Shoals. Broke and wallowing in self-pity, I let the answering machine pick up and was surprised to hear the voice of Harley Day. It seemed he'd accepted a commission from The Smithsonian to build a reproduction of an eighteenth-century Ruckers-Taskin harpsichord; a project that would leave him little time to deal with the steady stream of guitar orders and restoration work. He needed my help, he said, so would I please consider coming back to work at the shop.

Having few other options, and desperately in need of money to support my growing drug habit, I called him back. And after negotiating for a while, I accepted his offer of a raise and a percentage of the profits from guitar sales. By then I was on a roller-coaster ride of Quaaludes, cocaine, and speed, sometimes going days without sleep, and I dove into the work with a zeal that surprised even me.

The harpsichord, constructed using fragments of ancient schematics and drawings from Taskin's archives, was laden with intricate marquetry and featured a beautiful landscape scene painted in oils on the underside of the lid. Harley was a genius, not only as a craftsman, but as an artist and designer, and the finished product brought him and the workshop international acclaim. It also nearly doubled our commissions for Baroque instruments of all kinds, while adding to the demands by well-known musicians for custom guitars and repairs. I became so absorbed in the work that my young wife—the infatuated groupie who'd been the first person to hear ***Sunday Morning Sentinel***—hardly ever saw me. She would occasionally join me at the few gigs I managed to book as a single, but after those performances I was often too tired and drugged out for sex or intimacy of any kind. Before long she filed for divorce, and I had no desire to fight it.

I could easily have gotten lured into abandoning music altogether in favor of becoming a luthier, however, even as frustrated as I'd become with the constant rejections by my local producer, I couldn't let go of my obsession with writing. I was also falling deeper into drug use, and my early experiments with heroin were becoming less experimental and more habitual. I had started dealing as well, and between my work at the shop, the occasional singing engagement, and profits from drug sales, I had accumulated a substantial bankroll.

For years I'd harbored a dream of getting away from civilization: finding a place where I could leave the bedlam of city-life behind and concentrate solely on writing. But by the time I turned thirty, my life was so complicated and my mental equilibrium so dependent upon maintaining the cash flow necessary to keep myself in drugs, I had all but given up hope of ever realizing that dream. Fate, however, would soon intervene.

One night the cops came banging at my door yelling that they had a search warrant. Having become paranoid about the drugs and the dealing, I kept the majority of my stash in the trunk of my car, which—thankfully—their warrant did not cover. I managed to flush most of what was in the apartment down the toilet before they broke through the door, so all they found were some syringes and a little residue, plus a single roach I'd forgotten about in an ashtray. Still, they decided to arrest me, and I spent the night in jail awaiting my first appearance before the judge. My one phone call had been to Jimmy, who was well versed in dealing with drug charges, and he contacted his favorite attorney, who showed up at the hearing to defend me.

It turned out they didn't have enough evidence to impose bail, so they released me on my own recognizance, and a week later the charges were dropped. But the experience woke me up to the fact that I was in serious jeopardy of being arrested again and charged with more serious crimes. I spent the next few days gathering the tools I'd accumulated and selling most of my instruments, then packed everything I owned in a rental truck with a hookup for my VW Beetle and headed north. Jimmy had a friend who'd bought some undeveloped land in north Georgia with the idea of someday retiring there to grow marijuana, and he agreed to rent me a small cabin that was on the land when he bought it.

Even though he was upset about my leaving, Harley graciously allowed me to take the workbench I'd built, so I arrived at the cabin with all the trappings of a small woodshop, plus a few sticks of furniture, half an ounce of uncut coke, 500mg of nearly pure heroin, and a little over $20,000 in cash.

Had I possessed any measure of sanity, I would have realized my exodus represented a perfect opportunity to kick the drug habit and go legit. After all, I was in a place I'd always dreamed of being: away from the confusion of civilization, in an awesome natural setting where I could commune with nature and write, and with enough money to see me through at least a year of relative comfort without the need to generate any additional income. The drugs, however, preempted common sense, and instead of cleaning up my act, I took whatever gigs I could find, while blowing through the coke and heroin and cash like a tornado on steroids. I awoke six months later lying in a pool of bloody vomit, with a lovely young woman slapping my face in an attempt to revive me.

22
Robin's Song

Robin Barbary worked as a waitress at the club where I'd apparently passed out on stage. I'd tried to hit on her a few times, but she'd always rebuffed my advances, so I was surprised to find her in my tiny cabin playing the Good Samaritan. Over the next two weeks, she nursed me through the severe dysphoria of withdrawal, force-feeding me liquids and dealing with the nausea and diarrhea like a professional nurse. She never once complained about the messes I made or the burden of cleaning up after me, and she even seemed embarrassed to ask if I had any money so she could buy groceries, because she'd quit her job in order to stay with me twenty-four/seven.

We went through the cabin and scraped together a couple of hundred bucks, but we both knew that wasn't going to last long. So as soon as I'd dried out enough to be left alone, Robin took a part-time job waiting tables in a truck stop at the nearest exit on I-85. Though not bedridden, I was still feeling a little woozy and confused, especially when it came to making sense of this mysterious intervention by someone I barely knew. We'd spoken several times at the club, but other than her patient and sometimes apologetic rejections, I couldn't recall anything that might have suggested she would sacrifice her job to be my savior. And that was apparently all she intended to be, since she continued to rebuff my sexual advances, even though we were sleeping in the same bed.

Despite her obvious devotion to my wellbeing, our personal interactions were limited to brief conversations about practical matters. And although she was affectionate, her concern seemed more like what she might feel for an injured puppy than a human being with complex feelings. I tried several times to draw her out, get her to explain her reasons, not only for refusing to have sex with me, but for being there at all. Her responses were sketchy and evasive, mostly designed to redirect the conversation to questions about me and my past. And over the course of a few weeks she managed to coax me into relating most of my life story, the good and the bad.

I often wondered if I was imagining things, if my drug-addled brain hadn't conjured her up out of thin air. But as time went on and she didn't disappear, I realized she was not a manifestation of some psychotic break, but a real, live person. So real, in fact, so fascinating and enigmatic, I soon gave in to the feelings I'd been trying to hold in check and admitted to myself I was falling in love with her. I held these feelings inside, however, not wanting to chance the rejection I felt sure would come if I told her how I felt. But one night, as we sat on the rickety front steps of the cabin under a sliver of moon shining through the trees, I decided the romantic atmosphere was too good to pass up.

"You know," I said, "other than through my music, I'm not very good at expressing my feelings, which is why I haven't found a way to thank you for everything. Maybe, when I'm feeling a little better, I'll write you a song. In the meantime, though, at the risk of sounding corny, I wanted to tell you … I wanted to say that I'm pretty sure I've fallen in love with you."

She looked up into the trees, her face silhouetted against the glow of the new moon. For a moment I thought she wasn't going to answer, but then she shook her head, slowly, as if preparing to admonish a child. "Don't mistake gratitude for love, Rix," she said, staring straight ahead. "You owe me nothing. I'm not doing this for you, I'm doing it for me."

"But what the hell do you get out of it?" I said, a little angrier than I intended. "If you refuse to let things go any further, or to even explore the possibility, what's the point?"

She turned to look at me then, her eyes conveying sympathy and something I chose to interpret as poorly disguised longing. Finally, she took my hands in hers. "I never said I didn't want to explore the possibility," she said. "But there are things that have to happen first, the most important being that you have to convince me you're through with drugs."

"But ... but I am. I haven't taken anything in over six weeks, not even a drink."

"Yes," she said, "and that's mainly because I threw everything away and I'm in control of the money now. Don't get me wrong, I'm proud of you for making it this far, hopeful even. But I've been through this scene dozens of times before, and I've learned that six weeks is nothing more than a blip on the scale when it comes to kicking a drug habit, especially if it includes heroin."

"Dozens of times?" I said. "What are you, some kind of undercover drug counselor, disguising yourself as a waitress and looking for addicts to cure?"

"Don't be angry with me, Rix. I have not tried to deceive you in any way. I made it clear from the start that I wasn't interested in having an affair. And whether or not you want to believe it, that was a difficult decision for me. After all, you're an extremely talented and good looking guy, and underneath all that ego and seductive horse manure, I could sense there was a nice person struggling to get out."

"I don't know about the nice-guy stuff, but if that's the case, why do you keep avoiding me? And I'm not talking about sex here. I can deal with that. What I mean is you won't tell me anything about yourself, so how are we supposed to, I don't know, explore the possibility? You know almost everything there is to know about me, but all I know is your name and that you quit your job to take care of me. I appreciate what you've done, I do. But if we're going to get to know each other, try to get past this caretaker-patient relationship, you need to stop being so evasive."

She looked down and closed her eyes.

"Come on, Robin," I said, lowering my voice. "This is killing me, this mystery woman shit you're pulling. Don't you see how unfair it is?"

"I know it's unfair," she said, "and I'm sorry. There's a lot of pain involved in my life story, and talking about it brings that pain to the surface again. But maybe just this once, if there's something specific you want to know ..."

I could see the reluctance in her body language, feel it in the moistness of her fingers. But I could also sense a chance for intimacy.

And even if it had nothing to do with sex, I knew I couldn't pass up the opportunity.

"Okay," I said, "let's go back to that 'dozens of times' comment you made. What did you mean by that?"

More silence, then a deep sigh and a nervous cough. "I was a flower child," she murmured, her voice distant, almost too soft to hear. "My parents were both musicians, and I grew up during the Beat Generation. You know, Kerouac and Ginsberg and the rest of that New York gang? We moved to California when I turned sixteen, and I eventually joined the so-called counterculture: free love and drugs and all that. I stuck with it for a while, thinking I could help save the world, but when my friends started dropping like flies from overdoses and psychotic episodes, I decided I'd better get out while I still had the chance. That's what I meant about having been through the drug-withdrawal thing many times before. Not only myself, but with my friends."

Her eyes were closed now, tears dripping from the corners. I squeezed her hands and waited, knowing there was more she needed to get out.

"I lost five of them to overdoses." she said, finally. "Most of the others ended up in jail or in psycho wards, and every single one had quit at one time or another. Some for weeks, others for many months. But they all went back. Promises meant nothing. Swearing they were done with drugs, flushing their stash down the toilet, voluntarily admitting themselves into rehab programs—none of it meant a thing. I loved some of those people, Rix. And I'm scared to death of loving you."

I waited until her body stopped shivering, then said, "So, what happened after that? I mean, how did you end up waiting tables in Atlanta?"

"That's a long, sordid story, and it's not something I want to talk about, so please don't ask me to tell you. I'm here now, and I'm going to give it one last shot with you. I have no illusions about what might happen, but I've made a commitment and I intend to see it through, no matter how painful the outcome. I know my refusal to have sex with you seems cruel, but that's the way things have to be, at least for now. So please, let's drop the subject."

And that was that. She left no room for discussion. Argument, maybe, but I knew I couldn't win, so I didn't even try. The fact that she'd finally opened up a little did, however, release a lot of the tension between us, and after that she would occasionally—very occasionally—offer me little tidbits of her life story, though she always used those opportunities to emphasize the pitfalls of drugs. She tried to be encouraging and upbeat about my recovery, but there was an underlying current of doubt in her words, and I could tell she had little confidence in my ability to stay clean. I soon came to understand that nothing I could say was going to convince her I was different from the others, so I resolved to keep my mouth shut and let my actions speak for themselves.

I'd never tried to give up drugs before. I'd thought about it from time to time, and I felt confident I could quit whenever I wanted, but I always managed to convince myself there was no good reason. Now, however, there *was* a good reason, perhaps the most persuasive reason I would ever have.

AS SOON AS I felt steady enough to work without fear of cutting off a finger or two, I started organizing the shop in hopes of drumming up some repair business. I had no desire to perform anymore, and Robin accepted this without complaint. Meanwhile she continued to refuse my sexual advances. She did, however, promise that once I'd convinced her I was through with drugs, she would "reconsider" having sex with me. How long that was going to take, she wouldn't say, and not knowing nearly drove me crazy.

A week or so after she made that somewhat nebulous promise, we were sitting on the front steps during what had become a daily ritual of watching twilight descend among the trees, when I told her I knew there was more to her reluctance than my giving up drugs.

"I'm not trying to push you, Robin," I said. "But I'm also not blind. I can tell you're having a hard time with this and, well ... Look, I told you I love you, and I meant it. I've never felt this way about anyone before in my life, and I'm finding that there are new feelings, new emotions that go along with it. One of them is compassion, or maybe empathy would be a better word. Whatever it is, it means that I know you're fighting against your desires just as I am. And I know there's more to it than the drug thing. Nothing you can ever say is going to change the way I feel about you, if that's what you're worried about. So please tell me what's really going on."

She looked away, and for a moment I thought I'd made her angry. But then she sighed. "You have to understand something, Rix," she said. "For me, sex used to be as thoughtless and routine as brushing my teeth or taking a walk. I was smoking pot before I hit puberty, and I lost my virginity when I was twelve. I've had so many lovers I couldn't count them if I wanted to. Hell, I can't remember more than five or ten of them, and even those relationships were so casual they were meaningless except for the friendships involved."

"So, what? Are you saying you've decided to swear off sex because you got laid a lot when you were younger? That doesn't make a lot of sense to me."

"I'm sure it wouldn't," she said, smiling. "Not to point out the obvious, but you happen to be a male, so you're predisposed by nature to have as many partners as you can manage. Besides, I'm not talking about remaining celibate for the rest of my life. What I'm saying is there's a big difference between getting laid and making love. I was lucky enough to find out about that difference a few years ago, and I'm never going to go back to having sex simply for recreation or physical pleasure."

We both knew what my next question would be, but before I could get it out she turned to me and held up a finger. "Don't ask," she said. "That's part of the pain, and if you have any respect for my feelings, you'll leave it alone. The point is, after that I decided sex was going to have to have meaning beyond animal desire or procreation. In your case, that meaning—my purpose for being here—is to try and save you from yourself."

"How noble of you," I said, immediately regretting it. "Sorry, I didn't mean that. The thing is—and please don't take this as a come-on. The thing is ... Oh, shit, I don't know what the thing is. I mean, it's not just because I'm horny as hell, although since we're finally talking about it, I have to admit that I am. What I'm trying to say is there's a lot more going on here than physical attraction. At least for me, there is. No one's ever crawled into my psyche like you have, and for once in my life I'm dead sober, so it can't be drugs or booze making me feel this way."

"Feel what way?" she said, turning to look at me.

"I don't know, like I'm being swallowed up by something I can't control. Something I don't *want* to control. Like I've found the last piece of a puzzle I've been trying all my life to complete. But when I reach for it—for you—it's like reaching for that ring on the merry-go-round I could never quite touch."

"But you can touch it, Rix. All you have to do is be willing to get off the merry-go-round and come back into the real world for good. You're already halfway there. You've fallen off the painted pony and now you have to get back up and climb into the saddle on a real live horse. And I don't mean the horse that group America sings about. Drugs aren't the answer, they're the problem, and until you convince me you've accepted that as a fact, my job won't be finished."

"But I have," I said. "I swear it."

"Don't swear to something you're only hoping for," she said, touching my hand. For the first time her touch felt like more than that of a caretaker's, and the feeling reverberated through my body like the tremors of an earthquake. "I'll know when you've finally committed, and nothing you say before then will persuade me."

It would be three months—three agonizing months of complete abstinence from drugs and alcohol—before she gave in. And when she did I realized what she'd said about there being a difference between getting laid and making love was true. It wasn't a matter of technique or physical compatibility; it was an all-encompassing experience: quiet and graceful, like the sighing of wind in the trees. And it was followed by a preternatural calm, during which we held hands and listened to the sounds of the forest as it came alive in the early dawn.

That morning—as we lay quietly awaiting the sunrise, with the lingering fragrance of night-blooming jasmine wafting in from an open window—would change my life in more ways than one. As if obeying some unheard command, a robin perched on the windowsill and began to sing; then another, somewhere in the trees, answering. Soon the air was filled with the music of springtime: the rustling of squirrels and chipmunks; the plaintive cry of a mourning dove; sounds I'd no-doubt heard a thousand times, but that had always been obscured by the ambient noise of civilization. Here, however, there was nothing to dampen those sounds, and among them I heard the strains of melody lines, the poetry of nature in all its pristine and lyrical beauty.

It would be some time before this experience would manifest itself in my music, but whenever I think back to where it all started, what led to the compositions that would define my career as a singer-songwriter, I always end up at that morning, and the miraculous awakening of my soul to nature's symphony. Until that epiphany I had lived in an emotional cocoon, insulated from the real world by the hustle and bustle of civilization and nurtured only by the marketing dictates of a heartless entertainment industry. For the first time I learned to be still, to bask in the quiet security of love and open myself up to the spiritual richness of the world around me.

Although I would struggle at first to translate these revelations into music, Robin's unwavering confidence in my talents led me through the wilderness of self-doubt into a new landscape of creative freedom, from which would emerge the songbook of my life. Among the pages of that book was the song that eventually propelled me from anonymity to international recognition. However, even though nourished by my growing love for the woman who had become my savior, ***Robin's Song*** was one piece I would never play for her, since I only managed to finish it in the melancholy wake of her disappearance from my world.

But on that morning, the thought of losing her stood no chance of intruding on the sanctity of our newfound love; a love so sensually overwhelming it left no room for doubt or worry of any kind. No longer plagued by the anxiety of waiting and wondering, I experienced a surprising burst of energy that immediately obliterated the lethargy of withdrawal and set me on a new course of action. After all, there was work to be done, discoveries to make, a new level of intimacy to explore. And I set about these tasks with a renewed sense of purpose and a clarity of mind I had not known since I was a teenager.

First, I needed to set up the shop and make some contacts in the music community. Being basically in the middle of nowhere, I had to travel south to Atlanta, where I approached several music stores with an offer to do stringed-instrument repairs. Many of the larger stores had their own in-house repairmen, but I managed to get an occasional job from the smaller ones. With little money to spare for gas, the travel back and forth became burdensome, so I came up with a plan to carry some tools and supplies with me. This saved time by allowing me to handle the less complicated repairs right in the stores. Still, the jobs were scarce, requiring only a couple of days work each week, plus a trip into the city every ten days or so. I felt bad about Robin being the main breadwinner, but she ignored my apologies, encouraging me use the free time to try and write some music.

We were sometimes so broke we couldn't pay the power bill or buy heating oil, so I learned how to chop wood and feed the fireplace, which sometimes also served as source of heat for cooking. And since our water supply came from a well, when they turned the electricity off, I had to use the hand pump and haul water in buckets for drinking, bathing, and filling the toilet. It was a primitive existence, made bearable only by our deepening love for each other and Robin's upbeat attitude and gentle encouragement for me to write. She even managed to sneak enough from her tips to buy me a used typewriter, and her patience in teaching me how to touch-type bordered on the miraculous.

I soon began to explore the property in search of ideas for songs, wandering through the woods and following an ancient Indian trail to a fast-running stream, where I would sit on a granite outcropping and contemplate the unspoiled beauty of the wilderness. I became so attuned to the nuances of my surroundings I could sense subtle changes in the environment: slight alterations in temperature and humidity signaling an oncoming storm, or a whisper in the underbrush that indicated the presence of animals whose habitats I'd become familiar with. Other than the occasional flyover by an airplane, the only sounds were those of nature, and I began to wonder how I'd ever been able to tolerate life in the city.

Still, I was having trouble putting these things into words and setting them to music. Then one evening, while Robin and I were conducting our ritual of sitting on the steps in the early twilight, I started complaining about not being able to write.

"This place is so fantastic," I said, fiddling around with a new fingerstyle riff on the guitar. "I ought to be writing reams of music. But for some reason, I can't really *be* here."

"But you *are* here," she said. "I like that a lot, by the way. That thing you're doing on the guitar."

"Thanks," I said. "Anyway, I guess what I'm trying to say is there's something making me feel like I don't belong here. As much as I want to, I can't seem to stop thinking of myself as an intruder: a city boy who doesn't fit in. It's like there's some kind of invisible string tying me to the past."

"Well," she said, "why don't you write about it—that string, I mean? Maybe about trying to break it."

And in a flash, my career as a successful singer-songwriter was born. It would be more than a year before my first national release, and it would not be the song I wrote the next day while she was at work. But ***City Strings*** served as the confidence builder that allowed me to write fearlessly, from my heart instead of my mind. I didn't think much of it at the time, but when I played it for Robin the following evening she went crazy over it.

"I wrote something," I said as we, again, sat on the steps in the growing twilight.

"Something?" she said, getting up to turn on the light over the front door. When I didn't answer, she stared down at me, raising an eyebrow in mock impatience.

Surprised by the nervous stammer in my voice, I mumbled, "It's nothing great, but at least it's ... well, it's something."

"I see," she said. She must have sensed my anxiety, because she dropped the impatient look and returned to her seat next to me.

I tried to waste a little time by pretending to tune my guitar—which was already in perfect tune. And when I could think of no other way to stall, I sighed and began to play the intro.

Her face lit up as she recognized the riff from the night before, but after I'd stretched it out for a while with several variations, she said, "That's nice, Rix. Does it have words?"

"Yeah," I said, resigning myself to the inevitable. "I don't know if they're any good, but—"

"Would you please drop the introductory apologies and just sing?"

"Right," I said. "Sing. Okay, it goes like this ..."

Well I found me a place to sit
So I think I'm gonna sing a bit
About how I came to be here
I'll start at the very end
And work my way back again
And watch yesterday disappear

I was born a city boy in the land of the sun
Where livin' right meant stayin' tight
Lookin' out for number one
Like a puppet in a puppet show, with plastic tears to cry
And city strings around my mind
To hold me ... till I die

"What do you think?" I asked.

"I think," she said, the words coming out slow and deliberate. "I think you'd better play the rest of it."

"Okay. Hold on a sec." I played long refrain on the guitar, watching an indignant look spread across her face. And just when I thought she was about to complain, I continued ...

Well the strings turned into cables, and the cables into chains
With links made out of ego trips, and locks made out of games
Till one day I found a way to leave it all behind
Now I'm breakin' chains with every step
And man I'm feelin' fine

Another short guitar break, then ...

I cut me a walkin' stick and found me a trail
And left all the ego trips behind
And I built me a cabin with my own two hands
From what God left for me to find

And I'll touch only what I need to touch
And leave the rest just as it was
And lay back by a stream somewhere
And make sure that I take care
To break the strings as they unwind

As the last strains of guitar music faded away, she remained silent. I was thinking she hated it and didn't know what to say, when she jumped up and almost knocked me off the stairs with a hug.

"Oh, Rix," she cried. "It's wonderful."

"Whoa, there," I said, scrambling to keep my guitar from being crushed. "Slow down a little, will you? It's not *that* good."

"It *is*, Rix. And I'm not just saying that to be nice. It may not sell a million records, but it represents something important. I heard most of your other songs at the club, and they were pretty and well-written, but they were all about other people and love affairs and things songwriters usually write about. This was about *you*, how you feel, what you're struggling with. It's authentic, and nothing beats authenticity. Besides, it's the first thing you've written since I've been here, probably the first thing you've ever written sober. And that in and of itself is enough to celebrate. I'm so proud of you."

"Okay, okay," I said, as she untangled herself from the guitar strap. "But I can't take all the credit. It was your idea, you know, the breaking strings to the city bit?"

"Those were your words, Rix. Not mine. All I did was suggest you use them in a song. Now we'd better get inside before the mosquitoes eat us alive."

Whether or not she wanted to believe it, the song *had* been her idea. In fact, she was the inspiration for half the songs on my first album, and that album didn't even include ***City Strings***. No, the song that would lead to my first record contract was hers and hers alone, written from the memory of that morning after we first made love. ***Robin's Song*** would be my first hit single, but unfortunately, Robin would not be around to share in my success.

IT TOOK ANOTHER NINE months or so for me to convince Robin I was serious about getting married, and even then she seemed doubtful. In the meantime, I spent every spare moment walking the woods and writing fragments of lyrical poetry. Eventually, some of those lyrics started coming together, and before long I had a dozen or so compositions set to music. The only thing I couldn't seem to write was the song I'd promised her early on. Writing *about* things was easy, but writing *to* someone was a different story, especially someone I was so in love with I often found it difficult to express that love even to her. Finally, one evening, I confessed my frustration.

"I just can't find the words," I said. "In fact, what I feel for you ... hell, I don't think they've even made the words."

"Listen," she said, "you need to stop obsessing over this. You're on a roll now, but you're letting that promise you thought you made get in the way. You didn't actually promise, by the way. All you said was *maybe* one day you would write me a song. So what if that day hasn't yet arrived? More important by far is for you to keep on writing. Speaking of which, you've been so wrapped up in your quest to write *my* song, you're closing your mind to other possibilities. You probably don't even realize it, but you just came up with a great idea for another one."

"I did?"

"You did. Think about it: ***City Strings*** came out of your trying to do something you were struggling with, so why not write about your frustration with writing a song to me?"

I sat in silence while what she said sank in and an idea began to coalesce in my head. After a few minutes, she leaned over and whispered in my ear: "Hello? Anybody home in there?"

"Uh, yeah," I said, reaching back to grab my notebook off the top step. "Turn the light on will you." Fifteen minutes later, I had the song roughed out.

I was experimenting with the chord arrangement and humming along, when she said, "Hey! Are you going to sit there all night goofing off and mumbling, or are you going to play it for me?" I didn't answer, just smiled and started singing …

It's a waste of time I know
I've tried it a thousand times before
But a mocking bird outside my door
Said to come and try it just once more

So I grabbed my old guitar,
And walked out to watch the sun go down
Tried to sort the lines that were runnin' 'round
In my head –

But they just ain't made the words for me
To write a song to you
And all them silly poets lines
Well Babe they just won't do
They just ain't made the words to say
The things I feel inside
And though you know I've often tried
The words sound old and cracked and dried
And that's what led me to decide
They just ain't made the words

I stopped and looked at her. "Go on," she said. "I hope that's not all."

"Nope," I said. Then my standard caveat: "It's still rough, though, so—"

"Shut up and sing!"
So I did …

Well it's springtime in the country now
There's inspiration all around
I can feel the happiness we've found
In everything that's goin' down

And if all I had to say
Was I love you more than night and day
Or more than the smell of new-mown hay
I think I could probably find a way

But they just ain't made the words for me
To write a song to you
And all the thoughts that springtime brings
Well Babe they just won't do
They just ain't made the words to say
The things I feel inside
It isn't just that I can't find 'em
It isn't that I couldn't rhyme 'em
I wrote a thousand songs to you and never signed 'em
'Cause they just ain't made the words

It *was* rough; that would become evident several months later when the producer demanded I make many changes before he would allow ***They Just Ain't Made The Words*** to be used as the flip side of ***Robin's Song***. But the saddest thing about it was that by the time I signed the record contract, Robin was gone.

WE WERE MARRIED A month after I wrote ***They Just Ain't Made The Words***, in a small civil ceremony, and for two weeks I was in heaven. The music was flowing, and my confidence had never been higher. Too high, as it turned out.

It was only a little marijuana plant, stunted for lack of care and cultivation. I discovered it growing in a clearing near the trail I walked almost daily, and I felt sure that even if she found out it wouldn't be a big deal. I was wrong, of course, not only about keeping it secret, but about how ironclad her drug ban would be.

After hanging the plant up for a while to let the THC drain into the buds and leaves, I smoked my first joint in over a year, and I was still a little stoned when she got home from work that afternoon. The next morning she said I should keep the car for the day in case I got a call and had to go into the city to do some repairs. I thought that was kind of strange, since the few work calls I got were never emergencies, but I didn't argue. When I went to pick her up from work she was gone. The manager told me she'd left right after I dropped her off, saying only that she was sorry for leaving him in the lurch. She left no note, no message for me, and I never saw her again.

A month later I got the annulment papers in the mail. The pending decree cited fraud and mental incompetence as the reasons for requesting dissolution. I called her attorney in Atlanta, and he said I was welcome to attend the hearing and argue the case, but he advised against it, especially if I couldn't afford legal representation, which I couldn't. He also said Robin would not be at the hearing, so if my purpose was to see her, I would be disappointed. He wouldn't tell me where she was, except to say she had moved out of state and wanted no further contact with me.

Six weeks after the final decree arrived in the mail, I got a postcard, a touristy one with a photo of Cypress Gardens in Florida. A short note on the back said: "You won't find me, so don't even try." No signature; postmark illegible.

As my depression deepened, I found it impossible to write. That is, until I realized my only hope of ever seeing her again was to somehow finish ***Robin's Song*** and get it released nationally. Maybe then, I thought, she'd hear it on the radio and try to contact me. I'd been working on the song for over a year, aiming for a perfect ending that always seemed just out of reach. And, ironically, it was my sadness that eventually provided me with the final verse.

Excited again, for the first time in weeks, I sold all my tools and two of my guitars, and drove to Muscle Shoals, hoping my short visit with the three producers while trying to peddle ***Sunday Morning Sentinel*** would gain me another audience. It took a lot of patience, and many hours sitting in waiting rooms, but I finally managed to outwait one of them. And when I played ***Robin's Song*** for him, he immediately signed me, this time with no talk about having someone else sing it.

I watched my first national release climb the charts, while I worked on the album. And I called Robin's lawyer to let him know where I was, in case she had a change of heart. The song peaked at number nineteen on Billboard's Top 100, and I remained hopeful. But after my second album came out three years later, I finally accepted the fact that she was never going to contact me. It probably wouldn't have mattered anyway, because by then I was deep into heroin again, unrepentant and cynical and dealing with anger issues that would plague me for the rest of my life.

The pain lingered, though, hanging like a shadow over my personal life; a cautionary tale that drew an impenetrable curtain around my heart and kept me at arm's length from any future emotional involvement with a woman. That curtain remained closed for more than thirty years, until it was finally ripped away by the only woman I'd ever loved more than Robin. And even that turned out to be nothing more than a cruel joke; a twist of fate destined to break my heart for a second time.

It seemed ironic that Heyoka, the man who hoped to be my savior, would also serve as my executioner. Not only would his experiment lead to my physical demise in this dimension, but the demise of my relationship with Aurélie as well, a loss for which even the prospect of a second chance at life could not adequately compensate.

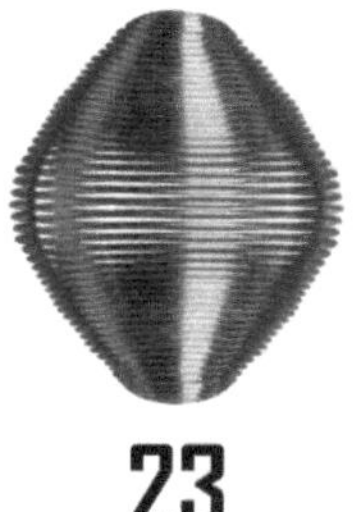

23
A Change Of Plans

The memory of my time in Georgia and the years that followed ended abruptly when Aurélie knocked on the door and peeked in.

"You're awake," she said.

"Sort of," I groaned. "Why? Did you think I died or something?"

"Well, I was certainly hoping you hadn't." She pushed my feet over so she could sit on the bed. "I've been checking on you every so often to make sure. You've been out for ten hours."

"Guess I fell asleep. Maybe that's why it seemed like years. That damned brain juice has turned me into a human time machine. I just had the most vivid flashback yet."

She lifted my arm and pressed two fingers against my wrist. "Mmmn," she said. "Pulse feels like you've run a marathon. Was it that bad?"

"Good and bad. Mostly bad. Things always start out good, but then they turn to shit. I seem to have a talent for turning good things into shit."

"You have many talents, Rix," she said, brushing a wayward strand of hair from my forehead. "What you're talking about are the ups and downs of life. We all go through them. If there were no downs, we wouldn't be able to enjoy the ups. It's like God needing the devil, because without him there wouldn't be much use for a god."

"Very profound," I said. "The problem with your theory is there's supposed to be that balance you talked about. You know, the yin-yang thing? Except in my case the scale seems to be way out of kilter."

"Right, and that's why you get another chance. So, are you reconsidering your third trip?"

"I am. In fact, I don't think I need it."

The memory had ended when I was thirty-four, the same year I had scheduled for my next trip back in time. By then my body would already be chemically addicted, not only to heroin, but to booze. And although I'd eventually managed to kick the heroin, I knew the alcohol addiction was something I probably couldn't give up at that late date.

"So, what made you change your mind?" she asked.

"Lots of things. For one, I'd been worried about not being able to write without drugs, but my sharpened memory reminded me of something important." I pulled her down until our lips were close, and, surprisingly, she let me kiss her.

She seemed to have forgotten about her decision not to make love, stretching out beside me and pressing her body against mine. But before things got too hot and heavy, she pulled back. "Sorry about that," she said, caressing my cheek. "I was worried about you and I forgot myself there for a minute."

"Yeah, well, what am I supposed to do with this?" I grabbed her hand and put it between my legs.

"Let's see," she said, giving me a quick squeeze. "Maybe I could rustle up some potassium nitrate."

"You guys have a chemical solution for everything," I said. "Okay, I give up, what would potassium nitrate do, make me fall out of love with you or something?"

"Heaven forbid. No, it's what you probably think of as saltpeter. And in the right dose, it can … uh, soften things up a bit, if you get my drift. The problem is, it also causes high blood pressure, anemia, kidney problems, and has a depressive effect on the heart. So not only would you not be able to get it up, chances are you wouldn't be able to get up, period. On second thought, the best thing would be a cold shower."

"I think the best thing would be for you to take off your clothes," I said, reaching for her zipper.

"If you only knew how much I want to," she said, pushing my hand away. "But if anything happened to you before the transfer, I would never forgive myself. Now stop it and tell me about this memory. You said it reminded you of something?"

I turned on my back and closed my eyes. "It reminded me what falling in love can do for creativity. Kind of like now, with you. I'm actually getting the urge to write again. I *am* in love with you, you know."

"Yes, I believe you've mentioned that a few hundred times. And I love you. Which is why I refuse to kill you. Now please stop brooding and tell me what changed your mind."

So I told her about the flashback. As the story unfolded, I could tell she was having a hard time maintaining her scientific objectivity. To say she was jealous of Robin might have been a stretch, but there was definitely more going on than simple curiosity.

"You see?" she said when I finally wound down. "You're only thinking about the bad part. About losing Robin. I understand how difficult that was for you, but the short time you had with her was probably the most creative period in your life. There was value in that, Rix. Tremendous value."

"Maybe so, but the thing is it seems to be a pattern with me. No matter how great things are, I always find a way to fuck them up. Or maybe it's destiny, because it's happening again with you, and this time I don't think I've done anything to deserve it. Have I?"

"No, you haven't. It's just an odd convergence of circumstances. There's no one to blame. And believe me when I say this is no easier for me. I'm sorry if I seem so analytic about it sometimes, but I can't help it. I try to see the facts and weigh the good against the bad. In this case, the potential good for you far outweighs the pain either of us has to endure. And it *is* painful for me too, Rix. More painful than you could possibly know."

"Jesus!" I said. "Why can't things ever work out the way I want them to? It's like I'm cursed or something. Here I am looking at an opportunity any normal person would cut off an arm for, yet in order to take advantage of it I have to lose the thing I want most. Isn't there some way to fix this? Some way I—we—can have both?"

"Not that I can see," she said. "Our only priority right now is making sure the transfer is successful."

"So, what? Are you saying there might be a chance for us after that?"

"I'm not saying anything of the kind. Sorry if I made it sound that way. I've told you before it's impossible for me to inject myself into your new reality without committing murder, and there's no way I'm going to do that."

"I understand. But you also said the project might continue after I'm sent back. So maybe you could figure out a way."

"I wasn't talking about anything like that," she said. "The next phase, if there is one, will probably concentrate on doing something similar in this dimension, though it wouldn't involve mind transference, at least in the same way. Since we'd be restricted by the forward progression of this timeline, there would be no younger version of someone to transfer a mind into, so the objective would be preservation of consciousness for the future."

"Preservation? You mean Cryogenics?"

"We've looked into cryogenics, and Heyoka doesn't think there's any chance of it ever working like people expect it to. Even if we were able to freeze and revive a physical brain—which is highly unlikely—his calculations show the personality would not survive. What I'm talking about is holographic brain imaging."

"I've read some things about that," I said. "The idea of making a digital copy of someone's mind. I thought we were decades away from developing computers capable of duplicating the structure and capacity of the human brain."

"*We*—meaning the computer-science community in general—probably are. On the other hand, *we*—meaning our team of researchers, working under the guidance of possibly the most brilliant scientist in the world ... Well, you've seen some of the things we can do. And those represent only the tip of a very large iceberg."

"Right. So this iceberg, it includes a quantum leap in computer technology?"

"Of course it does. How do you think we're able to do the computations necessary for all our experiments? The human brain is an incredible machine, but it would take thousands, maybe millions of brains to handle the complex problems we've been tackling. Human neurons exchange electrochemical signals at about 150 meters per second, whereas the speed at which data is exchanged in a computer—the speed of light—is about 300 million meters per second, something like two million times faster."

"Oh ...kay." I said. "So what have you done, built some kind of super computer?"

"The supercomputers you're probably thinking of are stone-age stuff to us. We've developed computational systems that use quibits—quantum bits— to represent data, instead of the ones and zeros digital computers use. This gives our computers incredible capacity, enough to emulate the biological nervous system, including the way neurons connect with each other, how those neurons react to stimuli, and how they learn to adapt. Our systems don't just store and retrieve data, they learn and improve themselves without our intervention. In other words, they evolve, and they do so at an exponential rate. That evolution has already resulted in a power and capacity far greater than the capabilities of the human brain."

"Sounds encouraging," I said. "But what do you plan to do with all that power? Conquer the world or something?"

"If that were Heyoka's goal, I'm sure he'd figure a way. But it's not. We're using it to advance our research into things like quantum teleportation, energy production, genetic engineering, and many other branches of technology. In the case of brain imaging, the objective would be to preserve the minds of extraordinary thinkers and talented artists, so we will never again lose another Einstein or da Vinci or Mozart."

"What about an Aurélie?" I said.

"I'm not anywhere near important enough to waste time on," she said. "You, on the other hand ..."

"Sorry, but I don't get it. If you're not important enough, I'm not even in the ballpark. So what would be the point?"

"The point is we need a backup plan. Interdimensional transfer involves some unproven and rather nebulous techniques, and even though our calculations tell us the chances of failure are miniscule, we're going to make a backup copy of your mind just in case."

"A backup copy of my mind," I said. "You mean I'm going to exist in two places at once?"

"I guess you could look at it that way, though the copy will be for storage only. It won't be activated unless absolutely necessary."

"Uh, huh," I said. "So instead of storing the brain, you store the information it contains. That sounds pretty cool, but let me ask you about something else. You've mentioned quantum teleportation a couple of times now, and I'm wondering if you're talking about what they did in that old sci-fi movie, ***The Fly***. You might remember it from the remake with Jeff Goldblum and Geena Davis. Anyway, the idea is they have these things called telepods, and they use them to send objects instantaneously from one pod to another, supposedly over any distance."

"That would be the ultimate goal," she said. "But so far, we haven't been able to send what you're probably thinking of as objects. What we're working on now is something similar, though not quite as magical sounding. It involves sending quantized digital information in the form of instructions for building *copies* of objects. Instead of sending the objects themselves, their molecular structure is mapped and instructions for building exact duplicates are sent to a receiving machine that recreates them. The technology is relatively new, and it may be decades before we can do this with complex living organisms. However, considering the exponential rate at which our computational systems are evolving, you never know."

You never know, I thought, wondering what those exponential possibilities might be. It felt like bits of data were trying to assemble themselves in my head, as if once everything fit together, my brain would start spitting out answers. Answers to what, I didn't know, because I had no idea what questions to ask. Still, there seemed to be something important lurking in the shadows just beyond the limits of my understanding.

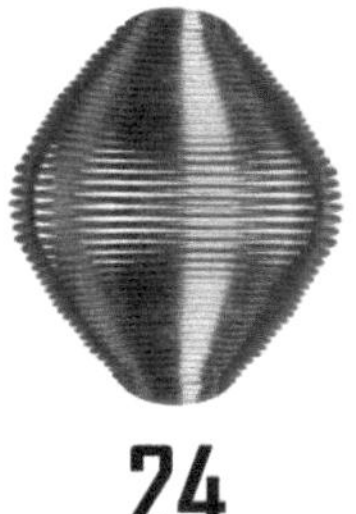

24
Swan Song

The brain imaging operation reminded me of an old *Outer Limits* episode: a platform that slid into a glass-enclosed coffin-like tube, then a lot of lasers and other sci-fi crap that struck me as a poor special-effects production. I had to stay awake during the process, but there was no pain or discomfort of any kind, and I emerged wondering if it hadn't all been for show; something to reassure me that if the transfer failed, at least the essence of my personality would survive so future generations could wonder what the big deal was about preserving Rix Vaughn. After that, it was supposed to be all downhill towards the transfer, but there was one more unexpected revelation for me to deal with.

The three of us were sitting beside a flickering fire in the Great Room as rain battered the tall windows. I'd brought my guitar and was experimenting with a new chord arrangement, while Heyoka went over some of the things I should be prepared for during the transfer procedure. I wasn't paying much attention until I heard him mention something about the memory enhancements I'd been experiencing. When I tuned into the conversation, he was looking at me apologetically.

"Unfortunately," he said, "Those improvements were only applied to your physical brain as it exists today. Since the transfer will be of your persona, without the improved function of the organ itself, I'm afraid your memory will be as it was before you met us."

"So, more-or-less fucked," I grumbled, setting my guitar aside. "That's just great. How the hell am I supposed to improve my life if all I have to work with is a mind that functions like a worn-out Model-T running on dried-up oil and needing a hand-crank to get it started?"

"It won't be as bad as all that, Rix," Aurélie said. "The wisdom you've accumulated over the years will still be intact. The only things that might be a little murky are some details of your past, and that's common for anyone your age. It's not like you're going to be starting out with a blank slate."

"Hey," I said. "You don't live in my old brain, so how the hell do you know what's left in there? I do, and I can tell you that without the magic Jack juice there ain't much."

She looked shocked at my anger, and for a moment no one spoke. Finally, Heyoka broke the silence. "I understand your trepidation," he said, "but much of it is unwarranted. As Aurélie said, your accumulated wisdom will still be there, as will the mental aspects of your matured talents and musical acumen, all of which should serve you well. As for the memories, one of the reasons we've been refreshing them with the overviews and the trips back is so you will have those more recent experiences to call on. Certainly your recollections will not be as sharp and clear as they are now, but they won't be gone altogether."

"Okay. Okay, I get it," I said. "So, any more warnings?"

"Other than the things we've already discussed about the conflict between your older mind and your younger body, I can't think of any," Heyoka said. "Although, I do need to reiterate the fact that this is an experiment. We've done all the calculations possible, and the data tell us everything should go according to plan. But since nothing like this has ever been tried before, we can't be absolutely certain about the ultimate outcome. I can assure you of one thing, though: you *will* go back and become a younger version of yourself. And since the current version has very little time left, you should be—"

"I should be grateful," I interjected. "And I am. But I'm also terrified, so forgive me if I sound a little unappreciative at times. Neither one of you two geniuses has the slightest idea what I'm going through right now. I'm not only about to embark on a journey into the unknown, but I'm also about to say goodbye to a woman I love more than anything on this earth."

Even though my feelings for Aurélie were no secret, I could tell Heyoka was embarrassed when I turned to her and we embraced. "I'll leave you two alone for a while," he mumbled, rising and shuffling across the room toward the hallway.

As soon as he was out of sight, the grief I'd been holding back for weeks exploded in a torrent. Aurélie held me tight, and although she didn't make a sound, I soon realized the tears were mutual. Like me, she was far from being an overly emotional person, and her sudden loss of control surprised me. We stayed like that for a long time while our mutual anguish was slowly mollified by the anesthetizing monotony of rain pounding on the windows.

Finally, we managed to compose ourselves, and after we'd destroyed half a dozen tissues I said, "Sorry. I tried not to let that happen, but I couldn't help it. As I'm sure you know by now, I'm not much of a crier. I mostly convey my feelings through music, which is why I haven't written anything in decades; because, frankly, I haven't felt anything in decades. At least anything worth writing about."

She blinked at me, her eyes going wide each time they opened, as if she expected me to continue. When I didn't she said, "You should take that back with you, Rix. The emotion, I mean. The ability to show it outside your music."

"I'd love to, Aurie. But without you ..." I started to choke up again, so she put her arms around me.

After I regained my composure I kissed her, then reached over to pick up my guitar. "Anyway," I said, playing a few bars of the song I'd been working on, "I've been thinking."

She looked apprehensive, perhaps wondering if I'd decided not to go ahead with the transfer. I let my words hang in the air for a while, but I'd already made up my mind.

"I want to go back to when I was twelve," I said. "Before most of the stupidity and the drugs and the alcohol. I know I'm going to be carrying the mental addictions with me, even the heroin—you know, once an addict, always an addict, and all that. But maybe if I start over before the physical dependence began I can marshal enough will power to stay away from all the shit that fucked up my life."

"You can, Rix. I know you can. Not only will you be free of the physical addictions, but you'll also carry with you the knowledge of how devastating they can be. So what made you stop worrying about the loss of creativity without the drugs?"

"Remember when you told me I was recalling only the bad part of my time with Robin?" I said. She looked at me curiously, then nodded. "Well, that may have been what stood out in my mind, but after a while I *did* start thinking about the good things that happened while I was in Georgia. Specifically the burst of creativity that led to all those songs." I played the intro to ***Robin's Song***.

"Anyway, I knew it couldn't have come from drugs, because I wasn't taking any at the time. I'm sure a lot of it had to do with the natural setting and getting away from all the distractions of city life. But those things only served as an environmental incubator. There had to have been something else, something undefinable. A catalyst of some sort."

"Robin," she said. "And what you're talking about is a muse."

"Right," I said. "A muse. Once I remembered it was Robin who inspired most of that musical bonanza, I started going back over all the other times I'd come up with ideas for songs. Not the run-of-the-mill tunes, but the ones I considered to be my best. And what I realized was that in almost all cases they were inspired by women I cared about. Which explains why I haven't written anything worthwhile since Robin left me and I swore off all future emotional involvements."

"Are you serious?" she asked. "No affairs or serious relationships of any kind?"

"Oh, there were tons of affairs, if you call getting laid having an affair. But, as one young woman I met many years ago put it, I was 'emotionally unavailable.' And I was. Right up until the moment I first saw you standing here in this room."

She went quiet then, staring out at the darkened forest, where a half moon peeked through wisps of dissipating storm clouds. It soon became obvious she wasn't going to respond, so I decided to fill the silence by playing the new arrangement I'd been working on. As my fingers flew over the strings, I said, "You know what finally convinced me my best work required a muse?"

She didn't answer, except with a quick shake of her head. Then, as if compelled by the music, she turned and looked down at my hands. "That's ... That's new," she said, her voice quivering with emotion. "It's beautiful, Rix. Are there words?"

I smiled. "Some," I said, softening my touch until the guitar was barely audible. "I haven't finished it yet, but here's what I've got so far …

She left me with an empty page
Of tomorrow's history
She took all of my yesterdays
And gave them back to me
She left me thinkin' everything
I felt for her was wrong
But at least the lady left me with a song

Lonesome empty feelin'
Rollin' round my days
Memories and reveries
I'm goin' down to stay
But I've still got my music
And I've still got my pen
There always seems to be a song
When love comes to an end

A memory, a teardrop
A broken dream or two
A fantasy you realize
Can never quite come true
And all that's left are paper words
And melody and rhyme
The epitaph in written verse
And lonely chorus lines

She left me with an empty page
Of tomorrow's history
She took all of my yesterdays
And gave them back to me
She left me thinkin' everything
I did for her was wrong
But at least the lady left me with a song

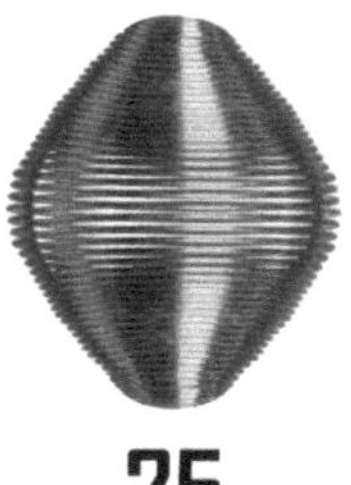

25
Transmigration

Despite the anxiety meds and comforting assurances Aurélie gave me, I almost backed out when we entered the transfer chamber. The first thing that hit me was the noise, which sounded like the screeching of a thousand tortured banshees, and was barely dampened by the molded earplugs we wore. Next there was the intimidating size of the room itself. The walls on either side of the entrance disappeared into the surrounding gloom, making it impossible to discern the chamber's overall volume other than by the intuitive sense that it was enormous.

In the center, suspended high above the floor, hung the huge beehive-like accelerator she'd shown me a holographic image of back when we first toured the lab. The only other feature visible from where we stood at the perimeter was a tiny circular glow beneath the accelerator. As we followed a narrow walkway toward the glowing circle, I realized we must have been hundreds of yards away, because it took us the better part of twenty minutes to approach it. Before we were halfway there, the accelerator could no longer be viewed as an object with specific shape; instead it hovered over us like a second ceiling, defined only by its boundary line around the edge.

Another element of intimidating discomfort was the intense cold. We'd both been injected with some kind of human antifreeze; however, the fact that we were naked made the temperature almost unbearable.

Earlier, she'd tried to explain the reasons why we both had to be naked, but I couldn't comprehend a bit of it. She'd also warned me not to become aroused, which turned out to be unnecessary, since the cold and my fear made any thought of sex impossible. Besides, my libido was sated, because the night before, she had finally given in, and we'd spent a glorious five hours making love, talking, crying, and making love again, until I'd fallen into an exhausted sleep.

About ten yards short of the center, the floor fell off into a circular indentation with three descending shelves around the perimeter that provided step-down access to the staging area. Seeing how cold I was, she stopped at the bottom shelf and signaled for me to sit. The noise eliminated any possibility of conversation, so all she could do was hold me while I tried to stop shaking.

After the chemically-enhanced warmth of our touching bodies had subdued the worst of the shakes, she took my hand and pulled me to my feet, giving me one last hug before leading me to the glowing circle beneath the accelerator. Following her instructions of the night before, I removed the earplugs and tried to hand them to her, but the auditory blast buckled my knees, and I fell on the icy platform. Signaling me to cup my hands over my ears, she helped me up, making sure I was steady before climbing the perimeter shelves to stand outside the recessed circle.

As the platform rose into the inky bowels of the accelerator, I kept my eyes on her face, watching her forced expression of bravado fade into contortions of anxiety. The last thing I saw before being swallowed into the screaming darkness, was her hand, fingers outstretched, raised in a solemn gesture of farewell.

THE IMAGE OF AURÉLIE'S hand would sear itself into my memory, but I didn't have time to give it much thought, because seconds after she disappeared, something exploded in my head, and my first life came to an end.

Part Three

Then Again

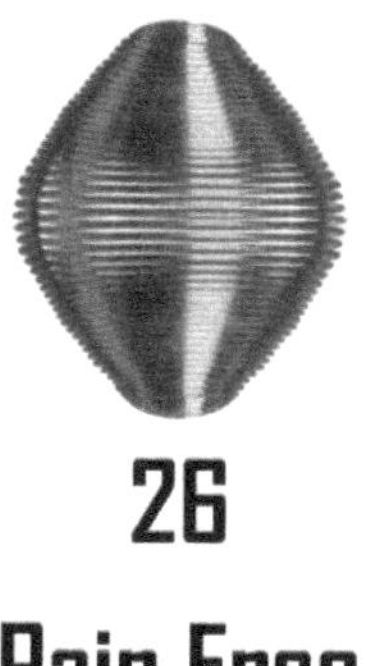

26

Pain Free

The first thing I noticed was the absence of pain. Over the years, as my body slowly decomposed under the onslaught of a lifestyle that would have challenged Wolverine's healing powers, I'd apparently adapted to the accumulating deterioration and learned to accept it as a part of daily life. Only when I awoke completely pain free was I able to appreciate the extent to which I had been dealing with an increasing cacophony of discomfort. The relief was palpable, giving me a weightless feeling, as if I could pull back the covers and float to the ceiling.

For several minutes I tried not to move, savoring the sensation of residing in a body that seemed almost hollow, since there was no longer a way for my organs, bones or muscles to announce their presence. Taking inventory, I started at my feet, noting that the morning cramps and gout that had tortured me for years now resided only in my memory; then the left ankle, where nothing remained of the chronic ache from a fall some two years before. *Two years before?* What did that mean? In this life, I would have been ten years old two years before.

Confusing.

Back to the inventory.

Next was the left knee and the cartilage I had destroyed while attempting to impress a couple of female admirers with youthful vigor I no longer possessed. I'd agreed to participate in a softball game and ended up on crutches for six weeks. No longer any pain there, nor higher up, as I realized the sciatica that had plagued me for decades was gone, along with the lower back pain, the constant sting of hemorrhoids, the groaning indigestion, the chest twinge from my heart attack, and the sore shoulder from years of supporting a guitar strap. Dozens of other minor injuries and metabolic insults had no-doubt added to my overall suffering, but the only way to discern them now was by the vacuum left in the wake of their disappearance.

I was contemplating this new-found physical fitness when I noticed my hands were opening and closing as if squeezing two invisible breasts. Once conscious of this apparently involuntary exercise, I tried one finger at a time, curling them tightly into my palm, then stretching them out until they were almost bent backwards. No pain! Not even a hint of the arthritic deterioration that had threatened for years to put an end to my guitar playing. Fascinated with the slender, unwrinkled youth of those now-flexible appendages, I had resumed my air massage when Mom came bustling through the door with an armful of folded t-shirts.

"Something wrong with your hands?" she asked, as she opened a dresser drawer and began rearranging the contents to make room for the shirts. For a moment, I couldn't speak, remembering the morning ritual my mother always employed to make sure I was awake in time to get ready for school, or, in this case, church. After I turned ten or so, Mom never simply came in to wake me in the mornings; instead, she would find some pretense, whether it be to put away clothes, or bring me a cup of cocoa, or deliver a tidbit of news she'd read in the morning paper. Once I was old enough to look after myself, it seemed she thought it would be insulting to insinuate that I didn't have enough self -discipline to respond to my alarm clock. That small display of thoughtfulness nearly overwhelmed me with emotion. It wasn't so much the act itself, but that it made me realize there must have been thousands of other tiny examples I'd ignored in my first life; little things kids never think about: sacrifices, anticipations, subtle, almost secretive gestures of emotional support.

"Uh, no," I finally managed to croak. And a croak it was, a two-toned bleat, reminding me I was in that voice-changing stage of puberty. "I was just … thinking about my fingers. I mean, if they're ever going to be strong enough to play guitar like I want to."

"I don't think you have to worry about that," she said, closing the drawer and coming over to sit on the bed. "As much time as you put in whacking away on that old Stella, they'll probably be as strong as Superman's before long." She leaned over to kiss me on the forehead. "Happy birthday, honey. Now, why don't you get moving? There's pancakes and bacon and scrambled eggs for breakfast, and your dad's got a little surprise for you."

I knew what the surprise was, but, thinking quickly, I reacted with a curious widening of the eyes, as if I had no idea my first electric guitar—that iconic Les Paul Junior—was at that very moment leaning against a chair in the breakfast room.

As I brushed my teeth, staring in the mirror at the smooth, unstubbled skin of my 12-year-old face, I realized for the first time how complicated it was going to be to pull off the acting job I now faced. How did pre-teen boys behave in 1956? Certainly not like those of the early twenty-first century. There would be less freedom when it came to bad language, less individual autonomy for kids, more respect for parents and other authority figures. Also, I would have to be considerably dumber than the older version of Rix Vaughn, and I had to remember not to know about certain events before they happened.

Dressing wasn't a problem because I had to wear the clothes in my younger self's wardrobe. And, before the transfer, I had checked online to determine that my twelfth birthday had fallen on a Sunday, so that meant a suit and tie for today. As I rummaged around in my closet, choosing a white dress shirt, a solid blue tie, and a gray suit, I thought about other things, like asking permission instead of simply doing what I wanted; remembering to say "Yes sir" and Yes ma'am" when addressing adults; operating primitive devices like ancient TVs and record players; riding a bicycle, (which I had not done in over fifty years); and interacting with teachers and friends, many of whom I probably would not remember. By the time I got to the breakfast table I was so nervous I had to wipe the sweat from my forehead with a napkin.

I made it through breakfast, doing, I thought, a pretty good job of acting surprised when I saw the guitar, and begging to try it out before Church. This request was denied, as I assumed it would be, and I even managed a little pout to convey how I probably would have reacted at that age. Church was pretty easy, since Sunday school didn't involve much more than listening, and the service required only silence and joining in on hymns I mostly remembered. Staring up at the choir loft, I was initially perplexed by the familiar face of the music director, until I realized it was Carol Henderson. Seeing my old friend and musical mentor brought back a flood of memories, forcing me to swallow a large lump that lodged itself in my throat. Those memories were, however, misty and fragmented, and I began to wonder how I was going to interact with Carol and others without sounding like a nut case.

The monotony of our minister's hell-fire-and-damnation sermon gave me additional time to think, and I soon came up with a plan: if I could somehow have a minor accident, preferably a fall that would involve a slight head injury, I could feign mild amnesia for a few weeks. What I needed was an excuse for being unable to remember things like names, schoolwork, recent events, and the status of various relationships. Less than a month remained before school let out for the summer, and with a little help from my "mental impairment" I could probably make it through without raising too much suspicion.

After we shook hands with the minister on our way out, I approached the broad staircase that led down to the sidewalk. The crowd was thick and jostling, and when I reached the top step, I considered faking a fall down the stairs. But I chickened out at the last moment. *Chickened out?* I couldn't remember using that phrase since I was a kid. Maybe I was already beginning to think like a twelve-year-old.

Contemplating this possibility helped me relax a little and open my mind to the vague familiarity of the scene around me. And the first thing I noticed was Dad inviting several people out to lunch. This, I remembered, was a weekly after-church ritual: if he was in a good mood, Dad would often ask a dozen or more folks to join us at one of the local restaurants, where he would always pick up the tab.

As the crowd thinned, Mom and I walked hand-in-hand to the car, and before long the warmth of her grip and the serenity of her smile began to spark more memories. Sunday had always been Mom's favorite day of the week. As long as Dad wasn't called away on some emergency, it was a time when the family could be together for the whole day and she got to socialize with friends at church and during lunch. The rest of the afternoon she and Dad would spend relaxing, while he read medical journals and the Sunday paper, and she read the latest ***Look*** or ***Life Magazine***. Sunday dinner usually involved something simple for her to prepare, like grilled cheese sandwiches and tomato soup, which we would eat on folding TV trays in front of the round-screened TV, watching ***Lassie, Jack Benny,*** and ***Ed Sullivan,*** and constantly adjusting the rabbit ears and vertical hold.

Caught up in the nostalgia, I was startled when the car jerked to a stop in front of our favorite Chinese eatery. Dad had apparently called ahead, because when we arrived, several tables had been pushed together to accommodate the large group that accompanied us. After we were all seated, a steaming array of oriental dishes was served family style, including my favorites: egg foo young, fried rice, and eggrolls. I was so delighted by the taste of those long-forgotten delicacies, I got a reprimand from Mom to watch my manners, but that didn't seem to be anything unusual.

As the meal wound down, I saw Dad raise his eyebrows in my direction, a signal I remembered as his way of telling me it was time to settle the bill. And this brought back another memory: that it was not only my responsibility—privilege actually—to pay the bill, but that I was allowed to keep whatever change there might be. It was a kind of secret between Dad and me, since the money would be over and above my weekly allowance, and Mom wasn't supposed to know about it. When he handed me two twenty-dollar bills, I wondered what he was thinking, but then I remembered it was the fifties. And when I paid the bill I was surprised to pocket five dollars and change.

On the way back to the house, I realized that these sense memories had begun to accumulate, filling in gaps and giving me more confidence in my ability to act the part of my younger self. We were getting out of the car when I heard a long, loud whistle coming from across the street and looked over to see Sam running toward us. Recognizing Sam was easy, since I'd recently relived the ***Skip School Flu*** era. As we fell in together, I excitedly told him about my new guitar, and was surprised at the comfortable way I seemed able to slip into my old persona. The two of us spent most of the afternoon in my room, adjusting the action on the guitar and learning how to use the Gibson GA-90 amp Dad had bought me to go with it. It wasn't until around 4:30 that I made my first mistake.

It was a hot, muggy afternoon, and the only air conditioner in the house at that time was in Mom and Dad's bedroom downstairs. We were sometimes allowed to use their room during the day, and Sam suggested we take the equipment down there where it was more comfortable. By then, my fingers were sore from trying to play stuff I had yet to master at that age, and I needed a break. So I suggested an alternative.

"Let's just go for a swim," I said.

"Right. Where?" Sam asked.

"In the pool, idiot," I said, attempting to sound like a typical, sarcastic kid.

"What pool?"

"My pool, of course," I said. Sam scratched his head and looked at me like I'd lost my mind, so I wandered over to the window and pulled back the curtains—and found myself staring out at a wide expanse of grass where our swimming pool should have been.

"You nuts?" he said, walking up to look over my shoulder.

My first thought was that Heyoka had screwed up and sent me to the wrong dimension. I was about to panic, when I remembered that our pool did not exist until that coming Christmas. Dad wanted it to be a surprise, so he had it installed while Mom and I were away in Indiana. In order to allow enough time for the installation, they'd arranged for me to take an extra couple of weeks off from school prior to Christmas vacation so we could enjoy an extended visit with our northern relatives. I wasn't too thrilled with the idea, until Mom enticed me with the possibility of seeing snow for the first time in my life. Unfortunately, there was no snow, but my disappointment was immediately forgotten when we got home on Christmas Eve and I saw the large, kidney-shaped pool in our side yard.

I was momentarily speechless while the memories began to fill in, and before I could answer, Sam said, "Are you feeling okay, Ricky? You've been acting a little strange. When did you learn to play all that stuff on the guitar, anyway? And what is this crap about a pool? You dreamin' or something?"

"Uh, yeah," I stammered. "Just wishful thinking, I guess. Sure would be nice to have a pool, though." I turned to see him backing away slowly.

"Hey, I gotta go," he said. "Mom's gonna have dinner ready before long. I'll see you at school tomorrow." And with that, he disappeared into the hall, tramping quickly down the stairs and yelling "Bye Mrs. Voniossi" as the screen door slammed behind him.

So my act wasn't as convincing as I'd imagined. Well, then, back to Plan A.

After giving it a little thought, I decided the perfect place for an accident would be the huge banyan tree in our side yard. Sam and I were in the process of building a tree house among its thick branches, and we'd both suffered minor cuts and bruises while working on it, so I figured a slightly more serious injury might not seem too suspicious. Carefully placing my new guitar back in its case, I changed into shorts and a t-shirt, then ran downstairs and headed for the side door.

Seeing the direction I was headed in, Mom grabbed me by the arm as I passed her. "If you're going tree climbing, you be careful," she said. "And don't get all dirty, or you'll have to take a bath and change your clothes before dinner."

"Okay," I said, wrestling my arm free. I let the screen door slam behind me and scrambled up the rope ladder to the half-constructed tree house. I was trying to figure out how to stage an accident without injuring myself too badly when I heard the screen door slam again and looked out to see my dad jump in his 1956 Ford and back out of the driveway. The tires screeched as he drove off, indicating a medical emergency. Dad was always on call at the hospital, and he also made daily house calls, mostly to the elderly patients that constituted about eighty percent of his practice. *Good,* I thought, *at least he won't be here to see through whatever ruse I come up with.*

I decided there would have to be some genuine head trauma if I wanted to make things believable. And if it was going to involve a faked fall, there should be some bruises and scrapes as well. This realization gave me pause, but after that stupid comment about the pool and Sam's inquiries concerning my strange behavior, I knew I had to do something to justify my imperfect memory and lame attempts to act like a preteen. Though the idea of purposely injuring myself would have been anathema to the boy I remembered, my pain tolerance had, over decades of life in a deteriorating body, increased considerably, so I set about to the make damage appear as realistic as possible.

Finding a chunk of two-by-four left over from our latest construction efforts, I first tried hitting myself on the leg, and was shocked at how much it hurt. Apparently, my young body was more sensitive than I had estimated. I waited to see if there would be any visible evidence, but nothing more than a little pinkness appeared. I was rubbing at the minimal bruise, when I heard Mom calling me, and I leaned over to peer through an open space between two large limbs.

"What?" I yelled, hanging on with one hand and swinging out to see her standing in the doorway. And just then Mother Nature stepped in to help me out, though it wasn't exactly the kind of help I might have wished for.

"You need to get down from there," Mom screamed, as if she'd discovered me standing on a railroad track in front of a speeding train. I opened my mouth to answer, but before I could get a word out, a deafening crack of thunder shook the tree.

I would later realize I'd been ignoring the soft rumbles and occasional flickers of lightning from an oncoming afternoon thunderstorm, though it didn't take being struck by lightning to initiate a more severe version of my original plan. All it took was the brain-rattling concussion of that thunderbolt to momentarily loosen my casual handhold on the tree limb and send me plunging through the tangle of branches below.

I felt the first impact on my right shoulder, a thud that spun me around in midair and slammed my back against another limb. For a second or two my momentum was stopped, and I grabbed at what turned out to be only a clump of leaves. As I felt the warm smack of raindrops hit my upturned face, the limb gave way, and I fell, catching another branch with one leg and flipping head-over-heels toward the ground. The last thing I remembered before awakening in the backseat of Mom's Cadillac, was feeling my ear smash against the hard, unyielding earth.

I LEARNED MANY VALUABLE lessons from that fall, the most important of which was not, it turned out, how perilous it could be living in a world where, for a stupid twelve-year-old, danger lurked around every corner. The most poignant of those lessons would not come until a day later when I woke up in the hospital, although I would experience its origin the moment I regained consciousness in the backseat of Mom's car. I was trying to rise up on an elbow, when the car swerved and threw me against the door. Then a loud thump and another swerve sent me sliding back across the seat. And when my head collided with the opposite door, I passed out again.

THE FOLLOWING TWENTY-FOUR hours were blurry, as I went in and out of consciousness, finally awakening with a tremendous headache in the semi-dark of a hospital room. Mom was there, looking shaken and distraught, and when I'd made it back to full consciousness I remembered my original plan and pretended I couldn't speak. I did try, however, to express curiosity through facial expressions and eye movements. And after a few minutes of this, Mom decided she should fill me in on what happened.

I had suffered a concussion, she said, plus a broken right clavicle and humerus. There were a few other scrapes and cuts, but I should be good as new in a few weeks. Then she went on to explain what had happened in the car on the way to the hospital. She'd been driving pretty fast, she admitted, but the girl on the bicycle seemed to come out of nowhere. "I swerved to avoid her," she said, "and it's a good thing I did, or she might have been killed. She's still in intensive care, but your dad says she's going to be okay."

I widened my eyes to try and get across that I wanted to know more, and after a while she seemed to get the message. I was thinking the accident must have happened close to our house, but my sense of time was off due to the fact that I'd been unconscious for most of the trip.

"It happened here on the south side," Mom continued, indicating the low-income area surrounding the hospital. "You might know her, though. She older than you, but she goes to your school. Her name is Patricia. Patricia Williams."

IT TOOK ME AWHILE to figure things out. I thought back to my first life, trying to remember if Pat had ever had a serious accident. I'd known her since my first day in seventh-grade chorus class, although it wasn't until later in the school year that I'd worked up the nerve to start bugging her with love notes. And after we got together, there had never been any mention of an accident. It came to me then that the instant I arrived in this dimension, unless my actions were a precise duplicate of what I'd done the first time around, things would be different from that moment on. Had it not been for my dumb plan to injure myself, I wouldn't have been in the tree, which meant there would have been no fall, no trip to the hospital, no causing Pat a brush with death, not to mention the suffering she must be going through.

This realization made me wish with all my heart that I could talk to Aurélie; that even if we couldn't be together, I could somehow slip out of this dimension and meet her on another plane, where we could have one of our intimate, philosophical conversations. Although I had known what I was in for in a general sense, experiencing firsthand the devastating consequences of my own stupid actions was sobering. And I was now officially terrified of the future.

27
The Les-Paul Solution

I went to see Pat in her hospital room as soon as I was allowed to get up, bringing flowers and hoping to apologize. But she wasn't in the mood for visitors, especially anyone from my family. Her anger was, I suppose, justified, though from what I could gather the accident really had been her fault; she'd apparently run a stop sign and darted out into the path of Mom's car in the early twilight. Of course, the fault ultimately lay with me, so I accepted her rebuff and left her alone after that.

I agonized over the whole thing for days, but after a while I started imagining I could hear Aurélie's voice in my head, reassuring me that there was no way I could have anticipated the consequences of my actions. I knew it was only a trick of the mind, but I found the dreamlike hallucination so comforting I decided to pretend it was real. After all, it did sound like something she might say. *Little Miss Practical*, I thought, hearing her sharp, logical retort to my playful sarcasm reverberate in my rattled brain.

One consequence of the accident was that it essentially put an end to any chance I might have eventually had with Pat. I was so intimidated by her anger that I never gave any consideration to developing a personal relationship with her, which meant I should be able to avoid the alcohol and drugs she'd introduced me to in my other life. I would miss those things, yearn for them actually, but the yearning was something I found I could handle, certainly far easier than the addictions that would have resulted. Forgoing the sex, however, was another matter, one that became more and more difficult as I began to experience the explosion of desire that came with adolescence.

But, at least for a while after the accident, there were other things to occupy my mind. One of these was how to continue my progress on the guitar while dealing with the huge cast that would soon encase my entire shoulder and arm. Dad said the breaks were clean, so there was no need to insert pins or screws, but in those days doctors tended to overdo the immobilization of broken limbs, both in cast size and the time necessary to insure healing. So while I was waiting for him to come in and apply the cast, I tried to think of a way to get him to go easy with the thick plaster.

In trying to convince everyone that my memory had been negatively affected by the concussion, I decided it should come and go, allowing me snippets here and there, then fading back into a mishmash of confusion. Thankfully, Dad bought this act, so he wasn't surprised when I remembered my birthday present and asked if he could design the cast so my right arm would be in a position that allowed me to play while my bones healed. The idea wasn't new, I told him; it had first been done years earlier for none other than the man whose name graced my new guitar. And Les Paul's injuries were far more serious than mine.

A world-renowned guitarist and inventor, Les Paul was instrumental in the development of the first practical solid-body electric guitar. He was at the high point of his recording career when his right arm and elbow were shattered in a near-fatal automobile accident. The doctors told him their only option was to amputate his arm, but Les refused to let them because it would have put an end to his guitar playing. After several consultations and experimental surgeries, a bone specialist suggested they replace the elbow with a piece of bone from his leg. This would mean that, once set, his arm would remain frozen in one position, so he had them set it at an angle that allowed him to cradle and pick the guitar. It took him nearly eighteen months to recover from all his injuries, but he went on to have a successful career as a guitarist and recording engineer, eventually pioneering innovations like multi-track recording, and producing several hit records with his wife, Mary.

Dad reluctantly agreed to my plan, and he even brought my new guitar in so I could determine the best angle for my right arm. The process was incredibly painful and had to be hurried so the bones would not have time to begin setting until we had the positioning right. But in the end it turned out to be one of the best ideas I would ever have, because for the next several weeks about the only thing I could do was practice the guitar. And by the time they removed the cast I had strengthened my hands and fingers and trained them to do things I never would have been able to accomplish at that age in my first life.

During this time, Sam became my constant companion, accompanying me on the bass and helping me recapture the bluesy folk style I had developed as Rix Vaughn. We also began tinkering with ideas for recording and creating sound effects, with Sam using his innate mechanical and electronics expertise to design and construct innovative devices and circuitry. Sympathizing with the restrictions of my temporary disability, Dad agreed to finance these endeavors by opening a charge account for us at Alcorn Electric, a local Electronics and hi-fi supply and repair house. Mike Alcorn was a patient of Dad's and a close family friend, so we were also given access to what Mike called their "Parts Graveyard," a small room in the back of the building where they stored cast-off remnants of equipment they'd repaired.

Before long our collaboration suggested that my new life was going to take an entirely different direction, and I began to wonder why I had not seen the enormous potential of Sam's multiple talents the first time around. I'd always thought of him as a sort of simpleton, with his heavy southern accent and unassuming attitude. But now I realized that underneath that quiet demeanor lay some extraordinary talents. He not only had a gift for music and a natural feel for rhythm and blues, he was a genius when it came to electronics. And, as an extra bonus, he had a lovely older sister.

Sarah was fifteen, an auburn-haired beauty whose shy, self-conscious manner and child-like naiveté made her particularly alluring. She wore no makeup and her naturally wavy hair was allowed to fall around her freckled, country-girl face without benefit of styling. The youngest of Sam's four sisters, she doted on him as if he were her own child. She'd never paid me much mind in my first life, but in this one she seemed, if not interested, at least more inclined to accompany Sam when he came to the house. When she did, she would sit quietly, listening and occasionally humming along with our music. I could tell she had a beautiful voice, though it took me a long time to convince her of that fact.

Eventually, as Sarah's comfort level with me grew, she would sometimes come over by herself for a swim in our new pool, often staying afterward when I asked her to give me her opinion on a new song I was trying to learn. At first these visits were a little awkward, because she wasn't much of a talker, wanting only to listen to me play and sing. After a while, though, I got her to open up a little by asking her to tell me about Sam and their family before they moved to St. Pete. It was clear that she idolized her younger brother, and when I made this request, she surprised me by launching into a detailed narrative of his early life.

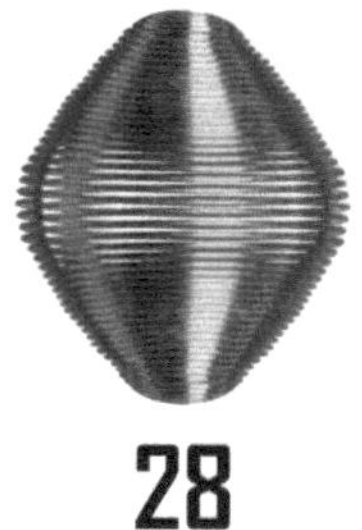

28

Sam The Man

Born Samuel Josiah Smith in Two Egg, Florida, Sam was the youngest of five children. Eunice and Gideon Smith had always wanted a boy and, after four pregnancies resulting in four girls, their efforts were finally rewarded. Sam was a skinny, reddish mouse of a thing that no one ever bounced on a knee for fear he might fall and stick right into the wooden floor like the tine of a pitchfork.

Sam came into the world with one thought on his mind: he wanted to know how things worked. At the age of two, Eunice found him disassembling the toilet, which was the most mechanical thing in the house at the time. Six months later, he somehow managed to get the flimsy, paperboard back off the new, round-shouldered radio and had neatly laid out over half of the electronic parts before his father found him. Gideon scolded Sam for his handiwork and, after the radio was repaired, he devised a crude, wooden back for it and screwed it on with forty countersunk brass screws.

It took Sam three weeks to learn to use a screwdriver well enough to get the back off again (he had to sneak into his dad's toolbox and practice secretly on the screws that held together the family's ancient steamer trunk). When he finally did get all forty screws out, the heavy wooden back fell on him and broke his right wrist, which, though it healed slightly crooked, did not affect in the least the unparalleled dexterity of his curious fingers.

Gideon then nailed the radio to the wall.

Sam did not speak until the age of seven, by which time he had disassembled every mechanical device on the thirty-acre dirt farm. And, to his father's relief, learned how to put them back together again. The occasion of his first word was during a rare trip to the "Big City" of Marianna (population 5,284) to attend the Jackson County Fair. His father had raised what he believed to be a prize-winning hog, and had consented to take the family along to witness the awards ceremony. When they arrived at the fair and Sam caught his first glimpse of the colorful, animated mechanical rides, his mouth dropped open and he stood without moving until Gideon finally asked him what was wrong.

Sam pointed at the Ferris wheel and said, "Wow!"

The hog came in third, and the next day Gideon discovered his toolbox missing. A thorough search of the farm confirmed his worst fear: Sam was nowhere to be found. Quick thinking led them back to the fair, where, after a few inquiries, they found Sam being looked after by one Bugger McGraw and his wife Emily. Bugger, otherwise known as The Amazing Pretzel Man, had spotted Sam early that morning sitting next to one of the Tilt-A-Whirl cars with parts spread out all around him.

"I was 'bout to grab 'im," Bugger told them. "But he's a workin' so fast and concentratin' so hard, it stopped me in my tracks. And before I got to movin' again, he had the dang thing all put back together."

Sam showed no remorse as Gideon thanked the McGraws, grabbed him by the ear, and dragged him to the truck. Before they drove off, Bugger yelled after them: "Car works perfect, so don't be too hard on him. Got yerself a good'n there. Don't talk much, but that's one smart boy. Y'aughta send him to school."

The Smiths had not considered sending Sam to the two-room schoolhouse in the nearby town of Dellwood, mostly because they needed him to work around the farm. They both knew he was special, however, and later that night they had a long talk about it and decided Bugger was right. So the next morning they got Sam all spiffed up and sent him off to school with the girls.

Sam was thrilled, and for the next two years he studied diligently, quickly learning to read and devouring every book in the school's tiny library. He also kept up with his chores at the farm, helping maintain the machinery and eventually acting as a tutor to his older sisters.

Every year, Gideon took the family back to the fair, mostly so they could show Bugger how far Sam had come since he'd suggested they should send him to school. It was on their second trip back, while the girls were out wandering the fairgrounds and Gideon and Sam were visiting with Bugger in his trailer, when Sam happened to pick up a dog-eared copy of Popular Mechanics from the coffee table.

While Gideon and Bugger shot the breeze, Sam read, and when he came upon an article about the new computer at MIT, he was transfixed. He'd never heard of such a thing before, and his mind almost exploded trying to imagine all the possibilities. These thoughts haunted him all the way home, and it wasn't long before he made a decision.

After they'd eaten dinner that evening, he worked up his courage and confronted his parents. He told them he had learned everything there was to learn from the teacher at the school in Dellwood, that he'd read every book in the school library and was now actually helping teach the other students math and science.

"Problem is, Mom and Dad, I'm stuck," he said, putting on a grave face and smacking a fist into his palm for emphasis. "There's so much more out there to know, but I don't stand a chance of learning it unless I can go to a *real* school with a big library and lots of smart teachers. Ask Mrs. Davison, if you don't believe me. She's told me the same thing."

Eunice had spoken to his teacher, Mrs. Davison, so she knew what Sam said was true. She'd discussed the dilemma with Gideon, but they couldn't come up with a solution. The farm was their only livelihood; they'd bought it shortly after Gideon suffered an accident at the cigarette factory where he worked in Winston Salem, North Carolina. He'd been blinded in one eye, and the settlement gave them enough money to move to Florida and buy the farm, plus a hefty chunk of extra cash to keep in the bank. But farming was now the only thing they knew, and the idea of giving it up and moving to the city seemed far too risky.

They explained this to Sam, who considered it for about thirty seconds, then said, "Okay. I understand. But if I can come up with a plan, will you at least listen to it?"

"You bet we will, Sam," said Gideon, thinking even his genius son couldn't figure out a solution that would be both practical and safe enough to keep them secure.

Of course, he was wrong.

By then Sam had started bringing in his own money doing repair work for other farmers, and he had a good bit saved up. It was summertime, so he used some of his savings to chip in for gas and hitch rides with neighbors whenever they drove down to Marianna to buy supplies. He also made it a point to accompany Gideon on such trips, and while there he would spend hours at the public library, researching various Florida towns and cities, reading their newspapers and checking reference books to determine things like population growth, economic stability, and local business potential. He also made inquiries into the real-estate value of the land surrounding their property, and went through Gideon's records to work up a financial evaluation of the farm's income.

Though never formally educated, Gideon was not dumb. He had grown up on a farm and learned how to turn crops and stay abreast of trends in the marketplace. One thing he determined right away was that weather patterns and disease were driving the citrus crop southward, so the first thing he did upon buying the farm was hire some immigrant laborers to clear the ten acres or so of orange trees. In place of the fruit he took a chance on a new onion variety that was yet to enjoy widespread popularity. It was a simple crop to grow and maintain, resistant to disease and drought, and drawing high prices because of its relative scarceness outside a certain area of Georgia, where the low sulfur content of the soil contributed to its unique sweetness. Testing had revealed that the soil on the Smith farm was also low in sulfur, so even though it seemed a little risky, he decided to try one of the Georgia hybrids. Little did he know the Vidalia onion would one day become a sensation, leading to a boom in sweet onion varieties like the one he had planted. He called his onions Dellwood Sweets, thinking Two Egg Sweets sounded a little too whacky.

By the time Sam got through with his investigations, he'd put together a plan that not only gave them a substantial profit on the farm, but would provide them with a nice home in the northeast section of St. Petersburg. It was an income-producing property, which meant Gideon would no longer have to work, except for managing several rental units and overseeing their maintenance. The apartment building was only four blocks from my house, and it was shortly after they moved in that Mom, who always paid new neighbors a visit, asked me to tag along and carry the chocolate layer cake she'd baked for the Smiths.

I recalled being smitten by Sam's youngest sister on that visit, though in my first life Sarah had paid me little attention. In this one, however, I had the feeling we might eventually become more than casual friends, since she seemed to have conquered her shyness and was willing to spend time alone with me. As she was finishing her story about Sam, some of that shyness returned when she realized how much she'd told me.

Stopping abruptly in the middle of a sentence, she blushed and shook her head. "I don't know what got into me," she said. "I didn't mean to tell so much. I know Sam wouldn't want anyone outside the family to know some of that stuff, so please don't mention this to him. I'd hate it if anything I did messed up your friendship. He's never had any real close friends, you know, other than us girls."

"Really?" I said. "That's hard to believe. I mean he's so smart and talented, I can't imagine him not being popular."

"Oh, everybody likes him, alright, but he's always been kind of a loner. It's like he doesn't have time for the silly things kids his age do. Not that he's conceited or anything, he's always treated me and my sisters like equals, even though we're nowhere near him in the brains department. Heck, if it weren't for him, I would never have learned much of anything except how to milk a cow, slop the hogs, and gather eggs. It's just that he was so far ahead of everyone, and I think it bored him to hang around with the other kids. You, on the other hand ..."

She stopped then, apparently searching for the right words. When she seemed unable to find them, I spoke up. "I think it's the music," I said. "I'm no Brainiac, but he seems to love the music we make together."

"Oh, yes," she said. "He does. And so do I, Ricky. So do I."

"You know," I said, "you really should try joining in sometimes. I've told you before you have a beautiful voice, and I meant it. Maybe we could form a trio or something."

"Oh, I could never do that," she said, her voice betraying an attempt to subdue the longing that lay behind her fear. "Not in front of people. I'd be too embarrassed. Anyway, I don't know anything about singing."

"Well, I do," I said. "I've had three years of voice lessons, so maybe I could teach you. I know what you mean about being embarrassed. I was scared the first time I sang in public. But once you get past the first time, it gets a lot easier. Besides, at least for now, we would only be singing into a tape recorder, right here in the privacy of this room."

She looked down at her hands, which were rubbing together, as if she were washing them under an invisible stream of water. "I don't know, Ricky," she said finally. "I—"

"Listen, just think about it, okay?" Then I offered what I felt would be the clincher. "Sam would be thrilled to have you sing with us. We've talked about it," I lied, "but he didn't want to push you."

"Really?" she said, her eyes lighting up like sparklers.

"Really," I said. "I promise."

AND SO BEGAN AN entirely different musical track for me. I spent the next year teaching Sarah some simple techniques on the guitar (turned out she didn't need much vocal training—she was a natural), while I worked with Sam on electronic projects. At the time, multi-track recording was in its infancy, and the only recording studios anywhere near us were the fairly primitive operations housed at local radio stations. What I wanted was at least a four-track setup, and when I explained what I could remember of these machines to Sam, he went right to work.

Using our new charge account, and cannibalizing parts from Alcorn Electric's Parts Graveyard, Sam cobbled together a bizarre-looking contraption that would synchronize and record six tracks at once. We didn't have access to the wider magnetic tapes and reels just beginning to be used at the major studios, so he had to stack six quarter-inch recording heads and reel mechanisms one above the other. It took him a while to figure out how to synchronize them, but he eventually decided to run all six off a geared-down motor we salvaged from Mom's old vacuum cleaner. Then, employing an ingenious combination of cams and gears, he even managed to come up with a tape-delayed echo system that allowed us to add reverberation effects to our recordings. This put us light-years ahead of the local radio stations, since that kind of technology could still only be found at studios in New York and Nashville.

Ever since Sam had seen the article about the computer at MIT, he'd studied everything he could find about computers. He was already putting together flip-flop circuits, the original building blocks of computer circuitry, and learning things like binary math and Boolean algebra. But the technology was so elemental at that time I realized we would be restricted to analog devices in our recording efforts. I felt sure, however, that with Sam's genius, we would remain ahead of the technological curve as the digital age approached.

Our efforts soon outgrew the space in my bedroom, so I petitioned Dad to let us use one of the storage rooms under our garage apartment for a combination studio/workshop. Before long we'd filled shelves and workbenches with an assortment of Sam's paraphernalia, and walled off a cubicle, which we soundproofed with acoustical tile to use as a recording booth.

Meanwhile, I had decided to give up my beautiful new electric guitar and amplifier, in favor of buying two acoustics. Having advanced knowledge of the marketplace, I scanned the want ads and searched the music stores and pawn shops, until I found a couple of used Martins: a small-body 00-17 classical for Sarah, and a D-18 for me. I was shocked at the obscenely low prices I paid for these instruments, but thrilled that I actually had enough from the sale and my savings to purchase them. By then Sam was working on building us a sound system for vocals, and when I mentioned the idea of amplifying the instruments, he began designing magnetic pickups for the guitars and bass, attuning the windings to match their widely varied frequencies.

I was in no hurry to develop the trio, knowing the so-called "folk revolution" would not reach its peak of popularity until the mid '60s. What I wanted was to create something unique, not simply imitate artists like Bob Dylan, Joan Baez, Peter Paul &Mary, or the dozen or so others who formed the foundation of that revolution. With Sarah and me playing guitar, Sam on the bass fiddle, and the three of us singing in harmony, we had all the ingredients of a modern folk group.

Sarah caught on quickly to the guitar and her vocals were as pure and fresh as a mountain waterfall. I went to work writing songs and was happily surprised to find that many of the lyrics I'd written before began to come back to me. I included Sam and Sarah in the writing process, and soon their Appalachian influence started to come through, giving us a distinctive country/folk/rock sound. It was a little like a combination of Jackson Browne, Jim Croce, and The Carter Family, with a hint of bluegrass juxtaposed against my more contemporary fingerstyle arrangements. We made our public debut at the same school talent show where I'd sung ***You Are My Special Angel*** to express my undying love for Pat, but by then I'd developed a crush on Sarah and had practically forgotten Pat existed. I did happen to see her in the audience, however, and that started to bring back memories, one of which was that my parents would soon be getting a divorce.

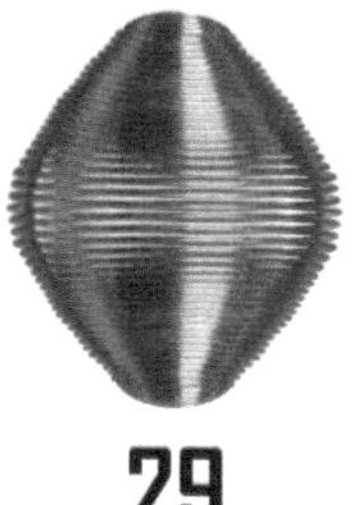

29
Charlotte's Web

In my first life, Mom and Dad had divorced shortly after my fifteenth birthday, and I remembered the tremendous heartbreak Mom suffered when they split up. Dad was the love of her life and, she would tell me years later, finding out he'd been unfaithful was the most devastating thing that ever happened to her. Not only that, but we were both convinced his infidelity had been a prime cause of his eventual death.

My father was a devoutly religious man, who grew up dirt poor on a farm in North Dakota and worked his way through college and med school. Though highly intelligent, in many ways he was simple and naïve, and Mom told me the two of them were sexually inexperienced when they met. So she wasn't really surprised that he'd been vulnerable to the devious flirting of his pretty young receptionist.

Charlotte, we would find out later from her roommate, had set her sights on the wealthy, middle-aged doctor from the moment she was hired, and the conflict between Dad's religious beliefs and his adultery must have been enormous. This was evidenced by the fact that, shortly after he married Charlotte, his health began to go downhill dramatically. And the most telling thing was that he refused to do anything about it.

The lifestyle changes that came with being married to a lusty, high-spirited young woman, whose tastes ran to drinking, smoking, nightclubbing, and gambling in the Bahamas, were substantial. And, being a doctor, there was no way Dad could not have known what he was doing to his body by joining her in these activities. We later learned that his good friend, Dr. Prather, a neurosurgeon, had begged him on many occasions to clean up his act or at least to begin taking medications for his high blood pressure and other ailments. But it seemed he was determined to continue living the life Charlotte dictated, even though he had to know what the consequences would be. This, Mom and I agreed, was a deliberate attempt to atone for his sins by essentially committing a slow act of suicide.

Five years after the divorce, he was delivering a baby in the middle of the night when he suffered a massive cerebral hemorrhage, during which, Dr. Prather said, practically every blood vessel in his head had burst. He was brain dead before we arrived at the hospital, and when they finally took him off life support it was clear that his young wife's insincere sadness could not hold a candle to my mother's genuine grief.

But that was in my first life. In this one, Dad's five-year slog toward heaven's waiting room had not yet begun, and I began to wonder if I could prevent it from happening, or if it was inevitable—written in the stars, so to speak. After causing the accident that nearly killed Pat, I'd tried to calculate as best I could what the consequences of any important decision I made would be, even though I'd learned back at the villa that trying to extrapolate the effects of a particular action was an exercise in futility. On the other hand, I *had* done several things that appeared to be altering the future course of my life, and these decisions—even though made on the fly—seemed to have woven themselves fairly smoothly into the fabric of this dimension. However, the idea of attempting something as momentous as saving a life or even a marriage was another matter.

By now, Dad's affair with Charlotte would already be in full swing, so it might be too late to change the outcome anyway. In any case, what could I possibly do about it? I could not imagine confronting him myself for several reasons, not the least of which was coming up with an explanation for how I knew about his adultery. Besides, Dad and I never had the kind of relationship that included heart-to-heart talks. Being a somewhat hard-nosed Midwesterner, he was not at all the touchy-feely type. Instead, he tried to show his love for me in monetary ways, which is why he seldom if ever denied me anything material. If something I wanted could be bought and did not pose an undue risk to my health or wellbeing, he always seemed to find a way to make sure I had it. And he always saw to it that I had spending money. But talking, at least the kind that involved serious emotional interaction, was out of the question.

The only thing keeping me from formulating a plan of action was my reluctance to do anything at all for fear of causing some unforeseen disaster. Still, I couldn't get the thought out of my mind. And, after hours of contemplation during which I tried to approach the problem from every angle I could think of, the only solution that seemed feasible was to somehow find a way to remove Charlotte from the picture. If she were to simply disappear, Dad might come to his senses in time to salvage his relationship with Mom. I was trying to think how this might be accomplished, when I got a call from Carol Henderson that gave me an idea.

Since I hadn't jumped headlong into rock 'n' roll as I had in my first life, Carol still held out the hope that I might someday return to the fold and continue my studies in classical music. And, to make sure I didn't drift too far toward "that trash being perpetrated on the American public," she would occasionally call to ask if I would sing a solo at church or for some special event she was promoting.

In the twelve years or so since she'd introduced me to fried mush and discovered my musical talents, Carol had climbed the social ladder in St. Pete and was now one of the most respected and connected women in town. She had not only become the music director at our church—which boasted the city's largest congregation—she also directed the Municipal Boy Choir, was the only female member on the city council, and served as president of the Pinellas County Women's Club. This time, the event at which she wanted me to perform was the annual Woman's Club Ball, the crown jewel of yearly social affairs, always attended by the cream of St. Petersburg's rich and powerful. It was the type of soiree I hated, and I was trying to think of a good reason to refuse, when it occurred to me that I might be able to use her help.

"There will be a full orchestra," she said when I hesitated, "and everybody who's anybody will be there. It would mean a lot to me, Ricky."

I vaguely recalled turning her down before, but that was at the height of the Nite Cats' popularity, when ***Skip School Flu*** was all over the airwaves and I didn't want to perpetuate my earlier image as a classical vocalist. "Okay," I said, with what I hoped was a clear lack of enthusiasm. "But no opera this time. And I'm going to need a favor from you in return."

"As long as it's legal and doesn't involve heavy lifting, you got it. Now, about the song: it doesn't have to be opera, but it's going to be the highlight of the night, so we need something powerful. How about something from Broadway, like ***Bali Ha'I***? Or maybe traditional, like ***Danny Boy***?"

I remembered having covered Conway Twitty's version of ***Danny Boy*** back when I was with The Madisons. It was a dynamic and emotional rendition that made use of my full range, so I told Carol that's what I wanted to sing. She agreed, and we set up a date for rehearsal at her place.

WHEN WE'D MOVED TO the big house some seven years before, Carol made arrangements with Dad to buy our old one, and after church the following Sunday I rode home with her for the rehearsal session. I knew the song well, so about all we had to do was decide on a key. We ran through it a few times until she was comfortable with the arrangement I wanted, and I was still trying to figure out how to broach the subject of Dad and Charlotte when we were ready to wind things up.

"So," she said, making a couple of last-minute notations on the sheet music, "what's this big favor you were talking about?"

Carol, I knew, had always admired my dad, not only for his dedication as a doctor, but because of his generous contributions to the church. He'd also been instrumental in seeing to it she was hired as the music director, so convincing her he was having a secret affair with a younger woman was going to be difficult. One thing I had going for me, though, was that she'd become close friends with Mom, and I was hoping the strength of their friendship would be enough to rouse her anger.

She listened attentively to my story, which began with my accidental discovery of a love note from Charlotte in the backseat of Dad's car. I followed this with another fiction about approaching his nurse, Doris, who roomed with Charlotte. I said that after I confronted Doris with the evidence, she broke down and told me about Charlotte's master plan to seduce Dad, so I had it more-or-less from the horse's mouth. I watched Carol's reaction slowly change from skepticism to shock to concern, and when I got teary-eyed talking about how devastated Mom was going to be, that concern turned to red-faced, speechless anger. While she was trying to come up with words to vent her outrage, I hit her with my request.

"I don't know what to do, Carol," I said, my voice cracking with emotion. "I mean, I'm just a kid and nobody's going to listen to me. Heck, I don't even want Mom to find out about it. All I want is for that little slut to disappear from Dad's life. So I was hoping you might be able to help."

What happened next seemed to start out as a distant, inaudible rumble, though the only evidence of it was in her eyes. I watched the smoldering anger gradually transform into tiny flashes of conspiratorial calculation, imagining I could hear gears grinding and cogs falling into place one after the other. After a while, she picked up a notepad and began to scribble, nodding from time to time as if she'd written something satisfying.

"Yes," she said finally. "I'm going to handle this. I can't tell you what I'm planning, but I *will* need your help."

"Anything. Just say the word," I said, unaware that my carefully constructed lies would lead to an assignment I had no desire to take on.

"You're going to have to get Doris away from Charlotte," she said. "From what you told me, she's already disgusted about the affair, so you shouldn't have any trouble convincing her she needs to move out of the house they share."

"Me?" I said, "But—"

"No buts about it, Ricky. I don't know her personally, other than seeing her at your dad's office a few times. She's already confided in you, so it's going to be your responsibility to make sure she gets out of that house as soon as possible."

I was getting a weird feeling about this. Carol had started sounding like a character from ***The Godfather***, and I was beginning to think she might be planning to have the house burnt to the ground, or perhaps have Charlotte murdered and didn't want Doris to be implicated.

Seeing the fear in my eyes, she chuckled. "Don't worry, honey, I'm not going to do anything crazy. A little fraudulent, maybe, and certainly unethical, but in this case, we have to fight fire with fire. Like I said, I can't go into the details, but if I'm successful, which I'm sure I will be, Charlotte will disappear like a puff of smoke on the breeze. You will need to talk to Doris in person, not on a party-line phone, so maybe you should call her after I get you home and see if she will meet you somewhere."

I couldn't tell Carol I hadn't really spoken to Doris, as that would blow my whole story out of the water. The problem was, I had no idea how to approach Doris with the fact that I knew about the affair. I did know from my talks with Mom that in my first life Doris had been so angry with Charlotte for stealing Dad away she'd terminated their friendship, so at least I had that. But how the hell was I going to talk her into moving out before it actually happened?

"You've got to give me something to work with," I said as we pulled up in front of my house. "She's never going to move out simply because I tell her to, at least not without some practical reason."

Carol stared straight ahead, tapping her fingers on the steering wheel for a full minute before turning to look at me. "Okay," she said. "I've got an idea."

CAROL'S IDEA WAS, I thought, pretty brilliant. The upstairs apartment she'd rented from us when we owned the house happened to be vacant, and—as if to emulate my ***Godfather*** analogy—she was willing to make Doris an offer she couldn't refuse. It was a nice apartment, clean and furnished. Plus, it was only five blocks from Dad's office, as opposed to Charlotte's house, which was easily ten miles away in Pinellas Park. Carol usually rented it to snowbirds for a couple of months during the winter, but she would offer a substantial discount if Doris agreed to sign a 6-month lease. The rent would be far below market value and include all the utilities, so the total monthly cost would probably be less than what she was paying Charlotte. Considering Doris's anger over the affair, she should jump at the chance to move, while also saving money and being within walking distance of work.

My job, then, became much simpler: all I had to do was mention the opportunity to Doris, and she would surely take advantage of it. Unfortunately, it didn't turn out to be as simple as I'd hoped.

When I called her that evening, she was, understandably, surprised to hear my voice. I did my best, telling her Carol had asked me if I might know someone who would be interested in renting the apartment. But since I was only a teenager who should have had no idea about her housing situation, she was skeptical from the get go. I told her Dad had mentioned that she lived pretty far from the office, but that didn't quite cut it.

"Why would he mention that to you?" she asked.

"Oh, I don't know," I said. "It came up in conversation, I guess."

"Ricky," she said, clearly unconvinced by my irrational explanation. "What's going on?"

Doris was a smart lady who'd always joked around with me when I was at the office. She was the one who stabbed my finger for blood counts, took my blood pressure, and gave me vaccine boosters. Occasionally, if she wasn't too busy, she would let me look through the microscope or test my own urine with litmus strips. I'd known her since I was five, and she obviously knew me better than I realized.

"Nothing's going on," I said. "I was over at Carol's to rehearse this afternoon, and she asked me if I might know someone who would want to rent her apartment is all."

"Uh, huh," she said. "Sounds pretty good, but I'm not buying it. There's something you're not telling me here. And until you do, I'm not going to even consider this seemingly unbelievable offer."

I was beaten, and I knew it. But somehow I had to get her to agree, so I decided to try a different tact. "Look," I said, "you're right. There *is* something I'm not telling you. I *will* tell you, though, just not on the phone, because someone might be listening in on the party line. Maybe I could come by the office after school tomorrow so we can talk about it?"

"Mmnnn," she said. "Mysterious. Okay, you have me intrigued now, so I guess I'll see you tomorrow."

The next day, after sneaking past Charlotte and poking my head in to say Hi to Dad, I found Doris in the lab. She was busy with the centrifuge and didn't acknowledge my presence, so I waited, breathing in the familiar smell of alcohol and listening to Sam Cooke sing ***You Send Me***.

Finally, she turned the radio down and spun around on the lab stool. "Well, if it isn't the mystery man. So, tell me, what is all this crap you're trying to feed me?"

"Can you take a break for a few minutes?" I said, ignoring her question. "I'd like to talk to you in private."

"About renting an apartment? Come on, Ricky, you can't be serious."

"I am, though. Real serious. What I have to say is for your ears only, and I don't want anybody interrupting us or overhearing. Maybe we could go for a walk or something."

"Sounds a little overdramatic to me," she said, "but I guess I could use a breather. Give me a couple of minutes." She turned back to the bench, took a couple of test tubes out of the centrifuge, and held them up to the light. Then she corked and labeled both tubes and inserted them into a rack alongside several others.

"Okay, sonny," she said, removing her lab coat and laying it on the stool. "Lead the way." It was the first time I'd ever seen her without the shapeless white coat, and I was surprised to find she had a nice figure. I'd always thought of her as a sort of female version of my dad; an efficient, yet friendly technician whose humorous manner and quick wit kept my fear of needles and other medical procedures at bay until the last possible moment. Now, however, I saw a different version, one that was not only sexually attractive, but whose smile and quirky attitude lent a certain element of intrigue to my childhood image of her as an untouchable adult. Of course, these were the thoughts of an old man residing in a horny teenage body, and I remembered Heyoka warning me not to let my adolescent desires override my common sense.

"Uh, Ricky?" she said. "Are we going or not?"

"Sure. Sure," I mumbled, pushing open the heavy back door and starting through. Then, remembering my manners, I stood aside and held it for her.

"My, my," she said as she walked out into the parking lot, "Since when did you learn to be so polite?"

"Been practicing," I said catching up with her and striding alongside. We crossed the dirt lot to the sidewalk, and when we reached the corner, I pointed to a bus-stop bench. We both sat down and I immediately found myself tongue-tied. I'd planned to use the story about finding a love note in Dad's car, but at the last moment I decided against it.

"Look," I said, "the thing is, I know all about Dad and Charlotte."

I'd expected shock, or at least a little wide-eyed curiosity, but she showed no outward emotion. "Oh, really?" she said with a hint of sarcasm. "And exactly what is it you think you know?"

"I understand you're trying to protect me," I said. "And I appreciate that. But I really do know what's been going on. And I also know you're not the type of person who would approve of what Charlotte's doing. The reason I'm bringing this up now is because it's getting to a critical stage, and if it goes on much longer, Dad's going to leave Mom, and that would kill her. How I learned about the affair is another matter, one I'd rather not talk about because it's embarrassing. I'm telling you something you already know is true, so that by itself should be enough to convince you I'm not kidding around."

"Oh, Ricky," she groaned, looking at the ground between her feet. "I'm so, so sorry. I've been torn about this. I've threatened to tell your mom, but Charlotte said she'd kick me out if I did, and I didn't have any place else to go. I can't afford to live on my own, and—"

"But you can now. Don't you see? In fact, you're going to have to."

"What do you mean, I have to?"

That was a good question, one I didn't have an answer for because Carol hadn't told me what her plans were. And that's when something else Heyoka said came back to me. *Being able to think on your feet will be a great asset when it comes to confronting situations that arise unexpectedly,* he'd said. *After all, you've been playing it by ear all your life.* Suddenly, my mind went into overdrive, spewing out ideas so fast I didn't have time sort through them.

"I hate to perpetuate the mystery thing," I said, stalling for time, "but I can't tell you what I mean. All I can say is something's going to go down, something pretty serious that will rectify the situation with Charlotte. And you shouldn't be around her when it happens."

Now she was staring at me with narrowed eyes. "You know," she said after a moment of silent scrutiny, "the really mysterious thing is how you're talking. 'Perpetuate?' 'Rectify?' Since when did you start paying attention in English class? And what the heck does 'go down' mean?"

I realized too late that I'd been using words my younger self would never have uttered, and adding to the problem by employing idioms not yet in common use. I'd slipped up like this before with Sam and Mom, but had always been able to brush it off by quickly changing the subject or telling some white lie. Doris, however, was probably not going to buy that kind of avoidance tactic.

I was trying to come up with a plausible answer when I remembered an old John Cusack movie where he played a professional hit man attending his ten-year high-school reunion. Oddly, whenever any of his old classmates asked what he did for a living, he told them the truth. Everyone thought he was kidding, but his bizarre answer always served to move the conversation past that question, which is what I needed to do here.

"If you want to know the truth," I said, "I've been reincarnated from a previous life in which I was an old man about to die. This was in a parallel dimension, far in the future, so I was not only older and more knowledgeable, but I knew slang that hasn't yet been used in this dimension. Anyway, that's beside the point. The important thing is that I know you need to be out of the picture when whatever it is … well, goes down."

She reacted to this outrageous claim with a completely blank expression, as if what I'd said had momentarily paralyzed her. But then the Mount-Rushmore look melted and she chuckled. "Had me going for a minute there. I have to say you do sound an awful lot more mature than the last time we talked, but it's been a couple of months and you *are* growing up pretty fast. In any case, it's clear you're not going to tell me the truth, so let's drop it. I do need to know what this is all about, however, so you tell Carol—whom I assume is in on whatever plan you have in mind—I'll have to talk to her about it first."

I didn't know if Carol would be willing to tell Doris any more than she had told me, but I now knew I had to get the two of them together, which meant my little lie about Doris having confirmed the affair would be revealed.

"I can do that," I said, "if you'll agree to do me a big favor." I waited for a reaction, and when there didn't seem to be one in the offing, I continued. "Like I said, I don't want to tell you how I found out about Dad and Charlotte, and I also didn't want Carol to know. So I told her you were the one who told me about the affair."

"What!" she shrieked. "You had no right to do that, Ricky! You're making me look like a cheap gossip who has no regard for your feelings. I … I—"

"Not true," I said holding up a hand. "What I'm making you look like is a responsible, caring adult who felt she had an obligation to intervene and help remedy the situation if she could. Or, if it couldn't be remedied, at least spare a young, emotionally-vulnerable adolescent the shock and heartache of finding out too late." When I saw her eyes go wide, I realized I had again stepped out of my teenage persona, and I began to wonder if I might be able to convince her of the truth. I'd talked to Aurélie about the advisability of confiding in someone, and when I remembered this, I heard her voice echo in my mind. *I can understand that it would be comforting to have a confidant,* she'd said, *although telling anyone is likely to get you thrown in the loony bin. On the other hand, if you can make someone believe you, I really don't see any reason not to.*

Doris was still sitting there with a dumbfounded look on her face, so I decided to test the waters a little more deeply. "I know you think I was kidding about the reincarnation thing, and I don't blame you for that. Hell, I wouldn't believe me either."

"Hey," she said, interrupting me. "Watch your language."

"Sorry," I said, smiling. "Old habit. Where I come from—or maybe I should say, 'when I come from,'—'hell' isn't considered much of a swearword anymore. Society has—will—become far more tolerant of what you consider bad language by the end of the twentieth century."

"Oh, really?" she said with a sneer. "And just what else will be tolerated?"

I reached out and cupped her chin in my hand, as if I were an adult commanding the attention of a child. At first I thought she might pull away, but the insistent look in my eyes must have stopped her. "Many things, Doris," I said. "There will be much greater sexual freedom, for one. It won't be long now before they come out with a pill that prevents pregnancy, which will allow women more autonomy in managing their own sex lives. And there will be other dramatic changes as well. The doomsday shadow of the atomic bomb will eventually be lifted and the Soviet Union will dissolve, allowing democracy to spread across the planet. We will land astronauts on the moon and build a permanent manned space station to orbit the earth. And one day, practically everyone in the developed countries will have an electronic device that links wirelessly to a worldwide network and provides instant access to an almost limitless source of information."

Throughout my soliloquy her eyes remained riveted on my face, as if searching for any sign that might betray some hidden agenda I had for making all this up. Finally, she snapped out of it. "Right," she said, though this time the sarcasm seemed to have faded. "So you're a science fiction fan. And I know about the contraception pill. It's in trials right now. Perhaps you read about that somewhere. I'm not sure why you're going to so much trouble to convince me of this fantasy, but I don't want to argue about it anymore. You set up a meeting with Carol, and I'll go along with your little story if the question ever arises. Now I have to get back to work."

I followed her to the office door, which she opened without my help. Once inside she donned her lab coat, then leaned back against the workbench. "You know," she said, "I really am sorry about all this."

I nodded. "It's not your fault, so don't beat yourself up over it. Dad's pretty vulnerable right now: middle aged, overweight, probably feeling unappreciated because his family takes him for granted. He's not a bad person, though, as I'm sure you know from having worked with him for so long. He's a little naïve when it comes to sex, but that's certainly forgivable. As for Charlotte, she's nothing but a shallow, good looking gold digger with no conscience and the morals of a black widow spider. I don't know if we can stop this thing before it goes too far, but I think we have to at least give it our best shot."

I waited for a response, but all I got was a bewildered look, so I shrugged and headed for the lobby.

"Hold on a minute," she said as I turned into the hall. I stopped halfway around the corner and leaned back in. When our eyes met, she remained silent, her expression seeming to vacillate between curiosity and skepticism. Finally, she let out a long sigh. "I'm not sure what to make of all this, Ricky. Don't get me wrong, I'll do my best to help out in any way I can, but ..."

"I know," I said. "It's just as weird for me as it is for you. We can talk again if you like, but right now I need to get out of here and convince Carol to call you before it's too late."

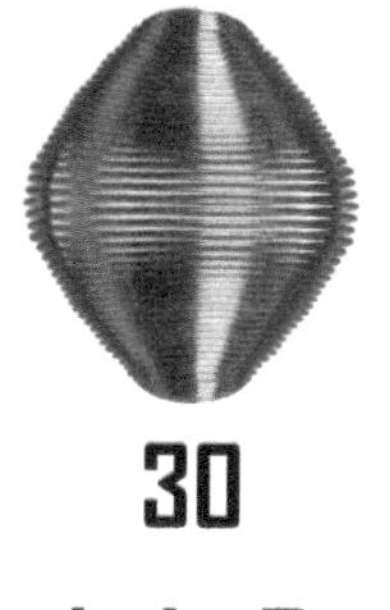

30

Twilight Time

I never found out exactly what Carol did, but shortly after Doris moved into her upstairs apartment, Dad hired a new receptionist, and the constant house calls that had often kept him away from home in the evenings slacked off considerably. I overheard some fragments of gossip at church about Charlotte having legal problems; something to do with a loan being called in and a fraud investigation. And a smattering of vague references appeared in the local society columns about her leaving town. But there was nothing that implicated Dad in any kind of scandal, nor was there any mention of Carol being involved in Charlotte's sudden exodus.

After the dust settled, Doris surprised me by showing up at church one Sunday. She sat in our pew next to Mom, and by the time the service was over it was clear they had struck up a friendship. That afternoon Dad was holding his annual swim party and barbecue for new the interns at the hospital, so Mom asked Doris to join us. She showed up around two-o'clock wearing a frilly red sundress, and when she walked out of the cabana in a tight-fitting bathing suit, the dozen or so young interns tracked her with their eyes until she dived in and disappeared under the water.

My first detailed look at Doris, unadorned by her nurse's uniform, revealed a body unlike those from my era, where six-pack-abs and lean, athletic figures were considered sexy. No, this was a body from the fifties, hourglass shaped, with a narrow waist and beautifully proportioned hips and breasts. When she emerged from the water and shook out her short, blond hair, she seemed to unabashedly revel in the attention she received, laughing and splashing with the boys, who gathered around her in an embarrassing attempt to outdo one another with their antics. I, on the other hand, kept my distance, admiring from afar her fresh-faced, pinup-girl looks and the uninhibited bubbly personality I'd never before been privy to.

Later in the afternoon, when the barbecue was served, she sat down across from me at one of the picnic tables, and I noticed her scrutinizing my face whenever I spoke. I was careful not to slip back into the more mature speech patterns I'd used during our earlier meeting, though I did wink at her a couple of times when I caught her looking at me.

Around six-thirty, while she was helping Mom and me clean up, she casually mentioned that, since her apartment was close, she had walked over. When Mom offered to drive her home, she declined, saying she enjoyed the walk, but that because it was turning dark, she might ask if I would accompany her. Doris's apartment was less than a mile from our house, and with twilight approaching, the fact that she would ask me to walk her home didn't seem out of the ordinary. So while she changed back into her sundress and said her goodbyes, I grabbed a flashlight and waited by the front door.

I could feel the tension rise between us like static electricity as we walked without talking for the first couple of blocks. And when we turned onto her street, she stopped and touched me on the arm, tilting her head toward a lot where a house was under construction. We made our way around the stacks of lumber and piles of brick until we reached the newly-poured front steps, then sat side-by-side in the fading twilight.

A sudden breeze kicked up around us, mingling the odors of sawed wood and fresh concrete with the scent of magnolias blooming on the low-hanging branches of a nearby tree. Augmented by a shimmer of moonlight, this mixture of aromas lent an odd ambience to the scene; not exactly romantic, but a little on the wistful side, as if we were a young couple anticipating completion of our first house.

"So, we're going up there, are we?" she said, nodding at the half moon as it flickered among windblown cloud fragments. "When?"

"I don't know, exactly," I said. "I'm not trying to dodge the question, it's just that I never was much good at remembering the dates of historical events."

"Uh, huh," she said. "Seems pretty convenient."

"It's the truth, though. I can remember big stuff, like the moon landing, and birth control pills, and music—especially music. But I can't pinpoint exactly when things happened. Or, in this dimension, when they *will* happen. I think the moon landing was—will be—sometime in the late sixties, and I do know the first person to set foot on the surface will be a guy by the name of Neil Armstrong."

"Interesting. But that's a little far off. What about something coming up soon, so I won't have to wait a decade to see if you're right?"

"I don't know," I said. "Let me think." I drew a blank, so I pointed the flashlight at the jumble of construction debris and swept it around in hopes of finding some inspiration. I was about to give up, when the beam fell on a yellow cement bag with a round logo on the front, and suddenly, something clicked. I walked over to get a better look, then returned and stood in front of Doris, smoothing the dirt at her feet with my shoe. I looked around for a stick, and when I found one, I handed her the flashlight and drew a circle in the dirt, adding two oval eyes and a broad, curved smile below. "Ever seen that before?" I asked.

She pointed the flashlight at my drawing, which, in the yellow glow, looked pretty close to the real thing. "What, a cartoon face?" she said. "I've seen hundreds of them."

"No, what I mean is that face exactly. It will be yellow with black eyes and a black mouth. Simple. Kind of like this one."

She stared for a moment, then shook her head. "I guess not. What is it?"

"It's called a smiley face, and it's going to be a sensation. There will be t-shirts and stickers and all kinds of other products with that face on them."

"Come on, Ricky. Give me a break. That simple thing?" I didn't answer, and after a while she shook her head. "Okay, so when is all this smiley face stuff supposed to come out?"

"Like I said, it's hard for me to remember. But I think it was pretty early in the sixties, so maybe only three or four years from now."

"Too long to wait," she said. "Think of something else."

I was looking at my handiwork, when the circle gave me another idea. "Ever heard of a hula hoop?" I asked. I remembered getting one for Christmas, and I thought it might have been this year because Pat and I had a blast playing around with it.

"Can't say as I have," she said. "What is it?"

"It's this plastic hoop thing you put around your waist and spin. If you learn the right moves, like a hula dancer, you can spin it round and round without letting it fall. It's going to be one of the most popular toys ever, even with adults. There will be contests—even national competitions—to see who can keep it going around the longest, and they're going to sell millions of them."

"Boy, you are a weird one. So when is this hula thing going to hit the market?"

"Hula hoop. And if I'm remembering correctly, sometime soon. Before Christmas maybe."

"Okay, we'll see about that." She fell silent for a moment, then said, "You mentioned something about remembering music. What about a hit song I haven't heard yet?"

I concentrated, trying to remember something that might be coming out soon. I'd recently bought the Platters' latest album which featured the song ***Twilight Time***, and suddenly I realized there was one hit they hadn't released yet. Instead of saying the name, I decided to slip into my old cover-band persona and do my best Tony Williams impersonation.

They ... asked me how I knew
My true love was true
Oh ... Ohao
I of course replied
Something here inside
Cannot be denied

They ... said someday you'll find
All who love are blind
Oh ... Ohao
When your heart's on fire
You must realize
Smoke gets in your eyes

"That's beautiful, Ricky. You sound just like the guy with The Platters."

"Good guess," I said. "I don't know when ***Smoke Gets In Your Eyes*** is going to come out, but I'm pretty sure it won't be long. It will be a monster hit for them, number one on the Billboard Top 100 for many weeks.

"Okay," she said. "I'm not saying I believe any of this yet, but at least you've stuck your neck out, so we'll soon see if you're telling the truth. Now, I need to get home and feed my cats."

We walked the rest of the way without speaking, and when we reached the stairway that led up to her apartment, she stopped and waited while three cats came bounding down the stairs and wrapped themselves around our legs. "These are my lovers," she said, reaching down to scratch behind their ears. "Thomas, Richard, and Harold."

"Aha," I said. "I get it: Tom, Dick, and Harry." The vague sexual reference in those names, coupled with the fact that she'd called them her lovers, stimulated some wayward thoughts, and I was glad the dark wouldn't allow her to see what was happening behind my zipper.

"Well," she said, "I'd better get some food into these guys before they go crazy and start drawing blood. It's been, how shall I say, a fascinating evening. Thanks for walking me home." She leaned over to peck me on the cheek, but before she made it, I turned and brushed her lips with mine. There was a moment of uneasy surprise during which she didn't move, and when I pulled her toward me, she let me kiss her. It started out nervy and a little stiff, but then her lips softened, and soon we were kissing like desperate lovers.

"Jesus," she whispered when we finally parted. "That was, uh ... unexpected."

"Sorry," I said, nuzzling into her neck. "I've been, I guess you could say, deprived ever since I got back." By then I knew she could feel the growing bulge in my pants. "I really am older, you know, so it's not like you're robbing the cradle or anything."

"Uh, huh," she said, pushing back and holding me by the shoulders. "Maybe. I guess we'll find out shortly. Okay. I've got to get inside now. I'll, uh, see you around."

I watched as she trudged up the stairs, fighting against the tangle of cat bodies that threatened to trip her. She opened the screen door, then stopped and turned back, and in the dim light above the landing, I thought I caught a fleeting smile."

Whoa, I thought, as the door closed behind her. *What the hell am I doing?*

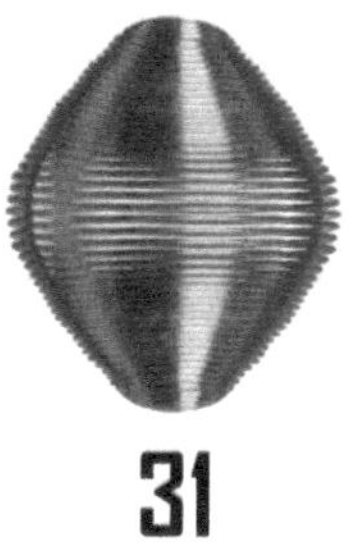

31
Changing Direction

After I got back from walking Doris home and relieved myself in the shower—during which exercise I noted that I had matured considerably in the size department—I stood in front of the full-length door mirror and examined my body. The growth spurt I remembered was nearly complete, and the results of my daily weight-lifting sessions were evident in the hardened muscles of my arms and chest. I hadn't been paying much attention to these changes, and when I took a good look at my face, I was surprised to see a pretty handsome fellow looking back. That Paul-Newman look was beginning to appear in my slightly dimpled chin and downturned eyes, and the many hours of swimming and sun had turned my skin a burnished bronze. Due, I assumed, to sun and chlorine exposure, my eyes had faded from their original hazel to a misty aquiline blue that appeared even lighter framed by my deep tan. Though there was still a whisper of adolescence in my youthful posture and smile, all-in-all it wasn't a bad look, which was probably one reason why Doris had been momentarily confused enough to return my kiss.

Still wondering what had possessed me to be so aggressive, I dried off and changed into pajamas, then lay in bed and contemplated how confusing that scene must have been for her. Here was this sixteen-year -old kid who claimed to be a mature adult trapped in a teenage body, and who kissed like an experienced lover, talked like a grown man, and told incredible stories about the future. It was a wonder she hadn't called my folks and recommended they send me to a shrink. The encouraging thing was that, even though she had to be perplexed by what was happening, I could tell some part of her wanted to believe me. I could also tell that the chronological age difference had done nothing to override the sexual chemistry between us. What I didn't know was how to handle it.

For one thing, there was Sarah to think about, although my prurient interest in her now seemed almost pedophilic, and whenever I was around her I had to keep reminding myself I was a teenager. Still, the illusion of having sex with a nineteen-year-old was hard to shake. That illusion, however, could very well remain a fantasy because she seemed determined not to give up her virginity until she married. And even though I cared for her, marriage was not something I was ready to consider any time in the foreseeable future—if ever. The prospect of deflowering her was intriguing, but one thing I didn't want to do was damage our friendship and endanger our musical collaboration. So, other than a little playful teasing, I hadn't argued the point.

At first, the idea of abstaining from sex was hard to accept. After all, in my other life, Pat and I were screwing like rabbits when I was only thirteen. Even stranger was the fact that my libido didn't seem to be as uncontrollable as it had been the first time around. Granted, I'd come a little unglued over my encounter with Doris, but since I'd been back I had not experienced the same intense adolescent frustration that had once kept me lusting after every pretty girl I came in contact with. Sex in general had become a somewhat secondary pursuit, taking a backseat to music and working with Sam to develop new and better recording techniques.

I'd also been able to avoid alcohol, which seriously curtailed other activities, like raising hell and partying. Sam had never been much of a drinker, and Sarah wouldn't touch the stuff. And because I spent almost all my time with them, I wasn't influenced by the kids I'd hung around with in my first life. Nor was I skipping school.

As for the lowered sex drive, I knew a lot of that had to do with memories of Aurélie, who continued to dominate my fantasies, although Doris was now coming in a close second. In many ways Doris reminded me of Aurie: intelligent, clever, playfully sarcastic, not to mention sexually alluring. I also think the decades I spent hopping from one bed to another might have been enough to satisfy my formerly insatiable hunger for sex and the ego satisfaction that went along with it. In fact, I didn't seem to have the same desperate need to feed my ego at all. I could easily have followed the old path, becoming a local rock star and enjoying the sexual benefits and accolades of that lifestyle, but I was apparently choosing to go another route.

In my time alone, I thought a lot about what I wanted to do with my life, and was surprised to find that becoming famous wasn't high on the list. I had applied myself far better at school, and my years of living experience allowed me to master subjects I'd once hated. Consequently, college became a choice I hadn't had before. I'd always been interested in science, but I wasn't all that enamored with academia, so higher education took a back seat to other possibilities, one of which was trying my hand at music production. For several months now, Sam and I had been refining our equipment with more sophisticated circuitry and mechanical designs, and we really were pretty advanced when it came to recording technology.

After decades of busting my ass in my other life seeking fame and fortune, I no longer felt up to the task. For one thing, I wasn't interested in being constantly on the road, doing drugs and drinking and screwing every female in sight. And I certainly didn't want to have to grovel at the feet of agents and producers and record company executives while they enriched themselves using me as a human ATM machine. But if I could somehow manage to be the one in control …

I knew I could recognize talent, and I had years of experience writing, arranging and recording my own songs. I'd also become an expert at using digitized samples of my own instrumentation and vocals to remix and re-master my earlier studio albums for release on CD and as MP3s. Even though it would be decades before computers were sophisticated enough for me to make use of that expertise, I had some ideas on ways Sam and I could do something similar with analog tape. Plus, if my memory didn't fail me, I could probably do a pretty good job of predicting trends and evaluating other artists. I was mulling this over when I realized I was already sitting on top of a potential gold mine. And I immediately decided to abandon the trio idea and start concentrating on developing Sarah as a solo artist.

The folk revolution and all the things that fueled it—Vietnam, the civil rights movement, nuclear disarmament, environmental activism—were still years in the future, which meant the trio wouldn't have those issues to draw on. But one thing that was right around the corner was a tremendous upsurge in the popularity of R&B. Artists like Ray Charles, B.B. King, and Hank Ballard were already becoming popular mainstream stars, as were Etta James, Martha Reeves, and a few other female blues singers. And it was in that category, I thought, where I might be able to create something new and unique with Sarah; a sound not only ahead of its time, but different from anything currently on the market.

Sarah's vocal quality and range had matured exponentially since we'd been working together, as had her stage presence and projection. And, although we were still mostly singing my folky songs in three-part harmony, whenever we took a break and started messing around with other genres, we always seemed to end up down in the music room, with me playing piano, Sam on the bull bass, and Sarah singing the blues. With a nearly four-octave range, she could do everything from crying heartbreak to soft, sexy come-hither type stuff. The really unique thing about her voice, though, was the way her deep-south country accent came through in her vocals, creating an odd fusion that might be referred to as Appalachian-Blues-Rock, or soul music with a twang. The only problem I could see was that she was a little ahead of her time when it came to white blues singers.

It was sometime in the mid '60s when I'd first seen The Righteous Brothers and was shocked by the fact that they were white. Janis Joplin wouldn't hit her stride until later in that decade, so the only female blues stars at that time were black, and I was worried Sarah might not be accepted. Still, with our advanced recording techniques and my decades of experience in the workings of the music industry, we might be able to break her in before anyone ever saw her in person.

I remembered a conversation I'd had with Aurélie, when we were talking about things I might do in my new life. And suddenly, I heard that little phantom voice again: *Maybe, with your knowledge of the industry, you could go back and ... I don't know, become a producer or something,* she'd said. *Sell that piece of your soul to get rich and be the benefactor of the unknown singer-songwriter. It's not written in stone that you would automatically turn into a scumbag as Lord Acton suggested.*

Of course, this wasn't going to be a singer-songwriter thing, but I was about to convince myself that I should forgo my own career in favor of molding artists and becoming a producer-promoter. As for selling my soul in the process, there might have to be a little of that as well. I knew that in the rough-and-tumble music business some ethical compromises would have to be made in order to achieve success, but maybe I could keep the old yin and yang in balance if my goals were not fame and fortune for myself, but for the artists I decided to nurture and promote. After all, the odds were stacked against them—all of them, at least at first. So drawing on my previous experience to do a little shaving of those odds didn't seem like a big swing toward the Dark Side.

32

Match Making

"But I love the trio, Ricky. Without you and Sam, I'd be lost." The three of us were sitting by the pool, and I was trying to explain my idea to them. Sarah had conquered her fear of singing in public, though she retained a hint of shyness; an undertone of timidity that contributed to her stage appeal. Rather than distracting from her performances, this peek into her soul added an element of innocence and authenticity to her on-stage persona.

We'd been performing sporadically at local coffee houses and talent shows for a couple of years, and, without realizing it, she had stolen the spotlight. When you combined her looks with that incredible voice and her haunting, emotional delivery, the audience didn't even know Sam and I were there.

"The trio is not going away," I said. "It's just going to change a little. Sam will be playing electric bass, and I'll be on keyboards instead of guitar. We'll always be the backbone of the group, but we're going to add other instruments and voices and maybe even strings. Eventually, if we play our cards right, you'll be singing in front of a full orchestra for thousands of fans."

"I don't know," she said. "Sounds kind of scary to me. What do you think, Sammy?"

Sam, always a man of few words, said, "He's right, Sarah. You're the one."

"Look," I said, "it's not like we'd be throwing you to the wolves. For one thing, it's going to take a lot of time and practice to develop your sound. For another, you won't be performing in public any time soon. We're going to start with recordings, testing the waters so to speak, before we do anything live. We both know you'd rather be singing the blues than the folky stuff we've been doing, and if we take our time and do this right, one day you're going to be a superstar."

"Yeah, well, I sure wouldn't bet on that ever happening," she said, though she couldn't hide the gleam of anticipation that flashed in her eyes.

I DECIDED THE FIRST step in the process of grooming Sarah for a solo career should be to stop pursuing her sexually. We'd engaged in some minor petting, and I knew I could probably break down her defenses if I kept working at it. But I now had a more important goal in mind and didn't need the distraction of constantly trying to get into her pants. I was trying to think of a way to let her down easy, when something unexpected happened that promised to make the job simple.

Call it serendipity, or maybe it was fate stepping in again, but in any case, my chance meeting with Jimmy seemed to coincide perfectly with my need to break things off with Sarah. Not only did Jimmy's arrival serve as a catalyst for our transition from lovers to friends, it also added an important element to my new undertaking. Sam and I had talked about how difficult it would be to find a drummer who would go along with what promised to be a slow, non-paying process of developing our studio sound. We could handle most of the other instrumentation ourselves, but when it came to drums, neither of us was adept enough to reach the standards I wanted.

In my first life, Jimmy and I had eventually joined forces, first with The Continentals, and later with The Madisons. But those groups wouldn't even be conceived until many years down the road, and even if they did come together in my new life, I now knew I would not be a part of them. I'd spoken to Jimmy a few times about our fledgling efforts in recording, but he hadn't shown much interest, so I was surprised when he asked how the project was coming along. I told him we were doing things he wouldn't believe, then invited him over to check out what we we'd accomplished so far.

Jimmy was a tall, handsome, clotheshorse, with curly blond hair and a suave, humorous demeanor that made him a natural ladies' man. He was around Sarah's age, and when she first set eyes on him I could almost hear her heart skip a beat. Sam and I spent the afternoon showing Jimmy what we were doing and explaining where we wanted to take things, while Sarah sat quietly, trying in vain not to fidget or stare. We were about to call it a day when I suggested we all go for a swim, and the moment Jimmy saw her in a bathing suit, I knew he was hooked.

Half an hour later I said I had an idea for a song and asked Sam to join me in the music room. When we were out of sight, I told him what I was up to. He didn't much care for the underhanded way I went about making sure Jimmy and Sarah would be alone, but he seemed to understand my reasoning. So for the rest of the afternoon, we piddled around with some music, while the two of them got better acquainted.

A couple of weeks after Jimmy's visit, Sarah took me aside and apologized for seeing him while we were still supposed to be dating. I tried to act saddened, though not devastated, assuring her that I understood and wasn't angry. I also told Jimmy the next time he came over that I was okay with the two of them hooking up, while at the same time petitioning him to join us in our recording efforts and help me develop Sarah as a solo artist. Whether he agreed because he felt guilty about stealing her away from me, or he was genuinely intrigued by the plan, I would never know. Whatever the reason, it turned out to be one of the best moves I'd made yet. Except, perhaps, for the fact that I suddenly found myself without a girlfriend.

To compensate for my loss, I dove headlong into the new project, hoping to smother my growing horniness with hard work. I was only partially successful in this effort, however, and seeing Jimmy and Sarah in their infatuated lovebird stage, starry-eyed and unable to keep their hands off each other, didn't help. Meanwhile, *my* hands, or at least one of them, became my only refuge, and when I received an unexpected call from Doris, I couldn't stop my mind from wandering into what I knew intellectually was forbidden territory. Adding to this potentially disastrous wishful thinking was the enormous popularity of the hula hoop and the steady rise of ***Smoke Gets In Your Eyes*** toward number one on the charts.

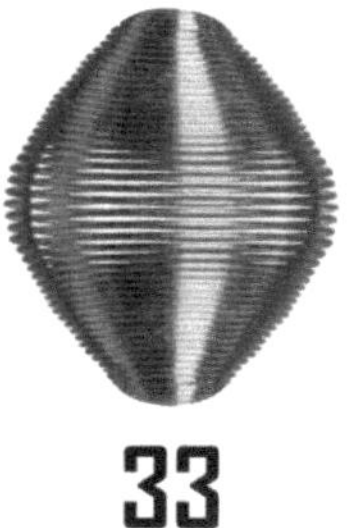

33

Back To The Future

When I answered the phone that Saturday morning, my cheerful 'Hello' was greeted with silence. Seconds ticked by, and I was about to hang up when Doris cleared her throat and blurted out, "Hey. It's me."

I thought about pretending not to recognize her voice, but I knew she would see right through that silliness, so instead I said, "Why, hello there Nurse Shelton. How've you been?"

"What's with the formality, Ricky? Are you angry with me for not staying in touch?"

"Not at all," I said, still in formal mode. "I was just being respectful of my elders. So, what can I do for you?"

"I'm not sure there's anything you can *do* for me, but I'm also not sure anymore that I actually am one of your elders. So I thought we might get together and have another one of our little chats. That is, unless you'd rather leave things as they stand."

"And where do you think things stand right now?" I asked.

"Well, for me, they aren't doing a very good job of standing at all, so if you don't mind, I'd like to see if we can bring them to an upright position again."

"You sure you don't mean horizontal?" I said, realizing too late that I might be treading on thin ice. "Sorry about that. I used to be a rather ribald fellow and sometimes it's hard to let loose of my old persona, especially when I'm talking to a beautiful young lady."

"My, what a nice compliment. Thank you. Now, do you want to see me or not?"

"Can't think of anything I'd like better at the moment. Should I come over, or would you prefer neutral territory?"

"Why don't you meet me down at the bayou, and at least we can start off someplace neutral."

By 'the bayou' she meant a long stretch of seawall about seven blocks from my house surrounding an expanse of water called Coffee Pot Bayou. It was a pretty public place, bordered by a red-brick road lined with mansions. There were, however, a few small wooded parks that jutted out into the water, and I assumed she wanted to meet at one of these. "Okay," I said. "Where, exactly?"

"You know that little park with the wall and the big oak trees?"

"I do," I said. "See you there in fifteen."

I DECIDED TO WALK to the park, and when I arrived I located a bench sheltered by a copse of trees that hid it from the street. A yellowish morning fog strained to rise from the surface of the water, and couple of seagulls dived toward me, hoping for breadcrumbs. I didn't offer any, so they flew off in search of another morning snack. A sickly smell of dead fish drifted from the sand exposed by low tide, and I was about to look for a less malodorous spot, when I felt something touch my shoulder and turned to find Doris standing there in the same red sundress she'd worn to the pool party.

"Ugh," she said, "This place stinks. Maybe we should go somewhere else."

"It's up to you," I said. "Exactly what did you have in mind?"

"I don't have anything in mind, Ricky, so get those thoughts out of your head. I want to talk, is all? Just talk."

"Hey," I said, trying to sound hurt, "I didn't mean that the way it came out" (although I did). "I only wanted to know if you had an idea of where we might go."

"Sorry," she said, "I guess I'm a little jumpy. Frankly, I don't know what to make of all this … this weirdness. I mean, ***Smoke Gets In Your Eyes*** is number one on the charts, and the hula hoop is everywhere, so I have to think something out of the ordinary is going on with you.

Either you're some kind of seer or you really are from the future. In any case, this is not normal, and I'm having a hard time figuring out how to deal with that."

"Listen," I said, "let's forget the smell for a moment. The fog is lifting and the tide is rising, so things should be tolerable before long. Come on, sit down. I promise not to do anything indecent."

She hesitated, but when I turned back and looked out over the water, she came around and sat beside me. We watched the fog swirl and tear apart in fragments while we both tried to think of how to begin. Finally, I reached over and she let me take her hand.

"First off," I said, "I'm no seer, nor am I from the future, at least not in this dimension. Where I *am* from and why I'm here would be difficult to explain to anyone with a smattering of common sense. Frankly, I don't even understand it myself, at least not how it worked. All I do know is that I came from something physicists call a parallel universe—a universe identical to this one—with a chance to live my life over again and make any changes I choose to make. In one sense, I did come from the future, but that future was in the other universe. In this one, the future won't be exactly the same because I'm back here with the ability to alter things in my own life and in the lives of people who are affected by my new choices.

"For example, the reason I knew about Dad and Charlotte is that in my other life he divorced Mom and married her. Then he went a little crazy and killed himself because what he'd done conflicted with his religious beliefs and he couldn't handle the guilt—that's why I went out on a limb and tried to stop the affair before it became unstoppable. I lied to Carol and to you, and took a real chance, because something bad could have happened that I didn't foresee. Fortunately, things seem to have worked out, though I can't know for sure if that will end up being the case. Anything I do or don't do will have ripple effects that could go on for years before they cause other problems, so there's no way I can predict the overall impact of any action I take."

I stopped then, realizing I'd already said too much for her to digest, let alone accept as anything more than the ravings of a lunatic. But when I looked at her, she didn't appear to be unnerved. Instead she seemed to be trying to work something out in her mind. Finally, she squeezed my hand.

"I don't understand," she said, staring at our entwined fingers. "But for some reason, I want to believe you. Maybe if you told me the whole story, all the details and scientific stuff, I could get a better grasp on things."

So I did. From the beginning when I met Heyoka at the club, to a description of the Villa and the early demonstrations that convinced me something extraordinary was going on. I embellished nothing, nor did I try to simplify Heyoka's explanations, though most of those had been so complicated I couldn't remember all the specifics. I didn't go into detail about the flashbacks and my early life, but I did tell her that part of the process had been for me to relive certain episodes in order to choose the age at which I wanted to start over. I briefly described my failing health and the heart attack, and I gave a pretty comprehensive overview of the lab complex and its fantastic equipment and capabilities.

The only thing I bent the truth on a little was Aurie, whom I decided not to mention at all. Instead, I put Fred in her place as the person who'd been in charge of taking care of me. I justified this minor falsehood by telling myself that admitting I'd fallen in love would only lead to a lot of personal questions, the answers to which were irrelevant to the story.

I ended my chronicle with the harrowing scene under the accelerator, describing the intense cold and how unbearable the noise had been. When I finished, exhausted from reliving those months, I leaned back against the bench and closed my eyes, hoping she wouldn't run away screaming.

A long period of silence ensued, during which she continued to hold my hand. And when she gave it another squeeze, I opened my eyes to see her smiling at me. "I believe you," she said in a near whisper. "No one could make all that up on the spur of the moment. Plus there's the Platters and the hula hoop and the thing with your Dad. I don't understand it, but then again, neither do you, so I guess we're even on that point. My only question is, why me? Why did you choose me to confide in?"

"I'm not sure I did choose you," I said. "I think it was more a matter of opportunity than conscious choice. That and the fact that you were always nice to me and I felt I could trust you." *Not to mention that I found you attractive and would love to take you to bed,* I thought, though I managed to keep those words from reaching my lips.

"Thanks for being honest with me," she said. "I was hoping there might have been some preordained connection between us, but I guess not. So, what do we do now?"

"I don't know that we should do anything, really. Stay in touch, I guess. Maybe, if you're up to it, you could act as a sort of sounding board for me. I've been so confused about things, wondering if what I do might cause some major catastrophe or alter the course of history in a negative way, so I could really use someone to talk to. You're intelligent and clever and you live in this era, where I've only lived for five years. I don't mean to put you on the spot or anything, but since we've come this far, I thought I would at least ask."

"Are you kidding? Of course I want to stay in touch. This is like being offered a chance to visit another planet, or see the future of this one. I'm not sure how much help I can be, but I'd be an idiot to pass up the opportunity."

"Great!" I said. "Now, there's just one other thing."

"Uh, oh, here it comes," she groaned. "You want to have sex with me, right?"

"That wasn't what I was going to say, but since you mention it ..."

I could feel her tremble as she turned away and looked up into the trees. I knew it was too quick, that she hadn't had enough time to absorb everything, let alone sort out her feelings. I was about to let her off the hook and say I was kidding, when she shook her head and said, "You have to understand that things are a little out of focus for me right now. I'm attracted to you, there's no getting around it. But that attraction might only be because this is all so fascinating, because you're like an alien being with super powers, or the second coming of Christ. I don't know if I'm being seduced by an over-romanticized fantasy or if there's something more meaningful going on here. And even if there *is* more to it than a starry-eyed reaction to who and what you are, the first thing I'd have to ask myself is would I be committing a crime against nature by having sexual relations with a teenager eight years my junior? I'm not going to say no, Ricky, but right now, I'm not going to say yes either."

"I do understand," I said. "I've had the same problem with a girl I know. She's older than me by a couple of years in this life, but younger than me by decades in my other one. And every time I think about calling on my many years of experience to seduce her, I start feeling like a pedophile, wondering if I have the right to prey on her innocence when it's clear I would have the upper hand."

"So, have you ...?"

"No, I haven't. In fact, I recently pawned her off on a friend of mine. Actually, I haven't had sex—intercourse, that is—with anyone since I got back. And that's been a conscious choice."

"Well," she said, "I don't know what things are like where you come from, but that isn't unusual for a sixteen-year-old in this era."

"I know that, Doris. But what you're forgetting is that, in my mind, I'm not really sixteen—I'm about to turn seventeen in this life, by the way. Nor am I immune to the sexual desires any man of my mental age would feel toward an attractive younger woman. I've been able to deal with those desires, but only by constantly reminding myself I have no right to take advantage of someone young enough to be my great granddaughter."

"What about someone only young enough to be your granddaughter? Apparently that's not a problem for you."

"Look, I don't want to argue with you about this. I will say, however, that I don't find it abhorrent to think of making love to someone with experience, especially since I am actually younger than you from a chronological—or I guess I should say a physical standpoint. I would not be robbing you of your innocence, nor would I be conning you into anything. I've been completely honest with you, and I will continue to be so no matter what you decide. But I cannot—will not—deny my feelings. The decision, however, will be yours and yours alone."

"That's funny," she said, shaking her head.

"What's funny?"

"Your naiveté in assuming I'm not a virgin."

"Oh, right. I didn't mean to be presumptuous, but where I come from, the only beautiful adult virgins left are kept in museums. You're not seriously telling me you've never had sex, are you?"

"Ha! Wouldn't you like to know? I refuse to answer that extremely personal question, other than to say you're forgetting where you are again. Twenty-four-year-old virgins in this day and age are not all that hard to find, and they certainly wouldn't be candidates for museum displays."

"Touché," I said. "Sorry I asked."

"Consider yourself forgiven. Now what I'd really like to do is spend some time with you and ask about a million questions."

"I thought your only question was—"

"Cut the literal interpretations, will you? I'm serious. So, what did you have planned for the rest of the day?"

"I did have some plans with my friend, Sam, but I can call and cancel. Exactly what did you have in—oops, there I go again. Let me rephrase: uh, how should we work this out?"

"I guess you could come over to my apartment," she said. "But we'll need to be careful. We don't want to start any rumors. Carol usually grocery shops on Saturday morning, so let me go first and make sure the coast is clear. You drive by and if you see my porch light on you'll know it's okay to come up. On second thought, maybe you should walk over and come in from the alley. That way there'll be less chance any of the neighbors will see you and you won't have to worry about hiding your car."

AFTER WALKING BY IN front to make sure the light was on, I snuck in from the alley and climbed the stairs to Doris's apartment. As a precaution, I carried an empty box I'd taped shut, to make it look as if I were a delivery boy. The only person I saw was a neighbor mowing his lawn with a push mower, but he didn't seem to notice me.

Safely inside, I followed her to the couch, where we sat side-by-side. She handed me a glass of tea and pointed at a plate of brownies on the coffee table, so I picked one up and took a bite, chewing slowly while I waited for her to break the ice. She fiddled around for a while, straightening the magazines on the table, then sipping her tea and nibbling at the corner of a brownie. Finally, she leaned back against the cushions and closed her eyes.

"There's so much I want to know," she said. "But I can't figure out where to start. Maybe you could tell me about your first life, what college you went to, what you did for a living, that kind of thing."

"Sure," I said, "but you're probably going to be disappointed."

"Why so?"

"Well, for one thing, I didn't go to college. In fact, I never even graduated from high school."

"You have to be kidding. Someone as bright as you? What did your dad have to say about your dropping out?"

"My dad wasn't around to say anything," I said. "I was a teenager when he and Mom got divorced, and after that Mom couldn't control me. And Dad was too preoccupied with Charlotte to worry much about what was going on in my life. After they were married, she led him down a completely different road, one paved with booze and cigarettes and bar hopping, and obviously involving some pretty outrageous sexual activity for a man of his age. His health started to decline, but he wouldn't slow down or treat his high blood pressure, which was getting out of control. Mom and I talked about it years later, and we both agreed he was intentionally committing a slow act of suicide because he couldn't handle the conflict between his immoral behavior and his religious beliefs."

"I'm sorry, Ricky. That must have been devastating."

"It was," I said, "but hopefully we've stopped it from happening in this dimension. Anyway, it wasn't long after the divorce before I had my own career, one that did not require higher learning."

"What kind of career?"

"I was a musician. A singer mainly. I worked with several rock bands in my teens and twenties, and then went on to develop a solo act."

"Were you famous?"

"Not really. I was a singer-songwriter, playing guitar and singing my own compositions. I had a couple of top-forty hits and released three albums, but I never was what you'd call famous. Then, after the last album flopped, everything went downhill. In fact, I fucked up pretty bad in that life."

"Language!" she growled.

"Listen," I said, "we need to lay down some ground rules here. I understand your objection to certain words, but if you want to hear the story of my first life there's an awful lot you're going find hard to listen to. And I don't mean only bad language. Like I said, things were different where I came from, just as things will be different here in the future. If I'm going to be honest about everything—as I fully intend to be—you're not only going to have to deal with words you're not used to hearing, you're going to learn some things about me that aren't very pretty. So please try to set aside your conservative idealism and keep an open mind. Things change, Doris. Society evolves. What's considered unspeakable or immoral in this era will be accepted as commonplace in the future."

She looked crestfallen, as if she'd been scolded by a parent, and I realized we had switched roles; that now she was accepting me as the adult—the teacher—and she was assuming the role of student.

"I'm sorry, honey," I said, hoping the endearment wasn't too presumptuous. "I didn't mean to shout, and I'm not angry. But if I'm going to tell you my life story, I'll have to talk about a lot of things you might find uncomfortable, including sex and illegal drugs and selfishness and alcohol abuse, and a host of other crap that screwed up my first life and caused me all kinds of pain and regret. If you don't want to hear the details, then say so, and we'll move on to some other subject. But if you do, I'm not going to candy coat it or pretend I was anything but an egotistical, amoral bad guy."

"I can't imagine you being a bad guy," she said. "And I do want to hear the whole story. I'm not really a prude, you know? It's just that it's hard for me not to feel as if it's my ethical responsibility to admonish someone your age when he says something that's considered obscene in today's society. And when I hear things like ... like that f-word coming from the mouth of a teenager, it's difficult not to react negatively."

"Oh, man, would you be lost in my world. The f-word, as you call it, will become so common in the future you wouldn't believe it. Women and teens will use it liberally. You'll read it in books, hear it in movies and plays. Couples will say it—scream it even—while they're making love. It will essentially become a standard part of everyday language in the early twenty-first century, as will dozens of other words and phrases considered to be taboo today, words that describe genitals or acts of perversion, phrases that insult or degrade, novels and films that depict intimate sex acts in graphic detail. What you have to try and understand is that they're only words, words used to express emotion, to emphasize things like anger, lust, humor, disgust, happiness, and even joy.

"Anyway, I don't mean to lecture you, and this is all beside the point. What I'm trying to get across is that if I censure myself, you won't get the true story in all its lurid, yet authentic detail, which I'm assuming is what you want."

"Boy," she said. "That's a lot to think about. But I guess I can handle it. Just don't be surprised if I jerk a little now and then. So tell me about this long career as a singer. When did it begin?"

"It began much as it has in this dimension. I only started over when I was twelve, so what came before was identical to my first life. Carol was the person who first introduced me to music, right here in this room."

I went on to relate my entire history, from my early classical training, to my life as a rock singer and my transition to a single. I spared no details, telling her about my sexual debauchery and exploitation of young female fans, my three botched marriages, and my drug and alcohol abuse. By the time I finished, she was leaning against my shoulder, holding my arm and blinking back tears.

I looked at her and grinned sheepishly. "I told you it wasn't going to be pretty. The only positive thing I can say is that I seem to be moving in another direction in this life. It's like I wore out the selfish asshole persona and now I want to do something entirely different. In a way, I guess I'm trying to make amends for all my bad behavior before, though that's not really possible because I'm doing it in a different dimension, and all the people I hurt in the other one are still hurt, still living with the repercussions of what I did or didn't do."

"But you did do some good things, Ricky. Or should I call you Rix?"

"Rix is over with. I'm not sure I like Ricky, so maybe I'll start going by Rich. But Rix is no longer an option: too many bad memories."

"Okay, Ricky—uh, Rich. But like I said, you did do some good things. You brought joy into people's lives with your music. You helped friends along the way, like Carol and Harley and those guys in The Madisons. You gave many women and girls the thrill of a lifetime by taking them as lovers, even though it might have been only temporary. You took care of your Mom later in her life. Maybe the bad outweighed the good, but that doesn't mean your life was a total waste. At least you were willing to take a chance on righting some of those wrongs by giving it another try."

"That's a nice whitewash job," I said, 'But it won't cut it. I know what I did, and there wasn't much of anything to be proud of. Maybe I never killed anybody or stole money or did anything fraudulent—though there are a few girls who might dispute that last statement. But I did spend my life as an egotistical, self-centered, ass, drugged out and drunk, thinking I was God's gift to women, and being irresponsible when it came to the possible harm I might cause by my thoughtless actions. No, kiddo, this is not a nice guy you're looking at. Or at least it wasn't. Far from it."

"God's gift to women, huh? I wonder. Are you saying you were abusive or uncaring? Did you rape anyone or lie or use violence?"

I thought about that for a moment, but I couldn't recall ever doing any of those things. "I don't think so," I said, still trying to remember. "In the first place, I'm not capable of committing rape. Not only would I never consciously force a woman to have sex, it wasn't necessary: women came to me. It was an occupational hazard—a perk, some might say—of being on stage. As for lying, I did my share of that, but only to feed my ego, not to get into any girl's pants. And violence? Other than destroying a few pieces of furniture, or maybe making a threat or two when I was drunk or stoned, no. I'm not the violent type. Never have been. But that doesn't mean—"

"Rich! Shut up! I'm tired of hearing you degrade yourself. What I see is a kid who never grew up, a kid whose ego got in the way of common sense. I'm sure your behavior was influenced by drugs and alcohol, but I think even that was part of your struggle for recognition. A lot of your conduct most likely had to do with your relationship with your father, who we both know is a fairly stolid, unapproachable man, a man who can't show love except by throwing money around. The lack of an emotional connection with him probably led to your trying to prove yourself valuable by becoming successful, not only musically, but with women who would show you the kind of respect you couldn't get from your Dad. Everything has a cause, Rich, even those things we think of as our worst sins."

"Interesting analysis," I said. "Are you studying to be a psychiatrist or something?"

"Believe it or not, I've thought about it. I took a few courses in psychology and counseling while I was in nursing school. But there's a lot of resistance to women becoming MDs, so that's probably out of the question."

"You'll be happy to know that's going to change soon. In fact, there will be many positive changes for women in the future. When I left, there was actually a woman running for President of the United States, and it looked like she might win. So don't sell yourself short."

"This is so cool," she said, laying her head on my shoulder. "It's like having a time machine. Tell me, what was our relationship like in your other life? I can't imagine we would ever have gotten together like this without your being, you know, who you are now."

"Actually, we did," I lied. "You fell in love with me after I took you to bed and ended your virginity. Then we got married and had four kids, and—"

"Yeah, right," she said. "In the first place, I would never have even considered going to bed with you. In the second place, I'm ... oh, stupid me. I almost fell for that one. Sneaky."

"Almost was close enough," I said. "I think you let the cat out of the bag there."

"Riiickeee," she said when I nibbled on her earlobe. "I haven't made up my—" but by then my mouth had found hers, and her feeble attempts to resist didn't last for long. When we finally came up for air, her face was flushed and she was breathing heavily. "My god," she whispered, touching my lips with shaky finger. "Oh my dear god."

I'M STILL NOT SURE about this," she murmured as I laid her on the bed and stretched out beside her. "I mean, I want to and all, but it's just so ... strange."

"What's strange about it? Two people who are attracted to each other making love? Seems pretty natural to me." I reached down and caressed her thigh, determined not to go any further until she let me know it was okay.

"You know what I mean," she said. "Besides, I'm not all that experienced, regardless of what I almost said earlier."

"So, you *are* a virgin?"

"No. Well, not exactly. I mean, maybe."

"I don't think there's such a thing as maybe when it comes to virginity. Either you are or you aren't." I could feel heat rising in her skin, and the way she was moving seemed encouraging, so I inched my fingers a little farther up."

"What I mean is," she said, tightening her leg muscles. "What I mean is, I'm not really sure. I know that sounds stupid, but—hey, hold on a minute will you. I want to talk about this first."

"As long as there's a second after the first," I said, removing my hand and laying it on the starched cotton of her sundress. "Okay, let's talk."

She played with the hair on the back of my arm for a moment, then said, "I guess it won't come as a surprise if I tell you I've had a few boyfriends. But, except for some innocent necking, only a couple of those relationships were what you might call serious. One was in high school, the other in college. The high-school thing was a little juvenile, a constant silent battle, if you know what I mean."

"I know precisely what you mean," I said. "Went through it many times in my former youth. And the college one?"

"That was a little more intense: lots of intimate, you know, contact, and ... Oh, this is embarrassing."

"Look," I said, leaning up on an elbow, "I know things are different here, and you're not used to talking to a guy about sexual matters. But nobody's ever going to know what goes on between us except you and me, and that includes anything we say. If you can somehow manage to think of me as, I don't know, your diary or maybe a close girlfriend, and forget all the societal taboos, I guarantee you will eventually find the freedom refreshing. Where I come from, lovers—even potential lovers—tell each other all kinds of personal things about their past sex lives and their feelings and fears and desires. And believe me, it turns out better in the long run for both partners, a lot better than the old Victorian crap that often led to unspoken problems and years of silent frustration for the woman."

She looked at me like I'd asked her to run naked in the streets. Her face turned lobster red, and what I saw in her eyes was a combination of anxiety and the thrill of anticipation, as if she were on a rollercoaster, hovering at the apex of the first drop and staring down at what might be her last view of the world. Finally, just when it looked like her ears might burst into flames, she took a deep breath and let it out slowly.

"Okay," she said, reaching for my hand. She pressed it against her cheek, then sighed. "The thing is, I was drunk, and I don't remember what happened. He swore nothing did, so I let it drop. Shortly after that he left for law school and we lost touch."

"Was this guy honest? Do you believe what he told you?"

"I think so. He was a little insistent at times, but never physically forceful. I doubt he would take advantage of a situation like that, at least not without my permission. And I couldn't give him permission because I passed out before we'd gone very far. I should tell you that, in a way, I wanted it to happen, but that must have been the alcohol. Ever since then I've been scared to take more than one drink, and I've never let my guard down again."

"Your guard?" I said. "How long do you plan to wait? Until some Prince Charming rides in on a white horse and sweeps you off your feet? Sorry to break the news, but that only happens in fairy tales. Look, I'm not going to try and talk you into anything, least of all giving up your possible virginity. But I'm also not going to lie to you. You are a mature woman, a beautiful, funny, sexy adult female. Even if it isn't with me, you need to climb down off that pedestal of perceived virtue and get yourself laid before you miss out on the most vibrant and erogenous time of your young life."

"I know that, idiot! Why do you think I'm lying here beside you in this bed? If anyone's going to be my Prince Charming, who better than a handsome time traveler with all the experience in the world and a knack for deflowering young virgins? Maybe you weren't a superstar in your first life, but to me you're the closest thing to it. So, Sir Lancelot, let's stop all the chatter and get on with it."

Suddenly, she hopped off the bed and stood with her legs spread. Then, closing her eyes, she slowly lifted the dress over her head. I watched in fascination as she unfastened her bra and let it fall to the floor, then slipped out of her panties and straightened up, resisting an instinctive effort to cover herself with her hands. I was stunned into silence as I examined her body; a body even more exquisite than I'd imagined when I first saw her in a bathing suit.

"Well?" she said, opening her eyes and giving me an indignant look. "You're the one who wanted me to let loose of my inhibitions."

THAT EVENING WOULD PROVE to be one of the scariest and most worrisome of my new life. Not only had I been charged with the responsibility of deflowering a twenty-four-year-old virgin, but I had none of the excuses I'd always had to fall back on should I screw up: I wasn't drunk or stoned or trying to satisfy an overzealous ego; I was with a lovely, inexperienced woman, whose fascination with a mature time traveler encased in a handsome young body was tantamount to being hypnotized.

"Are you sure about this?" I asked, after she'd climbed back in beside me. Still fully clothed, I wondered how to handle getting undressed without dampening the mood.

"I'm sure." She said. "I'm a little nervous, but I'm a big girl and I know what I want." When I didn't move, she started to unbutton my shirt. "What's the matter, Rich? Your body is stiff as a board."

"Sorry," I said. "It's just that this is a major responsibility, and I'm worried about fu—messing things up for you."

She giggled. "Who's being the prude now? Is this okay?" she said, unsnapped my jeans and lowering my zipper. "I'm not being too forward am I?"

"Uh, no. Not at all," I said, trying not to shudder when her fingers slid inside my underwear.

THE PROCESS TOOK A while, and things didn't go very well in the beginning. I did my best to prepare her, but her anxiety kept her from becoming fully aroused. When I refused to continue for fear of hurting her, she begged me not to stop, and after some initial trauma, she managed to relax. From there on out, we talked and adjusted until she seemed comfortable. I took it slow, encouraging her to tell me exactly how she wanted to proceed, and in the end, though it wasn't perfect, I thought it worked out pretty good considering it was her first time. Afterward, I waited for her to say something, and when she remained silent I started to get up.

"Don't you dare," she said. Her eyes were still closed, but I could tell by her grimace that my seeming indifference had upset her. "Just hold me for a minute, will you? Please?

I slid back in beside her and kissed her on the cheek. "Sorry," I whispered. "I thought you might want a little time alone to, you know …"

"No, I don't know!" she opened her eyes and stared at the ceiling. When I reached across her chest and turned her toward me, she hesitated for a moment, then melted into my embrace.

"You're mad at me," I said. "Was it that bad?"

"No," she said. "It wasn't great, but it wasn't all that bad either. I am not mad at you because of how it was. I'm mad because you didn't want to stay with me."

"But that's not true, I only …"

"What?"

"I don't know. It was stupid of me. I shouldn't have—"

"You're damned right, you shouldn't have. But I forgive you. Now, if you don't mind, could we please try it again? We've apparently gotten past the hard part, so I'd like to see if it's going to get any better."

And it did. So much better she could hardly breathe by the time we finished. And this time when I rolled off, she didn't protest. I did not, however, make any attempt to leave. Instead I pulled her on top of me and rubbed her back, waiting while her body shivered in receding waves like an ebbing tide against my chest. When I felt her eyelashes flutter on my neck, I drew back and watched while she blinked and tried to focus on my face. Finally, she smacked her lips a couple of times, smiled sleepily, and said, "That was, how shall I say, otherworldly? Ethereal? Ungodly?"

"Stupendous? Sensational? Extraordinary?" I added.

"Okay, if you need an ego boost, all of those things. You may kiss me now."

It was a long, languorous kiss made even more sensual by her tear-softened lips. When we finally parted, I touched the smeared makeup on her cheek and asked, "Did I hurt you?"

She looked confused for a moment, then said, "Oh, you mean the tears. Those are, you know, the other kind. The good kind. And to answer your question: no, it didn't hurt at all. Or, I don't know, maybe it did. Either way, it doesn't matter because I obviously didn't care."

I watched as her composure slowly returned, and when she finally seemed to have shaken off the languid afterglow, she said, "I know you're probably worn out, but do you think we could maybe try it just one more time? I'd like to find out if what just happened was some kind of fluke."

"I'll see what I can do, but I'm probably going to need your help."

She obliged.

WHEN WE AWOKE ABOUT an hour later, cuddled together like two nesting spoons, I whispered in her ear, "Had enough?"

"Don't ask me that right now," she said, reaching back to pinch my leg. "My body feels like someone poured hot tar into it, and my brain is so muddled I can't think."

We lay like that for a long time, and I was about to fall asleep again when she turned on her back and looked at the ceiling. "You know," she said, "this is still pretty scary."

"What?" I said. "Having sex? By now you should be well over your fears."

"I'm not talking about the sex itself. What I'm talking about is keeping it a secret. I assume you didn't want this to be our first and last time. I sure don't."

"That's good to hear," I said. "Any suggestions?"

"Nothing specific, only that we need to be extremely selective about when and where. As much as I'd like to do it every day, if you keep showing up here, someone is bound to see you sooner or later, and then there will be rumors and questions and all kinds of speculation to deal with."

"Just Saturdays, then?"

"I guess," she said. "But not every Saturday. Any repetitive pattern will increase the chances of our being caught."

"We could do the typical teenage thing and go parking out at Weedon Island, or maybe get a motel room occasionally. And in between we can have phone sex."

"I don't think I'm up for parking in the woods or risking being seen checking in and out of motel rooms. And what do you mean, 'phone sex?'"

"Hard to explain," I said. "It wouldn't work anyway. I forgot about the primitive phone technology here, the party lines. We shouldn't even talk about any of this on the phone. What about at the office? You could stay late to work in the lab, and we could use the cot in the exam room."

"Maybe," she said. "God, this is so weird. Never in my wildest dreams did I think I'd be sneaking around having sex with a teenager. It makes me feel slutty."

"Nothing wrong with feeling a little slutty now and then," I said, climbing on top of her. "As for being with a teenager, there are benefits."

"Don't tell me you … Oh, I guess you can."

DORIS AND I WERE careful, alternating Saturdays at her place with an occasional after-hours meeting at the office. The long intervals were frustrating, but the sneaking around and constant worry about being caught actually made our sporadic encounters more exciting.

Over the next few months our luck held out, but even though we managed to avoid being caught, fate always seemed to be lurking just outside the karmic door, ready to step in and shake things up. It would be some time, however, before the yang would once again catch up with the yin, and while the probability shit storm made its way steadily toward the whirling blades of that legendary fan, we would be lulled into complacency by a series of positive developments.

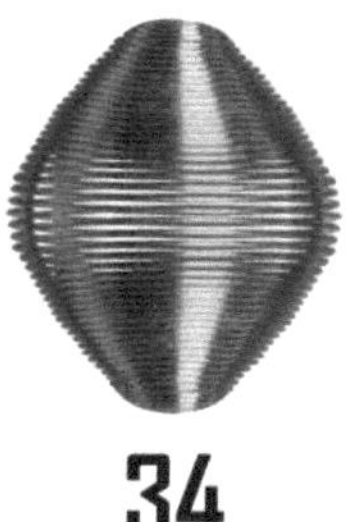

34

Blue Note Records

By the time I decided to take Doris into my confidence, I'd become somewhat of a star in the Voniossi family. I was making excellent grades, about to graduate with honors, and Dad had even hinted at sending me to medical school. I had no intention of following in his footsteps, however, and I knew it was going to be a hard sell to convince him that a career in medicine was not for me. Fortunately, he had one soft spot I felt I could exploit.

Having grown up poor, once he'd established his medical practice and the money began rolling in, Dad started spending like he'd won the Reader's Digest sweepstakes. He was always picking up tabs, and he usually carried hundreds of dollars in cash, often flashing his overstuffed wallet in public. He also became the epitome of a keep-up-with-the-Jones kind of guy, wanting to be the first to have the most modern versions of everything, including whatever new technology was coming down the pike. His friendship with Mike Alcorn led to our owning the latest and best in electronic equipment; not only were we first in our neighborhood to own a TV, when Stereophonic sound came out, he and Mike put together a state-of-the-art stereo set up and had it built into the wall on our back porch. This included a three-way speaker system with a tuner and amplifier, plus a two-track tape deck and turntable that slid out from behind panels at the touch of a button.

Playing on his personality quirk, I'd kept Dad abreast of our innovations in recording technology, and when I invited him and Mike out to the studio we'd built in the storage room, Mike turned out to be an important ally in my quest to expand the operation. Fascinated by our multi-track capabilities, the two of them listened to some of our early recordings of the trio, then paid close attention while I explained what we wanted to do. I concluded with a demonstration of our latest endeavor, which was to try and duplicate in analog some of the digital aspects of recording that were still decades down the road.

"I don't know if you've heard of it, Mike," I said, pointing at a small unit Sam had recently put together, "but there's a new technique called tape looping. It's still in the early stages of development and has only been used in a few isolated experiments, but we have some ideas that I think will prove to be the basis for a revolutionary new recording platform." I hit a switch and the sound of a single violin note rang out from the speakers. "This is what we're calling a sample. It's a note Sam played on the violin, recorded on a continuous loop of tape so we can play it over and over again anytime we want. But the really unique thing is this." I nodded at Sam, who turned a knob, raising the pitch of the note a half step. He continued to turn, raising it several additional semitones, then reversed the process, lowering the pitch until it was an octave below the original. "What Sam's come up with is a way to electronically alter the frequency of the note without changing its clarity or the authenticity of its sound."

"Interesting," Mike said. "But what use would it be?"

"I'll get to that in a minute," I said, again nodding at Sam. "First, let me show you something else." Sam hit another switch and Sarah's voice joined the violin, singing a note in harmony. "The point is we can do this with any sound, from horns, to strings, to the human voice. And we can stack them, meaning we can record multiple frequencies by overdubbing them on top of each other. Consequently, we'll be able to create any group of sounds we want, from guitar chords and keyboard accompaniment, to strings, horn sections, and even vocal background harmonies. We've got a long way to go yet, but the potential is virtually limitless.

"Once we've catalogued a library of samples, we can put them together in any number of configurations to emulate anything from a small combo to an entire orchestra or choir. What this means is that, right here in this room, we can build complex musical productions without having to hire musicians to play together or pay for studio time at one of the big recording facilities in New York or Nashville."

"Won't that come off sounding artificial?" Mike said. "I mean, the idea is good, and what you've done here is impressive, but I can't imagine it being of high enough quality to compete with the real thing."

"For now, you're right, it won't be good enough to replace the real thing altogether. At first I want to use it mainly to develop and perfect full-scale arrangements without having to hire an orchestra or a choir. Then after we have everything in place, we can spend minimal time recording live versions. However, for things like strings and other background elements, it already works quite well as a stand-alone substitute. Sam?"

Sam shut off the two loops, then cranked up the main tape system, playing our first complete experiment, which featured Sarah singing ***Summertime***, accompanied by me on the piano, Sam on the bass, and Jimmy on drums. It started out simple, with only the three instruments and Sarah on vocals, but in the middle of the first verse, the strings came in, then a little later, the horns. By the time Sarah hit the last note, these had been joined by a choral background, and the sound was so full I could see it was having a powerful effect on Dad and Mike.

I waited until the song faded, then said, "We put that together right here with only three musicians and Sarah. It's still a little rough around the edges, but I think you can hear the potential." They looked at each other and Dad shrugged, so I went on.

"The reason I wanted to explain all this to you both, is that we're going to need some help getting it off the ground before others jump in and beat us to the punch."

"And by help, I suppose you mean money," Dad said. He tried to sound skeptical and reluctant, but I could see a smile crack the corner of his mouth.

"Well, yes," I said. "But more than that. We could also use Mike's expertise and advice, plus his connections in the electronics supply industry. And I'd like your permission to expand our operation into the other storage room so we can have space for a larger recording booth."

Again, they looked at each other, and after a moment Mike glanced back at me and nodded. "I think they've got something here, Al," he said. "This could represent a major breakthrough in recording technology. It's given me some ideas as well, ways I might be able to help. You're always asking me to keep my eye out for investment opportunities, and quite frankly, I can't think of a better one."

So, with Mike—a successful businessman—as our adult advisor, and Dad as our venture capitalist, we founded Blue Note Studios, a combination recording studio, production company, and incubator for new talent. We eventually took over the entire garage complex, knocking out walls, enclosing the front where the garage door had been, and installing an air conditioning system. While Sam and Mike worked on refining the recording technology, I spent hours with Sarah, writing songs and choosing others, and nurturing her stage persona.

Meanwhile, I set about trying to locate Kenny and Billy. That job would have been a lot easier in the Internet age, but the musicians' grapevine served almost as well. When I found them, I sent Jimmy to make the initial contacts, and he talked them into coming over to check out some of our recording capabilities. After I introduced them to Sam and Sarah, the five of us jammed for a while, and, not surprisingly, things clicked much as they had when we'd met at the Skyway Lounge in my first life. This time, however, instead of forming a band, my goal was to bring them on board as part of our core group of studio musicians and creative advisors. I spent the rest of the afternoon demonstrating some of our production techniques and talking about our vision for the future, then asked if they'd like to join us.

My offer did not include money, only a promise to let them in on the ground floor, with salaries to come and maybe even a small percentage of the company. I explained the creative autonomy we would have by being in control of production, distribution, and promotion, and by the time I finished they were so excited about the potential they agreed on the spot. So, in a roundabout way we did bring The Madisons together after all.

Before they left, we had a little brainstorming session, and one thing everyone agreed on was that we wanted to create a different kind of operation, one that would treat visiting musicians and artists like family instead of hired hands and celebrities. The only studio I knew of with a similar philosophy was a place called Sound City in California. Sound City would not be up and running for another decade in this dimension, but I'd recorded my second album as Rix Vaughn there, and I wanted to model our operation on theirs.

Unlike other studios of the day, which could be cold and technical, with strict rules and authoritarian producers and engineers, Sound City was a homey place, where musicians were free to fully participate in the entire production process. I'd been impressed by the way everyone—from the stars to the side men, and sometimes even invited guests—was encouraged to offer their creative input. The atmosphere was laid back and unpretentious, allowing for a free flow of ideas that often resulted in productions of unprecedented authenticity and quality. Add to this the fact that they had state-of-the-art equipment and the best engineers in the business, and it was easy to see why some of the most famous acts in rock had recorded there, producing more than a hundred certified gold and platinum albums.

One piece of equipment for which the studio became famous was an incredible analog mixing console built by the British engineer, Rupert Neve. The Neve console was one of only four in the world at the time, and I already had Sam working on building our own version.

Another thing that had impressed me about Sound City was the way they treated traveling musicians, making sure they were comfortable and often providing temporary accommodations, including rooms and food, at no cost. This, I felt, added something special to the down-home feel of the operation, and one of my ideas was to try and duplicate that same feel at Blue Note Studios.

Before we started remodeling, the garage complex had contained a space for three cars and a workshop on one side, plus two large storage rooms and a half bath on the other. Above this was a three bedroom apartment, with a kitchen, living room, dining room and full bath; perfect for what I had in mind. All I had to do was talk Dad into letting us use the apartment as a place to put up our guests, which I figured would be a piece of cake.

I also started working on building a network of contacts in the radio industry, sending out short demo tapes, not intended for airplay, but as teasers. With each tape, I included a gift; sometimes a bottle of scotch—bought by Jimmy who had recently turned twenty one—and sometimes an expensive diamond stylus for the DJ's turntables that Mike provided at wholesale. The Congressional Payola Investigations were just getting underway in Washington, but Dad's lawyer advised us that since we were not asking for airplay, our promotional gifts wouldn't fall into that category.

We continued to expand our library of looped samples, though for our final recordings—except for the strings and some choral background vocals—we used only live, overdubbed performances. Sam and Mike eventually abandoned the cumbersome, multi-level tape machine in favor of four Ampex 8-track recorders, synchronizing them perfectly to give us one of the first 32-track systems in the world. And Sam's mixing console was far and away more sophisticated and versatile than anything on the market at that time.

To help with the financing, we started booking outside jobs, mostly writing and recording jingles for car dealerships and retail stores and working with ad agencies to create signature audio logos and commercials for a few corporations. I also began searching for local and regional talent, enticing the artists and bands I felt had promise with offers of lucrative recording contracts once we had perfected their acts.

We soon became self-supporting, which gave us a little breathing time to perfect our sound and copyright a number of songs before releasing what I hoped would be the first of a long list of top-forty hits. Finally, after months of intense work and long hours in the studio, I announced that Blue Note Records was about to burst onto the music scene with the introduction of Miss Sarah Love as the first white female R&B artist to hit the airwaves. I was still worried about her being accepted as a white blues singer, but since I did not plan to have her make any personal appearances for a while, I figured no one needed to know about her ethnicity until I decided the time was right.

Sarah's first single, a tune I wrote called ***I Think I'm Ready***, was a bluesy, double-meaning song that played on the subtle sexual innuendo that would one day sell Gary Puckett a few million records. It told the story of a young girl on the brink of womanhood, as she finally gave in to her lover's demands for sex. Of course, there was nothing said about sex or deflowering or anything else the censors could object to. But as with Puckett's ***This Girl Is a Woman Now*** and Neil Diamond's ***Girl, You'll Be a Woman Soon***, the meaning was clear. And when I sent the 45 out to the two-dozen big-city radio stations I'd been teasing with advanced tapes and gifts, it got so much airplay we were caught off guard.

I had set up a small record pressing operation and distribution network, but the demand was so strong, I had to quickly negotiate a deal with EMI in London to handle worldwide distribution. This necessitated the first plane trip of my new life, on a Boeing 707 that rattled and shook and reminded me of the prop plane I'd flown home in from Muscle Shoals after that botched effort to sell ***Sunday Morning Sentinel***. Thankful to have survived, I hailed a taxi at the airport, looking forward to my meeting with the EMI executives. Unfortunately, that meeting turned out to be even more stressful than the plane ride.

The sticking point came when I demanded our own private label imprint, which was unprecedented at the time. It took several hours of contentious negotiation, but with the instant popularity of ***I Think I'm Ready*** as a bargaining chip, I finally convinced them that Blue Note Records should become one of the first independent record labels on the planet. The song had already hit the US charts at number 36 with a bullet, and five weeks after I signed the deal with EMI, ***I Think I'm Ready*** made it to number one and was rapidly gaining international exposure. The year was 1962, and we were right up there with Ray Charles, Chubby Checker, and Elvis. And I was working frantically to finish mastering Sarah's first album.

Before long, the day-to-day details of the business were taking up far too much of my creative energy and time, and even though Mom had been helping out where she could with bookkeeping and other financial matters, I knew I was going to need someone to take over and manage the entire operation. And I also knew who I wanted that someone to be.

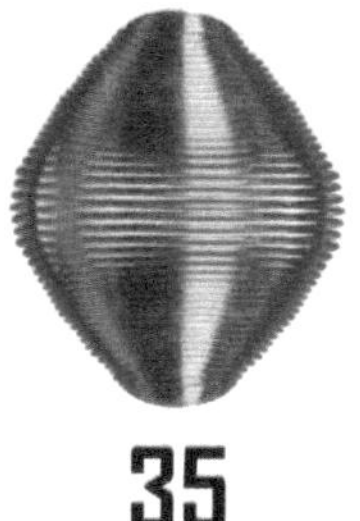

35
Vatican Roulette

Doris and I had continued our affair, miraculously managing to keep it a secret, while enjoying a few more platonic encounters when Mom would invite her over for dinner or a swim. During these visits I made it a point to talk enthusiastically about the business, so it didn't seem out of the ordinary for Doris to take an interest in what we were doing. After a while, she started coming to the studio, listening and commenting on our progress, and often making creative suggestions and offering constructive criticism. Her opinions were always insightful, and I soon began wonder how we'd ever gotten along without her.

One day, while we were working on an exceptionally challenging arrangement, I found myself wishing she were there to add her input. It was then that I came up with a plan I thought might turn out to be valuable in more ways than one. I knew a career in medicine was first on her list of priorities, so when I hit her with the idea of becoming our general manager, I fully expected her to turn me down flat. Instead, she went silent, and I could tell she was considering the idea. We were lying in bed on a Saturday morning, after a particularly varietal and passionate exchange of bodily fluids, and before she had a chance to answer, I decided to sweeten the pot with the other half of my idea.

"You know," I said, "I'm thinking we've been going about this affair of ours all wrong."

"Mmmm," she murmured, obviously still contemplating my proposal.

"Hey!" I said. "Pay attention for a minute, will you?"

She turned toward me and blinked. "Sorry, what did you say?"

"I said, I think we should reconsider how we're handling our affair."

"Oh?" she said, scratching her head. "How so?"

"I know this is going to sound a little crazy at first, but please hear me out before you jump in with any objections. What I'm thinking is, instead of all this skulking around and trying to hide, maybe we should make it so obvious that no one would suspect. I'm working sixteen hours a day trying to hold the production company together, and the only breaks I get are when you and I steal a few minutes here and there to have sex. Not only do I need help managing things, but I'd like to be able to spend more time alone with you. Mom and Dad both know how much you've been contributing to the business without getting paid, so if I tell them I want to hire you, and that I need you close by, I don't think they would suspect anything out of sorts was going on."

"What reason would they have to suspect something out of sorts was going on?" she asked.

"Because I'm going to suggest that you move in with us."

She looked at me and frowned. "You're nuts. What makes you think they would agree to something like that? More importantly, what makes you think *I* would?"

"*They* are not going to be a problem. I'll take care of that. As for you, I think you'd love being an official part of the operation. And then there's the minor fact that we'd be paying you at least three times what you make now, plus a percentage of the profits."

By then she'd gone glassy eyed, and I wondered if she'd grasped the full implications of what I was proposing. So I decided to go ahead and put the icing on the cake. "You do realize, don't you, that we'd be living less than twenty paces from each other, isolated up here about as far from Mom and Dad as you can get in this house? From what I can tell, no one has even begun to suspect anything's going on between us other than friendship and an exchange of creative ideas, so we'll pretty much be free to do whatever we want whenever we want."

Dad had originally bought the house, with its four large upstairs bedrooms, so we could bring Grandpa Voniossi and Grandma Davis down from Indiana to live with us and still have one room free for guests. But Grandpa had died of a stroke three years earlier, and Grandma was in a nursing home, so three of the four rooms—one of which had a private bath—were now vacant.

"Listen," I said. "The reason I'm sure Mom and Dad wouldn't object to my hiring you and having you move in with us is that the only other option would be to hire a full-time business manager from outside the company, someone who wouldn't have one tenth of your brains, creativity, or insight into the business. Not only that, but he would be a nine-to-fiver, and that's not what I want. I want someone whose going to be dedicated to what I'm trying to do, someone who'll be available twenty-four/seven if need be. You've been in on things almost from the start, and you've helped out in so many ways already, it's a shame you're not being paid for your efforts. What I need is a partner, Doris, not an employee, and there isn't anyone on the planet I can trust as much as I do you to put their heart and soul into the business."

"But what about my medical career?" she said, sounding a little whiny, as if she were arguing with herself over the two possibilities.

"Put it on hold for a couple of years," I said. "Just until I get this thing going full speed. Then if you still want to pursue a career in medicine, you should have enough money saved up to put yourself through med school in style. And don't forget, we'll be right down the hall from each other."

"Well, then, what about your Dad. He's not going to like the idea of me leaving the office."

"Not to belittle what you do for him," I said, "but you and I both know there's no shortage of nurses around here. And when I get through explaining to him how important this is, I guarantee he'll go along with it. I've already talked to the rest of the gang, and they're all for it. Everybody loves you, kiddo, you know that, don't you?"

Although she tried to make it seem like pulling teeth, I could tell she was thrilled with the prospect. And when she finally agreed, I presented the idea to Mom and Dad. Dad went through all the objections he could think of, but I was ready, countering each one with my own talking points and rhetoric. Eventually, Mom came over to my side, and, together we beat down his arguments so thoroughly that later on he would claim the whole thing had been his idea in the first place.

As soon as Doris was settled in the room next to mine, we set up an office for her in one of the other bedrooms. Sam installed an intercom system that connected to the studio, and we finally got private phone lines with extensions in both locations. Mom took over as our combination hospitality director and concierge, seeing to it that visiting artists were well fed and cared for, and before long we had gained a reputation as the most musician-friendly studio in the south. Sarah's next two singles went gold, and the album was on its way to becoming platinum, while we worked on several new releases for the other artists we'd signed.

The work was grueling, even after we hired an operations manager to handle scheduling and serve as my personal assistant, but at least Doris and I could wind down with sex at the end of the day. After we'd worn each other out, we always spent a little time talking quietly, though not in the way infatuated lovers talk after satisfying sex. On the contrary, our conversations were almost exclusively about the business, or industry trends, or some new idea one of us had for promotion. And this was indicative of the rather unemotional relationship that had evolved between us.

Even though Doris seemed at times to worship me like a god, we were not at all what you would call a loving couple. The sex was sensational, and we'd become so familiar with each other's needs and desires our physical compatibility bordered on the miraculous. Still, we were more like what would one day be referred to as 'friends with benefits.' Why this was, I couldn't quite figure out, although it suited me fine.

Perhaps our lack of a deep spiritual connection had to do with the fact that I was—as one woman in my past had put it—emotionally unavailable. I'd never been able to get over losing Aurélie, and although I didn't speak of her, Doris could probably sense that my true emotional allegiance lay elsewhere. Or maybe our spiritual disconnect had to do with the difference in our ages and the impossibility, at least in her mind, of our ever being openly together as a couple. Whatever it was, the words "I love you" never crossed our lips, nor did phrases like "You're my one and only," or "I want this moment to last forever." We did love each other, of that there was no doubt, but our love felt more familial than romantic, which at times made having sex with her seem almost incestuous.

The unspoken distance between us often struck me as contradictory, because in almost all other respects we were extraordinarily compatible. We both had quick wits and humorous, sarcastic verbal styles. And, like Aurélie, Doris was extremely intelligent and opinionated. In short, we got along famously, though the interaction of these similar traits often led to some pretty spirited debates. One of those debates had to do with my reluctance to use my knowledge of the future for personal gain or to intervene in ways she thought would be beneficial to the world at large. This particular subject had come up several times, and it was when I mentioned Kennedy's assassination that it really came to a head.

Kennedy had recently solved the Cuban Missile Crisis, and his popularity was at a high point. I'd already made the mistake of telling Doris that Marilyn Monroe would be found dead, and she'd asked me if there wasn't something we could do to save her life. I said no, that it wouldn't be a good idea to even try, but she didn't understand. And later, when I slipped up again and mentioned that Kennedy was going to be assassinated the following year, she nearly went ballistic.

"What do you mean you can't do anything?" she shouted. "Tell someone. Call the White House. Call the FBI. You can't just stand by and let it happen."

"Keep your voice down," I said. We were in her bedroom after finishing a long recording session at around 5:00 AM. "You're going to wake everybody up."

"Okay," she said, lowering her voice to a loud whisper. "But we're going to talk about this whether you want to or not."

"The problem with talking about it," I said, "is that you don't seem to grasp the complexity and danger involved in messing around with major events. I told you I almost killed an old girlfriend of mine—not to mention myself—by trying to pull off some idiotic scheme I thought would only have affected me. And what you're suggesting is that I try to alter an incident that changed the course of human history."

"What about saving your dad's life? I wouldn't call that minor."

"We lucked out there," I said. "So far, at least. Not only could any number of things have gone wrong, but we won't know the ultimate outcome for years, maybe decades. What you need to understand is that some things are so deeply woven into the fabric of the future, any attempt to change them could lead to disastrous results in the long run. Besides, I'm nobody. I have no clout, no credibility, no access to celebrities or politicians. Even if I found a way to warn people, no one would believe the predictions of an obscure record producer."

"Well then, maybe you *should* have that kind of access and clout," she said. "You know, don't you, if things keep going the way they are now, you're going to be a rich man before long? And who's to say you have to restrict your creative endeavors to the music business. The patents we've applied for on several of the inventions you and Sam have come up with should be bringing in a lot of additional revenue soon. So, for a start, I was going to suggest we set up a separate company or division dedicated to engineering innovations. Jimmy's become so valuable as your right-hand-man, he could eventually take over the production company with only occasional creative input from you, and that should free you up to do other things."

"What other things?" I asked. "More sex? Aren't you getting enough as it is?"

"Now that you mention it, I am. And that's something else we need to discuss. But what I'm talking about is branching out into other areas: inventions, TV, movies, concert tours. And speaking of concert tours, this crap of keeping Sarah under wraps with those photos and album covers that make the color of her skin ambiguous is going to have to come to an end soon. We're looking at tens of thousands of dollars in concerts and TV appearances that we can't tap into as long as she remains out of public view. Sullivan's already offered us five grand for one performance, and there are half a dozen others who'd pay big bucks for her to be on their shows. Not to mention that TV exposure, plus a tour, would probably triple her record sales. My point is, once we expand the operation, there's no limit to the possibilities, and in the end, you could become a very powerful and influential man."

I was trying to think of a rebuttal, when I remembered my conversation with Aurélie about how easily power can corrupt. "What if I don't want to be powerful and influential?" I said. "Right now, I'm doing fine in my little niche, and if I'm careful, I can probably help some people without stepping on too many toes or making a lot of compromises that end up hurting others. Power corrupts, you know. And the more a person has the more corrupt he's likely to become."

"That may be true," she said, "but you're forgetting that power can also be used for good. Look at Gandhi, or Martin Luther King, or even FDR: all powerful men who used their clout to help make the world a better place."

"Don't even think about comparing me to those people," I said. "I couldn't lick their boots when it comes to virtue or value to the world.

It's all I can do to resist the temptation of using what little advantage I have to screw others."

"Yes," she said, "and that's exactly why you probably wouldn't abuse whatever power you acquire. Besides, I'll be here to rein you in if you ever get out of line. Which brings me back to the subject of sex."

"It does?"

"It does. I don't mean to throw a wet blanket on such a stimulating conversation, but we're going to have to talk about the possibility of making our arrangement a little more permanent."

"What? You want a new contract or something?"

"Sort of," she said, reaching over and grabbing my crotch. "One that involves this and our future together. As I've mentioned before, often to your chagrin, I've used my knowledge of ovulation and timing to try and keep things between us less, shall we say, obligatory. But playing Vatican Roulette is, after all, only another form of gambling, and depending upon how you look at it, we've either hit the jackpot, or we've just lost the biggest bet of our lives."

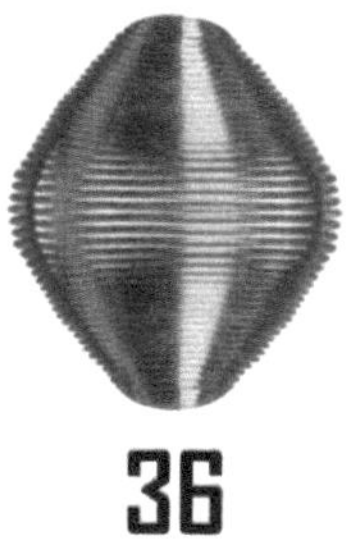

36
Karmageddon

A bruised cotton–candy sky hung low over Coffee Pot Bayou—an ominous dome of swollen clouds that obscured the approaching dawn. The threat of early morning rain matched our mood, as we sat together contemplating the crisis we now faced. Following Doris's announcement, we'd gone over our options: running away together, coming clean and dealing with the consequences, Doris quickly finding another lover then claiming he was the father. Finally, feeling trapped and claustrophobic, we decided to get some fresh air, only to find when we arrived at the small bayou park that the threatening sky compounded the feeling of impending doom.

One thing we had not discussed was abortion. Even if it hadn't been illegal at the time, I wasn't about to suggest it. And, apparently, Doris did not consider it an option or she would have brought it up herself.

Emotionally exhausted, we sat on the bench and watched the clouds bulge and droop, making no effort to move as the first fat drops of rain slapped our skin. "Appropriate, don't you think?" she said, huddling under my arm. "The rain, I mean."

I didn't answer, just hugged her and thought about the hopelessness of the situation. Finally, I tried to shake off the gloom and face reality. "We really don't have much choice, do we?" I said. "We can't give up the business and run away, too many people are depending on us now. And the bit about you finding someone else to pin the pregnancy on is just silly. Forgetting the repercussions, the question is, do you really want to get married? I mean, we both know our relationship isn't the kind of storybook romance every woman dreams of."

"Not every woman, necessarily," she said, sitting up and shaking raindrops from her hair. "Oh, I've had my romantic fantasies—mostly about you by the way. But I'm not blind, Rich. I know there's someone else in your heart, someone who's miles ahead of me. My only compensation has been that I'm sure she's from your previous life, so she doesn't represent much of a practical challenge in this one. I also know that you care for me, maybe even love me a little, so I'm willing to take what I can get. In case you hadn't noticed, I'm a very practical girl. If I wasn't, the business would have gone to pot a long time ago, not to mention that your sex life would be a lot less exciting."

"Oh, hell," I said. "I'm sorry Doris. I know how hard it's been for you. If I could do anything to change things—"

"You'd do it in a flash. I'm sure of that. But even you can't change the past, so we need to concentrate on the future. As for your question, the answer is, yes, I'll marry you if that's what it's going to take. Nothing much will change anyway, other than the fact that we won't have to hide anymore. We'll have to weather a minor tornado of embarrassment, and I'll probably go down a few notches in your parents' eyes because I'm sure to take most of the blame. Older woman seduces younger boy, and all—"

"Not so," I said. "There's no way I'm going to stand for that. I'll make sure they know I'm the bad guy here."

"I doubt anything you say will convince them of that, but thanks for offering. What I need to know is if you can handle marrying *me*. I won't expect anything more than what we have now, except a sincere, lifelong commitment to the wellbeing of our child. Plus, I'd want to retain my financial independence, just in case things don't work out. I wouldn't want to end up dragging our offspring through a nasty court proceeding should you find someone else or decide you can't live with me somewhere down the line."

"Not gonna happen," I said, putting my arm around her. The rain had stopped, but I pulled her close as if to protect her from some invisible threat. "Still, if that's what you want, we can draw up a prenup."

"What's a prenup?"

"Something you're going to hear a lot about in the future. It's short for prenuptial agreement, a contract couples sign before they get married that spells out how the finances will be handled in case of a divorce. Even better, though, would be for me to sign over half the company to you right now. Or more than half, if you want. I don't really care, so long as I'm sure you and the baby will be provided for."

"Okay, if you say so," she said. "But there *is* one other option, one we haven't discussed."

"Oh?" I said, kissing her damp hair. "What's that?"

"I didn't want to bring it up because I thought you might be shocked, but there's always the possibility of ending the pregnancy. One of my old classmates knows a doctor in New York who handles that kind of thing, so I could call her and find out where to go."

I could hear the shakiness in her voice, feel her shiver in my embrace, and I knew it wasn't the rain causing it; clearly she was only putting the idea on the table for my sake. I also knew that the thought of it was tearing her up, and the fact that she would be willing to make that kind of sacrifice reached deep inside me and grabbed a piece of my soul.

"I do love you, you know," I said, pulling away and looking into her eyes. "And you can forget about an abortion. I have no idea what kind of parent I'll make, and the thought of it scares the hell out of me, but I would never forgive myself if I went along with something like that just to make things more convenient."

After that, there didn't seem to be anything more to say, so we leaned against each other in the slackening rain until the sun broke through and lit up the bayou with streaks of yellow and orange.

37

Crazy

"Ow!"

"What?

"He kicked me in the ear."

"Well, that's what you get for listening so much. And what do you mean 'he?'"

"I don't know," I said, touching the tiny bump on her stomach. "I just figure it's going to be a boy."

"Wishful thinking," she said, ruffling my hair. "It's that male ego of yours asserting itself again. Now come up here and give me a kiss."

Doris and I had weathered the storm of moral indignation that followed our announcement, accepting the beratement from our fathers and taking solace in the fact that our mothers were not nearly so outraged. It seemed the prospect of having a grandchild had, at least for the women, cast a magical aura around us that neutralized their anger. We'd spared everyone the embarrassment of a public wedding by sneaking off to Georgia to be married by a justice of the peace, with Sam and Jimmy standing up for me and Sarah serving as Doris's maid of honor.

We were now seven months into the pregnancy, and I was becoming frustrated with the primitive state of medical technology. "You know," I said, scrunching down to put my ear back on her stomach, "where I came from we would already know the gender, not to mention a lot of other more important things, like if there are any physical abnormalities or positioning problems. And if there *was* anything wrong, in many cases, they could fix it before the baby was born."

"You're kidding," she said. "I know some obstetricians in Scotland are experimenting with something called ultrasound, but that's only for *viewing* the fetus. Why would any competent doctor risk performing major abdominal surgery on a pregnant woman, let alone her unborn child?"

"It's complicated," I said. "And it doesn't involve major surgery. They use this thing called an endoscope, a thin tube with a light at the end and a high-resolution imaging device—like a movie camera that takes real-time moving pictures. It only requires a small incision and they watch the pictures on a TV screen while they guide the tube to the place they need to go. Then there are these miniaturized surgical instruments they insert through the tube and manipulate from outside the body."

She looked at me like I was crazy.

"I know," I said. "It's hard to believe, but it's true. They can do all kinds of things, from intricate surgery to delivering medications, with minimal trauma to the woman. But it all starts with an ultrasound exam that lets them see if there's anything that needs fixing. In fact, the ultrasound exam will be a standard part of obstetric care in the future, and one of the first things they find out is whether the baby is a boy or a girl."

"Sometimes I don't know about you," she said. "I can never figure out if you're making things up or telling the truth, what with all the fantastic stuff you describe. Computers so small you can hold them in your hand, recording devices that don't even need tape, this cloud thing that's supposed to be like some huge invisible brain floating around in the sky. I write all this down in my journal, you know, so if none of it ever happens I'm going to call you on it. Anyway, I haven't heard of anyone doing fetal ultrasound exams in this country. Does it really matter to you if it's a boy or a girl?"

"No, I guess not." She rolled her eyes at me, so I decided to change the subject. "What about names? Do you have any ideas yet?"

"Not really," she said, "I've thought about it, but I haven't come up with anything I like. I guess if it's a boy we could name him Llewellyn."

"Very funny," I said. She knew I hated my middle name. "What about naming him after your dad? David's a nice name."

"I don't know," she said. "I'll think about it. What if it's a girl?"

"Oh, that's easy. It has to be Doris."

"It does *not* have to be Doris! I wouldn't want to saddle her with such a commonplace name. I'd want something unusual, something pretty like Geneviève or maybe Antoinette."

"Do you particularly like French names?"

"I do," she said. "They're lyrical, kind of like one-word songs. How about you? If it's a boy we could call him François or Frédéric."

"Too stuffy," I said. "I like French names for girls, though."

"Okay. Any ideas?"

I hadn't realized it, but my subconscious must have been leading me in a particular direction. "I do know one French name for a girl," I said. "A pretty one that's also unusual."

"Well?" she said when I didn't continue. "Are you going to tell me?"

"I will, but you have to promise you won't say you like it just because I do."

"You have my word."

"Okay," I said, "it's Hortense, and we could call her Horty for short." I tried to keep a straight face, but when I saw her disgusted expression I couldn't stop myself from laughing.

"Right," she said. "Then if it's a boy we could call him Scrooge, after Scrooge McDuck. Hortense was his sister you know. Come on, get serious."

"Seriously?" I said. "How about Aurélie?"

"Aurélie," she said, pronouncing it slowly, in three distinct syllables. "I like it. And we could call her Ellie. One of my best friends growing up was an Ellie, Ellie Samuels. She died of leukemia when she was only sixteen, so it would be nice to memorialize her that way. And Aurélie Voniossi sounds great. It rolls off the tongue like butter. Yes, I think that's the one. Now, what about a boy's name?"

We kicked around a few ideas, finally agreeing on a combination of our fathers' first names. "David Albert Voniossi" also rolled well off the tongue, Doris said, but that decision became moot when, two months later, on the first day of September, 1962, she gave birth to a healthy six-pound, five-ounce baby girl. This was an unexpected and somewhat disconcerting turn of events; not only had I been expecting a boy, but I had no idea how I was going to raise a girl. The prospect seemed akin to skydiving without a parachute; however, once I caught a glimpse of my newborn daughter, my apprehension took a backseat to an overwhelming feeling of love.

ELLIE, WHOSE INTELLIGENCE AND beauty would one day outshine even her mother's, was referred to by the studio gang as "Super Baby." Jimmy and Sarah—who were now engaged to be married—agreed to be her godparents, though it seemed as if she had half a dozen parental guardians. Everyone at Blue Note Records made it a point to look after her, and no one ever complained about the fact that she spent almost all her waking hours—first crawling, then toddling—around the studio. When she wasn't on the move, she would sit quietly, watching Jimmy and Sam operate the huge console, or looking out through the glass partition at the musicians as they played. This silent scrutiny continued for several months, until one day she surprised us all by speaking her first word. Unfortunately, it was not "Momma" or "Da Da."

We were in the mixdown booth at the time, and Jimmy was counting off the intro to a rhythm-section track when Ellie loudly exclaimed, "Royape." Everyone froze, and after a couple of seconds she put her hands on her hips and glared at us. "Royape!" she repeated. Finally, Doris leaned over and pointed at the master control. "Do as she says, idiot," she whispered to Jimmy. "Roll Tape."

That was amazing, but it didn't hold a candle to her second word, which came a few days later while her mother and I were lying in bed next to her crib. The radio was on, and suddenly Ellie stood up and wailed, "Cayzeee." She didn't say it so much as sing it, in a quavering voice that faded away as Patsy Cline finished the line with "I'm crazy for feelin' so lonely."

"Far out," I said. Ellie smiled as if she knew we were impressed, and throughout the rest of the song, she repeated her trembling rendition of the word every time Patsy sang it. She was mostly off key and late in her delivery, but she didn't miss a one. When the song was over she plopped down on her butt and beamed that electric smile at us.

"Looks like we've got another singer in the family," Doris said. "I love Patsy Cline."

"So do I," I said. "It's too bad she's …" I stopped myself, but Doris was too sharp not to pick up on what I'd started to say.

"Too bad she's what?"

"Oh, nothing," I said. "Hey, Ellie has to have heard that song before, don't you think?"

"Rickeee," she growled, reverting back to my childhood name as she always did when she was angry. "Finish your sentence."

I knew I was letting myself in for another fight, but I couldn't think of any way to get out of it. "Patsy's going to die in a plane crash," I said.

"No!" she cried. "When? How?"

Unfortunately, that was one date I would always remember. In my first life, I'd had occasion to visit the Country Music Hall of Fame in Nashville, and at the Patsy Cline exhibit I'd read the story of the crash and seen the watch she was wearing when the plane went down. But it wasn't the watch that caught my interest, it was the date: March 5th, 1963, the day my father had passed away. Patsy's watch was frozen at 6:20 p.m.—presumably the moment the crash occurred—so I not only knew the date, but the approximate time she died.

"We have to do something," Doris said after I told her the story. "Maybe you couldn't do anything about Marilyn, but you've gained a lot of recognition and respect in the music industry since then, so I know you can find a way to warn Patsy. Besides, she's obviously your daughter's favorite singer, so if not for me and her fans, we should at least try to save her for Ellie's sake."

Saying Patsy was Ellie's favorite singer was a stretch, but arguing the point wasn't going to get me anywhere; this time I knew I was on the losing end of the battle. The next day, Doris managed to get in touch with Patsy's agent, who had apparently heard of Blue Note Records because he seemed exceptionally cooperative. He even offered to send us a lengthy telegram with a list of her upcoming concert bookings. Doris knew, however, that we only needed her schedule for the next few days, because it was already March 2nd. The agent told her that the only gig Patsy had scheduled over the next two weeks was a benefit to be held the next day at the Soldiers and Sailors Memorial Hall in Kansas City, Kansas. This meant that her plane trip must have been delayed, because the crash hadn't occurred until the fifth.

I tried to tell Doris it was crazy to think we could do anything in that short a time, but she was already on the phone with our travel agent, booking a convoluted schedule of flights that started in Tampa, then had us changing over in Atlanta and Nashville on our way to St. Louis, where we would take a chartered prop-plane to the Fairfax

Municipal Airport in Kansas City. The difficulties we encountered in booking the flights and the ensuing delays seemed to confirm my feeling that there was some kind of resistance in the space-time continuum to our making major alterations in the preordained flow of history. I mentioned this to Doris on the last leg of our trip, but she just kept telling me I was being paranoid. Her confidence in that diagnosis held until the pilot told us we would have to divert to a small airport in Springfield, Missouri because Fairfax Municipal was socked in with fog.

We landed in Springfield at 8:00 a.m. on March 5th, with no chance of flying to Kansas City. So we spent the next two hours trying to rent a car. Doris, who seemed almost psychic when it came to anticipating problems, had brought along a bundle of cash, and after paying an exorbitant fee to a private rental agency, we hit the road at 10:30 in a brand-new Chevy Impala and headed north. The thick fog slowed us as we approached Kansas City, and it was nearing noon by the time we reached the city limits.

The agent had told Doris Patsy would be staying at the Town House Motor Hotel, and we stopped at the first gas station we saw to ask for directions. The attendant—a young redneck we could barely understand—had no idea where the hotel was, so we had to look it up in the phone book and call from a pay phone for directions. After losing our way twice, we pulled up to the hotel office at 12:45, only to find that Patsy had left fifteen minutes earlier. By then the fog had lifted, and as we drove up to the small airport we saw Patsy and three other people—one wearing a pilot's cap—walk out on the tarmac toward a Piper Comanche prop plane. Ignoring the shouts from employees, we sprinted through the terminal and out the open gate, catching up with them as they were about to board.

Before I could stop her, Doris ran in front of the pilot waving her arms like a wild woman. I was still reluctant to interfere, but since we'd come this far, I decided the least I could do was try to help out. I joined her just as the pilot was trying to push her aside, and even though I'd never been much of a fighter, when I saw him roughly grab Doris's arm, something snapped.

"Take your hands off my wife," I shouted, catching him by the shoulder and pulling him away. He turned and took a swing at me, but his awkward roundhouse went wide, and when I dodged, his momentum carried him to the asphalt. He started to get up, but by then

Doris had taken over, placing her foot strategically between his legs. She pressed the heel of her shoe against his crotch and said in a calm, menacing voice, "If you're planning on having children, I would advise you not to move."

Meanwhile, the others had started backing away, all except Patsy, who remained stoically in place. I realized the full gravity of the situation when I looked over her shoulder and saw two uniformed policemen emerge from the terminal and head in our direction. I was about to grab Doris and make a run for it, when I heard that little voice in my head. *You can handle this, Rix,* it said. *Just calm down and play it by ear.* So I took a deep breath and gave Patsy my most sincere smile.

"I apologize for the intrusion, Miss Cline," I said. "And I can assure you we are not the reincarnation of Bonnie and Clyde. As you can see, we have no weapons, and the only violence you have observed was due to your pilot's aggressive behavior. We mean you no harm whatsoever. In fact, we are here to save your life."

The policemen arrived seconds later, but before they could draw their weapons, Patsy held up a hand to stop them. "It's alright, officers. Give us a minute, please." Then, turning to me she said, "Who the hell are you?"

"My name is Richard Voniossi," I said. "I am president of Blue Note Records. You may know us as the producers of Miss Sarah Love?"

For a moment she looked confused, then a light seemed to dawn in her eyes. "***I Think I'm Ready,***" she said. "Platinum album, three gold singles. Incredible voice. Sure, I know the label. So what the hell is this all about? You trying to sign me away from Decca or something?"

"Not at all," I said, "Though you should not take that as an insult. Were it conceivable, I'd sign you in a second. All I'm asking for is a few minutes of your time. I promise that if you speak to us in private, I will leave you alone after that and you can go about your business in any way you see fit."

"Look, Hoss," she said, "I don't need your permission to go about my business any way I see fit. Nobody owns me and nobody tells me what to do, so you can cut that crap. You do seem like a nice feller, though, so what say we retire to the coffee shop and talk about this ... whatever it is? A little delay won't be a problem, will it Randy?" she said to the prone pilot. Then, without waiting for an answer, she turned and headed for the terminal.

I smiled at the two police officers and nodded at Doris, who removed her foot from Randy's crotch and joined me as we strolled casually behind Patsy.

"What the fuck are we going to do now?" I whispered when we reached the terminal.

"I don't know," Doris said, "but whatever it is, we can't let her get on that plane. And please watch your language."

SO," PASTY SAID, AFTER the waitress had delivered our coffee, "what's this all about Mr. Voniossi?"

"It's Rich," I said. "And I know this is going to sound crazy, but you must not get on that plane."

"Oh?" she said, stirring her coffee then looking at me with a condescending grin. "And why is that?"

"Because it's going to crash and there will be no survivors."

"What are you, some sort of fortune teller? Are you planning to charge me a fee for this consultation, or are you only looking for publicity?"

"Neither," I said. "The reason I know what's going to happen is ..."

"Well?" she said.

Things were happening so fast, I hadn't had time to come up with a believable story. But I knew I had to say something, so I opened my mouth, hoping some brilliant explanation would come to me before I was forced to close it again. I was about to give up, when the memory of my visit to the Country Music Hall of Fame suddenly flashed in my mind. The details were as clear as one of those episodes Aurélie had put me through, and it gave me an idea. "It's my daughter," I said, as the story began to come together in my mind. "She's your biggest fan, and she also has this, uh, gift. The gift of prophecy, I guess you could say. I mean she has these premonitions. It's only happened a few times, but she's always been right."

"I see," Patsy said, obviously trying to suppress her cynicism. "So your daughter is the psychic in the family."

"She is," I said. "And two days ago, she went into one of her trances and saw the whole thing: the concert, the fog, your refusal to take Dottie West up on her offer to let you ride with her and her husband back to Nashville, the fact that your manager, Randy Hughes, would also be the pilot on this plane trip. Look, what's going to happen is you're going to fly out of here and stopover at a small airport in Dyersburg, Tennessee. The airfield manager there is going to advise you to stay the night because of high winds and the possibility of heavy rain, but Randy will refuse. I don't know if you are aware that Randy is not an instrument-rated pilot, which means he'll have to navigate visually. And that, of course, is impossible in driving rain. Anyway, ninety miles short of Nashville, he's going to lose control and the plane will crash, killing everyone on board."

Doris was staring at me as if my hair had caught on fire, but when I looked at Patsy, I could see she wasn't dismissing my story out of hand. She picked up her coffee cup, raised it to her lips, then set it down without taking a sip. "That's an interesting story," she said. "Even more so because I've been having some premonitions myself lately. And frankly, I don't expect to be around much longer. I even wrote a will recently, and just last week I told Ray Walker ... well, never mind what I told him, that's beside the point. What isn't beside the point is that I don't believe you for a minute. Although I may seem like a country bumpkin, I'm not nearly as gullible as most people think. I don't know what your motivation is, but I'm sure to find out one day, and maybe then we can sit down and talk business. In the meantime, I've got a plane to catch."

She stood and walked toward the door, and before I could move, Doris was on her feet running after her. "Please, Miss Cline," she said, as the door swung open. "Let us drive you to Nashville. We've got a nice car and we won't charge you a cent."

Patsy turned and looked over Doris's shoulder at me. "Boy," she said, shaking her head, "you folks are something else. Listen, the bottom line is, I've already had two close encounters with death, and the third one is bound to be the charm. I'm not worried about it and neither should you be. When it's my time to go, it's my time." And with that, she turned on her heel and headed for the plane.

"I told you," I said as we watched the four of them board. "Some things are too inevitable to change, especially when we try to move out of my particular cone of influence. My life has—had—nothing to do with Patsy's, so changing her destiny is like—I don't know, like trying to stop a freight train with my bare hands."

As the plane rose into the gloomy sky, Doris put her head on my shoulder and sobbed.

WE DIDN'T HEAR ABOUT the crash until we were driving home from the Tampa airport in our own blinding rainstorm. The report came on the radio, interspersed with static from the lightning. We heard enough, however: "Patsy Cline ... crash ... no survivors."

The next day, we were listening to the radio in Doris's office, when Willie Nelson's version of ***Crazy*** came on. Ellie was in her playpen, and when she heard Willie's gruff voice, she looked confused. She seemed to be trying to figure out if she should sing along, and right when she opened her mouth, the phone rang, startling us all. Doris seemed unable to move, so I answered the call.

"It's Patsy's agent," I said, handing her the receiver.

She put the phone to her ear and mumbled a greeting, squeezing her eyes shut to hold back the tears. But after a few seconds, her eyes snapped open and her jaw dropped. "It's ... for you," she said, handing the receiver back to me.

"Hey there Hoss," said a scratchy woman's voice. "Sorry 'bout the voice. I caught a little cold on the trip home. I just wanted to call and say thanks for the tip."

"Patsy?" I said, incredulous. "Is that you?"

"None other," she said. "Hope you're not too upset over that little talk we had. Anyway, didn't mean to scare you with the phone call, but I thought you should hear it from me personally."

"Hear what? How? I mean—"

"I'm not a ghost, if that's what you're thinking," she said with a chuckle. "I took the plane alright, but when we got to the airport in Dyersburg and the airfield guy tried to talk us into staying overnight, I figured something weird was going on. I begged Randy—God rest his soul—not to fly in that weather, but he wouldn't listen. I ended up catching a bus back to Nashville, so here I am, none the less for wear, except for a sore throat and the loss of my good buddy. Listen, once you catch your breath, I'd like to talk about visiting your studio. I've got some ideas for a new album, stuff I've been scribbling about fate and destiny and losing friends and such. But what I'd really like is to meet that psychic daughter of yours."

UNFORTUNATELY, THE FACT THAT we were able to save Patsy led Doris to believe we should continue to intervene in the flow of history whenever we could. And her belief in my ability to recall important events was bolstered later in the year when I assured her the Cuban missile crisis would not result in nuclear Armageddon. What I couldn't seem to convince her of was that I hadn't actually remembered the crisis until after it started, and that the only reason I'd known the date of Patsy's plane crash was because it happened to have occurred on the same day my father died. The discussion eventually ended without a resolution, but the issue did not go away. And when JFK was assassinated in November of '63, I once again had to suffer through her admonitions for not at least trying to warn him. I tried to explain the potential for disaster in attempting to alter events of such magnitude, but that was an argument I would never be able to win.

The next few years were so busy for us—building the business and raising our daughter—we didn't have time to worry much about the outside world. Blue Note Records continued to expand, eventually giving rise to Blue Note Enterprises, while Ellie grew into a beautiful young girl whose intellect far surpassed that of her peers. Then, in 1968, the controversy raised its ugly head again when I was caught off guard by the assassinations of Martin Luther King and Bobby Kennedy. After that, it took a couple of weeks for things to finally settle into an uneasy truce between us, but by then I knew Doris was never going to let loose of the conviction that I should use my prior knowledge to right the wrongs of the world. And her unshakable position on the subject would continue to be one of the few causes of discord in our otherwise nearly idyllic marriage.

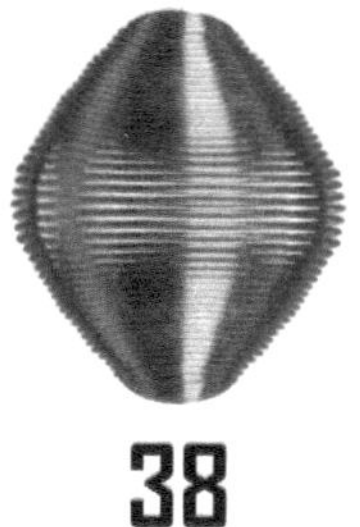

38

Another Prodigy

Daddy?" Ellie said, over breakfast one morning. "What's a con … glom … erate?" She was reading the newspaper, something that always fascinated me because I'd never cared much about the news when I was her age, especially the financial pages. Ellie, on the other hand, had been reading the paper since she was four, and now, at age seven, she was far more knowledgeable about the workings of the world than I was.

"It's a kind of big collection of businesses, all owned by the same corporation," I said. "You know what a corporation is?"

"Don't be silly." She laughed. "Of course I know what a corporation is. Blue Note Enterprises is a corporation, right?"

"Right."

"So, we're a conglomerate. I mean, we have lots of businesses and they're all owned by our corporation."

I hadn't thought of the business as being a conglomerate, but now that she'd mentioned it, I figured she was technically correct. Over the past six years, thanks in part to Patsy coming on board and enticing several other country stars to do the same, our growth had been exponential. We'd weathered a court battle with another label by the name of Blue Note, eventually buying them out, which gave us a star-studded Jazz division; and Blue Note Records was now second in worldwide sales only to EMI. We had a division that produced an array of recording equipment, an intercontinental record distribution network, one of the largest entertainment agencies in the world, a concert promotion operation, and were in the process of starting an independent film company. Most exciting of all was Sam's baby: our computer division. Sam had recently signed a deal with IBM to manufacture the first practical PC, and he was working with Paul Baran and others to develop the Arpanet, with the goal—at my suggestion—of turning it into the Internet and eventually the World Wide Web.

"I guess we are, honey," I said.

"Good," she said. "Because I want us to be billionaires one day."

"Why is that important to you?" I asked. "There's only so much you can buy with a lot of money, and you'd never be able to spend a billion dollars."

"Oh, I don't want to buy things." She sniffed as if reprimanding me for the thought. "I want to stop all this war and stuff, and maybe figure out a way to keep people from starving all over the world."

"Well," I said, "I hate to break the news, but that would cost a lot more than a billion dollars. It would cost so much that only big governments could afford it, and you can't make big governments do anything unless you become a powerful politician with millions of people supporting you."

"Okay then, I guess that's what I'll have to do."

"If you want to do that, you'll have to start working harder on your geography and history and social studies, instead of spending all your time on math and science."

"But those are boring subjects, Daddy," she whined. "And all I have to do is look things up when I need to know something about them."

Ellie's naïve confidence was refreshing in a humorous sort of way, although that humor was always tempered by periodic demonstrations of her uncanny intellect and logic. Before she turned six she was helping Sam in the lab, coming up with simple solutions to problems only evident to a mind unencumbered by the concept of impossibility. She'd also inherited my talent for instant memorization, though in her case it was not restricted to music. And her near-photographic memory and genius-level IQ had already allowed her to skip two grades. Doris had resisted this, claiming her emotional development would be compromised by rushing her into an environment that would turn her into a social outcast. Ellie, on the other hand, seemed not to care where she was or how the older kids treated her, so long as she had a good-sized library to go to and could spend her free time working with Sam and occasionally helping Jimmy out in the studio. Still, when her teachers recommended she be placed in a special school for gifted mathematics students, Doris flatly refused.

Ellie had also become the darling of many of our artists, who sought her opinions on everything from lyrics to arrangements. And Patsy, with whom she shared a mutual love affair, refused to book a recording date unless we could guarantee that Ellie would be free to spend at least some time with her in the studio. Their friendship, however—as well as Patsy's with Doris and me—did not exactly start out on the right foot.

When Patsy first visited the studio a couple of months after the phone conversation that seemed to have raised her from the dead, we had no choice but to introduce her to our nine-month-old daughter, which necessitated an explanation of the fictional psychic I'd told her about. I ended up taking on the role of soothsayer myself, apologizing for the elaborate story I'd made up and telling her it had all started with a dream I'd had. And, no, I said, I wasn't really a psychic; it was the first and last time I'd ever had such a dream, but it had been so vivid and detailed I felt I had to try my best to stop her from taking that plane trip.

The part about Ellie being her biggest fan, however, was true, I told her. To prove it, I played a tape of ***Crazy***, chuckling at Patsy's astonishment when Ellie sang along with it word-for word. And when I picked up my guitar and asked Patsy to sing it in person, Ellie nearly went into hysterics, hugging Patsy's leg and refusing to let go until she sang it again.

That was the beginning of a relationship so strong that Ellie cried for hours when Patsy had to leave. After that, Patsy would call at least once a week, regardless of whether she was in Nashville or Germany or even Australia. At first their conversations were a little one-sided, but it wasn't long before they were gabbing like sisters. And they always ended each call with a duet of Crazy.

Oddly, Ellie had shown no interest in performing, even though she did have a lovely singing voice with—no surprise—a twang not unlike Patsy's. She was thrilled, however, when, on her sixth birthday, Patsy asked her to sing harmony on one of her records. The song was ***Parable***, a tune I wrote in my first life that had ended up on the B side of my second album and was never released as a single. I found it somewhat ironic that it had been one of Aurélie's favorites and that Ellie chose to be billed as Aurélie on the record. Although Ellie was excited when the duet peaked at number five on the Country charts, it would be her first and last recording.

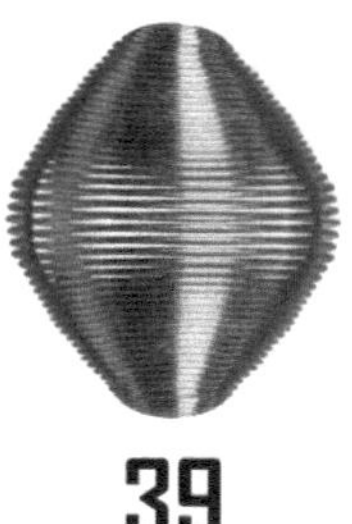

39

Sunday Morning Sentinel

As the Vietnam War began to wind down, I found myself facing a major decision. Up to that point I had not given much thought to performing myself—for one thing, I was too busy serving as CEO of Blue Note Enterprises; for another, I'd already made up my mind to remain in the background and was perfectly satisfied with my somewhat anonymous role. But when it came to ***Sunday Morning Sentinel,*** I had mixed feelings.

Although that fiasco now seemed decades in the past, the sting still lingered: an unquenchable psychic tapeworm that fed on the remnants of my previously overinflated ego. I'd even given a fleeting thought to exacting a measure of revenge on John Denny, the man I felt deserved most of the blame for the song's failure. But that old karmic balancing act continued to strike fear into my heart, keeping me from doing anything that carried even a faint odor of the unethical. Besides, having become a major country music producer, I'd found it necessary to befriend Denny, whose Cedarwood Publishing was the largest country publishing house in the world.

Another point of irony had to do with the fact that, like the producers who had refused to allow me to be the singer on ***Sunday Morning Sentinel,*** I now had several artists to whom I owed my loyalty. And I realized that if some unknown singer were to offer me the song, I would probably have the same response. I was mulling over my options when I got a call from David Geffen that, in effect, made up my mind for me.

Although I'd kept a pretty low public profile, I *had* accumulated a number of friends in the recording and entertainment industries, and one of these was Geffen, a producer-promoter whose star was rapidly rising. David's first label, Asylum Records, had recently been bought by his distributor, Atlantic, then later merged with Elektra to form Elektra/ Asylum. David had remained in charge through all these machinations, maintaining his reputation for signing little-known artists who'd had a hard time finding a record label. One of these was a young fellow by the name of Jackson Browne, whose struggles had been the impetus for David originally starting Asylum Records.

At the time, Jackson was riding a wave of popularity on the heels of his first big hit ***Doctor My Eyes***, and was in the studio working on his second album. Worried about the dreaded sophomore slump, David called me more-or-less to shoot the breeze and pick my brain about Jackson's career trajectory. I knew Jackson casually in this life, and in my former one he'd been one of my favorite singer-songwriters, mainly because he was a dedicated social activist who refused to compromise his ideals for commercial gain. David and I brainstormed for a while, and after listening to a few of his ideas a plan began to come together in my mind.

I knew Jackson preferred to record only his own songs, and I respected him for that, but with ***Sunday Morning Sentinel*** on my mind, I started to wonder if he might make an exception. Sarah and I had played around with the song, cutting a demo of it as a duet, and it came to me that pairing Jackson with Sarah could lead to a blockbuster collaboration. I didn't go into detail about my thoughts during our phone call, except to say I had an idea for a way to assure the success of Jackson's new album.

"Come on, Rich," David said when I wouldn't elaborate. "You can't tell me you have an idea then refuse to fill me in."

"Tell you what, David," I said. "Let me send you a little demo I've got here, then *you* can tell *me* if I'm on the right track."

I sent the tape via private courier, and David called the next day. His blasé attitude came off so transparent it was laughable. He clearly wanted the song, but I sensed that he was fishing for some kind of special deal. When I explained my idea of having Jackson sing it as a duet with Sarah, he balked.

"You know, don't you," he said, "Jackson's not going to like the idea of doing someone else's material."

"I do know that David," I said. "But I also know his stance on the war, and I think the prospect of working with one of the biggest R&B stars in the world might be enough to sway him."

"Who wrote this thing, anyway?" he asked, still trying to sound skeptical by referring to the song as a 'thing.'

"Oh, some obscure songwriter I've got on staff here by the name of Voniossi," I said.

"You wrote it?"

"I did, actually, a long, long time ago. Not only did I write it, but if you're interested in what I'm suggesting, I'll give it to you for nothing. I don't even want credit. For all I care Jackson can be listed as the writer. Or you, if you'd like to collect the few million bucks it's going to generate in writer's royalties. I'll even throw in the studio time, if you don't mind recording at Blue Note."

"Mind?" he said. "You've got to be kidding. Listen, let me talk this over with Jackson and get back to you."

"Okay," I said, "but you'd better make it quick. I'm sure I don't need to tell you that timing on this one is of utmost importance."

It took some convincing, but the art of persuasion was one of the primary reasons for David's success. In the end, Jackson agreed, and although they did take me up on my offer of free studio time, he demanded that I be credited as the writer. We decided to include it on both Jackson's second album and Sarah's sixth, releasing them simultaneously along with the single.

Sunday Morning Sentinel hit the charts at number fourteen with a bullet. Ten days later it was number one, and it stayed there for 15 weeks, breaking the current record of 11 weeks set in 1956 by Elvis with ***Hound Dog/Don't Be Cruel***. It remained in the top ten for 217 days, a record that would not be broken until the LeAnn Rimes hit ***How Do I Live*** surpassed it a quarter of a century later.

Both albums went double platinum within a year, and Jackson's would eventually beat out Sarah's by a few thousand copies (a minor victory David never ceased to rib me about). After that, Jackson refused to record at any other studio but Blue Note, and David and I went on to produce a dozen more albums together.

Even though I did not relish the minor upsurge in personal notoriety that came with being the writer of ***Sunday Morning Sentinel***, at least my original instincts were vindicated by the song's unparalleled success. Not only that, but I'd accomplished something I never could have in my first life: I'd become close friends with the incredible Mr. Jackson Browne.

Because of the stature of Blue Note Studios, I would also befriend several other of my earlier idols, including artists like James Taylor, Sarah McLachlan, John Denver, Dan Fogelberg, and Jim Croce. The latter three of these, I knew, would also die far too young, and after our apparent success in saving Patsy's life, I thought about the possibility of intervening in their fates as well. But since I couldn't remember the circumstances surrounding their untimely deaths, let alone the dates, there was little I could do.

It was too late to save Hendrix and Joplin, who had already succumbed to the same drugs and alcohol that had ruined my first life, and I was still wary of doing anything that might awaken the dreaded karmic referee. So, while Haight-Ashbury transitioned from a haven for hippie bohemia to the epicenter of new-age comedy, and fallout shelters that had once sprouted like root vegetables in the yards of nuclear survivalists were converted to rec rooms, Blue Note Enterprises rambled along, making beautiful music and bringing innovations to the world of technology.

Meanwhile, in those quiet moments between the exhausted oblivion brought on by sixteen-hour workdays and the first caffeine jolt of the morning, my thoughts would often stray to the people and events of my earlier life. It was during one of these waking dreams that I began to consider looking up some of those people and at least seeing how their lives were unfolding without Rix Vaughn there to screw things up. Or maybe even lending a hand if I thought a hand needed to be lent.

I'd already been of some help to Harley Day, commissioning him to build me a couple of guitars, which I encouraged visiting guitarists to try. That exposure had helped establish Harley's reputation as one of the best classical and flamenco guitar builders in the US. I experienced a slight longing every time I visited his shop, where I was surrounded by the sweet smell of sawdust and could watch master craftsmen at work. But I was far too busy to scratch that particular creative itch.

My world had been so full I'd hardly given a thought to the three wives from my earlier life. And I felt sure that if I chose to I could do some things to improve their lives. Anything I did would have to be anonymous, though, since I had no interest in personally interacting with them, not even Robin. The heart string once so loudly plucked by Robin's gentle fingers had long ago been silenced by Aurélie. And with Doris and Ellie now competing with Aurie for my love, there was no room left for even a fleeting sexual fantasy of Robin. I had, however, demonstrated a measure of respect for her by leaving ***Robin's Song*** to molder in the dustbin of my mind, foregoing the profits I felt sure I could generate by producing it for one of Blue Note's artists. Then again, if I was honest about it, that decision was probably more to punish myself than it was to honor her, since she would never know the song existed.

I was going over some ideas for locating my former wives, realizing that, in these pre-Internet days, I would probably have to hire a private investigator, when something happened that stopped me cold.

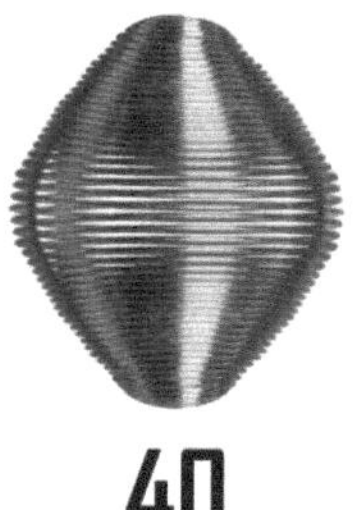

40

"Familiar" Advice

Tom, Dick and Harry had passed on to that great sandbox in the sky, though their legacy was evident all around us. Of the dozens of litters they must have sired, only three had been produced by our own cat, Jenny, a beautiful, long-haired calico who was herself now getting along in years. We'd found good homes for most of her offspring, but Mom and Doris always insisted on keeping a few of the more frisky and unusually colored kittens. These, of course, had grown up and continued to do what cats do, so we were constantly searching for adoptive parents we could trust to take good care of Jenny's extended family.

As a result of this serial procreation, we often had half a dozen or more cats wandering the premises, two or three of which would invariably choose our bedroom as their preferred sleeping chamber. My favorite of these interlopers—Cinnamon, a huge tomcat whose fur matched precisely the color of that far-eastern spice—hopped up on my chest one morning while I was wondering how to locate my three former wives. Jerked from my musings by his sudden arrival, I looked down to find him staring at me with his head tipped to one side and his eyes radiating what we humans often mistakenly think of as curiosity. I felt sure his expression was more indicative of hunger than inquisitiveness, but it had the effect of reminding me of that old saying about what killed the cat. And since I had only two lives to his nine, one of which I had already used up, that thought tempered my plans with a hefty dose of caution.

There was something else about Cinnamon's penetrating stare that gave me pause, something almost ghostly, as if I were looking into the soul of a departed spirit that hadn't quite managed to depart. It was then that I heard that phantom voice again, that cerebral consultant I'd chosen to believe was Aurélie. *Let sleeping dogs lie*, it said, choosing a canine, rather than feline metaphor, and a rather unimaginative one at that. I was thinking how little this sounded like something Aurie would say, when the voice continued: *Sorry about that. What I should have said was, there's no need to try and fix what isn't broken.*

Now I was really freaked. What had in the past been something I could easily chalk up to my imagination suddenly seemed to be responding directly to my mental criticism of its chosen metaphor.

Excuse me, I said, thinking rather than speaking, *but are we having a conversation here, or am I imagining things?*

Dammit, the voice said. *I'm not supposed to be doing this. Just ... Just give me a minute.*

No problem, I said. *Take your time.* Then, worried I might accidentally say something out loud and wake Doris, I added, *Do we really need Cinnamon for this? I'd kind of like to get out of here and go someplace where I—we—can be alone.*

No. I mean, yes, you can forget about the cat. I was only using him as a familiar to distract you from your ill-advised speculations. Go wherever you like. But don't be surprised if I can't get back to you. I have to talk to...

She stopped then, obviously not willing to say anything that would confirm her identity.

You wouldn't be referring to our Lakota Sioux friend, would you? I said.

Oh, shit, Rix. I'm really screwing up here. Look, I'll do my best, but I've probably let myself in for it, so this may be the last time you hear from me. Heyoka's going to be seriously pissed, and if he says 'no more,' that will be it.

Wait! I said. *If this might be the last time we talk, at least you can tell me what's going on. I assume you've been there all along. I mean you told me you were going to be monitoring things. So, how am I doing?*

You're doing okay. Except maybe for those interventions with your dad and Patsy Cline. Those were inadvisable. The reason I'm not supposed to be interfering is because things seem to be going reasonably well. Oh, and I love that you named your daughter after me. She's pretty incredible, by the way, and I like Doris a lot, too.

Listen, I said, *if Heyoka gets on your case about this, tell him I want to talk to him. I'll convince him I need to have you as an advisor.*

We'll see. Now I really have to go. But before I do, I want to warn you about something else.

I can use all the help I can get, so let's hear it.

Look, I know you've been incredibly busy, and I'm not trying to throw a guilt trip on you, but you need to keep a closer eye on Ellie. She's a beautiful girl, Rix, and I don't think you've noticed how fast she's growing up. That wouldn't be so much of a problem were it not for the fact that her intelligence makes her curious about everything, and it won't be long before her curiosity turns to sex. I'm sure I don't have to tell you that an emotionally immature, sexually ripe virgin rubbing elbows with musicians and famous rock stars will be particularly vulnerable.

She was right, I hadn't even begun to think about such things, nor had I paid much attention to Ellie's physical maturation. But now that I thought about it, there was the growth spurt and the recently appearing breasts; and just the other day she'd told me she'd popped her first pimple. I hadn't worried about her safety or wellbeing because of her intelligence and logical way of thinking. Plus, she had several dedicated protectors in the studio who'd been looking out for her almost since the day she was born. However, if she decided on her own to do something clandestine, she was so clever that no one would even suspect anything was going on.

But isn't that supposed to be Doris's department? I said, knowing the moment those words entered my mind that it was not only a copout, but that hoping Doris would discuss the subject of sex with Ellie was like hoping a bunch of hot young musicians would keep their cocks in their pants. Despite her expertise and creativity in bed, Doris had never been able to loosen up outside the bedroom.

You know better than that, Rix. Sure Doris should be responsible for seeing to it that Ellie is well informed and cautious, but we both know how uptight she is about discussing sex with anyone but you. If you want to prepare Ellie for dealing with a horde of mercenary rock stars, I'm afraid you'll have to talk to her yourself. And don't forget about drugs and alcohol. Even the smartest kids can become awfully dumb under the influence of mind-altering substances, especially when you combine them with adolescent hormones. I hate to say it, but you of all people should know what she's in for.

Unlike other studios of the day, we'd been fairly strict about drugs, though only in the sense that open use was not tolerated. Alcohol, on the other hand, was a different story. Had we banned drinking, we would have lost at least ninety percent of our clients. My stupidity in not seeing what was happening to my daughter and the influences she was being subjected to was worse than simple neglect; it bordered on aiding and abetting her potential predators. I'd been so fascinated by her intellectual skills, I had completely ignored her emotional development, and now I began to wonder if it might already be too late.

Okay, I said. *I guess I'll have to figure out some way to talk to her about it. I could sure use some help, though, so please try your best to stick around.*

She didn't respond.

Aurie? Are you there?

But there was nothing, not even in Cinnamon's eyes. In fact, after giving me a final, disinterested look, he stretched out on my chest, kneading my neck and purring like a nursing kitten.

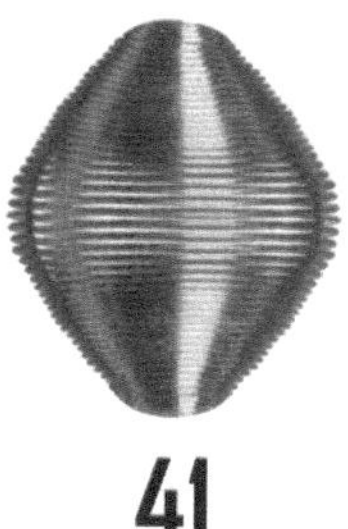

41

The Empress's New Clothes

I broached the subject with Doris as soon as she woke up, but when I pointed out how quickly Ellie was maturing and suggested it was time they had a talk about sex, you'd have thought I'd asked her to jump off the Empire State Building. I explained the dangers that lay ahead and how important it was for Ellie to understand how to deal with them, but all that did was drive Doris deeper into a state of abject terror, this time accompanied by tears of guilt over her reluctance to do what she knew should be her responsibility.

"I just can't, Rich," she whined. "I know it sounds selfish and irresponsible, and I'm worried sick about Ellie. But I wouldn't even know how to begin, let alone what to say. You've had a lifetime of experience, and you told me yourself that where you came from people talk openly about sex all the time. So please, *please* don't make me do it."

I could have feigned anger, but I wasn't about to play that kind of game with her, even though I, myself, had never been so terrified in my life—lives; either of them. Fortunately, Blue Note Enterprises was in the process of moving to a brand new facility, and we'd suspended all recording operations for the next couple of months, which meant there should be no immediate temptations for Ellie.

We'd been dealing with a mounting pile of complaints from neighbors about the traffic congestion, late hours, and noise caused by our growing operation. We'd started out before there were many strict zoning laws in place, so the business had been grandfathered in when it came to certain violations. But disturbing the peace was disturbing the peace, and we all understood that the neighbors had a valid point. Our move to a larger facility had been in the planning stages for some time, and it wasn't only because of the complaints. Fact was we'd outgrown the garage shortly after Sarah's second album went triple platinum, and our waiting list for studio time was now so long we were losing clients. Plus, our various other divisions were spread all over town, making it difficult for Doris to manage things.

After graduating high school at the tender age of fourteen, Ellie had decided to take a year off to evaluate the dozens of scholarship offers she'd received. With her schooling temporarily on hold, I'd asked her to help Doris oversee the planning and design of the new facility. They'd tackled the job with enthusiasm, working with the architects and interior designers to develop a sprawling complex that would include five recording studios, two labs and a machine shop for Sam, a cafeteria and attached fitness center, offices for our other divisions, and housing for visiting artists.

One idea Ellie came up with was to build a small performance hall or club, where artists could hone live performances in parallel with their studio sessions. It was a concept that never would have occurred to me, and when I ran her proposal by the rest of the gang, everyone agreed it was a great idea. Ellie suggested we called it the Shindig Club, and insisted that we not serve alcohol. This, she said, would make it a safe, politically acceptable destination for teenagers, who would be drawn not only by the talent, but because the club would have the look and feel of an adult cocktail lounge. And, with a clientele representative of the audiences most rock acts were targeting, we could offer our artists a convenient test venue for new material. We presented the idea to our team of lawyers, and they were unanimous in their approval, pointing out that it could help us get past some of the political hurdles we faced in our efforts to purchase a tract of city-owned property on which to build our expanded operation.

Situated on the banks of Tampa Bay, about half a mile from our house, the property included 20 acres of prime real estate just north of the abandoned Vinoy Park Hotel and the world-famous Million Dollar Pier. The pier, which had recently been remodeled, had always been an important destination for tourists who pumped hundreds of millions of dollars into the city's coffers every year. Needless to say, St. Pete was extremely protective of its waterfront, so gaining approval for our new complex was going to be a delicate matter.

To help garner public support for the project, our attorneys had suggested we designate half the land to be used as a municipal arts and entertainment complex, splitting the construction costs with the city. This would eventually house a theater in the round, a children's hands-on museum, an after-school arts-and-crafts learning center, and two Little League baseball fields. I couldn't have cared less about the city politics, but, as a favor to me, Carol Henderson had agreed to come on board to handle most of that, putting aside her disdain for rock 'n' roll and using her political influence to grease the wheels of government. However, everyone agreed it was the Shindig Club that tipped the balance. Ellie put together a stellar promotional campaign aimed at the region's teenagers, who, along with their parents, bombarded the city council with thousands of letters and phone calls in favor of the project.

The grand opening of Blue Note Enterprises' new complex was set for August 30th, two days before Ellie's fifteenth birthday. David, Jackson, and Patsy flew in, along with several other industry folks and artists, including Tony Orlando, B. J. Thomas, and Glen Frey of the Eagles, all of whom had recently cut tracks at the old Blue Note Studios. The formal ceremony—a boring litany of speeches by city officials—was capped by an elaborately staged ribbon cutting, at which Doris and Ellie shared the honors. Both wore identical designer outfits—slinky pant suits of silver lamé, with tight-fitting bodices that showed off their figures and made them look more like sisters than mother and daughter. I was marveling at how much they looked alike, when I realized I was undressing them with my eyes—both of them.

That realization was not only shocking, it added an exclamation point to what Aurélie had said: that Ellie was rapidly becoming a woman. And it was then that my planned talk with her—which I'd been putting off for weeks—took on a sense of urgency.

42
The Facts Of Life

When Ellie was eleven, she decided she wanted to check out some of the other churches around town. Mom didn't much care for the idea, but Doris and I convinced her that not allowing Ellie the freedom to choose her own religious path could very well lead her to rebel against religion in general. So with me as her chaperone, the two of us set out to make the rounds of several local churches.

Ellie soon realized that the similarities among Protestant churches were much greater than their differences, though she *was* intrigued by the high ceremony of the Catholic Mass we attended, particularly when the priest would swing the smoking thurible. On our way home that afternoon, she assumed her sweet-little-girl persona and begged me to buy her a thurible of her own, a request I dodged by employing the standard parental "We'll see." Knowing that "We'll see" almost always meant "yes," and being the crafty diplomat she was, she dropped the subject and waited. It took me a couple of months to find an elaborate brass model similar to the one she'd seen at the Mass, and I'm sure she was not surprised when she found it under the Christmas tree that year.

The thurible now hung in the corner of her bedroom, and the waning aroma of incense set an ominous tone when I snuck in to wake her on the morning of her fifteenth birthday. On any other day that lingering odor of sandalwood would have been a pleasant addition to the cozy, predawn atmosphere, but after having stayed up all night fretting over what I had to do, the thurible's religious symbolism only added to my sense of foreboding; as if I were being watched over and judged by an invisible priest.

"Happy fifteenth, honey," I said as I sat on the side of her bed.

"Hi, Daddy," she murmured. "What time is it?" Even crusty-eyed and disheveled, her sleepy smile illuminated the early darkness like a warm, glowing candle.

"I think it's time we had a little talk," I said. "Here." I handed her the slim book I'd brought with me.

She yawned, then reached out to take the book from my trembling hand. Scratching the sleep from her eyes, she read the title out loud: "Life and Love for Teenagers." She looked at me and started to giggle. "Oh," she said, "thaaaat talk. I thought moms were supposed handle the big sex lecture."

I started to answer, but she held up a hand. "Sorry, Dad," she said. "I didn't mean to belittle your brave attempt to do what you felt was your duty. I knew Mom would never have the guts to talk to me about the birds and the bees, so I really do appreciate you're caring enough to make the sacrifice. I've read this one, by the way, back when I was, let's see, maybe ten? It's not bad for preteens, but it doesn't hold a candle to the medical books in Grandpa's home library. Now, what can I help you with?"

My clever, sarcastic daughter had decided on a preemptive strike intended to sabotage my attempt to have a serious conversation. And although I knew I was no match for her intellect and needle-sharp wit, I did have a lifetime and a half of experience with things she could never find in Dad's medical books. One lesson she had yet to learn was that the *real* facts of life had little to do with a technical knowledge of anatomy.

"Okay," I said, "I guess you know more than I gave you credit for. So tell me, what do you know about rape, or how to protect yourself from sexual predators? What's the difference between having sexual intercourse and falling in love? Between dreamy fantasy and the reality of losing your virginity to some creep you've inadvertently let go too far? Is a kiss really just a kiss, like the song says, or a prelude to loss of innocence, emotional pain and irreversible consequences? And by the way, since we're being so honest with each other, when was the last time you had a tongue jammed down your throat, or a finger shoved up your vagina?"

By then, she'd lost her bravado and was staring at me open mouthed.

"Don't tell me you're shocked by these questions," I said. "It's obvious from your statements that you know a lot more than I expected. So, let's have it, the cold, unadulterated truth. Then maybe, just maybe, you'll want to listen to your old man and see if he has anything of value to add. And while we're at it, take a look at this." I handed her a Polaroid photo I'd taken of her and her mom at the ribbon -cutting ceremony. "I can't for the life of me decide which one is sexier. But if I weren't your father, I think I might go for the one on the left."

She fingered the photo, turning it toward the dim light from the window, then looked at me with sad, puppy-dog eyes. I could see her chin start to quiver, so I dropped the tough-guy act and put my arms around her. "Oh, honey," I said. "I'm sorry, but I'm not going to let you bully me into sidestepping what we both know is something you need to deal with, and deal with sooner rather than later. All I want is for you to—"

"Daddy?" she said, the word a breathy gasp.

"What, honey?"

She pulled away and leaned back against the pillows, closing her eyes, then opening them again and looking away. "Please don't hate me," she whispered barely loud enough for me to hear, "but I ... it's already too late."

ELLIE REFUSED TO TELL me who it was, even after I calmed down and promised not to kill him (although I crossed my fingers when I made that promise). It had happened after the grand opening, she said, while everyone was preoccupied partying and jamming.

"I guess you can gloat now," she said, wiping her tears on a corner of the sheet.

I was still in shock, but I managed a weak smile. "I'm not going to gloat, honey. I'm a little thunderstruck is all. Can you ... can we talk about it? I promise not to get angry, but I would like to know what happened, if you were forced or anything."

"I wasn't forced, Daddy. Except maybe a little right at the end when I got really scared. It wasn't rape, though, if that's what you're thinking. I wanted it to happen."

"But why, honey?" I said, sounding childishly whiney. "What could possibly lead you to make such a life-changing decision at your age? Was it something your mom and I did? Were you lashing out at us?"

"Don't be silly. It had nothing to do with you or Mom. It was something I needed to do for myself. And it wasn't one of those heat-of-the moment things. I didn't go all brain dead and lose my self-control. I'd been planning it for a long time, waiting for the right guy and the right opportunity."

"I see," I said, although I didn't. "Are you okay about it now? I mean, was it all you thought it would be?"

"No," she said. "In fact, it hurt like hell—heck, sorry. But that wasn't the point anyway."

So there was a point, I thought. "Listen, I'm sorry it didn't work out the way you hoped it would, and I hate to be redundant, but could we go back to the question of why? I'm not looking for reasons to chastise you. I swear. It's just that you're obviously not happy about it, and when you're unhappy it makes me unhappy. So I'd like to help if I can."

"Actually," she said, "I'm not all that unhappy. Oh, it would have been nice if things had gone a little smoother, if it had lived up to my naïve expectations. But I don't regret losing my so-called innocence. As for why, that's a little hard to explain. It's not that I don't want to tell you, I'm just not sure I can put it into words."

"Would you rather talk to your mom or Grandma about it? I mean, maybe it's, you know, a female thing, something too embarrassing to tell me."

"God no," she said with a grimace. "I'm not embarrassed at all. A little disappointed over the physical part maybe, but not ashamed or embarrassed. The problem with talking to Mom or Grandma is that they could never understand what's going on inside my head. You're the only person I've ever been able to talk to about serious stuff, so I'll be glad to fill you in on all the details if you think you can handle it. By the way, we did use a prophylactic—a condom—so you don't have to worry about any 'irreversible consequences.'"

"Well, that's one positive thing," I said. "Are you in love with him? Is that what this is all about?"

"Not a chance," she said. "I wouldn't have done it with anyone I cared about in that way."

"I'm confused," I said.

"I don't blame you. It's so complicated and personal I don't even know if I can explain it so someone else can understand."

"Look," I said, "We both know I'm not the smartest guy on the planet, but I've got a lot of living under my belt, and as long as it doesn't involve higher math or physics, I might be able to figure out a way to help. Why don't you take a deep breath and give it your best shot?"

"Okay," she said, sliding back until she was propped up on the pillows and pulling the covers up to her neck. "The thing is, I'm kind of lost, and I need to—pardon the cliché, but I need to find myself, to find out what is uniquely me. I've been Sam's calculator, Jimmy's side kick, Mom's pride and joy, your little girl, Patsy's muse, the school's award winner, an advisor to half a dozen musicians. But don't you see? None of those things are me alone. They're all me as part of somebody or something else. I wanted to do one thing just for me, to feel something that was only mine. I'm getting ready to go out into the big wide world, and I need an identity. I need to be somebody unique, not an appendage or a support mechanism."

"But you are, honey. You're one of the most unique individuals on the face of the earth."

"You don't get it, Daddy. Not that I expected you to. Look, the sex thing was painful and disappointing, but at least it was my pain, my disappointment. For the first time in my life I felt really alive. It was only a start, but I can move on from there. I want to put *my* name, *my* stamp on the world. Not as the famous Rich Voniossi's brainy kid or that pretty little girl at Blue Note Studios. I want to be me, Aurélie, a singular entity with her own identity."

"Then why don't you sing? Let me produce some stuff for you. I guarantee I can make you a star. Then it will be you out there, on your own."

"But don't you understand? Don't you hear what you just said? *You* would be doing it, not me. I'm not really star material anyway. Without a lot of promotion and writers and production, I'm no better than your average teenage shower singer. Besides, fame is not what I'm after. What I *am* after is my own personal fulfillment. I want to do something important, and if nobody else ever knows it was me, that's fine."

Her determination seemed unshakable, and even though she was wrong about not being seen as an individual with her own unique accomplishments, I realized she wasn't going to buy that argument. The hardest part about all this was that I knew she was still a kid inside, that Doris had been right about not letting her skip all those grades. Emotionally she was as confused and vulnerable as any adolescent, despite the fact that she had the brains of a forty-year-old physics professor. There was a point at which every parent had to let go, but we seemed to have reached that point with Ellie far too early.

"I know you probably think I'm being overprotective," I said, "and the last thing I want to do is hold you back. But I'm scared, honey. You're trying to cut the ties way too early, before your emotional maturity catches up with your intellectual development. You're still at the stage where impulse and hormones take precedence over common sense and logic. When a teenage crush can seem like true love. When conquering the world looks as easy as passing a math test. If you think the physical pain and disappointment of being inexpertly deflowered is as bad as its going to get, you'd better think again, because that's nothing compared to what you're going to experience as an attractive, emotionally immature kid alone in the cruel, uncaring world out there."

"Maybe," she said. "Maybe not. Did you ever stop to consider that I'm also one of the most logical persons you've ever known? I understand what you're saying, and you're right on one level. But what you don't seem to get is that I already know all that. I've examined myself from every angle you could think of, and I've studied adolescent psychology and the hormonal influences of puberty. So I've got a pretty good idea of what's going on inside me. Why do you think I chose someone I could never fall in love with to deflower me?"

"I give up, why?"

"Because it was the logical thing to do. Believe me, I've had more than one crush, starting long before I hit puberty. What girl wouldn't, being around all those older guys, some of whom are so sexy and famous any teenager would give her eyeteeth just to be in the same room with them? Hell, before I came to my senses, I would have jumped Jackson in a second, and he knew it."

"He knew it? Does that mean ...?"

"It means I tried," she said, with a suggestive smirk. "Oh, don't worry Daddy. You know Jackson's too much of a gentleman to even consider taking advantage of a kid. There were others, though, who weren't quite so reluctant. Probably the only thing that stopped them was who I am—you know, the boss's daughter and all. What I'm getting at is that I've experienced adolescent infatuation of the first degree, but once I began to analyze things, I came to the conclusion that I needed to take control of my emotions. And I did."

"You did?" I said, wondering what she thought she'd taken control of. "So what was Friday night all about then?"

"Like I said, that wasn't a matter of infatuation or adolescent rebellion or any of the other diagnoses your average psychologist might come up with. It was a conscious decision made with forethought and careful planning. By the way, in case you're wondering why we could never be together as a couple, it's because he's homosexual—he prefers gay actually. We've been friends for years, and he did it as a favor to me, so don't get the idea he seduced your sweet little innocent daughter."

I must have gone pale, because she looked at me with alarm. "Don't go having a stroke on me, Daddy," she said, sitting up and taking my face in her hands. "God, you're white as a sheet. Look, things haven't changed from ten seconds ago, unless you've suddenly turned into a homophobe, which I can't imagine. You know a lot of gay musicians and I've never known you to discriminate against any of them. Tom's not even a musician. He's a shy, straight-A student who's a bit of a nerd, if you want to know the truth, but a really nice guy. Come on Dad, buck up. Everything's going to be okay. I promise."

Tom, I thought, wondering why I wasn't already planning his brutal demise. It was probably because her matter-of-fact way of telling me had caught me off guard and left me wondering how to react. Actually, once the initial shock wore off, I'd been worrying more about how cold and analytical she was being. And she was right about my moronic reaction to her choice of partners, which, now that I thought about it, was a fairly logical decision from her perspective.

"Give me a second here," I said, trying to catch my breath. I took her hands from my face and held them between us until my heart stopped pounding. *Forget the gay guy,* I told myself. *There's something far more serious going on here.* Her attitude reminded me of mine during those decades of emotional detachment following Robin's disappearance; those years of lonely, self-centered sexual conquests that left me unfulfilled and spiritually crippled.

"So," I said when I'd calmed down enough to think clearly, "What about love, marriage, kids, the joy of sharing your life with someone? You seem to have closed yourself off to those possibilities."

"I don't know," she said. "Maybe I have in a way. At least for now. I need space, Dad. Time and space to figure out what I want to do, how I want to attack my life. I can't really share that space and time with anyone until I've become someone myself. Even then, I'm not sure I'd want to trade my independence for the security of a one-on-one relationship."

I was in over my head and I knew it. I couldn't counter her arguments with logic; she was way ahead of me on that front. So I fell back on the only thing I could think of. "I love you, honey," I said. "I love you more than life itself, and I'd hate to see you let one bad experience influence the rest of your life. Don't get me wrong, I'm not suggesting you should keep experimenting, not until you're older. What I'm saying is that when everything goes right, and you're with someone you really love, it can be the most wonderful thing you will ever experience. If that weren't the case, kiddo, you wouldn't even be here."

"I love you too Dad, and I don't want you to worry about me. I have no plans to do any more experimenting, at least for a while. And I am not shutting out the possibility of falling in love. I just need a little time. Now please get out of here and let me get dressed. In case you've forgotten, I've got a surprise birthday party coming up this afternoon, and I have to practice looking surprised."

"To be continued?" I said.

"Sure. Anytime. I may come off as a smart-mouthed know-it-all sometimes, but I do know how valuable real life experience can be. And you've got it all over me in that department. The only thing I ask is that we keep this between the two of us. It's not that I want to be dishonest or anything, but if Mom found out it would kill her, not to mention really screwing up our relationship. You know how she is about stuff like this."

"Don't worry," I said. "I don't think I could tell her if I wanted to."

"Great! Thanks, Dad. Nice talk."

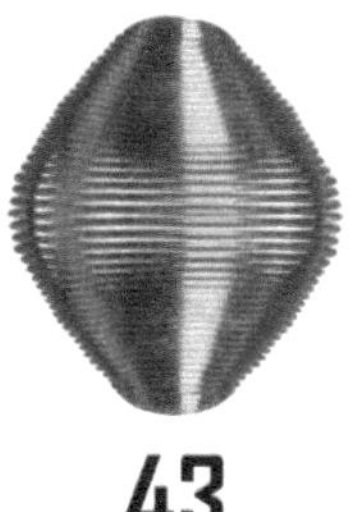

43
Pons Asinorum

W*ell, how'd I do?* I thought, after I left Ellie's bedroom. I tried my best to project the words out into the subethric, but there was no response. Not that I'd expected one; it had been weeks since I'd heard from Aurélie, and I'd begun to wonder if she would ever contact me again.

As much as I'd wanted to continue my talk with Ellie, I realized there wasn't a whole lot more to say on the subject of love and sex and relationships. Unless, that is, I wanted to get into the more physical and erotic aspects of love making, which I didn't; I couldn't imagine discussing the mechanics of sexual arousal with her. Surely, I told myself, fathers didn't talk about those kinds of things with their teenage daughters in 1977.

Except for her apparent determination not to fall in love, Ellie seemed to have a pretty good handle on things; at least she was far more realistic and thoughtful than I'd been at her age. Because of that, and because I'd seen no evidence of them, I didn't think I had to worry about drugs or alcohol either. As for love, I knew matters of the heart had little respect for logic or resolve; when love happened, it happened, and all the calculated planning in the world couldn't stop it. Aurie had proven that by breaking through the barrier I'd hidden my heart behind for nearly forty years.

ELLIE'S BIRTHDAY PARTY TURNED out to be a rather star-studded event. All the musicians stuck around to attend, and she acted appropriately surprised. Most of her gifts were of the humorous variety: Jimmy and Sarah gave her a mediaeval chastity belt they'd found at an antique store, while Sam and a bunch of the engineers had made her a compilation tape that included a medley of three Gary Puckett songs. The cautionary medley began with ***Young Girl*** and ***Lady Willpower***, and ended with ***Don't Give In To Him***, all separated by goofy Spike Jones instrumental breaks. Glen, who had flown in from California where The Eagles were recording at the time, brought her a lingerie box from the newly-opened Victoria's Secret in San Francisco, though when she lifted the lid, she found only a pink t-shirt with the words "OFF LIMITS!" printed in large block letters across the chest. About the only serious gift she got, other than ours, was a beautiful Hopi turquoise necklace from Jackson.

Over Doris's objections, Patsy and I had gone in together and bought her a Volvo 262C—a top-of-the-line, limited edition; metallic silver with black leather upholstery and hardwood panels in the doors. Ever since she'd gotten her learner's permit she'd been begging for a car, even though she wouldn't be able to drive on her own until she was sixteen. As part of her not-so-subtle campaign, she'd collected promises from Sam, Jimmy, and Sarah to ride with her whenever they could. And, she pointed out, when you added me, Doris, and Mom to the mix, she would have six licensed adult supervisors to choose from. She was a little disappointed with our choice of cars—she'd been hinting at a Corvette or a Mustang, but we both agreed we wanted safety not muscle, and Volvo had the best safety record of any car manufacturer in the world at that time.

The evening ended in typical musician fashion, with everybody jamming and trying out new material. Jackson was working on a new song he said he'd written for Ellie called ***That Girl Could Sing***, and when he played it for her I could tell she was having a hard time keeping her emotions in check. She'd never been an overly emotional child, and I got the feeling there was more to her reaction than the remnants of a teenage crush.

ELLIE STILL HADN'T DECIDED where she wanted to go to college, which was fine with me. Even as mature and sensible as she seemed to be, I didn't want her moving far away until she was at least sixteen and had her unrestricted driver's license. I did, however, encourage her to do whatever she felt she had to in her quest to, as she put it, 'find herself.' She'd always been frugal with her money, saving most of what we paid her and never touching the royalties from ***Parable***, so when she said she'd like to support herself and live on her own for a while, there didn't seem to be any way to refuse her. After all, she would be leaving for college soon and she only wanted to move into Sam's family's apartment complex a few blocks from home.

About a month after she moved into her new apartment, she invited us over for dinner to show off her domestic skills, which, it turned out, lacked a little in the cooking department. Still, we spent a pleasant evening talking about her scholarship offers and helping her hang some curtains. The pleasant part of the evening ended abruptly, however, when we were driving home and the news of Elvis's death came on the radio. The announcement caught me by surprise, and again, Doris complained that I hadn't told her or tried to do anything to intervene. I reminded her that it was almost impossible for me to remember exactly when certain events had occurred, but that didn't stop her.

"You told me long ago you could remember the big stuff," she said. "So you could at least tell me about some things that haven't happened yet, even if they're years away."

I reiterated my objection to interfering with the flow of history, but she fell back on her standard claim that the only reason she wanted to know was so she could record the events in her journal for future reference. Even though I doubted she would leave it at that, I couldn't very well call her a liar, so I did my best to recall a few things in the hope of satisfying her curiosity.

Unfortunately, my memories of what went on in the world during my tumultuous thirties were blurred by heroin and booze and the whirlwind of my early recording career, appearing in my mind's eye like blurry impressionist paintings—wispy, undetailed renderings of things I'd spent most of my time trying to ignore. Back then, all that mattered to me was getting laid, staying high, and feeding my insatiable ego, which left little room for concern about the world at large.

The only important events I could recall from that era were those that had dominated the headlines and conversations of the time, and even that list was pitifully short. Other than Elvis's death, there were things like the Jonestown massacre, the Iran hostage crisis, John Lennon's assassination, and the eruption of Mount St. Helens. There was a smattering of trivia: Michael Jackson's huge success with the album ***Thriller***, the first ***Star Wars*** movie, and the popularity of Rubik's Cube. But that wasn't what Doris was after. So I ran through the more historic incidents, explaining each one as best I could and pointing out the impossibility of doing anything about them.

"We can't stop a volcano from erupting, or convince a bunch of religious fanatics their leader is a nut case." I said. "Besides, I don't remember the exact dates any of these things happened, and warning people years in advance would only make us sound like delusional alarmists. Then, when they do happen, we would probably be investigated by the CIA or the FBI because of our prior knowledge."

She didn't say anything in response, and I was thinking maybe I'd finally gotten through to her. But when I pulled into the driveway and turned off the engine, she made no move to get out of the car. She stared straight ahead for a couple of minutes, then turned and gave me a steely-eyed look. "We *cannot* let John die," she said with a finality that left no room for argument. "Ellie would be devastated."

We'd met Lennon two years earlier when David Bowie booked the studio through EMI to record his number one hit, ***Fame***. John had co-written the song with Bowie, and he played guitar and helped out with background vocals during the session. After we wrapped, John, David and Yoko joined us for dinner at Bern's Steakhouse in Tampa.

The evening's conversation was dominated by Ellie and John discussing social issues ranging from war to famine to civil rights. And by the end of the night, the two of them had become fast friends. John even drew a quick sketch of her on one of Burns' linen napkins, then politely called the maître d' over and offered to pay for the napkin so he could give it to Ellie.

Since then, Ellie and John had stayed in touch, and I realized what Doris said—that Ellie would be devastated by his death—was true. Still, I was reluctant to interfere. Even if I'd wanted to, my memory of the shooting was too fragmented to be of much help. About all I could remember was that it had happened outside his hotel in New York and that the shooter was some religious crackpot by the name of Mark David Chapman.

When I told this to Doris, she thought for a moment, then said, "Mark David Chapman is not a terribly common name. Do you remember anything else about him?"

"Not much," I said. "Born-again Christian. Insanity defense. I think he eventually pled guilty, though. And there was something about him being pissed at John for claiming the Beatles were more popular than Jesus."

"So, you don't have any idea when it happened?" she said. "Even something unrelated we could use as a time reference?"

"Maybe," I said. "I'm not sure, but I think it was around the time Reagan was elected President. Whenever that was."

"Reagan? You mean that crummy actor, the one who was governor of California?"

"Yeah, Ronald Regan. I remember because his election was all tied up with the Iran hostage thing I told you about. The Iranians held the hostages until the election was over then released them, and lot of people thought Carter was defeated because he couldn't get them released. I think the shooting happened shortly after the election."

"Carter only served one term?" she asked.

"Yep."

"That's too bad," she said. "I like Carter. Wait! That means Reagan will be elected in November of 1980, almost three years from now. So we have lots of time."

Right. I thought. *Lots of time to do something stupid.*

DORIS DIDN'T MENTION THE shooting for a long time after that, which only added to my anxiety. Silence, I knew, did not mean she had forgotten about it; more likely it meant she had something up her sleeve that she didn't want to talk about yet. Meanwhile, I kept trying to contact Aurie, pleading for advice because Doris's calculation of the approximate date John was killed had me worried. Ellie and John had been talking about organizing some sort of charity concert tour, and I couldn't help wondering how that might alter the sequence of events.

ELLIE EVENTUALLY DECIDED TO accept a scholarship to Florida State University, where she could study under the Nobel Prize Winning physicist Paul Dirac. And a week after she passed her driving test,

Doris and I stood in the middle of the street, choking back tears as we watched her car disappear into the early morning mist.

A year had passed since our conversation about John's assassination, and so many things were happening with the business I had a hard time thinking of anything else. Managing the avalanche of money that accompanied our growth was a full-time job in itself—when I wasn't sequestered in the office, I was bouncing around like a pinball between stock brokers and attorneys, or playing golf (which I hated and was no good at) with some politico or corporate bigwig. The job had become ... well, a *Job*, robbing me of the time to do the creative things I enjoyed, and I often found myself entertaining the fantasy of grabbing my guitar and hitting the road. Unfortunately, that would have to remain a fantasy, because by then, too many people were dependent upon me for their livelihood.

As for doing something about John's shooting, thoughts of that had been squeezed into a small space at the back of my mind, although they would occasionally tickle my conscience like the irritating buzz of a lone mosquito. I tried to ignore that mosquito, just as I'd tried not to use what little I remembered from my first life to grow the business. I could not, however, stop myself from making suggestions, many of which, I would later realize, had been based on my knowledge of what was to come.

At my urging, Sam had developed a computer operating system that was challenging Bill Gates' MS-DOS, and the success of our computer division had spawned an embryonic version of Silicon Valley along the I-4 corridor between Tampa and Orlando. Miniaturization and artificial intelligence were Sam's top priorities now, and I had convinced him that the next *Big Thing* would be wireless communication, though I didn't have any idea how that was going to work or when it would be introduced. I vaguely recalled that some of the earliest cell phones had been made by Motorola, so I suggested he talk to some of his engineer friends over there and see if we might be able to get in on the ground floor of that technology.

After I made that suggestion, I decided to take a step back and try to evaluate what, if any, impact my foreknowledge was having on the world at large. I had not stolen any specific inventions—I couldn't have even if I'd wanted to, because I didn't have the technical expertise—however, I *had* occasionally mentioned concepts and ideas in a broad, simplistic way, and I wondered if that was any different than outright theft. In the early days, when I was deeply involved with the music and production end of the business, I was determined not to use even a hint of the lyrics or arrangements from hit songs I remembered. But my knowledge of trends in the music market had definitely influenced my writing and arranging, and had been an important factor in choosing the artists and songs we produced.

The more I thought about it, the more I began to wonder if the potential for disaster might be dependent on how heavy-handed my interference was. Perhaps if I didn't set out to deliberately change the course of world history or profit from what I knew, I wouldn't be disturbing the space-time continuum enough to cause devastating consequences. The problem—as it had always been—was that I had no way of knowing, nor would I ever know, what the ultimate outcome of anything I did might be. I simply could not predict how far into the future the ripple effects would reach, or what other events they might trigger along the way.

I tried to talk this over with Doris one afternoon, but her response was the same as always: that I worried too much about things not worth worrying about. No matter how carefully I explained the reasons for my apprehension, she didn't seem to get it. And when she again brought up the subject of John's assassination, the discussion threatened to deteriorate into an angry argument. I was too mentally exhausted for another debate, and I finally decided to come clean and tell her about my growing frustration with work.

"I'm sorry, honey, but I can't think clearly right now," I said, pacing back and forth in front of her desk. "This damned business is driving me crazy. I'm feeling trapped, like the walls are closing in on me."

"Take it easy, Rich," she said, coming around the desk and grabbing my wrist. "My God, your pulse is racing. Maybe you should see your dad. You need to have your blood pressure checked and get an EKG. Come on, sit down for a minute."

"What I *need* is to get out of here for a while. I'll be okay. I just need some space and time to think." I thought I was putting on a pretty good act, but when I felt my heart pounding and the vertigo set in, I realized what I'd said was true: I *did* need to get out of there, maybe for good.

She helped me down into a chair, then knelt in front of me, holding my hands and watching my face. "Your hands are cold," she said, rubbing my fingers. "And your cheeks are flushed. Please let me call your dad."

I closed my eyes and took a deep breath, counting to ten before opening them again. "I'm feeling better now," I lied. "Give me minute, and then I'm going for a walk. A long one. I'm alright, really."

"I wouldn't bet on that," she said. "Anyway, I'm calling your dad and you're going to see him as soon as he has an opening. And I'm going with you on that walk."

"I don't think so," I said, pointing at the flashing buttons on her phone. "One of us has to be here or there'll be hell to pay. There's nothing wrong with me that a little fresh air won't cure. Go ahead and call Dad if you want. He'll probably want to run a bunch of tests, so at least that will give me another reason to play hooky."

I stood up and waited while she pressed a finger against my neck. "Pulse is better," she said. "Are you sure you're okay?"

"I'm sure," I said. The vertigo had eased and my heart didn't feel as fluttery, so I took her by the hand and walked to the door. "Do me a favor and tell Janet to cancel my appointments. Say I was hit by a meteor or something." I stopped in the doorway and bent to kiss her. "I'll think about John, and we'll talk about it again soon. I promise."

I knew she would be evaluating my every move, so I turned and walked briskly down the corridor. When I reached the end, I looked back and smiled. "See?" I said. "I'm fine."

She shook her head. "You be careful, Ricky," she said. "I mean it!"

I did a little dance step, shuffling around the corner, then peeking back and tipping an imaginary hat before making my way toward the nearest exit.

I had to brush off a couple of engineers who tried to corner me in the hall, and once outside I jogged quickly across the parking lot and headed north along the seawall. Still a little shaky, I slowed to a walk, and by the time I passed the Little League fields, I was feeling steadier. Half a dozen teenagers were throwing Frisbees in the waterfront park, and a few older couples sat on benches facing the bay, so I hopped down to the narrow swatch of dry land that sloped from the seawall to the edge of the water. Duck walking to stay out of sight, I stumbled through a thicket of sea grapes until I came upon a gnarled tree trunk half buried in the sand.

A single leaf hung from a tiny branch on the trunk, the last vestige of life clinging to a dying host. And as I sat on the rotting bark a strong feeling of déjà vu came over me. Suddenly, Aurélie's voice echoed in my head: *If I were to speculate, I'd have to say there would be a price to pay. I have no idea what that price would be, but it seems to me you'd have to settle the account sooner or later.* I remembered then: we were sitting on a log in the woods behind the villa, talking about what the consequences might be if I used my knowledge of the future to get rich or steal hit songs in my new life.

"But you haven't done that, have you Rix?" she said. "Not on purpose, anyway." It took me a moment to realize the voice was not in my head, and when I turned toward it, there she was, sitting right next to me. I knew it was a hallucination, but that didn't keep my heart from resuming its impersonation of a Gene Krupa drum solo.

"Calm down," she said. "I refuse to take responsibility for another heart attack."

"Is that really you," I asked, reaching out to touch her.

"Sort of," she said as my fingers disappeared into her arm. "Sorry, but you can't touch me. Really sorry, actually. I'm a hologram. Or at least what you're seeing is a hologram. I'm real, I'm just not here in the flesh."

"Far out," I said, withdrawing my hand and watching my fingers reappear. "But you look ..." I was going to say older, but I figured that wouldn't be very diplomatic. "You look so, uh, solid. Where's all the flickering and transparency?"

"You're thinking of that CGI crap from ***Star Wars***," she said. "And the answer to your unspoken question is I look older because I am. It's been over twenty years since you last saw me, remember? I'm fifty-eight now, Rix. Kind of an ironic role reversal, huh?"

"You look fantastic," I said, and she did. A little more maturity in her face, a few soft laugh wrinkles around the eyes, but all-in-all the years hadn't detracted a bit from her beauty. "So, does Heyoka ... did you get his permission?"

"We came to an understanding," she said. "When I told him you were about to have a stroke from all the anxiety over your workload and your argument with Doris, he caved. He didn't like the idea, and it took some serious persuading on my part. But you know me. I can be a pretty stubborn bitch when I want to."

"That's great," I said, reaching for her again, then snatching my hand back. "Sorry, I can't help it. Can anybody else see you?" I glanced at the seawall to make sure nobody was watching us.

"Everyone can see me," she said. "That's one reason I had to wait until you were somewhere alone and we were not likely to be interrupted. Although now that I think about it, being seen wouldn't cause much of a stir unless someone tried to touch me."

"How long can you stay? I mean, is there a witching hour or something?"

"This is not a fantasy, Rix. There's no fairy godmother to enforce a curfew. Heyoka has agreed to let me stay as long as I feel is necessary, but I've got a job I have to get back to, so I can't stick around too long."

"Can you come back?"

"I can, but it's not going to be easy. Like I said, Heyoka doesn't like the idea at all. Probably the only reason he gave in this time is because we've been developing this interdimensional holographic projection system in the lab, and I convinced him this would be a good time to field test it."

"But, if he doesn't like the idea, why are you developing new systems like this? And, by the way, where is all the research leading? I mean, what's the ultimate goal?"

"There really isn't what I'd call an ultimate goal," she said. "Nor is this procedure new. We had it in place years ago. We never got around to field testing it because there was no immediate need. Like I told you back at the villa, our plan was to monitor you for a while before we moved ahead with any new experiments. We probably would have finished with the monitoring phase if it weren't for the fact that you kept doing things that could have a significant negative impact, and we needed to wait and see what that impact would be. Look, I'm not supposed to be talking about this stuff, so we need to move on to you and your problems."

"Right. Well, since you've been monitoring things, you probably know what's been going on."

"I don't monitor you twenty-four/seven," she said. "I have a life to live and other work to do. I check in every so often, and I can always backtrack if I think I might have missed something important. I also have an alarm system that alerts me whenever your metabolism goes haywire, like it did today and when you had that talk with Ellie. I thought you handled the news about Ellie pretty well, by the way. And I don't think you should worry about her attitude toward falling in love. That will change one day when she least expects it. I just hope it doesn't take as long as it did for me. If you hadn't come along I might still be waiting."

"Yeah," I said. "Me too. God, I wish I could touch you."

"Listen, we need to get off this and talk about some of the things that have been bothering you. For example," she said, "I don't think you should do anything to try and save Lennon."

"Oh? Why not?"

"Because Ellie's presence in his life will be enough to substantially alter his future. Think about it, he never met Ellie in your first life because she didn't exist. And you know the two of them have been talking about organizing a charity tour with Jackson Brown and some other big-name stars. This will cause significant changes in John's schedule, so it's doubtful he will be in the same place at the same time on December 8th, 1980. That's the date he was shot, by the way."

"I have thought about it," I said. "In fact, I've thought a lot about how what's happened might change things. The problem with your theory is that you're not looking past the first level of ripple effects. I know you don't have time to worry about extrapolating all the possibilities, but that's been my main focus ever since Doris talked me into that harebrained, eleventh-hour attempt to save Patsy. I don't ever want to do anything like that again without first considering all the things that might go wrong."

"Okay," she said. "Enlighten me."

"Well, I don't have any answers, but the way I see it, the situation is even more problematic than it was before. Just because John might not be there on that date doesn't mean Chapman won't still try to kill him. In fact, he was so obsessed with the idea I think we can count on it. And now that we've changed John's future, we no longer know when or where it will happen. To make matters worse, John and Ellie are apparently going to be working closely with each other for some time, and if she is with him when the shooting takes place she could be in jeopardy as well."

Thunder rolled in the distance and a few threads of lightning flashed from a rapidly approaching bank of clouds. "Looks like rain," she said, staring out over the bay. "I don't know, Rix. You're right that I didn't think this through, but there must be millions of possible permutations. And when you consider the way they could intertwine, the variables become almost infinite. We couldn't possibly predict the scenario that will ultimately emerge."

"That's exactly my point. It's what I've been worried about all along. We apparently lucked out with my dad and Patsy, but now we're looking at something that could end up getting Ellie killed, and there's no way to know how to intervene and make sure she's safe. Forget about John. It's Ellie I'm worried about now."

We watched in silence as the rain moved closer, and when the first drops slapped the sand at our feet, she sighed and shook her head.

"Pons asinorum," she said.

"Sorry?"

"It's a term used in Euclidean geometry for the isosceles triangle theorem. Translated from the Latin it means 'bridge of donkeys.'"

"Great. That explains everything," I said, a little angrier than I'd intended.

"It's also used as a metaphor for finding the middle term of a syllogism."

"Oh, well in that case—"

"Or to describe a problem that severely tests the ability of an inexperienced person to solve or extrapolate."

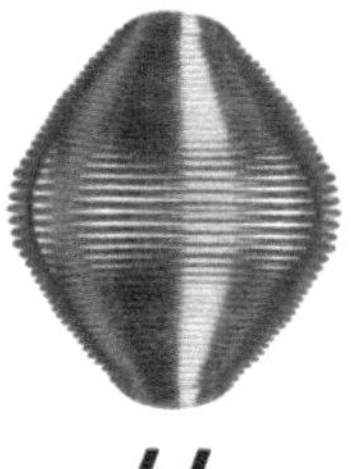

44

Running On Empty

In west-central Florida, afternoon rains do not glide across the landscape like misty bridal-veils; they roll in like giant exploding water balloons, often moving so fast they're gone before you can open your umbrella. If you have an umbrella. Which I didn't. This particular downpour emptied the park in a matter of seconds, then passed as quickly as it had come, leaving me drenched and steaming under the late-day sun. Had anyone looked closely, they might have noticed the raindrops disappearing into Aurie as if she were a human sponge, but they were all too busy running for shelter when we scrambled back over the seawall.

"How do you interact with this environment and make it look so real when you can't actually touch anything?" I asked as we walked across the wide expanse of grass toward the road.

"What you're seeing is a holograph projected from a virtual-reality system," she said. "I'm wearing a helmet, inside which your environment is visible in 3D all around me. I don't have to move, I manipulate my virtual double using mental imaging. It's not perfect—if you watch my feet, you can tell they're not compressing the blades of grass—but most people won't notice the flaws."

"Awesome," I said. Another clap of thunder threatened more rain, so I sprinted ahead and started across the street.

"Where are we going?" she said.

"Just follow me," I yelled, dodging a UPS truck and hitting the far sidewalk at a full run. I glanced back to make sure she was with me, then stopped dead. She had followed me, alright, directly into the path of the truck. The driver slammed on his breaks, but not before her trailing leg disappeared into his left front fender. Fortunately, the broad body of the panel truck obscured his view, and since he felt no impact, he drove on, honking his horn and shouting something unintelligible. Worried someone else might have seen what happened, I picked up the pace, pausing only when we approached the house.

Mom's car was parked out front, so I headed down the driveway to the old recording suite. I fumbled through the dozen or so keys I'd accumulated since moving to the new complex, found the one I was looking for, jammed it in the lock, and swung the door open. After locking the door behind us, I spun the rheostat and waited while the fluorescent bulbs flickered and came to life.

The squish of my sodden shoes echoed in the silence as we made our way through the empty reception area and into the abandoned studio. I adjusted the track lights, bathing the room in a dim saffron glow that illuminated the checkerboard of carpet-covered sound baffles Sam had strategically positioned around the walls. All that remained in the dusty chamber were a few scattered pieces of obsolete equipment: a microphone stand, a broken bass pedal, a hi-hat with one warped cymbal, and a wooden stool standing alone on the stained and mildewed Persian rug. I caught a glint of something metallic in the shadows near one wall, and when I went to investigate, I saw it was a reflection off the gold tuners of my old Ramirez flamenco. Thinking how strange it was that I hadn't touched my favorite instrument since before the move, I lifted the guitar and cradled it reverently, as if handling an ancient artifact from the museum of my past.

"How long has it been, Rix?" Aurie asked.

I set the instrument back on its stand and held my left hand up in the dim light, examining the smooth, uncalloused fingertips. "Too damn long," I said.

"Maybe you should do something about that."

"Wish I could," I sighed. "But I don't have the time or mental energy anymore."

"Really?" she said. "Seems to me someone in your position should be able to make the time. Surely there are key people you trust enough to delegate some of your responsibilities to."

"A couple," I said. "Problem is they don't have the time either. Sam's up to his neck managing the computer group, and Jimmy's working so many hours coordinating the studios I don't know when he finds time to sleep. The rest of my top people are specialists in their fields. None of them know enough about the parent corporation, nor could they command the respect my job calls for. Not that I deserve that respect—it's the position, not the person. But there are people—CEOs, politicians, industry leaders—who would be insulted if they were asked to deal with anyone other than the president of Blue Note Enterprises."

I picked up the guitar again and played a quick arpeggio on the open strings. "What's funny," I said, "is that all I really am is a glorified PR person, an executive inkslinger. I sign papers and move money around, deciding which projects to fund and how to invest the profits. My phone literally never stops ringing, and half my life is spent massaging egos and pretending to be someone I'd hate if I met him on the street. Doris does the important work, coordinating things and handling all the details. She's the glue that holds the company together. Without her I'd be dead in the water."

"But Rix," she said, "look at what you've accomplished. Think of the people you've helped, the fortune you've amassed. Those things have to count for something."

"Sure, there's a certain amount of satisfaction," I said, tuning the strings in rapid succession. "Although it has nothing to do with being rich. You know I've never cared about money. But now I have to because so much depends on me. I make decisions every day that could affect the lives of hundreds of people. It's a vicious circle, Aurie, a trap. And once you're in it there's no way out. For a while in the early days it was fun, then it seemed to take on a momentum of its own, and all I've done since then is hang on for dear life. It's almost as if I'm being punished for having known some things in advance. After all, that's what set the stage for everything."

"I don't think so," she said. "I'm sure it's just the natural outcome of the choices you've made. And I still say you could find a way to reduce your workload. In fact, if you don't you're liable to end up dead anyway, and I don't mean metaphorically. Have you thought about selling off some of the company so you can get back to the things you love—the music and working in the studio?"

"I have, but I feel like I'd be letting too many people down." I wandered over and stared up at my reflection in the darkened glass front of the mixdown booth. "Besides, I'm no longer needed in the studio. We've got a dozen of the best producers in the business on staff now, along with some excellent writers and extremely talented session people. Even when I do steal a few minutes to spend down there, I only get in the way. Everybody stiffens up when I'm around, as if I'm there to judge them. I don't think I could ever recapture the laid-back comradery of those early days."

"I'll bet you could if you acted the part," she said. "Stay out of the booth. Pick up your guitar and work as a sideman. Play some local gigs. Go on the road with Patsy or Jackson. You know they'd love to have you."

"I've thought about that, believe me." I turned and walked to the center of the room. "In fact, Jackson asked me to sit in back when he was laying down the tracks for ***Running on Empty***. Everything was all set when I got called away to New York for a conference about a possible acquisition. From there I had to fly to LA and meet with the principals of this independent film company, then fly back to New York for a bargaining session with a bunch of lawyers and accountants in order to finalize the deal. By the time I got home, the album was in post -production. Talk about running on empty. I don't know, Aurie, things are too damned complicated now. My whole goddamned life is too complicated. Hey, you should sit down," I said, nodding at the empty stool.

"I am sitting, remember? And the hologram doesn't need any rest. Why don't *you* sit down and play something?"

I shrugged, then sat on the stool, hooking my heels on the second rung and resting the guitar on my knee. I fooled around with some chords, but my heart wasn't in it. "Fingers don't work so good anymore," I said. "Anyway, let's forget about me and try to figure out what to do about stopping this Chapman character."

"I don't *know* what to do, Rix," She said. "Except try to look out for John and Ellie. Maybe you could hire some bodyguards."

"I seem to remember reading that John fired his bodyguards shortly before the shooting, so maybe he has a philosophical problem with that. Besides, as determined as Chapman was, I doubt a few musclemen would stop him. He's probably nuts enough to try a suicide bombing."

"You're right about John firing his bodyguards," she said. "It was three weeks before the shooting. And another thing, Chapman may be nuts but he's not stupid. He has an IQ of 121, which is considered in the superior range, a couple of notches above normal."

"Yeah, I—wait a minute. You looked him up. You looked both of them up. That's how you knew the date of the shooting. You've been thinking about this all along."

"So I did some Googling," she said with a smirk. "That doesn't mean I came up with anything useful. Even if I had, I don't think it would be a good idea to use the information in order to conduct some kind of history-changing intervention. John's death was a major event and the reverberations were felt worldwide. Who knows what might happen if we interfere and he lives another thirty or forty years?"

I noted she was now using the word "we," which suggested that the hard line she was taking probably wasn't quite as hard as she wanted me to believe. "Look," I said, "if it was anyone else—a scientist, say, or a political leader—I might agree with you, because someone like that would have a chance of changing the world for the worse. But Lennon? I can't see how prolonging his life could possibly lead to a negative outcome. He's a pacifist, for Christ's sake, a peacenik whose philosophy is centered around love and tolerance. If anything, his continued presence should have a positive effect on the world." I played a few bars of ***Give Peace a Chance*** to emphasize my point.

"I know that, Rix," she said. "But there's still no way to predict what would happen. He's already a controversial figure, and Yoko even more so. People change, you know. John's living proof of that. What if his next revelation turns him into a religious fanatic? Remember what happened with Cat Stevens? What if somewhere down the line John decides to embrace Islam and support the Taliban? Think of how his influence could affect world opinion."

"I seriously doubt that, Aurie," I said, transitioning smoothly to an instrumental rendition of ***Imagine***. "Look at what he's planning with Ellie. From what I gather it will be similar to Live Aid, and it's going to happen long before Bob Geldolf comes up with the idea, before the famine in Ethiopia gets out of hand. Bob's efforts were commendable, but they addressed situations only after they had become critical. Ellie and John could end up confronting the same problems in their early stages, focusing world attention on the famine and other matters in time to keep them from becoming full-blown disasters."

"I don't know," she said. "I still say it's a risky proposition"

"Maybe so," I said, "but given the circumstances, I think the risk to Ellie makes it imperative that we do something. And with your help, we should be able to come up with a plan that will minimize that risk, if not eliminate it altogether."

"My help?" she said. "Oh, no. Anyway, what could I do? Have you forgotten that I'm not really here?"

"Have *you* forgotten where you *are*, the tools you have at your disposal? All I have is a name and a date we can no longer rely on. You, on the other hand, have access to a huge store of historical data. I would bet there have been books written on Chapman, or at least news articles and published papers that include interviews with him and transcripts of his psychological evaluations. With that type of information we could not only locate him, but we might be able to figure out what he's going to do before he even knows for sure himself."

"Heyoka won't like it," she said.

"You can handle Heyoka," I said. "All you have to do is put on your stubborn-little-bitch persona—your words, not mine. Even if it takes a while, we've still got two years. Although I *will* need some time to come up with a plan. All you'd have to do is compile as much information on Chapman as possible and get it to me as soon as you can."

"Mmmnn," she murmured. "I don't know. I'll have to think about it."

"Think about it all you want. Just make sure you don't wait too long, because with or without your help, I'm going to do something. And if I'm wandering around in the dark, the possibility of disaster increases exponentially."

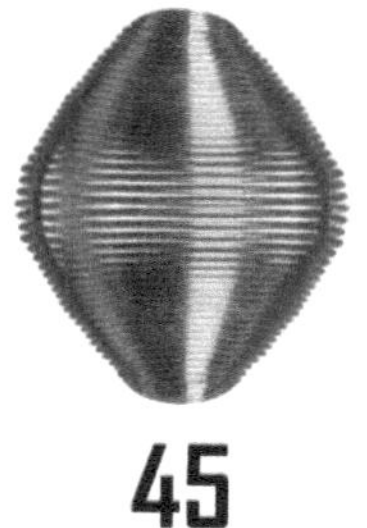

45
Homecoming

Aurélie didn't agree to lend a hand in researching Chapman. Instead, she steered the conversation back around to me and how disappointed she was that I'd decided to sacrifice my musical career for the business.

"It makes no sense to give up what you love in order to do things you hate," she said.

She was right, of course, but the fact that it made no sense didn't change the situation; I was still caught in a trap from which there seemed to be no escape. I did, however, promise her I would give it some serious thought. And when she again asked me to play something, I decided it would be a good way to get her off the subject.

Ignoring the pain in my fingertips, I managed a fair rendition of ***Parable***, and was winding up the closing guitar riff on ***The Lady Left Me With A Song*** when she began to shimmer and disappear. In the short time we'd been together I had allowed myself to get lost in the fantasy of her presence, and seeing her dematerialize before my eyes was devastating. I was staring at the empty space, dreading a return to the harsh reality of my life, when a crack of thunder shook the building and the room was plunged into darkness.

Unable to see in the pitch black, my thoughts turned inward, threatening to drive me deeper into depression. Desperate for some way to maintain control of my emotions, I tried to channel the anger and frustration through my fingers, attacking the guitar with every ounce of energy I had. I played through the pain with astonishing speed and intensity, challenging the thunder with song after song until the lights flickered and sprung back to life.

OVER THE NEXT FEW days I walked around in a fog, performing my job like a robot and waiting for Aurélie to contact me. But as the days turned into weeks and the weeks into months, I began to lose hope. Meanwhile, thoughts of Chapman were once again pushed to the back of my mind by an endless barrage of mind-numbing meetings, ass-kissing negotiations, and financial headaches that threatened to drive me back to the house of Jack Daniels. I might have taken that drive were it not for the fact that I had no time to deal with drunkenness or hangovers.

The only bright spots in the months following Aurélie's visit were Ellie's weekly phone calls, during which she would give me a brief update on school ("Dirac is weird ... grades are perfect ... social life is minimal.") then light into an excited report on her plans with John. By the summer of 1978, she'd secured commitments from Jackson, Stevie Wonder, and Ray Charles, while cajoling Patsy to use her Nashville connections to draw in Willie Nelson, Dolly Parton, and a slew of other country stars. Though she never came right out and said it, I could tell Ellie's enthusiasm for academia was waning, and it didn't surprise me at all when she decided to skip the summer trimester and come home to work on the logistics of the charity tour.

She arrived a week before her seventeenth birthday, full of energy and as feisty and beautiful as ever. I did, however, occasionally catch a glimpse of a more contemplative Ellie, one who seemed restless and a little confused. We hadn't spoken at length about her personal life since our talk on her fifteenth birthday, so after giving her a few of weeks to get reacquainted with the studio gang and check out what Sam was up to, I suggested we take a walk.

The air was humid as we strolled hand-in-hand along the waterfront, dodging yellow flies and slapping at mosquitoes in the early twilight. We made small talk at first, but after a while we ran out of trivia and I decided to broach the subject of her future.

"I haven't made up my mind yet, Dad," she said when I asked what her long-range plans were. "I've got a lot of ideas, and I need to get them sorted out before I make any concrete plans. The tour is a start, but after that there are so many problems that need to be addressed it's going to be hard to set priorities."

It fascinated me how she'd never lost that little-girl desire to take on the problems of the world. Although, thankfully, she'd matured enough to realize she couldn't fix everything and would have to do some prioritizing. I didn't press her on that, but I couldn't keep from inquiring about her love life.

"I got the physical kinks worked out a few months ago," she said, watching my face for a reaction. I managed to maintain a neutral expression, so she shrugged. "Thing is, I don't have much time to devote to intimate relationships. I've had a couple of lovers, but there isn't anyone special. Finding someone who's good in bed and who's also on my mental wavelength is not easy. Especially when he has to deal with my somewhat unemotional approach to lovemaking. For now I think of sex as entertainment, like going to an art museum or listening to good music."

Her attitude still worried me, but she seemed so well-adjusted and sure of herself, I couldn't think of any way to argue. She acted—at least outwardly—like a typical 17-year-old girl, shopping with her mother, joking around with the guys in the studio, even flirting a little with some of the newer musicians. And she apparently felt comfortable enough with her own identity not to need the isolation she'd once craved, because she'd moved back into her old room at the big house.

Dad retired a month before Ellie came home, and after he and Mom spent a little time with her, they took off with Doris's parents for an extended trip to Europe and Asia. Maybe it was because the house now seemed so empty with only the three of us there, or maybe Ellie and Doris had entered some sort of mother-daughter phase where their relationship underwent a natural change—whatever it was, the two of them spent a lot more time together than they ever had when Ellie was growing up. Before, Doris had always seemed intimidated by Ellie's intellect, but now they were almost joined at the hip, working together on financial aspects of the tour, and sometimes shutting themselves off behind closed doors.

This new and seemingly more intimate connection between them, while certainly welcome, was also a little disconcerting, bringing on an irrational feeling of jealousy and sometimes leading me to wonder what they were talking about that required so much privacy. I didn't have to wonder for long, however, because one day Ellie came into my office, locked the door behind her, and proceeded to knock my socks off with the answer.

46

Conspiracy

I was on the phone with Sam when Ellie showed up at my office. She listened for a few minutes to my side of the conversation, pretending to read the sports page I'd left open on the desk. When her patience ran out, she folded the paper, dropped it in the wastebasket, and walked over to take the receiver from my hand.

"Hey, Sam," she said. "It's Ellie. Listen, I hate to interrupt you guys, especially when you're talking football, but I've got something I need to talk to Dad about, so could you give us a half hour or so? Yes, I understand Doug Williams is going to be out for the rest of the season, but this is a little more important than news about the Bucs. Thanks, buddy, I owe you one." She handed the receiver back to me, then sat on the edge of the desk.

"What's up, kiddo?" I said.

She raised an eyebrow and smiled. "The jig," she said. "The jig is what's up Dad."

"And what jig would that be?" I said, thinking this was some kind of joke. "Don't tell me you finally found out I'm an imposter and that your real dad was Jimmy Hoffa?"

Shaking her head slowly, as if admonishing a child, she said, "I'd love to keep up this banter, but I'm afraid what I need to tell you doesn't lend itself very well to humor."

"Oh, God. Please don't tell me you're pregnant. I can't handle another—"

"Dad!" she said, "I'm not pregnant, I'm not getting married, I don't have a venereal disease, and I don't have cancer. Unfortunately, this is far more serious than that."

"More serious than cancer?" I said. "What could be more serious than cancer?"

"I found Mom's diaries, Dad—her journals, as she calls them. Four volumes full of single-spaced, typewritten pages chronicling everything, starting from that day in 1960 when you two met at the park on Coffee Pot Bayou."

"I see," I said. I knew about Doris's journals, but the significance of what Ellie was saying hadn't quite sunk in yet. "So, was there anything embarrassing? I can't imagine your mother writing any graphic details about our sex life. I mean, you know how she ..." When I saw the look in Ellie's eyes, it suddenly dawned on me what she was talking about. "Oh, holy shit," I said, "You don't mean—"

"That's exactly what I mean, Mr. Vaughn. So I think—how did you put it? Oh, yeah, I think it's time we had a little talk."

OUR 'LITTLE TALK' ENDED up being nothing of the kind. For one thing, Doris's journals turned out to be incredibly detailed. Not only had she faithfully chronicled the evolution of our relationship, she'd transcribed my narrative confessions as if she'd been taking shorthand while I spoke. When Ellie confronted her, Doris lost it, breaking down in tears and screaming at Ellie for invading her privacy. After she calmed down, she tried to claim that the journal entries were notes she was making for a novel she intended to write.

"She swore that's what they were," Ellie said, "and she made me promise not to tell you because she said you might get upset with her. But why would you be upset with her for writing a novel? Besides, they explained a lot of things—how you, as a teenager, managed to seduce an older woman, the little bugs you put in Sam's ear about recording innovations and computers, your ability to write and arrange at such a young age. Even what happened with Patsy. Anyway, after I convinced her I wasn't buying that story, we had a long talk, and she said she'd planned to tell me when I was older. Turns out she'd always thought I should know, but she wanted to tell me in her own words, not have me find out by reading her journals."

"What difference would that make?" I said, still trying to figure out how to deal with the news. "Obviously the journals were far more detailed than any conversation would be."

"Yes," she said, "and that was the problem. She didn't mind so much my learning the truth about you. What she did mind was that I'd read all the intimate stuff about you guys. And boy that was some read. She may be shy about openly discussing sex, but she spared nothing in describing what went on between you two in the bedroom. And when she found out I'd read all that, she was so embarrassed and angry she went off on me."

Ellie's revelation hit me like a sledgehammer. My first impulse was to deny everything, but when I saw that familiar look of unyielding determination in her eyes, I knew there was no chance I could lie my way out of this one. My sudden brain freeze must have been evident, because she reached out to hug me.

"Everything's going to be okay, Dad," she said. "I'm not mad at you, and I can certainly understand why you didn't want me to know. Mom and I talked it over after she calmed down, and we both think it was for the best. In fact, you'd be amazed at how much she's loosened up with me now that we have no secrets. We've been getting along famously ever since, talking about things we never would have before and brainstorming about the future. By the way, I know quite a bit about quantum mechanics and the theory of alternate universes, although I'm a little lean on Native American religious rituals. I plan to do some research on the subject so I can get a better grip on this Heyoka character. Sounds like a pretty eccentric fellow to me."

"He was—is, I guess. I'm sure you'd find him fascinating."

"And his sidekick sounds a lot like me. Math whiz and all. Extremely logical. I'd love to meet him someday, though I guess that's impossible."

"Her," I said.

"Her? I thought the guy's name was Fred.

I was wondering what she meant, until I remembered that in my narrative I'd substituted Fred for Aurélie. Ellie didn't know it, but she was actually talking about her namesake. "Yeah," I said, "Fred. It's short for, uh ... Frederica. You'd be amazed at how much you two are alike. So, okay, now you know. It doesn't change anything, though. I mean, I'm still your dad and I still love you. All the other stuff is water under the bridge. We can put it behind us and move on, right?"

I didn't like the look in her eyes; it suggested that all the water had not quite passed under the proverbial bridge. In fact, it looked downright conspiratorial.

"Well," she said, "I don't think so. You see, Mom and I talked about a lot of other stuff, too. Like how reluctant you've been to use your knowledge of the future to stop bad things from happening. We both think you're being too conservative, especially when it comes to saving John's life."

I wasn't sure how to respond, but I figured since she already knew what was going on there was no reason to avoid the subject. "I've changed my mind about that," I said. "I don't have a definite plan in place, but I'm not going to let it happen. Things are going to unfold differently now that you're in the picture, and that will introduce a whole new set of variables, making it almost impossible to predict what Chapman will do. I'm working on it, though."

"Can I help?" she asked.

"Maybe," I said. "I'll let you know if I think of anything you can do. Meanwhile, I want to work on it myself, at least until I come up with a basic plan."

"Okay," she said. "Now there are a few other things we need to talk about."

"Oh, no," I groaned. "Don't do this to me Ellie. I know what you—"

"Hear me out, Dad. Please. Mom told me about your fear of not being able to forecast the overall impact of changes you might choose to make in the flow of history. So I've spent the last couple of months researching the science of forecasting, studying the work of experts in the field like Willi Dansgaard, John Nash, Eric Siegel and others. I've been working on this from a mathematical perspective, and I've developed some pretty exciting algorithms that can create highly reliable, long-term forecasts for almost any set of circumstances."

I realized that now I was really in for it. Doris had been a formidable opponent, but with Ellie on her side I would be seriously outgunned.

"You're messing with Sasquatch," I said.

"I'm what?" she asked. "This has nothing to do with mythology."

"Sorry, that was a euphemism. What I meant was you're playing with fire. You and your mom have no idea what the consequences of intervening in history will be. Some things are going to happen that all your scientific algorithms and naïve theories couldn't begin to foresee in detail, and there's no way to predict the consequences when something we do interacts with those events."

"Not necessarily," she said. "Look, I know this is probably going to be way over your head, but maybe you can grasp a little of it. My algorithms are based on a technique called logistic regression. Using this, I can analyze available statistical data to conduct what mathematicians and futurists call predictive modeling. It's not perfect, I'll admit that, but it's really only restricted by the size of the data base and the fact that we don't have specific known target events to analyze. With your help, however, we *will* have those target events, plus information about how things originally evolved. And with Sam's advances in computing power, we can build data bases large enough to make reasonable predictions about the impact of any intervention we decide to make. We could accomplish a lot, Dad. Maybe save millions of lives. Maybe even change the course of human history for the better."

"Regardless of whether or not I understand what you're talking about, the key word here is 'reasonable,'" I said. "Millions of *reasonable* assumptions have been proven wrong in the past. What you're not taking into consideration is a little thing called chaos theory, otherwise known as the butterfly effect. There's an element of randomness in the way things evolve, and that randomness is impossible to anticipate. Playing around with future events means experimenting, Ellie, and experimenting by definition means taking actions for which you do not know the ultimate outcome."

"That's true," she said. "Certain aftereffects may be impossible to predict precisely, but they are not impossible to predict in a general sense. Granted, there's some gambling involved, but every decision we make is a type of gamble. When you see someone drowning and you dive in to save that person, you're gambling your own life to change an outcome. Do you let that stop you? There are never any guarantees, Dad, only educated guesses, and those guesses are based on how we analyze the available data."

Her words were startlingly similar to something Aurélie had said. The difference was that Aurie would not be arguing *for* large-scale intervention; she would be arguing *against* it. At least I assumed she would. Her reluctance to help me deal with Chapman seemed to confirm that.

"I see what you're saying," I said. "But you're forgetting one small detail."

"Oh, what's that?"

"Scale," I said. "You're not taking into consideration the potential impact of interventions that could affect large numbers of people. If I jump in to save someone from drowning and I die trying, that only involves two people. But when you scale that up to, say, attempting to do something that will save millions of lives, as you suggest, the potential impact is exponentially larger, and a larger scale means a wider butterfly effect. What if one of those people you save kills someone who was slated to do something earthshaking, like inventing a cold-fusion power generator or discovering a cure for cancer? Even using the largest data base in the universe you wouldn't be able to predict every possible outcome."

"That may be true," she said, "but the same thing applies at any scale, and it works both ways. For example, what if that one person you saved from drowning turns out to be a mass murderer or the carrier of a new communicable disease that causes a worldwide epidemic? Anticipating the worst is one thing, but there's a difference between anticipation and paranoia. Based on your timorous theory of non-intervention, no one should ever do anything to intervene in even a single person's fate."

Her disease example reminded me that I'd failed to mention the AIDs pandemic when I was listing major events for Doris. Having lived under the shadow of HIV for so long in my first life, I'd forgotten that the crisis was yet to come in this one. And when I realized this, I began to wonder if there was any way I could warn the medical community of the looming threat. Obviously Ellie's arguments were getting to me or I wouldn't even be entertaining such an idea, and the fact that I *had* made it clear that I needed time to think before continuing the debate. I was trying to come up with a plausible reason to postpone our conversation when my eyes were drawn to the flashing lights on my phone.

"We're going to have to continue this another time," I said, pointing at the phone, which was lit up like a Christmas tree. "Janet will kill me if I don't start taking some of these calls. I'll think about what you've said, and maybe we can come up with a compromise. But right now, I have to get back to work."

"You're not getting out of this by putting it off," she said, kissing me on the forehead and ruffling my hair affectionately. "I'll let you off the hook for now, but I want to talk about it again soon." She was halfway to the door when she stopped and looked back. "Oh, and that traffic jam of a phone? That's something else we need to discuss. Mom and I both think you need to back off before you have a nervous breakdown."

After she left, I reached up to smooth my hair, and was shocked when my fingers touched bare skin. In my first life I'd kept a full head of hair into my late sixties, and now I was losing it in my thirties? I jerked my hand away and hesitated for a moment before reluctantly lowering it toward the row of flashing buttons. But instead of pressing one, I found myself lifting the phone off the desk. I held it in the air for a moment, then jerked the wires loose and threw it across the room. Janet opened the door just as I let it fly, and she watched calmly as it crashed against the wall and landed at her feet.

"Phone's broke," I said.

"Yes. I see," she said, staring at the jumble of wires and splintered plastic. "Well, you weren't answering it anyway. I'll call the phone company. Meanwhile, you have some visitors."

"Tell them I died. And cancel the rest of my appointments."

"They didn't have an appointment, but you might want to reconsider," she said.

"I don't care if it's the King and Queen of England, I'm not seeing anyone."

"Odd looking couple," she said, ignoring me. "Grizzled old Indian with a twinkle in his eye and smile like a neon sign. Wife looks a little like Brigitte Bardot. Said they'd like to take you to Coney Island for lunch, so I figured they must know you pretty well."

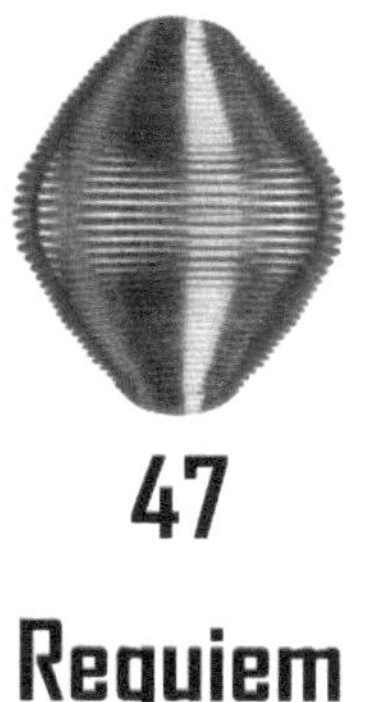

47
Requiem

Morning sunlight painted a pastel kaleidoscope on the majestic cupola above the choir loft. Sculpted to resemble the cupped hands of God, the once-chalk-white façade had yellowed over time, transforming the stained-glass reflections into an undulating, milky smear. As Carol Henderson's fingers fluttered over the three-tiered keyboard below, somber notes from unseen pipes rumbled through the sanctuary like melodic thunder.

It had been nearly two years since I'd sat in these time-burnished mahogany pews; two years, in fact, since I'd given more than a fleeting thought to things religious. My parents had fallen in love with the Mediterranean on their trip overseas, eventually deciding to return and live out their retirement in a small house on the coast of Italy. So I'd taken the opportunity to stop attending church, since my adherence to that ritual had been maintained only for their sake. Primarily out of respect for her mother, Ellie had continued to accompany Doris on Sunday mornings, while I took those precious few hours of relief from the business to sleep in.

My daughter now sat beside me, our fingers intertwined in a moist, fretful grasp, as we fought against the grief that threatened to overpower us at any moment. Though flanked on either side by my folks and Ellie's maternal grandparents, and surrounded by friends and extended family members, we nonetheless seemed isolated, as if imprisoned in our own private world of despair.

Reminded by the brick-hard, butt-numbing contours of the unpadded bench, I recalled those Sundays of my youth when I was forced to sit—without fidgeting or making a sound—and listen to the scary, hellfire-and-damnation ranting of our evangelic minister. I'd learned back then to concentrate on the wavering colors as they mingled with reflections from the water of the baptistery. And so far this morning I had managed to remain stoic by doing just that. But as Carol led the choir in a powerful, tear-jerking rendition of ***Amazing Grace***, Ellie's grip tightened, and I found I could no longer avoid glancing down at the velvet-draped bier that stood in front of the podium. Once my eyes came to rest on the gold-trimmed, alabaster casket, covered in a profusion of candy-striped carnations, my emotional control dissolved like so much tissue paper in a churning whitewater of sadness and remorse.

I'd tried without success to forgive myself, not only for being unable to anticipate the depth of Chapman's lunacy, but for the years I'd spent perpetuating the self-serving fantasy of loving two women without slighting one. I'd justified this by telling myself they were different kinds of love: one a spontaneous, uncontrollable infatuation that grew and strengthened until it became an inseparable part of my soul; the other born of friendship and sexual desire, leavened over the years by loyalty and respect and appreciation. Had there been any choice, I would certainly have chosen Aurélie, but knowing the impossibility of that relationship, I'd done my best to dedicate myself to Doris.

It wasn't as if I'd attempted to deceive her; she'd been aware early on that there was someone else. And she had accepted this dichotomy without a trace of bitterness, resigning herself to the fact that she would have to share my affection with another. Oh, she would occasionally refer to it in a jokingly sarcastic—though never spiteful or quarrelsome—way: "That mysterious woman from your former life, what was her name again?" she'd say, knowing I would never answer the question. Then she would smile and add some mildly threatening declaration, like, "Well, if I ever have an affair, I won't tell you his name either." At times, I almost wished she had taken a lover; at least that would have evened the score a bit and alleviated some of my guilt. But that wasn't Doris. Despite those flippant and mildly acerbic comments, her commitment to the marriage had never wavered from the day she'd accepted my somewhat awkward proposal.

"I'm not blind," she'd said. "I know there's someone else in your heart, someone who's miles ahead of me." Then, as if to justify her decision to marry me, she added, "I also know that you care for me, maybe even love me a little, so I'm willing to take what I can get."

From that moment on, I'd tried to devote my life to Doris, and later to both her and Ellie. In a way, I'd succeeded, at least when it came to outward appearances and my conduct within the closed circle of our family. Inside, however, Aurélie continued to hold first chair in the orchestra that played privately to my heart. It was an affair without fulfillment, one that not only frustrated, but that often left me feeling as if I were in love with a ghost or was plagued by a phantom limb that itched but could never be scratched. And now, as I stared at my wife's closed casket, the guilt I'd carried for that silent betrayal tortured me with unrelenting shame.

The last two years had been the hardest.

Shortly after Aurélie and Heyoka surprised me by showing up at the office, Aurélie had made her virtual self available to me almost any time I'd needed her. Unfortunately, this new, unrestricted access was precipitated by a tragic turn of events in their world, one that seemed destined to result in catastrophe. Still, I cherished every moment Aurie and I were together, even though not being able to touch her was exasperating. But the worst part, the thing that threatened to destroy what little remained of my self-esteem, was being forced to tell Ellie and Doris the truth.

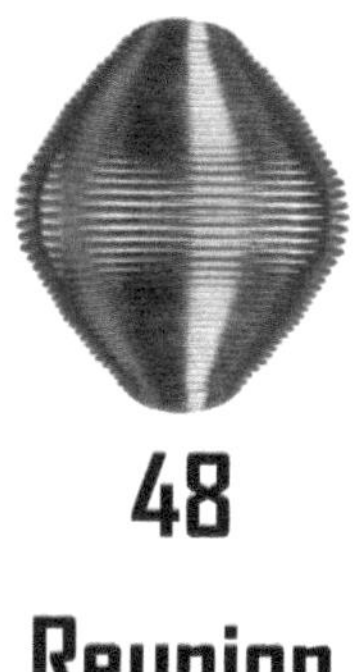

48

Reunion

After ushering Heyoka and Aurélie into my office, Janet lingered in the open doorway pretending to examine her nails. "Thank you Janet," I growled. "That will be all. And please hold my calls."

"Don't have to," she said as she shut the door behind her. "Phone's broke, remember?"

Heyoka glanced at the remnants of the phone, then gave me an inquiring look.

"Little accident," I said with a shrug. "Got run over by an attitude adjustment." Even though deep down I was thrilled to see both of them, the anger and frustration that led to the phone's demise had not yet subsided. "Sorry," I added, forcing a smile. "Caught me at a bad time. Come in. Come in."

"Hello Rix," Heyoka said. "How've you been?"

"How have I been," I mused. "Well, if you mean fiscally, I've been fine. Hell, I've got more money than Scrooge McDuck, for all the good it does me. Other than that, I'd say I'm hovering somewhere between a jail cell and a mental hospital. How about you? I must say you're looking good. Haven't aged a bit. Have you come up with some kind of anti-aging concoction?"

"Actually," he said, "that's one of the things we've been working on in our genetics division, though it's still in the experimental stages. As for me, ugly old red men don't tend to get much uglier with age. I was wondering if we could go somewhere more private so we can talk for a while without worrying about being interrupted. Aurélie is a little more adept at this virtual projection thing than I am, and I'd hate for someone to burst in and find me floating six inches off the floor with my leg stuck through a chair."

"I guess that means Coney Island is out," I said. "Why didn't you just pop in here directly and bypass Janet?"

"We wanted to avoid the shock factor," said Aurélie. "Seeing as how you were already approaching basket-case status."

"Right. Okay, how about if we try the old studio again? There's nobody at the house now. Mom and Dad are in Europe, and Doris is stuck in her office as usual. Not sure where Ellie is, but she's not likely to show up at the empty studio. Of course, you'll have to walk out of here with me, or Janet will wonder what happened to you. Think you can handle that?"

Heyoka looked a little uneasy, but Aurélie said, "Come on, old man. You made it in, you can make it out."

As we passed Janet's desk, I said, "We're going to Coney Island. And then I want to take these folks on a little tour around town. Probably won't be back this afternoon so—"

"I know. I know." She flashed a plastic smile at Heyoka and Aurélie. "If anybody asks, you got hit by a meteor."

YOU'LL HAVE TO HOLD the door open for us again," Aurélie said as I led them down the hall to the nearest exit. Once outside, Heyoka finally seemed to relax, and we made our way to the house without incident. Still nursing nightmare memories of my last visit to the abandoned studio, I suggested we stop off in the reception area, where an ancient couch and a few overstuffed chairs remained.

"I know you guys don't need to sit," I said as I settled into one of the chairs, "but I'd feel a lot more comfortable if you could fake it for me." Aurélie waited while Heyoka did his best to assume a realistic-looking posture on the couch, then she came over and 'sat' on the arm of my chair.

"Great," I said. "Much better. Now to what do I owe this joint visitation?"

"It's a little complicated to explain," Heyoka said, "so let me start back a ways. As you know, I've been reluctant to let Aurélie interfere with your new life, mainly because I wanted to keep the initial phase of the experiment clean, letting things evolve without our influence. But now we both feel it's time we moved to a more advanced stage."

"Advanced stage?" I said.

"What he means," said Aurélie, "is we want to see if we can help you make some deliberate alterations in the course of history. Starting with the Lennon situation."

"Why the sudden change of heart?" I asked.

She glanced at Heyoka, then back at me. "Well," she said, "for one thing, this isn't really a change of heart, nor is it sudden. The thing is, we haven't been totally honest with you, Rix. There were good reasons, though, and once you hear them I think—I hope—you'll understand."

"Hope springs infernal," I said, deliberately adulterating the tired cliché. "Can't wait."

"Okay." She looked at the floor and cleared her throat. "Here it is. You've asked me many times where all this research was leading, and I've always claimed it was more-or-less intended to gather data, with no specific goal in mind. But things have changed somewhat dramatically over the past few years. The compiling of data has worked out better than we could have hoped. We've been able to observe the changes you've made and compare the results to your first life, which we mapped from your memories while you were with us."

I gave a noncommittal shrug.

"The part I failed to mention," she continued, "was that another objective was to use the data to help us develop reliable methods of predicting how certain deliberate actions would interact with and change the future. Then we hoped to use those methods to forecast the impact our scientific and technological advancements might have on the future of our own world. Unfortunately, the actions you've taken so far have not been of sufficient magnitude to provide us with the information we need. And that's where you can be of help to us. Not only you, but Ellie as well."

"Ellie?" I said. "You're kidding."

"Not at all. You may not realize it, but your daughter has some unique talents, not only in the realm of theoretical mathematics, but in the pristine way her mind works, never dismissing an idea simply because it might appear impossible given the scientific parameters dictated by currently accepted theories. Anyway, it appears she has been able to do what we have failed to do so far by coming up with some advanced algorithms for forecasting the long-term impact of specific events."

"Far out," I said. "She told me a little about that, but I blew it off as so much wishful thinking. And what do you mean my actions have not been of sufficient magnitude? I thought you were worried about some of them being just the opposite."

"Another minor deception, I'm afraid," said Heyoka, "intended to keep you from going off half-cocked and doing something earthshaking before we were capable of evaluating the potential consequences. Now, however, with you seemingly intent on saving Lennon's life, we feel this is something that could have major repercussions. Frankly, I wasn't aware of the influence he'd had on a large portion of the worldwide populace. His passivity—swaying opinions at the grass-roots level with his music and educating more-or-less by example, rather than establishing a broad, political powerbase—led me to believe he was far less influential that he was, or would be if he were to live longer. But Aurélie has convinced me I was mistaken."

"So, are you saying Aurélie was right, that saving Lennon could have a significant effect on the future?" I looked at Aurie. "And what about you? Weren't you worried about John morphing into some sort of Islamic militant."

"Not really," she said. "I was only arguing with you in order to stall. At the time, we had yet to produce a reliable formula for predicting long-term ramifications. In fact, until I saw what Ellie was up to, we hadn't come up with anything that would provide us with more than a list of vague probabilities. She really is incredible, Rix. In a very short time, she's pulled together dozens of ideas and techniques, discarded some, refined others, and merged the results into an amalgam that's led to an astonishing set of predictive algorithms. What we need to do now is test those algorithms, not only by conducting experiments here in this dimension, but by creating computer simulations. With our computing capabilities, we can do complex modeling impossible at this time in your world. But in order to proceed, I'm going to have to consult with Ellie in person."

"In person?" I said. "That's going to be awkward. She doesn't even know you exist. I told her—"

"I know what you told her, Rix. She thinks I'm Fred. But that's going to have to change, which is why we wanted to talk to you first."

"Frederica," I said. The thought of Ellie learning about my relationship with the woman whose name she shared shot cold ribbons of fear up my spine. Not only was that prospect terrifying, it also meant Doris would find out I'd been secretly meeting with Aurie. "Is that absolutely necessary right now?" I asked, hoping for a way to at least delay things while I figured out how to deal with this unexpected twist of fate.

"I'm afraid so, Rix," Heyoka said. "We're at a critical time—a watershed moment, you might say—in our universe. And we're in urgent need of your and Ellie's help."

"Critical? Watershed? Those are pretty powerful words, but they don't really tell me much. Maybe you could explain what's happening in a little more detail?"

Heyoka looked at Aurie, obviously hoping she would step up to the plate. When she gave a quick jerk of her head to indicate he should take this one, he waited a few seconds to make sure she wasn't going to change her mind, then pinched the bridge of his gigantic nose and sighed. "I hate to bore you with another one of my long stories, but a comprehensive explanation is going to require a foundation, so please don't think I'm being condescending if I start with some basics."

"Condescend all you like," I said. "I never argue with simplicity."

"Yes, well then ... Let's see. Say we look at the unfolding narrative of reality as a river." He swept a hand through the air, wiggling his fingers in a childish imitation of flowing water. "Time, like the water, flows in one direction, from the past through the present into the future, creating a continuum that is constantly being shaped and reshaped by events, both naturally occurring and those that originate with human intelligence and creativity. I draw this dividing line because, were it not for the development of human intelligence, what we think of as the *natural* world would have evolved quite differently. So we might look at human-created events as being outside the norm, perhaps analogous to colorful, flavored pebbles tossed into the natural flow at different points, where they interact with the water and with each other, slowly dissolving and adding their colors and flavors to the overall mix." He hesitated to see if I was following.

"Got it," I said. "Go on."

"Okay. Good. Now if the pebbles are small enough, their impact on the continuum will be minimal, in some cases disappearing with hardly a trace and leaving little or no evidence of their existence. The larger they are, however, the longer and more powerfully they exert their influence on the future, and the more potential they have to cause negative or positive consequences. The really big ones, say the size of boulders instead of pebbles, can actually divert the flow, steering it away from its original trajectory, sometimes with catastrophic results."

"Examples?" I said.

"Examples," he repeated. "Well, a few of the more consequential events might include things like the discovery of the wheel, or the evolution of the opposable thumb, or the splitting of the atom."

"Don't see any catastrophes there."

"No, not yet. In your world at least. But take the splitting of the atom. On one hand, it seemed to be a boon to humankind, providing new methods of energy production and insights into the nature of matter that laid the groundwork for the computer age. On the other, it nearly led to nuclear holocaust, not to mention that the hope for an unlimited, safe source of energy turned out to be overly optimistic. And you are still left with a looming shadow of nuclear devastation. Even the wheel. Although its discovery did, in part, lead to the industrial revolution, the ramifications of that revolution have threatened to turn the planet into an uninhabitable hunk of rock by destroying the entire ecosphere."

"Not to go all Zen on you," I said, "but isn't that sort of the way of the world, so to speak? You know, the yin-yang factor? That balancing act Aurie's always talking about?"

"It is," he said. "But let me go back to the idea that human intelligence is—in some views at least—an aberration, not part of the natural flow of things. At any rate, our technology is advancing at such a rapid pace that anticipating its possible negative impacts has become more important and more difficult than ever before. What's happened in our universe—and may eventually happen in yours—is that most of the scientific community was too busy inventing and discovering and innovating to worry much about the downside.

"For the most part, this didn't pose a great problem, because of the incremental advancement of science and technology. But every once in a while, something comes along that represents a leap for which society is not adequately prepared. For example, Crick and Watson's discovery of the helical structure of DNA, which led to genetic mapping and a host of exciting innovations in medical science, genetic engineering, and so on. The problem was, too few scientists and politicians were willing to look on the dark side, and now we are paying the price."

"We are? In what way?'

"He doesn't mean you, Rix," Aurélie said. "He means us. You keep forgetting that we are many years ahead of you. The fact is, things aren't going so good in our universe, and some of that is our fault. We've been guilty of the same kind of blind disregard, not taking time to develop the means for calculating the consequences before releasing some of our findings to the public. That's why we need Ellie's help. And yours as well."

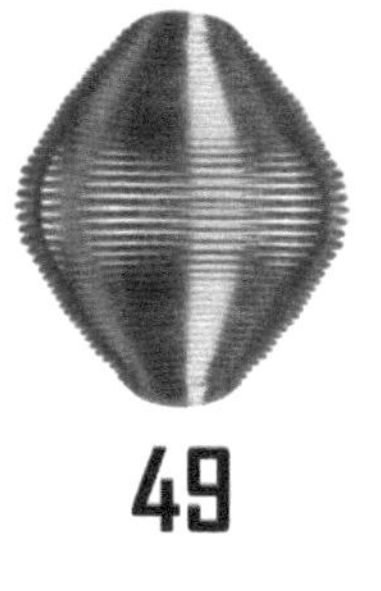

49

Terra Infirma

The picture Aurélie and Heyoka drew of their world could have come from any of a hundred science fiction films: a dark, barren landscape, littered with the remnants of a once-promising, technologically-advanced society; a society that, because of the unrestrained exploitation of scientific discoveries and the failure of its leaders to act expediently, eventually imploded, leaving in its wake a social and ecological nightmare. Heyoka's description of the world I left behind wasn't quite that bleak, though there was no doubt it was well on its way. And all the hoped-for remedies, the promises that somehow science would figure things out in time, were turning out to be too little too late.

International squabbles had kept solutions to catastrophic climate change from being implemented; genetic engineering had led to a reduction in biodiversity, allowing plant diseases to cripple crop yields across the planet; portable nuclear weapons and tactical human pathogen attacks had transformed terrorism from a manageable threat into a global phenomenon of devastating proportions. Even the digital revolution and the worldwide proliferation of social media had its downside, with terrorists building their ranks through the Internet, and state-sponsored hackers wreaking havoc by shutting down power grids, water supplies, and financial systems around the world.

The thrust of Heyoka's research had long ago turned from technological innovation to strategies for ameliorating the results of government complacency and the rise of corporate power. However, in light of the unforeseen consequences of unbridled scientific advancement, he had withheld many of his breakthroughs for fear they might prove catastrophic in the long run. It was the lack of a reliable method of forecasting that altered his original intentions for the interdimensional research that had led to my resurrection. Though at first designed only to explore the parameters of his unique insights and abilities, and to observe and document the results of my actions, the urgency of the moment had taken precedence over simple data collection. And now, with Ellie's apparent accomplishments in the science of forecasting, he wanted to use our dimension as an active, global laboratory, in which to conduct real-time, empirical studies.

Although they tried to make me feel as if my cooperation would be essential, it was clear to me that my role would be miniscule when compared to Ellie's. I could do specific things, and the short-term results could be analyzed, but from the way they described the situation in their world, there wasn't time to wait for long-term consequences to evolve. The data collected would be valuable in helping prove or disprove the validity of Ellie's methodologies; however, refining her algorithms and testing them with computer modeling was obviously the most important part of the plan.

"I guess you could look at it that way," Heyoka said in response to my suggestion that I would continue to serve as little more than a lab rat. "Although you should know that my original intentions were not quite as mercenary as you seem to be suggesting. We never hid the fact that this was an experiment, Rix. Nor did we hide our intention to monitor you in order to document the impact of your actions. And my choice of you as our subject was not based solely on our needs, but yours as well. You are, by the way, still in control of the situation. You can choose to help us or not. We couldn't forcibly interfere with your life if we wanted to. We can suggest, advise, even cajole a little, but we have no physical presence in this universe, so we cannot make you do anything, or cause anything to happen ourselves."

He was right, of course, but for some reason I still felt used. It was similar to the way I felt about the business: that it was in control of my present and therefore my future; the tail wagging the dog, so to speak.

"So," I said, trying to quell my growing anger, "what do you want from me? I mean, you're obviously trying to make me feel important, as if I have something wonderful to contribute. But I don't really see it. If what you're saying about Ellie is true, then what good am I in this scenario?"

"Without you, Rix," Aurie said, "There would be no real-time results to evaluate. Although it was not in our original plans—couldn't have been because we had no idea how your life would turn out—the fact that you have become such a wealthy and influential person makes you indispensable. You can do things few others can, things that could have an enormous sociopolitical impact on the future of your world. Ellie is a genius, and we need her to help us forecast the repercussions of your actions so we can compare them to the actual outcomes, but only you can provide the raw material to be evaluated. The short-term results will form a baseline from which we can use Ellie's algorithms and our computer modeling to extrapolate the long-term effects. And the first of these experiments will be your efforts—along with my help—to save Lennon's life."

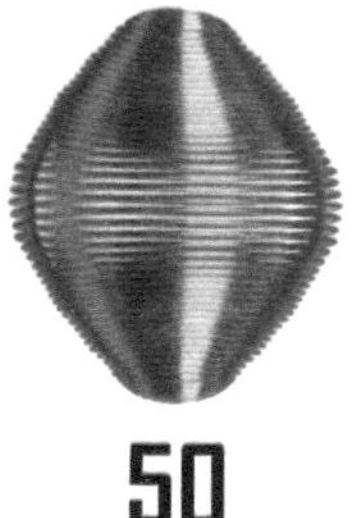

50
The Confession

What's up, Dad," Ellie said, yawning and squinting through half-opened eyes. "You know, ever since that sex talk when I was fifteen, I always worry when you sneak in to wake me up in the morning."

Once again overseen by the antique thurible and its suggestion of a ghostlike priest sitting in judgment, I felt as if I were about to subject myself to the intimidating ritual of Catholic confession. Though I knew it was only a construct of my imagination, the feeling rendered me momentarily tongue tied. I had practiced my speech a dozen times before entering Ellie's room, but I couldn't seem to get my mouth in gear.

"'S'matter, Dad?" she mumbled, rising up on her elbows and blinking sleep from her eyes. "Cat got your tongue?"

"Sorry, honey," I said, "I'm trying to figure out how to say what I have to say."

"Mmnnn, sounds serious. Are we going to talk about deep, dark secrets? Because if we are, I've got one of my own, so maybe we can do a tit-for-tat thing."

"Really? What's yours? Good news or bad?"

"Oh, no. You started this. You go first."

"Well," I said, "mine is both. You want the good news first or the bad?"

"Always the bad first," she said. "That way I have something to look forward to."

"Okay," I said, "give me a second here." I tried to clear my throat and ended up in a nervous coughing fit. When I finally managed to catch my breath, Ellie was holding my hands and staring anxiously into my watery eyes.

"Come on, Dad. It can't be as bad as all that."

"Yes it can, honey," I said. "Yes it can. I have to tell you something I'm ashamed of. It's ... it's a betrayal of your mother that I've carried on for years."

The shock in her eyes was accompanied by an open-mouthed gasp, and I realized what I'd said suggested a physical affair. "It's not what you're thinking," I said quickly. "I mean, I haven't been committing adultery, at least not in the classic sense. But there *is* someone else, always has been. So in some ways it's even worse than being physically unfaithful. It has to do with my former life. You see, I've—"

"Oh, *that*," she said with obvious relief. "Sheesh, I thought you were going to tell me you got some bimbo pregnant or something."

"That?" I said. "You make it sound like *that* is no big deal. But it is, honey. What I'm trying to tell you—"

"Dad!" she interrupted. "I know all about *that*. I read Mom's journals, remember? And one of the things she often lamented was this 'other woman' from your first life. She didn't obsess over it, though. We've talked about it a couple of times, and other than admitting to a little curiosity, she never expressed anger or regret. I guess it's hard for her to worry about a rival you will never be able to interact with in this world."

The way she stated it provided the perfect entrée for what I had to say, although it wasn't going to make saying it any easier. "Unfortunately," I said, hesitating a moment and taking a deep breath, "that's not exactly true. And therein lies not only the bad news—the betrayal I spoke of—but the good news as well. You see, honey, I *have* been able to interact with her, and you can, too. In fact, it's going to be extremely important for you to do so."

MY EXPLANATION WAS SO inexpert and simplified I was sure Ellie wouldn't understand. But she did. I answered the few questions she had as best I could, and when she seemed satisfied, I waited for her reaction, which turned out to be far less judgmental than I had expected.

"So," she said, "you get to see and talk, but not touch. Is it that Frederica person you told me about? What's-his-name's sidekick?"

"Heyoka," I said. "And it is. But—and here's something else I've been lying about all along—her name is not Frederica."

"Okay, so she has a different name. I don't see the big—"

"Her name is Aurélie, honey."

That stopped her. She opened her mouth, but nothing came out, and when she dropped my hands and looked at the ceiling, a hollow cavern opened up in my chest. "I don't know what to say, Dad," she said, finally. "I mean, I love my name, and I guess I should be proud that you named me after someone you care for, but ... what about Mom? You never told her?"

"No, I didn't. She's going to have to know now, though, because Aurélie is going to become a part of our lives. She and Heyoka are in desperate need of our help, and we need theirs if we're going to save John." She didn't say anything, so I decided to forge ahead. "They want to learn more about your ideas. You know, those methods of forecasting the impact certain events will have on the future. They are really impressed with what you've accomplished, and Aurélie wants to meet you and talk to you about it."

"So they've been spying on me? Reading my thoughts?" The anger in her voice seemed forced, as if she were trying to conceal a growing excitement.

"It's not like that at all," I said. "They've monitored my progress from day one, which was part of the deal to begin with. I'm an experiment, Ellie, the first person they ever tried this interdimensional transfer stuff with. And in the process of their monitoring they've been privy to the lives of people close to me. I suppose you could call it spying, but there was nothing sinister about it, believe me. Their knowledge of your ideas was a byproduct of the research, a serendipitous one, it turns out."

She looked down from the ceiling, her eyes widening with curiosity. "Serendipitous?" she said, "In what way?"

"It's hard to explain," I said. "But if you think about what I said earlier, you should realize that because I went back in time in this universe, their timeline is different from ours. In fact, they're years ahead of us, which means they are experiencing our future. Or what would be our future if I hadn't come back and changed things."

"Right, I get that. So, the serendipity?"

"The serendipity has to do with the fact that things are not going so well in their universe, and they need your to help to determine the long -term effects of certain scientific advances they've come up with, advancements that could help reverse the trends that are leading their world toward a potentially disastrous end. But first they want to do some experimenting in this universe to see if they can calculate how accurate your forecasts are."

She was now sitting straight up in bed. "Wow!" she said in a near whisper. "That's ... unbelievable. You mean I'm going to get to meet them and work with them and, I don't know, maybe even visit their universe?"

"I'm not sure about the visitation part, but yes, if you're willing to help, you will have to meet them and work with them. And the first thing they want to do—the first real-time experiment they want to try—is to see if they can help us save John's life."

I could tell by the faraway look in her eyes that she was still trying to absorb all this and put it in some kind of mental order. I waited, sure she was going to ask a dozen questions I couldn't answer, but I'd forgotten how smart she was. In the end, she had only one.

"How can they help us with John?" she asked. And before I could speak, she answered her own question: "Oh, right. It's all history to them. They can read up on Chapman, maybe find out where he was at any given time, what his plans might have been, and other details that would help us find and track him. Boy, this is exciting."

"For you, maybe," I said, "but not so much for me."

"Why not for you?"

"Because before any of this can happen, I have to explain it all to your mom."

"Oh," she said. "Yeah, I guess that's not going to be much fun. Tell you what, I'll go with you and break my news at the same time. Maybe that will take some of the sting out of yours."

"And what might your news be?"

"Okay, hang on to your hat," she said, grabbing my hands again and squeezing them. "Jackson asked me to marry him. And, guess what? I said yes!"

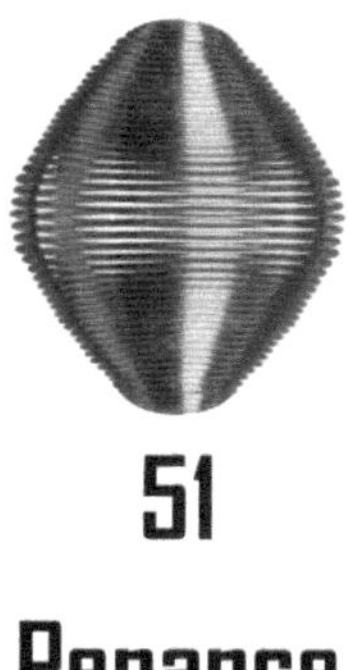

51

Penance

So, you've been seeing her all along?" Doris said after I finished my soul-crushing confession. The three of us were sitting around the breakfast-room table, picking at plates of half-eaten eggs, cheese grits, and French toast.

"No, not all along," I said, raising my coffee cup in a shaky hand. "It started around the time Ellie turned fifteen. And for a while, she was only a voice in my head, advising me from time to time." I glanced at Ellie, then replaced my cup without taking a sip. "The holographic projection thing started more recently, and it's only happened twice. The first was that afternoon when you and I were arguing about Lennon and I took a walk to cool off. Then a couple of weeks ago she and Heyoka showed up at my office. That's when they asked to meet with Ellie."

"And you're okay with this?" she said, looking at Ellie, obviously hoping for some indication of disapproval.

Ellie stiffened, and I realized what a compromising position I'd put her in. "Look, Mom," she said, staring at her plate, "I don't want to say I'm okay with it. I'm angry and confused and disappointed in Dad, but there are bigger things at stake here. Besides, it's not like he's been screwing some mistress or anything. I understand this is a shock. Hell, nobody could be more shocked than I was. The thing is, they need our help and we need theirs if we're going to do anything about saving

John. Not to mention the fact that they are living our future, and from what Dad says, that future is looking pretty bleak right now."

Doris rubbed her forehead while my breakfast rose in the back of my throat, threatening to spill out onto my plate. Finally, she pushed back from the table and stood. "I've got to get to the office," she said, grabbing her purse and heading for the back door. She stopped halfway through and turned back. "You two do what you think you have to, but leave me out of it. I don't want to see these people or hear any more about them, okay?" She didn't wait for an answer, and when the door slammed behind her it felt like it had slammed on our future as well.

ELLIE'S FIRST MEETING WITH Heyoka and Aurélie was awkward to say the least. I think she was a little taken aback by Heyoka's size and appearance, which frankly does not suggest a person of his scientific stature. But her attention soon became riveted on Aurie, whom she unabashedly scrutinized as if examining a specimen under a microscope. For her part, Aurie showed no nervousness or embarrassment; she just smiled and waited until the examination appeared to be over, then said, "Hi, Ellie. I'd shake your hand if I could, but I can't. I know this is probably uncomfortable for you, but I'm hoping we can be friends. We have a lot more in common than our names, you know."

We had again chosen the reception area in the old studio. This would become our regular meeting spot, though it would mostly be used only by Ellie and Aurie. After that first appearance, Heyoka restricted his visits to once every two or three months, times when he felt his presence might be important. As I'd expected, my role became almost peripheral, although every once in a while Aurie would show up when we could be alone and talk. And, despite the guilt that continued to gnaw away at my crumbling self-esteem, I treasured every second we were together.

On that first evening, after the awkwardness subsided and a certain level of tepid comfort set in, Heyoka and Ellie began to carry on a more-or-less one-on-one conversation about the problems they faced in their dimension, while Aurie and I concentrated on the Chapman situation. Because she could not carry any written materials into our dimension, she had instructed me to bring several legal pads. And while she read from a comprehensive report she had compiled, I scribbled as fast as I could.

Much of the report was like a life story, intended to familiarize me with Chapman's background and personality traits as they evolved over time. The image that slowly emerged was not much different from the one I already had in my head: a weirdo, born-again Christian with an abusive father, who suffered from paranoia and delusions of grandeur. Chapman was using drugs by age fourteen, was bullied in school for lack of athletic ability, and started having suicidal thoughts while in college. After dropping out, he made a failed attempt to take his own life and was admitted to a psych ward for clinical depression. Early on he had been a big Beatles fan, idolizing Lennon, but had later turned on the superstar, obsessing over contradictions between John's wealth and the lyrics to some of his songs. And it apparently wasn't only John we had to worry about, because Aurie had discovered a little-known list Chapman had compiled of others he planned to kill. That list included celebrities like Johnny Carson, Marlon Brando, Walter Cronkite, Elizabeth Taylor, George C. Scott, and Jackie Kennedy. So the task of stopping him became even more urgent.

Toward that end, the most important information she provided concerned Chapman's whereabouts at various times during the two years leading up to the assassination. The information was sketchy in parts, but at least it gave me more than I could have discovered on my own. By the time we finished I had filled an entire legal pad and half of another with my nearly indecipherable chicken scratchings.

Later that night, as Doris and I lay in bed, I tried to make a belated apology. Feeling a renewed sense of guilt from the meeting, I stumbled through a nervous soliloquy, sounding, I thought, more like a kid who'd been caught shoplifting than a truly remorseful husband. She listened silently, and when I ran out of words, she turned to me and touched my cheek with a finger. I thought for a moment she was going to say something, if not that she forgave me, then maybe that she understood my side. But she just gave me a stiff, resigned smile, then turned away and switched off her reading lamp.

It would be several weeks before Doris spoke to me in private, although when others were present she acted no different from before. And when she finally did break her silence, she surprised me with her concern and insight into my personal struggles.

"You know, Rich," she said one night while we were undressing for bed. "As soon as you're finished with this Lennon thing, you need to think long and hard about your future."

I was a little alarmed that she'd referred to it as *my* future, not *ours*, but I didn't mention my concern for fear she would stop talking. "Okay," I said. "You have any thoughts on that yourself?"

"I do," she said, looking at me in the mirror above her dressing table. "I think you need to get away from the business. I haven't wanted to mention it because you've got so many other things to worry about right now, but we've had several offers for buyouts of various divisions. Attractive offers, I should say. And Geffen's been hinting at wanting you to merge the music division with his operation. He's getting ready to form a new production company, and he thinks you two would make a great fit. But if you want to know what I think, I think you'd be better off getting out of the business altogether."

"Oh?" I said. "And what makes you think that?"

"Don't be obtuse, Rich," She said. "We both know you hate things as they stand. Look, I understand you think you're responsible for holding everything together, but that's really not the case anymore. Sam's handling the computer division, turning it into a dynasty, actually. And Jimmy's got the music division churning out hits faster than any production company in history. The other facets of the company are so diverse and individualized, there's nothing you can do for them other than act as a cheerleader and a PR person. And the holding company is run by our brokers, with a little oversight by me and our financial team. Still, it all seems to keep you running around like a corporate Keystone Kop, putting out fires that don't exist. Ellie and I have talked about it, and we both think you need to get out before you end up in the morgue. Besides, aren't you two supposed to be concentrating on saving the world?" This last was said with a heavy dose of sarcasm, which I chose to ignore.

"What about you?" I said. "I assume you're suggesting we sell everything, but if we cash out, what are you going to do with your time? I can't imagine you as a wealthy society matron, attending cocktail parties with Carol and sucking up to the rich and famous while you dedicate museum wings."

"Glad you asked," she said. "Now let me ask *you* something. Do you have any idea how much we're worth right now?"

"Not really," I said.

I'd never cared much about the bottom-line, and she knew it. I'd once been interviewed for a Wall Street Journal article, and the reporter asked me what my net worth was. Since Blue Note Enterprises was privately-held, our finances were not a matter of public record, but I wasn't trying to hide anything when I told him I had no idea. "Well," he said, "now that Hunt and Getty and Hughes are gone, rumor has it that you're one of the ten richest men in the world, though I must say you don't live like it." Doris later told me the guy was trying to get rise out of me by subtly insulting our blue-collar lifestyle, but at the time what he said sounded silly to me.

Doris didn't seem to be following up on her question, so I shrugged and said, "I guess it would be a few hundred million, right?"

"Jesus," she said, "you need to get your head out of the sand. The holding company alone is worth over a billion."

"Yeah, right," I said, laughing. "What exactly is this holding company thing anyway?"

She looked at me and rolled her eyes. "I've explained that to you half a dozen times. You do realize our flagship businesses make a ton of profit, don't you?"

"Yeah. So?"

"Well, we have to do something with that profit, don't we? We hardly spend any of it ourselves, and we can't stuff the rest in a mattress. So we invest it in other companies, buying their stock, and in some cases gaining controlling interest. You negotiated many of those deals yourself, and approved the rest."

"You know I don't pay much attention to that kind of stuff, at least when it comes to the details. I listen to you and the finance people, decide if I think it's a good idea, then turn on the charm and start haggling. Mostly I go along with what you think, and when I'm through I try to put it out of my mind because there's always a new bag of shit to worry about. To me it's all simply moving money from one place to another, for reasons I never really understood. Anyway, what are you saying, that we're some kind of new Rockefellers or something?"

"I can't be precise," she admitted, "because at any given moment the value of our holdings could be up or down by quite a bit. But a ballpark figure would be in the neighborhood of four billion. A cash out could be a little less or a little more, depending on where things stand at the time."

"Bullshit!" I said. She had to be joking, although I couldn't help but think back to what Ellie had said at age seven about wanting us to become billionaires.

"It's not bullshit, Rich. It's a fact." For the first time she cracked a smile. It was a sly smile, as if she'd lured me into a trap. And it wasn't long before I found out she had done precisely that.

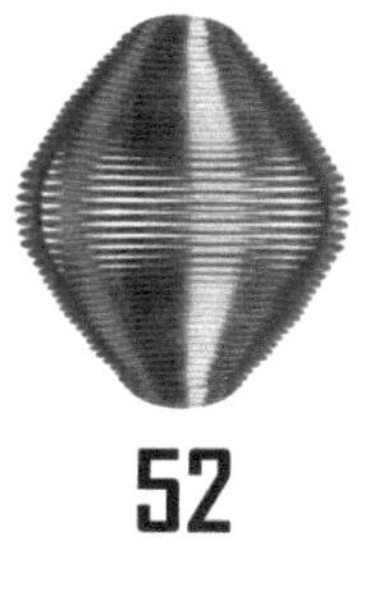

52

Intervention

Okay, here's the deal," Ellie said, spreading a bunch of papers and charts out on the dining-room table. I would soon realize I'd been ambushed, and when it dawned on me what was happening, all I could do was sit there and look from face to face. The mind-numbing thing was that two of those faces belonged to Aurélie and Doris. Apparently Ellie had managed to broker a peace between the two, and they now sat side-by-side, clearly amused by my confusion. The other conspirators included Heyoka, Jackson, Sam, Jimmy, and David Geffen. It almost seemed like one of those drug or alcohol interventions, though I couldn't think of any reason for such a thing. Except for an occasional beer or glass of wine, I wasn't a drinker, and the only drugs I took were a couple for my blood pressure and a non-prescription sleeping pill.

"Dad?" Ellie said, peering into my eyes, which I'm sure resembled those of a deer caught in the headlights. "Are you with us?" I wasn't, but I nodded anyway, hoping I was about to be let in on the joke. "Good. Now try to concentrate, because there's a lot you're going to have to absorb before we're through here tonight."

ALTHOUGH DORIS AND I had continued to discuss her proposal, without my knowledge or consent, she and Ellie had started putting together a plan for liquidating the company. They'd let me in on it a couple of months before the ambush, and the passion of my protests had slowly faded as the prospect of freeing myself from the shackles that had held me captive for so long began to seem like a real possibility. As time went on, the debate evolved into a negotiation, during which my arguments were reduced to only a couple of demands. One was that Sam and Jimmy had to be on board with any plan; the other was that no one in the organization would lose their job. Unless, of course, they chose to quit, in which case they were to be compensated with more-than-generous severance packages. I was prepared to fight for these conditions, but as it turned out, I didn't have to.

Doris and the financial folks had structured things so that Sam could assume ownership of the computer division, with the financing arranged in such a way that we received fair market value without saddling him with too much of an immediate financial burden. She had also negotiated a collaboration between Jimmy and Geffen that involved a buyout of the music division and a partnership between the two; the only condition being that I would agree to serve in an advisory capacity and as a member of the corporate board. I feigned reluctance at this, even though I was somewhat intrigued by the idea. There was a lot of financial stuff Ellie tried to explain to me during the meeting, but all that did was cause my eyes to glaze over again. Sam and Jimmy were apparently satisfied with everything, so in the end, I made Ellie and Doris swear things would be handled exactly as they had described, and left it at that.

The job-retention language, I was assured, would be written into any and all contracts for sale of the company's other assets. These did not include the small division that handled legal and bookkeeping for the holding company, because that division would not be sold.

The liquidation was going to take some time, most likely six months or more. But in the end—in addition to retaining the holding company, which was valued at over a billion dollars—we would come out with nearly three billion in cash and/or negotiable securities, whatever that meant. One thing it was supposed to mean was that I would soon be free of any responsibilities related to Blue Note Enterprises, with the exception of a minor obligation to the music end of things. And as this realization began to sink in, it felt like I was being released from a long stint at hard labor in a Siberian work camp. That is, until the meeting began to break up and Ellie pulled me aside. "We're not through here," she whispered.

Jimmy and David said their goodbyes, and as the door closed behind them, I noticed Heyoka and Aurélie had not moved. Then I realized they couldn't even stand up unless someone pulled their chairs out for them. I was about to help Aurie with her chair, when Heyoka—who had done a fine job of imitating a corporeal human until then—stood as if to stretch his non-corporeal legs. This would not have been a big deal, except for the fact that he walked right through the arm of his chair and then through the corner of the table. I looked at Sam and Jackson, who had clearly observed this ghostly phenomenon, and when Ellie saw my concern she squeezed my arm. "It's okay, Dad," she said. "They know everything." I was still trying to absorb this news, when she raised her voice and said, "Okay, gang, now let's move on to the more important business."

Letting Sam in on the truth seemed logical. After all, he'd been suspicious since that first day when I suggested we go swimming in my non-existent pool. And even though he'd never broached the subject again, I'd often seen a glimmer of skepticism in his eyes. That Ellie had confided in Jackson, however, came as a shock. I didn't have time to dwell on it, though, because she immediately launched into a long and detailed presentation of the "more important business." This, it turned out, concerned how our soon-to-be-liquid wealth should be reinvested and used. I hadn't given much thought to that, even though Doris had reminded me earlier that large chunks of money could not simply be left lying around. Or, as she'd put it, "stuffed in a mattress."

To my way of thinking, the best thing to do would be to just stick it in the bank, live off some of the interest, and let the rest grow. But she was quick to point out things like the limits on FDIC insurance coverage (which for us would have meant using literally thousands of federally insured banks and savings & loans), and the fact that savings-account interest rates were only running around seven-percent. I assumed this meant we would have to do a lot of complicated reinvesting, but she said that would not be the case. At the time, her convoluted explanation of how the money would be allocated had left me seriously confused. Now, however, I was about to learn that their real intent was to implement an elaborate plan they'd devised and cultivated behind my back.

THINKING IT WOULD MEAN a return to some kind of corporate slog for me, I objected strongly at first to Ellie's proposal. But as the details of the plan became clearer, I began to lose my footing in the debate. For one thing, she said I would only be required to participate in whatever way I chose, even if that meant no participation at all. For another, there were apparently all manner of tax breaks and exemptions involved in forming a non-profit foundation and financing it through grants and endowments. The holding company would be retained to provide a modest income for us and operating cash flow for the proposed foundation, whose public activities would include donations to various charities and causes, plus support of organizations working to effect sociopolitical change. What would not be known to the public was that the foundation would serve as a front for implementing Heyoka and Aurélie's efforts to use our universe as a testing ground for actions that might rescue their world from impending devastation. And, hopefully, to save our own from the same future fate.

My only mandate in this scenario was to coordinate and direct our efforts to neutralize the threat to Lennon and Chapman's other potential victims. Doris, Ellie, Sam, and Jackson had agreed to act as the primary operatives for Heyoka's plans in this dimension, so all they needed was my permission to allocate the money as the group saw fit. Of course, there was the more-or-less honorary role as advisor and board member for the new entertainment business, but those obligations were not in writing, so could be manipulated to fit my chosen lifestyle. What that lifestyle would be was a question I had yet to even consider.

Unbeknownst to me, however, the intervention wasn't over, not by a long shot. In fact, it was about to move into its second phase, a phase intended to answer that question for me. This part of the conspiracy was subtly woven into the evening's business, and the bit of amateur theater they managed to pull off was performed with surprising expertise and perfect timing by all.

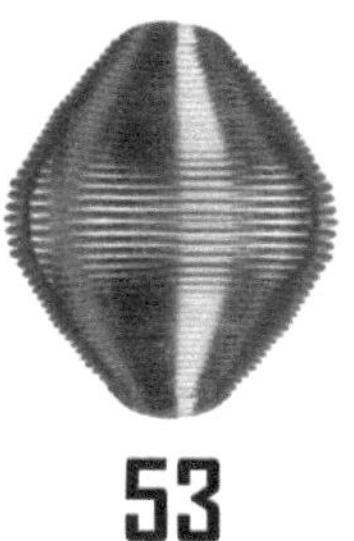

53
The Foundation

Once I'd agreed to the terms of the liquidation, we celebrated with champagne toasts, then moved on to a brainstorming session to select a name for the foundation. Suggestions ranged from the tedious (The Foundation for Benevolent and Transformative Intervention), to the nebulous (The Millennium Foundation, The Star Foundation, etc.). Without thinking, I suggested "Dreamworks," but after a stern look from Aurélie, I remembered that was going to be the name of Geffen's future collaboration with Steven Spielberg and Jeffrey Katzenberg. Unfortunately, everybody liked the suggestion, so Aurie, who had an implant that gave her instantaneous access to the Internet in her dimension, bent the truth a little, saying she'd checked and found that the name was already protected by copyright.

We were mulling over some other ideas, when I remembered Heyoka's comparison of the flow of time to a river into which pebbles of change were thrown. But when I said we should try incorporate pebbles in the name, no one understood the significance of the word. I thought about trying to explain, but decided it would be best to ask Heyoka to repeat his metaphorical analogy. Not only to justify my suggestion, but to give everyone a better idea of how important and potentially dangerous the foundation's work would be. He did so in his typically eloquent style, and when he finished there was general agreement that we should try to include at least some reference to pebbles in the name.

The champagne was soon gone, but by then the gathering had taken on an excited, optimistic tone, so Jackson offered to run up to the liquor store for a case of beer. Meanwhile, Doris called out for pizza, and by the time Jackson got back we had all the makings of a party. We felt bad for Heyoka and Aurélie, who could not partake of the refreshments, but they seemed to catch the spirit of things, and soon we were all laughing and joking and kicking around absurd ideas for names. Because Heyoka had described the pebbles as colorful and flavorful, Sam said we should call it The M&M Society. This was followed by Jackson suggesting the Swedish Fish Foundation. And, picking up on the river reference, Doris chimed in with The Gurgling Brook Foundation. All of these drew collective groans, and, finally, Ellie demanded we stop goofing around and get serious.

Among a dozen or so pebble names eventually rejected were "Pebbles of Change" and "Sand Pebbles" (nixed because it was the name of a well-known Steve McQueen movie). "Rainbow Pebbles" came close, but just as we were all about to agree, Ellie pointed out that it would conjure up images of the colorful children's cereal. The final death knell for the word came when Doris suggested that any use of it might bring to mind not only the cereal, but the Flintstone's character as well. After another few minutes of debate, we all agreed that something more ambiguous would be best and settled on The Millennium Foundation.

After that, the conversation turned reflective and the mood grew somber as everyone began to realize the magnitude of the tasks that lay ahead. Before long, Jackson seemed to tire of the humorless atmosphere, so he wandered over to the piano and began tapping out the opening notes to the theme from Dragnet. The ominous *Dum de Dum Dum* was clearly intended to add a note of levity, but when he sat down to play he ended up transitioning into the prelude to ***Before the Deluge***. And as he began to sing, Ellie joined in, singing in harmony with the bleak, disheartening lyrics.

The song, from his 1974 album ***Late for the Sky***, told a sobering story about the once-promising 'Hippie' and 'New Age' movements. It was a cautionary tale, written, it now seemed, with uncanny foresight, since the much ballyhooed Age of Aquarius was on the decline and would soon be overtaken by the age of I-me-me-I materialism. And if the fate of Heyoka and Aurélie's dimension turned out to be true for ours, those movements would end up being little more than historical footnotes, rather than leading to world peace and ecological balance. But even though the song's prediction of a coming deluge was depressing, it did contain one subtle, upbeat message: that music was the one thing that could help us get through the worst of times.

After the final piano notes faded, Jackson spun around on the stool and looked at me. "Aurélie tells me you wrote something similar in your first life," he said. "Why don't you play it for us, Rich?" And before I could protest, Ellie produced my Ramirez and placed it in my lap.

"Man, I can't perform any more," I said. "My voice and fingers are as rusty as the cars in a redneck's front yard. Besides, I don't remember writing anything that would even approach ***Before the Deluge***."

"Come on, Dad," Ellie said, looking at Aurélie. "What song is Jackson talking about Aurie?"

"It's that post-apocalyptic one from your first album," she said. "I don't recall the title, but it was about the artist and the writer who can only paint or write from memories."

"***Baptism***," I said. "Hell, I can't remember the chords, let alone the words." But something stirred in my memory, and without meaning to, I started picking at the strings. As the arrangement began to take shape, the room went silent, and I realized I was humming the melody. Soon Jackson joined in on the piano with a murmuring bass line and a tinkling cascade of high notes that so perfectly matched the song's melancholy spirit, I was transported back to Georgia and that wintery morning on the banks of the creek when the lyrics had come to me, it seemed, out of nowhere.

We had run through it a couple of times, making subtle adjustments to the arrangement, when Ellie let out an exasperated sigh. "Dad!" she said. "You can't leave us hanging like that. Quit humming and sing, dammit!" I tried to come up with an acceptable excuse, but before I could think of one Jackson played an elaborate intro so inviting that the words began to spill out of their own accord:

In the clear and crystal morning
As the autumn sun paints rainbows on the weary trees
See the artist's brush performing
Spreading colors on the canvas in the gentle breeze

And the painter is the only one who knows
But if you look upon his face
You'll see his eyes are closed

For the painter cannot paint the things he sees
The painter only paints from memories

From the poet's gentle verses spring
The memories left sleeping in a long past day
Recalling how it first was
In the fantasies of woven rhyme his pen displays

And the poems written yesterday live on
While the hand that writes today must tell
Of days that long are gone

For the poet cannot write of things he sees
The poet only writes from memories

While Jackson improvised an instrumental break, I stretched my aching fingers and glanced at the smiling faces all around me. Then, closing my eyes, I tried to recapture the emotion I'd once put into the closing words.

Everyone must pay the price
The waters will run still
Nature's wrath will fall upon
The universe until . . .

The tender tears of promise fall
From paradise to cleanse the earth of man's great sin
And on the wind the breath of God
To wash the heavens clean and bring the sun again

And the sun will lift the oceans to the sky
And purify the waters with the tears the angels cry

And once again the songs we sing
Will be of things we see
Beginning once again
We shall be free

The applause was a little overdone, I thought. Even Heyoka and Aurie joined in with silent but enthusiastic handclaps. I probably should have been suspicious, but my ego must have kicked in, because I got a hint of that familiar, warm feeling I remembered from my days on the stage.

"Damn, man, you need to record that," said Jackson. "In fact, you need to climb out of that cocoon you've woven around yourself and start playing again. You'll have the time now, and you've easily got a couple of albums worth of songs just in the stuff you've written for Sarah and Patsy, not to mention yours truly."

There was encouragement all around, but I wasn't about to climb out on that particular limb. I no longer felt confident in my ability to perform, and I could not imagine risking humiliation by appearing before an audience of strangers. "I appreciate the sentiment," I said, "but I think it's a little too late for that."

"Horseshit," Jackson said. "Despite what Carole King said, it's never 'too late, baby.' And Carole should know. Remember what happened when James took her on tour with him? Nobody knew her from Adam's housecat, but all it took was JT telling the audience that all the songs she was going to play were her own compositions. And when they heard those familiar hits, she brought down the house at every stop. That tour launched ***Tapestry***, you know, and practically everyone on the face of the earth now owns a copy."

"Yeah, but I'm no Carole King," I said. "I'm a stogy old business man who hasn't seen a stage since Sam and Sarah and I were diddling around with a folk trio that never went anywhere. I appreciate the compliment, but I just don't have the chops for that kind of thing anymore."

This elicited a few moans and murmured disagreements, but I knew these were colored by love and friendship, and were not an objective response to my performance. So I stuck to my guns, gently deflecting their arguments until things calmed down and the party began to break up.

I was looking around for my guitar case when Jackson came up beside me. "Listen," he said. "We need to talk. It's not that late, so why don't we go somewhere and get a drink?"

Not having had much experience in this life with alcohol, I was feeling the effects of the champagne and beer, and the mild high brought back a long-forgotten desire to continue. For the first time in decades I was in a position of freedom, and with that freedom—influenced no doubt by the alcohol—came an almost angry, fuck-it attitude. Heyoka and Aurélie had dematerialized, and Ellie, Sam, and Doris were in deep conversation about financial crap that didn't interest me in the least, so I decided to accept Jackson's offer.

We were heading for the door, when Doris looked up. "And where do you two think you're going?" she said, though her tone wasn't quite as admonishing as she tried to make it sound.

I looked at Jackson, then we both turned to her. "Out!" we said in unison. And before she could object, we were gone.

I KNEW OF HALF a dozen fancy cocktail lounges downtown, but I had a feeling this might turn out to be more than a two-drink night, with the potential to result in embarrassing rumors about the man who was still CEO of Blue Note Enterprises. So I suggested we go to a little bar off the beaten path called Jerry's.

I'd been a loyal patron of Jerry's place in my first life, and he and I knew each other casually in this one. Jerry was the kind of old-school bartender who would tell phoning wives and girlfriends their significant others had just left, or deny they'd even been there if that was called for. The interior of the bar was dark, with several booths that provided privacy and a juke box kept just loud enough to obscure private conversations without damaging eardrums.

For food, Jerry offered the standard assortment of Slim Jims, pickled pigs feet, and beef jerky. But his signature culinary offering was free roasted peanuts, the shells of which carpeted the floor. The bar's olfactory ambience was reminiscent of a football locker room that had been set on fire by smoldering cigarette butts then extinguished with a splash of stale beer and urine. Needless to say, Jerry's attracted a 'select' clientele, and was the perfect venue for patrons who wanted to be left alone to drink, talk sports or politics, and hook up with the two or three working girls who were always hanging around.

Jackson and I found an empty booth, and Helen—the bar's only waitress—showed up seconds later. Helen was one of those fixtures you see characterized in TV sitcoms set in Miami or California: frazzled reddish-gray hair with the requisite pencil stuck in it; animated facial features surrounding a tired but sincere smile; and a skinny, sun-browned body that looked like it had been carved from a hunk of rusty angle iron.

Jackson ordered a draft, and I was about to do the same, when I suddenly changed my mind. "Double Jack on the rocks," I said, mentally savoring the prospect of tasting whiskey for the first time in over twenty-three years.

"Didn't know you were a hard-liquor man," Jackson said.

"Never touch the stuff," I said. "Not in this life, anyway. In my other one I singlehandedly kept the legend of Jasper Newton Daniel alive, ruining a couple of kidneys, a liver, and half a heart in the process."

"Here ya go, boys," Helen said, setting our drinks down in front of us along with a bowl of peanuts. "Gimmie a yell when you're ready for more."

Remembering the 'good old days,' I thought about ordering another one right then, but common sense got the better of me. "To emancipation," I said, raising my glass. Jackson clinked it with his, and we both took a drink. For a second, the taste brought back fond memories, but when I swallowed it felt like molten lava had been poured down my throat. I managed to keep from regurgitating, but I could feel my eyes trying to burst from their sockets as the liquor seared its way down my esophagus.

When things came back into focus, Jackson was staring at me with a concerned look on his face. "You all right?" he asked. "Here, have a sip of my beer." He handed me his glass and signaled to Helen for another.

I slurped hungrily at the cool liquid, which did help put out some of the fire, and I had almost regained my ability to speak when Helen arrived with another round. I thought about asking her to take mine back, but just then the alcohol started to hit my brain, and I decided to keep my mouth shut. Many things went through my head as I set the beer down between the two whiskey glasses, not the least of which was an echo of that old saw, "once an alcoholic, always an alcoholic." But this was different: I hadn't had a drop of liquor since the transfer so I was in control, wasn't I? All I wanted was one night of freedom, a few hours of relaxation during which I could let loose of the inhibitions and anxiety that had dominated my second life and be … well, be me again.

I recalled my first taste of whisky as a teen, and how it had scorched my throat in much the same way. But then there was the aftermath, when Pat had urged me to quickly take another drink, and the burning began to be overpowered by that lightheaded feeling I'd eventually become addicted to. I'd lost my virginity that night in more ways than one, and forever thereafter I'd associated sex with alcohol, as if it were some kind of Willy-Wonka golden ticket that allowed me to enter a new world of sensual pleasure. The only exception to this combination was the year I'd spent sober with Robin, but that hadn't lasted.

"So," Jackson said, interrupting my reverie. "Tell me about your first career. From what I hear, you were quite the star."

I was still trying to figure out how to deal with the pallet-scalding, when I had an idea. Raising the half-full whisky glass, I held my fingers over the top to keep the ice cubes from falling out, and poured the remaining liquor into the beer. "Boilermaker," I said, in answer to his curious stare, then tilted the glass up and drained it. This time it went down so smooth I immediately waved at Helen and mouthed the word "beer."

"I'm going to have to have a serious talk with my daughter," I said. "How much did she tell you?"

"Quite a bit, actually," he said. "You shouldn't be angry with Ellie, though. It wasn't her fault. When she first told me what was going on with you, I thought she was joking, but once I got past the disbelief factor all I really wanted to hear about was your music. If it hadn't been for my bugging her all the time she wouldn't have gone into so much detail—you know, boy prodigy, perfect pitch, the hits and all that."

"Yeah, well, there's a lot more to it than she knows—than anyone knows, for that matter. Except maybe Aurie, and even she doesn't know everything." Helen arrived with my beer, and before she left I told her to bring me another one, plus another double shot of Jack—without ice this time. I mixed my second boilermaker and drank half of it while Jackson waited for me to elaborate.

"So," he said when I didn't continue, "I can't help but wonder why you didn't go the same route in this life. I mean, it's no secret that you could have—still could, if you wanted to. And don't give me that crap about not having the chops. You might just be the best damned guitarist I've ever heard, not to mention the fact that you can write and sing rings around most of the artists I know. Maybe there's a little rust, but I didn't hear it. Doesn't it drive you up the wall having to watch from the sidelines?"

"Drive me up the wall?" I said, wondering if that was an accurate description of how I felt. "I don't know, Jackson. I really don't. It's hard for me to describe my feelings about that." The alcohol was loosening up my tongue, and I didn't seem to be able to do anything about it. "I guess the only thing that's really driven me up the wall is the fact that I let Blue Note Enterprises take over my life."

"Okay, I get that. But the question is, take it over from what? Aren't you saying it kept you from doing what you wanted to do? And wouldn't that be making music yourself rather than producing it for others?"

Helen delivered the makings of my third boilermaker, and I ordered us another round. Meanwhile, the question of what I would have done had I not gotten so involved in the business rattled around in my brain, poking at my memory and evoking all kinds of emotions. "Bear with me, here," I said, pouring the whiskey into the beer and stirring it with a finger. I took a long, satisfying drink, then set the glass down and spread my hands out flat on the table. "You know, to be honest, I haven't given that much thought—the question of what I really want. My first inclination is to say sure, I'd like to write and sing my own music. Problem is, that would be an emotional response, a knee-jerk reaction, and I've learned to be careful about making significant changes in my life without first trying to evaluate their long-term impact, not only on me, but on the people I care about."

"What if the people you care about want you to get back up on the stage because they know it's the only thing that will make you happy?" he asked.

"Well, then, they would have to understand that it would mean a lot of travel and time spent away from them."

"Not necessarily. For one thing, Ellie and I are going to be married soon, and then we'll be hitting the road with the tour, so she's not going to be around much anyway. And who's to say Doris wouldn't want to travel with you? Seems to me like you're just looking for excuses, though I can't understand why."

He was right about the excuses, and it didn't take me long to realize that the 'why' was all about fear. There was the fear of failure, because for some reason my self-confidence had long-ago taken a hike. Given my life-and-a-half of experience that particular fear didn't make much sense, but it was there nonetheless. Far more frightening, however, was the looming possibility—probability, actually—of falling back into my old lifestyle. I was already half drunk on boilermakers with no intention of slowing down, and I knew what was likely to happen if I went back on the road, not only with alcohol, but with women as well. Doris would be busy running the foundation and would probably not be traveling with me much if at all, so I would be free to resume my old debauchery, while once again destroying my health. And this time, I wouldn't have Heyoka and Aurie to bail me out.

I didn't want to get into all that with Jackson, but there was one other aspect of returning to the stage that had been preying on my mind. And since we were apparently having one of those honest, heart-to-heart talks, I decided to mention it.

"Maybe you're right," I said. "Maybe it won't be much of a problem when it comes to Ellie and Doris. But I still have to think about myself, and when I do—when I start to look at what my own motivations would be—I don't like what I see. Whether I like it or not, part of making that kind of decision has to involve asking myself why? What would I be looking to get out of it?"

"That's easy," he said, "the satisfaction of doing something pure, something that has nothing to do with making money. Isn't that what every musician craves? You know, Rich, some of us were given a gift, and not sharing that gift with the world is, I don't know, like blasphemy, like throwing it back in nature's face. You've used your talents to help other artists, but that's a sort of dilution. In a way, it's selfish—denying others the benefit of enjoying your undiluted talents."

"Very philosophical," I said. "You trying to make me feel guilty?"

"No, man. Well, maybe a little. Why? Do you?"

"I ... okay, yeah, now that you mention it. A little, anyway. The thing is, when I look back at my other life and how I felt about music, it wasn't anything like that, all the purity and obligation stuff. In fact, if I'm honest about it, my attitude was pretty mercenary."

"Mercenary? How do you mean?"

I hadn't really meant to say that, but apparently the booze was acting like a truth serum. So, what did I mean by saying my attitude was mercenary? I thought for a minute, then said, "I guess what I mean is that music came so easy to me. I never had to work hard at it, except maybe to develop some of the physical things. The mental stuff was just

… there. I took it for granted, like being able to walk or breathe. I didn't appreciate it and I don't think I ever actually loved it, at least not in the pure sense you're talking about. If I had I would have studied, pursued it academically, gone to Julliard or something. Helen got me started on the piano and gave me some voice lessons, but hell, man, I never even took the time to learn how to sight read."

"Sounds like me," He said. "I took some lessons when I was real young, played the trumpet for a while. After that I picked most everything up on my own."

"Yeah, but you *did* something with your talents, all the activism and political stuff. Me, I used music as a tool to get what I wanted, not like it was a gift I was obligated to share with the world."

"And what was it you wanted, exactly?"

"Nothing noble or valuable, that's for sure. It was mainly an ego thing. I craved the recognition, the applause, the sex and drugs and booze. And the money was nice, though after my two so-called hits, I never made much of that. But, truth be told, I never was that good of a musician. Most of the time I didn't know what I was doing, I just did it. I was so good at faking stuff, I sometimes look back and all I see is a clever con man who happened to be blessed with an ear for music and decent singing voice."

"And the ability to write," he added. "So what is your reluctance now? You've still got the talent, and now you don't even have to worry about money, so you can do just about anything you want. Maybe make up for some of that stuff you seem to be feeling guilty about."

Helen delivered another round while I considered his question. She wasn't very good about cleaning tables, and as I watched her finally clear ours, I counted five pairs of empty glasses being removed from my side of the table. The room hadn't started to spin yet, but if I kept drinking at this rate I knew it wouldn't be long.

"Look," I said, as soon as Helen was out of earshot, "I've got a lot to do before I can even consider what I want for myself. For one thing, there's going to be a lot of crap involved in the liquidation, making sure everyone is properly taken care of and approving the buyouts and other deals. But most importantly I have to figure out how to get rid of this Chapman lunatic before Lennon exposes himself on the international stage promoting your charity tour. And speaking of that, Ellie's been hassling me about using my influence to get a bunch of other acts on board. I managed to get commitments from Springsteen and Stevie Wonder, and now she wants me to approach McCartney, but you and I both know there's about as much chance of him getting involved as there is building a snowman in hell. The point is, I don't really have time to think about anything else, at least for a while."

"Get rid of Chapman?" He said, frowning. "What does that mean?"

"I don't know what it means, Jackson. I wish I did. Things have changed from the way they were in my first life, and now the danger is not only to John, but to everybody involved in the tour, including Ellie and even you. I've got a couple of private investigators working on it, and we're still more than a year away from the original date of the shooting, but there's no way to know exactly how much time we have, given the new situation and the fact that we're dealing with a crazy person. So if you're asking if I'm considering some kind of drastic action, you're damned right I am."

"Drastic?" he said. "You're not suggesting—"

"Taking him out? Yes, I've given that some thought. It would be a simple solution to an incredibly complex problem, one I have yet to figure out how to handle. Thing is, I don't think I'm capable of having someone killed. Oh, I could do it, probably pretty cleanly, in a way that would never be traced back to me. But as much as I might want to, it's just not in my nature to take a human life."

"Well, that's good to hear," he said. "So what *are* you going to do?"

"I wish I knew, my friend. I wish I knew."

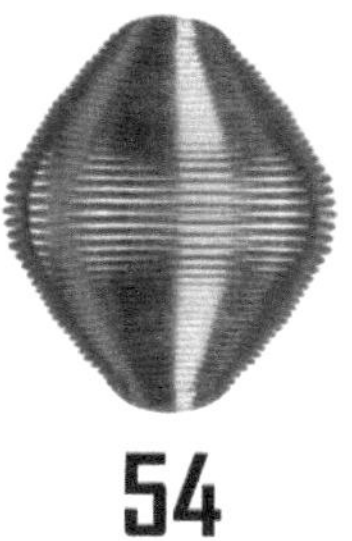

54
The Morning After

The last hangover I'd experienced was at the villa, but that had been the result of drinking Heyoka's fake Jack with its simulated aftereffects. This one, however, was the real thing, featuring all the typical miseries; the only untypical thing being that each of those miseries was amplified by a factor of approximately ten-thousand. The result was an exquisitely-vicious migraine; hours of throat-tearing, fire-hose vomiting; and a severe case of intestinal tsunami; all followed by a seemingly endless round of dry heaves that threatened to rip my stomach from its moorings.

Doris and Ellie served as my nursemaids, although Ellie stopped short of accompanying me to the bathroom, which was where I spent most of the morning. Her contribution to my recovery was limited to the afternoon, during which I drifted in and out of consciousness, sipped chicken broth from the spoon she managed to occasionally squeeze through my clamped lips, and was forced to listen to her continuation of Jackson's arguments in favor of my return to the stage. Even though my brain had all the functionality of a squashed grape, I soon came to realize that the musical finale to the previous night's meeting had been part of a carefully-planned setup.

My anger over the conspiracy was no-doubt influenced by the pain and nausea; however, the seed had been planted. And in my dreamlike, post-inebriated muddle, I began to imagine a scenario in which I could, as Jackson had suggested, do something 'pure' with my music; something disassociated from ego or money or stardom. Even though I'd thought of my earlier songwriting as being rebellious when it came to compromising its integrity for the sake of commercialism, I knew much of what I'd written had been influenced by the "rules" that had been drummed into my head over the years by producers—producers not unlike the one I'd become in this life. As I thought about this apparent contradiction, snippets of the previous night's conversation began to come back to me.

"I don't see what's wrong with trying to reach as many people as possible with your music," Jackson had said in response to my insistence that commercial compromise was the harbinger of artificiality. "It's no different from a journalist adhering to the rules of grammar and punctuation so that what they write can be understood and appreciated by the public. It doesn't mean you can't be innovative or that your music won't have value. It only means you're using those rules to make what you write more accessible. I think you overemphasize the downside of commercialization."

"Ah," I said, "so you admit there's a downside."

"Of course there is. When a song's commercial viability is due only to repetition, or pathos, or hook lines, with no emotional appeal other than jerking a tear or suggesting something sexual or violent, then, sure, it's like a plastic imitation of reality. Even though it may sell a million records, that doesn't mean it has lyrical or compositional integrity. On the other hand, just because a song has those elements doesn't mean it is valueless, especially if it has a message or comes from the heart or tells a story based on some real experience others can identify with."

He'd gone on to admit that he thought he'd been guilty of commercial compromise himself at times, though he'd never consciously written with sales as a goal. "There's always a seed of something real and personal in my lyrics," he said. "And the music itself is never compromised. I'll admit that I sometimes think about how a song is going to go over and make adjustments accordingly. But if it means being emotionally dishonest or sacrificing the true essence of the story I'm trying to tell, I'll shut it down, maybe put it on the shelf for a while and see if something more authentic comes out of the idea later on."

After that, the conversation had devolved into a blur of senseless, drunken rhetoric, until he brought up the subject of Chapman again. Because of the looming urgency and my growing fear of failure, the change of subject once again awakening the dread I'd been living with for months. And while we discussed various ideas, discarding most as impractical or too dangerous, I continued to drink myself into a catatonic stupor. My reward was this stupendous hangover, which had me promising myself I would never take another drink of liquor, a promise I'd made—and broken—hundreds of times in my first life.

Around four o'clock that afternoon I noticed a slight lowering of the pain index, while the cesspool in my stomach seemed to have dissipated somewhat. As the brain fog began to lift, I heard the sound of guitar music; a soft, distant, fingerstyle arrangement being played on an acoustic. I had started to relax and enjoy the soothing sound, when I realized my imagination must be playing tricks on me, because I was listening to music that did not exist in this dimension. In fact, I was listening to a song from my last album, one I had never played—let alone recorded—in this life.

As the music increased in volume, I took a chance on opening my eyes, expecting a stab of light-induced pain that—thankfully—never came. Blocked by the thick canopy of our banyan tree, the afternoon sunlight was muted, though not enough to hide Ellie's self-satisfied smile. Her expression reminded me of our cat, Jenny, on one of the many occasions when she had proudly presented me with a dead mouse.

"Where did you get that recording?" I croaked. "I thought they couldn't bring anything material into this universe."

"They can't," she said. "Not yet, at least. But they do project their non-material images and voices into our world. So I asked Aurie if she could play your albums for me, and I made the recordings on this end. You know, Dad, there are some really great songs on those albums, and I'm not talking only about the ones you've produced for Blue Note's artists."

"Look, Ellie," I said, "I know what's going on here, though I sure don't understand what all the fuss is about. It's not like the world is going to be a better place just because there's one more singer-songwriter to listen to. I appreciate the thought, but I've got a lot more important stuff to worry about right now, so please stop hassling me about this."

"I will if you promise me you'll give it a shot once we're through with the liquidation and you've taken care of the Chapman situation. And I'm not saying that because I think the world is going to be a better place. I don't mean to get all mushy about it, but I love you, Dad, and I want you to be happy. When you're not, I worry, and I'm getting tired of worrying about you all the damn time."

Hearing her say those words nearly choked me up. We weren't the kind of family that openly expressed our feelings to one another, and I knew this was my fault, probably because I took after Dad in that regard. I often regretted it and wanted to change, but over the years I'd come to realize that you really can't teach an old dog new tricks. About all I could come up with was a nervous smile, before turning the subject back to the daunting reality we faced.

"If you're going to worry about something," I said, squeezing the words past the lump in my throat, "you'd better make it Chapman. From what Jackson told me, your target date for the inaugural concert is Saturday, December sixth, which is two days before the original assassination. Obviously John is going to be the headliner at that one, and according to your mom, the publicity will be unprecedented. So Aurie and I are thinking Chapman might take advantage of the confusion and the crowds to carry out his plan."

"Aren't you having him followed, though?" she asked. "Won't we know where he is and what he's doing as the date approaches?"

"We are, and we may, but there's no way to know for sure. Chapman is proving to be an awfully erratic fellow, and predicting where he's going to be or what he's going to be doing at any particular time is turning out to be more difficult than we expected. Over the past twelve months he's been all over the place, from Geneva, Switzerland to London to Hawaii, where he married a Japanese-American girl last year. So far, his movements have been similar to what Aurie was able to find out through her research, and it's been fairly easy for our investigators to keep tabs on him. The problem is, John's schedule is going to change drastically with all the tour preparations and plans, so we have no idea what Chapman is going to do from here on out."

"So, what's the plan?" she said.

"I don't know, honey. It has to remain pretty fluid because things are still evolving. What we do know from the two shrinks we hired to work with the investigators is that he's apparently starting to fall apart mentally. He checked himself in and out of a psychiatric hospital there in Hawaii, then ended up working for the same hospital as a maintenance man and later in the print shop. He quit that job to work in maintenance at a big condo near Waikiki Beach, but that didn't last long. And now he seems to have disappeared, which means his previous pattern has already been broken. We know he was drinking heavily and that he suffers from severe paranoia, so maybe he caught on to the fact that he was being followed. Aurie keeps reminding me that even though he's nuts, he's no dummy, and right now our guys are scrambling to pick up his trail again. In fact, I was thinking you might be able to help, maybe use some of your predictive techniques to see if you can figure out where he might be or where he's likely to go."

"I've talked to Aurie about that," she said, shaking her head, "but, unfortunately, there isn't enough data to work with. Even though she was able to find dozens of news stories and short bios, they were all pretty murky when it came to exact details, and many of them contradicted each other about dates and locations and activities. If I had detailed, reliable data to work with, I might be able to integrate that information with the current changes in John's schedule and come up with some sort of probability timeline. But I don't have that kind of data, so all I could do is guess. And if I guess wrong, we could end up chasing our tails while he's out there planning some kind of elaborate, unpredictable attack. My job right now is to concentrate on forecasting the sociopolitical impact that prolonging John's life will have on the future of our world, and believe me that is no small task itself."

"Great," I said. "Not that I think what you're doing isn't worthy and important, but if I can't manage to keep John alive, that all becomes moot. And that puts a shitload of pressure on me, Ellie. I'm no goddamned Jason Bourne, you know. Hell, I don't even own a gun, and I wouldn't know how to use one if I did."

"Maybe you should consider buying one and getting some training," she said. "And who the hell is Jason Bourne?"

"Long story. I guess you could think of him as the James Bond of the twenty-first century. But my point is I'm not really cut out for this kind of spy crap. And the whole damned thing is scaring the shit out of me."

"Don't get discouraged, Dad," she said, squeezing my hand. "I have all the faith in the world in you, and so does everyone else. You'll figure something out, I'm sure of it. Besides, we've got bodyguards now and all manner of security for the shows, so even if he shows up at one of the concerts he'll be faced with a phalanx of professionals whose sole job will be to protect John and the rest of us."

"Boy, I wish we could let John in on all this," I said. "Things would be a lot easier if he knew what was going on and we had his cooperation."

"I know," she said, "and I've discussed the idea with Aurie. But she and Heyoka worry that if too many people are made aware of what we're doing, of what the foundation is really all about, it could compromise our effectiveness. Much of what we want to do in the future will require absolute secrecy in order to succeed, and the more people who know about it, the more likely it will be for someone to let the cat out of the bag, either accidentally or on purpose. Right now, except for Sam, it's all family here in this dimension. At least it will be shortly. And we've all agreed that it should stay that way."

"Shortly, huh. When is the Big Day anyway?"

"We haven't decided yet, but you shouldn't get your hopes up for a 'Big Day.' We don't have time for a fancy wedding, nor do either of us want one. I know it's going to piss off the grandparents, but we'll probably just stop off at a justice of the peace somewhere and do a quickie. Right now we're trying to coordinate Jackson's travel schedule with stops at some major cities we're hoping to book as venues for the tour. And along the way we're going to be recruiting more performers. Meanwhile, Mom will be handling logistics and publicity with a team of agents and promoters she's putting together, and Jackson and I are going to be doing fundraising for the tour during our travels. So if you want to talk about full plates, all you have to do is look at ours."

"Fundraising? I thought this thing was going to be financed by the foundation."

"Sponsored by," she said. "We'll need a little funding at first—seed money—but if my plan works out, the expenses will be covered by donations and grants, plus the proceeds from sales of live albums, videos, and other merchandise. So all the profits will go straight to the causes we've chosen without being diluted by operating and administrative costs. I've got my own team of producers, road managers, and finance people working on developing the tour, and in addition to several stadiums here in the US, we're hoping to stage concerts in major venues around the world, including the UK, Hong Kong, Taipei, Prague, and even Sydney."

"Far out," I said, and I meant it. I had no idea they were planning anything of that magnitude. "So what about artists? You're going to need a lot more than the few you've recruited if you're going to fill that many venues."

"Well, once you got Stevie Wonder and Springsteen for us, the walls came tumbling down, so to speak. We already have commitments from over 30 of the top acts in the world, and believe it or not, we're even talking to The Stones. The cool thing is that not only are all of the ones we've signed so far playing for free, many are making substantial donations as well. This thing is going to be a monster, Dad, and we're going to save lots of lives. In fact, if things work out like we hope, we should be able to stave off the coming famine in Ethiopia and have enough left over to fund several other projects. Willie and Mellencamp are talking about doing something for farmers here in this country, so we'll probably get involved with that. And from there the sky really is the limit."

My daughter never ceased to amaze me. Her energy level was so far above mine, it was hard to believe she carried my genetic lineage. Of course, a lot of that came from Doris, whose workload was such that it would take ten people to replace her. That is, if you could find ten people with her brains and drive, which was doubtful.

The conversation had exhausted me, and Ellie must have realized this because she reached over and touched my drooping eyelids. "Get some sleep now, Dad," she whispered, gently closing my eyes with her fingers. "Everything's going to be okay. I promise."

Her cheerful optimism was often infectious, but on that somber afternoon it failed to raise my spirits. At the time I chalked this up to the waning effects of the hangover, however, I would later look back and wonder if it wasn't my intuition telling me that her prediction was destined to miss the mark by a wide margin.

As I dozed off, the final words of the last song I'd ever recorded drifted across the room. It was the song I'd written to my father long after his death in my first life; the one I'd recalled as I drove away from Heyoka's villa, only to stop and return:

Be there no graves in the fields of your memory
No end where there is no beginning
For passing before you the lives of your people
Must drown in the sea of their sinning

Nobody's winning
We're all just beginning
Beginning again

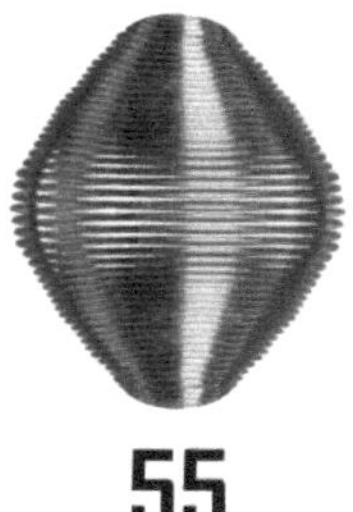

55
Best Laid Plans

"Have you thought any more about the music thing?" Aurélie asked me. She'd just finished a lengthy session with Sam and had called me down to the old studio to go over some newly discovered details on Chapman's life.

"I wish you'd leave that alone," I said. "I'm sick of everyone harassing me about getting back up on stage."

"Sorry. I was just—"

"Chapman's off the radar again," I said, interrupting her. "He flew back to the states about a month ago, leaving his wife in Hawaii. My people lost him in LA—he ditched them in Chinatown of all places. He's carrying a wad of cash he borrowed from his father-in-law, so he's not using credit cards, which makes his movements even harder to trace."

"That matches the timeline I have for him, except that his destination in the states was New York. Another thing I found out was that, for some reason, he'd become obsessed with the novel ***The Catcher in the Rye***. He even considered legally changing his name to Holden Caulfield."

"Our PIs mentioned something about that. They said he was splicing together reasons for killing John from the lyrics of Beatles songs, the soundtrack of ***The Wizard of Oz***, and quotations from the Caulfield book. This guy is really around the bend, but he's apparently got everyone fooled. And we can't touch him unless he does something illegal, which he hasn't even come close to doing so far."

"Is the tour kickoff still scheduled for next month?" she asked.

"Unfortunately, it is. I've tried to get Ellie to postpone the whole thing, but too much has gone into the planning. They have contractual obligations with dozens of acts, hundreds of support staff, and several major venues. About all we can do now is make sure John and Ellie and the rest of the artists slated for the first concert are blanketed with protection. We'll have agents stationed all over the place, and everyone who enters will be scrutinized as they pass through the gates. Plus, we've warned John that there have been numerous recent death threats against him and Yoko, and despite their objections, we managed to convince them they should get out of New York and move in with us at least a week before the event. We've also hired doubles who will take their place in the New York apartment, then fly to Tampa the day before the concert."

I had talked Ellie and Doris into holding the inaugural event at the Tampa Stadium, which had recently been remodeled and could now accommodate around 65,000 plus standing room when configured for a concert. I argued that the location wouldn't matter because of the worldwide publicity and international TV coverage, and that because our people would be familiar with the layout, security would be far simpler than at some huge open venue like Central Park or Watkins Glen. In addition, Sam had been working with Motorola on accelerating the implementation of cellular technology, and after a lengthy battle with the FCC, they'd joined with AT&T to gain approval for a test program in the Tampa Bay area. So our team would be equipped with wireless, handheld phones for instant communication throughout the region.

"Sounds like you've got all the bases covered," she said. "Heyoka and I are going to be looking in as well. If we can manage it."

"What do you mean, if you can manage it?" I asked.

"Well, I haven't wanted to burden you with any additional worries, but I guess it's time you knew that things are getting pretty critical for us. We're okay for now, although we've had to move into the lab on a more-or-less permanent basis because of the atmospheric toxicity and roaming gangs of survivalists and religious fanatics."

"I thought you guys had come up with some ideas to stabilize things," I said.

"We had, but there comes a point at which so many interdependent systems are failing—social, economic, technological, agricultural—the underlying structure of society itself begins to crumble. If Ellie's calculations are correct, that point is rapidly approaching, and the slope has become too slippery to hope for a reversal. There for a while we thought we were making some progress, but in order to institute widespread change we had to have the cooperation of governments and corporate entities, most of which have now either lost their authority or have simply collapsed."

"What are you going to do, then?" I said. "I mean, there has to be something, some kind of plan. What about the space program? Can't you somehow get off the planet?"

"We might have been able to a few years ago, when there was still something that vaguely resembled a space *program*. But Virgin, SpaceX, and the other private carriers have fallen apart along with the remnants of NASA, which long ago turned into an ineffective, bureaucratic coordinating entity. Once space exploration was turned over to private industry, cooperation became secondary to competition and profit generation, and the whole thing went the way of all the other privatized public services, which was essentially straight to hell. About all that's left are a dozen or so isolated settlements scattered throughout the solar system, with little or no connection to Earth other than the occasional audiovisual broadcast."

"But ... but you have to do something," I said. "You can't just go down with the ship like loyal sea captains. For one thing, we need you to help us avoid the same fate. For another, I don't want to lose—"

"We're working on it, Rix. The foundation will play a major role, and Heyoka has already made contact with his counterpart—his younger self—in your dimension, so he'll have a head start on some of our research. The problem there is that technology has to advance enough to facilitate things. Materials science, organic chemistry, computers, nanotechnology, and a dozen other disciplines have to mature before what we've been doing can be accomplished here. And that maturation can't be instant, it can only be accelerated somewhat by the introduction of new ideas. It's the same kind of limitation you've had to deal with in the recording field. You know, the lack of computer sophistication that kept you working in analog rather than digital. Sam has done wonders, but because of the slow pace of full-scale technological systems development, he's only been able to advance things by a few years."

I really wasn't that worried about us. Whatever happened, it would be decades before our world reached the critical stage theirs was going through. What I *was* worried about was Aurie disappearing on me forever. Even though I might never be able to have her here in the flesh, the thought of losing her—of not being able to talk to her, see her, hear her voice—was tearing me up inside. My brain had started to take on that old cement-mixer feeling when I suddenly had an idea.

"Have you contacted *your* counterpart here?" I asked. "Couldn't you transfer your mind into her? I know you said it would be like murder, but in this case, it wouldn't. No more than my reincarnation was."

She chuckled. "I know what you're thinking. That then you and I could hook up for real. But you're forgetting a couple of things."

"Oh? And what might those be?"

"For one," she said with reprimanding scowl, "you're married, and I would never do anything to interfere with your relationship. Doris is a friend, Rix, a close friend. And so is Ellie. Then there's the minor fact that, in your world, I'm less than a year old, which means you'd have to wait at least another fifteen years or so. And even if you did, in addition to committing adultery, you'd have to become a pedophile as well."

"Great," I said. "Just what I needed to hear. Isn't there anything else? You said if this experiment worked out, you might be looking into other possibilities for the technology. And it sure looks like it's working out, doesn't it?"

"It does, and we *were* planning an expansion of the program. But we had to go into survival mode some time ago, so other than the foundation and working with Ellie on forecasting, we've put most of that on hold. We *are* working on one thing that may turn out to be important, though."

"Yes?" I said, when she didn't elaborate.

"Uh ... hold on a sec." She seemed to have mentally gone somewhere else, then she blinked a couple of times and came back. "I explained a little of this before, that day back at the villa when you were asking about our progress in developing quantum teleportation. It has to do with a highly advanced version of 3D printing. You know what that is?"

I'd read some things about 3D printers in my first life, so I had an idea of the basic concept. "Sort of," I said. "They take instructions from a program that tells them how to build things from layers of fast-hardening liquid plastics. Right?"

"Right. That's where the technology stood before you left. It's come a long way since then, and we've been on the cutting edge. We now have machines that can print almost anything in any combination of materials we choose, with an accuracy down to the atomic level."

"That sounds ... interesting," I said, "but what does it have to do with—"

"If you'll please let me finish?" she said, suddenly seeming impatient with my questions. "We've ... wait a minute." She looked distracted again, but after a few seconds she sighed and continued. "We've been talking with Sam about building a state-of-the-art 3D printer here. There are many hurdles to overcome, but Sam is an incredibly bright and resourceful fellow, so we may be able to jump over some of those hurdles quicker than we'd originally hoped."

I started to ask another question, but she held up a finger to silence me.

"If we're successful, it should allow us to reconstruct material objects from our dimension by sending instructions to a printer in yours. We can't transfer the actual objects, but we *can* send information in the form of binary data, which is all I am here in this dimension, a holographic image scanned and converted to a bunch of ones and zeros, then sent here much like a television transmission. And, of course, computer programs and files already *are* binary data, so we can send the instructions for building any object we scan and convert here. If we have a 3D printer on your end and can duplicate the necessary elemental materials, we should be able to print exact copies of almost any object that exists in our dimension."

It took a moment for this to sink in, and once it did I began to wonder about the possibilities. I was trying to formulate some questions that wouldn't sound too stupid, when she shook her head in exasperation. "Dammit," she said, "the alarm's going off again. I've got to run."

"Alarm?" I said, as her image began to waver. "Wait ... Please." But before I could get another word out she dissolved into a billion translucent pixels and disappeared with an almost audible pop.

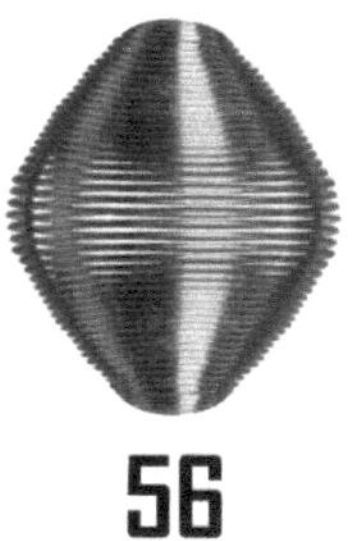

56
Collateral Damage

Coined in early 1961 by economist T. C. Schelling, the term "collateral damage" would soon become the military's favorite euphemism for the killing of innocent men, women, and children. Since then, it has been used (and misused) to describe a wide range of indiscriminant, reckless killings, one example of which appeared in a particularly gruesome newspaper article published on Pearl-Harbor Day in 1980. In this report, the term was misused to describe the deaths of five teenagers, two preteens, and four adults at the hands of a lunatic by the name of Mark David Chapman. I say misused, because in order for there to have been "collateral" damage, a successful attack on an intended target would have to have occurred. In this case, however, that intended target, one John Ono Lennon, escaped unharmed. The "damage," therefore, should have been described, not as collateral, but as the deliberate, senseless murder of eleven innocent persons.

TO SAY THE PRE-CONCERT scene on the eve of Pearl Harbor Day was chaotic would be a vast understatement. Much like the frantic confusion preceding a formal wedding, the combination of last-minute adjustments, petty arguments, late arrivals, and technical problems created an atmosphere of frenzied pandemonium that only the calm, guiding hands of my wife and daughter could have steered to a successful conclusion. I, on the other hand, found myself drowning in a quagmire of near-paralytic confusion as I attempted to coordinate the several-dozen members of our security team.

As if dealing with a standing-room-only crowd of over 70,000 unruly fans wasn't enough, a dozen major broadcast and cable networks showed up, each with its own trucks and wires and pea-brained spokesmodels, all jockeying for position with a swarm of radio crews, print journalists, and freelance photographers.

We had awarded the primary contract for live coverage and documentary filming to CBS. And, in addition to a worldwide satellite broadcast of the concert, David Geffen had put together a concept that would later become the format for the syndicated TV show Entertainment Tonight. The first syndicated program ever to be distributed via satellite, this bit of overenthusiastic theater would eventually become the most watched entertainment show in the world. But on the night of December sixth, 1980 it served only as one more irritating distraction.

We had picked up Chapman's trail again when he used the alias David Caulfield to buy a plane ticket from LA to New York. By then we were sure he was aware of being followed, because he had made several attempts to elude the tails we put on him. In New York, the PIs observed him loitering near the entrance to John and Yoko's apartment building, and at first we thought the doubles were fooling him. Then, three days before the concert, he stopped showing up, and that afternoon they lost track of him. We had tried to get the FBI involved, but even though the antipathy toward Lennon bred in the Nixon-J. Edgar Hoover era had mellowed somewhat, a latent residue of hostility remained, and they refused to offer us any help.

Chapman had checked out of the shabby hotel where he'd been staying, leaving on foot and employing several switchbacks and dangerous maneuvers in heavy traffic in an attempt to evade our surveillance team. They managed to keep him in their sights until he entered Central Park, where they finally lost him. After a mad scramble, during which they checked airports, bus terminals, train stations, and even car-rental agencies, we were forced to assume he had somehow managed to leave the city undetected and was on his way south, perhaps in a vehicle he'd paid cash for at a used-car lot.

This was long before law enforcement had a nationwide computer network for tracking the movement of criminals and suspects, so we were going to have to rely solely on our security plan for the stadium and the access routes we'd determined to be the safest. By the afternoon of the sixth I was in state of sheer panic, though I tried to project calm confidence as I went about coordinating the dozens of armed agents, unarmed spotters, and off-duty cops we'd stationed in and around the enormous stadium complex.

The doubles charade appeared to be working when crowds began to gather outside the Floridian Hotel in downtown Tampa, where the two impersonators had been delivered by stretch limo a day before the concert. We checked them into the same suite Elvis had occupied during a concert tour in 1955, then strategically "leaked" their location to the press. Meanwhile, John and Yoko were safely ensconced in one of the upstairs bedrooms at our house in St. Pete. And since there was no unusual increase in traffic around the house, we assumed we'd managed to fool the public. However, the fact that Chapman had abandoned his surveillance of the New York apartment three days earlier suggested to me that he'd caught on to our attempted diversion. And when he was not seen following the limo to the stadium, or spotted among the crowds surrounding the entrance where the actors were dropped off, I felt sure he'd caught on to our ruse.

The concert was scheduled to begin at eight o'clock, and by six the stadium was nearly full, with only a few dozen nosebleed seats and standing room remaining. I had begun to think Chapman was planning to attempt the assassination somewhere other than at the event, when one of our agents reported seeing someone who looked suspicious. I made my way to the ticket booth where the agent was stationed, calling half a dozen other security staff members to meet me. And when I arrived, sure enough, there he was, standing about twenty spots back in the line. His disguise was amateurish: fake mustache and beard, with a Bogart Fedora pulled low across his face and a heavy overcoat inappropriate for the mild Florida weather. The bulk of the coat suggested he was carrying a weapon, perhaps a shotgun or some kind of semiautomatic military rifle.

We had no authority to detain him or even to legally refuse him entry; however, since it seemed clear he was hiding something, I walked over to one of the off-duty policemen we'd hired and told him of my suspicions. By the time Chapman made it through the turnstile, six cops had joined with eight security guards to form a loose semicircular barricade inside the gate. At my signal, the cop I'd spoken to approached him and politely asked if he would mind opening his coat. His mouth dropped open, and for a couple of seconds he seemed bewildered. But then the bewildered look changed to one of outrage, and he proceeded to go ballistic.

It would be another twenty-plus years before the events of 9/11 would lead to a change in the accepted behavior of law enforcement, and on that night there was much more tolerance displayed than there probably would have been in the twenty-first century. Despite the fact that Chapman was yelling at the top of his lungs, everyone kept their distance while he screamed about his rights and the constitution and police harassment. He did not, however, make any specific threats or aggressive physical moves, so there was little the cop could do other than try to reason with him. And he did an admirable job, remaining calm and apologizing, while pleading for cooperation so they could resolve things before the concert began. He even made up a story about someone reporting that Chapman was carrying a gun, saying that stadium security rules would not allow him to be seated until he proved he was unarmed.

The confrontation went on for five minutes or so, while the cops and security guards slowly closed ranks. And just when it looked like Chapman was about to give up, a loud series of sharp explosions rang out, freezing everyone in place. We would later determine that the machinegun-like clatter had come from a string of firecrackers some kid had thrown from a passing car, but at the time it incited panic among the officers, many of whom fell to their knees with weapons drawn.

A look of terror spread across Chapman's face as he backed toward the ticket booth with hands raised. "Alright, alright," he yelled. Then, before anyone could move, he turned and vaulted the iron railing, flailing his arms as he approached the confused patrons outside the gate. The ensuing chase was hindered by the milling crowd, into which Chapman had vanished like the ghostly baseball players in Kevin Costner's ***Field of Dreams***. After a half-hour of futile searching, I realized we had left a large portion of the stadium unguarded, and reluctantly called everyone back to their posts. It took a while, but once the crowd calmed down and some semblance of order was restored, everything went so smoothly I began to worry that we were all being lulled to sleep by the lack of action.

The concert itself went off without a hitch, and judging by the crowds lined up at the sales booths, the merchandise must have been flying off the shelves. At around two in the morning, the remaining patrons gathered at the side exit, waiting patiently for the stars to appear. We had announced several times that security concerns would not allow any of the performers to sign autographs, but that hadn't deterred the two-hundred or so loyal fans.

A perimeter of security guards stood behind a line of low concrete barriers, and the anxious fans were pressing against their outstretched arms when Springsteen and his band members emerged from the tunnel. They waved to the crowd as they climbed into a line of station wagons, and before the screams died down, Stevie Wonder and his group appeared, piling into three vans and waving from the windows as they drove away. Next came Jackson Browne, Miss Sarah Love, Patsy Cline, and James Taylor, followed by Danny Kortchmar, Leland Sklar, Russ Kunkel, David Lindley, and the rest of the all-star house band Ellie and Jackson had assembled for the concert.

A determined group of fans still lingered, as our John and Yoko doubles strolled out wearing dark shades and ducking quickly into a stretch limo. The Lennons were staying with us, and we were determined to wait as long as possible before leaving. Finally, when only about fifty fans remained, the five of us, all dressed in scruffy cutoffs and t-shirts in order to look like straggling roadies, shuffled slowly from the tunnel.

On the far side of the stadium, the real roadies were loading semi-trucks, and an occasional screech or thud from equipment being moved echoed in the empty parking lot, along with yells from the load-out crews as they tried to make themselves heard over the rumble of diesel engines. It was this reverberating commotion that momentarily disguised the squeal of tires and the crunch of bodies being hit when Chapman drove the rusty '56 Chevy he'd bought through the remaining crowd and into the concrete barrier. Unfortunately, instead of impeding the car's forward progress, the knee-high barrier leaned inward, becoming a nearly perfect launching ramp.

Twisted bodies bounced from the hood and fenders as the car rose into the air, where it appeared to hang suspended for a moment. Then it tilted slightly to one side, slammed into the driveway, and skidded toward Doris and Ellie. After that everything seemed to happen in slow motion: cops running, people screaming, the sickening sound of metal scraping asphalt. The last thing I remember seeing—the image that would haunt me for the rest of my days—was Doris's face, eyes wide with fright, as she looked over at me an instant before the car pinned her against the stadium wall in a bloody mass of torn flesh and mangled body parts.

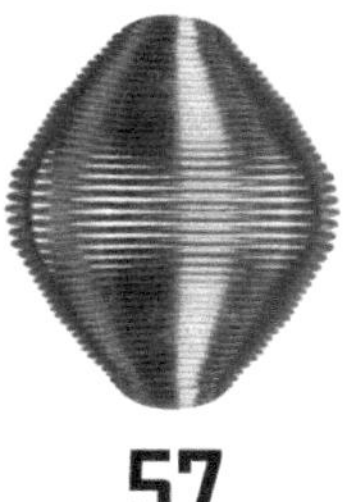

57
Suicide Is Painless

I replayed the scene in my mind for the thousandth time as we watched Doris's coffin disappear into the ground. Ellie had to lean on me for support because she'd insisted on leaving her crutches in the car. Fortunately, her injuries had been repairable: a broken fibula, some cuts and bruises, and three cracked ribs. The fibula required a bulky cast, but in a few weeks she'd be good as new—physically. Emotionally, it was hard to tell. So far she appeared to be doing a lot better than me in that department. Then again, now that Chapman was out of the picture, she had much more to occupy her mind than I did, with the tour and the foundation and her work with Aurie and Heyoka. And without Doris's help her workload would be even heavier.

Later that evening, as we sat at the dining-room table staring over the remnants of casseroles and deserts, we both seemed too exhausted to speak. The initial shock and trauma had been dulled by the confusion of coordinating Doris's funeral arrangements, while at the same time fielding hundreds of sympathetic phone calls and dealing with a whirlwind of press inquiries. Now it felt as if we'd been left drenched in the wake of a passing storm. Though in some ways the silence was a relief, it also created a void, into which the tidal wave of our dammed-up grief threatened to explode. I was trying to think of some way to avoid a shared emotional breakdown, when Ellie beat me to it.

"We need to talk," she said, straightening up in her chair and squaring her shoulders. "And not about Mom or the past." Her transformation was uncannily swift: the sadness melted from her face and within seconds her expression hardened into one of stubborn determination. "There's too much important stuff going on to waste time feeling sorry for ourselves."

"Okay," I said, thinking how much she sounded like Doris. "So what do you—"

"To begin with," she interrupted, "you need to catch up with what's been happening. You've been so busy trying to stop Chapman, we haven't wanted to bother you with a bunch of progress reports, but a lot has happened over the past year."

"No shit," I said. "Not the least of which is that I fucked up royally."

"Stop it, goddammit!" The anger in her voice startled me. "No one could have anticipated what happened, and you know it. If Mom were here she'd probably slap you silly for thinking any of this was your fault. So get over it, Dad. We don't have time for that crap. Now shut up and listen!"

ELLIE WAS RIGHT; A lot *had* happened since I'd last heard from anyone about the foundation's activities. Whenever she or Aurie had spent time with me, the discussion always centered on the tour and Chapman, with an occasional allusion to my getting back into writing and performing. That was a subject I had continued to sidestep, citing my need to concentrate on the security situation. Now, however, I no longer had that excuse.

"First," she said, "you should know that the foundation's focus has changed. Combining some of my research with the computing capabilities Heyoka's developed, we've been able to extrapolate the efficacy of several models, each based on the influences of numerous variables."

"English, please," I said.

"Listen, Aurie is going to be here later to fill you in on some of the details. And she's a lot better at breaking things down into understandable language. So if you want simple explanations, ask her. Bottom line is that we've run numerous models, and the data tell us that the major problem—the reason things are falling apart in their dimension—is not due exclusively to the misuse of technological advances, as we first thought. In fact, the primary influences are sociopolitical, ingrained cultural and religious belief systems and corporate gluttony that inevitably lead to chaos and anarchy, no matter how scientifically advanced the society becomes. What we run into at every turn is, for lack of a better term, human nature—the incredible stupidity, stubbornness, and greed of the human animal."

"Duh. Tell me something I don't already know."

"Don't worry, there'll be a lot of that when Aurie gets here. What I'm trying to do is give you an overview of what we're up against. All this time we've been worrying about the impact of technology, when it wasn't the scientific advances that were the root of the problem. It was how they were used by radical fringe groups, governments—including our own—and multinational corporations. And the only way to affect long-term, positive change in those areas is by altering the basic attitude of society toward things like the concentration of power in the corporate sector, weakening of governmental regulation over the business community, ecological indifference, and the rise of militant religious fundamentalism."

"Tall order," I said. "Sounds like a return to the hippie philosophy. Unfortunately, that movement didn't have the earthshaking effect we all thought it would. At least not in the world I came from. The old Gandhi bit about being the change you want to see in the world didn't seem to work out very well once it was drowned out by Reagan's philosophy of materialism, and Gordon Gekko's 'Greed is Good' became the motto of the late twentieth century."

"Gordon Gekko?" she said.

"Character in a movie. Sorry, I guess that one won't hit the theaters for a while. My point is that the movement to alter the so-called sociopolitical landscape has already failed, despite a valiant effort by millions of dedicated activists. Or, maybe I should say it *will* ultimately fail. You've seen what's happening in Heyoka and Aurie's world. And if, as you say, technology isn't the problem, then it probably can't bail us out either. So what do you scientific wizards plan to do about it?"

"There isn't much we can do by ourselves," she said. "That's not to say the kind of scientific advancements they've come up with can't play a role. They can, if they are properly introduced and utilized. But it's going to take a serious alteration of public sentiment to redirect the course of history. And that's where you come in."

"Me? What the hell do I have to do with any of this?"

"Not a lot," she said. "Not yet, anyway. And I don't mean only you. I mean anyone who's in a position to sway the emotions and political beliefs of large portions of the populace."

"You sure you're talking to me?" I said, turning to look over my shoulder. I got up and peered into the empty kitchen. "Nope. Nobody in there."

"Very funny," she said. "Come back in here and sit down."

"Getting pretty bossy in your old age," I said, flipping my chair around and straddling it backwards. I rested my chin on the top rung and grinned at her.

"What I'm getting at," she said, "is that it all comes down to effective communication, making the kind of emotional connection that goes deeper than mere words or fiery rhetoric and connects with the public in ways so subtle they don't even realize what's happening."

"Ah, you're talking about subliminal advertising. Kind of unethical, don't you think?"

"Actually, I *am* talking about something subliminal, but not in the way you're thinking. And, no, I don't think it's unethical. There's nothing hidden or clandestine about it. It's simply a way of openly expressing ideas and concepts to a broad spectrum of the public, a method of communication that transcends ethnic barriers and geographical borders, that communicates on a level so fundamental it can speak directly to the collective psyche."

"I assume this something new you guys have developed?"

"Boy, Dad, how dense can you be? Okay, before we start playing Twenty Questions, let me give you another hint. Think ***Close Encounters of the Third Kind***.

My density was, of course, an act. I had a pretty good idea of where all this was leading, but I really was hoping they'd come up with some super new communication device. At the risk of pissing her off, I decided to carry the act one step further. "Oh, I get it," I said, "you've made contact with aliens and they've agreed to help us mass-hypnotize the entire population of the planet."

"I'm going to ignore that," she said. "You know what I'm talking about. Look, you say the movements of the sixties and seventies were failures, but that's only partially true. The so-called hippies and their philosophy of peace and love eventually put an end to the Vietnam War, not to mention the influence they had on the civil rights movement, ecological preservation, and nuclear disarmament. And in all those endeavors it was music that led the way. Starting with Bob Dylan, Peter, Paul & Mary, Joni Mitchell, and others from the folk era, then moving into mainstream pop and rock with Denver, Lennon, Jackson, and Springsteen, among many others, it was music that kept the message alive. Problem was, too many of the hippies grew up and joined the so-called "real world," changing their priorities from promoting peace and equality and ecological balance to accumulating money and becoming part of the traditional political establishment."

"Maybe so, but that's only stating the obvious," I said. "It's a little too late to do anything about it now."

"Not so" she said. "You're forgetting where we are in that progression. In our world there's still time. And if anyone has the talent to do what's necessary, it's you. I'm not saying music is the only answer, but it *can* be an integral part—a significant part—of the solution. And with the foundation's money and support, we have a good chance of stemming the tide."

"You know," I said, "I've put up with this poorly-disguised conspiracy you guys have been trying to shove down my throat, but laying some sort of savior guilt trip on me is stooping pretty low." I slammed my fist down on the table, rattling the dishes. "Doesn't anybody give a shit about what I want? I'm not a goddamned politician, for Christ's sake. Nor do I want to be. Basically, I just want to be left alone."

"To do what?" she shouted, "crawl in a hole and lick your wounds while the rest of the world goes down the tubes?" Seeing my shock at her harsh tone, she hesitated for a moment, then lowered her voice. "Nobody's trying to put a guilt trip on you, Dad. We're all just trying to survive. And I don't care what you think, we need your help. Besides, you need something to drag you out of this downward spiral you're in before you lose it and slit your wrists or something."

Without thinking, I glanced down at my arm. I quickly looked away, but by then she was limping around the table.

"I read about that in Mom's journals," she whispered, leaning awkwardly to touch the smooth skin. "We talked about it, and although I'm sure she never mentioned it to you, she always worried that one day depression might get the better of you again. It's one of the reasons she finally decided to talk you into liquidating the business."

In this life there were no visible scars, no fading ribbons of white; only the flickering memory of that night when I'd sat on the seawall and tried to carve death from my veins with a chisel. I wondered if Ellie's fears were justified; the guilt and pain were obviously enough to bring the possibility to mind. And now she was adding another layer of stress by suggesting I could play a role in changing the course of history. It was silly, of course; I knew that intellectually. But emotionally, it only exacerbated my growing depression. With Doris gone and Aurélie's world on the brink of annihilation, I didn't have much to live for anyway. Ellie would be fine, I knew. She was far beyond needing my help or even my guidance, which meant my parental obligations had essentially been fulfilled …

"Dad?" she said.

As the room slowly rematerialized around me, I managed a smile. "Don't worry about that, honey," I said. "I'll be fine. I just need some time to get my head together." I stood and lifted her to her feet. "Now we'd better clean up this mess before it turns into a roach banquet." I could see the skepticism in her eyes, so I held her gently by the shoulders and nodded toward the table. "Come on, kiddo. Give me a hand here."

After we'd stored the leftovers in Tupperware and loaded the dishwasher, Ellie went upstairs to change and wake Jackson, who'd flown in from a gig in Montreal for the funeral and hadn't gotten much sleep in the past 36 hours. The two of them were scheduled to fly to Quebec City later that night for another of his tour stops, and I began to dread the idea of being left alone. Solitude, I knew, would inevitably lead to retrospect, and in my fragile state of mind I didn't think I could handle a lot of forced hindsight.

Later, as I watched them drive off, my grip on reality seemed to weaken with the dwindling glow of their tail lights. I stood for a long time in the middle of the road, while the world around me wavered and melted like a Dali painting.

I MUST HAVE LOST a significant chunk of time because the next thing I knew my surroundings were abruptly resolved into clarity by the ring of a cash register.

"You know, my friend," Jerry said as he laid some bills and coins on the counter, "you could save a lot of money at Ace Liquors down the street. Not that I'm complaining, mind you. Here, let me see if I can find you something to carry those in."

I waited while he rummaged around under the bar and came up with a wrinkled, brown grocery bag, into which he put the two quarts of Jack Daniels I had apparently bought. "You okay, buddy?" he asked when I picked up the bag and stood without moving. Still confused, I nodded and turned toward the door, nearly colliding with Helen on her way back to the bar with a tray of empty glasses.

"Sorry," I mumbled, shifting the bag to secure it under one arm.

"No problem, honey," she said. She set the tray on the counter and picked up my change. "Hey, don't you want this?"

Shouldering the door open, I waved my free hand to indicate that I didn't care about the money.

A chill December breeze swept across the parking lot as I leaned against the car and rifled through my pockets in search of the keys. Coming up empty, I peered through the window and saw them hanging from the ignition. Fortunately the door was unlocked, but once behind the wheel, I realized the really fortunate thing was that the car was still there at all. Not only had I left the keys in the ignition, I'd forgotten to lock the door, oversights that were just plain stupid in this neighborhood.

The drive home was shrouded in a misty montage of memories: disconnected flashes from both my lives, strung together like random movie clips with no discernable association.

Another time lapse found me sitting on the patio with a glass of whiskey in my hand, squinting at a blurry apparition of Aurélie. A shimmering glow from the underwater pool light had drawn insects that attracted our resident bats, and it was only when one of the flying rodents startled her by dive-bombing toward the water that I realized she wasn't an alcoholic hallucination. Twilight had faded into a moonless night, but there was still enough light from the pool to illuminate her face.

"Bats," I said. "They're drawn by the bugs. You look ... younger."

"You look drunk."

"Why do you look younger?"

"Why are you drinking?"

"I was thirsty. Why do you look younger?" Our silly banter joined with the early winter chill to sharpen my senses, and I was determined to wait for an answer.

Finally, she sighed. "It's experimental—genetics stuff. Heyoka mention it to you before. Now what's up with the booze?"

"The booze?" I said, raising my glass in a mock salute. "The booze is keeping me warm. As for what's up, I guess you could say my patience is up." My tongue felt like a swollen hockey puck, and a quick glance at the half-empty bottle on the table told me why. When I looked back at Aurie, she was rubbing her forehead.

"I … I can understand that, Rix" she said. "So is mine. So is Heyoka's. But at least we're not throwing in the towel."

"Who says I'm—"

"Don't try to bullshit me! I know you too well. Look, we have a lot to talk about, and I need for you to be fully cognizant, not half in the bag."

When I didn't respond, she stared up at the trees. After a few seconds she looked back down, and the dim light reflected from her eyes in tiny sparkles. She blinked, and two of the sparkles fell, leaving glistening streaks as they slid down her cheeks. It was unusual for her to openly display emotion, and the sight was both heart-wrenching and somehow perversely reassuring.

"You know," she said, flipping the tears away with a finger, "I do love you. I'm sorry I don't say it very often, but it's true. And I hate that I can't touch you, or wake up in the morning in your bed. Or—right now—beat you over the head until you come to your goddamned senses." The words came out in breathy spurts, and when she finished her eyes were red and swollen.

Over time I had learned to quell my instinctive desire to reach for her, but I knew I had to do something. So I set my glass down and, holding onto the table for support, rose unsteadily to my feet. "Give me a minute," I said. I shuffled to the edge of the pool, took a deep breath, and dove in. The icy water provided a jolt of adrenalin that instantly counteracted the alcohol high, replacing it with the shock of sudden circulatory distress. I emerged on the other side, gasping for air and shivering, but nearly sober. I slogged back around the pool in my sodden shoes and stood in front of her, dripping like a wet sponge. "Okay," I said, "let me find a towel. Then I'll listen."

COULD YOU PLEASE PUT some clothes on?"

I was standing in the music room, just inside the glass doors to the patio, drying myself. I'd long ago stopped being embarrassed about Aurie seeing me naked, although this, I realized, was the first time I'd undressed in front of her since the transfer. "Why?" I said. "Nobody's here to see me."

"Oh, so I'm nobody," she said. "How would you like it if I took off *my* clothes?" Seeing my smirk, she rolled her eyes. "Don't answer that. The point is ... well, frankly, I'm dealing with a bit of an overactive libido, at the moment."

"A bit of an overactive libido," I mused. "Are you trying to say you're horny?"

"I've never much cared for that word. At least when it's applied to me." She looked away to hide her reddening cheeks. "It sounds so, I don't know, irrational. But in this case, I guess ... okay, the truth is I've been pretty seriously horny for years now."

"You don't mean to tell me you've been celibate all this time. I find that hard to believe."

"What would make you say that?" she said. "Before I met you, I'd gone over a decade without having sex—without even *wanting* to have sex. And since you've been away I've been too absorbed in my work to give it much thought."

"Apparently not," I said, wrapping the towel around my waist.

"I didn't mean ... what I meant was ... Oh, hell, it's probably this damned age-regression thing. Not that I haven't wanted you all along. But you know I don't dwell on impossibilities. And right now neither of us needs the distraction. There are more important things going on in both our lives."

"If you say so," I said, sitting on the piano stool and shoving the towel down between my knees. "Is this acceptable, or are you going to make me go upstairs and actually get dressed?"

"No, no. That's fine. Now let me bring you up to date."

AURIE'S UPDATE WAS CLEARLY intended to lift my spirits, and it probably would have if only I'd been able to get the word "impossibilities" out of my head. To make matters worse, she refused to discuss anything that might give me hope of one day having her with me in the flesh. Instead, it sounded more like she was delivering a scientific paper.

Although she admitted that things had continued to deteriorate in their dimension, other than being isolated, they were, she claimed, doing pretty well. The lab had always been a self-contained compound, generating its own power, while scrubbing and recirculating water and a breathable atmosphere. To that they had added a food-production operation that relied in part on the 3D printing technology she'd described to me earlier. They could now reproduce almost anything using the basic chemical building blocks found in nature, including structures as small as bacteria and viruses.

The Large Hadron Collider had long ago been shut down; however, their own accelerator was now self-sufficient, no longer requiring the sympathetic influence of the LHC. I hadn't realized how important the accelerator was to their research efforts, thinking its main purpose was to facilitate the interdimensional transfer experiment. Turned out that was only one of its many functions, the most important being its contribution to basic R&D.

On our end, using their instructions, Sam had built a rudimentary 3D printer that was constantly being upgraded by printing the parts needed for each incremental improvement. The process was slow and fraught with technical problems, but progress was steady, with the hope of one day being able to duplicate organic structures and compounds that could help in the fight against disease, plus various nanoparticles and the basic components of quantum cybernetics, whatever that meant.

When it came to the foundation, as Ellie had said, its work had shifted from an exclusive focus on experiments concerning the impact of scientific innovations, to developing plans for strategic social and political intervention. These were being orchestrated and guided by computer-enhanced versions of Ellie's algorithms, which would eventually lay the groundwork for predicting the potential ramifications of each carefully considered course of action.

"I know you don't want to hear it," she said, "but what Ellie said about our needing your help is true. It's complicated to explain, and you're probably not going to like it …" She waited, and when I didn't respond she continued.

"What we've come up with is a long-term strategy that, among other things, involves subtly influencing politics by altering public perception. Some of this can be accomplished through traditional methods—information campaigns, money to support the right social causes, both domestically and abroad, international economic manipulations and the like. However, in order for these to work, there has to be a common thread that connects everything conceptually and reaches the broader populace on an emotional level."

"Sounds to me like you guys have gone off the deep end," I said. "I mean, sure, music might have played a small role in some social changes in the past, but those didn't last. And we both know how much more influential money and political power will turn out to be. All you have to do is look at what the Koch brothers and Murdoch and a few other demigods did in your world. Besides, what about all the terrorists? Music is not going to change the minds of religious fanatics or their ignorant followers who believe in fantasies like the Apocalypse or the promise of 72 virgins awaiting them in heaven."

"You'd be surprised," she said. "You have to stop thinking so narrowly about subcategories like terrorism or politics or economics. What we're talking about is something much broader, something that not only includes those things, but transcends them. Think of it as analogous to the slow movement of tectonic plates as opposed to the localized phenomenon of earthquakes. Or maybe the difference between millennial climate change and seasonal weather patterns. It will require decades of subtle maneuvering, and the struggle will be ongoing. The first phase will be to build a base, a permanent, unshakable foundation from which we and our descendants can continue to watch over and support the metamorphosis. But for any of this to be effective in the long run, we first have to create a universal atmosphere in which such an emotional and psychological transformation can occur. And that's where you come in."

"*Our* descendants?" I said. "Does that mean—"

"Sorry. Slip of the tongue. What I meant was that, for now at least, we are in this together. Heyoka and I are dedicated to the project, and as long as we're still around, we'll be doing our best to help out. Hopefully we can train other researchers in your dimension to replace our team, and if all goes as planned, the young Heyoka can eventually take over leadership of the technological branch. But that's beside the point. What I was trying to get across is that each facet of the project is important—indispensable, actually. Without everything working together, it falls on its face. And whether you want to believe it or not, music *is* one of those facets, a powerful one that all the money and science and political maneuvering in the world cannot hope to duplicate."

"Excuse me," I said. "This is a little much to take in all at once. I need a drink." I was preparing to argue my case when she surprised me.

"Okay," she said, "but not that crap you've been drinking. There's a bottle in the cabinet above the fridge. It's been there for months. We had Sam put it together just in case *you* decided to go off the deep end."

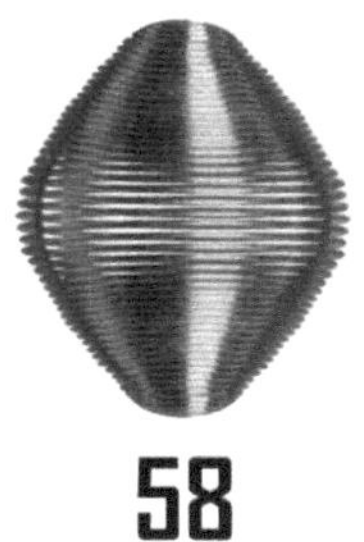

58
Capitulation

The intriguing thing about Aurie's sales spiel was how much it reminded me of a sexual seduction. Not that there was any suggestion of such a possibility; only that all the elements combined to resemble a scenario not unlike those I'd relied on in my first life to help me worm my way into the pants of several young girls.

First, there was the innate but unspoken desire a randy young man can sense in a reluctant virgin. The analogous urge for me lay in a long-suppressed desire for another taste of the recognition I'd once enjoyed—for public acknowledgment that my musical talents were appreciated and respected.

A second enticement—for the girls—was the promise of a new kind of pleasure. For me, this was echoed in the prospect of doing what Jackson had referred to as something pure, something I'd seldom experienced in my first life because I'd been too tied up in the quest for fame and monetary reward. Of course, it was absurd for Aurie to suggest that my participation could serve as anything more than an insignificant adjunct to their grand plan. Still, the possibility of doing something even minimally altruistic was intriguing.

Finally, there was a third similarity: the compelling desire to please someone I loved. In the girls' case, this would have been due more to a naïve infatuation than anything approaching what I felt for Aurie. But the same imperative applied: when asked to surrender by someone with an almost mystical power over your emotions—someone whose disappointment you wished to avoid at all costs—refusing became nearly impossible.

I can't say for certain if her platonic seduction was planned or if she was even consciously aware of the power she wielded over me, but there was no denying her sincerity. Before she was halfway through with her presentation, my previously impenetrable wall of resistance had begun to crumble, the only thing left to shore it up being fear. As irrational as it seemed, I was terrified by the prospect of exposing my deteriorating skills on the public stage.

AFTER I RETRIEVED THE bottle of fake Jack and donned a terrycloth robe, we moved back to the patio, where the constant whine of a thousand tree frogs provided a backdrop of mind-numbing white noise. The soothing, almost hypnotic sound, like a coating of auditory honey, further softened my resolve, leaving me grasping at flimsy straws of rebuttal that snapped one by one under the onslaught of her carefully constructed argument. Even my fear did not escape her notice.

"I know you're scared," she said when she concluded her speech and I remained silent. "But I also know your fear is based on emotion, not logic or reality. As far as I can tell, you haven't lost a beat when it comes to performing, though I'll admit I'm not musically competent enough to notice any minor flaws. What I do know—what we both know—is that even if those flaws exist, they can easily be eliminated with a little practice. You still have a beautiful voice, Rix. And if Jackson is to be believed, your guitar technique ranks above almost anyone's. Not only that—and most importantly—you're an incredible writer, adept at turning ideas and stories into soul-stirring, commercially viable songs."

My surrender had evolved so slowly I wasn't aware I'd begun to capitulate until I heard myself say, "So what exactly do you want me to do?"

"First," she said, "you have to become a superstar."

AFTER ANOTHER QUICK ROUND of feeble objections, I gave up and let Aurie explain the plan Ellie and Jackson had devised. Jackson had actually mentioned it over a year ago, during what I'd come to think of as the 'Intervention,' though at the time I'd been so dead set against performing it hadn't registered. Now, however, I saw that, from a promotional and marketing standpoint, it just might work. The strategy involved introducing me to the public as the writer of a couple of dozen top-ten hits—songs first recorded by some of the most famous artists in pop music. These included several number ones, a few Grammy winners, ten gold records, and numerous popular cuts on platinum albums. Aurie referred to it as the "Taylor-King" plan, in reference to the way James had transformed Carole from an obscure song writer into an international superstar by introducing her on his now-legendary ***You've Got a Friend*** tour. For my introduction, we had the triple whammy of Jackson Browne, Patsy Cline, and the one and only Miss Sarah Love.

Jimmy had already committed to act as my producer, and Geffen—who had recently agreed to take over logistics for the charity tour—would handle promotion and distribution of my records. The plan was to introduce me during the tour's final concert, which was scheduled for September at Watkins Glen, a venue that still held the all-time concert-attendance record of 600,000 at its 1973 Summer Jam.

"So you'll have at least nine months to scrape off the rust and start writing," she said. "The initial phase will be to establish your new career, and Geffen feels sure we can do that based on your previous writings, with perhaps one or two new songs. After that, we'll be working closely with you to develop material that will complement our ongoing efforts. The reason your participation is so important is that even if there were some other artist with your musical talents and song-writing abilities—which there isn't—we couldn't approach them with our own ideas for subject matter. We have Jackson, of course, and he's already working on some things, but we need a fresh face, someone who can explode onto the scene and capture the attention of a worldwide audience."

"So, you're going to tell me what to write?" I said, trying to quiet the anger that suddenly arose in my chest.

"Not *exactly* what to write," she said. "If we could do that we wouldn't need you for anything more than performing. What we want to do is provide you with some concepts, ideas that will integrate with and support what we're trying to accomplish. It won't be easy, Rix. You're going to have to suppress that ego of yours—stop thinking about yourself and start worrying about the next generation, the one your daughter and her kids will be struggling to survive in. And if you want to accuse me of laying a guilt trip on you, go right ahead, because that's precisely what I'm doing."

IT TOOK ME A while to calm down and let Aurie's words sink in. Thankfully, she seemed to sense my growing angst, and instead of pressing the matter, she remained silent while I tried to straighten things out in my head.

I definitely wasn't convinced about the viability of the Grand Social Experiment—it sounded impossibly complicated and the expected results were, I thought, naïvely optimistic. But I had already committed to my small part in it, and I realized she was right about the selfish way I'd been thinking. I hadn't given much thought to a future I didn't intend to stick around for, nor had I considered the possibility that Ellie and Jackson might have a family, in which case I would have to think of my grandkids' quality of life, not to mention that of my friends and their families.

I still had many questions. So while I silently worked on my grumbling ego, I grilled her about the other facets of the project. I did my best to play devil's advocate, though now it was more an attempt to understand and point out flaws than to shoot the whole thing down. My main concern had to do with money: even with the foundation's substantial resources, I knew it didn't stand a chance pitted against the enormous fortunes of ultra-conservative billionaires and the tyranny of international corporate power.

"The foundation is only in its embryonic stage," she told me. "As I mentioned, Heyoka is already working with his counterpart in this dimension to get a head start on some of the inventions that made him a multi-billionaire in our world. We'll be setting up a base of operations soon, a massive complex that will include space for an investment arm, a technology incubator, a social sciences and media center, and, eventually, a duplication of our lab and the accelerator. The income potential is astronomical, not only from the products and processes we generate in house, but from our investment strategies. Obviously, we will have an advantage there, though we'll have to be careful because the existence of Blue Note Enterprises has already had a significant economic impact on the future, as will the activities of the foundation itself. Unfortunately, the plan has become so vast and multi-faceted it has outpaced Ellie's ability to precisely calculate specific long-term results. Consequently, we're having to rely more on historical evaluations and computer modeling than algorithmic predictions alone."

"So," I said, "we're going to have a lot of money to work with. That's good. But I still don't get what makes music such a vitally important part of this huge, multifaceted scenario."

"Neither did we at first," she said. "In fact, we didn't even consider it. But when we started brainstorming on how to manipulate societal and cultural trends, Ellie rewrote her algorithms and programming to look for even the most subtle historical influences. Eventually this led to an in-depth study of the evolution of human communication, from the earliest Stone-Age storytellers, to the Internet. And the one thing that consistently stood out—the kind of communication that most effectively carried ideas and beliefs from generation to generation—was music."

"I thought that was supposed to have been the evolution of writing and the invention of the printing press," I said. "And what about the great philosophical and political orators?"

"They were historically important, but over time the spoken word and even writing were subject to alterations in meaning and interpretation, both inadvertent and deliberate. However, when written stories and ideas were simplified and put to music, they became memorable in a way that bypassed the intellect and spoke directly to the collective subconscious. Think about it—how many people remember all the words of a speech or the rhetoric of even the most famous politician? They may remember a few sound bites, or lines from the Gettysburg Address, but how many can sing from memory songs like ***Amazing Grace***, or ***Blowin' in the Wind***, or even ***Sunday Morning Sentinel***?"

She had a point, but I still wasn't convinced that music could be all that important in redirecting the course of history. "Okay," I said, "I'll grant you that music has a way of making things stick in the mind, but that's mostly because of its repetitive nature and simplicity. And, dare I say it, catchy tunes and hook lines. I still don't see how any of that could have an earthshaking influence on worldwide society."

"That's where you're wrong," she said. "In fact, when it comes to music's influence on cultural evolution, not only did it facilitate some of the most important social changes in modern history, it augmented and enhanced the most pervasive philosophical movement the world has ever seen." She raised an eyebrow, waiting for the dawn to break in my mind. Unfortunately, it didn't.

"I give up," I said.

"Well," she said, "how about a little thing called religion? From the earliest chants in primitive societies, to the songs of Jewish cantors and hymns of Christianity and other organized religions, music has served as the single most effective way to embed spiritual and religious concepts in the minds of the people. And that continues to this day. In fact, the majority of songs that have been committed to memory in the history of humankind are religious in nature. Even rock 'n' roll had its origins in religious music. The emotion of gospel gave rise to the blues, which was then combined with country and folk to create the genre you and thousands of others have made your living on. And how about Woody Guthrie's music and its impact on the labor movement and the proliferation of unions? Or the so-called folk revival of the '60s and '70s and its pervasive influence on politics and various social causes?"

She had me there. I'd run out of arguments and was about to admit she was right, when she hit me with the clincher.

"Anyway, let's put all that aside for a moment and get back to the current situation, which is that not only are you in need of some creative activity to counteract the depression you're dealing with, but we're offering you one of the most complex and interesting challenges you've ever faced. And, if you need any more incentive, there's the fact that you and I will be spending more time together over the next nine months than we have since you've been in this dimension."

59
The Getaway

"I need to think about this," I said, though I didn't, really. At least not in so far as the decision was concerned. What I needed was breathing room: mental space to allow the idea to gel and give me time to adjust to the new reality I was facing. Again, Aurie seemed to read my thoughts.

"What you need," she said, "is to get out of this mausoleum of a house and go someplace that doesn't constantly remind you of what happened to Doris."

"Get away?" I said. "Where? How?"

"The how is easy. Money's not a problem, so you can go wherever you want. Isn't there someplace you'd like to go other than to the nearest bar?"

"Haven't thought about it," I said.

"Well, you need to *start* thinking about it."

"Damn!" I said, "Why is it that all the women in my life have suddenly gotten so bossy?" I put my hands behind my head, leaned back in my chair, and closed my eyes. I was trying my best not to give in, but I couldn't keep my mind from working; and after a minute or so of silent contemplation, it became clear there was only one place that fit the bill. "Georgia," I said, shocked at my sudden candor.

"Georgia," she repeated.

"There's this secluded tract of land up there north of Atlanta. About a hundred acres of virgin hardwoods with a cabin—"

"I know all about Georgia, Rix." I caught a hint of petulance in her voice, but it quickly disappeared. "It's perfect," she said. "So, what should we do?"

"I don't know. Find it, I guess. See if it's still like I remember. If it hasn't been run over by urban sprawl, maybe I could rent the cabin."

"Better yet, why don't we just buy the whole thing?"

"Get serious," I said. "Even if the land is still undeveloped, it would cost an arm and a leg."

"So? It's not like we can't afford it. Whatever the cost, it would be a drop in the bucket for us, certainly worth it if it provides you with an environment where you can work in peace. Besides, it would probably be a good long-term investment. Do you know who owns it?"

"Friend of Jimmy's," I said." Or they *were* friends. We both knew the guy back in junior high, but things have evolved differently here. Jimmy doesn't even resemble the drugged out musician he was in my first life. That all changed when he fell in love with Sarah. Chip, on the other hand, was a drug dealer, and he probably still is in this dimension."

"But you both knew him in school?"

"Sort of," I said. "Jimmy more than me. I don't even remember his last name."

"Well then, you should talk to Jimmy. Meanwhile we can have someone from the foundation's legal department check on the cost of undeveloped land up there. Do you remember anything that might help us locate it?"

"I never had an address for the property. I got my mail through General Delivery at the post office in Lawrenceville. But even that was over thirty miles south. I'm telling you, the place was really isolated back then. That's what was so great about it."

"Back then would be what, around 1974?" She said.

"Yeah, '74, '75. Something like that."

"Okay, I'll get Ellie on it as soon as she's back from Canada. Meanwhile, you give Jimmy a call and see if he knows where to find this Chip character."

I CALLED JIMMY THE next day, but when I mentioned Chip, he drew a blank. "My friend Chip?" he said.

"Not your friend, exactly," I said. "We knew him back in junior high. I think he did a lot of drugs."

"You don't mean that sleazebag Chip Salazar, do you?"

"Salazar," I said. "Yeah, that's it."

"What's this about, Rich?"

I didn't want to get into a long explanation, so I dodged the question. "Nothing, really. It was just one of those tip-of-the-tongue things. I got to thinking about him and I couldn't for the life of me remember his last name. Didn't the two of you used to hang around together?"

"I guess we did, a little, but I haven't spoken to the guy in over twenty years. What do you want with him anyway?"

"Long story. I'll fill you in later. Thanks, buddy. Talk to you soon." I hung up before he could answer.

I DECIDED TO PUT off my search for Chip until I'd heard from our lawyers about the relative value of undeveloped land in north-central Georgia—which, they said, varied widely depending upon its proximity to highways and the northern tendrils of Atlanta's rapidly expanding suburbs. Best they could figure from knowing the property's general location was that it would probably sell for one or two-thousand an acre. With that information in hand, and wishing for the umpteenth time that the Internet was up and running, I flipped clumsily through the tissue-thin pages of our local phone book.

There were seven Salazars listed, but no Chip. I was hoping the name hadn't been short for a chip off the old block, but even if it wasn't, I didn't have any idea what Chip might be a nickname for. The closest name among the seven was a Christopher, so I called that one—and hit the jackpot. He didn't remember me until I mentioned Jimmy and Blue Note Enterprises, and he was skeptical when I asked him about the land. I finally convinced him I'd heard about it when I ran into some old classmates at a party.

"Okay," he said, "So?"

"Do you still own it," I asked.

"Yeah. What the fuck do you care?"

"I want to buy it," I said.

"People in hell want ice water," he said, laughing.

"I'll give you half-a-million cash."

That did it. Not only was it over twice what the land was worth, but I knew how fond drug dealers were of cash transactions.

It took Ellie a few days to put the money together, and the closing was a little awkward because the payment was in cash. But we eventually got things wrapped up. We were leaving the attorney's office when Chip pulled me aside.

"You're fucking nuts, you know that, don't you?" He said. "It's hard to figure. I mean, guys as rich as you don't get that way making bad deals like this."

"Maybe not," I said. "But I always try to look on the positive side. And that side says rich guys like me get to do whatever the fuck we want."

SO NOW I OWNED 100 acres and a cabin in the north-Georgia woods. That was nice, but I still didn't know if things were going to pan out like I wanted them to. The last time I'd seen the property was in 1975—over five years ago in this timeline—and for all I knew it was now surrounded by tacky housing developments. Ellie had shown me a few photos taken by some of our 'people' so I knew the cabin was still there. And the land itself seemed to have changed little if at all. In fact, she said, there were several thousand acres of mostly wooded property surrounding it.

Later that night, I was sitting alone on the patio, sipping the last of the fake Jack, when the trees began to sway violently. The abrupt blast of icy wind reminded me of those freezing nights in Georgia—of chopping wood and shivering under threadbare blankets. And I thought how, in this life, I'd become a sedentary slug, taking for granted the comforts of civilization. Did I really want to do the Walden-Pond thing again—the back-to-nature trip I'd already been through once? Ellie had suggested I build a comfortable, weather-tight house to replace the broken-down cabin. But somehow that seemed like it would be an insult to the primitive setting, or at least to my memories of it. Maybe I could just fix up the cabin a little; plug the leaks and install a decent heating system. Or … maybe not.

Whatever I did, I would still have to deal with the problem of solitude. Aurie had promised she would be spending more time with me, but that wouldn't be right away. Before we could start working on new material, I needed time to get my hands and voice back in shape, and that was something I had to do on my own. Not only would her presence be of no help, it would be a hindrance, at least until I'd regained some degree of confidence in my ability to entertain anything other than an audience of chipmunks and squirrels.

A Buddhist monk would no-doubt advise me to see this as a perfect opportunity to seek enlightenment. But other than practicing transcendental meditation, I'd never given much credence to that kind of stuff. During my first go-'round, when Robin was there to support me and cheer me on, I'd used the solitude to get in touch with nature and write. This time, however, I would be on my own much of the time.

Thinking of Robin, I couldn't help but wonder how things had turned out for her without Rix Vaughn around to screw up her life. Maybe she would still be waiting tables at the Black Orchid Lounge in Roswell, where I was working when we met. That was doubtful, but if I was going to hone my new act, I would eventually need a place to perform in public, and the Orchid seemed like an ideal venue.

60
Georgia

The room's ambience was familiar: subdued light, a crisp aroma of broiling steak, the clink of glasses and silverware—all overlaid with a combination of soft piano music, stale tobacco smoke, and the muted fragrance of expensive perfumes and colognes. The familiarity wasn't from my time at the Black Orchid—I'd been far too wasted back then to remember much of anything—but from wispy memories of a hundred other supper clubs, the last being LeMusique, where I'd first encountered Heyoka. Other than the architecture and a murmur of southern-accented conversations, the atmosphere here was essentially the same.

Unlike LeMusique, where the restaurant and concert area were separate, here they occupied a single expansive room. Semicircular in design, the two-tiered floor plan centered on a cozy, amphitheater section with a small stage set in a domed alcove. A perimeter of booths surrounded what was originally a dance floor, but that now held a dozen or so tall cocktail tables. The restaurant and piano bar occupied a second tier that rose above and beyond the booths, creating an acoustic configuration that helped insulate the amphitheater from the clatter and conversations of dinner guests. Two short staircases allowed diners to migrate to the lower level after they'd finished their meals, and on a busy night the vacated tables could accommodate additional spectators.

At the piano bar, a white-haired gentleman, imitating Dean Martin in both vocal style and liquor consumption, fielded requests from a few old timers. On the lower level, the stage stood empty, awaiting the nine o'clock arrival of the night's featured performer. This would probably be some up-and-coming local talent with a small backup band; or maybe a single doing cover songs and repeating jokes from yesterday's late-night TV shows.

It was my first visit to the club since I'd taken up residence in the cabin where Robin and I had spent that glorious but ill-fated year together. Despite my objections, Ellie had insisted on making several improvements to the cabin, though I *had* managed to convince her that I did not want it torn down and replaced with a comfy example of modern, suburban housing. I'd eventually agreed to a compromise, settling for a new roof and paint job, plus a few modest pieces of furniture salvaged, at my insistence, from local thrift shops. I had patched most of the leaks myself and installed electric baseboard heating, along with a slightly-used stove and refrigerator. In spite of these upgrades, the structure retained a somewhat unpolished, woodsy charm, insulated from the outside world by dense forest and accessible only by negotiating a long and somewhat treacherous dirt road.

When I wasn't working on the cabin, I spent most of the daylight hours sitting in my favorite spot: a diving-board-shaped granite outcropping overlooking the fast-running stream, where I'd come up with most of the ideas for the songs that had eventually filled my three albums. This time, however, instead of writing, I'd concentrated on mundane tasks, like running scales on the guitar to rebuild the callouses on my tender fingertips and regain the dexterity I'd once had. As for my voice, there was a lot of work to do there. Lack of practice had severely reduced my vocal range, and the break between tenor and falsetto that I'd worked so hard to eliminate after puberty was once again pronounced. I'd asked Carol Henderson for some exercises to help me reestablish a smooth transition from the lows to the highs, and when I wasn't working on my guitar technique, I would sing at the top of my lungs to an audience of curious wildlife.

Evenings were spent in the cabin, refining the lyrics and music to some of the songs I'd never published in this dimension, and creating new fingerstyle arrangements for the hits I'd written while at Blue Note Studios. When I tired of these activities, I would call Jimmy to discuss recording ideas, or Sam to talk about his progress with the 3D printing technology, which, he said, was coming along faster than they had originally anticipated.

"We're getting closer every day to equaling the capabilities of the printers Heyoka and his team have developed," he said. "We can now print everything from microscopic circuitry, to advanced composite materials, and even organics—plants, foodstuffs, and the like."

"Living organisms?" I said. I was thinking, of course, about humans, Aurie in particular. "What about animals—mammals?"

"We haven't gotten that far yet. Actually, Heyoka says there's been a problem with printing higher life forms. They print fine, but the copies are inanimate—perfect duplications, just not alive. They can be jump started electrically and brought to life, but even though the brain is functional, the mind, or maybe I should say the personality, disappears. It's like they start over from scratch, having to learn everything as if they'd just been born."

"That's ... disappointing."

"Yeah," he said. "I guess we've all been thinking the same thing. The good news is they haven't given up. Hey, how about that tour? Looks like Ellie's setting the world on fire."

Ellie had been calling me several times a week ever since I moved into the cabin, so I knew about the tour. It was obvious that these calls were her way of checking to make sure I wasn't slitting my wrists or drinking myself into oblivion, but she always tried to cover that up by giving me detailed progress reports on the tour.

Other than that, my only respite from the loneliness and solitude was when Aurélie showed up to provide encouragement. As if she thought seeing her might be too intimidating, she would often revert back to the voice-in-the-head thing. Sometimes, though, when I was wandering through the woods, she would appear beside me, saying little and seeming to enjoy our being together in a setting not unlike the forest surrounding Heyoka's villa. It was during one of these visits that she broached the subject of my getting back in front of an audience, and she surprised me by suggesting I take my first shot at the Black Orchid.

"It's a perfect spot, Rix," she said as we approached the cabin. "Besides, I know you're curious about Robin, so why not at least stop by some evening and talk to her?"

"Talk to her?" I said. "How do you know she's even there?"

She looked off into the trees, where a few lightning bugs twinkled among the budding springtime leaves. "Don't be mad at me," she said, "but I did a little investigating."

"Oh, really?" I said. "And?"

"She's still there. In fact, she's managing the place now. It was really weird. You know, like seeing myself in a mirror. I didn't let her see *me*, of course, but you were right about us looking alike. I followed her around for a while, watched her interact with employees and customers. And, well, she seems really sweet and kindhearted, so I can understand why you fell in love with her."

I was a little freaked out by this; it sounded almost like she was encouraging me to hook up with Robin, which I had no intention of doing.

"What's going on, Aurie?" I said. "You know as well as I do there are dozens of clubs around Atlanta I could try. I may be curious to find out how Robin's doing, but curious is all I am. If there was anything more to it I would have checked out the Orchid myself a long time ago."

It wasn't like Aurie to show nervousness or lose her composure, but my question had obviously made her uncomfortable.

"I wasn't suggesting anything of the kind!" she said, her defensive tone indicating that, in fact, she was. "I just thought since you were familiar with the club and all …"

"And all what?"

"Like I said, it seems perfect to me. It's a nice-sized room. Not too big, not too small. And it draws a more laid-back clientele than the fancier clubs in Atlanta. Plus, they often feature little-known singer-songwriters. The fact that you'd get to see Robin would just be a bonus."

"A bonus?"

"You know, kind of killing two birds with one—oh, sorry. Bad idiom. Anyway, I'll bet if you auditioned and played ***Robin's Song***, she'd hire you on the spot."

"Do you really think I'll need a gimmick like that?" I said. "If I'm going to have a problem getting hired, then maybe we should just buy the place and offer free liquor so people won't leave when they hear how bad I am. It would only be another drop in the bucket, right?" I was getting a perverse kick out of watching her squirm. Not only was it unprecedented, but she was clearly trying—and failing—to convince me without sounding condescending.

"I wasn't saying you needed a gimmick, Rix, only that it would be a good spot to help you ease back into live performing. Plus, it's the closest club of its kind in the area, so there wouldn't be a lot of travel time involved. And, I don't know, I just thought you might like to see how Robin is doing."

We went back-and-forth like that for a while, until I started to feel sorry for her and eased up on my cross-examination. In the end, I agreed, which is why I was sitting here at the Black Orchid, nursing an after-dinner beer and waiting for the main act to take the stage before moving to the lower level. I had yet to catch a glimpse of Robin, and I'd begun to wonder if Aurie had made up the story, when a small commotion arose a few tables away from me. Within seconds, Robin emerged from the back room and strolled to the problem table. She put her arm around the frazzled waitress's shoulder and waited while the customer vented like a whining child, nodding and shaking her head in sympathy until he finally wound down. Then, all smiles and apologies, she took control of the conversation.

She spoke softly, but the nearby crowd had quieted, and I was suddenly transported back in time as I heard that familiar, gentle voice calming the angry patrons and assuring them there would be no charge for their dinner. Problem solved, she turned to leave, but her progress was impeded by several diners who stopped her to shake hands and exchange pleasantries. She was clearly well-liked, and as I watched her interact with the crowd, I realized how little she had changed from the kind, patient woman I'd once known.

She had almost extricated herself from the last group of admirers, when someone behind me yelled, "Hey, Robin. Come over here for a second, will you?" She turned and looked in my direction, then, without showing a trace of frustration, walked back into the fray, dodging a couple of busboys on her way toward the table next to mine. Trying not to be too obvious, I swiveled in my chair and did a quick visual inventory as she passed by.

She wore loose, tan slacks and a cream-colored, masculine-style blouse; and she didn't look a day older than the last time I'd seen her. I remembered, then, how she'd always dressed in fairly nondescript clothes in order to downplay her sexuality, and how that made her all the more alluring to me. The only difference I could see was the way she did her hair. Though still a radiant shade of auburn, instead of being cropped short, it was parted down the middle and styled in a casual sort of bob that curled below her ears.

She stopped at the table next to mine and began talking quietly with the young man who had called her over. The ambient restaurant noise had returned to full volume, making it hard to hear them distinctly, but I got the impression he'd made up some excuse to draw her over so he could hit on her. I watched as she bantered amiably with him and his two companions, thinking that an animator would probably have depicted them as dogs with their tongues hanging out.

When she turned to leave, I caught her eye and she smiled at me. It was the noncommittal smile of a manager being attentive to a new customer, and as she approached my table, she touched me lightly on the shoulder. "Everything alright here?" she said, nodding at my near-empty beer glass.

"I guess I could use another beer," I said. "And I was wondering if I could talk to you for a few moments. Not right now. I can see that you're busy."

"I'm never too busy for a new patron," she said. "You *are* new, aren't you? I'd hate to find out you've been here before and I didn't notice." Though still somewhat formal, I could sense a vague stirring of non-professional curiosity in her demeanor.

"I'm new," I said. "Not only to the Orchid, but to Georgia."

"Well, then," she said, sliding into the chair opposite me, "welcome to the Peach State. What can I do for you? I'm Robin, by the way. And you are …?"

I started to answer truthfully, but caught myself, realizing my name might be recognized by someone whose business involved working with musicians. "Rix," I said, after what I hoped was an unnoticed hesitation. "Rix Vaughn."

"Nice to meet you, Rix," she said, holding out a hand. I shook it stiffly, expecting a jolt of libidinous electricity that didn't materialize. "You know, now that I think about it, you do look familiar. Have we met?"

"Not likely," I said, "unless you've spent some time in the west-central Florida area. I used to work at Blue Note Studios in St. Petersburg as a session guitarist."

"Can't say that I have. What brings you to Georgia?"

"That's what I wanted to talk to you about," I said. "I've been doing the standard, frustrated studio-musician thing. You know, trying to write some songs and put together my own act? I've played a few small gigs around central Florida where I'm fairly well known, and I've got a commitment from Blue Note to produce my first album. But first I need to test some of my songs in front of an audience of strangers."

"I see," she said. A wayward curl of hair fell across her eyes and she brushed it away, whereupon it immediately fell back and was joined by another. She continued to repeat this futile exercise, as if she had long ago stopped giving it conscious thought. Finally, she said, "Look, Rix, I hate to throw cold water on your aspirations, but I should tell you that I see at least a dozen wannabes a month, maybe one out of a hundred with the talent necessary to make it as a single. And even those few will probably never get past playing at flea markets or local talent shows."

"Believe me," I said, "I know the odds. You should see how many kids camp out in the waiting room down at Blue Note. I have no illusions, Robin, only a hatful of naïve ambition, a little talent, and a decade or so of studio experience. I hear you used to have an open-mike thing on Sunday afternoons."

"We did, but it got overrun by rowdy, talentless drunks. We were losing customers, so we cancelled it about a year ago."

Tell her you'll write her a song. It was Aurie, invading my brain again.

"Cheap shot," I said, without thinking.

"What?" Robin said.

"Sorry, I didn't mean ... what I mean was that I would be cheap. I'm not asking for a paying gig or anything. Just a shot." I was determined not to take advantage of my former position, but I had to come up with something that would be hard to refuse. "Tell you what," I said, "pick the slowest time. Say, Tuesday before the main act goes on. Give me thirty minutes, and if the audience doesn't like me, I promise I'll leave without a word and never bother you again."

She continued to fiddle with her uncooperative hair, reminding me of those CNN field reporters who stood in the wind doing the same thing over and over. After a while she signaled to a waitress and pointed at my glass. Then, with an audible sigh, she looked me in the eye and said, "Okay. It's against my better judgment, but you seem like a nice enough fellow. Be here at 8:30 on Tuesday, and I'll give you your shot. Don't get your hopes up, though. We may not be a big-city club, but our clientele can be pretty tough on newcomers."

After she left, I hung around to catch a few minutes of the featured act, and was surprised to find myself listening to a young John Berry, who I knew would go on to chart many country hits. Even this early in his career, he was damned good, with a soulful tenor voice and a unique guitar style. So good, in fact, that I left after his first set—not because I wasn't enjoying the music, but because hearing it and seeing the audience's enthusiastic response was messing with my already shaky confidence.

I HAD ONLY THREE days to prepare for my big debut, and suddenly Aurélie seemed to be with me every waking hour. We argued about what songs I should sing, what clothes I should wear, and even whether I should use my Ramirez or my Martin. By Monday evening, I'd had enough, and for the first time ever I actually asked her to leave me alone.

"It isn't that I don't want to be with you," I said. "I do. It's just that I need some private time to get my head together and practice without anyone looking over my shoulder."

"Do you not want me there on Tuesday either?" she pouted.

"Of course I want you there," I said, though I wasn't sure about that either. "But you have to promise me you won't climb into my head while I'm on stage. I'm thinking about playing your song, by the way."

The Lady Left Me With a Song was the last thing I'd written in my former life, and I'd never even considered letting one of Blue Note's artists record it. In fact, I'd never played it for anyone other than Aurie. There were good reasons for this, one being that the song was so personal I couldn't objectively evaluate its potential. But probably the most important reason was something I'd only recently admitted to myself—as self-indulgent as it seemed, I really didn't want anyone else singing it.

"I promise," she said, "but I still think you should do ***Robin's Song***. You know they'll love it."

"You mean Robin will love it. Look, no matter what you think, I'm not doing this to impress Robin, I'm doing it to see if I can command the attention of an audience. Using a song we already know was a hit won't prove much of anything. I need to find out if I can still hold my own as an entertainer, and playing proven hits, especially one written specifically for the person who might hire me, would give me an advantage I don't want and shouldn't need. Now please do me a favor and give me the next twenty-four hours alone to see if I can work up enough courage not to be a no-show."

That shut her up. And even though I knew she was upset, she did a pretty good job of hiding it, smiling and wishing me luck, before vanishing into the dark like a windblown wisp of smoke.

As adamant as I'd been about being alone, I wasn't prepared for the rush of anxiety that came over me once she was gone. Sitting in the sallow glow of the porch light, it felt like the trees were closing in on me, and my hands were sweating so badly I could barely hold on to my guitar.

I'd managed to keep my drinking to a minimum since I'd been in Georgia, but those last couple of binges in St. Pete had reignited the old cravings, making even semi-abstinence difficult. And at that moment, all I could think about was how much I wanted a drink. I was on my way to the kitchen, when it occurred to me that I couldn't remember ever performing as single without being drunk, or at least well on my way. That thought lingered in my mind as I drank from a carton of orange juice, wishing it was quart of Jack.

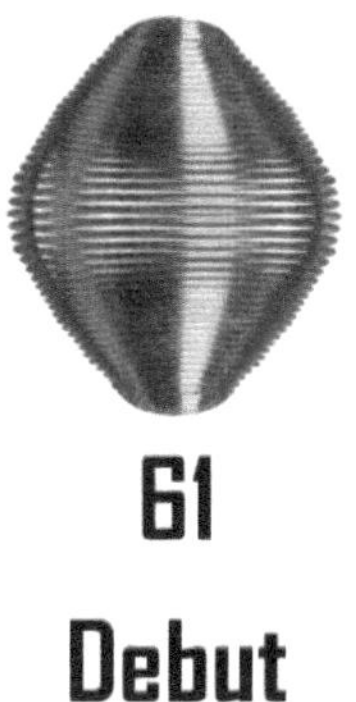

61
Debut

There is an art to garnering the attention of a tiny, disinterested audience. And, as a matter of necessity, I'd spent the later years of my first life perfecting that art. Using humor was one method—a scary one, though not quite as scary as standup comedy. A guy with a guitar wasn't expected to be George Carlin, so laughs were easier to elicit, much like they would be for a politician or a well-known athlete. Another trick was to shock the audience into paying attention. This could be accomplished with a pratfall or maybe an odd opening statement—anything unexpected that would jerk them out of their conversations and alcoholic indifference.

Finally, there was a subtle, less offbeat approach I sometimes used if a room had the proper seating configuration and acoustics. This involved starting out with an instrumental rendition of a recognizable tune, then steadily increasing the volume and tempo in coordination with a gradual expansion and brightening of the spotlight. Under the right circumstances, the mounting drama would slowly draw the audience's attention toward the stage. Keeping it there, however, was another matter altogether.

If you were a nobody—or, as in the case of my later career, a little-known has-been—it often took more to hold an audience than playing a few songs they'd never heard, no matter how good the songs might be. One thing I had going for me in that regard came from the many years

I'd spent adjusting my presentation to compensate for my deteriorating skills.

As my vocal quality faded and the arthritis in my hands grew worse, I began to pad my performances with short monologues and expanded introductions, repeating the ones that drew chuckles and nods while eliminating or refining those that met with yawns. This process of elimination soon taught me that what people enjoyed almost as much as the music was learning the meaning behind the songs. So, unlike James Taylor and a few other artists who preferred not to reveal what their songs were about, I started introducing mine with emotional or humorous background stories. The advantage in doing this was twofold: first, it reduced the time I was required to sing and play; and second, if an audience knew the intimate circumstances that led to each song's creation, they tended to be less critical of my musical performances.

With all this journeyman expertise under my belt, I should have been confident in my ability to capture and hold the attention of even the smallest audience. However, not only had it been nearly a quarter century since I'd last performed as a single, tonight I would be playing stone cold sober to a handful of strangers anxiously awaiting the appearance of local favorite, John Berry.

After taking stock of the Black Orchid's design and acoustics, I'd decided to open with drama rather than shock or humor. I had met with the kid handling the lights—a busboy in his other life—hoping he was competent enough to follow my instructions, which were to train the spotlight on my empty stool, lock it in place, turn it off, and wait until he heard the first soft notes of my guitar solo. Then, he should try to synchronize a gradual increase in the beam's size and intensity with the rising volume and tempo of my performance.

I wanted to open with something familiar rather than something original, and had settled on a complex arrangement of the Flamenco favorite, Malagueña, from which I would transition into an acoustic version of the Eagles' megahit, ***Hotel California***. In a way, this was cheating, because the group had recently split up, and I would essentially be copying a rendition introduced on their 1994 reunion album. But I was sure no one would remember my interpretation of it thirteen years down the road.

As I took my place on the darkened stage and surveyed the near-empty lower level, I saw that only one couple had chosen to sit at a table near the front, while the others were scattered among the perimeter booths. The restaurant level, however, looked to be about half full, so if I played my cards right, I might be able to entice a few of the diners down, or at least grab their attention before they finished their meals. On the other hand, as nervous as I was, I might drive them all away. With this thought looming in my head, I decided to concentrate on the couple in front, as if they were the only customers in the place.

I played the first notes so softly I was afraid the spotlight operator wouldn't hear me. But as I slowly increased the volume and tempo, I saw a dim circle of light begin to glow in the distance and sighed with relief. Unfortunately, this somewhat loud exhalation was picked up by the voice mike and broadcast for all to hear, reminding me how much I'd forgotten about the nuances of performing live. To make matters worse, my two-person audience appeared to find my gaffe amusing, smiling and nodding at each other as if I'd confirmed their suspicion that I was a rank amateur.

Fighting a wave of anxiety, I closed my eyes and tried to lose myself in the music, interspersing machine-gun falsetas with powerful rasgueado as I moved toward a crescendo of loud, brash strumming. I stretched the high-spirited finale out, then slowed to a soft finger roll and squinted into the now-bright spotlight. Fortunately the beam was elevated enough to allow a misty view of the room, and I saw that the couple now seemed, if not mesmerized, at least courteously attentive. Encouraged by this minor victory, I eased into the intro for ***Hotel California***, and when I next looked up I saw two other couples abandon their booths and head toward the front tables.

The small surge of confidence this provided allowed me to relax, and I finished the intro with a flourish. From there it was like I'd become possessed by a much younger version of myself (that cocky front man for The Madisons, whose claim to fame was an ability to precisely imitate the voices of popular rock and blues singers) and I dove into the vocals, performing a near perfect impersonation of Don Henley.

I tried to keep an eye on the room to see if any of the other patrons were moving to the front, but the ending—a difficult duplication of the synchronized guitar solos played by Don Felder and Joe Walsh—required all my concentration, and I didn't raise my head until the last notes were fading away. When I finally did look up, I saw that the number of occupied tables had more than doubled, and after a nervy moment of silence, a flutter of applause started at the back and flowed through the small crowd. The applause wasn't loud—there were, after all, only a couple of dozen hands clapping—but at least they weren't booing.

It was then that I noticed Robin. She had descended one of the stairways that led down from the restaurant and was standing at the bottom with a hand resting casually on one hip. I couldn't read her expression in the dim light, but her body language seemed to say, "Not bad. What's next?" I saw Aurie, too, smiling at me from where she'd materialized near one of the exits, and it wasn't long before all the scrutiny brought on another surge of anxiety. I had managed to make it through my opening without any major screw-ups, but the response had been less than enthusiastic. And now I had to do something that would keep everyone in their seats.

When the applause died down, I looked out at the sparse crowd. "Thank you. Thank you. Thank you," I said, as if I'd just brought down the house. "I have to say that of all the ovations I've ever received, that was by far the most … recent." This was met with a communal groan. "But seriously," I continued, "it's nice to be here at the Black Orchid on a Tuesday. I don't usually perform on Tuesdays. I usually go to my AA meeting."—nervous chuckles—"No, really, as of tonight I've been sober for 100 days. Not in a row or anything. Since I was twelve."—a smattering of genuine laughter— "I'm Rix Vaughn, by the way. And Robin has asked me to entertain you for the next half hour or so. I should warn you, though, that I've never done this without having a few drinks under my belt, so what you're about to hear might make you want to throw some at me. That's fine, so long as you give me time to open my mouth." This time, the laughter was louder, and suddenly I knew I had them.

The only sticking point was that I had inadvertently altered the mood, which meant that starting off with something serious was not going to hack it. Fortunately, being sober allowed me to quickly switch gears and come up with a new plan. After assessing the makeup of my small audience—mostly redneck, informally dressed, many cowboy hats and pitchers of beer—I put the Ramirez back on its stand and picked up my Martin.

"Here's a little thing I wrote one chilly Georgia morning," I said while I D-tuned the guitar. "I was sittin' on my front porch, dead broke and suffering from a colossal hangover, when one of them fine fellers from Georgia Power & Light showed up to turn off my electricity. I thought about sicc'n my old hound dog, Betsy, on him, but she was already down for her daily twelve-hour nap, so I just sat there and watched him do his thing. And when he left, I got this brilliant idea for a hit song. It took me the rest of the morning to write the thing, and I knew right away it was a good'n. Only problem is, the 'hit' part hasn't happened yet, so I was thinkin' maybe you could help me out. Anyway, best I can recall, it goes *exactly* like this." I improvised a twangy, country intro, then slipped into my best Garth Brooks voice …

They just turned off the power and fuel is runnin' low
There's two eggs in the icebox and they say it's gonna snow
I'm told to grin and bear it, that my faith will keep me warm
That there's a silver linin' on the back side of the storm

Politicians say tomorrow will be better than today
But they ain't told me how to pay the bills I cannot pay
I've heard it all called rhetoric, that it's just a game they play
So I think I'll make an omelet and get on my knees and pray

And ask the Lord to find me room and board
And take the preacher all my bills and have him fix my Ford
And when the congregation says there's no more they can do
I'll find a place to sell this song and leave it up to you

For the instrumental break I did a little showing off, flat picking a variation of Roy Clark's ***Rocky Top*** guitar solo. And I was happy to hear a flutter of applause as I swung into the last verse …

The few things that I've mentioned here can't begin to tell it all
I've never felt so helpless, no I've never felt so small
I think I'll take a shower, catch a cold and maybe die
But that would be too easy so I'll give it one more try

Well, I asked the Lord to help me, yes I got down on my knees
I told him I was hungry and that I was gonna freeze
He hasn't called me back as yet, so there's nothing left to do
But find a place to sell this song and leave it up to you

I asked the Lord to find me room and board
And I took the preacher all my bills and helped him fix my Ford
And when the congregation said there's no more we can do
I found a place to sell this song, and now it's up to you!

This time, the applause was generous; even some of the diners were clapping as they came down to take seats at the remaining tables and vacated booths. I fiddled around on the guitar while everyone got settled, and once they'd quieted down, I said, "Thanks again, folks. I really appreciate it. In fact, after that ovation, I can't wait to hear what I'm going to play next. Unfortunately I won't be singing too many songs tonight because of my throat. The last time I sang too many, someone threatened to cut it."

The friendly laughter, punctuated by a loud whoop here and there, was reassuring, and I figured I could now move on to something a little more serious.

"I hate to admit it," I said, "but I'm not a native Georgian. I'm from Florida."—subdued grumbling—"Now wait a minute, I didn't say I was in love with the state—all that flat land and sunshine and them nasty gators. Of course, I'm referring to the University of Florida Gators."—cheers and hoots—"Actually, I moved to the woods up north of here to get away from all that and try to write some decent country songs."

"Smart move," someone yelled over a general murmur of agreement.

"Yes it was," I said, "And man, let me tell you, the women up here are something else. In fact, it was one of those women who inspired this next song." I began an extended intro to ***They Just Ain't Made The Words***, playing softly and speaking over the music.

"She and I met in a supper club a lot like this one, and she sort of took me under her wing. You see, I was on the verge of killing myself with alcohol and drugs, and this lovely lady—let's call her Rusty—sacrificed everything to save me from my own stupidity."

The laughter gradually faded into a curious, shuffling silence. Even Robin—who had moved closer to the stage—now seemed more interested than judgmental. Of course, she couldn't know the story was about her, but, since 'Rusty' was being depicted as the savior of a drug-addicted alcoholic, it was probably hitting a little close to home.

"Anyway, as might be expected, I fell head over heels for Rusty, and the one thing I wanted to do more than anything was write a song for her. But she was so incredible, and I was so in love with her, nothing I wrote even came close to describing how I felt. I was complaining about this one evening, apologizing to her for my failure, when she came to my rescue a second time."

I stopped talking but continued to play, milking the suspense as long as I could before lightening up on the guitar and continuing.

"Rusty was not only a beautiful person, she was smart as a whip, and she saw something I couldn't, even though it was right in front of my nose. I was floundering around, trying to come up with excuses for my inability to find the right words, when I made the silly claim that it wasn't my fault—that the words simply did not exist. She laughed at that, then said, 'Okay, if the words really don't exist, why don't you write about that?' It took me a while to figure out what she meant, and when I did, I wrote this song . . ."

Judging by the crowd's wide-eyed anticipation, my setup appeared to have worked perfectly, and I proceeded to pull off one of the most emotional interpretations of ***They Just Ain't Made The Words*** I'd ever performed. In some respects it was an act, because I used every skill I'd learned over two lifetimes to make it sound spontaneous and from the heart. But it was also a long-overdue tribute to Robin—a 'thank you' of sorts—and the emotion was not totally fabricated. The audience's response was enthusiastic, though it almost seemed like a footnote, because all I really cared about was the quick thumbs up I got from Robin.

As I scanned the rest of the room, trying to convey a measure of humble appreciation, I began to wonder if this was what Jackson was talking about when he said I could do something pure with my music—something not for monetary gain or recognition, but for the simple joy of using my talent to pay some dues and maybe fulfill the mandate of having been given that talent by whatever entity or force of nature had provided it.

The only other time I'd performed with such unfabricated sincerity was that last evening at the villa, when I played Aurélie the song I'd written for her. That performance had nothing to do with ego or money; it was simply an attempt to convey my feelings. Which, at the time, were regret and heartbreak and anger at having to leave her. Now I was about to play that song again, and I suddenly realized how easily it could be misinterpreted—not by the audience, but by Aurie. She'd already been subtly pushing me toward Robin, no doubt because she didn't want me to live my life without some kind of physical love. And much as I hated to admit it, I was sorely tempted.

The irony of these conflicting emotions seemed like some sort of karmic justice, but that didn't stop it from being emotionally confusing. Considering my feelings for Aurie, the fact that I would entertain the idea of a liaison with Robin was unsettling. Not to mention that I had already begun to speculate on my chances. Even though I was nowhere near the basket case she had rescued in my first life, I *had* sensed some primal chemistry between us during our first meeting, which was probably why I was experiencing this unwelcome craving.

It was the old, oversexed Rix Vaughn rearing his ugly head again. And, as if I needed more grief, I had stupidly painted myself into a corner. I thought I was being clever by telling the story of ***They Just Ain't Made The Words***, then following up with a fictionalized, tear-jerking break-up tale as a prelude to ***The Lady Left Me With A Song***. It seemed like a perfect plan, until I realized it would sound to Aurélie like I'd been thinking of Robin when I wrote the song. But the crowd was already getting restless, and I couldn't think of any other way to handle things, so I decided I would just have to explain it all to Aurie later.

A hush fell over the room as I cleared my throat and leaned into the mike. "Sadly," I said with a frown, "Rusty and I broke up a year later." A rumble of sympathetic moans swept through the crowd. "It was my fault, of course. I just don't seem to have a lot of luck with the ladies, especially when I keep falling off the wagon. But even though she broke my heart, she left me with one last gift. It goes like this ..."

THAT WAS PRETTY IMPRESSIVE," Robin said, peering suspiciously at me over a small desk cluttered with schedules and bills and trade magazines. "To be honest, I'm surprised. It sounded to me like you've been performing professionally for years. And, as I said before, you do look familiar."

She was absentmindedly thumbing the corner of an issue of ***Variety***, and I suddenly remembered the magazine had covered the sale of Blue Note Enterprises. Over the years I'd managed to remain out of the limelight, refusing most interviews and photo ops, but I knew a few shots of me had appeared in business journals and trades. I couldn't recall if ***Variety*** was among them; if so, that was probably where she'd seen my face.

"The folks over at Blue Note used to say I was a dead ringer for their boss," I said. "You know, Rich Voni ... I never could pronounce his last name."

"Voniossi," she said, still sounding skeptical. "So, Mr. *Vaughn,* do you have an agent? And are you an AMF member. We're a union shop you know."

"Please call me Rix. I haven't checked in with the local AMF office yet, but I'll take care of that right away. As for an agent, you're looking at him."

"Okay, Rix," she said. "Let's talk turkey. I can move some things around and get you in here in about a month. What are you expecting in terms of money?"

"To tell you the truth, Robin, I'm not much interested in money, nor do I want a full-time gig. For the next few months, I'm going to be spending most of my time writing songs and working on arrangements for my album. What I'm thinking about is that Sunday afternoon slot, since you don't have anything going on there now. I need a place to try out some of my material, and I'll be happy to work for tips, if that's alright with you."

"Mmnnn," she said, "I don't know. If things go anything like they did tonight—I mean, if that wasn't some weird stroke of luck—my customers are going to want to see you more than once a week. How long before you'll be ready to work a six-night gig?"

Hopefully, it would be decades before I was relegated to playing in supper clubs. Though when I thought about it, if she went along with my proposal, I should probably return the favor. "Tell you what," I said, "give me a couple of months to put this album together, and if you still want to book me for a week or two, I'll take you up on that offer."

She stared at me without speaking, and I could almost hear the gears turning in her mind. Finally, she shrugged. "Well, if that's the way it has to be. But I'm going to at least pay you union scale. Tell me something, was all that stuff about drugs and alcohol part of the act, or is it true?"

And here was my opportunity. I couldn't have planned it better if I'd wanted to. All I had to do was play the remorseful, recidivist addict and I would tap into her most vulnerable personality trait. But not only would that be using my prior knowledge to take unfair advantage, it was an idea I knew was being generated by shallow, animal desire rather than a latent resurrection of the love I'd once felt for her. And for the first time I could remember, my conscious won out.

"I'll have to ask that you keep this between just you and me," I said, as if I were letting her in on an important secret. "It's something I've been working on that I think might become a permanent part of my act. Playing a not-so-stable recovering alcoholic opens up all kinds of possibilities for humor and heart-rending story telling. And if tonight was any example, I think it's going to work pretty well as an underlying premise for my on-stage persona. I've done my share of drugs and booze, so I know whereof I speak, but that was in what I like to refer to as my prior life. Although I do indulge in an occasional beer or glass of wine, nowadays about the only things I'm addicted to are chocolate and peanut butter."

This brought a smile and a nod, though I could still detect a shadow of suspicion lurking behind her eyes. Whether she was suspicious of my sobriety declaration, or my claim of being an inexperienced stage performer, I couldn't tell. Whatever it was, I wanted to wind things up and get out of there before she had time to probe any deeper. Unfortunately, she wasn't through.

"What about Rusty?" she asked. "Was she real or just a part of the act?"

I thought for a second, then said, "A little of both. She was a part of the former life I mentioned, and our breakup did inspire that last song. We're still friends, and I see her from time to time, although circumstances have made it impossible for us to ever be a couple again."

"Circumstances?"

"It's complicated," I said, hoping my reluctance to elaborate would end the conversation.

"Sorry," she said. "Didn't mean to pry. But I find those stories you tell intriguing."

Her interest in my love life seemed uncharacteristically aggressive, and I had the feeling she might be trying to determine if I was available. I could have been imagining this, but true or not, she'd once again awakened those erotic urges I thought I'd put to rest. I was about to turn down that forbidden path, when I caught myself. "No problem," I said. "What I meant was there's someone else in the picture now."

"Oh," she said. "Well, that's good. I was afraid you were alone and still dealing with a lot of heartbreak. Anyway, I guess we'll see you Sunday. It's three-to-eight, so you should be here around two-thirty to set up."

Our handshake was warm, though not suggestive in any way, and I left with mixed feelings, the strongest of which was satisfaction in knowing I'd made the right decision.

AURÉLIE WAS WAITING FOR me when I got back to the cabin.

"You twit," she said the moment I opened the door. "You're a flesh-and-blood human being with a future. I'm a ghost whose future is limited at best. You need to start facing reality here, Rix."

"So, you *did* climb into my mind," I said. "I thought I asked you not to."

"You asked me to stay out while you were on stage, and I did. But I couldn't resist seeing how you made out with Robin."

"I didn't *make out* with Robin, Aurie. I told you, I have no intention of getting emotionally involved with anyone other than you. Ever!" She seemed somewhat taken aback at this, though I also thought I saw a glimmer of relief in her eyes. When she didn't respond, I sat down at the folding table I used as a desk and leaned on the closed lid of my typewriter. "Anyway, I've done about all I can to get back in shape musically, so please, let's drop the subject and get on with this project of yours. Isn't it time we started my *training*?"

"I wish you wouldn't call it *my* project," she said. "And I don't like the suggestion that we are going to be *training* you. It's not as if I could teach you anything about performing or writing. All I want is to give you a detailed explanation of what we're trying to accomplish. But first you need to understand some sociological cause-and-effect realities you might have misconceptions about. After that, you'll be on your own, unless you ask for my help or criticisms."

"Okay," I said, "so no training, just a course in sociology. Sounds like fun."

"It may not be fun, but hopefully you'll find it interesting, if not enlightening. And I'm not putting you down by insinuating that you don't know everything you should about the origin and evolution of some of the major problems your world will face in the near future. Very few people do."

"Oh? And why is that, do you suppose?"

"Because, like you, they prefer simple sound-bite explanations to facing the complexities of reality. Of course, most people don't have the time or resources or intellectual capacity to do the kind of analysis necessary to reveal those underlying complexities. And even those few who care enough to think beyond their own immediate wants and needs are far too fixated on short-term solutions—metaphorically speaking, Band-Aids instead of vaccines or cures—which often do little more than push the problems further into the future and expand their eventual impact."

"Uh, right," I said, scratching my bald spot. "I hope you have some innovative way of injecting these things directly into my brain, because I can barely grasp what you just said."

"I do," she said with a sly smile. "You may even have heard of it. It's called reading, and it's pretty magical the way it injects knowledge directly into the brain. I'm sure you'll be thrilled with the couple of dozen books you're going to have to read."

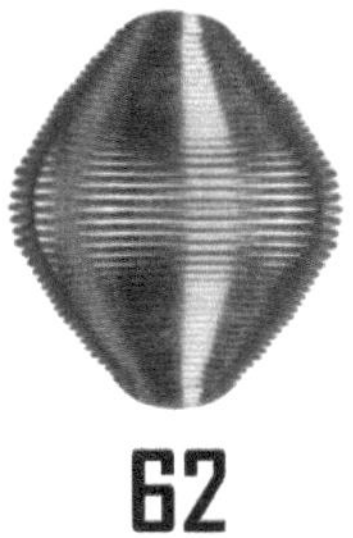

62
Secondary Education

Most of the books Aurélie and Heyoka insisted I read had not yet been published in this dimension, so they'd transferred them electronically and Sam had printed them out on an old dot-matrix printer. This made for an awkward reading process because they were delivered to me in accordion stacks of connected sheets with the punch-hole side strips still attached. I complained about that—actually, I complained about the entire process, since I'd never been much of a book reader in this life. In my first one, I was a somewhat voracious reader of science and science fiction, but my second incarnation had been such a whirlwind that, even though I'd learned to speed read, I'd hardly had time to read the newspaper, let alone thick tomes of history, philosophy, anthropology, theoretical sociology, and other subjects I had little interest in.

One exception to this uncomfortable reading exercise was a small stack of older books written by Native Americans, recounting their allegorical legends of origin and explaining the ethical mandates of North-American tribal life. These surprised me with their easy-to-grasp symbology that seemed to encompass ideals and concepts the other authors went to great lengths to break down and complicate. Not only were they more comfortable to read, they were a welcomed respite from the convoluted theoretical treatises on things like systems theory, the history of religion, the evolution of tribal and feudal societies, and the long-reverberating effects of colonialism, fascism, and so-called 'democracies.' The latter, I learned, instead of fulfilling the promise of 'power to the people,' simply gave rise to the unbridled growth and domination of international corporate power, triggering a catastrophic backlash from the economically depressed underclasses and less-democratized societies.

The purpose of all this reading, according to Aurie, was to steer me away from common misconceptions about cause-and-effect and start me thinking in a more sociologically holistic manner—to view the movement of history and social evolution, not through a microscope, but through a wide-angle lens.

"The old adage about not seeing the forest for the trees is true for most people," she said. "It's kind of like the difference between Newtonian physics and quantum mechanics. One is mostly observational, based on human senses and simple mathematics, while the other delves far deeper into cause-and-effect through the development of abstract mathematical structures."

I spent three weeks reading twelve or more hours a day, but when I finished with the books, it seemed I still had more questions than answers. I did, however, notice a somewhat slow, seismic shift in the way I viewed the world and its problems. For one thing, I began to see a wavering mental picture of what the Douglas Adams character, Dirk Gently referred to as the "fundamental interconnectedness of all things." And this brought to mind that old butterfly effect: the idea that a butterfly flapping its wings could actually affect the development and intensity of a hurricane hundreds of miles away. The point was that everything—no matter how seemingly insignificant or disconnected—mattered, even, perhaps, the influence of music on the evolution of human behavior.

Applying this more analytical, global viewpoint to the Gordian knot of interwoven problems that had devastated the world I left behind was no easy task. And I soon began to realize the vast differences in how even superior intellects—which Aurie insisted I possessed—could be influenced by the way they processed information and by their ingrained prejudices and perceived self-interests. Letting loose of the self was, she said, the first step to enlightenment. But for me, an ego-driven, stubborn individualist, raised in a society dominated by self-aggrandizing demigods, it was hard to quickly metamorphose into an altruistic, contemplative, world-empathetic parody of all I once believed to be true. Fortunately, Aurie was patient with me, taking an inordinate amount of time to explain things, while addressing my naïve arguments with carefully constructed, easily-understood metaphorical examples.

What I eventually came to understand was that things like global warming, the rise of fanatical religious fundamentalism, destruction of the rain forests, the widening disparity between haves and have-nots, plus dozens of other global crises were all tied together by a nearly invisible web of interrelated sociopolitical crosscurrents so vast and complex that even the most learned scientists and philosophers were hard pressed to sort out their underlying causes. Making things even more difficult to analyze was the fact that each of these categories had an almost infinite number of offshoots that, themselves, intertwined. So, if you tweaked one thing you were liable to affect many if not all the others.

The complexity was mind boggling, and by the time I finished reading I was doubtful that anything could be done to repair the existing damage and stop the doomsday clock from ticking.

"How," I asked her, "can you possibly know when, where, and how to intervene?"

"We can't know with one-hundred-percent certainty," she said. "However, our computer modeling—which is light-years ahead of where it was when you left—coupled with refined versions of Ellie's algorithmic equations, has allowed us to develop holographic representations of possible futures based on experimental interventions. Give me a second and I'll show you what I'm talking about."

She dematerialized, then returned almost immediately and drew my attention to a three-dimensional image that appeared above our heads. At first, it looked like a fuzzy, amorphous cloud, a blob of iridescent cotton candy glowing with a shifting rainbow of colors.

"This is the web you were talking about," she said. "And you're right, the complexity is mind boggling. Without the development of quantum computing and advanced artificial intelligence, we wouldn't stand a chance of even beginning to map the intricate minutiae. The model looks solid, because at this size, the interconnected filaments are packed so tight you can't see them individually. But if we move closer ..." The cloud began to grow, eventually blotting out the entire room and surrounding us in a fog that gradually resolved into a tangled mass of colored threads connecting tiny blobs. "Seen close up, it bears a striking resemblance to the human brain with its billions of neurons connected by synapses. Here, the blobs are significant events, while the threads represent the interconnecting pathways. Interrupting or redirecting those connections can alter the outcome of individual events or even the entire network, which, in this case, means reshaping the future."

"What are those darker regions?" I asked.

"We like to think of those as a kind of social cancer," she said. "They're actually areas of accumulating negativity that we've programmed our models to identify as potential trouble spots. The trick is to extrapolate the consequences of different ways we might attack them and alter their influence on the flow of history. Such interventions could involve something as simple as a suggestion whispered in the ear of a powerful leader, or as complicated as influencing large social, political, and environmental movements. Because of our starting point in history, we can anticipate and work more effectively with the development of the Internet and social media, accelerating innovations and communication techniques to spread new, positive ideas and beneficial technologies. One of those, by the way, will involve the introduction of Internet-based music sharing."

"You don't mean to tell me that pirating music is a positive thing. That damned Napster took money out of the pockets of every songwriter and recording artist on the planet, including yours truly."

"Yes, but you have to understand that, as distasteful as it might have seemed, it was inevitable, just as was the BitTorrent protocol for sharing pirated software. As you know, the development of digitized music and concepts like Napster revolutionized the recording industry, which is why controlling the introduction and growth of those technologies will be crucial to our use of innovative communication tools—including music sharing—as adjuncts to our overall plan."

"So some of the bad stuff has to happen in order for the Grand Plan to work?" I said.

She shook her head. "You have to stop thinking of good and bad as separate things. They each contain the seed of the other, and together they make up the whole. Yin-yang, remember? Throughout the entire process, a balance has to be maintained, which is another reason it's so complicated. Often, an attempt to right some wrong or eliminate something negative will yield unintended results and throw the larger plan into chaos."

"What about things like infectious diseases, famine, war, terrorism—can't we do something about them?"

"At this stage, very little," she said, "other than to support and guide efforts that are or were already underway, like the charity tour, Doctors Without Borders, and many others. Artificial intervention must be handled delicately, always with the long-term goal in mind. Plus, there are mechanisms in place that make some near-future problems unavoidable. For example, famine and the spread of disease in the Third World will continue for the time being, due to conditions like drought, poor sanitation, unclean drinking water, and the negative agricultural impact of genetically modified organisms. These problems can be remedied, or at least ameliorated; however, it will have to happen gradually, in concert with everything else. As for war, terrorism, religious conflicts, and the greed-based objectives of the military-industrial complex, these can only be addressed through sociological pressures that bring about regional and international political change."

"Terminal diseases, medical advances? You guys have to have come up with some cures and treatments"

"In some areas we—meaning the scientific community—have, although such discoveries and inventions slowed to a stop many years ago in our world with the disintegration of society. Research here at the lab, however, has continued to move ahead at a slow, but steady pace. That said, some of the things you might have hoped for, such as universal cures for all types of cancer, heart disease, diabetes and the like, did not happen. Instead, these have become manageable disease states, treated mostly through lifestyle changes and the use of implants that constantly administer low-dose drug cocktails. We have, however, made several advances in the fields of immunotherapy and genetic engineering, which reduce the occurrence of disease, and may lead to important breakthroughs in the future. It might be possible to introduce some of these therapies and treatments earlier in your dimension, however, there are roadblocks.

"For example, an AIDs vaccine became available here many years ago, but introducing it into a society that has yet to even acknowledge the existence of the disease would be impossible for obvious reasons. Only now are your scientists beginning to observe clusters of

Pneumocystis pneumonia, which will become the first harbinger of HIV infection. From there, it must be identified as a blood-born, sexually transmitted pathogen, and only then will the medical community be prepared to consider methods of treatment and prevention. We may be able to speed the process up a little; however, we are talking about a major pandemic that changed the world in many ways, so we have to be extremely careful not to do something that upsets the apple cart, so to speak."

"This is crazy," I said. "How the hell do you expect to coordinate everything and keep it moving in the right direction without screwing up at some point?"

"*We* can't, because humans are prone to what is euphemistically referred to as 'operator error.' But *we* won't be running things, at least not when it comes to the incredibly complex detail work—the sort of separating-fly-shit-from-pepper part. That will be handled by computers. Just as cars and airplanes will eventually be driven and flown exclusively by computers, most of what we want to accomplish will happen on autopilot. The tasks left to us will be the ones that rely on human creativity and ingenuity, which are the only areas where our brain power remains superior to even the most sophisticated artificial intelligence programming. Essentially, computers will determine when and what should be done, then it will be up to us to decide exactly how to intervene. And one of those avenues of intervention will be through music."

By then, my head was spinning. It felt like I was staring at a million-piece puzzle dumped out of a box whose cover showed only a blurry, abstract painting. There was no tranquil farm scene or mountain landscape to guide me, so I had no idea what pieces to start with. "How am I going to figure out what to write about?" I asked.

"Don't worry about that," she said. "When the time comes, we'll give you some general ideas to work with, and I'll help in any way I can. We've already delineated several areas and times where specific subjects and attitudes will need to be addressed. We've also written programming that can translate what you write into different languages and cultural music styles, and we'll be looking for indigenous artists in various countries to record and perform the songs. This will parallel other efforts to alter the sociopolitical landscape and influence attitudes in the public sector around the world. But you needn't concern yourself with those things right now. First you need to finish the arrangements for your album and get together with Jimmy and Geffen on the recording date and preparations for the concert at Watkins Glen."

THE ENORMITY OF THE task that lay ahead dwarfed my initial anxiety over performing after all these years, and the warm reception I was getting at the Black Orchid left me with little to worry about other than how I could possibly meet Aurélie's lofty expectations. That worry was almost—though not quite—drowned out by the fact that, by the third week, my Sunday shows were packing the place. Unfortunately, it didn't take long for Robin to figure out who I was, and I was forced to admit my identity and beg her not to let the cat out of the bag.

"Why all the secrecy and the name change?" she asked after I confessed.

"It's the result of a conspiracy," I said. "When I sold the company I was planning to retire, but all my friends ganged up on me and more-or-less ordered me to try my hand at performing. I put up a fight, but when everyone from your daughter, to Jackson Browne and David Geffen are hammering you, it's hard to tell them all to go to hell. As I alluded to before, I want to try my stuff out on an audience that doesn't know me, and even though my reputation is not as a performer, if *you* found out who I am, others might as well."

"Well," she said, "if you want to remain anonymous maybe you should grow some face fuzz or something, because somebody's bound to recognize you sooner or later. And, by the way, I don't care if you're the reincarnation of Elvis, I'm going to hold you to that promise of at least two weeks as our main act."

Aurie had continued to drop hints and subtle suggestions about my getting involved with Robin, but in spite of an occasional jolt of sexual desire, I'd managed to keep our relationship completely platonic. We were, however, becoming more comfortable with each other as the weeks passed, and I was even helping her out by suggesting she book artists Jimmy had told me would soon be releasing their first albums. These gestures didn't make a lot of sense, but I still felt like I was repaying an old debt; and after Ellie started nagging me to let her come to Atlanta and check out my show, I had another idea.

"You can come on one condition," I told her.

"Name it," she said.

"You have to schedule a stop-over and bring Jackson with you."

"Hell, I'll not only bring Jackson, I'll bring Sarah and Patsy and Geffen if they're available. Everybody's been dying to see your act anyway."

"That would be nice," I said. "Oh, and before I forget, there's one more thing. It's really strange, but Robin, the manager at the club? She's the spitting image of Aurélie, so you should be prepared for that. And tell Jackson, too. I don't want anyone accidentally saying something about it."

"Really?" she said. "That's … interesting. Are you two—?"

"No! We're not! So don't go getting any ideas. You'll like her, though. She's a sweetie."

GEFFEN WAS TOO BUSY with the tour, but Ellie managed to coordinate things so that Patsy and Sarah could join them. And when I told Robin, she could barely contain her excitement. "Can I leak it?" she asked. "I know they won't be performing or anything, but just the fact that they're going to be here …. Well, you know."

I did know, but I was worried about what might happen if word spread too far. "Okay," I said, "but just to some of our regular customers. Not to the media. These folks are looking to relax for a change, and I don't want them mobbed by a bunch of fans and reporters."

"No problem," she said. "I like the mustache, by the way."

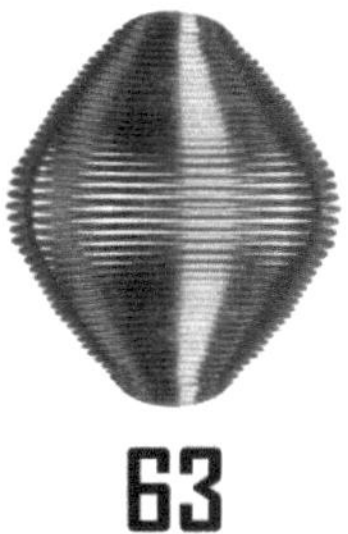

63

Old Home Week

Not only did Sarah and Patsy fly in with Ellie and Jackson, Sam, Jimmy, Billy, and Kenny came along as well. I expected them to meet me at the club, but they surprised me that Sunday morning at the cabin, which nearly burst at the seams with the nine of us crammed in it. My Spartan furniture collection was no match for the group, so we ended up sitting around on a couple of folding chairs, some floor pillows, and my unmade bed. A few jokes were made about my new facial hair and the goofy southern drawl I'd let seep over into my everyday speech. And after everyone filled me in on their lives since I'd been gone, we all went out to lunch at a fancy restaurant down the street from the Orchid.

Ellie had sprung for a stretch limo so we could ride together, and after the disgruntled driver managed to negotiate my primitive dirt driveway for a second time, we headed across to US-19, then down toward Roswell. We had jogged over to Old Roswell Road and were passing the club, when Patsy glanced out the window.

"Wow, Hoss," she said, "Is that the place?"

"Holy shit," Ellie said. "You don't go on 'til, what, three?"

It was only twelve-fifteen, but the parking lot was already overflowing and a line had begun to form at the main entrance.

"Sorry, gang," I said. "I tried to keep it as quiet as I could, but I guess word got around." Surprisingly, there were no complaints, only a few sardonic groans and an elbow in the ribs from Ellie.

"Don't be so modest, bud," Jimmy said. "From what we've heard, this is pretty much the norm when you're performing."

If it had been two-thirty, I might have agreed with him, but with nearly three hours to go, I knew we were looking at a potential human horde. "Not really," I said. "I've been drawing pretty good crowds, but this looks like the beginnings of a mob."

"You might be right about that," Jackson said. "And considering the location, they're probably only interested in seeing one of us."

Everyone turned and looked at Patsy.

"I doubt that," she said. "You and Sarah are international superstars, I'm just an old country girl with a few hits that never crossed over." Everyone started to protest, but Patsy held up a hand. "I appreciate your support, kids, but let's not waste time arguing the point. What I'm thinking is that we should swallow our pride and give 'em a thrill. With all the hoopla they're liable to wreck the place if we don't. How 'bout it, Rich? Wanna try a duet?"

"Got a better idea," I said, grabbing Ellie around the shoulders and squeezing. "Since Ellie's here, why don't you two do your famous phone duet of ***Crazy***?"

"Oh, no," Ellie screeched. "I haven't sung a note in years."

"Not so," said Jackson. "I hear you singing in the shower every morning."

The argument continued as we exited the limo and snuck in the side door of the restaurant. Ellie had reserved us a private room so we wouldn't be bothered, and while we ate, we debated who was going to do what. Before we settled anything, I asked the waitress to bring me a phone so I could call the club. When Robin came on the line, I listened to her repeated apologies, then told her we were talking about possibly working up something that would satisfy the fans.

"Listen," she said, "the fire marshal has already been here, and we're going to have to limit the crowd or they'll shut us down. So it's not like you'll be dealing with a thousand deranged groupies or anything. Plus, I called in a few favors, and there will be at least a dozen off-duty cops here to control things and make sure you guys get inside without having your clothes torn off. I really appreciate this, Rich. It's going to do wonders for us—the publicity, I mean."

After I hung up we kicked around some more ideas, and before long, instead of grumbling, everyone was looking at the situation as an opportunity to have some fun.

"Wish we'd brought our instruments," Kenny said. "We could have a reunion of the old studio group."

"Well," I said, "there's a cheap Pearl drum kit and an old Baldwin upright on the stage. And I've got a Korg PE-1000 keyboard and a vintage Strat back at the cabin. I know you're a Gibson man, but ..." Kenny and I had been arguing the comparative merits of Fender over Gibson for years.

"No sweat," he said. "Haven't touched a Fender since I grew a brain and came to my senses, but I guess I can make do."

"What about a bass?" Sam asked.

"Don't know," I said. "If it wasn't Sunday, we could run into the city and buy one. But ... wait a minute."

I called Robin back and had to wait several minutes for her to get to the phone. "Sorry about that," she said, catching her breath. "Things are getting a little crazy here."

"I can imagine," I said. "Hey, You couldn't' rustle us up a bass guitar, could you?"

"I sure could," she said. "In fact, I've got a Fender Precision and a Bassman amp in the back room. I'm holding them for a friend who happens to be vacationing in the county jail at the moment. The strings are a little old, but I've kept them oiled, so they shouldn't be too bad."

"Great!" I said. "Now here's what I want you to do ..."

I told her to move one of the big, round restaurant tables down to the lower level and set it up in front of the stage, then have somebody get the bass and amp up and running. "But the most important thing," I said, "is I want you to make a deal with the audience. Tell them Sarah and Patsy and Jackson had hoped to relax and watch the show without being bothered, but that won't be possible without some cooperation. So the deal is this: they've consented to do a few songs on the condition that afterward they'll be left in peace. Say that if we have to we can station some cops around the table, though we're hoping that won't be necessary."

"Right," she said. "Tell you what, I'll arrange things so that only our most loyal regulars are seated near the table, and I'll make it clear that any shenanigans will result in a six-month ban from the club."

"Sounds good. Make sure the curtains are closed and have the cops watch for a stretch limo. We'll pull around back and come in through the service entrance. We've got to run up to my place first, but we should still be able to make it before three."

WE WOULD ALL LOOK back on that evening as one of the most enjoyable musical experiences of our lives. Because it was totally impromptu, the audience—which was miniscule in comparison to what the three stars were used to—had no preconceived expectations, so we could have screwed up royally without fear of undue criticism. As it turned out, the lack of pressure created a uniquely relaxed atmosphere that allowed us to be spontaneous and uninhibited, resulting in what would later be described by one of the reporters who managed to sneak in as a once-in-a-lifetime, superstar jam session.

Imagine paying nothing (other than the standard, two-drink minimum) to see Jackson Browne, Patsy Cline, and Miss Sarah Love on the same bill, backed up by some of the most talented studio musicians ever assembled. Before we finished our lunch, Sam had committed to playing bass; and—after a lot of ragging—Ellie gave in and agreed to sing. With Sam on bass, Jimmy on drums, Kenny on electric, me on acoustic, and Billy on the Korg, all backing up Jackson, Sarah, Patsy and Ellie on vocals, we had the equivalent of a super group.

We didn't have any idea what we were going to play, but after everyone tuned up, Jackson sat down at the piano and started pounding out the opening chords to ***Running on Empty***. And as Robin pulled the curtain, we all joined in one-by-one, until the tiny stage was rocking like a calliope on steroids. The three ladies handled the background vocals as if they'd been singing together for years, and by the time Kenny was tearing the neck off the Strat with the final, screaming guitar lead, everyone in the club was on their feet.

The applause was thunderous, but Jackson quieted them with a smooth key-and-tempo-change, improvising a lead-in to ***Sunday Morning Sentinel***. Everyone immediately picked up on the unexpected maneuver, and we pulled off a seamless transition between the two songs, while Jackson and Sarah sang the opening lines to another round of spontaneous applause. The moment they finished the final verse, Billy took over on the Korg, sliding into the intro for ***Crazy*** without missing a beat. Kenny did a flawless duplication of the original guitar part, and I added a polyphonic counterpoint on the Ramirez to complement Patsy and Ellie's duet. Doris and I had heard Ellie sing her part many times over the phone, but that couldn't begin to compare to hearing it in its full harmonic glory. Not only was it beautiful, the emotions it stirred brought back memories of those carefree early days with Doris.

Next, it was Sarah's turn, and by the time she finished the bluesy ***I Think I'm Ready***, you could tell by the sniffles and coughs that accompanied the loud ovation there wasn't a dry eye in the place.

On and on we went, linking song after song with elaborate melodic turnarounds, even between the most complicated arrangements. We continued far beyond the standard set length of forty-five minutes, sometimes adding prolonged improvisational solos and new twists on familiar hits. But after ninety-minutes of non-stop playing, everyone was exhausted and we were beginning to wind down. Then, as if we hadn't already exploited every possible ounce of drama, Jackson decided we should end with his famous tribute to the unsung heroes of life on the road. Slowing things down, he proceeded to turn what had been a loud, raucous medley into a gentle piano solo, setting the stage for his dual anthem dedicated to roadies and fans.

Performed live, ***The Load Out*** and ***Stay*** were arguably the most popular of his many hits, and when the audience recognized the opening chords, they immediately rose to their feet, screaming and clapping. They remained standing throughout, and when Sarah ended with an imitation of Maurice William's soaring falsetto vocal on ***Stay***, the walls literally shook with applause. Billy did an incredible interpretation of the final sax solo on the Korg, and as we thanked the crowd over a long fadeout, I signaled Robin to draw the curtains.

Undeterred by our attempt at a finale, the crowd continued clapping, stomping, and yelling "Encore." And, after five minutes of this seemingly tireless pandemonium I realized we were going to have to do at least one more song.

Everyone seemed to be waiting for me to make a decision, and it was Ellie who finally spoke up. "You have to sing something, Dad," she said. "You're the only one who hasn't."

"I'm the only one who doesn't have a hit," I said. "Besides, I've got at least three more sets to do, so it's not like they're going to miss anything of mine."

"One set," Robin said from the wings. "You guys have already played nearly two hours straight, and it's almost five o'clock anyway. I'm going to have a hard enough time clearing the place out as it is, so I'd like to wind things up early. Play one more song to placate them, take a thirty-minute break, then Rix can do a forty-five-minute set. Meanwhile, I'll have somebody find Benny and get him in here to work the piano bar. That should calm things down so I can close up and get out of here at a reasonable hour."

Robin's Song! It was Aurélie whispering in my brain again. *After blowing them away with that medley, you're going to need something awesome to follow up with, and it's the only song of yours they haven't heard.*

I was still reluctant. It wasn't that I didn't want to go public with the song—I'd already decided to include it on my first album—but it was a love song, and I was afraid Robin would get the wrong impression. Plus, with the crowd this pumped up, I wasn't sure a slow tearjerker would placate them.

"Dad?" Ellie said.

The noise had not abated, so I made a decision. "Okay," I said, turning to Jimmy. "This is a new one, slow, soft, so brushes only. In fact, I should probably do the first verse alone. It's a simple chord arrangement everyone should be able to pick up on. There's a build on each chorus, but a fade as we approach—oh, hell, I don't need to tell you guys anything. Just do whatever feels right."

I pulled my stool over to center stage and signaled Robin to open the curtains. As they parted, the audience noise faded to a restless murmur.

"That was something else, wasn't it?" I said as I tuned a couple of strings.

"Damned right it was!" somebody yelled. This was followed by a chorus of agreement and another round of cheers and whistles.

"Tell you what," I said, after things calmed down, "as you might imagine, we're all pretty worn out up here, but because you've been so nice, we're going to do one more song. Only one, though, and then we need to let these folks relax for a while."

The few scattered protests quickly died out as I began to play the intro to ***Robin's Song***.

"Anyway, since y'all have been bugging me about when I'm going to record some of my music, I wanted you to be the first to know that I will be releasing an album in September." This started up the hoots and catcalls again, which surprised me. "If I had my druthers," I said, "this is one of the songs I'd like to release as a single. But before I play it for you, I want you to put your hands together for our lovely hostess." I turned to where Robin stood behind the curtain. "Come on out here, Robin." She gave me a quizzical look, putting her hand to her chest as if to say "Me?" When she didn't move, Ellie grabbed her by the hand and led her out to center stage.

"Of course we all love Miss Robin here," I said. "And I want you to know that if it hadn't been for her, the extraordinary show you just witnessed would never have happened." The applause was so loud I had to yell to quiet them. "Also, I should tell you that I owe her a special debt of gratitude for giving me the opportunity to work here at the Orchid and use y'all as a test audience for my music." The roar that followed lasted a full minute. "So," I said after they settled down, "I wrote this song as a kind of thank-you note to her, and I wanted all my friends here to be the first to hear it."

The pandemonium resumed, but when they realized they wouldn't be able to hear the music, it faded as if someone had turned down a master volume control. In the ensuing silence, I played the last few notes of the intro and began to sing.

Halfway through the first verse, Jackson added a soft, tinkling piano part, and soon everyone had joined in, sweetening the arrangement with vocal and instrumental contributions that enhanced the emotional impact without drawing attention away from the simple, poignant lyrics.

I watched Robin's face first turn scarlet with embarrassment then slowly lose its color as the shock melted into a kind of fascinated wonder. By the time I got to the closing verse that wonder had turned to melancholy sadness, and as the final guitar notes faded, an eerie stillness fell over the room. Several seconds passed before a single handclap lit the fuse of pent-up emotion and ignited the air with a deafening ovation.

THE REST OF THE evening turned out to be surprisingly calm. Even though the standing-room crowd remained, everyone seemed to remember the promise they'd made, keeping their distance from us while straining to watch our every move from afar. For the first time I could remember, I was thankful the World Wide Web and smart phones had yet to be invented, or the news, accompanied by dozens of cell-phone photos, would have been spread to every media outlet in Atlanta. There was an occasional flash from a few cameras smuggled in by customers, but no one approached to ask for a pose. Autograph requests were allowed if delivered by waitstaff, but the three stars were so used to this, they hardly seemed to notice, absentmindedly signing napkins and autograph books without so much as a pause in their conversations.

After the break, I returned to the stage and went into my now-familiar routine, interspersing humor and stories with several of the songs I planned to include on my debut album. The reception was typically warm, with the most enthusiastic response always coming from the round table. Robin had taken my empty seat, ordering free drinks and food for all and basking in the reflected limelight.

There was much moaning and complaining when she announced that the club would be closing early, but the off-duty cops handled the situation with class, easing stragglers out the doors and maintaining a vigil until the parking lot was cleared. Ellie had booked rooms at the Ritz Carlton in Atlanta, and rather than have them take the time to drive me all the way back to the cabin, I said I would call a cab. This was met with a half-hearted protest, but everyone was so tired and sated with food and drink, the objections faded quickly. They were scheduled to fly out in the morning, so we said our goodbyes in the parking lot, and Robin and I watched the limo disappear into the night.

A rumble of thunder signaled an oncoming summer storm, and we hurried back to the entrance, ducking under the portico for shelter.

"Is she the one?" Robin asked as we watched the wind whip sheets of rain across the empty lot.

"Is who the what?" I said

"That pretty young singer. Ellie, isn't it? I was just wondering if she was the 'someone else in the picture now.'"

"My God, woman," I said. "Do you think I'm a cradle robber?"

"Not at all," she said. "She's not that young and you're not that old. Besides, being who you are, you're bound to have tons of young singers clamoring for your attention."

"What if I told you she wasn't a singer, at least not professionally?"

"I'd find that pretty hard to believe after hearing her voice."

"Okay, what if I told you she was an international concert promoter, in charge of the Millennium Foundation's worldwide hunger tour? And that she's engaged to Mr. Jackson Browne?"

"I'd say you were pulling my leg," she said.

"Well, since we're on a roll here, what if I told you she was my daughter?"

"More leg pulling. You're not old enough to be her father."

I thought about toying with her a little longer but decided against it. "Her mother and I were married when I was a teenager," I said. "And I am *not* pulling your leg. She and Jackson are engaged and she *is* the principal promoter—along with David Geffen—for the Millennium Foundation's concert tours."

She grabbed my arm and spun me around so she could see my face in the dim light of the entrance. As she examined my eyes, I remembered how—in my former life—she had seen through my feeble attempt at deception. The memory brought a twinge of pain, but this time I was telling the truth, and I was betting she could see that as easily as her twin had detected my dishonesty.

"You're serious," she said. It wasn't a question. "You never told me you were married."

"I'm not. Not anymore. Doris passed away last December."

"Oh my God," she said, putting a hand to her cheek. "I ... I am so sorry. But I thought—"

"That was part of the Rix Vaughn story. Before you knew who I was."

"I feel like such an idiot," she said, staring out into the rain. "I hope it wasn't ... I mean, did she—?"

"It was an accident. A bizarre thing, too complicated to explain." I was getting myself backed into a corner, and I needed to change the subject. "So," I said, "what did you think of the song?"

She looked back at me, obviously relieved to be talking about something else. "It was beautiful, Rich. Sad, but beautiful. Did you really write it for me?"

"I did. At least the name part. The story, of course, was made up."

"I'm impressed," she said. "It sounded so real. It's hard to believe you could make up something that emotional, that personal sounding."

"Yeah, well, I've had my share of heartbreaks, even before I lost Doris. If you listen closely, you can hear echoes of them in many of my songs." A warm flutter in my chest warned me of the chemistry flowing between us, and I realized I was treading on thin ice. "Listen," I said, "I don't mean to run off on you, but I am really beat. I need to call a cab and get myself home before I pass out."

"If you can wait a few minutes, I'll be happy to drive you," she said.

Things seemed to be falling into place according to some cosmic screenplay. Here I was again, a damaged single man in need of someone to help me recover. The only difference was that this time the recovery was from heartbreak and bereavement instead of drugs and alcohol. Like an idiot I'd let Aurélie talk me into playing ***Robin's Song***, and now that Robin knew the real story, I no longer had that 'someone else in the picture' to run interference for me.

"Oh, no," I said. "I couldn't ask you to do that. I live way up north, at the end of a nasty dirt road full of potholes that are probably flooded by now."

"Well, you're in luck," she said, reaching for the door. "I've got a four-wheel-drive Jeep CJ-5, so you'll be a lot better off with me than in a cab. Just let me take care of a few things here and I'll get you home safe and dry."

I was trying to come up with a credible way to turn her down, when I heard that niggling voice in my head: *Go ahead, Rix. Don't be an idiot. Whatever happens, it won't change how I feel about you, I swear! Nothing will ever change that. And I promise this is the last time I'll be listening in, so you don't have to worry about your privacy.*

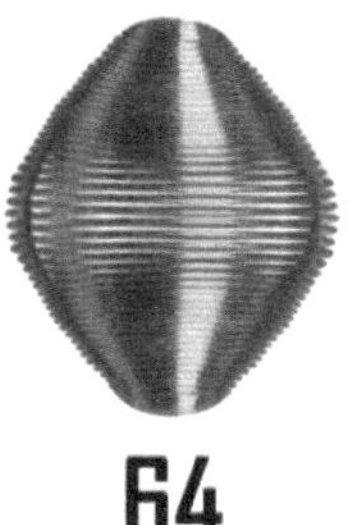

64
My Place Or Yours?

We didn't talk much on the ride home because navigating the storm required all of Robin's concentration. It occurred to me that once we arrived I should invite her in, rather than making her drive back alone in what now appeared to be considerably more than a brief summer squall. Under any other circumstances, the situation would have been perfect for a romantic encounter, but I had no conscious intention of using it for that purpose. Then again, my conscious mind might not be in complete control here. These were the thoughts running through my mind as we crept slowly over the crest of a hill and saw the blinking lights of a cop car ahead.

"Flash flood," yelled the cop. The windows on the CJ-5 didn't roll down, so Robin had opened her door about two inches. Still, the near vertical rain threw stinging drops far enough to smack my arm and face. Quickly closing the door, she wiped her face with a fistful of fast-food napkins snatched from a stack on the dashboard, then made a U-turn and headed back south. We crawled along, averaging maybe ten miles an hour, and when we came upon an abandoned gas station with a broad awning, she pulled off the road and under the rickety shelter. Fortunately, the wind was blowing from behind the building, so most of the rain was blocked. And after we rolled to a stop, she leaned her head on the steering wheel.

"Boy," she said, "this is one serious storm. What should we do?"

I'd run into flash floods up here a couple of times during my first life, and I knew it would be a minimum of twenty-four hours before they opened the road again. "Don't know," I said. "But that road won't be passable until tomorrow at the earliest."

"Is there a way around it?"

"There is," I said, "but it's likely to be blocked by the same flood."

"Well then, I guess we should find the nearest motel. Or, we *could* drive back to my place. It's not as far as Roswell, and you're welcome to stay there for the night."

Another dilemma: neither option was safe. The motel idea implied the possibility of intimate contact, even if we got separate rooms; while the alternative brought to mind the sexually-suggestive "Your place or mine?" proposition. Problem was, I couldn't think of any way to gracefully refuse. Thankfully, Aurie had promised to stay out of my head, so I didn't have to put up with her harassment. But that didn't do anything to offset the fact that nature had suddenly put me in checkmate.

"You sure it's not a problem?" I asked. "I mean, short notice and all."

"What, my place? No problem at all, as long as you can overlook the mess. I'll even feed you. And I I've got a bottle of wine—Bordeaux, I think. A Christmas gift—somewhere in the back of my pantry."

The storm's fury suddenly increased, coming in slashing blasts of wind and rain that pounded the aluminum awning like stampeding elephants. At first, this was a welcome break in what was turning out to be an extremely stressful conversation. But as the interior of the Jeep steamed up, our exhaled breath fogged the windows, creating an atmosphere so ripe with possibilities, the anticipatory tension crackled between us like static electricity. I told myself it was all in my imagination, most likely a fantasy emanating from my long-neglected libido. And when the noise finally let up, I was relieved to see nothing more than grim determination in Robin's eyes.

"Ready?" she said, releasing the emergency brake. Without waiting for an answer, she jostled us out onto the deserted road. "I'm turning on the defrosters, so it's going to get a little hot in here. How's your distance vision?"

I ducked down to look through the growing crescent of dried glass. "Not too bad now," I said.

"Good, then you can be my lookout. I'll concentrate on the road just ahead, and you watch out for fallen trees or power lines in the distance."

Our concentration on potential road hazards paid off—more than once she swerved to avoid some bit of debris, while I spotted two downed trees long before we came close to them. One of the trees blocked the road, and I was obliged to brave the battering rain in order to drag it far enough to the side for us to drive around. We arrived at her apartment after two hours of slow, emotionally draining travel, with the storm still raging around us, though not quite as violently as it had been farther north.

The apartment was above a three-car garage, and after parking in the attached carport, we made our way up the exposed stairway to the minimal shelter of her tiny porch. She fumbled in her purse for the keys, and once inside we stood dripping in the close confines of a narrow hallway.

"Bathroom's down the hall on the left," she said, squeezing water from her hair. "You get out of those wet clothes and take a hot shower. I'll bring you some towels and a robe."

"What about you?" I said.

"I'm fine. Not nearly as drenched as you. I'll light a fire and get dinner started. When you're done, we can switch."

Oh, boy, I thought as I removed my shoes and started down the hall. *Nothing like dinner by firelight to keep my sex drive in check.*

65

Inquiring Minds ...

I sat on the front steps and watched Robin's Jeep bump and splash through the flooded potholes in my storm-ravaged driveway. She had not even made it out of sight when Aurie materialized beside me.

"Well?" she said.

"Well what?"

"You know," she whined. "It's none of my business, but, well ..."

"You really didn't eavesdrop?"

"I said I wouldn't, and you should know by now that I don't say things unless I mean them."

"Good." I said. "What you don't know won't hurt you. Not jealous, are you?"

"Curious," she said. "There's a difference."

"Oh, just curious. I see." It did my heart good to see that, even with all her verbal skills and superior intellect, she was unable to hide her jealousy behind a claim of innocent curiosity. I decided to let her stew for a while over my sarcastic reply, but after a few moments of silent pouting, during which she tried—and failed—to keep her emotions from showing, I gave in. "Okay," I said, "you win. But you have to promise not to be angry."

"Why would I be angry?" she said. "After all, I was the one who—"

"Set me up? Gave me permission? Gee, thanks Mom."

That struck a nerve. And when the tears started to flow, it was all I could do to keep from reaching out for her. "Hey," I said. "Buck up there, kiddo. You're making me feel like a jerk."

"It's … It's just. I mean, it's hard, you know?" she blubbered. "I want you to be happy. More than anything in the world, I want you to have a full and happy life. But I can't help the way I feel. I only—"

"Nothing happened." I said.

"What? Oh, Rix, I'm so sorry. I didn't mean to …"

"You didn't do anything, Aurie. I tried to tell you it wasn't what I wanted, but you wouldn't listen. Not that I wasn't temped. I'd be lying if I said there was no desire. But that desire wasn't for Robin. I can't help it if sometimes when I look at her I see you. And it wasn't a resurrection of my old feelings for her either. Those died the moment I met you. She and I are friends. That's all we are and all we ever will be."

"But, what about, uh, the other thing"

"Sex? Why do you have such a hard time talking about sex? If you weren't so inhibited, I would have been talking about it all along. I've even thought about suggesting some kind of interdimensional holographic phone-type sex, but I was afraid that would freak you out."

Her eyes went wide and her cheeks started to color.

"Okay, okay," I said, "Don't go losing it on me again."

"I am *not* losing it!" she said. "It's just a little awkward for me. I need some time to process the idea is all. Meanwhile, why don't you tell me what actually happened last night? And this time, I can assure you that all I am is curious."

THE NIGHT BEFORE HAD started off pretty much as I'd expected. The shower relaxed me and I decided that since there was nothing I could do to alter the circumstances, I would play it by ear and take whatever came. Up until then, things had happened in such rapid succession I hadn't been able to do much more than worry about the storm. But while Robin took her shower I had time to think, and that's when I began to realize my longing for Aurélie had become totally confused with my sexual attraction to her virtual twin. Once I came to that realization, I knew I had to figure a way to nip things in the bud without hurting Robin's feelings. What I didn't know was that she was thinking the same thing.

Her intention to keep things platonic was evident when she emerged from the bathroom dressed in a dingy, flannel muumuu that covered her shapelessly from neck to ankles. She wore no makeup, and her hair, wrapped carelessly in a towel, capped off an obvious attempt to present a totally unsexy image. This subtle show of passive resistance was reinforced by the straightforward, non-suggestive eye contact she made with me during our conversation over dinner.

While I was in the shower, she'd thrown together a simple stir fry, which she served over wild rice, along with the wine and some crisp garlic bread. As we sat in front of the fire, eating off TV tables, we rehashed the harrowing trip back, finally able to find some humor in the ordeal now that we were safe and dry.

After I helped her clean up, we returned to the fire with our wine glasses, and the conversation became more personal. Remembering how reluctant she once was to talk about her past, I was surprised when she told me she'd been engaged for over a year to a musician she'd met at the club, and how tough it had been for her when they separated. She didn't go into much detail about the reason for the separation, though I heard enough to surmise that it had something to do with drugs. In fact, she told me it was Phillip's Fender bass and amp she'd let Sam use, which I understood to mean he was currently in jail. She must have mellowed over the past five years, because she said she had not completely given up on him—something her counterpart would never have considered, seeing as how she had dropped me like a hot potato over a few tokes of grass. And that thought suggested another possibility: that maybe Phillip had something I didn't have back then, like common sense and an honest heart.

Since she had been willing to tell me her story, I felt I had to come up with something about my personal life, so I bent the truth a little and told her I'd been involved in a long-distance relationship with a mathematician I'd met shortly after Doris died. Aurélie, I said, had taken a position at a famous laboratory in Geneva Switzerland, the name of which I couldn't even pronounce. Because of this we were only able to see each other on those rare occasions when our schedules allowed us both to travel at the same time and meet for a day or two at some mutually agreed upon location. Other than that, I said, our relationship was restricted to long, international phone conversations.

We spent the remainder of the evening talking about the music business and our personal ambitions for the future. Mine, I said, was to make it as a recording artist without using my real name or former position as leverage, which was why I was calling myself Rix Vaughn instead of Rich Voniossi. She thought that was pretty silly ("Noble, but silly," she said) so I decided to let her in on the plan to introduce me at the final stop on the hunger tour. After that, I said, it would be up to the public to decide whether or not I had deserved the opportunity.

"Oh, you deserve it, alright," she said. "Take my word for it, you will knock 'em dead."

When I asked what her goals were, she first seemed reluctant to tell me. But after a little prodding, she shrugged and said, "They're not nearly as grandiose as yours, but one day I'd like to buy the Black Orchid. I think I've become a pretty good judge of talent, and I like the idea of offering young artists a place where they can learn the ropes and maybe make some connections that could benefit them down the road."

I offered to help her out, but she apparently saw that as a threat to her independence and turned me down. So I made a mental note to keep an eye on things and see if there was some way I might be able to facilitate the purchase without her knowing, perhaps by making sure she was approved for a loan. I also decided to hook her up directly with Jimmy so she could continue to take advantage of the constant parade of new artists coming out of Blue Note Studios.

The evening ended when exhaustion from the day's activities finally got the better of us and we began to nod off. The closest we came to intimacy was a warm hug, after which she made up the couch for me, kissed me chastely on the cheek, and disappeared into her bedroom.

AURIE LISTENED TO THE story without betraying any emotion, though I could see the relief in her eyes when she realized there had been nothing more physical than a hug and an innocent peck on the cheek. As much as she wanted me to have an outlet for my physical needs, it was clear that she would have had a hard time coping if things had turned out differently. And that, as much as anything, told me how deeply she cared for me.

"I know how frustrated you must be, Rix," she said when I finished. "And I'm going to think about what you proposed. I can't promise anything yet because the thought is still alien to me, but maybe if we talk about it some more I'll become more comfortable with the idea."

Even though it was one of the many reasons I'd fallen in love with her, I had to laugh at the familiar, analytical way she approached even the most intimate of subjects.

"What's so funny?" she asked when she caught me smiling.

"Oh, nothing," I said. "Just that you are without a doubt the most fascinating person I've ever met, and sometimes the things you say are so incongruous—if that's the right word—I find them amusing."

"I see," she said with a frown. "Well, since I'm being incongruous, let me take things a step further and change the subject entirely. I could be mistaken, but I think you've just about perfected your stage act, so maybe it's time we started talking about some concepts for new songs."

"And just what might that entail?" I said. "More incomprehensible books and history lessons?"

"No more reading, if that's what's worrying you. From here on out it's mostly going to be just you and me discussing things. And I promise to use as much down-to-earth language as I can manage. Heyoka might join in from time to time, and maybe Ellie, if and when she gets the chance. What I want most of all is for you to understand and believe in what we've learned, because you are going to be one of our most important salesmen. And everyone knows the most effective salesmen are the ones who sincerely believe in the products they have to sell."

"Heavy," I said. "A great burden to put on a small mind. I wonder if I might have a few days to prepare my feeble brain for this intellectual onslaught."

"You may," she said. "In fact, first you need to finish the songs you've been working on and get into the studio so we can have your debut album ready in time for the concert. We can talk when you're not working, as long as it doesn't distract you. After the concert and the release of your album, you'll have some personal TV appearances to deal with, but Geffen has agreed to wait until we have your second album ready before booking you on your own tour. Not only are we going to need time to get the new material together, but the minimal exposure will create an aura of mystery around your public persona and increase the public's hunger for more from you. Meanwhile, you'll be composing songs for the second album, which will be one of the most challenging tasks you've ever had to face."

"Really?" I said. "Why's that?"

"Because the songs will not only have to be commercial hits, they will have to incorporate concepts that may be totally new to you. Those concepts must be skillfully transformed into lyrics and music that will plant seeds of change in the hearts and minds of the public, where they can grow and influence the direction of generations to come."

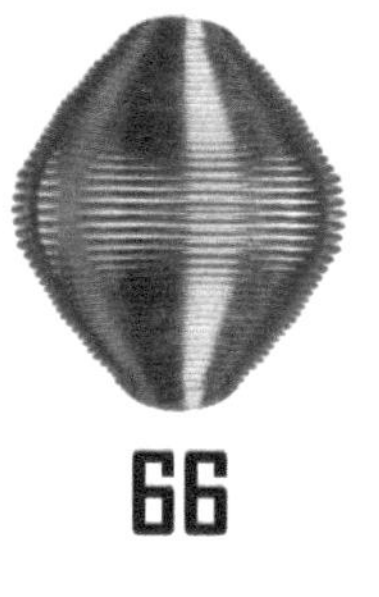

66

Millennium Park

I didn't tell Aurélie I was almost finished with the rewrites and arrangements for the album, hoping to buy a little extra time before we got into the brain-twisting exercise I knew was coming. But after a week or so of polishing, I sent Jimmy the demo tape and suddenly found myself with nothing to do. Relaxing was out of the question, so I ended up bugging people with meaningless phone calls. I could tell Sam and Jimmy were making an effort not to let on that they were too busy to talk, but Ellie would always make time for me, no matter how trivial my inquiries were. She and Geffen had turned over management of the tour to our old friend Bill Graham, whose resume included the famous Summer Jam at Watkins Glen, and Ellie was now spending the majority of her time directing the foundation's activities and planning construction of the new operations center.

"We're calling it Millennium Park," she said when I asked for a progress report. "We're in the process of—hold on a sec." This was typical of our recent phone conversations. Her work schedule had begun to resemble mine when I was CEO of Blue Note Enterprises, though she handled the multitasking much more efficiency. Like one of those circus performers who keeps dozens of plates spinning on wobbly poles, she juggled phone calls and meetings and snap decisions as if she'd been born for the job.

"Sorry," she said when she came back on the line. "Another brush fire. Anyway, I don't know if Aurie told you, but we're in the process of buying several thousand acres up there."

"Up where?" I said.

"Up where you are. We've already purchased the land bordering yours on the north and west, and we're in negotiations for several additional tracts. It's going to be really something. Kind of like the research triangle in North Carolina, only bigger and far more scientifically advanced. Heyoka is generating all the architectural and technical plans, and H2 is supervising development on this end."

"H2?"

"Oh, yeah," she said, "I guess you two haven't met yet. Everything's been happening so fast. H2 is what we're calling Heyoka's counterpart in this dimension—his younger self. We had to give him a different moniker to avoid confusion. He's cool, by the way. Brainy as hell. Only twenty-seven and he's already got all these degrees and awards. Not big headed or anything—treats me like an equal. He's working on the first phase of the lab, and we'll be moving Sam's operation up there in a few months so they can get started on the accelerator. They've really come a long way with the 3D printing and this quantum computing stuff. You'd be amazed at what they're able to do."

"I'm sure I would," I said. "This is all news to me. How did I get so far out of the loop?"

"You didn't want to be *in* the loop, remember? Besides, Aurie said she didn't want you bothered while you were working on your music. She'll probably be pissed at me for letting it slip. Listen, why don't you talk to her about all this? I really have to get back to work."

LATER THAT EVENING, I was drinking wine and watching Dan Rather report on Mount St. Helens, when Aurélie materialized in the chair next to me. "Hey there," she said. "Where's Cronkite?"

"Rather's sitting in," I grabbed the remote and turned down the volume. "I hear a lot's been going on since I moved up here. Want to bring me up to date?"

"Ellie seems to have taken care of that. Against my wishes, I should say."

"Wasn't her fault," I said. "I asked, she answered. So, when do I get to meet the young Heyoka? From what I gather, we're going to be neighbors."

"That's true, but the two of you are also going to be busy as hell for a while, and I didn't think it would be a good idea to bother either of you with unnecessary distractions. Speaking of distractions ..." She eyed the half-empty wine bottle I'd left on the table.

"What?" I said, "You want some? Oh, I forgot, you're not really here." The sarcasm was uncalled for, but I wasn't in the mood to give a damn. We had a little staring contest, which I won when she broke eye contact. "If you want to know what's really distracting me," I said, refilling my glass, "it's the fact that with all your goddamned advanced technology, you can't seem to come up with a way to—"

"Stop it, Rix! Just stop it," she said, her voice trembling with emotion. She stood and walked across the room, then turned to face me. "Don't you think we've tried? Don't you think Heyoka and I would both be here if we could? Our world is coming apart at the seams right now, and we're using all our ingenuity and remaining resources to try and survive long enough to help the foundation get off to a solid start. It's all we have left."

I tilted my glass and spun it slowly, coating the inside with a thin film of amber liquid. I felt like screaming, but I managed to reduce the urge to a shake of the head. Up until that moment, I'd hung on to a sliver of hope, but now, not only had that hope been dashed, she was telling me that even the little we had could be coming to an end soon. I felt like I was standing at her death bed, waiting for someone to turn off the machines.

When it became obvious I wasn't going to speak, she shuffled around and cleared her throat. "I've been thinking about your idea," she said.

She seemed to be making some kind of peace offering, so I did my best to swallow my anger and force a smile. "What idea might that be?"

"You know." She stared at the floor. "The, uh ... the sex thing." Her hands picked nervously at the bottom of her t-shirt, as if she was trying to work up the nerve to remove it. "I'm not sure what to do, but I'll do anything you want, Rix. Just please don't be angry with me."

"I'm not angry with *you*," I said, "I'm angry at ... I don't know, fate, I guess. Destiny. Life. And just where the hell is the so-called karma in this scenario? You haven't done a damned thing to deserve what's happening. If anyone deserves to be in your situation it's me, yet I'm here with a second chance, and you're there with no chance at all."

I could see by her sagging shoulders that my words had cut deep. None of this was her fault, and I'd stupidly made it sound like I was blaming her. "Hey," I said, "Forget all that, okay? I'm just frustrated. It didn't have anything to do with you."

A flash on the silent TV drew our attention, and we both turned to watch a video replay of the explosion that obliterated the north face of Mount St. Helens. Was that fate? Destiny? Maybe the eruption itself, but not the deaths. The nearby residents had been warned and were given ample time to evacuate. Even so, many chose to stay. It was choice, not fate that killed them.

Aurie must have been on the same wavelength. "Some things are inevitable," she said. "Even if we know about them beforehand, certain outcomes can't be altered. In our dimension, the warning signs were there, but the world refused to heed them until it was too late. Or maybe we just didn't see them in time. In any case, we all share some level of guilt."

"Not really," I said. "It was the greed and stupidity of people in power—billionaires, dictators, plutocrats, religious fanatics—that caused all the problems. You and thousands of other scientists and environmentalists did everything you could."

"Not everything," she said. "More could have been done if only we'd known exactly what to do—if we hadn't been so caught up in our own research, trying to come up with incremental scientific advancements instead of concentrating on the big picture. That's why we've been working so hard to figure out how to deal effectively with the situation here. And one thing we've learned is that the solution cannot be found in gadgets or innovations, it has to come from broad, unhurried intervention that will alter societal attitudes over the long term. We can't worry about saving individual lives or even populations. We have to focus on halting society's relentless march toward that tipping point our world passed long ago."

She seemed to have forgotten all about the sex bit, which was fine with me. I knew it was something she was having a hard time with, so I wanted to forget it anyway. I was about to say as much when she turned to face me, and with a shy smile, reached back and pulled the t-shirt over her head. "I hate to contradict myself," she said, holding the wadded shirt against her chest, "but with all this doomsday talk, I'm thinking you could probably use some distraction right now."

"Wait!" I said.

She looked at me and frowned, then loosened her grip, letting the wrinkles fall out of the shirt until it covered her from shoulders to waist. "But I thought ... I mean, I don't know exactly what you—"

"I changed my mind." For a split second, I'd considered letting her continue. After all, giving my most cherished sexual fantasy a virtual life was something I'd dreamt about for years. But the last thing I wanted to do was make her any more uncomfortable than I already had. "You know," I said, hoping to change the subject, "that's the same Dude Lebowski t-shirt you were wearing the first time I saw you at the Villa. I never saw the movie, so why don't you put the shirt back on and tell me about it?"

"I never saw it either," she said, turning around and slipping the shirt over her head. "I picked this up at a consignment shop in Lyon. I've been a Jeff Bridges fan ever since I saw him and Karen Allen in a rerun of ***Starman*** on TV. But ***The Big Lebowski*** got such horrible early reviews, I gave it a pass. I never was much of a movie goer anyway. What's wrong, Rix? I *can* handle this. I'm a little skittish about it is all."

"Nothing's wrong, Aurie. I just know it's something you don't want to do. I feel like a dirtbag for even suggesting it, so let's drop the subject. We've got a lot more important stuff to take care of."

She turned back, but couldn't bring herself to look me in the eye. "I love you," she whispered.

When I tried to answer, the words caught in my throat.

THE NEXT FEW WEEKS were not what I'd expected. Our conversations were more philosophical than technical, and I was surprised at how easy the themes were to follow. Much of the material I'd read had seemed incomprehensible, but some of it must have lodged in my subconscious because I was able to easily grasp the concepts she espoused and understand her sometimes-complex answers to my questions. By the second week, I was jotting down thoughts on a legal pad as we talked. It was as if the process had opened a conduit to an intellectual alter ego I never knew existed.

After those initial discussions, she suggested we explore several holographic models similar to the one she'd shown me before, the difference being that the events would be identified so I could better understand the relationships between them. We would also be able to test various interventions to demonstrate that what seemed to be the most logical action—eliminating a dictator, destroying the profits of a corrupt corporation, introducing a new technology—would often end up causing more problems than it remedied. During these experiments, I was surprised to find my brain silently churning out bits and pieces of what I felt sure would one day become the songs she wanted me to compose.

Our forays through the labyrinths of space-time eventually became almost like hallucinatory drug trips, during which I was able to envision a sweeping panorama of human evolution as it moved from the past through the present and into the future. This brought to mind Heyoka's stories of his early vision quests, and as I recalled his descriptions, I felt my ties to the temporal world dissolve, allowing me to step away and observe the universe in its entirety. And when I began to hear—or maybe imagine—the cosmic symphony he had spoken of as the music or harmony of the spheres, I started to wonder if Aurélie's ideas concerning the importance of music throughout history might not have been so far-fetched after all.

In one sense, it seemed, the universe was speaking my language. And, I thought, if I could learn to influence that vast concerto in some small way, it was possible that my contribution to the Grand Plan would be more significant than I'd previously imagined. Aurie had been adamant about maintaining a balance when it came to any kind of intervention, and I could now see a musical correlative to that balance in its similarity to melodic harmony. Whether this was a manifestation of my overactive imagination, or there really was some sort of orchestral score guiding our journey through space-time, didn't really matter; what mattered was that I suddenly saw with clarity what my role would be and how to attack it. As if to reinforce that realization, I began to hear melody lines—fragments of tunes I knew would eventually accompany the lyrics that came to mind as we observed the long-term consequences of mankind's foibles.

As I abandoned my vantage point and reentered the maelstrom of space-time, there was a sensation of unconditional acceptance, of instantly being absorbed into the marrow of the universe. My conversion from skeptic to believer happened so fast I felt like one of those gullible penitents being slapped on the head by a tent-show healer. A fundamentalist Christian would probably describe the experience as being born again, and even my agnosticism couldn't stop me from thinking of it as a kind of spiritual awakening.

I often came out of these trance-like states so overwhelmed with ideas I would have to shush Aurie so I could scribble them down while they were still fresh in my mind. At first, she tried to read my sloppy shorthand, but there was no context or flow to what I wrote, only random snippets—scattered, unrelated thoughts in no particular order that even I would need days to sort through and decipher. Eventually I put together a few verses and compiled a couple of rough lyric sets, and when I let her see them she seemed duly impressed.

As I became more and more absorbed in the writing process, Aurie gradually realized that her input was no longer required, and she started making excuses to leave me alone for prolonged periods. What I didn't know at the time was that these absences were the harbinger of approaching disaster.

I'd become almost manically obsessed with the project, working all hours of the day and night, often ignoring the phone and forgetting to eat. When I did manage a few hours of sleep, I was plagued by convoluted dreams; streams of consciousness that started out with creative ideas, then devolved into ominous warnings and nightmare visions of failure. It was three o'clock in the afternoon when I awoke from one of these dreams to find Ellie staring at me. She had apparently been slapping my face, and when I finally opened my eyes she seemed shocked, as if I'd risen from the dead.

"What the hell?" I mumbled.

"Sorry," she said. "I thought you might have had a stroke or something. I've got some bad news. Are you awake enough to listen?"

I scratched my stubbled chin and looked at her through bleary eyes. "Maybe," I said. "Can't really tell yet. What's up?"

"We haven't heard from Aurélie or Heyoka now for over a week. Have you?"

I took her hand and she helped pull me up. "Don't know," I said, swinging my legs over to sit on the edge of the bed. "What day is it?"

"It's Saturday. How long have you been out?"

"If you mean asleep, not long. Haven't been sleeping much lately. Been working, writing stuff for Aurie."

"Try to think," she said. "When was the last time you saw her?"

I rubbed sleep from my eyes then looked at my feet and tried to focus. "I guess it's been a few days. What's going on?"

"I was afraid of that." She rubbed the back of my neck. "I think it's over, Dad. Last time we saw her, she was in the middle of a sentence when she started to flicker and disappear. That was a week ago, and we haven't heard from either of them since. Then on Sunday morning, all the data transmissions stopped, including a set of instructions going directly to the printer. And that was really gross."

My brain was slowly coming back to life, and when I glanced up I saw that Ellie was trying to hold back tears. "What do you mean, 'gross?'"

"They've been sending instructions to print more complex organic stuff," she said. "You know, plants and insects and the like? They'd decided to move up to small mammals, but something must have gone wrong, because they sent instructions for a marmoset, and it was halfway done printing when things went berserk. You can't imagine … God, it was horrible."

The implications were beginning to sink in. If the connection was lost, that obviously meant things had shut-down on their end. Aurie had tried to forewarn me, but I was concentrating so hard on the writing process I hadn't paid much attention. "I need a drink," I said.

"No you don't!" she cried, smacking the back of my head. "That's the last thing you need right now. I know how hard this is for you, Dad. Hell, it's going to be hard on all of us. But we're on our own, now, and we have to start dealing with that reality as best we can. H2 will take over the scientific end, and Sam's got the computer division cranked up to near the point where theirs was. We've catalogued thousands of instruction sets, and we're doing our own modeling projections, so it's not like we'll be starting from scratch. This won't do anything to slow the development of Millennium Park or alter any of our other plans. What *you* need to do is concentrate on getting your album recorded and preparing for the concert."

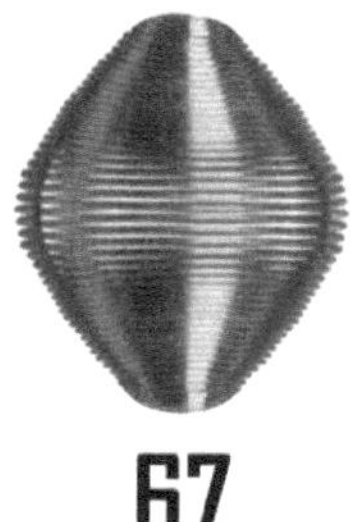

67
The Message

I tried to convince Ellie that I would be okay, that all I needed was a little time to get my head straight. But she didn't buy it. "We're still deciphering the last few digital transmissions," she said, "so I have to meet with Sam and go over them. But I'll be back to check on you, and I'm going to call every day. If you want to honor Aurélie's legacy, you *have* to follow through with the plan."

"You can call," I said, "but don't expect me to answer. I need some time to process all this, and I can't do that sitting here waiting for the phone to ring. If you want to talk, your best bet would be to look for me down at the stream. If I'm not there, I'll probably be somewhere in the woods, and your chances of finding me will be slim-to-none. As for my contribution to the Grand Plan, you can forget about that. You know as well I do it was bullshit anyway."

The conversation degenerated into a heated argument, ending only when I walked out on her. She tried to follow, but I knew the surrounding forest like the fingerboard of my guitar, and I lost her within seconds. The last thing I heard was her voice in the distance. "I'm coming back as soon as I can," she yelled. "You can't do this to us, Dad."

I sat on a fallen log and waited until I heard her car start. Then I gave in to the grief that had been pounding at my psyche. For hours, I wandered aimlessly through the woods, occasionally stopping to bloody my knuckles on a tree and yell curses at the darkening sky.

Back at the cabin, I washed the dried blood off my hands, retrieved the two bottles of real Jack I'd kept hidden in my tool box for emergencies, and proceeded to drink myself into an alcoholic fugue.

I AWOKE TO THE sound of cannonballs pounding on the walls. I rolled over and wrapped a pillow around my aching head, hoping it was a nightmare that would go away now that I was awake. I had almost convinced myself of this, when a loud crash reverberated through the cabin, and I turned to see Sam, Jimmy, and a younger version of Heyoka climbing over what remained of my shattered door. They were followed by Ellie and Robin, and a couple of guys wearing green scrubs.

The scrubs, who I thought at first might be nut-house orderlies, pushed past the others and started doing EMT stuff, checking my eyes and pulse, wrapping a blood-pressure cuff around my arm, and pressing a cold stethoscope against my neck and chest. I had no energy to protest or resist, but I wasn't about to help either, so I let my body go limp and waited until they finished.

"Wouldn't happen to have any morphine, would you?" I said as they straightened up and turned to Ellie, shaking their heads to indicate that I wasn't dying. There followed a period of angry recriminations, the volume of which amplified the excruciating pain in my head. While this was going on, Sam, Jimmy, and the young Heyoka slunk out the door, leaving only Ellie and Robin and the two scrubs, who hovered in the background until Ellie dismissed them with a wave of her hand.

"I'm going to make some coffee," Robin said, stepping into my tiny kitchen.

"There's aspirin in the cabinet above the sink," I bleated over the shattered glass in my throat. "Bring me a dozen, will you?" Then, looking up at Ellie's still-smoldering eyes, I said, "Were you through, or did you want to continue trying to commit verbal homicide?"

She seemed to have run out of gas, and when the teakettle started to whistle, she slumped into a chair and shook her head. "I don't know what to do," she said. "I can't babysit you. There's too much going on right now. I wish you'd stop being so selfish and start thinking about the rest of us for a change. We're all going through the same grief. Only difference is we don't have time to wallow in it like you."

Robin returned from the kitchen with a steaming mug of coffee and three aspirin. She set the mug down on the bedside table and handed me the pills. "They told me about Aurélie's plane crash," she said. "I'm so, so sorry."

For a moment I was confused, but then I remembered I had told Ellie about my imaginary girlfriend in Switzerland, in case the subject ever came up while Robin was present. "Thanks," I said. "What are you doing here anyway?"

"You didn't show up at the club yesterday, and I got worried. So I called down to Blue Note, and they put me in touch with Ellie. Turns out I wasn't the only one who was worried."

"Yesterday?"

"It's Monday, Dad," Ellie said.

"Monday, huh? No wonder I feel like road kill. Sorry Robin, I didn't mean to get you involved in this family stuff. I'm okay. Really. I'm just done with music, and Ellie here can't seem to get that through her thick skull.

"I'm sorry to hear that," Robin said. "And so will a few hundred of my customers be. What about your album and the big concert? You can't blow those things off, can you?"

"I'm a big boy. Got my own fortune and everything, so I guess I can do whatever I want." I put the aspirin on my tongue and looked at the steam rising from the coffee mug. Deciding it was too hot, I closed my mouth and started to chew. The acrid, chalky taste made me grimace, and seeing this, Robin ran back to the kitchen. She returned a moment later and handed me a glass of water.

"Thanks," I said, and drank it in one long gulp. "Look, I'm not feeling too swell right now, so don't pay any attention to my smart mouth, okay?"

"I understand," she looked at Ellie. "If you don't need me for anything else, I've got to get back to the club."

"Go. Go," Ellie said. "I can handle things now that we know my dipshit father is probably going to live."

Robin looked at me and flashed a pained smile, then turned to leave. "Well," she said, as she stumbled over the remnants of my ruined door, "have a good life, I guess. Maybe I'll see you around sometime."

Ellie waited until we heard Robin's Jeep start, then reached into her purse. "Here," she said, holding out a folded sheet of paper. "It's from Aurélie."

"Yeah, right," I said, snatching it from her hand. "If you think I'm going to fall for that crap, you'd better think again." I crumpled it into a ball and threw it across the room.

She stood and walked over to retrieve it. "Believe what you want, Dad," she said, tossing it on the bed beside me. "But at least read the damned thing. I've got to hit the head." She spun on her heels and left the room.

I looked at the wadded sheet, then picked it up. I knew what was going on: Ellie had decided the only way get to me was to fake a message from Aurélie; it would probably be a tear-jerking farewell, with a plea for me to continue with the plan for her sake. Holding it cupped in one hand, I picked at a protruding corner with the other until it came loose. A little more picking, and I saw part of a word, then another and another. Finally, I spread it out on the bed, smoothed the wrinkles with my palm, and started to read.

> *Rix,*
>
> *I'm hoping this gets through before we have to shut down completely. You've been so caught up in your writing for the last few weeks, I didn't want to bother you with what was happening here. I don't have time to go into detail, but our situation has become dire, and if this message makes it through, it might be the last you hear from me.*
>
> *I wanted you to know how proud I am of the way you immersed yourself in the project and tell you that the lyrics you showed me were incredible. I really hadn't expected so much so quick, nor had I expected your ideas to be quite so masterfully attuned to the specific themes and phases we talked about. As you know, the plan's success depends in large part on its flexibility, and if we are unable to stabilize things here, it will be up to Sam and Ellie and H2 to make future adjustments. The foundation now has the tools to keep things moving in the right direction, and I hope you will add your input to the plan's ongoing evolution. Until you shed your skepticism and committed to the program, there was an emotional element missing, something the rest of us couldn't tap into because of our objective*

attitudes and analytical way of looking at things. It's that element that you can bring to the table.

Speaking of emotional deficits, I wanted to apologize for my own shortcomings in that department and say how much I regret not being able to properly express my feelings for you. Though I might never have been able to say it in the right way, you should know that our relationship has meant the world to me. Even as I write these words, I can hear the coldness coming through, and it infuriates me that I can't seem to do anything to change that. I guess we could call it my own personal pons asinorum, because it severely tests my emotional inexperience to solve. So please, please try to read beyond the stiff prose and know that underneath it all is a simple girl who loves you with all her heart, and has since the day we met.

There's a lot more on my mind, but I'm going to have to cut this short. I did want to say, though, that if things continue to deteriorate here and I am unable to contact you again, I don't want you to think of me as being gone, because no matter where I am or what form I take I will always be with you (I know that sounds a little too spiritual for me, but I do believe it to be true). That said, I want you to start thinking of yourself for a change. Try to stay away from the alcohol; let loose of the anger you are sure to be feeling right now; and as a special favor to me, please give some thought to deepening your relationship with Robin. She's a wonderful person, Rix, and you would be an idiot to let that opportunity pass you by.

One last thing: I've been meaning to talk to you about my counterpart in your dimension, but so much has been going on lately I haven't had the chance. My initial feeling was that we should not try to intervene in her life, but I've been having second thoughts about that lately, especially since we've been working with H2 and things seem to be going so well. She's going to have a miserable childhood, and she won't be meeting Heyoka in her teens as I did, because he'll be down there in Georgia working with the foundation. You don't have to worry about her for a while because she's only two years old, but her life is going to be turned upside down a year from now when her parents divorce and she is sent to live with her alcoholic aunt. I'm not sure what you could do about that, but I'd appreciate it if you would at least keep an eye on her, perhaps until she meets my old high-school physics teacher. Then maybe you could offer her some sort of internship at Millennium Park, where you and the others can encourage her development as a physicist.

Finally, although I know you will suffer some pain and bitterness over what's happened, you mustn't grieve for me. I've had a good life all in all, and I have few complaints. Other than not being able to join you there, my only regret is that I won't be around to hear the music.

Anyway, take care of yourself and tr …

I looked up from the page to see Ellie standing there with her hands on her hips. "Well?" she said. "Believe me now?"

I wiped my eyes on the sleeve of my t-shirt, and held up the sheet. "Is that all?" I said. "It ends in the middle of a word."

"It ended without any warning, and that was the last transmission. What's does her reference to pons asinorum mean?"

"You read it?"

"Somebody had to transcribe it, Dad. And I thought you'd rather it be me than Sam. So, pons asinorum?"

"It's some obscure geometry thing—"

"I know what pons asinorum is. I was just wondering why she would use it when talking to someone who couldn't possibly understand what it means. She actually sort of misused the term, but you wouldn't know that."

I thought for a moment, then smiled. "She mentioned it once during one of our private conversations, so maybe it was code, something she knew only I would get."

"Okay," she said, "what's the verdict? Am I going to have to Baker Act you or are you going to come to your senses."

"The Baker Act is only good in Florida," I said. "But to answer your question, no, I don't think you need to have me committed. Give me a couple of days to get the alcohol out of my system, and I'll try to pick up where I left off."

She looked at me skeptically. "You sure about the booze? I don't want to have to scrape you off the wall next time I stop by."

"I'm sure," I said. "I've got some apologizing to do, and I'm going to need a couple of backstage passes for the concert to help me with that. So see what you can do. And I guess I'd better put the writing project on hold and get down to the studio. Call Geffen and tell him I'm going to book the session for two weeks from now, and see if Jackson can make it. If he's not available, we'll have to change things to fit his schedule, because I am *not* cutting this album without him. Meanwhile, I'm going to have a good cry, take a twenty-four-hour nap, and see if I can salvage what's left of my brain."

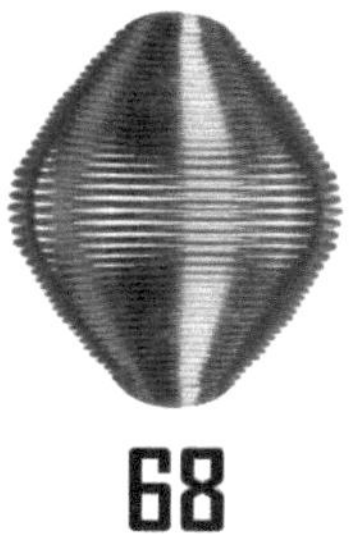

68

The Second Time Around

Back in the familiar confines of Blue Note Studios, Jimmy, Geffen, Jackson, and I worked on the arrangements for my first album. The sessions were long and often confrontational, but we were all so familiar with each other's nit pics and idiosyncrasies, the conflicts tended to work themselves out, if not amiably, then as a result of grudging compromise. In the end, we produced what everybody but me thought was some pretty fantastic stuff (my opinions on the final product were summarily dismissed as an overly paranoid quest for unachievable perfection).

We had all the tracks ready for mastering a month before the concert, and with nothing left to do, I drove back to Georgia in time to fulfill my promise to Robin. I'd made amends with the help of a couple of backstage passes to the concert, and I'd worked the two Sundays before I had to leave for the recording session. She wanted to book me as the featured act for the full month after I retuned, but I told her I needed a couple of free weeks to prepare psychologically for the most important performance of my life. To assuage her disappointment, I said I would have Geffen ship her a few dozen free copies of my album as soon as it was pressed, and that if there was time, I would sign them all so she could pass them out to our most loyal regulars.

"They'll be the first people on the planet to own signed copies of Rix Vaughn's debut album," I said. "It will probably turn out to be a flop, but those copies should still become collector's items, if for no other reason than there will be so few of them ever sold."

"Yeah, right," she said. "By the way, I never thanked you properly for the backstage tickets, so maybe you'll let me cook you dinner again sometime. It's the least I could do for the opportunity to witness the birth of a superstar."

I laughed at that. Even though the dual clout of Blue Note Studios' reputation and Geffen's dominance in the broadcast industry would insure an initial sales surge, that early bounce would only serve as a first step. All the hype and connections in the world could not guarantee stardom. Long-term success would depend entirely on the public's acceptance of me as a performer, and I was about to test that acceptance in front of more than half a million die-hard rock fans—knowledgeable aficionados who'd paid good money to see established stars, not unknown wannabes.

"Maybe I'll take you up on that," I said. "Who are you bringing to the concert?"

"Oh, I didn't tell you. Phillip got out of jail last week, so I'm going to bring him, if that's alright."

"If course it's alright," I said. And I meant it. Despite Aurie's admonitions, I had no intention of getting emotionally involved with Robin. "You guys can fly up with me if you want, but you'd better lower your expectations. I've been in this business a long time, and as I'm sure you know, for every success story there are a thousand talented musicians out there still playing for union scale and tips stuffed in a mason jar."

I WORRIED MYSELF SICK during the two weeks before the concert, fighting through bouts of intense sadness and remorse while entertaining my woodland friends with hours of rehearsal. Even with all that preparation, when I finally hit the stage, I damned near froze up. The largest audience I'd ever faced was something like 10,000, back when I was touring with Danny O'Donnell in my first life, and as I peered out from behind the curtain at that sea of humanity, my first instinct was to run for the exit.

Jackson handled my introduction, flanked by Sarah and Patsy. He said I was an old friend of theirs who rarely appeared in public. Then he told the audience they were in for a surprise.

"Many of the songs you are about to hear will be familiar to you," he said, his voice echoing over the huge crowd. "But Rix here will not be simply offering his interpretations of those classic hits. On the contrary, the versions you've already heard were the interpretations, because the fact is, he wrote every one of the songs he's going to sing tonight."

As I walked out on stage and took my place on the spot-lit stool, a curious murmur rolled through the crowd, accompanied by tentative, scattered applause. I remembered attending one of those famous concerts where James Taylor had introduced Carole King in the same way, and how the audience had been similarly reticent until they heard the first strains of ***Will You Still Love Me Tomorrow***. But my solo arrangements bore little resemblance to the heavily produced gold and platinum records this audience was familiar with, and it wasn't until I finished the first verse of ***Sunday Morning Sentinel*** that the crowd began to stir.

Jackson had suggested we duplicate the all-star band that had played at the Orchid, in order to add some star power to my performance. But I wanted to live or die on my own merits, so I'd told them to let me have the stage to myself for the first song. As I started the second verse, the seething mass of humanity grew increasingly quiet, and I realized the solo idea had been a mistake.

I played the closing guitar solo with fingers shaking so badly I could barely control them, and as the final notes drifted into the surrounding hills, it seemed my performance had bored the audience into catatonia. Except for a few coughs and whispers, the crowd remained silent for what seemed like an eternity, until finally, like the sound of approaching summer rain, a soft ripple of applause began to swell. It was as if they were having a hard time accepting the fact that this nobody—someone they'd never seen or heard of—had actually written the megahit that dominated the charts a few years before. And only as that realization began to sink in, were they able to appreciate what they'd just heard.

I'd never before experienced first-hand such a massive acknowledgement of my talents. I'd watched my songs climb the charts, seen them performed by others, listened to the applause they generated; but I'd shunned the limelight myself, refusing to personally accept the Grammys or publically receive the gold and platinum records. Those awards, along with all the civic citations and certificates of thanks for charity work, resided in the trophy room at Blue Note Enterprises, and that's where they would stay. I'd always felt that I didn't deserve the recognition; that I'd been given an unfair advantage by being allowed to cheat death and enjoy the benefits of having a second chance. Aurélie had berated me about this, as had Ellie and Doris, but I'd stuck to my guns. Until, that is, I'd let them convince me that my success could have far-reaching repercussions. I still wasn't convinced of that, but one thing I had to admit was that being admired and appreciated by hundreds of thousands of fans felt damned good.

I finished my performance that night floating on cloud nine. After a six-song set, with the best band anyone could hope for backing me, the crowd wouldn't stop screaming for more. So I obliged them with a solo rendition of ***Robin's Song***, walking off the stage with a feeling reminiscent of the first time I'd experienced applause that day at William's Park when Carol Henderson had given a seven-year-old his first taste of stardom. My elation, however, was short lived.

I walked off stage to another, smaller round of applause, plus high-fives and back slaps from crew members, roadies, and a dozen or so of the most famous rock artists on the planet. But that adulation did nothing to ease the pain and loneliness that rose in my chest as I stumbled through the gauntlet of well-wishers. Although I'd learned to exert a kind of makeshift, temporary control over the mind-shattering shocks of grief that struck me whenever I thought of Aurélie, searching the far walls backstage and not seeing her apparition was devastating. Behind me, chants of "More" and "Encore" were rising, but my knees had turned to rubber. And when Ellie reached out to hug me, I collapsed into her arms, knocking her to the floor.

"Take it easy, Dad," she said, as I buried my head in her lap. "You did great. Just listen to that crowd."

Yes you did, Rix. You were wonderful.

The sound of Aurélie's voice was, I knew, a figment of my deranged imagination, assembled from my memory banks as a defense mechanism against the thunderclap of grief. Still, my kneejerk reaction was to look up and search the cluster of concerned faces staring down at me. Squinting through a swirl of spots that warned of impending unconsciousness, I thought I saw Aurie and Heyoka at the edge of that cluster. But Heyoka looked too young and Aurie's hairdo was all wrong. And when I realized I was looking at H2 and Robin, the room began to spin out of control.

I AWOKE IN A hospital bed, thinking that somehow I'd traveled back in time to the day I'd had the heart attack at Heyoka's villa. But, unlike that awakening, there was no log in my throat or dried goo holding my eyes closed. To further confirm that I was still in my second life, Ellie and Jackson were at my bedside.

An IV tube dangled above one of my arms, and a blood pressure cuff was wrapped around the other. Out of the corner of my eye I could see a monitor and that flickering green light I remembered from my first visit to death's doorway. When I tried to speak, my throat was so dry all I could manage was a weak grunt.

"It's okay, Dad," Ellie said. "Don't panic. You had what they're calling a blood-pressure incident, not a stroke or heart attack or anything. Apparently you haven't been taking your BP meds, and that, plus all the stress pushed your pressure way up. It was around 300 over 200 when we checked you in, which they said meant you were a walking dead man. But they've got it back under control. All they need to do now is come up with an oral drug regimen that will keep it that way without your having to be hooked up to an IV for the rest of your life."

IT TOOK THEM A couple of weeks to get me off the IV, during which time I fell deeper and deeper into depression. It had been almost three months since Aurie's last transmission, and other than a few sporadic bursts of unintelligible data, there were no further messages or meaningful communications from their dimension. I tried to hang on to tiny bits of hope I thought I'd found in the now-dog-eared copy of her last message—the "might's" and "if's" and other equivocations that suggested they had not yet given up. But that, I knew, was only wishful thinking.

I left the hospital with six bottles of pills and orders to take various combinations of them three times a day to keep my blood pressure in check. One of the prescriptions was for an antidepressant, and between that and the side effects of the other drugs, my motor skills and brain function had deteriorated to the point of making me feel like a drunk on LSD wandering through a side-show House of Mirrors. Not only was I unsteady on my feet, there seemed to be a short circuit in the connection between my brain and my mouth that sometimes caused an embarrassing delay in verbalizing even the simplest of thoughts. The doctors assured me these side effects would ease and eventually disappear, though they said it would likely take several weeks for my system to fully adapt to the new chemical onslaught.

Back at the cabin, with a day nurse to monitor me and make sure I took my meds, I was subjected to a steady stream of visitors, whose efforts to cheer me failed miserably. Most of the foundation's operations had been moved to the Georgia site, so everyone was nearby. To make matters worse, Mom and Dad flew in from overseas for the sole purpose, it seemed, to berate me for not sticking to the drug regimen Dad had put me on earlier. Though happy to see them, I was not terribly disappointed when they left after a couple of days to travel to St. Pete and visit with friends before flying back to Italy.

The only positive thing about all this visitation was that I finally got to spend some time with H2. In spite of his busy schedule, he managed to drop by occasionally, and his presence was comforting because he reminded me so much of his older self. On his first visit, he seemed dismayed that I had not been told of the grave situation Heyoka and Aurélie had faced before we lost contact with them. They had kept everyone else in our small circle abreast of what was happening, but I had been excluded on the premise that my emotional state and mental attitude had to remain upbeat, at least until after the concert.

Although I was aware of their world's steady march toward Armageddon, at times Aurélie had assured me they were handling things and were still relatively safe. What she failed to mention was the extent to which their underground sanctuary was being increasingly threatened by marauding hoards of anarchists who were taking advantage of instability in the surrounding bedrock that had been caused years before by commercial mining of the area's natural gas reserves.

"You may recall a process called hydraulic fracturing, or fracking," H2 said during our first meeting. "The technique was relatively new when you left their dimension, and the scientific community was only beginning to understand the dangers it presented. There was a strong grass-roots movement to stop it, but that effort didn't stand a chance against the money and influence of huge multinational energy producers and their billionaire supporters. And, like many other ecologically unsound practices championed by corrupt politicians and greedy corporations, fracking operations flourished in the years that followed, creating devastating pockets of earthquake activity around the globe. One of those pockets was near Saint-Genis-Pouilly, and the resulting destabilization lingered, eventually weakening the defense system they'd built to protect the lab complex from invaders."

Over the years, he said, they had constructed several reinforced barriers, like nested shells, around the underground lab. These fortifications had been damaged by residual earthquake activity, and as the economic and social framework of society crumbled, access to outside labor and the materials needed to maintain their structural integrity was cut off. This forced them to retreat into isolation along with a core group of researchers. From then on, much of their energy and time was spent protecting the complex from savage gangs of mutant refugees who constantly attempted to break in and help themselves to the extensive, renewable supplies of food, clean water, breathable air, and medicine.

Of course, having regressed to a near stone-age existence, these marauders would have had no idea how to operate or maintain the sophisticated generation and conversion systems. But that ignorance had never stopped them before, nor would it stop them once they discovered the world's last remaining treasure trove of life-sustaining resources.

Damage was done and repaired; fissures were sealed only to be broken open again by improvised explosive devices. Force fields and chemical barriers, reinforced by googolplexians of microscopic nanowarriers, were deployed for protection. The battle soon became a war of attrition, as the gangs—once-hostile to each other but now frustrated—agreed to join forces.

In the midst of all this chaos, Heyoka, Aurélie, and their small group of dedicated colleagues worked frantically to help establish the foundation and complete development of the most sophisticated 3D printing operation ever conceived—a technology not only capable of printing complex living organisms, but of doing so interdimensionally. Because there was little hope for the future of their planet, the goal was to perfect the technology in time to send instructions to our dimension for printing copies of the lab's human personnel. Sam had said that higher life forms were coming through with blank minds, but H2 assured me they were close to remedying that problem when they apparently had to shut things down.

"That was true of the first few attempts," he said. "However, you are forgetting one of their monumental scientific achievements, an achievement validated by your participation in their first full-scale experiment."

I waited for my drugged brain to process this, but nothing came to mind. "Sorry," I said, "I'm not thinking too clearly since I've been on all these meds."

"Ah, yes," he said with nod. "Well, let's look at the situation a little more closely. Here we have, say, one Rix Vaughn, whose body has been copied and printed in another dimension. And we have the ability to animate that body so that it comes to life in the other dimension, but with no memories or personality. If we wanted to turn that body into a complete copy of Rix Vaughn, personality and all, how, then, could we do that?"

And suddenly I got it. "The same way they transferred my mind into my younger self."

"Correct!" he said. "And that's where the technology stood when we lost contact with them. In fact, it seemed like a foregone conclusion that they would be able to accomplish this, but only if the accelerator remained functional. Unfortunately, the accelerator and its ancillary components were what allowed them to communicate with us, and that communication has obviously ceased. This could be due to a number of factors, the worst being damage to the accelerator that rendered it permanently inoperable. However, it could also be that we are looking at something less-severe, such as a temporary interruption in their efforts due to the ongoing battle to protect the lab."

"So ..." I stopped to allow my mouth to catch up with my brain. "So, are you saying there might still be hope?"

"There's no way to know. However, the sporadic, unintelligible transmissions we've been receiving could indicate efforts to resume communications. Unfortunately, they could also be due to other factors, such as leftover static interference in the space-time continuum, or something else beyond our capability to understand at this time. The fact that we don't know what's happening leaves room for hope, but we can't expend a lot of mental energy speculating on what might or might not happen. Our primary mandate is to complete the development of Millennium Park and continue to deal with the looming prospect of worldwide disaster. And that's going to require all the time and intellectual resources we have."

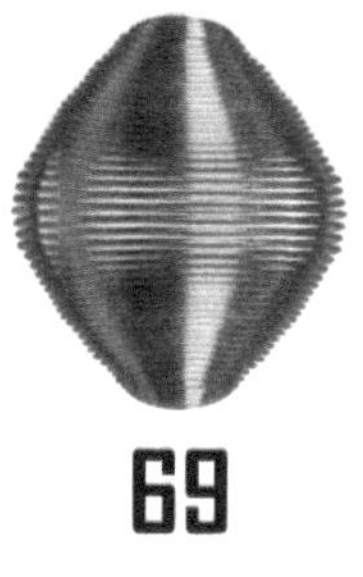

69

A Star Is Born

In the spaced-out aftermath of my collapse, I hadn't thought much about the concert or its impact on my future. And no one had mentioned record sales or chart positions, probably because they'd been ordered not to do anything that might aggravate my condition. But when the doctors said they were satisfied with the stabilization of my blood pressure, and that excitement was no longer a risk factor, David Geffen came by to fill me in. It had been six weeks since the album's release and already three singles had cracked the top ten on Billboard, with ***Robin's Song*** topping the list now for 27 days and the other two on the rise. Meanwhile, the album was well on its way to going double platinum, with no end in sight.

"We've purposely held back a little on distribution in order to create a false impression of shortages due to unexpected sales volume," said Geffen. "Interestingly, the rumor—purposely spread by our publicists—that you have gone into hiding, is adding an aura of mystery to your sudden popularity, and people are clamoring for any tidbit of news about your disappearance. The gossip weeklies are eating the story up, as are the celebrity rags and tabloids. Speculation has run from an alien abduction to a drug overdose, and everything in between. You're hot, my friend. Especially for an invisible man."

If he'd expected an exuberant response, I'm sure he was disappointed; I could barely muster a smile, let alone any overt display of happiness. My lack of enthusiasm was due in part to the fact that I—with some conceit—was not really surprised the album was doing so well. But the main reason was my ever-deepening depression over losing Aurélie. The antidepressant had not helped; on the contrary, its stupefying effects had made things worse, so I'd quit taking it after a couple of weeks. Fortunately, the original marketing plan had called for me to remain out of the public eye until they were ready to release my second album. Of course, I would have to finish writing the songs before we could even start recording the album, and that now seemed like it might take years.

Because of my supposedly delicate emotional status, no one was bugging me to complete the album, so I didn't have to worry about writing for a while. What I did worry about was finding some kind of motivation. I had never been convinced that my role in the Grand Plan was all that important, so there was little incentive on that score. I tried my best to recapture the thrill I'd experienced on stage at the concert, but that feeling had been so brief I could barely remember it, let alone use it as a creative stimulant. Fortune and fame, as James Taylor once wrote, is a curious game; it takes a strong desire and a considerable amount of energy to manage, and I had neither.

Ellie had been surprisingly undemanding and sympathetic. When she came by—which was more often I than would have expected given her work load—instead of berating me for my seeming laziness, she would read to me from the fan magazines and entertainment trades in the hope of raising my spirits. I was grateful for her show of tolerance, but she wouldn't have known, because I continued to act like a spoiled child, often refusing to get out of bed or eat, and never touching my guitar.

Periodic examinations by several medical specialists revealed no lingering physical problems. And even though I knew I was in a psychological tailspin, when Ellie finally got up the nerve to suggest I see a shrink, I flatly refused. Then, just as I was about to hit rock bottom, fate stepped in and threw me a lifeline.

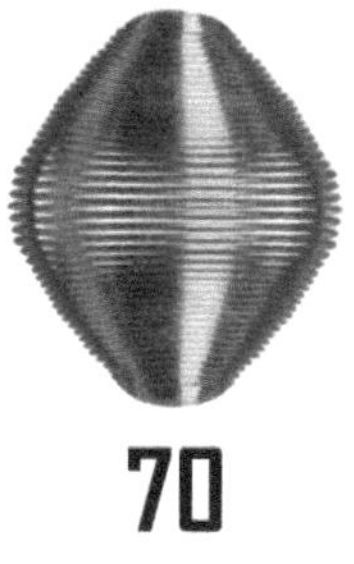

70
Special Delivery

Sunrise shot silver splinters of light through the cabin's ice-crusted windows as I huddled under a pile of blankets on that cold winter morning. The baseboard heating was struggling—and failing—to warm the house, when the phone jerked me out of a shivering half-sleep. Knowing Ellie was the only person who would call this early, I tried to ignore the brain-rattling clamor. But after the sixth ring, I knew it wouldn't stop until I answered, so I snaked an arm out and grabbed the receiver. Sure enough, it was Ellie, calling to warn me that she would be over in a few minutes with a surprise. Wrapping myself in a blanket, I crawled out of bed to turn on the coffeepot and light a fire, then climbed back under the covers to await another tedious visit from my daughter.

Ellie's surprises usually involved some news about the album, or maybe a delicacy from the bakery they'd recently opened at Millennium Park, so when she walked in carrying a puppy I was caught off-guard. I knew the bit about therapeutic pets, and I wasn't about to go for that. But the tiny chocolate lab was so feisty and cute, I decided not to say anything until she had a chance to explain herself.

"Meet Chance," she said, as the energetic ball of fur leaped from her arms and landed, legs akimbo, on the slick wooden floor. Together we watched it race around the room, slipping and sliding into walls and chairs before skidding to an awkward stop in front of the fire.

Cautiously backing away, it resumed its frantic investigation of the cabin, and when it made several unsuccessful attempts to jump on my bed, I reached down to lend a hand.

Ellie remained silent while the puppy snuggled up to my chin and licked my face, then slid off my chest to attack a pillow, snarling and tearing at the pillowcase as if protecting me from a vicious animal.

"Pretty cool, huh?" Ellie said. "Seems like a normal puppy, don't you think?"

"Yeah, so?" I grumbled.

"So ... it's a copy—She, I should say—She's a print."

I DIDN'T CATCH ON right away, but once my sluggish brain managed to put two-and-two together the implications became clear. Ellie, meanwhile, cautioned me against getting my hopes up.

"There was no message from Aurie," she said. "No status report or anything. It was a single unannounced transmission—a set of instructions sent directly to the printer. But, if you think about it, this actually says some things in and of itself. For one, it tells us the lab is still functional, though obviously with some limitations. For another, it tells us that they—at least some of them—might still be alive."

"What do you mean, might?" I said. "This obviously proves—"

"No it doesn't, Dad. H2 says the transmission could have been archived earlier and programmed to start automatically whenever the interdimensional link was reestablished. And the link could have opened up again due to something other than human intervention. The fact that there was no accompanying message suggests that might be the case."

"Whatever," I said. "At least it's ... Hey, wait a minute. She seems normal. Which means they must have solved the problem of transferring animals with their minds intact."

"Not necessarily," she said. "We estimate she's only about six weeks old, so even if she started out with no memories or personality, she would still be acting like a young puppy just getting acquainted with her new life and surroundings. There's no way to know one way or the other. The transmission came through yesterday morning, and since then there have been no further communications, not even a quick note of explanation."

"Still, it's—"

"Encouraging. I know. We named her Chance because that's what she represents, a chance. I don't mean to throw a wet blanket on things, but we have to be realistic. It's been months since Aurie's last message, so even if they *are* alive, it's clear they're still dealing with a lot of problems. Until we receive a direct communication—something we can confirm came from a living person—about all we can do is hope."

I didn't have the energy for a prolonged debate on the matter, but I wasn't about to let her pragmatic pessimism get to me. As far as I was concerned, their theory of some kind of automatic transmission was far less likely than the possibility that someone had been controlling things.

"I brought some food," Ellie said, holding up a bag. "Would you mind keeping her here for a while? She's a little hard to deal with over at the lab, and we don't want to put her in a cage."

I looked down at the now-exhausted puppy. She had scrunched up under my arm, and the warmth of her body against mine was somehow reassuring. "Chance, huh?" I said, scratching behind her ears. "Not a very hopeful sounding name. Tell you what, she can stay here for a while, but you need to find her a permanent home, so start asking around. And I'm probably going to change her name."

WHEN ELLIE TURNED TO leave that morning, the puppy jumped down and tried to follow, whining and scratching at the door as it closed. She soon realized this was hopeless and ran back to paw at the side of my bed. After I helped her up, the two of us fell asleep, and when we awoke, she seemed to have forgotten all about Ellie. From then on, she clung to me like a newborn to its mother, following me everywhere and begging for attention whenever I ate or watched TV.

I often wondered what made me decide to change her name, whether it was a flash of intuition or something less tangible, like Aurélie whispering to me across the space-time continuum. Common sense told me that couldn't have been the case, but there *was* something mysterious about the decision. Though it might have been only a coincidence, some surprisingly positive things began to happen shortly after I started calling her Hope.

As anyone who has ever trained a puppy knows, the process involves a lot of scolding, especially during the housebreaking phase. And that scolding almost always includes saying the puppy's name. In this case, that meant repeatedly saying the word "hope," and every time I said that word I was reminded of my conviction that Aurélie and Heyoka were still among the living. I can't discount the therapeutic value of having a joyful, loving, canine companion, but I'm inclined to believe it was the subliminal effect of repeating her name that slowly dragged me back from the brink of suicidal depression. Whatever it was, I soon found myself looking through the lyrics I'd written, scribbling notes and making changes. I also started playing around with chord arrangements, and before long I was putting together a portfolio of new material.

Hope turned out to be a fairly typical puppy (short memory, poor bladder control, and that pained puppy-dog expression whenever I yelled at her) so my first few attempts to convince her she should not pee in the house were frustrating. I finally decided to build her a doggie door, and after she conquered her initial fear of venturing outside alone, she caught on pretty quick. Once we had passed that milestone, I decided she was mature enough to negotiate the trail.

On our first trip to the stream she lagged behind for a while, but as she became more comfortable with the new environment, she began to dash ahead, snapping at insects and investigating every rustle she heard in the underbrush. That trip eventually became part of our daily routine, and when I started taking my guitar along, she would stare at me with tilted head, listening attentively while I sang and played.

ONE SIDE BENEFIT OF Hope's positive influence on my state of mind was that it put an end to the constant parade of visitors. Not only was I no longer showing signs of depression, Ellie said the demands of the foundation and the rapid expansion of Millennium Park had everyone working eighty-hour weeks just to keep things on track. Consequently, I rarely saw any of them, even Ellie. She did, however, call occasionally to check on me and see how the puppy was doing. I had managed to convince her not to wake me with her calls, but one morning in early spring, the phone rang before sunrise, and I knew it had to be her.

"You sitting down?" she said when I answered.

"No," I said. "It's five in the morning. I'm sleeping. What happened to your promise not to wake me?"

"Sorry, but I thought you might want to hear this sooner rather than later."

"What? Another report on my supposed superstar status?"

"A little more important than that."

The chuckle in her voice peaked my curiosity. "I give up," I said.

"Okay. I actually have two things to report. Both good, I think."

"You think?"

"Yeah. One for sure. The other ... well, it's going to complicate things a little for us is all. I just got the results of my first ultrasound."

"What?" I said, as my sleep-fogged brain tried to process this.

"Ultrasound, Dad. You know, fuzzy pictures of the baby in my tummy? You're gonna be a grandpa."

Still confused, all I could manage was a weak, "Grandpa?"

"Yep," she said. "It's a girl, and we're going to name her after Mom."

As my mind began to clear, I remembered that morning long ago, when Doris and I were discussing possible names for our unborn child. "That's ... That's fantastic!" I said, trying to hide the quaver in my voice. "I don't think I ever told you, but your mom wouldn't let me name you after her. So this is ... Wow! This is great! When? I mean, do you know—"

"I'm two months along, so she should be popping out around the middle of November."

"You mentioned something about complications," I said. "Is everything alright?"

"Everything's fine, Dad. A little morning sickness, but that's normal. What I meant was this is going to involve a lot of changes for us. Jackson will have to cut back on touring, and we'll probably need to hire a nanny. But we're both really happy."

"So am I, honey. So am I. And I can help, too, you know? Anything. Just say the word."

"Thanks," she said. "I'm sure we'll be taking you up on that. Now, are you ready for the second news bulletin?"

Still trying to get control of my emotions, I forgot we were on the phone and answered with a nod. After a moment of silence I realized she couldn't see me, so I coughed to dislodge the wad of gunk in my throat and said, "Sure."

Okay, then." She said. "Hold on to your hat. The real reason I called so early is because we got a message from Aurie. It came in about an hour ago. I would have called sooner, but it was a little scrambled, and Sam just finished cleaning up the static and interference."

For a moment, I was unable to speak.

"Dad?" she said. "Are you still there?"

I filled my lungs and breathed out a raspy, "Yeah."

"Good," she said. "Now I don't want you to get too excited. It's not much, really, just a few choppy sentences. I was hoping for—"

"Ellie!" I shouted. "Forget the qualifiers and read the damn thing!"

"You don't have to yell. Just give me a second. Okay, here it is ... 'Hope this gets through. Still many problems, but making some progress. Repairs going slow. Have to shut down to continue them. Expect long gaps between communications. Keep fingers crossed. Love to all.'

"That was it. Pretty cryptic, but at least it's something."

"Damned right it is," I said. "I want a copy. A framed copy."

"I'll see what I can do. By the way, how's Chance doing? Sorry I haven't been over lately."

"Growing like a weed. Chewing everything in sight. Hauling off anything that isn't nailed down. And please stop calling her Chance. Her name is *Hope!*"

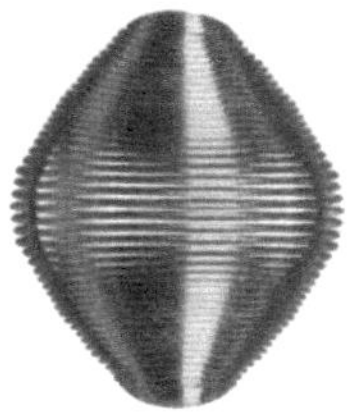

Epilogue

Hey, be careful there you two," Jackson yelled. We were watching our kids climb on the monkey bars at the Millennium Park playground, and Juju was holding Doris's legs, trying to help her swing from rung to rung on the overhead ladder.

"Can't get over how fast Doris is growing," I said. "By the way, how's Momma? I hardly ever get to talk to her anymore, what with the Foundation in full swing and all the new construction here at the park."

"Don't feel like the Lone Ranger," he said. "I've had to become chief cook and bottle washer lately. Ellie can't even get away to join me on the road anymore. Thank God for Janet."

My old secretary had become my granddaughter's nanny. And, oddly, that seemed to be working out fine. Apparently her acerbic personality had been reserved only for me.

We watched as the two girls tired of the rigorous exercise and came over to play in the sandbox near our bench. Juju smoothed a spot in the damp sand, and, scratching with a stick, wrote, "A ' A K U L U U J J U S I."

Doris touched one of the letters with a finger. "What is it?" she said.

"It's my real name. They only call me Juju because A'akuluujjusi is so long and hard to remember. Doris gave her a confused look, so Juju wiped the sand smooth again and started writing numbers. "Okay," she said. "Now, pay attention. This is one. This is two. This is three …"

"Wonder if she'll ever want to change her name," Jackson said.

"Don't know," I said. "Aurélie didn't change hers until she turned eighteen and was legally in control of her own life. But just because Juju is the same person doesn't mean she will do the same things Aurie did. Juju's future was altered from the moment I adopted her, so there's no way to know what, if anything, she'll want to do about her name."

"Well, at least she doesn't seem to have had any problem adjusting to her new life. I haven't noticed any outward signs of sadness or depression. Is there something I'm missing?"

"There may very well be something we're all missing," I said. "Juju is a strange duck. You can never know what's going on inside that head of hers, other than a tornado of numbers and equations. That's probably why she gets to spend more time with Ellie than you and I put together. But sad or depressed? I don't think so. She never got along with her parents, and when I adopted her, she seemed to accept it as nothing more than a change of venue. As long as she's got her calculator and the computer Sam built for her, she's content. The only thing that worries me is how cold and analytical she is. Makes me wonder if she's ever going to be able to open up and let her emotions come out."

"I wouldn't worry too much about that," he said. "If I recall correctly, you had the same concerns about Ellie, and I can guarantee you they were unfounded. She may be cold and calculating on the outside, but that is definitely *not* the case when we're ... you know, alone."

"Yeah. Aurélie was the same way. A little icy at times on the outside, but that covered up a smoldering bedroom volcano. I guess that's what half-wits like us get when they hook up with walking, talking supercomputers."

"Any change in their situation? Ellie doesn't talk a lot about them, and I haven't seen Aurie in a coon's age."

"Not much," I said. "They're still fighting the good fight, but it's tough, you know? The lab complex is constantly under attack, and they often have to suspend certain operations while they make repairs and refortify their defense systems. They haven't been using the holographic projection thing for a while now because it takes too much power, and they have to conserve wherever they can in order to keep the interdimensional printing platform up and running. Our face-to-face communications have been limited to two-dimensional telecasts, most of which are reserved for technical conferences with Sam, Ellie, and H2, so they can continue to help us duplicate their setup here at Millennium Park. That project, by the way, is really coming along. Sam's doing some incredible stuff with the computer division, and H2 should have the accelerator ready for a test run in a few months. After that … well, who knows?"

"Hey, Rix," Juju hollered. "I'm hungry."

"Think she'll ever start calling you Daddy?" Jackson asked.

"Funny thing," I said, "she used to. Actually almost right from the beginning. But her smarts got in the way of that."

"How so?"

"You know how it is when you're concentrating on writing? How you have to sort of tune the rest of the world out?"

"Oh, sure. I'm always catching flack for that. People think you're purposely ignoring them."

"Well, I don't know if Juju thought I was ignoring her on purpose, but after a few months of trying and failing to get my attention with 'Daddy, Daddy, Daddy,' one day she tried 'Rix,' and my head snapped around like I'd heard a gunshot. From then on 'Daddy' was out and 'Rix' was in."

"Does that bother you?" Juju said, tugging on my sleeve. "I can stop if you want."

"Doesn't bother me at all, sweetheart," I lied.

Doris waddled up and laid her head on Jackson's knee. "Looks like nap time," he said. "Guess we'd better head out. Come 'ere and give your Uncle Jackson a hug."

Juju dutifully administered the hug, then came back to sit on my lap as Jackson swept Doris up in his arms. He leaned over so she could give me a goodbye kiss, and the two of them headed for the trees. When they were gone, Juju grabbed my hand and pressed it on her stomach. "Feel that?" she said. "It's my hunger growling."

"Okay," I said, pretending to be exasperated. "Let's go see if we can find you some food. Come on, Hope. Bet you're hungry too."

I'VE BEEN WONDERING SOMETHING, honey," I said as Juju and I sat together on the granite diving board overlooking the stream. We'd brought a picnic lunch to what had become our favorite spot to spend time together when I was off the road and she wasn't with Ellie or her tutors.

"Yes?" she said in her typically brief, no-nonsense way.

"I was just wondering if you've ever thought about changing your name."

"Why would I want to do that? I like my name. Besides, Ellie says A'akuluujjusi Voniossi rolls off the tongue like butter."

"Oh she does, does she?" I said, wondering if Ellie had picked that phrase up from her mother. "I don't know. Maybe a buttered mouthful of jacks."

Juju looked up from her legal pad. "And what, pray tell, are Jacks? You're not saying a mouthful of boys, are you?"

"No, honey. Jacks are these sort of pointy star-shaped things used in a game called Jacks."

"I've never heard of that before. It's a game?"

"An old game. Ancient I think. Girls used to play it. I don't even think it's available anymore."

"Really? An ancient game. Sounds interesting. Does it involve numbers?"

"Numbers?" I said, thinking back. "I guess you could say it involves numbers. I mean you have to count the jacks. The way I remember it, you bounce a little rubber ball and try to pick up a certain number of jacks before you catch the ball again. Something like that. You could look it up in the Encyclopedia program if you want to know more."

"Mmmm," she said. "Maybe I will." She leaned back against Hope, who woke with a snuffle, then relaxed again, closing her eyes and slapping her tail on the smooth rock. "So, what you're saying is that my name sounds like someone spitting out a bunch of pointy star things. Do you really think I should change it?"

I thought for a moment, then realized I shouldn't even have brought it up. "Hey," I said, "it's no big deal. Forget I said it, okay? Tell you what, I'll see if I can find you a set of Jacks. Maybe one of the toy stores in Atlanta still carries them." I reached out and ruffled her kinky mop of hair."

"Stop it, Daddy," she whined.

"Sorry, pumpkin, I ..." That 'Daddy' had hit me like a punch in the chest.

"You what?"

"I … Uh … Give me a second here. Got something caught in my throat." I worked hard at coughing up the non-existent throat blockage, then grabbed a napkin to wipe my eyes. "I know you hate it when I do that," I finally managed to croak. "I'm sorry I keep forgetting. Guess it's because your hair looks so much like Aurélie's. That reminds me, we need to get over to the lab. She's going to be coming up on the viewer in about an hour, and we don't want to miss her."

"Okay," she said. She sat up and retrieved her legal pad. "Just let me finish this one equation. Why don't you play something on the guitar? It helps me concentrate. Maybe that one you wrote for Aurie?"

"Again?" I said

"Yes, please, Daddy," she said in a world-weary voice.

"Again."

The Missing

Lyrics

Robin's Song

Robin's song
Is music from the lady's fingers
Whispering for me to linger
Telling me how, if only for now
I can learn to sing it

Robin's song
Is honey from the tender rosebuds
Loving in a veil of soapsuds
Making a man
From a few grains of sand

And I know I've loved before
Given all I can
I'm only just a man
But I've given so much more
Than anyone could know
To make this feeling grow . . .

(Instrumental break)

A time for making promises
Initials in a tree
Dreaming of tomorrow
And longing to be free

Children born of innocence
Like flowers in the wind
A time filled with beginnings
Never thinking of the end

And then a time for growing up
And hearing nature's song
Of quiet days and simple ways
And time to sing along

(Instrumental break)

But Robin's song
Is passing with the changing seasons
Leaving me without a reason
An echo of June
That ended too soon
Fading to a whisper

Robin's song
A memory as my companion
A river flowing through a canyon
That's now running dry
And I'll never know why
We can't be together

'Cause I know I've loved before
Given all I can
I'm only just a man
But I've given so much more
Than anyone could know
To make this feeling grow . . .

Sunday Morning Sentinel

(© 1972 Rix Vaughn)

Along a dusty pathway past an old abandoned mine
I found a rustic cabin overgrown with weeds and vines
And as I stumbled over broken boards and through the door
I found a yellowed paper lying folded on the floor
And when I bent to try and read the news
There must have been 'least fifty years of dust around my shoes

And it said Sunday Morning Sentinel, as I folded out the crease
And I recall the biggest word upon the page ...
Was "Peace"

I wandered out the door again and down the dusty road
Pulled my coat up high around my ears against the cold
And deep inside I felt a warmth that I had felt before
When Mama said that Daddy would be coming home from War
And as the memories danced inside my head
I recalled the morning paper and the words that I had read

And it said Sunday Morning Sentinel, the fighting's going to cease
And I recall the biggest word upon the page ...
Was "Peace"

Reality had started to creep up inside my mind
And the tears I had been looking for, well they weren't hard to find.
And as I walked into the town, I bowed my head in prayer
For my brother who was crippled, and my son who was still there
And I said Lord, Lord, Lord, it isn't fair

But as I passed a newsboy on the street
I saw the headlines on the stack of papers at his feet

And it said Sunday Morning Sentinel
It's Over in the East
And I recall the biggest word upon the page ...
Was "Peace"

Acknowledgements

Acknowledgements

The author wishes to thank the following editors, critical readers, literary advisors, and supporters for their patience, suggestions, and uncanny ability to spot my often-egregious errors. Without their careful scrutiny and sometimes painfully-honest evaluations over the more than two years it took me to write this novel, it could never have been completed in a form that even vaguely resembles the story you have just read.

Elaine Smith, whose decades of experience as a mystery novelist (under the pen name ECS), editor, and creative-writing instructor, continue to prove invaluable in criticizing and correcting my work.

Burt Kempner, accomplished screen writer and author of the enormously successful ***Mild Wild Stories*** series of children's books, whose intimate knowledge of Native American culture and the worldwide impact of sociopolitical trends contributed greatly to the thematic development of this story.

Jonni Gill, long-time friend and literary critic, whose willingness to suffer through my fumbling attempts at a first-draft helped me turn a complex idea into an understandable and (I hope) entertaining bit of socially-relevant science fiction.

Martha Armstrong, childhood friend and emotional confidant, whose expertise in library science and voracious appetite for reading have made her one of my most trusted and reliable critical readers.

My Sister, Diana, whose generosity and encouragement over the years have not only been instrumental in assuring my survival, but have allowed me to continue my creative pursuits in the face of often extremely challenging circumstances.

Finally, I would like to thank my mother, the late ***Nina Belle Boling,*** without whose tolerance of my musical choices and unflagging support I would never have been able to establish the entertainment career from which the novel's characters and historical realism were derived.

www.ingramcontent.com/pod-product-compliance
Lightning Source LLC
Chambersburg PA
CBHW030827310726
48980CB00006B/670/J
* 9 7 8 0 6 9 2 5 5 4 8 0 7 *